LE CARRÉ

PERFECT
SPY

"LE CARRÉ IS SIMPLY THE WORLD'S
GREATEST FICTIONAL SPYMASTER."
—*Newsweek*

"A SERIOUS, VERY SERIOUS, WORK WITH
SOME OF LE CARRÉ's RICHEST WRIT-
ING. . . . This ambitious tale of betrayal and
its consequences cuts back and forth between
pursued and pursuer and between then and
now . . . By the last page, le Carré has peeled
away layers of secrets, in dark and dazzling
style."
—*New York Daily News*

"ABSORBING . . . LE CARRÉ HAS WRITTEN
A COMPLEX CASE STUDY OF A MAN
FOR WHOM LYING IS A JOY, LIKE DEEP
BREATHING. There are other marvelous people
too: Pym's socializing wife (who also works for
'the Firm'), his supervisor and especially the
amoral father who created this 'perfect spy.' "
—*People*

THE
PLAYERS

*RICK PYM is Magnus Pym's charismatic
father. A charming, unprincipled con man
who created a deadly, inescapable legacy
of treachery and deception to pass along
to his unsuspecting heir. . . .*

More . . .

LE CARRÉ

A
PERFECT
SPY

"A TWILIGHT WORLD WHERE NOTHING IS AS IT SEEMS, WHERE EACH ENCOUNTER POSES A RIDDLE. . . . The novel unexpectedly resembles a court of law in which Pym puts himself, his family, intimates and colleagues on the witness stand. It's a dangerous psychoanalytical endgame, with the marvelously charming, worldly Pym playing both doctor and patient."

—*The Washington Post*

"TO BE SAVORED . . . Skillfully manipulated, complex and probingly written."

—*Library Journal*

THE
PLAYERS

MARY PYM is Magnus's devoted wife and partner in tradecraft, bowed under the crushing weight of shocking revelations about the man she loved but never truly knew.

JACK BROTHERHOOD is Pym's superior, rival, mentor, friend. Like a modern-day Dr. Frankenstein, he is threatened with ruin at the hands of his own creation. . . .

More . . .

LE CARRÉ

A PERFECT SPY

"THE AUTHOR'S INTENSE FEELINGS, LINGUISTIC ARTISTRY AND STINGING WIT DRAW THE READER INTO THE STORY OF MAGNUS PYM, TRAITOR. . . . Le Carré again masterfully chronicles the dangerous game-playing world of international espionage."
—*Publishers Weekly*

"STIRRING, MAGICAL, GRAVELY JOYOUS."
—*Kirkus Reviews*

"EVEN MORE THAN THE HERALDED KARLA TRILOGY, IT EXPOSES THE HUMAN PRICE ONE PAYS FOR LIVING 'ON SEVERAL PLANES AT ONCE.' Far more than a thriller, *A Perfect Spy* is a meditation on the problem of identity in a complex world."
—*Booklist*

THE PLAYERS

MAGNUS PYM is the master operative. A perfect spy. Locked in furious combat with the conflicting demons of his twisted loyalties—an internal and external battle that may eventually tear him to pieces. . . .

Bantam Books by John le Carré
Ask your bookseller for the books you have missed

CALL FOR THE DEAD
THE HONOURABLE SCHOOLBOY
THE LITTLE DRUMMER GIRL
THE LOOKING GLASS WAR
A MURDER OF QUALITY
THE NAIVE AND SENTIMENTAL LOVER
SMILEY'S PEOPLE
THE SPY WHO CAME IN FROM THE COLD
TINKER, TAILOR, SOLDIER, SPY

A
PERFECT
SPY

John le Carré

BANTAM BOOKS
TORONTO · NEW YORK · LONDON · SYDNEY · AUCKLAND

A PERFECT SPY

A Bantam Book / published by arrangement with
Alfred A. Knopf, Inc.

PRINTING HISTORY

*Alfred A. Knopf edition published May 1986
A Book-of-the-Month Club Main Selection, May 1986
An excerpt of this book appeared in* The New York Times Magazine,
March 16, 1986, United Magazine, *June 1986, and* New Woman,
September 1986

Bantam edition / May 1987

Bantam Books are published by Bantam Books, Inc. Its trademark,
consisting of the words "Bantam Books" and the portrayal of a
rooster, is Registered in U.S. Patent and Trademark Office and in
other countries. Marca Registrada. Bantam Books, Inc., 666 Fifth
Avenue, New York, New York 10103.

PRINTED IN THE UNITED STATES OF AMERICA

KR   0 9 8 7 6 5 4 3 2 1

For R, who shared the journey, lent me his dog, and tossed me a few pieces of his life

A man who has two women loses his soul.
But a man who has two houses loses his head.

Proverb

1

In the small hours of a blustery October morning in a south Devon coastal town that seemed to have been deserted by its inhabitants, Magnus Pym got out of his elderly country taxi-cab and, having paid the driver and waited till he had left, struck out across the church square. His destination was a terrace of ill-lit Victorian boardinghouses with names like Bel-a-Vista, The Commodore and Eureka. In build he was powerful but stately, a representative of something. His stride was agile, his body forward-sloping in the best tradition of the Anglo-Saxon administrative class. In the same attitude, whether static or in motion, Englishmen have hoisted flags over distant colonies, discovered the sources of great rivers, stood on the decks of sinking ships. He had been travelling in one way or another for sixteen hours but he wore no overcoat or hat. He carried a fat black briefcase of the official kind and in the other hand a green Harrods bag. A strong sea wind lashed at his city suit, salt rain stung his eyes, balls of spume skimmed across his path. Pym ignored them. Reaching the porch of a house marked "No Vacancies" he pressed the bell and waited, first for the outside light to go on, then for the chains to be unfastened from inside. While he waited a church clock began striking five. As if in answer to its summons Pym turned on his heel and stared back at the square. At the graceless tower of the Baptist church posturing against the racing clouds. At the writhing monkey-puzzle trees, pride of the ornamental gardens. At the empty bandstand. At the bus shelter. At the dark patches of the side streets. At the doorways one by one.

"Why Mr. Canterbury, it's you," an old lady's voice objected sharply as the door opened behind him. "You bad man. You caught the night sleeper again, I can tell. Why ever didn't you telephone?"

"Hullo, Miss Dubber," said Pym. "How are you?"

1

"Never mind how I am, Mr. Canterbury. Come in at once. You'll catch your death."

But the ugly windswept square seemed to have locked Pym in its spell. "I thought Sea View was up for sale, Miss D," he remarked as she tried to pluck him into the house. "You told me Mr. Cook moved out when his wife died. Wouldn't set foot in the place, you said."

"Of course he wouldn't. He was allergic. Come in this instant, Mr. Canterbury, and wipe your feet before I make your tea."

"So what's a light doing in his upstairs bedroom window?" Pym asked as he allowed her to tug him up the steps.

Like many tyrants Miss Dubber was small. She was also old and powdery and lopsided, with a crooked back that rumpled her dressing-gown and made everything round her seem lopsided too.

"Mr. Cook has rented out the upper flat, Celia Venn has taken it to paint in. That's you all over." She slid a bolt. "Disappear for three months, come back in the middle of the night and worry about a light in someone's window." She slid another. "You'll never change, Mr. Canterbury. I don't know why I bother."

"Who on earth is Celia Venn?"

"Dr. Venn's daughter, silly. She wants to see the sea and paint it." Her voice changed abruptly. "Why Mr. Canterbury, how dare you? Take that off this instant."

With the last bolt in place Miss Dubber had straightened up as best she could and was preparing herself for a reluctant hug. But instead of her customary scowl, which nobody believed in for a moment, her poky little face had twisted in fright.

"Your horrid black tie, Mr. Canterbury. I won't have death in the house, I won't have you bring it. Who is it for?"

Pym was a handsome man, boyish but distinguished. In his early fifties he was in his prime, full of zeal and urgency in a place that knew none. But the best thing about him in Miss Dubber's view was his lovely smile that gave out so much warmth and truth and made her feel right.

"Just an old Whitehall colleague, Miss D. No one to flap about. No one close."

"Everyone's close at my age, Mr. Canterbury. What was his name?"

"I hardly knew the fellow," said Pym emphatically, unty-
ing his tie and slipping it into his pocket. "And I'm certainly
not going to tell you his name and have you hunting the
obituaries, so there." His eye as he said this fell on the
visitors' book, which lay open on the hall table beneath the
orange nightlight that he had fitted to her ceiling on his last
visit. "Any casuals at all, Miss D?" he asked as he scanned the
list. "Runaway couples, mystery princesses? What happened
to those two lover-boys who came at Easter?"

"They were not lover-boys," Miss Dubber corrected him
severely as she hobbled towards the kitchen. "They took
single rooms and in the evenings they watched football on the
television. What was that you said, Mr. Canterbury?"

But Pym had not spoken. Sometimes his gushes of
communication were like phone calls cut off by some inner
censorship before they could be completed. He turned back a
page and then another.

"I don't think I'll do casuals any more," Miss Dubber
said through the open kitchen doorway as she lit the gas.
"Sometimes when the doorbell goes I sit here with Toby and
I say: 'You answer it, Toby.' He doesn't of course. A tortoise-
shell cat can't answer a door. So we go on sitting here. We sit
and we wait and we hear the footsteps go away again." She
cast a sly glance at him. "You don't think our Mr. Canterbury is
smitten, do you, Toby?" she enquired archly of her cat.
"We're very *bright* this morning. Very *shiny*. Ten years
younger, by the look of our coat, Mr. Canterbury is." Receiving no helpful response from the cat, she addressed herself to
the canary. "Not that he'd ever tell us, would he, Dickie?
We'd be the last to know. Tzuktzuk? Tzuktzuk?"

"John and Sylvia Illegible of Wimbledon," said Pym, still
at the visitors' book.

"John makes computers, Sylvia programs them, and
they're leaving tomorrow," she told him sulkily. For Miss
Dubber hated to admit there was anyone in her world but
beloved Mr. Canterbury. "Now what have you done to me
this time?" she exclaimed angrily. "I won't have it. Take it
back."

But Miss Dubber was not angry; she would have it, and
Pym would not take it back: a thickly knitted cashmere shawl of
white and gold, still in its Harrods box and swathed in its
original Harrods tissue paper which she seemed to treasure

almost above their contents. For having taken out the shawl she first smoothed the paper and folded it along its creases before replacing it in the box, then put the box on the cupboard shelf where she kept her greatest treasures. Only then did she let him wrap the shawl round her shoulders and hug her in it, while she scolded him for his extravagance.

Pym drank tea with Miss Dubber, Pym appeased her, Pym ate a piece of her shortbread and praised it to the skies although she told him it was burned. Pym promised to mend the sink plug for her and unblock the waste-pipe and take a look at the cistern on the first floor while he was about it. Pym was swift and over-attentive and the brightness she had shrewdly remarked on did not leave him. He lifted Toby on to his lap and stroked him, a thing he had never done before, and which gave Toby no discernible pleasure. He received the latest news of Miss Dubber's ancient Aunt Al, when normally the mention of Aunt Al was enough to hurry him off to bed. He questioned her, as he always did, about the local goings-on since his last visit, and listened approvingly to the catalogue of Miss Dubber's complaints. And quite often, as he nodded her through her answers, he either smiled to himself for no clear reason or became drowsy and yawned behind his hand. Till suddenly he put down his teacup and stood up as if he had another train to catch.

"I'll be staying a decent length of time if it's all right with you, Miss D. I've a bit of heavy writing to do."

"That's what you always say. You were going to live here for ever last time. Then it's up first thing and back to Whitehall without your egg."

"Maybe as much as two weeks. I've taken some leave of absence so that I can work in peace."

Miss Dubber pretended to be appalled. "But whatever will happen to the country? How shall Toby and I stay safe, with no Mr. Canterbury at the helm to steer us?"

"So what are Miss D's plans?" he asked winningly, reaching for his briefcase, which by the effort he needed to lift it looked as heavy as a chunk of lead.

"Plans?" Miss Dubber echoed, smiling rather beautifully in her mystification. "I don't make plans at my age, Mr. Canterbury. I let God make them. He's better at them than I am, isn't he, Toby? More reliable."

"What about that cruise you're always talking about? It's time you gave yourself a treat, Miss D."

"Don't be daft. That was years ago. I've lost the urge."

"I'll still pay."

"I know you will, bless you."

"I'll do the phoning if you want. We'll go to the travel agent together. I looked one out for you as a matter of fact. There's the *Orient Explorer* leaves Southampton just a week away. They've got a cancellation. I asked."

"Are you trying to get rid of me, Mr. Canterbury?"

Pym took a moment to laugh. "God and me together couldn't dislodge you, Miss D," he said.

From the hall Miss Dubber watched him up the narrow stairs, admiring the youthful springiness of his tread despite the heavy briefcase. He's going to a high-level conference. A weighty one too. She listened to him step lightly along the corridor to room 8 overlooking the square, which was her longest let ever, in her whole long life. His loss has not affected him, she decided in relief as she heard him unlock the door and close it softly behind him. Just some old colleague from the Ministry, no one close. She wanted nothing to disturb him. He was to remain the same perfect gentleman who had appeared on her doorstep years ago, looking for what he had called a sanctuary without a telephone even though she had a perfectly good one in the kitchen. And had paid her in advance six-monthly ever since, cash-cash, no receipts. And had built the little stone wall beside the garden path for her, all in an afternoon to surprise her on her birthday, bullied the mason and the bricklayer. And had put the slates back on the roof with his own hands after the storm in March. And had sent her flowers and fruit and chocolates and souvenirs from amazing foreign places without properly explaining what he did there. And had helped her with the breakfasts when she had too many casuals, and listened to her about her nephew who had all the schemes for making money that never came to anything: the latest was starting up a bingo hall in Exeter but first he needed the capital for his overdraft. And received no mail or visitors and played no instrument except the wireless in foreign, and never used the telephone except for local tradesmen. And never told her anything about himself except that he lived in London and worked in Whitehall but travelled a lot, and that his name was Canterbury like the city. Children, wives, parents, sweethearts—not a soul on earth had he ever called his own, except his one Miss D.

"He could have a knighthood by now for all we know," she told Toby aloud as she held the shawl to her nose and inhaled its woolly smell. "He could be Prime Minister and we'd only ever hear it from the television."

Very faintly Miss Dubber heard above the rattle of the wind the sound of singing. A man's voice, tuneless but agreeable. First she thought it was "Greensleeves" from the garden, then she thought it was "Jerusalem" from the square, and she was halfway to the window to yell out. Only then did she realise it was Mr. Canterbury from upstairs, and this amazed her so much that when she opened her door to rebuke him, she paused instead to listen. The singing stopped of its own accord. Miss Dubber smiled. Now *he's* listening to *me*, she thought. That's my Mr. Canterbury all over.

In Vienna three hours earlier, Mary Pym, wife of Magnus, stood at her bedroom window and stared out upon a world which, in contrast to the one elected by her husband, was a marvel of serenity. She had neither closed the curtains nor switched on the light. She was dressed to receive, as her mother would have said, and she had been standing at the window in her blue twin-set for an hour, waiting for the car, waiting for the doorbell, waiting for the soft turn of her husband's key in the latch. And now in her mind it was an unfair race between Magnus and Jack Brotherhood which of them she would receive first. An early autumn snow still covered the hilltop, a full moon rode above it, filling the room with black and white bars. In elegant villas up and down the avenue, the last camp fires of diplomatic entertainment were going out one by one. Frau Minister Meierhof had been having a Force Reduction Talks dance with a four-piece band. Mary should have been there. The van Leymans had had a buffet dinner for old Prague hands, both sexes welcome and no *placement*. She should have gone, they both should, and swept up the stragglers for a scotch-and-soda afterwards, vodka for Magnus. And put on the gramophone, and danced till now or later—the swinging diplomatic Pyms, so popular—just the way they had entertained so famously in Washington when Magnus was Deputy Head of Station and everything was absolutely fine. And Mary would have made bacon and eggs while Magnus joked and picked people's brains and acquired new friends, which he was so tirelessly good at. For this was Vienna's high season, when people who have clammed up all year talked excitedly of Christmas and the Opera, and tossed out indiscretions like old clothes.

But all that was a thousand years ago. All that was until last Wednesday. The only thing that mattered now was that Magnus should drive up the avenue in the Metro he had left at the airport and beat Jack Brotherhood to the front door.

The telephone was ringing. By the bed. His side. Don't run, you idiot, you'll fall. Not too slowly or he'll ring off. Magnus, darling, oh dear God, let it be you, you've had an aberration and you're better, I'll never even ask what happened, I'll never doubt you again. She lifted the receiver and for some reason she couldn't work out sat in a heap on the duvet, plonk, grabbing the pad and pencil with her spare hand in case of phone numbers to take down, addresses, times, instructions. She didn't blurt "Magnus?" because that would show she was worried about him. She didn't say "Hullo" because she couldn't trust her voice not to sound excited. She said their whole number in German so that Magnus would know it was she, hear that she was normal and all right and not angry with him, and that everything was just fine to come back to. No fuss, no problems, I'm here and waiting for you like always.

"It's me," said a man's voice.

But it wasn't me. It was Jack Brotherhood.

"No word of that parcel, I suppose?" Brotherhood asked in the rich, confident English of the military classes.

"No word from anyone. Where are you?"

"Be there in about half an hour, less if I can. Wait for me, will you."

The fire, she thought suddenly. My God, the fire. She hastened downstairs, no longer capable of distinguishing between small and large disasters. She had sent the maid out for the night and forgotten to bank up the drawing-room fire. It was out for sure. But it was not. It was burning merrily; and all that was needed was another log to make the early morning hour less funereal. She put it on, then floated round the room prinking things—the flowers, the ashtrays, Jack's whisky tray—making everything outside herself perfect because nothing inside herself was perfect in the least. She lit a cigarette and puffed out the uninhaled smoke in angry kisses. Then she poured herself a very large whisky, which was what she had come down for in the first place. After all, if we were still dancing I'd be having several.

Mary's Englishness, like Pym's, was unmistakable. She was blonde and strong-jawed and forthright. Her one mannerism, inherited from her mother, was the slightly comic stoop from which she addressed the world, and foreigners in particular. Mary's life was a record of fine deaths. Her grandfather had died at Passchendaele, her one brother, Sam, more recently in Belfast, and for a month or more it had seemed to Mary that the bomb that had blown Sam's jeep to pieces had killed her soul too, but it was her father, not Mary, who had died of a broken heart. All of her men had been soldiers. Between them they had left her with a decent inheritance, a fiercely patriotic soul and a small manor house in Dorset. Mary was ambitious as well as intelligent, she could dream and lust and covet. But the rules of her life had been laid down for her before she entered it and had been entrenched with every death since: in Mary's family the men campaigned while the women lent succour, mourned and carried on. Her worship, her dinner parties, her life with Pym had all been conducted on this same sturdy principle.

Until last July. Until our holiday in Lesbos. Magnus, come home. I'm sorry I raised a stink at the airport when you didn't show up. I'm sorry I bellowed at the British Airways clerk in what you call my six-acre voice and I'm sorry I waved my diplomatic pass around. And I'm sorry—I'm terribly sorry—I phoned Jack to say where the hell's my husband? So please—just come home and tell me what to do. Nothing matters. Just be here. Now.

Finding herself standing before the double doors to the dining room, she pushed them open, switched on the chandeliers, and, whisky in hand, surveyed the long empty table glistening like a lake. Mahogany. Eighteenth-century repro. Counsellor's grade, nobody's taste. Seats fourteen with comfort, sixteen if you double up on the curved ends. That bloody burn mark, I've tried everything. Remember, she told herself. Force your mind back. Get the whole story straight in your stupid little head before Jack Brotherhood rings that doorbell. Step outside yourself and look in. *Now*. It is a night like this one was, crisp and exciting. It is Wednesday and our night for entertaining. And the moon is like the moon tonight except for a bite out of one side. In the bedroom, that fool Mary Pym who notched up one A-level and never went to university stands with her feet too wide apart putting on her family pearls while brilliant Magnus her husband, a First at Oxford and already in his dinner-jacket, kisses the nape of her neck and does his Balkan gigolo number to try to get her in the party mood. Magnus of course is in whatever mood he needs to be in.

"For God's sake," Mary snaps more roughly than she intends. "Stop fooling and fix this bloody clasp for me."

Sometimes my military family gets the better of my language.

And Magnus obliges. Magnus always obliges. Magnus mends and fixes and carries better than a butler.

And when he has obliged he puts his hands over my breasts and breathes hotly on my bare neck: "Please, my dullink, have we not time for most divine perfect moment? No? Yes?"

But Mary is, as usual, too nervous even to smile and orders him downstairs to make sure Herr Wenzel the hired manservant has fetched the ice from Weber's fish-shop. And Magnus goes. Magnus always goes. Even when a sharp smack across Mary's chops would be the wiser course, Magnus goes.

Pausing, Mary lifted her head and listened. A car engine. In this snow they come up on you like bad memories. But, unlike a bad memory, this one passed.

It is dinner; it is the diplomatic happy hour, it is as good as Georgetown in the days when Magnus was still an upwardly mobile Deputy Head of Station with the post of Chief of Service squarely in his sights and everything is mended between Magnus and Mary except for a black cloud that night and day hangs over Mary's heart, even when she is not thinking of it, and that cloud is called Lesbos, a Greek island in the Aegean wholly surrounded by monstrous memories. Mary Pym, wife to Magnus, Counsellor for Certain Unmentionable Matters at the British Embassy in Vienna and actually the Head of Station here as everyone unmentionable

knows, proudly faces her husband across Mary's silver candelabra while the servants hand round Mary's venison, jugged
according to her mother's recipe, to twelve unmentionably
distinguished members of the local intelligence community.

"Now you also have a daughter," Mary firmly reminds an
Oberregierungsrat Dinkel from the Austrian Ministry of Defence in her well-learned German. "Name Ursula—right?
She was studying piano at the Conservatorium when last
heard of. Tell me about her." And to the servant, quietly as
she passes: "Frau Wenzel. Mr. Lederer two down has no red
sauce. Fix."

It was a pretty night, Mary had decided as she listened
to a recitation of the Oberregierungsrat's family woes. It was
the sort of night she worked for, had worked for all her
married life, in Prague and Washington while they were
rising and now here where they were marking time. She was
happy, she was flying the flag, the black cloud of Lesbos was
as good as blown away. Tom was doing well at boarding-school
and would soon be home for the Christmas holidays, Magnus
had rented a chalet in Lech for skiing, the Lederers had said
they would join them. Magnus was so resourceful these days,
so attentive to her despite his father's illness. And before
Lech he would take her to Salzburg for *Parsifal* and, if she
pressed him, to the Opera ball because, as they liked to say
in Mary's family, a gal loves a hop. And with luck the
Lederers could join them for that too—the children could
spend the night together and share a baby-sitter—and somehow with Magnus these days extra people were a comfort.
Glimpsing Pym down the candlelight she darted a smile at
him just as he slipped away to engage a deaf mute on his left.
Sorry about being touchy earlier, she was saying. All forgotten, he was telling her. And when they've gone we'll make
love, she was saying, we'll stay sober and make love and
everything will be fine.

Which was when she heard the phone ring. Exactly
then. As she was transmitting those loving thoughts to Magnus
and having a desperately happy time with them. She heard it
ring twice, three times, she started to get cross, then to her
relief she heard Herr Wenzel answer it. Herr Pym will return
your call later unless it's urgent, she rehearsed in her mind.
Herr Pym should not be disturbed unless it is essential. Herr
Pym is far too busy telling a funny story in that perfect

German of his which so annoys the Embassy and surprises
the Austrians. Herr Pym can also do you an Austrian accent
on demand, or funnier still a Swiss one, from his days at
school there. Herr Pym can put you a row of bottles in a line,
and by pinging them with a table-knife, make them chime
like the bells of the old Swiss railway, while he chants the
stations between Interlaken and the Jungfraujoch in the tones
of a local stationmaster and his audience collapses in tears of
nostalgic mirth.

Mary lifted her gaze to the far end of the empty table.
And Magnus—how was he doing at that moment, apart from
flirting with Mary?

Going great guns was the answer. On his right sat the
dread Frau Oberregierungsrat Dinkel, a woman so plain and
rude, even by the standards of official wives, that some of the
toughest troopers in the Embassy had been reduced to
stunned silence by her. Yet Magnus had drawn her to him
like a flower to the sun and she could not get enough of him.
Sometimes, watching him perform like this, Mary was moved
to involuntary pity by the absoluteness of his dedication. She
wished him more ease, if only for a moment. She wanted him
to know that he had earned his peace whenever he chose to
take it, instead of giving, giving all the time. If he were a
real diplomat, he'd be an Ambassador easily, she thought. In
Washington, Grant Lederer had privately assured her, Magnus
had exerted more influence than either his Station Chief or
the perfectly awful Ambassador. Vienna—though of course he
was enormously respected here and enormously influential
too—was an anticlimax, obviously. Well it was meant to be,
but when the dust settled, Magnus would be back on course,
and the thing here was to be patient. Mary wished she was
not so young for him. Sometimes he tries to live down to me,
she thought. On Magnus's left, similarly mesmerised, sat
Frau Oberst Mohr, whose German husband was attached to
the Signals Bureau at Wiener Neustadt. But Magnus's real
conquest, as ever, was Grant Lederer III, "he of the little black
beard and little black eyes and little black thoughts," as
Magnus called him, who six months ago had taken over the
American Embassy's Legal Department, which meant of
course the reverse, for Grant was the Agency's new man,
though he was an old friend from Washington.

"Grant's a piss artist," Magnus would complain of him,

as he complained of all his friends. "He has us all round a big table once a week inventing words for things we've been doing perfectly well for twenty years without them."

"But he is fun, darling," Mary would remind him. "And Bee's *terribly* dishy."

"Grant's an alpinist," Magnus said another time. "He's stacking us all in a neat line so he can climb over our backs. You just wait and see."

"But at least he's bright, darling. At least he can keep up with you, can't he?"

For the truth was, of course, that given the limitations of any diplomatic friendship, the Pyms and the Lederers were one of the great quartets, and it was just Magnus's perverse way of liking people to kick at them and pick holes in them and swear he would never talk to them again. The Lederers' daughter Becky was the same age as Tom and they were practically lovers already; Bee and Mary got on like a house on fire. As to Bee and Magnus—well frankly Mary did wonder sometimes whether they weren't the tiniest bit *too* friendly. But, on the other hand, she had noticed that with quartets there was always one strong diagonal relationship even if it never came to anything. And if it ever *did* come to something between them—well, to be absolutely *totally* frank, Mary would be quite willing to take her revenge with Grant, whose lurking intensity she found increasingly to be rather a turn-on.

"Mary, cheers, okay? A great party. We're loving it."

It was Bee, for ever toasting everyone. She was wearing diamond earrings and a décolleté which Mary had been eying all evening. Three children and breasts like that: it was bloody unfair. Mary lifted her glass in return. Bee has typist's fingers, she noticed, crooked at the tips.

"Now Grant, old boy, come on now," Magnus was saying, in his half-serious banter. "Give us a break, be fair. If everything your gallant President tells us about the Communist countries is true, how the devil can we do a deal with any of them?"

Out of the corner of her eye Mary saw Grant's droll smile stretch until it looked like snapping in itchy admiration of Pym's wit.

"Magnus, if I had my way, we'd set you up on a big Embassy carpet with a shaker full of dry Martinis and an

American passport and magic you right back to Washington and have you pick up the Democratic ticket. I never heard a seditious case put so well."

"Draft Magnus for President?" Bee purred, sitting up straight and pressing out her breasts as if somebody had offered her a chocolate. "Oh goody."

At which point the ostentatiously menial Herr Wenzel appeared and, bowing elaborately over Magnus, murmured in his left ear that he was required urgently—forgive, Excellency—on the telephone from London—Herr Counsellor, excuse.

Magnus excused. Magnus excuses everybody. Magnus picked his way delicately between imaginary obstacles to the door, smiling and empathising and excusing, while Mary chatted all the more brightly to provide him with covering fire. But as the door closed behind him something unforeseen occurred. Grant Lederer glanced at Bee, and Bee Lederer glanced at Grant. And Mary caught them at it and her blood ran cold.

Why? What had passed between them in that one unguarded look? Was Magnus really sleeping with Bee—and had Bee *told* Grant? Were they momentarily joined, the two of them, in perplexed admiration of their departed host? In all the turmoil since, Mary's answer to those questions had not budged an inch. It wasn't sex, it wasn't love, it wasn't envy and it wasn't friendship. It was conspiracy. Mary was not fanciful. But Mary had seen and she knew. They were a pair of murderers telling each other "soon" and the soon was about Magnus. Soon we shall have him. Soon his hubris will be purged and our honour restored. I saw them hate him, thought Mary. She had thought it then, she thought it now.

"Grant is a Cassius looking for a Caesar," Magnus had said. "If he doesn't find a back to stab soon, the Agency will give his dagger to someone else."

Yet in diplomacy nothing lasts, nothing is absolute, a conspiracy to murder is no grounds for endangering the flow of conversation. Chatting busily, talking children and shopping—hunting frantically for an explanation for the Lederers' bad look—waiting, above all, for Magnus to return to the party and re-enchant his end of the table in two languages at once—Mary still found time to wonder whether this urgent telephone call from London might be the one her husband had been waiting for all these weeks. She had known for some while that he had something big going on, and she was praying it was the promised reinstatement.

And it was at this moment, as Mary remembered it while she was still chatting and still praying for her husband's luck to change, that she felt his fingertips skip knowingly over her naked shoulders as he returned to his place at the head of the table. She hadn't even heard the door, though she'd been listening for it.

"Everything all right, darling?" she called to him over the candelabra, playing it openly because the Pyms were so frightfully happily married.

"Her Maj in good shape, Magnus?" she heard Grant enquire in his insinuating drawl. "No rickets? Croup?"

Pym's smile was radiant and relaxed but that didn't always mean too much, as Mary knew. "Just one of Whitehall's little rumbles, Grant," he replied with magnificent casualness. "I think they must have a spy here who tells them when I'm giving a dinner party. Darling, are we out of claret? Jolly mingy rations, I must say."

Oh, Magnus, she had thought excitedly: you chancer.

It was time to get the women upstairs for a pee before coffee. The Frau Oberregierungsrat, who held herself to be modern, was inclined to resist. A scowl from her husband dislodged her. But Bee Lederer, who by this time in the evening was disposed to become the great American feminist—Bee left like a lamb, peremptorily handed out by her sexy little husband.

"Now comes the punch," says Jack Brotherhood contentedly, in Mary's imagination.

"There is no punch."

"Then why are we shaking, dear?" says Brotherhood.

"I'm not shaking. I'm just pouring myself a small drink waiting for you to arrive. You know I always shake."

"I'll have mine straight, please, same as you. Just give it me the way it happened. No ice, no fizz, no bullshit."

Very well then, damn you, have it.

The night is ending as perfectly as it began. In the hall Mary and Magnus help the guests to their coats and Mary cannot help noticing how Magnus, whose life is service, stiffens his arms and curls his fingers with each successfully negotiated sleeve. Magnus has invited the Lederers to linger but Mary has covertly countermanded this by telling Bee, with a giggle, that Magnus needs an early night. The hall empties. The diplomatic Pyms, ignoring the cold—they are English after all—stand valiantly on their doorstep and wave farewell. Mary has an arm around Pym's waist and she is secretly poking her thumb inside the waistband of his trousers at the back and down the partition of his buttocks. Magnus does not resist her. Magnus does not resist. Her head rests affectionately on his shoulder as she whispers sweet nothings into the same ear Herr Wenzel employed to summon him to the telephone and she hopes that Bee will notice their lovey-doveyness. Under the porch light—Mary luminously youthful in her long blue dress, Magnus so distinguished in his dinner-jacket—we must have looked the picture of harmonious married life. The Lederers leave last and are the most effusive. "Dammit, Magnus, I don't remember when I had such a good time," says Grant, with his quaint, rather faggy indignation. They are followed by their bodyguard in a second car. Side by side the very English Pyms enjoy a moment of shared disdain for the American way.

"Bee and Grant are terrific fun, really," says Mary. "But would *you* have a bodyguard if Jack offered you one?" There is more to her question than mere curiosity. She has been wondering recently about the odd people who seem to loiter outside the house with nothing to do.

"Not bloody likely," Pym retorts with a shudder. "Not unless he'll promise to protect me from Grant."

Mary extracts her thumb, they turn and arm in arm go indoors. "Is everything all right?" she asks, thinking of the phone call. Everything is absolutely fine, he replies. "I want you," Mary whispers boldly and lets her hand brush across his thighs. Smiling, Pym nods and pulls at his tie, loosening it apparently in preparation. In the kitchen the Wenzels are waiting to leave. Mary can smell cigarette smoke but decides to ignore it because they have worked so hard. On her deathbed she will remember that she took the conscious decision to ignore their cigarette smoke: that her life at that moment was so relaxed, Lesbos so far away, her sense of service so complete, that she was able to consider matters of such massive triviality. Pym has the Wenzels' money ready for them in an envelope plus a handsome tip. Magnus will tip with his last fiver, thinks Mary indulgently. His generosity is something she has learned to love even when her more frugal upper-class approach tells her he overdoes it: Magnus is so seldom vulgar. Even when at times she wonders whether he is overspending and she should offer him some from her private income. The Wenzels leave. Tomorrow night they will do another party at another house. The Pyms in close harmony move to the drawing-room, hands linking and breaking and ranging freely for the ritual foreplay of a nightcap and a gossipy post-mortem. Pym pours a scotch for Mary and a vodka for himself but unusually does not remove his jacket. Mary is fondling him explicitly. Sometimes in these cases they don't manage to get up the stairs.

"Super venison, Mabs," says Pym. Which was what he always does first: congratulate her. Magnus congratulates everyone all the time.

"They all thought Frau Wenzel cooked it," says Mary, feeling for the top of his zip.

"Then sod them," says Pym gallantly, rejecting the whole fatuous diplomatic world for her with a sweep of his forearm. For a moment Mary fears that Magnus has had one too many. She hopes not for she is not pretending: after the worries and fatuities of the evening she wants him very much. Handing Mary her glass, Magnus raises his own and drinks to her silently: well done, old girl. He is smiling straight down at her, his knees are almost touching hers and steady. Affected by the tension in him Mary wants him urgently here and now and gives him further clear evidence of this with her hands.

"If Grant Lederer is the *third*," she asks, thinking again for a moment of that murderous look, "what on earth were the first two like?"

"I'm free," says Pym.

Mary fails to understand. She thinks he is capping her joke in some way.

"I don't get it," she says a little shamefacedly. I'm so slow for him, poor love. A sudden awful thought. "You don't mean they've sacked you?" she says.

Magnus shakes his head. "Rick's dead," he explains.

"Who?" Which Rick does he mean? Rick from Berlin?

Rick from Langley? Which Rick is dead who can be setting
Magnus free and, who knows, making space for his promotion?

Magnus begins again. Perfectly reasonably. Clearly the
poor girl has not understood. She is tired from her long
evening. She's had a couple too many. "Rick, my father, is
dead. He died of a heart attack at six this evening while we
were changing. They thought he was okay after the last one
but it turns out he wasn't. Jack Brotherhood phoned from
London. Why the hell Personnel gave it to Jack to break to
me rather than break it to me themselves is a secret not ours
to share, presumably. But they did."

And Mary even then doesn't get it right.

"What do you mean—free?" she shouts wildly as all
constraint leaves her. "Free of what?" Then very sensibly she
bursts out weeping. Loud enough for both of them. Loud
enough to drown her own dreadful questions from Lesbos all
the way here.

And she has half a mind to weep again now, for Jack
Brotherhood, as the front doorbell sounds through the house
like a bugle call, three short peals as ever.

Pym briskly drew the curtains and switched on the light. He
had stopped singing. He felt nimble. Setting down his briefcase with a little grunt, he peered gratefully around him,
letting everything greet him in its own good time. The brass
bedstead. Good morning. The embroidery picture above it
exhorting him to love Jesus: I tried, but Rick always got in
the way. The roll-top desk. The bakelite wireless that had
listened to dear old Winston Churchill. Pym had imposed
nothing of himself on this room. He was its guest, not its
coloniser. What had drawn him here, back in those dark ages,
all those lives ago? Even now, with so much else clear to him,
a sleepiness came over him when he tried to make himself
remember. So many lonely journeys and aimless walks in
foreign cities led me here, so much fallow, solitary time. He
had been catching trains, looking for somewhere, escaping
from somewhere else. Mary was in Berlin—no, she was in
Prague—they had been transferred a couple of months earlier, and it was being made clear to him even then that if he
kept his nose clean in Prague, the Washington appointment
would be next on the list. Tom was—good God, Tom was

scarcely out of nappies. And Pym was in London for a conference—no, he wasn't, he was attending a three-day course on the latest methods of clandestine communication in a beastly little training house off Smith Square. The course over, he had taken a cab to Paddington. Mindlessly, the instinct guiding him. His head still crammed with useless knowledge about anodes and squash transmissions. He jumped on a train that was about to pull out and at Exeter crossed the platform and took another. What greater freedom than not knowing where you are going or why? Finding himself in the middle of nowhere, he spotted a bus bearing a vaguely familiar destination and boarded it.

This was granny-land. This was Sunday, when aunts rode to church with collection coins inside their gloves. From his spaceship on the upper deck, Pym gazed down fondly on chimney-pots, churches, dunes and slate roofs that looked as though they were waiting to be lifted up to Heaven by their topknots. The bus stopped, the conductor said "Far as we go, sir," and Pym alighted with a most curious sense of accomplishment. I'm there, he thought. I've found it at last, and I wasn't even looking for it. The very town, the very beach, exactly as I left them all those years ago. The day was sunny and the world empty. Probably it was lunchtime. He had lost count. What was certain was that Miss Dubber's steps were scrubbed so white it was a shame to tread on them, and a hymn tune issued from the house, together with a smell of roast chicken, blue bag, carbolic soap and godliness.

"Go away!" a thin voice shouted. "I'm on the top step and I can't reach the fuse and if I stretch any more I'll pop."

Five minutes later this room was his. His sanctuary. His safe house away from all the other safe houses. "Canterbury. The name is Canterbury," he heard himself say as, the fuse safely mended, he pressed a deposit on her. A city had found a home.

Stepping to the desk, Pym now slid back the top and began turning the contents of his pockets on to the leather-ette surface. As a stock-taking preparatory to a shift in personality and premises. As a retrospective examination of today's events till now. One passport in the style of Mr. Magnus Richard Pym, colour of eyes green, hair light brown, member of Her Majesty's Foreign Service, born far too long ago. There was always something rather shocking after a lifetime of symbols and codenames, about seeing his own name, naked and undisguised, splurged over a travel document. One calfskin wallet, a Christmas present from Mary. In the left side credit cards, in the right two thousand Austrian schillings and three hundred English pounds in various and elderly notes, his escape money cautiously assembled, more available in the desk. The Metro car keys. She's got the other set. Photo of family on Lesbos, everybody absolutely fine. Scribbled address of girl he had met somewhere and forgotten. He put the wallet aside and, continuing with his inventory, drew from the same pocket one green airport boarding-card still valid for last night's British Airways flight to Vienna. The sight and touch of it intrigued him. This was when Pym voted with his feet, he thought. In all his life till now, perhaps the first completely selfish gesture he had made, with the noble exception of the room where he now sat. The first time he had said "I want" rather than "I ought."

At the cremation in a silent suburb he had had a suspicion that the tiny number of mourners was unnaturally inflated by somebody's watchers. There was nothing he could prove. He could hardly as chief mourner stand at the door of the chapel challenging each of his nine guests to state his business. And it was true that Rick's erratic path through life had attracted a host of people Pym had never set eyes on and never wished to. All the same the suspicion remained with him and grew as he drove to London Airport, and became a near certainty when he returned his car to the hire company, where two grey men were taking much too long to fill in their contract forms. Undeterred, he checked his suitcase to Vienna and, with this very boarding-card in his hand, passed through immigration and sat himself in the insanitary lounge behind his *Times*. When his flight was delayed, he almost concealed his irritation, but still contrived to let it show. When it was called, he hurried obediently forward to join the straggling crowd on its walk to the departure gate, the very picture of a dutiful conformer. As he did so he could almost feel, if he could not see, the two men peel away for tea and ping-pong back at base: let the Vienna bastards have him and good riddance, they were saying to each other. He turned a corner and advanced towards a moving walkway but did not board it. Instead he ambled, peering behind him as if in search of a delayed companion, then imperceptibly allowing himself to be borne backward by the opposing flow of passengers. Moments later he was showing his passport at the arrivals desk and receiving the quiet "Welcome home, sir" that is reserved for those with certain serial numbers. As a last and spontaneous precaution he had taken himself to the domestic airlines counter and enquired in a loose and general way that was calculated to annoy the busier clerk about flights to Scotland. Not Glasgow, thank you, just Edinburgh. Well hang on, you'd better give me Glasgow as well. Ah, a printed timetable, fantastic. Look, thank you *very* much. And you can issue me with a ticket if I buy one? Oh I see. Over there. Great.

Pym tore the boarding-card into small pieces and put them in the ashtray. How much did I plan, how much was spontaneous? It scarcely mattered. I am here to act, not brood. One coach ticket, Heathrow–Reading. It had rained on the journey. One single rail ticket, Reading–London, unused, bought to deceive. One night-sleeper ticket, Reading–Exeter, issued on board the train. He had worn a beret and kept his face in shadow while buying it from the drunk attendant. Tearing these also into small pieces, Pym added them to the pile in the ashtray and, whether out of habit or for some more aggressive reason, set a match to them and gazed into the flames with an unblinking fixity. He'd half a mind to burn his passport, too, but a residual squeamishness restrained him, which he found quaint about himself and rather endearing. I planned it to the last detail—I who have never taken a conscious decision in my life. I planned it on the day I joined the Firm in a part of my head I never knew about until Rick died. I planned everything except Miss Dubber's cruise.

The flames dwindled, he broke up the ash, took off his coat and hung it over the back of the chair. From a chest of drawers he hauled an old cardigan, hand-knitted by Miss Dubber, and put it on.

I'll talk to her about it again, he thought. I'll think of something she'd like more. I'll pick my moment better. The important thing for her is to have a change of scene, he thought. Somewhere she doesn't have to worry.

Suddenly needing an activity, he switched out the lights, slipped quickly to the window, opened the curtains and set to work checking out the little square, life by life and window by window as the morning woke it, while he searched for tell-tale signs of watchers. In her kitchen, the wife of the Baptist minister, wearing her lovat dressing-gown, is unpegging her son's football gear from the washing line in preparation for today's match. Pym draws back swiftly. He has caught a glint of steel in the manse gateway, but it is only the minister's bicycle still chained to the trunk of a monkey-puzzle tree as a precaution against unchristian covetousness. In the frosted bathroom window of Sea View a woman in a grey slip is stooped over a handbasin soaping her hair. Celia Venn, the doctor's daughter who wants to paint the sea, is evidently expecting company today. Next door to her at number 8 Mr. Barlow the builder and his wife are watching breakfast television. Pym's eye passes methodically on, until a parked van holds his attention. The passenger door opens, a girlish figure flits stealthily through the central gardens and vanishes into number 28. Ella, the daughter of the undertaker, is discovering life.

Pym closed the curtains and put the lights back on. I will make my own daytime and my own night. The briefcase stood where he had left it, strangely rigid from its steel lining. Everybody carried cases, he remembered, as he stared at it. Rick's was pigskin, Lippsie's was cardboard, Poppy's was a scruffy grey thing with marks printed on it to look like hide. And Jack—dear Jack—you have your marvellous old attaché case, faithful as the dog you had to shoot.

Some people, you see, Tom, they leave their bodies to a teaching hospital. The hands go to this class, the heart to that one, the eyes to another, everyone gets something, everyone is grateful. Your father, however, has only his secrets. They're his provenance and his curse.

With a bump, he sat down at the desk.

To tell it straight, he rehearsed. Word for word the truth. No evasions, no fictions, no devices. Just my overpromised self set free.

To tell it to no one in particular, and to everyone. To tell it to all of you who own me, to whom I have given myself with such unthinking liberality. To my handlers and paymasters. To Mary and all the other Marys. To anyone who had a piece of me, was promised more and duly disappointed. And to whatever of myself remained after the great Pym share-out.

To all my creditors and co-owners incorporated, here once and for all the settlement of arrears that Rick so often dreamed of and that shall now be achieved in his only acknowledged son. Whoever Pym was to you, whoever you are or were, here is the last of many versions of the Pym you thought you knew.

Pym took a deep breath and puffed it out again.

You do it once. Once in your life and that's it. No rewrites, no polishing, no evasions. No would-it-be-better-this-ways. You're the male bee. You do it once, and die.

He took up a pen, then a single sheet of paper. He scribbled some lines, whatever came into his head. All work and no play makes Jack a dull spy. Poppy, Poppy, on the wall. Miss Dubber must a-cruising go. Eat good bread, poor Rickie's dead. Rickie-Tickie father. His hand ran smoothly, not a crossing-out. Sometimes, Tom, we have to do a thing in order to find out the reason for it. Sometimes our actions are questions, not answers.

2

A black and gusty day then, Tom, as sabbaths in these parts mostly are, I saw a crop of them as a child and I don't remember a sunny one. I hardly remember outdoors at all except when I was hurried through it like a child criminal on my way to church. But I am running ahead already, for Pym on this particular day was not yet born. The time is all your father's life ago plus half-a-dozen months, the place a seaboard town not too far from this one, with more of a slope to it and a thicker tower—but this one will do quite as well. A swirling, sopping doom-laden midmorning, take my word for it, and myself, as I say, an unborn ghost, not ordered, not delivered and certainly not paid for: myself a deaf microphone, planted but inactive in any but the biological meaning. Old leaves, old pine needles and old confetti stick to the wet church steps as the humble flow of worshippers files in for its weekly dose of perdition or salvation, though I never saw that much to choose between the two of them. And myself a mute and foetal spy, unconsciously fulfilling his first mission in a place normally devoid of targets.

Except that today something is up. There's a buzz around, and its name is Rick. There's a spark of mischief to their piety today they can't keep dim and it comes from inside themselves, from the smouldering centre of their dark little sphere, and Rick is its owner and its origin and its instigator. You can read it everywhere: in the portentous, rolling tread of the brown-suited deacon, in the fluttering and exhaling of the hatted women who arrive in a rush imagining they are late, then sit blushing through their white face-powder because they are early. Everyone agog, everyone on tiptoe and a first-class turn-out, as Rick would have remarked proudly, and probably he did, for he loved a full house whatever happened, never mind it was his own hanging. A few of them have come by car—such wonders of the day as Lanchesters and Singers—others by trolley-bus, and some have walked; and God's sea rain has given them beards of cold inside their cheap fox stoles, and God's sea wind is cutting through the threadbare serge of their Sunday best. Yet there is not one of them, however he has come, who does not brave the weather a second longer to pause and goggle at the notice-board and confirm with his own eyes what the bush telegraph has been telling him these several days. Two posters are fixed to it, both smeared by rain, both to the passer-by as dreary as cups of cold tea. Yet to those who know the code they transmit an electrifying signal. The first in orange proclaims the five-thousand-pound appeal, mounted by the Baptist Women's League, to provide a reading-room—though all of them know that no book will ever be read in it, that it will be a place to set out homemade cakes and photographs of leprous children in the Congo. A plywood thermometer, designed by Rick's best craftsmen, is fastened to the railings revealing that the first thousand has already been achieved. The second notice, green, declares that today's address will be given by the minister, all welcome. But this information has been corrected. A rigid bulletin has been pinned over it, typed in full like a legal warning, with the comically misplaced capital letters that in these parts signal omens.

Due to unforeseen Circumstances, Sir Makepeace Water-master, Justice of the Peace and Liberal Member of Parlia-

ment for this Constituency, will provide today's Message.
Appeal Committee please to Remain behind Afterwards for
an Extraordinary meeting.

Makepeace Watermaster himself! And they know why!

Elsewhere in the world, Hitler is winding himself up to
set fire to the universe, in America and Europe the miseries
of the Depression are spreading like an incurable plague, and
Jack Brotherhood's forebears are abetting them or not according to whatever spurious doctrine of the day prevails in the
deniable corridors of Whitehall. But the congregation doesn't
presume to hold opinions on these impenetrable aspects of
God's purpose. Theirs is the dissenting church and their
temporal overlord is Sir Makepeace Watermaster, the greatest
preacher and Liberal ever born, and one of the Highest in
the Land, who gave them this very building out of his own
purse. He didn't, of course. His father Goodman gave it to
them, but Makepeace, having succeeded to the fiefdom, has
a way of forgetting that his father existed. Old Goodman was
a Welshman, a preaching, singing, widowed, miserable
potteryman with two children twenty-five years apart of
whom Makepeace is the elder. Goodman came here, sampled
the clay, sniffed the sea air and built a pottery. A couple of
years later he built two more and imported cheap migrant
labour to man them, first Low Welsh like himself and afterwards and cheaper still and lower, the persecuted Irish.
Goodman lured them with his tied cottages, starved them
with his rotten wages, and beat the fear of Hell into them
from his pulpit before himself being taken off to Paradise,
witness the unassuming monument to him six thousand feet
high that stood in the pottery forecourt until a few years ago
when the whole lot was ripped down to make way for a
bungalow estate and good riddance.

And today *due to unforeseen Circumstances* that same
Makepeace, Goodman's only son, is coming down from his
mountain-top—though the circumstances have been foreseen
by everyone except himself, the circumstances are as palpa-
ble as the pews we wait in, as immovable as the Watermaster
tiles the pews are bolted to, as fateful as the rasping clock
that wheezes and whistles between every chime like a dying
sow fighting off the awful end. Picture the gloom of it—how it
stultified its young and dragged them down, its prohibition of
everything exciting that they cared about: from Sunday news-

papers to Popery, from psychology to art, from flimsy under-
wear to high spirits to low spirits, from love to laughter and
back again, I don't think there was a corner of the human
state where their disapproval did not fall. Because if you don't
understand the gloom of it, you'll not understand the world
that Rick was running away from or the world he was running
towards, or the twisting relish that buzzes and tickles like a
flea in every humble breast this dark sabbath as the last
chimes merge with the drumming of the rain and the first
great trial of young Rick's life begins. "Rick Pym's for the
high jump at last," says the word. And what more awesome
executioner than Makepeace himself, Highest in the Land,
Justice of the Peace and Liberal Member of Parliament, to
adjust the noose around his neck?

With the last chime of all, the strains of the voluntary die
also. The congregation holds its breath and starts counting to
a hundred while it seeks out its favourite actors. The two
Watermaster women have arrived early. They sit shoulder to
shoulder in the pew for notables directly beneath the pulpit.
On almost any other Sunday, Makepeace would have been
roosting there between them, all six foot six of him, his long
head cocked to one side while he listened to the voluntary
with his moist little rosebud ears. But not today because
today is extra, today Makepeace is in the wings conferring
with our Minister and certain worried trusties from the
Appeal Committee.

Makepeace's wife, known as Lady Nell, is not yet fifty
but already she is hunched and shrivelled like a witch, with a
habit of flicking her greying head without warning as if she
were shaking off flies. And next to her—a tiny, earnest statue
beside Nell's pecking and stupidity—perches Dorothy, rightly
called Dot, an immaculate speck of a lady, young enough to
be Nell's daughter instead of Makepeace's sister—and she is
praying, praying to her Maker, she is pushing her tiny
scrumpled fists into her eyes while she pledges her life and
death to Him if only He will hear her and make it right.
Baptists do not kneel before God, Tom. They squat. But my
Dorothy would have stretched herself flat on the Watermaster
tiles and kissed the Pope's big toe that day if God would have
let her off the hook.

*   *   *

I have one photograph of her and there have been times—
though no longer, I swear it, she is dead for me—when I
would have given my soul for just one more. I found it in an
old scuffed Bible when I was Tom's age, in a suburban
mansion we were hastily vacating. "To Dorothy with all my
special love, Makepeace," runs the inscription on the inside
page. One in all the world. One spotted sepia-brown photograph is all, taken like a pause in flight as she steps down
from the taxi, licence number not in frame, clutching a
homemade posy of small flowers that could be wild, and her
big eyes have too much behind them for our comfort. Is she
on her way to a wedding? To her own? Is she calling on a sick
relative—on Nell? Where is she? Where is she escaping to
this time? She has the flowers to her chin and her elbows
pressed together. Her forearms form a vertical line from waist
to neck. Long sleeves nipped at the wrist. Muslin gloves,
therefore no rings visible, though I have a suspicion of a
bulge in the third joint of the third finger of the left hand. A
cloche bonnet covers her hair and throws a shadow like a
mask across the scaring eyes. Shoulders on a slant, as if she is
on the point of losing her balance, and one tiny foot tipped
sideways to prevent her. Her pale stockings have the zigzag
sheen of silk; her shoes are of patent leather, pointed, buttoned.
And somehow I know they pinch her, that they were bought
against the clock like the rest of her outfit, in a shop where
she is not known and does not wish to be. Her lower face pale
as a plant grown in the dark—think of The Glades, the house
she was brought up in! An only child, as I was, you can see it
at a glance—never mind she has a brother twenty-five years
ahead of her.

Shall I tell you what I found once, in the summerhouse
in the Watermasters' great dark orchard, where I myself, a
child like her, was wandering? The colouring book she had
won at Bible class, *The Life of Our Saviour in Pictures*. And
do you know what my darling Dot had done with it? Scored
out every saintly face with savage crayoning. I was shocked at
first, until I understood. Those faces were the dreaded ones
from the real world she had no part of. They enjoyed all the
companionship and kindly smiles she never had. So she
coloured them out. Not in rage. Not in hate. Not even in
envy. But because their ease of living was beyond her grasp.
Look again at the photograph. The jaw. The stern unsmiling

jaw locking out expression. The little mouth clamped shut and downward to keep its secrets safe. That face cannot discard a single bad memory or experience, because it has nobody to share them with. It is condemned to store every one of them away until the day when it will break from overloading.

Enough. I'm running out ahead. Dot, a.k.a. Dorothy, family name Watermaster. No connection with any other firm. An abstraction. Mine. An unreal, empty woman permanently in flight. If she had had her back to me and not her face, I could not have known her less or loved her more.

And behind the Watermaster women, far behind, by chance as far as the great long aisle allows, at the very back of the church, in their chosen pew directly beside the closed doors, sits the flower of our young men, their neckties pulled up and outward from their stiff collars, their slicked hair parted in a razor slash. These are the Night School Boys, as they are affectionately known, our Tabernacle's apostles of tomorrow, our white hopes, our future ministers of religion, our doctors, missionaries, and philanthropists, our future Highest in the Land, who will one day go out into the world and Save it as it has never been Saved before. It is they who by their zeal have acquired the duties customarily entrusted to older men: the distributing of hymn books and special notices, the taking of collection money and the hanging up of overcoats. It is they who once a week, by bicycle, motorcycle and kindly parents' motorcars, distribute our church magazine to every god-fearing front door, including that of Sir Makepeace Watermaster himself, whose cook has standing orders that a piece of cake and a glass of lemon barley be always waiting for the bringer; they who collect the few shillings of rent from the church's poor cottages, who pilot the pleasure boats on Brinkley Mere at children's outings, host the Band of Hope's Christmas bunfights and put fire into Christian Endeavour action week. And it is they who have taken upon themselves as a direct commission from Jesus the burden of the Women's League Appeal, target five thousand pounds, at a time when two hundred would maintain a family for a year. Not a doorbell they have not pressed along their pilgrimage. Not a window they have not offered to

clean, flower-bed to weed and dig for Jesus. Day after day the
young troops have marched out, to return, reeking of peppermint, long after their parents are asleep. Sir Makepeace has
sung their praises, so has our minister. No sabbath is complete without a reminder to Our Father regarding their
devotion. And bravely the red line on the plywood thermometer at the church gates has climbed through the fifties, the
hundreds to the first thousand, where for a while now, for all
their efforts, it has seemed to stick. Not that they have lost
momentum, far from it. Failure is not in their thoughts. No
need for Makepeace Watermaster to remind them of Bruce's
spider, though he often does. The Night School Boys are
"crackerjack," as our saying goes. The Night School Boys are
Christ's own vanguard and they will be the Highest in the
Land.

There are five of them and at their centre sits Rick, their
founder, manager, guiding spirit and treasurer, still dreaming
of his first Bentley. Rick, full names Richard Thomas after his
dear old father, the beloved TP, who fought in the Great War
trenches before he became our mayor, and passed away these
seven years ago, though it seems like only yesterday, and
what a preacher *he* was before his Maker took him back!
Rick, your grandfather without portfolio, Tom, because I
would never let you meet him.

I have two versions of Makepeace's Message, both incomplete, both shorn of time or place or origin: yellowed press-
cuttings, hacked apparently with nail-scissors from the eccle-
siastical pages of the local press, which in those days reported
our preachers' doings as loyally as if they were our footballers. I
found them in Dorothy's same Bible with her photograph.
Makepeace accused nobody outright, Makepeace framed no
charge. This is the land of innuendo; straight speaking is
for sinners. "M.P. sounds Stern Warning against Youthful
Covetousness, Greed," sings the first. "Perils of young Ambition splendidly Highlighted." In Makepeace's imposing person, the anonymous writer declares, "are met the poet's
Celtic grace, the Statesman's eloquence, the lawgiver's Iron
sense of Justice." The congregation was "spellbound unto the
Meekest of its Members," and none more so than Rick
himself, who sits in an enraptured trance, nodding his broad

head to the cadences of Makepeace's rhetoric, even though every Welsh note of it—to the excited ears and eyes of those around him—is hurled at Rick personally down the length of the aisle, and rammed home with a botched stab of the lugubrious Watermaster forefinger.

The second version takes a less apocalyptic tone. The Highest in the Land was not ranting against youth's sinfulness, far from it. He was offering succour to the youthful falterer. He was extolling youth's ideals, likening them to stars. To believe this second version, you would suppose Makepeace had gone star crazy. He couldn't get away from the things, nor could the writer. Stars as our destiny. Stars that guide Wise Men across deserts to the very Cradle of Truth. Stars to lighten the darkness of our despair, yea even in the pit of sin. Stars of every shape, for every occasion. Shining above us like God's very light. The writer must have been Makepeace Watermaster's property, body and soul, if it wasn't Makepeace himself. Nobody else could have sweetened that awesome, forbidding apparition in the pulpit.

Though my eyes were not yet open on this day, I see him as clearly as I saw him later in the flesh, and shall see him always: tall as one of his own factory chimneys, and as tapered. Rubbery, with weak pinched shoulders and a wide bendy waist. One jointless arm tipped out at us like a railway signal, one baggy hand flapping on the end of it. And the wet, elastic little mouth that should have been a woman's, too small even to feed him by, stretching and contracting as it labours to deliver the indignant vowels. And when at long, long last, enough awesome warnings have been uttered, and the penalties of sin outlined in sufficient detail, I see him brace himself and lean back and moisten his lips for the kiss-off, which we children have been begging for these forty minutes while we crossed our legs and died for a pee however often we had peed before we left home. One cutting gives this final preposterous passage in full, and I will give it again now—their text, not mine—though no Watermaster sermon I ever heard later was complete without it, though the words became part of Rick's very nature, and remained with him all his life and consequently mine, and I would be amazed if they did not ring in his ears as he died, and accompany him as he strode towards his Maker, two pals reunited at last:

"Ideals, my young brethren . . ." I see Makepeace pause

here, shoot another glare at Rick and start again: "Ideals, my beloved brethren all, are to be likened unto those splendid stars above us"—I see him lift his sad, starless eyes to the pine roof—"we cannot reach them. Millions of miles separate us from them." I see him hold out his drooping arms as if to catch a falling sinner. "But oh my brethren, how greatly do we profit from their presence!"

Remember them, Tom. Jack, you'll think I'm mad, but those stars, however fatuous, are a crucial piece of operational intelligence, for they lend a first image to Rick's unquenchable conviction of his destiny, and it didn't stop with Rick either; how could it, for what is a prophet's son but himself a prophecy, even if nobody on God's earth ever discovers what either one of them is prophesying? Makepeace, like all great preachers, must do without a final curtain or applause. Nevertheless, quite audibly in the silence—I have witnesses who swear to it—Rick is heard to whisper "beautiful" twice over. Makepeace Watermaster hears it too—slurs his big feet and pauses on the pulpit steps, blinking round him as if somebody has called him a rude name. Makepeace sits down, the organ strikes up "what purpose burns within our hearts?" Makepeace stands again, unsure where to put his ridiculously tiny backside. The hymn is sung to its dreary end. Night School Boys, with Rick star-struck at their centre, process down the aisle and in a practised drill movement fan out to their appointed posts. Rick, smart as paint today and every Sunday, proffers the collecting plate to the Watermaster ladies, his blue eyes glistening with divine intelligence. How much will they give? How quickly? The silence lends tension to these massive questions. First comes Lady Nell, who keeps him waiting while she pecks in her handbag and curses, but Rick is all forbearance, all love, all stars today, and each lady regardless of age or beauty receives the benefit of his thrilled and saintly smile. But where daft Nell simpers at him and tries to muss his slicked hair and pull it forward over his broad, Christian brow, my little Dot is looking nowhere but at the ground, still praying, praying even while she stands, and Rick has actually to touch her forearm with his finger in order to alert her to his Godlike nearness. I can feel his touch now upon my own arm, and it sends a healer's charge through me of weak-kneed loathing and devotion. The boys line up before the Lord's table, the minister accepts the offerings, says a perfunctory blessing, then orders everyone but the Appeal Committee to leave at once and quietly. The unforeseen Circumstances are about to begin, and with them the first great trial of Richard T. Pym—the first of many, it is true, but this is the one that really whetted his appetite for Judgment.

I have seen him a hundred times as he stood that morning. Rick alone, brooding at the doorway of a crowded room. Rick his father's son, the glory of a great heritage creasing on his brow. Rick waiting, like Napoleon before the battle, for Destiny to sound the trumpets for his assault. He never made a lazy entrance in his life, he never fluffed his timing or his impact. Whatever you had in mind till then, you could forget it: the topic of the day had just walked in. So it is in the Tabernacle on this rainy sabbath, while God's wind booms in the pine rafters high above and the disconsolate huddle of humanity in the front pews waits awkwardly for Rick. But stars, we know, are like ideals and elusive. Heads begin to crane, chairs creak. Still no Rick. The Night School Boys, already in the dock, moisten their lips, tip nervously at their ties. Rickie's done a bunk. Rickie can't face the music. The deacon in his brown suit hobbles with an artisan's mysterious discomfort towards the vestry where Rick may have hidden. Then a thump. Round whips every head to the sound, till they stare straight back down the aisle at the great west door, which has been opened from outside by a mysterious hand. Silhouetted against the grey sea clouds of adversity, Rick T. Pym, until now David Livingstone's natural heir if ever we knew one, gravely bows to his judges and his Maker, closes the great door behind him, and all but vanishes once more against its blackness.

"Message from old Mrs. Harmann for you, Mr. Philpott." Philpott being the name of the minister. The voice being Rick's and everyone as usual remarking its beauty, rallying to it, loving it, scared and drawn by its unflinching self-assurance.

"Oh yes then?" says Philpott, very alarmed to be addressed so calmly from so far away. Philpott is a Welshman too.

"She'd be glad of a lift to Exeter General to see her husband before his operation tomorrow, Mr. Philpott," says Rick with just the tiniest note of a reproach. "She doesn't

seem to think he'll pull through. If it's any bother to you I'm
sure one of us can take care of her, can't we, Syd?"

Syd Lemon is a cockney whose father not long ago came
south for his arthritis and in Syd's view will shortly die of
boredom instead. Syd is Rick's best-loved lieutenant, a small,
punchy fighter with the townie's nimbleness and twinkle, and
Syd is Syd for ever to me, even now, and the nearest I ever
came to a confessor, excluding Poppy.

"Sit with her all night if we have to," Syd affirms with
strenuous rectitude. "All next day too, won't we, Rickie?"

"Be quiet," Makepeace Watermaster growls. But not to
Rick, who is bolting the church doors from the inside. We
can just make him out among the lights and darks of the
porch. Clang goes the first bolt, high up, he has to reach for
it. *Clang* the second, low down as he stoops to it. Finally, to
the visible relief of the susceptible, he consents to embark on
his forward journey to the scaffold. For by now the weaker of
us are dependent on him. By now in our hearts we are
begging a smile from him, the son of old TP, sending him
messages assuring him that there is nothing personal, enquiring
of him after the dear lady his poor mother—for the dear lady,
as everybody knows, does not feel sufficiently herself today
and nobody can budge her. She sits with a widow's majesty at
home in Airdale Road behind drawn curtains under the tinted
giant photograph of TP in his mayoral regalia, weeping and
praying one minute to have her late husband given back to
her, the next to have him stay put exactly where he is and be
spared the disgrace, and the next rooting for Rick like the old
punter she secretly is—"Hand it to them, son. Fight them
down before they do the same to you, same as your dad did
and better." By now the less worldly officers of our impro-
vised tribunal have been converted if not actually corrupted
to Rick's side. And as if to undermine their authority still
further, Welsh Philpott in his innocence has made the error
of placing Rick beside the pulpit in the very spot from which
in the past he has read us the day's lesson with such brio and
persuasion. Worse still, Welsh Philpott ushers Rick to this
position and twitches the chair for Rick to sit on. But Rick is
not so biddable. He remains standing, one hand rested
comfortingly on the chair's back as if he has decided to adopt
it. Meanwhile he engages Mr. Philpott in a few more easy
words of talk.

"I see Arsenal came a cropper Saturday, then," says Rick. Arsenal, in better times, being Mr. Philpott's second greatest love, as it was TP's.

"Never mind that now, Rick," says Mr. Philpott, all of a flurry. "We've business to discuss, as well you know."

Looking poorly the minister takes his place beside Makepeace Watermaster. But Rick's purpose is achieved. He has made a bond where Philpott wanted none; he has presented us with a feeling man instead of a villain. In recognition of his achievement Rick smiles. On all of us at once: grand of you to be among us here today. His smile sweeps over us; it is not impertinent, it is impressive in its compassion for the forces of human fallibility that have brought us to this unhappy pass. Only Sir Makepeace himself and Perce Loft the great solicitor from Dawlish, known as Perce the Writ, who sits beside him with the papers, preserve their granite disapproval. But Rick is not awed by them. Not by Makepeace and certainly not by Perce, with whom Rick has formed a fine relationship in recent months, based it is said on mutual respect and understanding. Perce wants Rick to read for the bar. Rick is bent upon it but meanwhile wants Perce to advise him on certain business transactions he is contemplating. Perce, ever an altruist, is supplying his services free.

"That was a wonderful sermon you gave us, Sir Makepeace," says Rick. "I never heard better. Those words of yours will ring inside my head like the bells of Heaven for as long as I'm spared, sir. Hullo, Mr. Loft."

Perce Loft is too official to reply. Sir Makepeace has had flattery before, and receives it as no more than his due.

"Sit down," says our Liberal Member of Parliament for this Constituency and Justice of the Peace.

Rick obeys at once. Rick is no enemy of authority. To the contrary he is a man of authority himself, as we waverers already know, a power and a justice in one.

"Where's the Appeal money gone?" Makepeace Watermaster demands without delay. "There was close on four hundred pound donated last month alone. Three hundred the month before, three hundred in August. Your accounts for the same period show one hundred and twelve pound received. Nothing put by and no cash in hand. What have you done with it, boy?"

"Bought a motor coach," says Rick, and Syd—to use his

own words—seated in the dock with all the rest of them, has a hard time not corpsing.

Rick spoke for twelve minutes by Syd's dad's watch and when he'd done only Makepeace Watermaster stood between him and victory, Syd is sure of it: "The minister, he was won over before your dad ever opened his mouth, Titch. Well he had to be, he gave TP his first pulpit. Old Perce Loft—well, Perce had fish to fry by then, didn't he? Rick had stitched him up. The rest of them, they was going up and down like a tart's knickers from waiting to see which way The Lord High Makewater's going to jump."

First of all, Rick magnanimously claims full responsibility for everything. Blame, says Rick, if blame there be, should be laid squarely at his own door. Stars and ideals are nothing to the metaphors he flings at us: "If a finger is to be pointed, point it here." A stab at his own breast. "If a price is to be paid, here's the address. Here I am. Send me the bill. And leave them to learn by his mistakes who got them into this, if such there have been," he challenges them, beating the English language into submission with the blade of his plump hand by way of an example. Women admired those hands till the end of Rick's days. They drew conclusions from the girth of his fingers, which never parted when he made a gesture.

"Where did he get his rhetoric from?" I once asked Syd reverently, enjoying what he and Meg called "a small wet" at their fireside in Surbiton. "Who were his models, apart from Makepeace?"

"Lloyd George, Hartley Shawcross, Avory, Marshall Hall, Norman Birkett and other great advocates of his day," replied Syd promptly, as if they were the runners and starters for the two-thirty at Newmarket. "Your dad had more respect for the law than any man I ever knew, Titch. Studied their speeches, followed their form better than what he did the geegees. He'd have been a top judge if TP had given him the opportunities, wouldn't he, Meg?"

"He'd have been Prime Minister," Meg affirms devoutly. "Who else was there but him and Winston?"

Rick next passes to his Theory of Property which I have since heard him expound many times in many different ways but I believe this was its unveiling. The burden is that any money passing through Rick's hands is subject to a redefinition of the laws of property, since whatever he does with it will improve mankind, whose principal representative he is. Rick, in a word, is not a taker but a giver and those who call him otherwise lack faith. The final challenge comes in a mounting bombardment of passionate, grammatically unnerving pseudo-Biblical phrases. "And if any one of you here present today— can find evidence of a single advantage—one single benefit— be it in the past, be it stored away for the future—directly or indirectly from this enterprise—which I have derived— ambitious though it may have been, make no two ways about it—let him come forward now, with a clear heart—and point the finger where it belongs."

From there it is but a step to that sublime vision of the Pym & Salvation Coach Company Ltd., which will bring profit to piety and worshippers to our beloved Tabernacle.

The magic box is unlocked. Flinging back the lid Rick displays a dazzling confusion of promises and statistics. The present bus fare from Farleigh Abbott to our Tabernacle is twopence. The trolley-bus from Tambercombe costs threepence, four-up in a cab from either spot costs sixpence, a Granville Hastings motor coach costs nine hundred and eight pounds discounted for cash, and seats thirty-two fully loaded, eight standing. On the sabbath alone—my assistants here have made a most thorough survey, gentlemen—more than six hundred people travel an aggregate of over four thousand miles to worship at this fine Tabernacle. Because they love the place. As Rick does. As we all do, every man and woman here present—let's make no bones about it. Because they want to feel *drawn from the circumference to the centre*, in the spirit of their faith. (This last is one of Makepeace Watermaster's own expressions and Syd says it was a bit cheeky of Rick to throw it back in his face.) On three other days in the week, gentlemen—Band of Hope, Christian Endeavour and Women's League Bible Group—another seven hundred miles are travelled leaving three days clear for normal commercial operation, and if you don't believe me watch my forearm as it beats the doubters from my path in a series of convulsive elbow blows, the cupped fingers never parting. From such figures it is suddenly clear there can be only one conclusion.

"Gentlemen, if we charge *half* the standard fare *and* give

a free ticket to every disabled and elderly person, to every
child under the age of eight—with full insurance—observing
all the fine regulations which rightly apply to the operation of
commercial transport carriages in this increasingly hectic age
of ours—with fully professional drivers with every awareness
of their responsibilities, god-fearing men recruited from our
own number—allowing for depreciation, garaging, mainte-
nance, fuel, ticketing and sundries, and assuming a fifty-
percent capacity on the three days of commercial operation—
there's a forty-percent clear profit for the Appeal and room
left over to see everybody right."

Makepeace Watermaster is asking questions. The others
are either too full or too empty to speak at all.

"And you've bought it?" says Makepeace.

"Yes, sir."

"You're not of age, half of you."

"We used an intermediary, sir. A fine lawyer of this
district who in his modesty wishes to remain anonymous."

Rick's reply draws a rare smile from the improbably tiny
lips of Sir Makepeace Watermaster. "I never knew a lawyer
who wished to remain anonymous," he says.

Perce Loft frowns distractedly at the wall.

"So where is it now?" Sir Makepeace continues.

"What, sir?"

"The coach, boy."

"They're painting it," says Rick. "Green with gold lettering."

"With whose permission, at any stage, have you embarked
on this project?" asks Watermaster.

"We're asking Miss Dorothy to cut the tape, Sir Makepeace. We've drafted the invite already."

"Who gave you permission? Did Mr. Philpott here? Did
the deacons? Did the committee? Did I? To spend nine
hundred and eight pounds of Appeal funds, widows' mites,
on a motor coach?"

"We wanted the element of surprise, Sir Makepeace. We
wanted to sweep the board with them. Once you spread the
word beforehand, talk it round town, you take the air out of
it. P.S.C. is going to be sprung upon an unsuspecting world."

Makepeace now enters what Syd calls the dicey part.

"Where are the books?"

"Books, sir? There's only one Book I know of—"

"Your files, boy. Your figures. You alone kept the accounts, we heard."

"Give me a week, Sir Makepeace. I'll account for every penny."

"That's not keeping accounts. That's fudging them. Did you learn nothing at all from your father, boy?"

"Rectitude, sir. Humbleness before Jesus."

"How much have you spent?"

"Not spent, sir. Invested."

"How much?"

"Fifteen hundred. Rounded up."

"Where's the coach at present?"

"I said, sir. Being painted."

"Where?"

"Balham's of Brinkley. Coach-builders. Some of the finest Liberals in the county. Christians to a man."

"I know Balham's. TP sold timber to Balham's for ten years."

"They're charging cost."

"You propose to ply for trade in public, you say?"

"Three days a week, sir."

"Using the public coach stages?"

"Certainly."

"Are you familiar with the likely attitude to be taken by the Dawlish & Tambercombe Transport Corporation of Devon to this venture?"

"A popular demand like this—those boys can't block it, Sir Makepeace. We've got God driving for us. Once they see the ground-swell, feel the pulse, they'll back away and give us our heads all the way to the top. They can't stop progress, Sir Makepeace, and they can't stop the march of Christian people."

"Can't they," says Sir Makepeace, and scribbles figures on a piece of paper in front of him. "There's eight hundred and fifty pound in rent money missing as well," he remarks as he writes.

"We invested the rent money too, sir."

"That's more than the fifteen hundred then."

"Call it two thousand. Rounded up. I thought you only meant the Appeal money."

"What about the collection money?"

"Some of it."

"Counting all monies from any source, what's the total capital? Rounded up."

"Including private investors, Sir Makepeace—"

Watermaster sat up straight: "So we've private investors too, have we? My gracious, boy, you've been going it a bit. Who are they?"

"Private clients."

"Of whom?"

Perce Loft looks as though he is about to fall asleep out of sheer boredom. His eyelids are two inches long, his goatish head has slipped forward on his neck.

"Sir Makepeace, I am not at liberty to reveal this. When P.S.C. promises confidentiality, that's what she delivers. Our watchword is integrity."

"Has the company been incorporated?"

"No, sir."

"Why not?"

"Security, sir. Keep it under wraps. Like I said."

Makepeace begins jotting again. Everybody waits for more questions. None come. An uncomfortable air of completeness settles over Makepeace, and Rick senses it faster than anybody. "It was like being up the old doctor's, Titch," Syd told me, "when he's made up his mind what you're dying of, only he's got to write out this prescription before he gives you the good news."

Rick speaks again. Unprompted. It was the voice he used when he was cornered. Syd heard it then, I heard it later only twice. It was not a pretty tone at all.

"I could bring those accounts up to you this evening, as a matter of fact, Sir Makepeace. They're in safekeeping, you see. I'll have to get them out."

"Give them to the police," says Makepeace, still writing. "We're not detectives here, we're churchmen."

"Miss Dorothy might think a bit different, though, mightn't she, Sir Makepeace?"

"Miss Dorothy has nothing to do with this."

"Ask her."

Then Makepeace stops writing and his head comes up a bit sharpish, says Syd, and they look at each other, Makepeace with his little baby eyes uncertain. And Rickie, suddenly his gaze has the glint of a flick-knife in the dark. Syd does not go as far as I shall in describing that stare because

Syd won't touch the black side of his lifelong hero. But I will. It looks out of him like a child through the eyeholes of a mask. It denies everything it stood for not a half-second earlier. It is pagan. It is amoral. It regrets your decision and your mortality. But it has no choice because you cannot go back.

"Are you telling me Miss Dorothy is an investor in this project?" says Makepeace.

"You can invest more than money, Sir Makepeace," says Rick, from far away but close.

Now the point is, says Syd rather hastily here, Makepeace should never have driven Rick to use that argument. Makepeace was a weak man acting hard and they're the worst, says Syd. If Makepeace had been reasonable, if he'd been a believer like the rest and thought a little better of poor TP's boy instead of lacking faith and undermining everybody else's into the bargain, things could have been settled in a friendly, positive way and everyone could have gone home happy, believing in Rick and his coach the way he needed them to. As it was, Makepeace was the last barrier and he left Rickie no alternative but to knock him down. So Rickie did, didn't he? Well he had to, Titch.

I strain and stretch, Tom, I shove with every muscle of my imagination as deep as I dare into the heavy shadows of my own pre-history. I put down my pen and stare at the hideous church tower across the square, and I can hear as plain as Miss Dubber's television downstairs the ill-contrasted voices of Rick and Sir Makepeace Watermaster matched against each other. I see the dark drawing-room of The Glades where I was so seldom admitted and I picture the two men closeted together there that evening alone, and my poor Dorothy trembling in our murky upper room reading the same hand-stitched homilies that now adorn Miss Dubber's landings as she tries to suck comfort from God's flowers, God's love, God's will. And I could tell you, I think near enough to a sentence or two, what passed between them by way of continuing their unfinished chat of that morning.

Rick's spirits are back, because the flick-knife never shows for long and because he has already achieved the object that is more important to him than any other in his human dealings, even if he himself does not yet know it. He has inspired Makepeace to hold two totally divergent opinions of him and perhaps more. He has shown him the official and unofficial versions of his identity. He has taught him to respect Rick in his complexity and to reckon as much with Rick's secret world as with his overt one. It is as if in the privacy of that room each player revealed the many cards, fake or real is of no account, that comprised his hand: and Makepeace was left without a chip in front of him. But the fact is, both men are dead, both took their secret to the grave, Sir Makepeace going ahead by thirty years. And the one person who may still know it cannot speak, because if she exists at all any more, then it is only as a ghost, haunting her own life and mine, killed long ago by the very consequences of the two men's fateful dialogue that evening.

History records two meetings between Rick and my Dorothy before that sabbath. The first when she made a royal visit to the Young Liberals Club, of which Rick was at that time an elected officer—I believe, God help them, treasurer. The second when Rick was captain of the Tabernacle's football team and one Morrie Washington, a Night School Boy and another of Rick's lieutenants, was goalie. Dorothy, as sister of the Sitting Member, was invited to present the cup. Morrie remembers the line-up ceremony, with Dorothy walking along the troops and pinning a medal to each victorious breast, starting with Rick himself as captain. It seems she fumbled the clasp, or that Rick pretended she did. Either way, he let out a playful cry of pain and went down on one knee, clutching his bosom and insisting she had pierced him to the heart. It was a bold and rather naughty number and I am surprised he took it so far. Even in burlesque, Rick was normally very protective of his dignity, and at fancy-dress balls, which were the rage until the war came, he preferred to go as Lloyd George rather than risk ridicule. But down he went, Morrie remembered it like yesterday, and Dorothy laughed, a thing nobody had ever seen her do: laugh. What assignations followed we can never know, except that, according to Morrie, Rick did once boast that there was more than cake and lemon barley waiting for him up at The Glades when he delivered the church magazine.

Syd, I think, knows more than Morrie. Syd saw a lot. And people tell him things because he keeps his counsel.

Syd, I believe, knows most of the secrets that lurked in the wooded house that Makepeace Watermaster called his home, even if in old age he has done his best to bury them six foot under. He knows why Lady Nell drank and why Makepeace was so ill-at-ease with himself, and why his damp little eyes were so tormented, and his mouth unequal to his appetites, and why he was able to castigate sin with such passionate familiarity. And why he wrote of a special love when he put his wretched name in my Dorothy's Bible. And why it was that Dorothy had taken herself to the furthest corner of the house to sleep, far from Lady Nell's rooms and further still from Makepeace's. And why Dorothy was so accessible to the smart-tongued upstart from the football team who spoke as if he could build her a road to anywhere, and drive her there in his coach. But Syd is a good man and a Mason. He loved Rick and gave the best years of his life, now to roistering with him, now to hanging on to his coat-tails. Syd would have a laugh, he would tell a story, provided it hurt nobody too much. But Syd won't touch the black side.

History records also that Rick took no account books to that meeting, though Mr. Muspole the great accountant, another Night School Boy, offered to help him write some and probably did. Muspole could invent accounts the way others can write postcards on holiday or rattle off anecdotes into a microphone. And that in order to prepare himself, Rick took a stroll over Brinkley Cliffs, alone, which I believe is the first known walk of this kind, though Rick, like myself after him, was always a one for striding out in search of a decision or a voice. And that he returned from The Glades wearing an air of high office not unlike Makepeace Watermaster's, except that it had more of the natural radiance in it that comes, we are told, of inner cleanliness. The matter of the Appeal had been attended to, he informed his courtiers. The problem of liquidity had been solved, he said. Everybody was going to be seen right. How? they begged him; how, Rickie? But Rick preferred to remain their magician and allowed nobody to look up his sleeve. Because I am blessed. Because I steer events. Because I am destined to become one of the Highest in the Land.

His other good news was not vouchsafed to them. This was a cheque drawn on Watermaster's personal account in the sum of five hundred pounds to set himself up in life—

presumably, said Syd, in outer Australia. Rick endorsed it, Syd cashed it, since Rick's own bank account, as so often in later years, was temporarily indisposed. A few days afterwards, on the strength of this subsidy, Rick presided over a lavish if sombre banquet at the Brinkley Towers Hotel, attended by the entire court as then composed and several local Lovelies who were always an off-screen feature. Syd recalls a mood of historic change pervading the occasion though no one knew precisely what was over or what was about to begin. Speeches were made, mostly on the theme of old pals sticking together and keeping a straight bat through life, but when Rick's health was drunk he responded with uncharacteristic brevity, and it was whispered that he was in the grip of an emotion, for he was seen to weep, which he did often, even in those days; he could weep buckets, on the drop of a handkerchief. Perce Loft, the great lawyer, attended the gathering to the surprise of some, and to their greater surprise brought with him a beautiful, if incongruous, young music student named Lippschitz, first name Annie, who put the other Lovelies in the shade even though she'd hardly a coat to cover her back. They dubbed her "Lippsie." She was a refugee from Germany who had come to Perce in some immigration matter, and Perce in his goodness had decided to extend a helping hand to her, much as he had extended one to Rick. To close proceedings Morrie Washington the court jester sang a song, and Lippsie joined the other women in the chorus, though she sang too well and didn't fully appreciate the dirty bits, being foreign. It was by then dawn. A sleek taxi took Rick away, and he was not seen in those parts for many years.

History records further that one Richard Thomas Pym, bachelor, and Dorothy Godchild Watermaster, spinster, both very temporarily of this parish, were the next day solemnly and discreetly married in the presence of two co-opted witnesses in a newly opened registry office off the Western by-pass, just where you turned left for Northolt Aerodrome. And that a little boy christened Magnus Richard and weighing in at very few pounds at all was born to them not six months later, whom the Lord protect. The Companies Registry, which I have consulted, also records the event, though in different terms. Within forty-eight hours of the birth, Rick had unveiled the Magnus Star Equitable Insurance Company

Ltd., with a share capital of two thousand pounds. Its stated
purpose was the Provision of life insurance to the Needy,
Disabled, and Elderly. Its accountant was Mr. Muspole, its
legal adviser Perce Loft. Morrie Washington was company
secretary, and the late Alderman Thomas Pym, affectionately
known as TP, its patron saint.

"So was there really a coach then or was it all flannel?" I ask
Syd.

Syd is always cautious in how he replies. "Now there *could*
have been a coach, Titch. I'm not saying there wasn't, I'd be a
liar if I did. I'm just saying I never heard about a coach till
your dad happened to mention it in church that morning. Put
it that way."

"So what had he done with the money—if there was no
coach?"

Syd really doesn't know. So many thousands of pounds
have floated under the bridge since then. So many great
visions come and gone. Maybe Rick gave it away, Syd says
awkwardly. Your dad couldn't say no to anyone, specially the
Lovelies. Never right with himself unless he was giving.
Maybe a con came and took it off him, your dad always loved
a con. Then to my amazement Syd blushes. And I hear faintly
but clearly from the side of his mouth the ratta-tat-tat he used
to make for me when I was a child and wanted him to do the
clip of horses' hoofs.

"You mean he used the Appeal money to lay bets?" I ask.

"Titch, I'm only saying that that coach of his could have
been horse-drawn. That's all I'm saying, isn't it, Meg?"

Oh but there was a coach all right! And it was not horse-
drawn at all. That coach was the most splendid, powerful ever
made. The golden lettering of the Pym & Salvation Coach
Company shone from its lustrous sides like the illuminated
chapter headings of all the Bibles of Rick's youth. Its green
was the racing green of England. Sir Malcolm Campbell
himself was going to drive it. The Highest in the Land would
ride in it. When the people of our town saw that coach they
were going to go down on their knees and put their hands
together and thank God and Rick in equal portion for it. The

grateful crowds would gather outside Rick's house and call him out on to his balcony till late into the night. I have seen him practising his wave in expectation of them. With both hands as if rocking me above his head, while he beams and weeps into the middle distance: "I owe it all to old TP." And if, as doubtless happened, it turned out that Balham's of Brinkley, some of the finest Liberals in the county, had never strictly speaking heard of Rick's coach, let alone painted it for cost out of the goodness of their hearts, then they were in the same state of provisional reality as the coach was. They were waiting for Rick's wand to beckon them into being. It was only when meddlesome unbelievers such as Makepeace Watermaster had difficulty accepting this state of affairs that Rick found himself with a religious war on his hands, and like others before him was compelled to defend his faith by unpleasant means. All he demanded was the totality of your love. The least you could do in return was give it to him blindly. And wait for him, as God's Banker, to double it over six months.

3

Mary had prepared herself for everything except for this. Except for the pace and urgency of the intrusion and the number of the intruders. Except for the sheer scale and complexity of Jack Brotherhood's anger, and for his bewilderment, which seemed greater than her own. And for the awful comfort of his being there.

Admitted to the hall he had barely looked at her. "Did you have any inkling of this?"

"If I had I'd have told you," she said, which was a quarrel before they had even begun.

"Has he phoned?"

"No."

"Has anybody else?"

"No."

"No word from *anyone*? No change?"

"No."

"Brought you a brace of house guests." He jabbed a thumb at two shadows behind him. "Relatives from London, come to console you for the duration. More to follow." Then he swept through her like a great ragged hawk on its journey to another prey, leaving her one frozen impression of his lined and punctured face and shaggy white forelock as he stormed towards the drawing-room.

"I'm Georgie from Head Office," said the girl on the doorstep. "This is Fergus. We're so sorry, Mary."

They had luggage and she showed them to the foot of the stairs. They seemed to know the way. Georgie was tall and sharp-edged, with straight, sensible hair. Fergus was not quite Georgie's class, which was the way the Office worked these days.

"Sorry about this, Mary," Fergus echoed as he followed Georgie up the stairs. "Don't mind if we take a look round, do you?"

In the drawing-room Brotherhood had switched out the lights and wrenched open the curtains to the French windows. "I need the key for this thing. The Chubb. The whatever they have here."

Mary hastened to the mantelpiece and groped for the silver rose bowl where she kept the security key. "Where is he?"

"He's anywhere in the world or out of it. He's using tradecraft. Ours. Who does he know in Edinburgh?"

"No one." The rose bowl was full of pot-pourri she had made with Tom. But no key.

"They think they've traced him there," said Brotherhood. "They think he took the five-o'clock shuttle from Heathrow. Tall man with a heavy briefcase. On the other hand, knowing our Magnus as we do, he might just be in Timbuctoo."

Looking for the key was like looking for Magnus. She didn't know where to begin. She seized the tea-caddy and shook it. She was getting sick with panic. She grabbed the silver Achievement Cup that Tom had won at school and heard something metal skid inside it. Taking the key to him, she barked her shin so hard her eyes blurred. That bloody piano stool.

"The Lederers ring?"

"No. I told you. No one did. I didn't get back from the airport till eleven."

"Where's the holes?"

She located the top keyhole for him and guided his hand to it. I should have done it myself then I wouldn't have had to touch him. She knelt and began fumbling for the lower one. I'm practically kissing his feet.

"Has he ever vanished before and you not told me?" Brotherhood demanded while she continued to grope.

"No."

"I want it level, Mary. I've got the whole of London at my throat. Bo's having the vapours and Nigel's cloistered with the Ambassador now. The RAF doesn't fly us out in the middle of the night for nothing."

Nigel is Bo Brammel's hangman, Magnus had said. Bo says three-bags-full to everyone and Nigel pads behind him chopping off their heads.

"Never. No. I swear," she said.

"Did he have a favourite place anywhere? Some hideaway he talked of going to?"

"He said once Ireland. He'd buy a croft overlooking the sea and write."

"North or south?"

"I don't know. South, I suppose. As long as it was sea. Then suddenly the Bahamas. That was more recent."

"Who does he have there?"

"Nobody. Not as far as I know."

"Did he ever talk of going over to the other side? Little dacha on the Black Sea?"

"Don't be a fool."

"So Ireland, then the Bahamas. When did he say the Bahamas?"

"He didn't. He just marked the property advertisements in *The Times* and left them for me to see."

"As a sign?"

"As a reproach, as a come-on, as a signal that he wanted to be somewhere else. Magnus has a lot of ways of talking."

"Has he ever talked about doing away with himself? They'll ask you, Mary. I might as well do it first."

"No. No, he hasn't."

"You don't sound sure."

"I'm not. I'll have to think."

"Has he ever been physically frightened for himself?"

"I can't answer it all at once, Jack! He's a complicated man—I've got to think!" She steadied herself. "In principle, no. No to all of it. It's all a total shock."

"But you still rang very fast from the airport. As soon as he wasn't on that plane, you were on the phone: 'Jack, Jack, where's Magnus?' You were right, he'd vanished."

"I saw his suitcase going round the bloody apron, didn't I? He'd checked himself in! Why wasn't he on the plane?"

"How about his drinking?"

"Less than before."

"Less than Lesbos?"

"Miles less."

"What about his headaches?"

"Gone."

"Other women?"

"I don't know. I wouldn't know. How could I? If he says he's out for the night, he's out for the night. It could be a woman, it could be a Joe. It could be Bee Lederer. She's always after him. Ask her."

"I thought wives could always tell the difference," said Brotherhood.

Not with Magnus they can't, she thought, beginning to settle to his pace.

"Does he still bring papers back at night to work on?" Brotherhood asked, peering into the snow-clad garden.

"Now and then."

"Any here now?"

"Not that I know of."

"American papers? Liaison stuff?"

"I don't read them, Jack, do I? So I don't know."

"Where does he keep them?"

"He brings them at night, takes them back in the morning. Just like everyone else."

"And keeps them where, Mary?"

"By the bed. In the desk. Wherever he's been working on them."

"And Lederer hasn't rung?"

"I told you. No."

Brotherhood stood back. Two men, muffled against the night, tumbled into the room. She recognised Lumsden, the Ambassador's private secretary. She had recently had a row

with his wife, Caroline, about starting a bottle-bank in the
Embassy forecourt as an example to the Viennese. Mary
thought it essential. Caroline Lumsden thought it irrelevant
and explained why in an angry outburst to an inner caucus of
the Diplomatic Wives Association: Mary was not a real Wife,
said Caroline. She was an Unmentionable, and the only
reason she was accepted as a Wife *at all* was to protect her
husband's half-baked cover.

They must have soldiered up the bridlepath from the
school, she thought. Waded through half a metre of snow in
order to be discreet about Magnus.

"Hail, Mary," Lumsden said brightly in his best scout-
master's voice. He was a Catholic but that was how he always
greeted her, so he did it tonight. To be normal.

"Did he bring any papers back on the night of the
party?" Brotherhood asked, closing the curtains once more.

"No." She put on the light.

"Know what's in this black briefcase of his that he's
carrying?"

"He didn't take it from here so he must have collected it
at the Embassy. All he took from here was the suitcase that's
at Schwechat."

"Was," said Brotherhood.

The second man was tall and sickly-looking. He carried a
bulging bag in each gloved hand. Enter the abortionist. It
was practically a full plane, she thought stupidly; Head Office
must have a permanent defection team on twenty-four-hour
standby.

"Meet Harry," Brotherhood said. "He's going to put
some clever boxes on your telephones. Use them normally.
Don't think of us. Any objection?"

"How can I?"

"You can't, you're right. I'm being polite, so why don't
you do the same? You've got two cars. Where are they?"

"The Rover's outside, the Metro's in the airport carpark
waiting for him to pick it up."

"Why did you go to the airport if he had a car there?"

"I just thought he might like me to be there so I took a
taxi and went."

"Why not take the Rover?"

"I wanted to ride back with him, not drive in convoy."

"Where's the Metro key?"

"In his pocket presumably."

"Got a spare?"

She searched her handbag till she found it. He dropped it in his pocket.

"I'll get it lost," he said. "If anybody asks, it's gone for repair. I don't want it kicking round the airport."

She heard a heavy thud from upstairs.

She watched Harry pull off his gumboots and place them neatly on the mat beside the French windows.

"His father died Wednesday. What's he been up to in London apart from burying him?" Brotherhood continued.

"I assumed he'd be dropping in at Head Office."

"He never did. He didn't ring, he didn't visit."

"Then probably he was busy."

"Did he have any plans for London—anything he told you of?"

"He said he'd go and see Tom at school."

"Well, he did that. He went. Anything else? Friends— dates—women?"

She was suddenly very tired of him. "He was burying his father and tidying up, Jack. The whole visit was one long date. If you'd had a father and he died, you'd know how it was."

"Did he phone you from London?"

"No."

"Steady, Mary. Think now. That's five days already."

"No. He didn't. Of course he didn't."

"Would he usually?"

"If he can use the Office phone, yes."

"And if he can't?"

She thought for him. She really tried. She had been thinking for so long. "Yes," she conceded. "He'd phone. He likes to know we're all right, all the time. He's a worrier. I suppose that's why I went off with such a bang when he didn't show up. I think I was worried already."

Lumsden was stalking round the room in his stockinged feet, pretending to admire Mary's water-colours of Greece.

"You're so, so talented," he marvelled, his face pressed against a view of Plomari. "Did you go to art school or simply do it?"

She ignored him. So did Brotherhood. It was a tacit

bond between them. The only decent diplomat is a deaf
Trappist, Jack liked to say. Mary was beginning to agree.

"Where's the servant?" said Brotherhood.

"You told me to get rid of her. On the phone. When I
rang."

"She smell a rat?"

"I don't think so."

"It mustn't get out, Mary. We've got to sit on it as long as
we possibly can. You know that, don't you?"

"I guessed."

"There's his Joes to think of, there's everything to think
of. Far more than you can know. London's stiff with theories
and begging for time. You quite sure Lederer hasn't phoned?"

"Jesus," she said.

His eye fell on Harry, who was unpacking his clever
boxes. They were grey-green and possessed no apparent
controls. "You can tell the servant they're transformers," he
said.

"*Umformer*," Lumsden piped helpfully from the wings.
"Transformer is *Umformer*. '*Die kleinen Büchsen sind
Umformer*.'"

Once again they ignored him. Jack's German was almost
as good as Magnus's, and about three hundred times better
than Lumsden's.

"When's she due back?" Brotherhood asked.

"Who?"

"Your servant, for God's sake."

"Tomorrow lunchtime."

"Be a good girl and see if you can get her to stay away a
couple more days."

She went to the kitchen and phoned Frau Bauer's moth-
er in Salzburg. Sorry about the outrageous hour but with a
death that's how it goes, she said. Herr Pym is remaining in
London for a few days, she said. Why don't you take advantage of Herr Pym's absence and have a nice rest? she said.
When she came back it was Lumsden's turn to say his piece.
She got his drift immediately and after that she deliberately
stopped hearing him. "Just to fill in any awkward blanks,
Mary... So that we're all speaking the same language,
Mary... While Nigel is still closeted with Ambass... In case,
which God forbid, the odious press gets on to it before it's all
cleared up, Mary..." Lumsden had a cliché for every occa-

sion and a reputation for being nimble-minded. "Anyway, that's
the route Ambass would like us all to go," he ended, using the
very latest in daring jargon. "Not unless we're asked, naturally. But if we are. And Mary he sends terrific love. He's with
you all the way. And with Magnus too naturally. Terrific
condolences, all that."

"Just nothing to Lederer's crowd," said Brotherhood.
"Nothing to anyone but for God's sake nothing to Lederer.
There's no disappearance, nothing abnormal. He's gone back
to London to bury his father, he's staying on for talks at Head
Office. End of message."

"It's the same route I've been going already," Mary said,
appealing to Brotherhood as if Lumsden didn't exist. "It's just
that Magnus didn't apply for compassionate leave before
taking it."

"Yes, well now I think that's the part Ambass wants us
not to say, if you don't mind," said Lumsden, showing the
steel. "So I think we won't, please."

Brotherhood squared to him. Mary was family. Nobody
messed her around in front of Brotherhood, least of all some
overeducated flunkey from the Foreign Office.

"You've done your job," said Brotherhood. "Fade away,
will you? Now."

Lumsden left the way he had come, but faster.

Brotherhood turned back to Mary. They were alone. He
was as broad as an old blockhouse and, when he wanted to
be, as rough. His white forelock had fallen across his brow.
He put his hands on her hips the way he used to, and drew
her into him. "God damn it, Mary," he said as he held her.
"Magnus is my best boy. What the devil have you done with
him?"

From upstairs she heard the squeak of castors and another
loud thud. It's the bow-fronted chest of drawers. No, it's our
bed. Georgie and Fergus are taking a look round.

The desk was in the old servants' room next to the kitchen, a
sprawling, spidery half-cellar to which no servant had been
consigned for forty years. Near the window among Mary's
plant pots stood her easel and water-colours. Against the
wall, the old black-and-white television and the agonising sofa
for watching it. "There's nothing like a little discomfort,"

Magnus liked to say primly, "for deciding whether a programme
is worth its salt." In an alcove under lanes of piping stood the
ping-pong table where Mary did her bookbinding and on it
lay her hides and buckram and glues and clamps and threads
and marbled end-papers and powering knives, and the bricks
in Magnus's old socks that she used instead of lead weights,
and the wrecked volumes she had bought for a few schillings
at the flea market. Beside it, next to the defunct boiler, stood
the desk, the great, crazy Hapsburg desk bought for a song at
a sale in Graz, sawn up to get it through the door and glued
together again all by clever Magnus. Brotherhood pulled at
the drawers.

"Key?"

"Magnus must have taken it."

Brotherhood lifted his head. "Harry!"

Harry kept his lock picks on a chain the way other men
keep keys, and held his breath to help him listen while he
probed.

"Does he do all his homework here or is there somewhere else?"

"Daddy left him his old campaign table. Sometimes he
uses that."

"Where is it?"

"Upstairs."

"Where upstairs?"

"Tom's room."

"Keep his documents there too, does he? . . . Firm's
papers?"

"I don't think so. I don't know where."

Harry walked out smiling with his head down. Brotherhood pulled open a drawer.

"That's for the book he was writing," she said as he
extracted a meagre file. Magnus keeps everything inside
something. Everything must wear a disguise in order to be
real.

"Is it though?" He was pulling on his glasses, one red ear
at a time. He knows about the novel too, she thought,
watching him. He's not even pretending to be surprised.

"Yes." And you can put his bloody papers back where
you got them from, she thought. She did not like how cold he
had become, how hard.

"Gave up his sketching, did he? I thought you two were in that together."

"It didn't satisfy him. He decided he preferred the written word."

"Doesn't seem to have written much here. When did he switch?"

"On Lesbos. On holiday. He's not writing it yet. He's preparing."

"Oh." He began another page.

"He calls it a matrix."

"Does he though?"—still reading—"I must show some of this to Bo. He's a literary man."

"And when we retire—when he does—if he takes early retirement, he'll write, I'll paint and bookbind. That's the plan."

Brotherhood turned a page. "In Dorset?"

"At Plush. Yes."

"Well, he's taken early retirement all right," he remarked not very nicely as he resumed his reading. "Wasn't there sculpture, too, at some point?"

"It wasn't practical."

"I shouldn't think it was."

"You encourage those things, Jack. The Firm does. You're always saying we should have hobbies and recreations."

"What's the book about, then? Anything special?"

"He's still finding the line. He likes to keep it to himself."

"Listen to this: 'When the most horrible gloom was over the household; when Edward himself was in agony and behaving as prettily as he knew how.' Not even a main verb, far as I can make out."

"He didn't write that."

"It's in his handwriting, Mary."

"It's from something he read. When he reads a book he underlines things in pencil. Then when he's finished it he writes out his favourite bits."

From upstairs she heard a sharp snap like the cracking of timber or the firing of a pistol back in the days when she had been taught.

"That's Tom's room," she said. "They don't need to go in there."

"Get me a bag, dear," Brotherhood said. "A bin bag will do. Will you find me one?"

She went to the kitchen. Why do I let him do this to me? Why do I let him march into my house, my marriage and my mind and help himself to everything he doesn't like? Mary was not usually compliant. Tradesmen did not rob her twice. In the English school, the English church, in the Diplomatic Wives Association, she was regarded as quite the little shrew. Yet one hard stare of Jack Brotherhood's pale eyes, one growl of his rich, careless voice, was enough to send her running to him.

It's because he's so like Daddy, she decided. He loves our kind of England and the rest can go hang.

It's because I worked for Jack in Berlin when I was an empty-headed schoolgirl with one small talent. Jack was my older lover at a time when I thought I needed one.

It's because he steered Magnus through his divorce for me when he was dithering and gave him to me "for afters" as he called it.

It's because he loves Magnus too.

Brotherhood was flipping the pages of her desk diary.

"Who's P?" he demanded, tapping a page. "Twenty-fifth September, six-thirty p.m. 'P.' There's a P on the sixteenth too, Mary. That's not 'P' for Pym, is it, or am I being stupid again? Who's this P he's meeting?"

She began to hear the scream inside herself and had no whisky left to quell it. Of all the entries, the dozens and dozens, and he has to pick that one. "I don't know. A Joe. I don't know."

"You wrote it, didn't you?"

"Magnus asked me to. 'Put down I'm meeting P.' He didn't keep a diary of his own. He said it was insecure."

"And he made you write the entries for him."

"He said if anybody looked, they wouldn't know which were his dates and which were mine. It was part of sharing." She felt Brotherhood's stare. He's making me speak, she thought. He wants to hear the quaver in my voice.

"Sharing what?"

"His work."

"Explain."

"He couldn't tell me what he was doing, but he could show me that he was doing it and when."

"Did he say that?"

"I could feel it."

"What could you feel?"

"That he was proud! He wanted me to know!"

"Know what?"

Brotherhood could drive her mad even when she knew he meant to. "Know that he had another life! An important one. That he was being used."

"By us?"

"By you, Jack. By the Firm! Who do you think—the Americans?"

"Why do you say that—the Americans? Did he have a thing about them?"

"Why should he? He served in Washington."

"Needn't stop him. Might even encourage him. Did you know the Lederers in Washington?"

"Of course we did."

"But better here, eh? I hear she's quite an armful."

He was turning forward to the days yet to be endured. Tomorrow and the day after. To the weekend, which was already gaping at her like a hole in her shattered universe.

"Mind if I keep this?" he asked.

Mary damn well did mind. She possessed no spare diary and no spare life either. She snatched it back and let him wait while she copied out her future on a sheet of paper: Drinks Lederer... dinner Dinkels... Tom's school term ends. ... She came to "meet P" and left it out.

"Why's this drawer empty?" he asked.

"I didn't know it was."

"So what was it full of?"

"Old photographs. Mementoes. Nothing."

"How long's it been empty?"

"I don't know, Jack. I don't know! Get off my back, will you?"

"Did he put papers in his suitcase?"

"I didn't watch him pack."

"Did you hear him down here while he was packing?"

"Yes."

The telephone rang. Mary's hand shot out to take it, but Brotherhood was already grasping her wrist. Still holding her, he leaned towards the door and yelled for Harry while the phone went on ringing. It was rising four a.m. already. Who the hell calls at four in the morning except Magnus? Inside herself Mary was praying so loud she hardly heard Brotherhood's shout. The phone kept calling her, and she knew now that nothing mattered except Magnus and her family.

"It might be Tom!" she shouted while she struggled. "Let go, damn you!"

"It might be Lederer, too."

Harry must have flown downstairs. She counted two more rings before he was standing in the doorway.

"Trig this call," Brotherhood ordered, loud and slow. Harry vanished. Brotherhood released Mary's hand. "Make it very, very long, Mary. Spread it right out. You know how to play those games. Do it."

She lifted the phone and said, "Pym residence."

Nobody answered. Brotherhood was conducting her with his powerful hands, willing her, pressing her to talk. She heard a metallic ping and crammed her hand over the mouthpiece. "It could be a call code," she breathed. She held up one finger for one ping. Then a second. Then a third. It was a call code. They had used them in Berlin: two for this, three for that. Private and prearranged between the Joe and base. She opened her eyes to Brotherhood to say what shall I do? He shook his head to say I don't know either.

Speak, he mouthed.

Mary drew a deep breath. "Hullo? Speak up, please." She took refuge in German. "This is the residence of Counsellor Magnus Pym of the British Embassy. Who is that? Will you speak, please? Mr. Pym is not here at the moment. If you wish to leave a message, you may do so. Otherwise, please call later. Hullo?"

More, Brotherhood was urging. Give me more. She recited her telephone number in German and again in English. The line was open and she could hear a noise like traffic and a noise like scratchy music played at half speed, but no more pings. She repeated the number in English. "Speak up, please. The line is dreadful. Hullo. Can you hear me? Who's that calling, please? Do—please—speak—up." Then she couldn't help herself. Her eyes closed and she screamed, "Magnus, for God's sake say where you are!" But Brotherhood was miles ahead of her. With a lover's knowledge he had felt her outburst coming and clapped his hand over the cradle.

"Too short, sir," Harry lamented from the doorway. "I'd need another minute at the least."

"Was it foreign?" Brotherhood said.

"Could be foreign, could be next door, sir."

"That was naughty, Mary. Don't do those things again. We're on the same side in this and I'm boss."

"Someone's kidnapped him," she said. "I know they have."

Everything froze: herself, his pale eyes, even Harry in the doorway. "Well, well," said Brotherhood at last. "That would make you feel better, would it? A kidnapping? Now why do you say that, dear? What's worse than kidnapping, I wonder?"

Trying to meet his gaze Mary experienced a violent time warp. I don't know anything. I want Plush. Give me back the land that Sam and Daddy died for. She saw herself as a school-leaver seated in front of the careers mistress in the middle of her last term. A second woman is with her, London and tough. "This lady is a recruiting officer for the Foreign Service, dear," says the careers mistress. "A special bit of it," says the tough woman. "She's terribly impressed by the way you *draw*, dear," says the careers mistress. "She so admires your draughtsmanship, as we all do. She wonders whether you'd be interested in taking your folder to London for a day or two, so that some other people can look at it." "It's for your country, dear," the tough woman says with meaning, to the child of English patriots.

She remembered the training house in East Anglia, girls like herself, our class. She remembered the jolly lessons in copying and engraving and colouring, in papers and cardboards and linens and threads, how to make watermarks and how to alter them, how to cut rubber stamps, how to make paper look older and how to make it look younger, and she tried to remember just when it was exactly that they had realised they were being taught to forge documents for British spies. And she saw herself standing before Jack Brotherhood in his rickety upstairs office in Berlin, not a stone's throw from the Wall, Jack the Stripper, Jack the Stoat, Jack the Black and all the other Jacks he was known as. Jack who had charge of Berlin Station and liked to meet all newcomers

personally, particularly if they were pretty girls of twenty.
She remembered his bleached gaze running slowly over her
body while he guessed her shape and sexual weight and she
remembered again hating him on sight, as she was trying to
hate him now as she watched him flip through a folder of
family correspondence he had pulled from the desk.

"You realise half of those are Tom's letters from boarding-
school, I suppose," she said.

"Why doesn't he write to both of you?"

"He does write to both of us, Jack. Tom and I have
one correspondence. Magnus and Tom have a separate
correspondence."

"No interconsciousness," said Brotherhood, using a bit of
trade talk he had taught her in Berlin. He lit one of his fat
yellow cigarettes and watched her theatrically through the
flame. There's a poseur in all of them, she thought. Magnus
and Grant included.

"You're absurd," she said in nervous anger.

"It's an absurd situation and Nigel will be here any
minute to make it more absurd still. What caused it?" He
opened another drawer.

"His father. If it's a situation at all."

"Whose camera's this?"

"Tom's. But we all use it."

"Any other cameras around?"

"No. If Magnus needs one for his work he brings it from
the Embassy."

"Any here from the Embassy now?"

"No."

"Maybe his father caused it or maybe a lot of things did.
Maybe a marital tiff I don't know about caused it."

He was examining the camera's settings, turning it over
in his big hands as if he were thinking of buying it.

"We don't have them," she said.

His knowing eyes lifted to her. "How do you manage
that?"

"He doesn't offer a fight, that's why."

"You do though. You're a right little demon when you get
going, Mary."

"Not any more," she said, mistrusting his charm.

"You never met his dad, did you?" said Brotherhood as

he wound the film through the camera. "There was something about him, I seem to remember."

"They were estranged."

"Ah."

"Nothing dramatic. They'd drifted apart. They're that sort of family."

"What sort, dear?"

"Scattered. Business people. He'd said he'd let them in on his first marriage and once was enough. We hardly talked about it."

"Tom go along with that?"

"Tom's a child."

"Tom was the last person Magnus saw before he vanished, Mary. Apart from the porter at his club."

"So arrest him," Mary suggested rudely.

Dropping the film into the bin bag Brotherhood picked up Magnus's little transistor radio.

"This the new one they do with all the shortwave on it?"

"I believe so."

"Take it with him on holiday, did he?"

"Yes, he did."

"Listen to it regularly?"

"Since, as you once told me, he runs Czechoslovakia single-handed out here, it would be fairly startling if he didn't."

He switched it on. A male voice was reading the news in Czech. Brotherhood stared blankly at the wall while he let it continue for what seemed like hours. He switched off the radio and put it in the bag. His gaze lifted to the uncurtained window, but it was still a long while before he spoke. "Not displaying too many lights for the time of morning, are we, Mary?" he asked distractedly. "Don't want to set neighbours chattering, do we?"

"They know Rick's dead. They know it's not a normal time."

"You can say that again."

I hate him. I always did. Even when I fell for him—when he was taking me up and down the scale and I was weeping and thanking him—I still hated him. Tell me about the night in question, he was saying. He meant the night they heard of Rick's death. She told it to him exactly as she had rehearsed it.

* * *

He had found the cloakroom and was standing before the
worn dufflecoat that hung between Tom's loden and Mary's
sheepskin. He was feeling in the pockets. The din from
upstairs was monotonous. He extracted a grimy handkerchief
and a half-consumed roll of Polo mints.

"You're teasing me," he said.

"All right, I'm teasing you."

"Two hours in the freezing snow in his dancing pumps,
Mary? In the middle of the night? Brother Nigel will think
I'm making it up. What did he do in them?"

"Walked."

"Where to, dear?"

"He didn't tell me."

"Ask him?"

"No, I didn't."

"Then how do you know he didn't take a cab?"

"He'd no money. His wallet and change were upstairs in
the dressing-room with his keys." Brotherhood replaced the
handkerchief and mints in the duffle.

"And none in here?"

"No."

"How d'you know?"

"He's methodical in those things."

"Maybe he paid the other end."

"No."

"Maybe someone picked him up."

"No."

"Why not?"

"He's a walker and he was in shock. That's why. His
father was dead, even if he didn't particularly like him. It
builds up in him. The tension or whatever it is. So he walks."
And I hugged him when he came back, she thought. I felt the
cold on his cheek and the trembling of his chest and the hot
sweat clean through his coat from his hours of walking. And
I'll hug him again, as soon as he comes through that door. "I
said to him: 'Don't go. Not tonight. Get drunk. We'll get
drunk together.' But he went. He had his look." She wished
she hadn't said that, but for a moment she was as cross with
Magnus as she was with Brotherhood.

"What look is that, Mary? 'Had his look.' I don't think I follow you."

"Empty. Like an actor without a part."

"A *part*? His father takes up and *dies* and Magnus doesn't have a *part* any more? What the hell does that mean?"

He's closing in on me, she thought, resolutely not answering. In a minute I'm going to feel his sure hands on me, and I'm going to lie back and let it happen because I can't think of any more excuses.

"Ask Grant," she said, trying to hurt him. "He's our tame psychologist. He'll know."

They had moved to the drawing-room. He was waiting for something. So was she. For Nigel, for Pym, for the telephone. For Georgie and Fergus upstairs.

"You're not doing too much of this, are you?" Brotherhood asked, pouring her another whisky.

"Of course not. When I'm alone, almost never."

"Well, don't. It's too damn easy. And when Brother Nigel's here, nothing. Keep it under wraps completely. Yes, Jack?"

"Yes, Jack." You're a lecherous priest scavenging the last of God's grace, she told him, watching his slow purposeful movements as he filled his own glass. First the wine, now the water. Now lower your eyelids and lift the chalice for a sanctimonious word with Him who sent you.

"And he's free," he remarked. "'I'm free.' Rick's dead, so Magnus is free. He's one of your Freudian types who can't say 'Father.'"

"It's perfectly normal at his age. To call a father by his Christian name. More normal still, if you haven't seen each other for fifteen years."

"I do like you to defend him," Brotherhood said. "I admire your loyalty. So will they. And you never let me down. I know you didn't."

Loyalty, she thought. Keeping my silly mouth shut round the Station in case your wife finds out.

"And you wept. Quite the old weeper, you are, Mary, I didn't know. Mary weeps, Magnus consoles her. Odd, that, to the casual observer, seeing as how Rick was *his* daddy, not yours. A rôle reversal with a vengeance, that is: you doing his mourning for him. Who were the tears for exactly? Any idea?"

"His father had died, Jack. I didn't sit down and say 'I'll cry for Rick, I'll cry for Magnus.' I just cried."

"I thought it might be for yourself."

"What's that supposed to mean?"

"You're the one person you didn't mention. That's all. Defensive: that's how you sound."

"I am not being defensive!"

She was too loud. She knew it and once more so did Brotherhood and he was interested.

"And when Magnus is done with consoling Mary," he continued, picking a book from the table and flipping through it, "he slips on his duffle and he goes for a walk in his dancing pumps. You try to restrain him—you beg him, which is hard for me to visualise, but I'll try—but no, he will go. Any phone calls before he leaves?"

"No."

"No incoming, no outgoing?"

"I said no!"

"Direct dial, after all, you'd think a bereaved man would want to share the bad news with other members of his family."

"They're not that kind of family. I told you."

"There's Tom for a start. What about him?"

"It was much too late to ring Tom and anyway Magnus thought it better to tell him himself."

He was looking at the book. "Another gem he's underlined. 'If I am not for myself who is for me; and being for my own self what am I? If not now when?' Well, well. I'm enlightened. Are you?"

"No."

"Nor am I. He's free." He closed the book and put it back on the table. "He didn't take anything with him on his walk, did he? Like a briefcase?"

"A newspaper."

You're going deaf. Admit it. You're worried that a hearing-aid will spoil your self-image. Speak, damn you!

She *had* said it. She knew she had. She had been waiting all evening to say it, prepared it from every possible angle, practised it, rehearsed it, denied it, forgotten it, revived it. And now it was echoing in her head like an explosion while she took a frightfully careless pull at her whisky. Yet his eyes, straight at her, were still waiting.

"A newspaper," she repeated. "Just a newspaper. What of it?"

"Which newspaper?"

"The *Presse*."

"That's a daily."

"Correct. *Die Presse* is a daily."

"A local daily newspaper. And Magnus took it with him. To read in the dark. Dressed in his dancing pumps. Tell me about it."

"I just did, Jack."

"No, you didn't. And you're going to have to, Mary, because when we get the heavy guns here you're going to need all the help you can get."

She had perfect recall. Magnus was standing by the door, a step from where Brotherhood stood now. He was pale and untouchable, the dufflecoat flung crookedly over his shoulders while he glared round in stiff phases: fireplace, wife, clock, books. She heard herself telling him the things she had already recounted to Brotherhood, but more of them. For God's sake, Magnus, stay. Don't get the blacks, stay. Don't sink into one of your moods. Stay. Make love. Get drunk. If you want company, I'll get Grant and Bee back, or we'll go there. She saw him smile his rigid, bright-lit smile. She heard him put on his awfully easy voice. His Lesbos voice. And she heard herself repeat his words exactly, to Brotherhood, now.

"He said, 'Mabs, where's the bloody paper, darling?' I thought he meant *The Times* for looking at the Scottish property market, so I said, 'Wherever you put it when you brought it back from the Embassy.'"

"But he didn't mean *The Times*," said Brotherhood.

"He went over to the rack—there—" She looked at it but didn't point, because she was terrified of giving too much importance to the gesture. "And helped himself. To *Die Presse*. From the rack, where the *Presse* is kept. Till the end of each week. He likes me to keep the back numbers. Then he walked out," she ended, making it all sound perfectly normal, which of course it was.

"Did he look at it at all when he took it out?"

"Just the date. To check."

"What did you suppose he wanted it for?"

"Maybe there was a late-night film." Magnus had never gone to a late-night film in his life. "Maybe he wanted something to read in the café." With no money on him, she thought, as she filled the void of Brotherhood's silence. "Maybe he was looking for distraction. As we all might be. Have been. Anyone might when they're bereaved."

"Or free," Brotherhood suggested. But he did not otherwise help her.

"Anyway, he was so upset he took the wrong day's," she said brightly, clinching the matter.

"You looked, did you, dear?"

"Only when I was throwing away."

"When were you doing that?"

"Yesterday."

"Which one did he take?"

"Monday's. It was all of three days old. So I mean obviously he was in considerable shock."

"Obviously."

"All right, his father wasn't the great love of his life. But he was still dead. Nobody's rational when a thing like that happens. Not even Magnus."

"So what did he do next? After he'd looked at the date and taken the wrong day's?"

"He went out. As I told you. For a walk. You don't listen. You never did."

"Did he fold it?"

"Really, Jack! What does it matter how somebody carries a newspaper?"

"Just tuck in your ego a minute and answer. What did he do with it?"

"Rolled it."

"And then?"

"Nothing. He carried it. In his hand."

"Did he carry it back again?"

"Here to the house? No."

"How do you know he didn't?"

"I was waiting for him in the hall."

"And you noticed: no newspaper. No rolled newspaper, you said to yourself."

"Purely incidentally, yes."

"Incidentally nothing, Mary. You had it in your mind to look. You knew he'd gone out with it and you spotted at once he'd come back without it. That's not incidental. That's spying on him."

"Please yourself."

He was angry. "It's you who's going to have to do the pleasing, Mary," he said, loud and slow. "You're going to have to please Brother Nigel in about five minutes from now. They're in spasm, Mary. They can see the ground opening up at their feet again and they do not know what to do. They literally do not know what to do." His anger passed. Jack could do that. "And later—as soon as you had a chance—you incidentally searched his pockets. And it wasn't there."

"I didn't *look* for it, I simply noticed it was missing. And yes, it wasn't there."

"Does he often go out with old newspapers?"

"When he needs to keep abreast—for his work—he's a conscientious officer—he takes a newspaper with him."

"Rolled up?"

"Sometimes."

"Bring them back ever?"

"Not that I remember."

"Ever remark on it to him?"

"No."

"He to you?"

"Jack. It's a habit he has. Look, I'm not going to have a marital row with you!"

"We're not married."

"He rolls up a newspaper and walks with it. The way a child carries a stick or something. As a comforter or something. Like his Polos. There. He had Polos in his pocket. It's the same thing."

"Always the wrong date?"

"Not always—don't make so much of everything!"

"And always loses it?"

"Jack, stop. Just stop. Okay?"

"Does he do it on any special occasion? Full moon? Last Wednesday of the month? Or only when his father dies? Have you noticed a pattern to it? Go on, Mary, you have!"

Beat me, she thought. Grab me. Anything is better than that ice-cold stare.

"It's sometimes when he meets P," she said, trying to sound as if she were pacifying a spoilt child. "Jack, for God's sake, he runs Joes, he lives that life, you trained him! I don't ask him what his tricks are, what he's doing with who. I'm trained too!"

"And when he came back—how was he?"

"He was absolutely fine. Calm, completely calm. He'd walked it out of himself, I could feel. He was absolutely fine in every way."

"No phone calls while he was out?"

"No."

"None after?"

"One. Very late. But we didn't answer it."

It was not often she had seen Jack surprised. Now he almost was. "You didn't answer it?"

"Why should we?"

"Why shouldn't you? It's his job, as you said. His father had just died. Why shouldn't you answer the phone?"

"Magnus said don't."

"*Why* did he say don't?"

"We were making love!" she said, and felt like the worst whore ever.

Harry was looming in the doorway again. He was wearing blue overalls and had a red face from his exertions. He was holding a long screwdriver in his hand and he looked shamefully joyful.

"Care to pop upstairs a jiffy, Mr. Brotherhood?" he said.

It's like our bedroom before the Diplomatic Wives' jumble sale, with our cast-off clothes all over the bed, she thought. "Magnus, darling, do you really need three worn-out cardigans?" Clothes over the chairs. Over the dressing-table and the towel-horse. My summer blazer that I haven't worn since Berlin. Magnus's dinner-jacket hung from the cheval mirror like a drying hide. There was nothing on the floor because there was no floor. Fergus and Georgie had removed the carpet and most of the floorboards underneath it, and stacked them like sandwiches beneath the window, leaving the joists and the odd plank for a walkway. They had taken the bedside lamps to pieces and the bedside furniture and the telephone and the wake-up wireless. In the bathroom, it was the floor again, and the panel to the bath, and the medicine chest, and the sloped attic door that led to the sloped attic where Tom had hidden for a whole half hour last Christmas playing

Murder, and nearly died of fright from being so brave. At the basin, Georgie was working her way through Mary's things. Her face-cream. Her diaphragm.

"What's yours is his, for them, dear, and vice versa," said Brotherhood as they paused to stare in from the doorless doorway. "There's no his and hers, not for them—there can't be."

"Not for you either," she said.

Tom's bedroom was across the corridor from theirs. His luminous Superman lay sprawled over the bed, together with his thirty-one Smurfs and three Tiggers. Her father's campaign table was folded against the wall. The toy chest had been pulled to the centre of the floor, revealing the marble fireplace behind. It was a fine fireplace. Works Department had wanted to board it over to reduce draughts but Magnus hadn't let them. Instead he had bought this old chest to put across the opening, leaving the mantel visible over it, so that Tom could have a bit of old Vienna all his own. Now the fireplace stood free and the girl Georgie knelt respectfully before it in her fifty-guinea freedom fighter's tunic. And before Georgie lay a white shoe box with its lid off, and inside the shoe box was a rag bundle, then several smaller bundles around it.

"We found it on the ledge up above the grate, sir," said Fergus. "Where it joins the main flue."

"Not a speck of dust on it," said Georgie.

"Reach up and it's there," said Fergus. "Dead handy."

"You don't even have to shove the chest out really, once you get the knack," said Georgie.

"Seen it before?" Brotherhood asked.

"It's obviously something of Tom's," said Mary. "Children will hide anything."

"Seen it before?" Brotherhood repeated.

"No."

"Know what's in it?"

"How could I if I haven't seen it?"

"Easily."

Brotherhood did not stoop but held his arms out. Georgie passed the box up to him and Brotherhood took it to the table where Tom did his Spirograph and his Lego and his endless drawings of German aeroplanes being shot down against a Plush sunset, with family in the background, everybody waving, everybody absolutely fine. Brotherhood picked out the biggest bundle first and they looked on while he started to unwrap it and changed his mind.

"Here," he said, handing it to Georgie. "Woman's fingers."

She's one of his mistresses, Mary suddenly realised. She wondered why on earth it hadn't dawned on her before.

Georgie rose elegantly to her full height, one leg, other leg, and having fixed her straight hair behind her ears, applied her woman's fingers to unwinding the strips of bedsheet that Magnus had said he wanted for the car, revealing at last a small, clever-looking camera with a clever steel harness round it. And after the camera a thing like a telescope with a bracket on it which, when you pulled it to its full length, made a stand that you could screw the camera to, face downwards and at a fixed distance, for photographing documents on your father-in-law's campaign table. After the telescope came a succession of films and lenses and filters and rings and other bits of equipment she could not identify offhand. And underneath these a pad of flimsy cloth-paper with columns of numbers on the top sheet and thickly rubberised edges so that you could only see the top page. Mary knew the type of paper. She had worked on it in Berlin. It shrivelled into fern the moment you put a match near it. The pad was half used. Underneath the pad again, an aged cardboard-backed military jotting pad marked "W.D. Property," standing for War Department and consisting of unwritten-on lined paper of blotchy wartime quality. And inside it, when Brotherhood continued searching, two pressed red flowers of great age, poppies, but just possibly roses, she was not entirely certain, and anyway by then she was shouting.

"It's for the Firm! It's for his work for you!"

"Of course it is. I'll tell Nigel. No problem."

"Just because he didn't tell me about it, it doesn't mean it's wrong! It's for in case he gets landed with documents in the house! At weekends!" And then, realising what she had said: "It's for his Joes—if they bring him documents, you fool! If Grant does, and he's got to turn them round at short notice! What's so fucking sinister about that?"

Fergus was fingering the half-used pad, turning it over and over, tilting it in the beam of Tom's Anglepoise lamp.

"Looks more like your Czech, sir, frankly," said Fergus, tilting the pad to the light. "It could be Russian but I think

Czech's more likely, frankly. Yes," he said pleasantly as his eye caught some unexplained feature of the rubber edge. "That's it. Czech. Mind you, that's only where they're made. Who's dishing them out is another matter. Specially these days."

Brotherhood was more interested in the pressed flowers. He had laid them on his palm and was staring at them as if they told his future.

"I think you're a bad girl, Mary," he said deliberately. "I think you know a lot more than you told me. I don't think he's in Ireland or the bloody Bahamas. I think that was a lot of smoke. I think he's a bad man and I'm wondering whether you're bad together."

All constraint left her. She screamed "You shit!" and hit at him with her open hand but he blocked her. He put an arm round her and swung her off the ground as if she had no legs left. He carted her across the corridor to Frau Bauer's bedroom which was the only room that hadn't so far been ripped apart. He dumped her on the bed and whisked her shoes off exactly as he used to in the squalid safe flat where he did his screwing. He rolled her into the eiderdown, making a straitjacket of it. Then he lay on her, grappling her into submission while Georgie and Fergus looked on. But somehow, amazingly, throughout all these antics and dramatics, Jack Brotherhood had still contrived to keep hold of the two pressed poppies in his left fist, and kept hold of them even when the doorbell went again, one long peal for authority.

4

"To be above the fray," Pym wrote to himself on a separate sheet of paper. "A writer is King. He should look down with love upon his subject, even when the subject is himself."

Life began with Lippsie, Tom, and Lippsie happened long before you came along or anyone else did, and long before Pym was what the Firm calls of marriageable age.

Before Lippsie all Pym remembered was an aimless trek through different-coloured houses and a lot of shouting. After her everything seemed to flow in the one unstoppable direction and all he had to do was sit in his boat and let the current carry him. From Lippsie to Poppy, from Rick to Jack, it was all one jolly stream, however much it wriggled and divided itself along the way. And not only life but death began with her as well, for it was actually Lippsie's dead body that got Pym going, though he never saw it. Others saw it, and Pym could have made the journey because it was in the bell yard and no one covered it for ages. But the little fellow was going through a squeamish and self-centred period at the time and had a notion that if he didn't see it she might not be dead after all, but pretending. Or that her death was a judgment upon himself for taking part in the recent killing of a squirrel in the empty swimming-pool. The hunt had been led by a wall-eyed maths master called Corbo the Crow. When the squirrel was safely trapped, Corbo sent three boys down the pool ladder with hockey sticks, and Pym was one. "On you go, Pymmie. Give it to him!" Corbo urged. Pym had watched the crippled creature limp towards him. Scared by its pain he had caught it a great swipe, harder than he meant. He had seen it catapult to the next player and lie still. "Good man, Pymmie! Good shot."

His other thought was that the Sefton Boyd gang had made the whole thing up to tease him, always possible. So as a stopgap Pym gave himself the desk job of gathering descriptions and forming, in that first rush before the school went silent, a mind's picture of her that was probably as clear as anybody's. She lay in a running position, sideways on the flagstones, her forward hand punched towards the finishing line and her rear foot pointing the wrong way. Sefton Boyd, who made the original sighting and alerted the Headmaster during school breakfast, actually thought she *was* running, he said, until he saw the wonky foot. He thought she was doing a special exercise on her side, a sort of kicking, bicycling exercise. And he thought the blood round her was a cape or a towel that she was lying on until he noticed how the old chestnut leaves stuck to it and wouldn't blow away. He didn't go close because bell yard was out of bounds, even to sixth-formers, on account of the dangerous roof above it. And he didn't throw up, he boasted, because us Sefton Boyds own simply masses of land and I've done a lot of shooting with my father and I'm accustomed to seeing blood and innards all the time. But he did run up sixth-form staircase to the tower window, which the police said later was where she had fallen from; she must have been leaning out to do something. And it must have been something urgent and important she was leaning out for because she had been wearing her nightdress, having bicycled up the mile-long drive from the Overflow House in the middle of the night. Her bicycle with its tartan cover on the saddle was still leaning against the dustbin shed behind the kitchens.

Sefton Boyd's theory, excitedly culled from his father's life-style, was that she was drunk. Except that he didn't call her "she" but "Shitlips," which was his gang's witty play on Lippschitz. But then again, as he had been suggesting for some time, Shitlips may have been a German spy who had slipped up the tower to send messages after blackout, sir. Because from tower window you can see right the way across the valley to the Brace of Partridges, so it would be a wizard place for signalling to German bombers, sir. The trouble was she had no light with her except her bike lamp, which was still securely on the handlebars. So perhaps she had hidden it in her vagina, which Sefton Boyd claimed to have seen clearly because the fall had ripped her nightdress off.

Thus the stories went round that morning while Pym stood on the fine wood seat of the staff lavatory which he had made his safe house after the first furore, and held his breath and blushed and turned white in front of the mirror in a series of puzzled efforts to make his face appropriate to his grief. Using the Swiss Army penknife from his pocket, he had sawn off a bit of his forelock as a sort of useless tribute, then loitered, fiddling with the taps and hoping someone was looking for him. Where's Pym? Pym's run away! Pym's dead, too! But Pym hadn't run away, nor was he dead, and in the chaos of having Lippsie's body lying in bell yard and ambulance and police arriving, nobody was looking for anybody, least of all in the staff lavatory which was the most out-of-bounds place in the school, so forbidden that Sefton Boyd himself was in awe of it. Classes were cancelled and what you were supposed to do after all the shouting and the clamour was go quietly to your form room and revise—unless, like Pym, you were in the second form which overlooked bell yard, in which case

you were to go to the arts hall. This was the converted Nissen
hut built by Canadian soldiers where Lippsie taught music
and painting and drama and held remedial exercises for boys
with flat feet. It was also where she did her typing and
paperwork in her capacity as school dogsbody: collecting
school fees, paying school bills for the Bursar, ordering taxis
for boys in confirmation class and, as such people do, just
about running the place single-handed and unthanked. But
Pym wouldn't go to the arts hall either, though he had a
half-finished balsa model of a Dornier to work on with his
penknife, as well as a half-made plan to copy out some
obscure poems from an old book there and claim they were
his own. What he had to do, when he found his courage and
the moment, was get back to the Overflow House where he
had lived till now with Lippsie and the eleven other Overflow
Boys. Until he had done that and done something about the
letters, he daren't go anywhere because Rick would go back
to prison.

How he had got himself into this pass, how he had
acquired the training that was to stand him in such fine stead
in this, his first clandestine operation, was pretty much the
story of his life this far, which was ten years and three terms
of boarding-school old.

Even today, trying to trace Lippsie through Pym's life is like
pursuing an errant light through an impenetrable thicket. For
Perce Loft, now dead himself, she was simply deniable—
"Titch's figment" he called her, meaning my invention, my
fabrication, my nothing. But Perce the great lawyer could have
made a figment out of the Eiffel Tower after he had banged
his nose on it, if he needed to. That was his job. And this
despite the testimony of Syd and others that it was Perce
himself who first had the use of her, Perce who had introduced her to the court back in the dark ages before Pym's
birth. Mr. Muspole, that marvel with the books—also now
passed on—understandably backed Perce up. He would. He
was up to his neck in the business himself. Even Syd, the one
surviving source, is not much more helpful. She was a German Four-by-Two, he said, using the affectionate cockney
rhyming slang for Jew. He thought she came from Munich,
could have been Vienna. She was lonely, Titch. Adored the

kids. Adored you. He didn't say she adored Rick but in the court that was taken for granted. She was a Lovely and in court ethic that was what Lovelies were there for: to be seen right by Rick and to bathe in his glory. And Rick in his goodness had her learn secretarial and qualify, says Syd. And your Dorothy, she thought the world of Lippsie and taught her English, which was meant, says Syd—after which he clams up, remarking only that it was a shame and we should all learn from it, and maybe your dad worked her a bit too hard because she never had your advantages. Yes, he admits, she was a looker. And she had a drop of class to her which some of the others, let's face it, didn't always have, Titch. And she loved a joke till she started to think of her poor family and what had been done to them by those Jerries.

My furtive record checks have not been more enlightening. Finding myself with the run of Registry during a stint as night duty officer not too many years back, I chased Lippschitz, first name Annie, right through the general index but drew a blank on all spellings. Old Dinkel in Vienna, who heads up the personnel side of the Austrian service, recently ran a similar search for me when I spun him a story; so, on another occasion, did his German counterpart in Cologne. Both reported no trace.

In my memory, however, she is anything but no trace. She is a tall, soft-haired, vital girl with large scared eyes and an air of flounce about her stride, nothing happening slowly. And I remember—it must have been a summer holiday in some house where we were temporarily sheltering—I remember how Pym longed more than anything to see her naked, and devoted his waking hours to contriving it. Which Lippsie must have guessed somehow for one afternoon she suggested he share her bath with her to save hot water. She even measured the water with her hand: patriots were allowed five inches and Lippsie was never less than a patriot. She stooped, naked, and let me watch her while she put her hand's span in the tub, I'm sure she did, and brought it out again: "See, Magnus!"—showing me the wet spread hand—"how we may be sure we do not help the Germans."

Or so I fervently believe, though try as I may I cannot to this day remember what she looked like. And I know that in the same house or one like it her room was opposite to Pym's own across a corridor, and that it contained her cardboard suitcase and photographs of her bearded brother and solemn sisters in black hats and silver frames which stood like tiny polished gravestones on her dressing-table. And there was the room where she screamed at Rick and warned him she would rather die than be a thief, and where Rick laughed his brown rich laugh, the one that went on longer than it needed and made everything all right again until next time. And though I do not remember a single lesson, she must have taught Pym German because years later when he came to learn the language formally he discovered that he possessed a repository of information about her—*Aaron war mein Bruder. Mein Vater war Architekt*—all in the same past tense to which she herself by then belonged. He also realised still later in life that when she had called him her *Mönchlein* she had meant her "little monk" and was referring to the hard path of Martin Luther—"little monk, go your own way"—whereas at the time he had thought she had cast him as the organ-grinder's tethered monkey and Rick as his organ-grinder. The discovery raised his self-respect no end, until he realised she had been telling him that he must get along without her.

And I know she was in Paradise with us because without Lippsie there was no Paradise. Paradise was a golden land between Gerrard's Cross and the sea, where Dorothy wore an angora pullover for her ironing and a blue ulster for her shopping. Paradise was where Rick and Dorothy fled after their runaway marriage, a Metroland of new beginnings and exciting futures, but I don't remember a day of it without Lippsie flouncing somewhere at the edge, or telling me what was right and wrong in a voice I didn't mind. One hour eastward by Bentley motorcar lay Town and in Town lay the West End and that was where Rick had his office; the office had a big tinted photograph of Granddad TP wearing his mayor's necklace, and the office was what kept Rick late at night, which was the infant Pym's best thing because he was allowed to climb into Dorothy's bed and keep her warm, she was so small and shivery even to a child. Sometimes Lippsie stayed behind with us, sometimes she went to London with Rick because she had to qualify and, as I now understand, justify her own survival when so many of her kind were dead.

Paradise was a string of shiny racehorses that Syd called "neverwozzers" and a succession of even shinier Bentleys which, like the houses, wore out as fast as the credit they were bought on and had to be changed with thrilling rapidity for yet newer and more expensive models. Sometimes the Bentleys were so precious they had actually to be driven round the side of the house and hidden in the back garden for fear they might become tarnished by the gaze of the Unfaithful. At other times Pym drove them at a thousand miles an hour sitting on Rick's lap, down sandy unmade roads lined with cement mixers, hammering the big deep horn at the builders while Rick shouted "How are you, boys?" and invited them all back to the house for a glass of bubbly. And Lippsie was there beside us in the passenger seat, straight as a coachman and as distant, until Rick chose to speak to her or make a joke. Then her smile was like holiday sunshine and she loved us both.

Paradise was also St. Moritz where Swiss Army penknives come from, though somehow the Bentleys and those two pre-war winters in Switzerland become fused in my memory as one place. Even today I have only to sniff the leather interior of a grand car and I am wafted willingly away to the great hotel drawing-rooms of St. Moritz in the wake of Rick's riotous love of festival. The Kulm, the Suvretta House, the Grand—Pym knew them as a single gigantic palace with different sets of servants but always the same court: Rick's private household of jesters, tumblers, counsellors, and jockeys; he barely went anywhere without them. In the daytime, Italian doormen with long brooms flipped the snow off your boots every time you went through the swing doors. In the evenings, while Rick and the court banqueted with local Lovelies and Dorothy was too tired, Pym would venture on Lippsie's hand through snowy alleys clutching his penknife in his pocket while he pretended to himself he was some kind of Russian prince protecting her from everyone who laughed at her for being serious. And in the morning after an early levee, he would tiptoe unescorted to the landing and gaze down through the banisters on his army of serfs toiling in the great hall below him, while he sniffed the stale cigar smoke and women's perfume and the wax polish that glistened like dew on the parquet as they buffed it with long sweeps of their mops. And that was how Rick's Bentleys smelt ever after: of the Lovelies, of beeswax, of the smoke of his millionaires' cigars. And very faintly, from sledge rides through the freezing forest at Lippsie's side, of the cold and the horse dung, while she chatted away in German to the coachman.

Back home again, and Paradise was pyramids of polished tangerines in silver paper, and pink chandeliers in the dining-room and roaring visits to distant racetracks to flash our Owners' badges and watch the neverwozzers lose, and a tiny black-and-white television set in a huge mahogany case that showed the boat race behind a sky of white spots, and when we watched the Grand National the horses were so far off that Pym wondered how they ever found their way home, but I'm afraid now that Rick's very often didn't which was why Syd called them neverwozzers. And cricket in the garden with Syd, sixpence if he didn't get Titch out in six balls. And boxing in the drawing-room with Morrie Washington, the court expert on the Fight Game, for Morrie was our Minister for the Arts: he had spoken to Bud Flanagan and shaken hands with Joe Louis, he had played conjuror's stooge for the Man with X-Ray Eyes. And having half-crowns pulled out of your ears by Mr. Muspole the great accountant, though Mr. Muspole was never my favourite; there was too much of making me do arithmetic in my head. And watching sugar-knobs vanish from under Perce Loft's legal Homburg: they were being turned to figments before my very eyes. And piggybacks round the garden on the waistcoated shoulders of the jockeys, who had names like Billie and Jimmy and Gordon and Charlie and were the best magic-makers in the world, the best elves, and read all my comics and left me theirs when they'd finished them.

But always somewhere in this pageant I can still find Lippsie, now mother, now typist, musician, cricketer and always Pym's own private moral tutor, flouncing through the outfield in pursuit of a high catch while everyone yelled "*Achtung!*" at her, and "Whoopsie, mind the flower-beds!" It was in Paradise too that Rick kicked a brand-new full-size football slap into Pym's young face, which was like being hit by the inside of all the Bentleys at once, the same leather travelling at the same breakneck speed. When he came round, Dorothy was bending over him with a handkerchief crammed between her teeth, whimpering "Oh, don't, please, dear God, don't," because the blood was everywhere. The football had only cut his forehead but Dorothy insisted it had shoved the whole eyeball deep into his head never to be got out again. The poor heart, she was too scared to dab away the blood so Lippsie had to do it for her, because Lippsie could touch me as she touched wounded animals and birds. I never met a woman since with so much touching in her hands. And I believe now that was what I meant to her: a thing to touch and cherish and protect, after everything else had been removed from her. I was her bit of hope and love in the gilded prison where Rick kept her.

In Paradise when Rick was in residence there was no night and nobody went to bed but Dorothy, the court's self-appointed Sleeping Beauty. Pym could join the festival any time he chose and there they all were, Rick and Syd and Morrie Washington and Perce Loft and Mr. Muspole and Lippsie and the jockeys, lying on the floor amid piles of money, watching the roulette ball hopping over the tin walls while TP in his regalia looked down on them, so there must have been a picture of him in the houses too. And I see us all dancing to the gramophone and telling stories about a chimpanzee called Little Audrey who laughed and laughed at jokes that were beyond Pym's intellectual reach. But he laughed louder than anyone because he was learning to be a pleaser, with funny voices, acts and anecdotes to make himself attractive. In Paradise everybody loved everybody because once Pym found Lippsie sitting on Rick's lap and another time he was dancing cheek to cheek with her, a cigar between his teeth, while he sang "Underneath the Arches" with his eyes shut. And it seemed a pity that Dorothy was once again too tired to put on the frilly dressing-gown Rick had bought her—pink for Dorothy, white for Lippsie—and come on down and have some fun. But the louder Rick yelled to her up the stairs the deeper Dorothy slept, as Pym discovered for himself when he was dispatched on Rick's instruction to talk her round. He knocked and had no answer. He tiptoed to the enormous bed and brushed what looked at first like cobwebs from her cheek. He whispered to her, then he tried shouting at her, but with no useful result. Dorothy was crying in her sleep, he reported when he returned downstairs. But next morning everything was all right again because there they were the three of them in bed together with Rick in the middle, and Pym was allowed to wriggle in beside Lippsie while Dorothy went down and made the toast and Lippsie held him gravely to her, and gave him her troubled, moral frown, which I suppose now was her way of telling me she was ashamed of her weakness and infatuation, and wished to cleanse it with her concern for me.

In Paradise, it was true, Rick roared but never at Pym. He never once raised his voice at me; his will was strong enough without it and his love was stronger still. He roared at Dorothy, he cajoled and warned her about things Pym could not understand. More than once he carted her bodily to the telephone and made her talk to people—to Uncle Makepeace, to shops, and to others who were threatening us somehow, and only Dorothy could appease them, because Lippsie refused to do that, and anyway her accent wasn't right. I believe now that this was the first time Pym heard the name Wentworth, for I remember Dorothy holding my hand for courage while she told Mrs. Wentworth it would be all right about the money if only everyone would stop pressing. So the name Wentworth was ugly to Pym from early. It became synonymous with fear and an end to things.

"Who's Wentworth?" Pym asked Lippsie, and it was the only time she told him to be quiet.

And I remember how Dorothy knew all the operators' names at the exchange, and what their husbands and fiancés did, and where their children were at school, because when she was alone with Pym and shaky in her angora pullover, she'd pick up the white phone and have a good chat with them, she seemed to find comfort in a world of disembodied voices. Rick roared at Lippsie too when she stood up to him, and I think now that she stood up to him more as I grew up. And sometimes he roared at Dorothy and Lippsie together, making them both weep at the same time until they all patched it up in the great bed where he had his toast for breakfast and dripped the butter on the pink sheets. But no one hurt Pym or made him cry. I think, even in those days, Pym understood that Rick measured his relationships with women against his relationship with Pym, and found them wanting by comparison. Sometimes Rick took Dorothy and Lippsie skating. Rick wore a black tail suit and a white tie, but Dorothy and Lippsie dressed like pantomime boys, each holding an arm of him and avoiding one another's eye.

*   *   *

The Fall occurred in darkness. We had been moving house a great deal recently, in what must have been a giddy ascent through the local real-estate market, and our palace of the day was a mansion on a hill and the day was a black winter afternoon near Christmas. Pym had been making paper decorations with Lippsie, and I have a notion that if I could ever find the place, if it is not a council estate or a bypass by now, they would still be hanging there exactly as we left them, stars of David and stars of Bethlehem—she taught me the difference precisely—twinkling in enormous empty rooms. First the lights went out in Pym's vast nursery, then the electric fire faded, then his brand-new ten-track, Hornby O electric train set wouldn't work, then Lippsie gave a kind of shriek and vanished. Pym went downstairs and pulled open the walnut lid of Rick's brand-new de-luxe cocktail cabinet. The mirrored interior refused to light up and it wouldn't play "Someone's in the Kitchen with Dinah."

Suddenly, in the whole house, the brass balls of the barometric perpetual clock were the only thing that had retained their energy. Pym ran to the kitchen. No Cookie and no Mr. Roley the gardener, whose children stole his toys but couldn't be blamed because they hadn't his advantages. He ran upstairs again and feeling very cold made an urgent reconnaissance of the long corridors, calling "Lippsie, Lippsie," but no one answered. From the arched landing window of stained glass, he glared into the garden and made out black cars in the drive. Not Bentleys but two police Wolseleys. And police drivers with peaked caps sitting at the wheel. And men in brown mackintoshes standing round them talking to Mr. Roley while Cookie twisted her handkerchief and wrung her hands like the dame in the Crazy Gang pantomime that Rick had taken the court to see only a week before. People under siege go upwards, I now know, which may explain why Pym's reaction was to race up the narrow staircase to the attic. There he found Rick in a great flurry, with files and papers on the floor all round him, and he was loading them by the armful into an old chipped green filing cabinet that Pym in all his explorations had never seen before.

"The electricity's broken and Lippsie's scared and the police have come and they're in the garden arresting Mr. Roley," Pym told Rick in one breath.

He said this several times, louder each time, because of

the great moment of his message. But Rick wouldn't hear
him. He was rushing between the papers and the cabinet,
loading up the drawers. So Pym went to him and punched him
hard on the upper arm, as hard as he could on the soft bit just
above the steel spring he wore to keep his silk shirt sleeve
straight, and Rick flung round on him and his hand went back to
strike him, and his face looked like Mr. Roley's when he was
about to make a huge last heave at a log to split it: red and
strained and damp. Then he dropped into a crouch and seized
Pym by each shoulder with his thick cupped hands. And his
face worried Pym much more than the axe-heave, because his
eyes were scared and crying without the rest of his face knowing
it and his voice was smooth and holy.

   "Don't ever hit me again, son. When I'm judged, as
judged we shall all be, God will judge me on how I treated
you, make no bones about it."

   "Why are the police here?" said Pym.

   "Your old man's got a temporary problem of liquidity.
Now clear a way to that cupboard and open the door for us
like a good chap. Quick."

   The cupboard was in a corner behind a pile of old clothes
and attic junk. Somehow Pym fought his way to the door and
hauled it open. With a series of crashes Rick was slamming
shut the drawers of the filing cabinet. He turned the lock,
grabbed Pym by the arm and poked the key deep into his
trouser pocket, which was small and woolly and only big
enough for a key and a small bag of sweets.

   "You give that to Mr. Muspole, you hear, son? Nobody
but Muspole. Then you show him where this cabinet is. You
bring him here and you show him. No one else. Do you love
your old man?"

   "Yes."

   "Well then."

   Proud as a sentry, Pym held back the door while Rick
swivelled and rolled the cabinet past him on its castors into
the cupboard, then into the dark wainscotting beyond. Then
he threw in a lot of junk after it, which hid it completely.

   "See where it went, son?"

   "Yes."

   "Close the door."

   Pym did so, then stomped downstairs with his chest out
because he wanted to take another look at the police cars.

Dorothy was in the kitchen dressed in her new fur coat and her new fluffy bedroom slippers, stirring a tin of tomato soup. She had one of those bubbles over her mouth that people get when they are too choked to speak. Pym loathed tomato soup, so did Rick.

"Rick's mending the water-pipes," he announced grandly, in order to keep his secret intact. This was the only meaning he could place on Rick's reference to liquidity. Yelling even louder for Lippsie he charged into the corridor, straight into the path of two policemen labouring under the weight of a great desk that was Rick's office when he was at home.

"That's my dad's," he said aggressively, putting a hand over the pocket where he had the key.

The first policeman is the only one I remember. He was kindly and had a white moustache like TP's, and he was taller than God.

"Yes, well, I'm afraid it's ours now, lad. Hold open that door for us, will you, and mind your toes."

Pym the official door-holder obliged.

"Your dad got any more desks, has he?" the tall policeman asked.

"No."

"Cupboards? Anywhere he keeps his papers?"

"They're all in there," said Pym, pointing firmly at the desk while he kept his other hand over the pocket.

"Do you want a wee then?"

"No."

"Where's some rope?"

"I don't know."

"Yes you do."

"It's in the stable. On a big saddle hook next to the new mower. It's a halter."

"What's your name?"

"Magnus. Where's Lippsie?"

"Who's Lippsie?"

"She's a lady."

"She work for your dad?"

"No."

"Slip and fetch the rope for us, will you, Magnus, there's a lad. Me and my friends here we're going to take your dad on a working holiday for a bit and we need his papers or nobody can work."

Pym raced off to the shed which was across the other side of the grounds between the pony paddock and Mr. Roley's cottage. On the shelf stood a green tea-tin where Mr. Roley kept his nails. Pym put the key into it, thinking: green tin, green filing cabinet. By the time he returned with the halter Rick was standing between two men in brown raincoats. And I picture it exactly: Rick so pale that not all the holidays in the world would see him right, commanding loyalty of me with his eyes. And the tall policeman letting Pym try his flat cap on and push the button that made the silver bell ring under the hood of the black Wolseley. And Dorothy looking as though she needed a holiday even more than Rick did, not choking any more, but standing still as an effigy with her white hands folded across her fur coat.

Memory is a great temptress, Tom. Paint the tragic tableau. The little group, the winter's day, Christmas in the air. The convoy of Wolseleys bumping away down the lane that Pym has spent so long patrolling with his new Harrods six-shooter. Rick's desk lashed to the last car with the aid of the halter from the stable. Motionless they stare after the cortège as it vanishes into the tunnel of the trees, taking our one Provider to Lord knows where. Mrs. Roley weeping. Cookie howling in Irish. Pym's little head pressed against his mother's bosom. A thousand violins playing "Will Ye No Come Back Again?"—there is no limit to the pathos I could squeeze out of that lemon if I worked on it. Yet the truth, when I make the effort to recall it, is different. With the departure of Rick a great calm descended over Pym. He felt refreshed and freed of an intolerable burden. He watched the cars leave, Rick's desk last. And he continued to stare anxiously after them, but only for fear that Rick would talk them into turning back. As he watched, Lippsie stepped out of the woods wearing her headscarf and struggled towards him weighed down by the cardboard suitcase that contained her life's possessions. The sight of her made Pym even more furious than he'd been when he'd found Dorothy making soup. You hid, he accused her in the secret dialogue he constantly conducted with her. You were so scared you hid in the woods and missed the fun. I realise now, of course, but could not at the time, that Lippsie had seen people taken away before: her brother Aaron and the architect her father, to mention only two. But Pym in common with the rest of the world cared little about pogroms in those days and all he could feel was a deep resentment that his life's love had failed to rise to a historic moment.

Muspole came that evening. He arrived at the side door with a cooked chicken for us and a rhubarb pie and thick custard and a thermos of hot tea, and he said he was making arrangements for us and everything would be fine tomorrow. To get him on his own, Pym said "Come and see my Hornby" and at once Dorothy cried because by then there was no Hornby: the distraining bailiffs had fought a pitched battle with the repossessing shopkeepers and the Hornby had been one of the first things to go. But Mr. Muspole went with Pym anyway and Pym took him to the shed and gave him the key, then led him to the attic and showed him the secret. And everybody watched again while Mr. Roley and Mr. Muspole heaved and puffed and loaded the cabinet on to Mr. Muspole's car. And waved again when Mr. Muspole drove into the twilight in his hat.

After the Fall came, very properly, Purgatory, and Purgatory possessed no Lippsies—I guess she was trying to make one of her breaks from me, using Rick's absence to cut herself off. Purgatory was where Dorothy and I served out our sentence, Tom, and Purgatory is just over the hill from here, a few of Rick's fare-stages along the coast, though the new time-share apartments have removed much of its sting. Purgatory was the same wooded hollow of clefts and chines and dripping laurels where Pym had been conceived, with red windswept beaches always out of season, and creaking swings and sodden sandpits that were closed to enjoyment on the sabbath and for Pym on any other day as well. Purgatory was Makepeace Watermaster's great sad house, The Glades, where Pym was forbidden to leave the walled orchard if it was dry or enter the main rooms if it was raining. Purgatory was the Tabernacle with the Night School Boys written clean out of the history books; and Makepeace Watermaster's frightful sermons; and Mr. Philpott's sermons; and sermons from every aunt, cousin and neighbourhood philosopher who felt moved to words by Rick's misfortune and saw the young criminal as the proper person to address.

Purgatory possessed no cocktail cabinets, television sets,

jockeys, Bentleys or neverwozzers, and served bread and
margarine instead of buttered toast. When we sang, we
droned, "There Is a Green Hill Far Away," and never "Underneath the Arches" or one of Lippsie's *Lieder*. Contemporary
photographs show a grinning toothy child, well grown and
well looking enough, but stooped as if from living under low
ceilings. All are out of focus; all have a furtive, stolen look
about them, and I try to love them only because I believe
Dorothy must have taken them, though it was Lippsie whom
Pym was missing. In a couple the child is tugging at the arm
of whatever mother happens to attend him, probably trying
to persuade her to come away with him. In one he is wearing
sloppy white gloves like puppets' hands, so I suppose he
suffered from some skin disease, unless Makepeace was worried about fingerprints. Or perhaps he was intending to
become a waiter.

The mothers, all large, all dressed in the same strict
uniform, have such an air of the wardress about them that I
seriously wonder whether Makepeace obtained them from
an agency specialising in the care of delinquents. One wears
a medal like an Iron Cross. I do not mean they are without
kindness. Their smiles are alight with pious optimism. But
there is something in their glance that assures me they are
alert at all times to the latent criminality of their charge.
Lippsie is not featured, and my poor Dorothy, Pym's one
cellmate in the dark rear wing to which the two of them were
confined, was even more useless than before. If Pym was
thrashed, Dorothy would dress his wounds but never question the need for them. If he was put into shameful nappies
as a punishment for wetting his bed, Dorothy would urge him
not to drink in the second part of the day. And if he was
denied tea altogether, Dorothy would save him her biscuits
and pass them to him in the privacy of their upper room,
poking them one by one between the invisible bars. In
Paradise on good days Pym and Dorothy had managed to
share the occasional joke together. Now the guilty silence of
her house reclaimed her. Each day drove her further into
herself and though he told her his best jokes and did his best
acts for her, and painted the best pictures for her that he
knew, nothing he could do was able to wake her smile for
long. At night she moaned and ground her teeth and when
she switched the light on, Pym lay awake beside her, thinking

of Lippsie and watching Dorothy's unblinking eyes staring up at the parchment star of Bethlehem that was their lampshade.

If Dorothy had been dying Pym could have gone on nursing her for ever, no question. But she wasn't so he resented her instead. In fact soon he began to weary of her altogether and wonder whether the wrong parent had gone on holiday, and whether Lippsie was his real mother and he had made an awful mistake, the one that accounted for everything. When war broke out Dorothy was incapable of rejoicing at the marvellous news. Makepeace turned on the wireless and Pym heard a solemn man saying he had done everything he could to prevent it. Makepeace turned off the wireless and Mr. Philpott, who had come for tea, asked mournfully where, oh where, would the battlefield be? Makepeace, never at a loss, replied that God would decide. But Pym, spilling over with excitement, for once presumed to question him.

"But Uncle Makepeace! If God can decide where the battlefield is, why doesn't He stop the battle altogether? He doesn't want to. He could if He wanted to, easy. He doesn't!" Even to this day, I do not know which was the greater sin: to question Makepeace or to question God. In either case the remedy was the same: put him on bread and water like his father.

But the worst monster in The Glades was not rubbery Uncle Makepeace with his little rose ears, but mad Aunt Nell in her liver-coloured spectacles, who chased after Pym with no reason, waving her stick at him and calling him "my little canary" because of the yellow pullover Dorothy had managed to knit him while she wept. Aunt Nell had a white stick for seeing with and a brown stick for walking with. She could see perfectly well, except when she carried her white stick.

"Aunt Nell gets her wobblies out of a bottle," Pym told Dorothy one day, thinking it might make her smile. "I've seen. She's got a bottle hidden in the greenhouse."

Dorothy did not smile but became very frightened, and made him swear never to say such a thing again. Aunt Nell was ill, she said. Her illness was a secret and she took secret medicine for it, and nobody must ever know or Aunt Nell would die and God would be very angry. For weeks afterwards Pym carried this wonderful knowledge round with him much as, briefly, he had carried Rick's, but this was better and more disgraceful. It was like the first money he had ever owned, his first piece of power. Who to spend it on? he wondered. Who to share it with? Shall I let Aunt Nell live or shall I kill her for calling me her little canary? He decided on Mrs. Bannister, the cook. "Aunt Nell gets her wobblies out of a bottle," he told Mrs. Bannister, careful to use exactly the form of words that had so appalled Dorothy. But Aunt Nell did not die, and Mrs. Bannister knew about the bottle already and cuffed him for his forwardness. Worse still, she must have taken his story to Uncle Makepeace who that night made a rare visit to the prison wing, swaying and roaring and sweating and pointing at Pym while he talked about the Devil who was Rick. When he had gone Pym made his bed across the door in case Makepeace decided to come back and do some more roaring, but he never did. Nevertheless the burgeoning spy had acquired an early lesson in the dangerous business of intelligence: everybody talks.

His next lesson was no less instructive and concerned the perils of communication in occupied territory. By now Pym was writing to Lippsie daily and posting his letters in a box that stood at the rear gate of the house. They contained to his later shame priceless information, almost none of it in code. How to break into The Glades at night. His hours of exercise. Maps. The character of his persecutors. The money he had saved. The precise location of the German guards. The route to be followed through the back garden and where the kitchen key was kept. "I have been kidnapped to a dangerous house, please get me quick," he wrote, and enclosed a drawing of Aunt Nell with canaries coming out of her mouth as a further warning of the hazards that surrounded him. But there was a snag. Having no address for Lippsie, Pym could only hope that somebody at the post office would know where she was to be found. His confidence was misplaced. One day the postman delivered the whole top-secret bundle to Makepeace personally, who summoned the prevailing mother, who summoned Pym, and led him like the convict he was to Makepeace for chastisement, though he simpered and begged and blandished him for all he was worth, for Pym somewhat unsportingly hated the lash and was seldom gallant about receiving it. After that he contented himself with looking for Lippsie on buses and, where he could do so deniably, asking people who happened to be passing the rear gate whether they had seen her. Particularly he asked policemen, whom he now smiled at richly wherever he found them.

"My father's got an old green box with secrets in," he told a constable one day, strolling in the memorial gardens with a mother.

"Has he then, son? Well, thanks for telling us," said the constable and pretended to write in his notebook.

Meanwhile word of Rick, though not of Lippsie, reached Pym like the unfinished whispers of a distant radio transmitter. Your father is well. His holiday is doing him good. He has lost weight, lots of good food, we're not to worry, he's getting exercise, reading his law books, he's gone back to school. The source of these priceless snippets was the Other House, which lay in a poorer part of Purgatory down by the coking station and must never be mentioned in front of Uncle Makepeace, since it was the house that had spawned Rick and brought disgrace on the great family of Watermaster, not to mention the memory of TP. Hand in hand, Dorothy and Pym rode there in fireside darkness, sticky mesh against bomb blast on the windows of the trolley-bus, and the lights inside burning blue to baffle German pilots. At the Other House, a steadfast little Irish lady with a rock jaw gave Pym half-a-crown out of a ginger jar and squeezed his arm muscles approvingly and called him "son" like Rick, and on the wall hung a copy of the same tinted photograph of TP, framed not in gold but in coffin wood. Jolly-faced aunts made sweets for Pym out of their sugar ration, and hugged and wept and treated Dorothy like the royalty she once had been, and hooted when Pym did his funny voices and clapped when he sang "Underneath the Arches." "Go on, Magnus, give us Sir Makepeace then!" But Pym dared not for fear of God's anger, which he knew from the Aunt Nell affair to be swift and awful.

The aunt he loved most was Bess. "Tell us, Magnus," whispered Aunt Bess to him, alone in the scullery, drawing his head close to her own. "Is it true your dad ever owned a racehorse called Prince Magnus, after you?"

"It's not true," said Pym without a second's thought, remembering the excitement as he sat beside Lippsie on her bed, listening to the commentary of Prince Magnus coming nowhere. "It is a lie made up by Uncle Makepeace to hurt my father."

Aunt Bess kissed him and laughed and wept in relief, and held him even tighter. "Never say I asked you. Promise."

"I promise," said Pym. "God's honour."

The same Aunt Bess, one glorious night, smuggled Pym out of The Glades and into the Theatre Pier, where they saw Max Miller and a row of girls with long bare legs like Lippsie's. On the trolley-bus back, brimming over with gratitude, Pym told her everything he knew in the world, and made up whatever he didn't. He said he had written a book by Shakespeare and it was in a green box in a secret house. One day he would find and print it and make a lot of money. He said he would be a policeman and an actor and a jockey, and drive a Bentley like Rick, and marry Lippsie and have six children all called TP like his granddad. This pleased Bess enormously, except for the bit about the jockey, and sent her home saying Magnus was a card, which was what he wanted most. His gratification was short-lived. This time Pym had made God very angry indeed, and as usual He was not slow to do something about it. On the very next day before breakfast the police came and took away his Dorothy for ever, though the reigning mother said they were only ambulance.

And once again—though Pym dutifully wept for Dorothy—and refused food for her, and flailed with his fists at the long-suffering mothers—he could not but see their rightness in removing her. They were taking her to a place where she would be happy, the mothers said. Pym envied her luck. Not to the same place as Rick, no, but somewhere nicer and quieter, with kind people to look after her. Pym planned to join her. Escape, till now a fantasy, became his serious aim. A celebrated epileptic at Sunday school acquainted him with his symptoms. Pym waited a day, ran into the kitchen with his eyes rolling, and collapsed dramatically before Mrs. Bannister, shoving his hands into his mouth and writhing for good measure. The doctor, who must have been a rare imbecile, prescribed a laxative. Next day in a further attempt to draw attention to himself, Pym hacked off his forelock with paper scissors. No one noticed. Improvising now, he released Mrs. Bannister's cockatoo from its cage, sprinkled soap flakes into the Aga cooker and blocked the lavatory with a feather boa belonging to Aunt Nell.

Nothing happened. He was beating the air. What he needed was a great dramatic crime. All night he waited, then early in the morning when his courage was highest, Pym walked the length of the house to Makepeace Watermaster's study in his dressing-gown and slippers and relieved himself prolifically over the centre of the white carpet. Terrified, he threw himself on to the patch he had created, hoping to dry it out with the heat of his body. A maid entered and screamed. A mother was summoned and from his anguished position on the carpet Pym was treated to a formative example of how history rewrites itself in a crisis. The mother touched his shoulder. He groaned. She asked him where it hurt. He indicated his groin, the literal cause of his distress. Makepeace Watermaster was fetched. What were you doing in my study in the first place? The pain, sir, the pain, I wanted to tell you about the pain. With a screech of tyres the doctor returned and now everything was remembered while he bent over Pym and probed his stomach with his stupid fingertips. The collapse before Mrs. Bannister. The nightly moans, the daily pallor. Dorothy's madness, discussed in hushed terms. Even Pym's bed-wetting was taken down and used in evidence on his behalf.

"Poor boy, it's got him here as well," said the mother as the patient was lifted cautiously to the sofa and the maid was hurried off to fetch Jeyes disinfectant and a floor-cloth. Pym's temperature was read and grimly observed to be normal. "Doesn't mean a thing," said the doctor, now battling to make good his earlier negligence, and ordered the mother to pack the poor boy's things. She did so and in the course of it must inevitably have discovered a number of small objects that Pym had taken from other people's lives in order to improve his own: Nell's jet earrings, Cook's letters from her son in Canada and Makepeace Watermaster's *Travels with a Donkey* which Pym had selected for its title, the only part he had read. In the crisis even this black evidence of his criminality was ignored.

The outcome was more effective than Pym could have hoped. Not a week later, in a hospital newly fitted to receive victims of the approaching blitz, Magnus Pym, aged eight and a half years, yielded up his appendix in the interests of operational cover. When he came round, the first thing he saw was a blue and black koala bear larger than himself seated on

the end of his bed. The second was a basket of fruit bigger
than the bear, which looked like a piece of St. Moritz that had
landed by mistake in wartime England. The third was Rick,
slim and smart as a sailor, standing to attention with his right
hand lifted in salute. Beside Rick again, like a scared ghost
dragged unwillingly from the shades of Pym's chloroformed
realm, came Lippsie, hunched at the shoulders by a new fur
cape, and supported by Syd Lemon looking like his own
younger brother.

Lippsie knelt to me. The two men looked on while we
embraced.

"That's the way then," Rick kept saying approvingly.
"Give him a good old English hug. That's the way."

Softly, like a bitch recovering her pup, Lippsie picked
me over, lifting the remains of my forelock and staring gravely
into my eyes as if fearing that bad things had got into them.

How they celebrated their release! Shorn of all possessions
except the clothes they stood up in and the credit they could
muster as they went along, Rick's reconstituted court took to
the open road and became crusaders through wartime Britain. Petrol was rationed, Bentleys had vanished for the
duration, all over the country posters asked "Is Your Journey
Really Necessary?" and every time they passed one they
slowed down to yell back, "Yes, it is!" in chorus through the
open windows of their cab. Drivers either became accom-
plices or left in a hurry. A Mr. Humphries threw them all into
the street in Aberdeen after a week, calling them crooks, and
drove away without his money, never to be seen again. But a
Mr. Cudlove whom Rick had met on holiday—and who got
the court a week's tick at the Imperial at Torquay on the
strength of an aunt who worked in the accounts department—
he stayed for ever, sharing their food and fortunes and
teaching Pym tricks with string. Sometimes they had one
taxi, sometimes Mr. Cudlove's special friend Ollie brought his
Humber and they had day-long races for Pym's sole benefit,
with Syd leaning out of the back window giving the car the
whip. Of mothers they had a dazzling and varying supply and
often acquired them at such short notice they had to cram
them into the back two deep, with Pym squeezed into an
exciting, unfamiliar lap. There was a lady called Topsie who

smelt of roses and made Pym dance with his head against her breast; there was Millie who let him sleep with her in her siren-suit because he was frightened of the black cupboard in his hotel bedroom, and who bestowed frank caresses on him while she bathed him. And Eileens and Mabels and Joans, and a Violet who got carsick on cider, some into her gas-mask case and the rest over Pym. And when they were all got out of the way, Lippsie materialised, standing motionless in the steam of a railway station, her cardboard suitcase hanging from her slim hand. Pym loved her more than ever, but her deepening melancholy was too much for him and in the whirl of the great crusade he resented being the object of it.

"Old Lippsie's got a touch of what's-its," Syd would say kindly, noting Pym's disappointment, and they'd heave a bit of a sigh of relief together when she left.

"Old Lippsie's on about her Jews again," said Syd sadly another time. "They keep telling her another lot's been done."

And once: "Old Lippsie's got the guilts she isn't dead like them."

Pym's intermittent enquiries after Dorothy led him nowhere. Your mum's poorly, Syd would say; she'll be back soon, and the best thing our Magnus here can do for her meantime is not fret over her, because it will only get to her and make her worse.

Rick took a wounded line. "You'll just have to put up with your old man for a while. I thought we were having fun then. Aren't we having fun?"

"All the fun in the world," said Pym.

On the subject of his recent absence Rick was as sparing as the rest of the court, so that soon Pym began to wonder whether they had ever been on holiday at all. Only the occasional hint convinced him that they had shared a cementing experience. Winchester had been worse than Reading because of those bloody gypsies off of Salisbury Plain, Pym once overheard Morrie Washington tell Perce Loft. Syd backed him up. "Those Winchester gyppos was rough you wouldn't believe," said Syd with feeling. "The screws was no better, either." And Pym noticed that their holiday had made hearty eaters of them. "Eat your peas now, Magnus," Syd urged him amid much laughter. "There's worse hotels than this one, *we* can tell you."

It wasn't till a year or more later, when Pym's vocabulary had grown equal to his intelligence gathering, that he realised they had been talking about prison.

But their leader did not share these jokes and they ceased abruptly, for Rick's *gravitas* was something no man tampered with lightly, least of all those appointed to uphold it. Rick's superiority was manifest in everything he did. In the way he dressed even when we were very broke, his clean laundry and clean shoes. In the food he required and the style to eat it in. The rooms he had in the hotel. In the way he needed brandy for his snooker, and scared everyone into silence with his brooding. In his preoccupation with good works, which involved visiting hospitals where people had taken bad knocks and seeing the old people right while their children were away at the war.

"Will you see Lippsie right too, when the war's over?" Pym asked one day.

"Old Lippsie's crackerjack," said Rick.

Meanwhile we traded. What in, Pym never rightly knew and nor do I now. Sometimes in rare commodities, such as hams and whisky, sometimes in promises, which the court called Faith. Other times in nothing more solid than the sunny horizons that sparkled ahead of us down the empty wartime roads. When Christmas approached somebody produced sheets of coloured crêpe paper, thousands of them. For days and nights on end, augmented by extra mothers recruited for this vital war-work, Pym and the court crouched in an empty railway carriage at Didcot, twisting the paper into crackers that contained no toys and would not crack, while they told each other wild stories and cooked toast by laying it on top of the paraffin stove. Some of the crackers, it was true, had little wooden soldiers inside them, but these were called "samples" and kept separate. The rest, Syd explained, was for decoration, Titch, like flowers when there isn't any. Pym believed it all. He was the most willing child labourer in the world, so long as there was approval waiting for him round the corner.

Another time they towed a trailer filled with crates of oranges which Pym refused to eat because he overheard Syd saying they were hot. They sold them to a pub on the road to Birmingham. Once they had a load of dead chickens that Syd said they could only move at night when it was cold enough, so perhaps that was what had gone wrong with the oranges. And there is a clip of film running forever in my memory. It shows a scraggy moonlit hilltop on the moors, and our two cabs with their lights out winding nervously to the crest. And the dark figures standing waiting for us on the back of their lorry. And the masked lamp that counted out the money for Mr. Muspole the great accountant while Syd unloaded the trailer. And though Pym watched from a distance because he hated feathers, no night frontier crossing later in his life was ever more exciting.

"Can we send the money to Lippsie now?" Pym asked. "She hasn't got any left."

"Now how do you know a thing like that, old son?"

From her letters to you, Pym thought. You left one in your pocket and I read it. But Rick's eyes had their flick-knife glint so he said "I made it up," and smiled.

Rick did not come on our adventures. He was saving himself. What for was a question nobody asked within Pym's hearing and certainly he never asked it for himself. Rick was devoting himself to his good works, his old people and his hospital visiting. "Is that suit of yours pressed, son?" Rick would say when as a special privilege father and son embarked together on one of these high errands. "God in heaven, Muspole, look at the boy's suit, it's a damned shame! Look at his hair!" Hastily a mother would be ordered to press the suit, another to polish his shoes and get his fingernails proper, a third to comb his hair till it was orderly and sensitive. With flimsy patience Mr. Cudlove tapped his keys on the car roof while Pym was given a final check-over for signs of unintentional irreverence. Then away at last they sped to the house or bedside of some elderly and worthy person, and Pym sat fascinated to see how swiftly Rick trimmed his manner to suit theirs, how naturally he slipped into the cadences and vernacular that put them most at ease, and how the love of God came into his good face when he talked about Liberalism and Masonry and his dear dead father, God rest him, and a first-class rate of return, ten percent guaranteed plus profits for as long as you're spared. Sometimes he brought a ham with him as a gift and was an angel in a hamless world. Sometimes a pair of silk stockings or a box of nectarines, for Rick was always the giver even when he was taking. When he was able Pym threw his own charm into the scales by reciting a prayer he had composed, or singing "Underneath the Arches," or telling a witty story with a range of regional accents that he had picked up in the course of the crusade. "The Germans are killing all the Jews," he said once, to great effect. "I've got a friend called Lippsie and all her other friends are dead." If his performance was wanting, Rick let him know this without brutality. "When somebody like Mrs. Ardmore asks you whether you remember her, son, don't scratch your old head and pull a face. Look her in the eye and smile and say, 'Yes.' That's the way to treat old people, *and* to be a credit to your father. Do you love your old man?"

"Of course I do."

"Well then. How was your steak last night?"

"It was super."

"There's not twenty boys in England ate steak last night, do you know that?"

"I know."

"Give us a kiss then."

Syd was less reverent. "If you're going to learn to shave people, Magnus," he said over a lot of winks, "you've got to learn how to rub the soap in first!"

Somewhere near Aberdeen, without warning, the court became interested only in chemists' shops. We were a limited company by then, which to Pym was as good as being a policeman. Rick had found a new banker with Faith, Mr. Cudlove's live-in friend Ollie signed the cheques. And our product was a concoction of dried fruit that we pulped with a handpress in the kitchens of a great country house belonging to a dashing new mother called Cherry. It was a large house with white pillars at the front door and white statues all like Lippsie in the garden. Even in Paradise the court had never stayed anywhere so grand. First we stewed the fruit and pulped it in the press, which was the best bit; then we added gelatine to make lozenges out of it, which Pym rolled round and round in Company sugar with his bare palm, licking it clean between batches. Cherry had evacuees and horses, and gave parties for American soldiers who presented her with cans of petrol in the tithe barn. She owned farms and a great park with deer, and an absent husband in the Navy whom Syd referred to as "the Admiral." In the evenings before dinner, a pack of King Charles spaniels was whipped by an old gamekeeper. They swarmed over the sofas yapping till they were whipped out again. At Cherry's, for the first time since St. Moritz, Pym saw silver candles on the dinner table lighting bare shoulders.

"There's a lady called Lippsie who's in love with my father and they're going to marry and have babies," Pym told Cherry helpfully one evening as they walked together down the ride; and was greatly impressed by how seriously Cherry took this news, and how intently she questioned Pym concerning Lippsie's accomplishments. "I've seen her in the bath and she's beautiful," said Pym.

And when they left a few days later, Rick took something of the dignity of the place with him, and something of its proprietor also, for I remember him striding down the great stone steps with a white hide suitcase in each hand—Rick always loved a fine suitcase—and sporting a smart country outfit of the sort no admiral would wear to sea. Syd and Mr. Muspole followed after him like circus midgets, clutching the chipped green filing cabinet between them and shouting, "Your end, Deirdre!" and "Gently down the stairs, Sybil!"

"Don't you ever talk to Cherry about Lippsie again, son," Rick warned him, in his heaviest moralistic tone. "It's high time you learned it's not polite to mention one woman to another. Because if you don't learn that, you'll waste your advantages and that's a fact."

It was through Cherry also, I suspect, that Rick formed the determination to turn Pym into a gentleman. Until now it has been assumed that Pym was already of the aristocracy. But Cherry, a forceful and superior woman, taught Rick that true English privilege was obtained by hardship, and that the best hardship was to be found at English boarding-schools. She also had a nephew at Mr. Grimble's academy by the name of Sefton Boyd, but better known to her as my darling Kenny. A second and less tender influence was the army. First Muspole became its casualty, then Morrie Washington, then Syd. Each with a rueful smile of failure packed his little suitcase and disappeared, returning only seldom and with very short hair. Then one day to his hurt surprise Rick himself was summoned to the flag. In later life he took a more tolerant view of the pettiness of the society entrusted to his care, but the sight of his call-up papers on the breakfast table provoked an outburst of righteous anger.

"God damn it, Loft, I thought we'd taken care of all that," he raged at Perce, who was exempt from everything.

"We did take care of it," said Perce, jabbing a thumb in my direction. "Delicate kid, mother in the nut-house, it's watertight compassion."

"Well where the devil's their compassion now then?" Rick demanded, shoving the buff document under Perce's nose. "It's a damn shame, Loft. That's what it is. Get after it."

"You never ought to have told old Cherry about Lippsie," Perce Loft fumed at Pym later. "She went and peached on your dad out of spite."

But the army declined to surrender, and the depleted court, consisting of Perce Loft, a clutch of mothers, Ollie and Mr. Cudlove, duly uprooted itself to a drab hotel in Bradford, where Rick was obliged to reconcile the ignominy of the parade ground with the burdens of financial generalship. Using the hotel's coin box and the hotel's credit, typing and filing in the hotel's bedrooms, storing their mysterious wares in the hotel's garage, the court fought a gallant rearguard action against dissolution, but in vain. It was Sunday evening in the hotel. Rick in his private's uniform, freshly pressed, was preparing to return to barracks. A new dartsboard was wedged under his arm, which he planned to present to the sergeants' mess, for Rick had his heart set on the post of catering clerk, which would enable him to see us right in the shortages.

"Son. It's time for you to set those fine feet of yours on the hard road of becoming Lord Chief Justice and a credit to your old man. There's been too much lazy fare about and you're part of it. Cudlove, look at his shirt. No man ever did business in a dirty shirt. Look at his hair. He'll be an airy-fairy before you can say Jack Robinson. It's boarding-school for you, son, and God bless you and God bless me too."

One more bear-hug, a final staunching of the tears, one noble handshake for the absent cameras as, dartsboard at the ready, the great man rode away to war. Pym watched him out of sight, then stealthily climbed the stairs to the provisional State Apartments. The door was unlocked. He smelt woman and talc. The double bed was in disarray. He pulled the pigskin briefcase from beneath it, tipped out the contents and, as he had often done before, puzzled over unintelligible files and correspondence. The Admiral's country suit, donned for a few hours and still warm, was hanging in the wardrobe. He poked in the pockets. The green filing cabinet, more chipped than ever, lurked in its habitual darkness. Why does he always keep it in cupboards? Pym tugged vainly at the locked drawers. Why does it travel separately from everything as if it had a disease?

"Looking for money, are we, Titch?" a woman's voice asked him, from the bathroom doorway. It was Doris, typist elect and good scout. "Spare yourself the trouble, I would. It's all tick with your dad. I've looked."

"He told me he'd left me a bar of chocolate in his room," Pym replied resolutely, and continued delving while she watched.

"There's three gross of army milk-and-nut sitting in the garage. Help yourself," Doris advised. "Petrol coupons too, if you're thirsty."

"It was a special kind of bar," said Pym.

I have never fathomed the machinations that sent Pym and Lippsie to the same school. Were they infiltrated singly or as a package, the one to be taught, the other to supply her labour in payment? I suspect as a package but have no proof beyond a general knowledge of Rick's methods. All his life, Rick maintained a work-force of devoted women whom he regularly discarded and revived. When they were not required in the court they were put out to work for him in the great world, easing his crusade with remittances they could ill afford, selling their jewellery for him, cashing their savings and lending their names to bank accounts from which Rick's name was banned. But Lippsie had no jewellery and no credit with the banks. She had only her lovely body and her music and her brooding guilt, and a little English schoolboy who held her to the world. I suspect now that Rick had already read the warning signs collecting in her, and decided to give her to me to look after. Nevertheless there was profit to our partnership and Rick was nothing if not an opportunist.

If Pym possessed any learning by the time he presented himself to Mr. Grimble's country academy for the sons of gentlemen, then he owed it to Lippsie and not to any of the dozen or so infant schools, Bible schools and kindergartens scattered along the hectic road of Rick's progress. Lippsie taught him writing, and to this day I write a German "t" and put a stroke through my small "z"s. She taught him spelling, and it was always a great joke between them that they could not remember how many "d"s there were in the English version of "address," and to this day I can't be sure of the answer until I have written out the German first. Whatever else Pym knew, apart from meaningless passages of the Scriptures, was contained in her cardboard suitcase, for she never came to see him anywhere without whisking him to her room and foisting some piece of geography or history on him, or making him play scales on her flute.

"See, Magnus, without informations we are nothing. But with informations we can go anywhere in the world, we are like turtles, our houses always on our backs. You learn to paint, you can paint anywhere. A sculptor, a musician, a painter, they need no permits. Only their heads. Our world must be inside our heads. That is the only safe way. Now you play Lippsie a nice tune."

The arrangement at Mr. Grimble's was the perfect flowering of this relationship. Their world was inside their heads, but it was also contained in a brick-and-flint gardener's cottage at the end of Mr. Grimble's long drive, designated the Overflow House and occupied by the Overflow Boys of whom Pym was the newest recruit. And Lippsie, his lovely lifelong Lippsie, their best and most attentive mother. They knew at once they were outcasts. If they didn't, the eighty boys up the drive made it plain to them. They had a pallid grocer's son without an "h" to his name, and tradesmen were ridiculous. They had three Jews whose speech was spattered with Polish, and a hopeless stammerer called M-M-Marlin, and an Indian with knock-knees whose father was killed when the Japanese took Singapore. They had Pym with his spots and wet beds. Yet under Lippsie they contrived to glory in all these disadvantages. If the boys up the drive were the crack regiment, the Overflow Boys were the irregulars who fought all the harder for their medals. For staff, Mr. Grimble took what he could get, and what he could get was whatever the country didn't need. A Mr. O'Mally punched a boy so hard across the ear he knocked him out cold, a Mr. Farbourne beat heads together and fractured someone's skull. A science master thought the marauding village boys were Bolsheviks and fired his shotgun into their retreating rumps. At Grimble's, boys were flogged for tardiness and flogged for untidiness, flogged for apathy and flogged for cheek, and flogged for not improving from the flogging. The fever of war encouraged brutality, the guilt of our non-combatant staff intensified it, the intricacies of the British hierarchical system provided a natural order for the exercise of sadism. Their God was the protector of English country gentlemen and their justice was the punishment of the ill-born and disadvantaged, and it was meted out with the collaboration of the strong, of whom Sefton Boyd was the strongest and most handsome. It is the saddest of all the ironies of Lippsie's death, as I see it now, that she died in the service of a Fascist state.

Each leave-out day, on Rick's standing orders, Pym presented himself at the entrance to the school drive in readiness for Mr. Cudlove's arrival. When nobody appeared, he hurried gratefully to the woods in search of privacy and wild strawberries. Come evening he returned to the school boasting of the great day he had had. Just occasionally the worst happened and a carload would appear—Rick, Mr. Cudlove, Syd in private's uniform, and a couple of jockeys crammed in anyhow—all well refreshed after a pause at the Brace of Partridges. If a school match was in progress they would roar support for the home side and hand round unheard-of oranges from a crate in the boot of the car. If none, then Syd and Morrie Washington would press-gang any boy who happened to be passing on his bicycle, and mount a handicap race round the playing fields while Syd belted out the commentary through his cupped hands. And Rick personally, dressed in the Admiral's suit, would start them off with a mayoral wave of his handkerchief, and Rick personally would present an unimaginable box of chocolates to the winner, while the pound notes changed hands around the court. And when evening came Rick never failed to install himself at the Overflow House, bringing a bottle of bubbly along to cheer old Lippsie up because she seemed so glum—"What's got into her, son?" And Rick cheered her up all right; Pym heard it going on, thump, creak and scream, while he crouched outside her door in his dressing-gown wondering whether they were fighting or pretending. Back in bed, he would hear Rick tiptoeing down the stairs, though Rick could tread as lightly as a cat.

Till a morning came when Rick did not leave quietly at all. Not for Pym, not for the rest of the Overflow Boys, who were greatly excited to be woken by the clamour. Lippsie was bawling and Rick was trying to quell her, but the nicer he was to her the more unreasonable she became. "You made me to be a *teef!*" she was yelling between great big whoops while she took another gulp of air. "You made me *teef* to punish me. You were bad priest, Rickie Pym. You made me to steal. I was honest woman. I was refugee but I was honest woman." Why did she speak as if it was all last year? "My father was honest man. My broder also was honest man. They was good men, not bad like me. You made me to steal until I was criminal like you. Maybe God punish you one day, Rickie Pym. Maybe He make you to weep, too. I hope He will. I hope, I hope!"

"Old Lippsie's having a touch of her wobblies, son," Rick explained to Pym, finding him on the stairs as he made to leave. "Slip in there and see if you can make her laugh with one of your stories. Is old Grimble feeding you up there?"

"It's super," said Pym.

"Your old man is seeing them right, know that? The healthiest school in Britain, this is. Ask them at the Ministry. Want a half-crown? Well then."

To reach Lippsie's bicycle Pym used a walk he had acquired from Sefton Boyd. You kept your hands lightly linked behind your back, shoved your head forward and fixed your eyes upon some vaguely pleasing object on the horizon. You stalked wide and high, smiling slightly, as if listening to other voices, which is how the flower of us wear authority. He was too small to sit on the tartan saddle but a lady's bicycle has a hole and not a bar, as Sefton Boyd was always happy to point out, and Pym swayed through the hole pumping his legs from side to side as he swung the handlebars between the rain-filled craters in the tarmac. I am the official bicycle collector. To his right was the kitchen garden where he and Lippsie had Dug for Victory, to his left the coppice where the German bomb had fallen, hurling bits of blackened twig against the window of the bedroom he shared with the Indian and the grocer's boy. But behind him in his terrified imagination was Sefton Boyd with his lictors in full cry, mimicking Lippsie at him because they knew he loved her: "Vere are you goink, mein little black market? Vot are you doink mit your sweetheart, mein little black market, now she be dead?" Ahead of him was the gate where he had waited for Mr. Cudlove, and to the left of the gate was the Overflow House with its iron railings ripped away for the war effort, and a policeman standing in the gap.

"I've been sent to collect my nature-study book," said Pym to the policeman, looking him straight in the eye as he leaned Lippsie's bicycle against a brick post. Pym had lied to policemen before and knew you must look honest.

"Your nature book, have you?" said the policeman. "What's your name, then?"

"Pym, sir. I live here."

"Pym who?"

"Magnus."

"Hop along then, Pym Magnus," said the policeman but Pym still walked slowly, refusing to show any sign of eagerness. Lippsie's silver-framed family was queued up on the bedside table, but Rick's heavy head dominated the lot of them, sensitive and political in its pigskin frame, and Rick's sage eyes followed him wherever he went. He opened Lippsie's wardrobe and breathed the smell of her, he shoved aside her frilly white dressing-gown, her fur cape and the camel-hair overcoat with the pixie's hood that Rick had bought her in St. Moritz. From the back of her wardrobe he pulled out her cardboard suitcase. He set it on the floor and opened it with the key she kept hidden in the Toby jug on the tiled mantelpiece next to the soft toy chimp who was Little Audrey who laughed and laughed and laughed. He took out the book like a Bible that was written in little black sword blades, and the music books and reading books he didn't understand and the passport with her picture in it when she was young, and the wads of letters in German from her sister Rachel, pronounced "Ra-ha-el," who no longer wrote to her, and from the very bottom of the case Rick's letters, tied into bundles with bits of harvest twine. Some he knew almost by heart, though he had difficulty unravelling the portent seething beneath their verbiage:

"It is a matter of weeks no days my darling before the present besetting clouds will be dispersed away as a permanency. Loft will have obtained my Discharge and you and I can enjoy our well-deserved Reward.... Look after that boy of mine who regards you as a Mother and make sure he doesn't turn out airy-fairy....

"Your doubts regarding Trust completely misplaced... you should not trouble your Head as it is a further worry to me here waiting for the Bugle's summons Perhaps never to Return... what is involved here will bring untold benefits to Many such as Wentworth... don't go on at me about W or his wife, that woman is a professional troublemaker of the worst kind out....

"My regards to Ted Grimble whom I consider a great Educationist and Headmaster. Tell him a further Hundred-weight of prunes on its way... he should prepare kitchen for Two gross best fresh oranges also. Loft has got me Out on three weeks compassionate which means I Recommence my basic from scratch if I am recalled. Regarding Another Matter, Muspole says to continue sending items as before. Please oblige quickly owing purely Temporary problem of liquidity this end which is preventing decent people like Wentworth being seen right....

"If you don't send more fee cheques immediately, you may as well send me back to Prison and all the Boys excepting Perce as usual and that's a Fact.... Talk about killing yourself is Foolishness with so many Killing each other round the World in this Senseless and Tragic war.... Muspole says if you send poste restaurant express Tomorrow he will be at P.O. when they open Saturday and send on to Wentworth immediately...."

Lippsie's letter, which he had left till last, was by contrast a marvel of conciseness:

"My dear darling Magnus,
"You must be good boy always, darling, play

your music and be strong like a man to your father, I
love you.

Lippsie"

Pym made a bundle of them, Lippsie's included, stuffed
them inside his nature book and the nature book inside his
belt. He rode past the policeman slowly, feeling cats' claws on
his back. The school boiler was a brick furnace built into the
basement, fed by a chute in the kitchen yard. To approach
the chute was a beatable offence, to burn paper was a
Quisling act and sailors would drown for it. A fierce rain was
blowing from the Downs, the chalk hills were olive against
the storm-clouds. Standing before the open chute, shoulders
high against his neck, Pym shoved the letters into it and
watched them disappear. A dozen people must have seen
him, staff and inmates, and some for sure were allies of Sefton
Boyd. But the openness with which he had proceeded convinced them he was acting on authority. Certainly it convinced Pym. He shoved in the last letter, which was the one
that told him to be strong, and walked away without once
turning to see if he was being noticed.

He needed the staff lavatory again. He needed his secret
St. Moritz with its panelled seclusion, he needed the secret
majesty of its brass taps and mahogany-framed mirror, for
Pym loved luxury as only those can who have had love taken
from them. He gained the forbidden staircase to the staffroom;
he reached the half-landing. The lavatory door was ajar. He
pushed it, slipped inside, locked it behind him. He was
alone. He stared at his face, making it harder, then softer,
then harder. He ran the taps and washed his cheeks till they
shone. His sudden isolation, added to the grandeur of his
achievement, made him unique in his own eyes. His mind
whirled with the vertigo of greatness. He was God. He was
Hitler. He was Wentworth. He was the king of the green
filing cabinet, TP's noble descendant. Henceforth, nothing on
earth need happen without his intervention. He took out his
penknife, opened it and held its big blade uppermost before
his face in the mirror, taking an Arthurian vow. By Excalibur I
swear. The lunch bell rang but there was no roll-call for lunch
and he was not hungry; he would never be hungry again, he
was an immortal knight. He thought of cutting his throat but
his mission was too important. He thought of names. Who

has the best family in school? I have. The Pyms are cracker-jack and Prince Magnus is the fastest horse in the world. He pressed his cheek against the wood panelling, smelling cricket bats and Swiss forests. The knife was still in his hand. His eyes went hot and blurred, his ears sang. The divine voice inside him told him to look, and he saw the initials "KS-B" carved very deeply into the best panel. Stooping, he gathered the splinters at his feet and put them into the lavatory where they floated. He pulled the plug but they still floated. He left them there, went to the arts hut and completed his Dornier bomber.

All afternoon he waited, confident nothing had happened. I didn't do it. If I went back it wouldn't be there. It was Maggs in third form. It was Jameson who owns a kukri, I saw him go in. An oik from the village did it, I saw him sneaking round the grounds with a dagger in his belt, his name is Wentworth. At evensong he prayed that a German bomb would destroy staff lavatory. None did. Next day, he presented Sefton Boyd with his greatest treasure, the koala bear Lippsie had given him after his appendix operation. In break he buried his penknife in the loose earth behind the cricket pavilion. Or as I would say today, cached it. It was not until evening line-up that the full name of the Honourable Kenneth Sefton Boyd was called out in a voice of doom by the duty master, the sadist O'Mally. Mystified, the young nobleman was led to Mr. Grimble's study. Mystified himself, Pym watched him go. Whatever can they want him for—my friend, my best friend, the owner of my koala bear? The mahogany door closed, eighty pairs of eyes fixed upon its fine workmanship, Pym's also. Pym heard Mr. Grimble's voice, then Sefton Boyd's raised in protest. Then a great silence while God's justice was administered, blow by blow. Counting, Pym felt cleansed and vindicated. So it wasn't Maggs, it wasn't Jameson and it wasn't me. Sefton Boyd did it himself, otherwise he would not have been beaten. Justice, he was beginning to learn, is only as good as her servants.

"It had a hyphen," Sefton Boyd told him next day. "Whoever did it gave us a hyphen when we haven't got one. If I ever find the sod I'll kill him."

"So will I," Pym promised loyally and meant every word. Like Rick he was learning to live on several planes at once. The art of it was to forget everything except the ground you stood on and the face you spoke from at that moment.

The effects of Lippsie's death upon the young Pym were many and not by any means all negative. Her demise entrenched him as a self-reliant person, confirming him in his knowledge that women were fickle and liable to sudden disappearances. He learned the great lesson of Rick's example, namely the importance of a respectable appearance. He learned that the only safety was in seeming legitimacy. He developed his determination to be a secret mover of life's events. It was Pym, for instance, who let down Mr. Grimble's tyres and poured three six-pound bags of cooking salt into the swimming-pool. But it was Pym who led the hunt for the culprit too, throwing up many tantalising clues and casting doubt on many solid reputations. With Lippsie gone, his love for Rick became once more unobstructed and, better, he could love him from a distance, for Rick had once more disappeared.

Had he gone back to prison, as he had promised Lippsie that he would? Had the police found the green filing cabinet? Pym did not know then and Syd, I suspect by choice, does not know now. Army records grant Rick an abrupt discharge six months before the period in question, referring the reader to the Criminal Records Office for an explanation. None is available, perhaps because that Perce had a friend who worked there, a lady who thought the world of him. Whatever the reason Pym floated out alone once more, and had a fair amount of fun. For weekend leave Ollie and Mr. Cudlove received him at their basement flat in Fulham and pampered him in every imaginable way. Mr. Cudlove, fit as ever from his exercises, taught him how to wrestle, and when they all went out for a toot on the river together, Ollie wore ladies' clothes and did a squeaky voice so well that only Pym and Mr. Cudlove in all the world ever knew there was a man inside them. For his longer holidays, Pym was obliged to trek over Cherry's vast estates with Sefton Boyd, listening to ever more awful stories about the great public school of which he would soon become a member: how new boys were tied into laundry baskets and flung down flights of stone stairs, how they were harnessed to pony traps with fish-hooks through their ears and made to haul the prefect round school yard.

"My father's gone to prison and escaped," Pym told him in return. "He's got a pet jackdaw that looks after him." He imagined Rick in a cave on Dartmoor, with Syd and Meg taking him pies wrapped in a handkerchief while the hounds sniffed his trail.

"My father's in the Secret Service," Pym told him another time. "He's been tortured to death by the Gestapo but I'm not allowed to say. His real name is Wentworth."

Having surprised himself by this pronouncement Pym worked on it. A different name and a gallant death suited Rick excellently. They gave him the class Pym was beginning to suspect he lacked and made things right with Lippsie. So when Rick came bouncing back one day, not tortured or altered in any way, but accompanied by two jockeys, a box of nectarines and a brand-new mother with a feather in her hat, Pym thought seriously of working for the Gestapo and wondered how you joined. And would have done so, too, for sure, had not the peace ungraciously robbed him of the chance.

A last word is also needed here about Pym's politics during this instructive period. Churchill sulked and was too popular. De Gaulle, with his tilted pineapple head, was too much like Uncle Makepeace, while Roosevelt, with his stick and spectacles and wheelchair, was clearly Aunt Nell in disguise. Hitler was so wretchedly unloved that Pym had more than a fair regard for him, but it was Joseph Stalin whom he appointed to be his proxy father. Stalin neither sulked nor preached. He spent his time chuckling, and playing with dogs, and picking roses in news cinemas while his loyal troops won the war for him in the snows of St. Moritz.

Putting down his pen, Pym stared at what he had written, first in fear, then gradually in relief. Finally he laughed.

"I didn't break," he whispered. "I stayed above the fray."

And poured himself a Poppy-sized vodka for old times' sake.

5

Frau Bauer's bed was as narrow and lumpy as a servant's bed in a fairy-tale and Mary lay in it exactly as Brotherhood had dumped her there, roly-polyed in the eiderdown, knees drawn up in self-protection, clutching her shoulders with her hands. He had slid off her, she could no longer smell his sweat and breath. But she could feel his bulk at the foot of the bed and sometimes she had a hard time remembering that they had not made love a few moments earlier, for his habit in those days had been to leave her dozing while he sat as he was sitting now, making his phone calls, checking his expenses or doing whatever else served to restore the order of his all-male life. He had found a tape-recorder somewhere and Georgie had a second in case his didn't work.

For a hangman Nigel was small but extremely dapper. He wore a waisted pinstripe suit and a silk handkerchief in his sleeve.

"Ask Mary to make a voluntary statement, will you, Jack?" Nigel said, as if he did this every week. "Voluntary but formal is the tone. Could be used, I'm afraid. The decision is not Bo's alone."

"Who the hell says voluntary?" said Brotherhood. "She signed the Official Secrets Act when she joined, she signed it again when she left. She signed it again when she married Pym. Everything you know is ours, Mary. Whether you heard it on top of a bus or saw the smoking gun in his hand."

"And your nice Georgie can witness it," said Nigel.

Mary heard herself talking but didn't understand a lot of what she said because she had one ear in the pillow and the other was listening to the morning sounds of Lesbos through the open window of their little brown terrace house halfway up the hill that Plomari was built on, to the clatter of mopeds and boats and bouzouki music and lorries revving in the alleys. To the scream of sheep having their throats cut at the butcher's and the slither of donkey hoofs on cobble and the yells of the vendors in the harbour market. If she squeezed her eyes tight enough, she could look over the orange rooftops across the street, past the chimneys and the clotheslines and the roof gardens full of geraniums, down to the waterfront and out to the long jetty with its red light winking on the point and its evil ginger cats soaking themselves in the sunshine while they watched the tramper putter out of the mist.

And that was how Mary saw her story henceforth as she told it to Jack Brotherhood: as a nightmarish film she dared look at only piecemeal, with herself as the meanest villain ever. The tramper draws alongside, the cats stretch, the gangway is lowered, the English family Pym—Magnus, Mary and son Thomas—file ashore in search of yet another perfect place away from it all. Because nowhere is far enough any more, nowhere is remote enough. The Pyms have become the Flying Dutchmen of the Aegean, scarcely landing before they pack again, changing boats and islands like driven souls, though only Magnus knows the curse, only Magnus knows who is pursuing them and why, and Magnus has locked that secret behind his smile with all his others. She sees him striding gaily ahead of her, clutching his straw hat against the breeze and his briefcase dangling from his other hand. She sees Tom stalking after him in the long grey flannels and school blazer with his Cub colours on the pocket, which he insists on wearing even when the temperature is in the eighties. And she sees herself still doped with last night's drink and oil fumes, already planning to betray them both. And following them in their bare feet she sees the native bearers with the Pyms' too-much-luggage, the towels and bed linen and Tom's Weetabix and all the other junk she packed in Vienna for their great sabbatical, as Magnus calls this once-in-a-lifetime family holiday they have all apparently been dreaming of, though Mary cannot remember it being mentioned until a few days before they left, and to be honest she would rather have gone back to England, collected the dogs from the gardener and the long-haired Siamese from Aunt Tab, and spent the time in Plush.

The bearers set down their burdens. Magnus, generous as ever, tips each of them from Mary's handbag while she holds it open for him. Stooped gawkily over the reception

committee of Lesbos cats, Tom declares they have ears like
celery. A whistle sounds, the bearers hop up the gangway,
the tramper is returned to the mist. Magnus, Tom and Mary
the traitor stare after it like every sad story of the sea, their
life's luggage dumped around them and the red beacon
dripping slow fire on their heads.

"Can we go back to Vienna after this?" asks Tom. "I'd
like to see Becky Lederer."

Magnus does not answer him. Magnus is too busy being
enthusiastic. He will be enthusiastic for his own funeral and
Mary loves him for this as she loves him for too much else,
does still. Sometimes his sheer goodness accuses me.

"This is it, Mabs!" he cries, waving an arm grandly at the
treeless conical hill of brown houses that is their newest
home. "We've found it. Plush-sur-mer." And he turns to her
with the smile she has not seen until this very holiday—so
gallant, so tired-bright in its despair. "We're safe here, Mabs.
We're okay."

He throws an arm around her, she lets him. He draws
her to him, they hug. Tom squeezes between, an arm round
each of them. "Hey, let *me* have some of that," he says.
Locked together like the closest allies in the world, the three
move off down the jetty, leaving their luggage till they have
found a place to put it. Which they achieve within the hour,
for clever Magnus knows just the right taverna to go to first
time, whom to charm and whom to recruit in the surprisingly
passable Greek identity he has somehow cobbled together for
himself on their journeying. But there is the evening yet to
come and the evenings are getting worse and worse, they
hang over her from when she wakes, she can feel them
creeping up on her all through her day. To celebrate their
new home Magnus has brought a bottle of scotch though they
have agreed several times in the last few days to lay off the
hard stuff and stick to local wine. The bottle is nearly empty
and Tom, thank God, is finally asleep in his new bedroom. Or
so Mary prays, for Tom has recently become a fag-ender, as
her father would have said, hanging around them for whatever he can pick up.

"Hey, come on, Mabs, that's a bit of a bad face, isn't it?"
says Magnus, jollying her up. "Don't you like our new *Schloss*?"

"You were being funny and I smiled."

"Didn't look like a smile," says Magnus, smiling himself

to show her how. "More like a bit of a grimace from where I sits, m'dear."

But Mary's blood is rising and as usual she cannot stop herself. The prospect of her uncommitted crime is already laying its guilt on her.

"That's what you're writing about, is it?" she snaps. "How you waste your wit on the wrong woman?"

Appalled by her own unpleasantness Mary bursts out weeping and drives her fists on to the arms of the rush chair. But Magnus is not appalled at all. Magnus puts down his glass and comes to her, he taps her gently on the arm with his fingertips, waiting to be let in. He puts her glass delicately out of reach. Moments later the springs of their new bed are pinging and whining like a brass band tuning up, for a desperate erotic fervour has latterly come to Magnus's aid. He makes love to her as if he will never see her again. He buries himself in her as if she is his only refuge and Mary goes with him blindly. She climbs, he draws her after him, she is shouting at him—"Please, oh Christ!" He hits the mark for her, and for a blessed moment Mary can kiss the whole bloody world goodbye.

"We're using Pembroke, by the way," Magnus says later but not quite late enough. "I'm sure it's unnecessary but I want to be on the safe side in case."

Pembroke is one of Magnus's worknames. He keeps the Pembroke passport in his briefcase, she has already located it. It has an artfully muddy photograph that might be Magnus or might not. In the forgery workshop in Berlin they used to call photographs like that floaters.

"What do I tell Tom?" she asks.

"Why tell him anything?"

"Our son's name is Pym. He might take a little oddly to being told he's Pembroke."

She waits, hating herself for her intractability. It is not often that Magnus has to hunt for an answer even when it concerns guidance on how to deceive their child. But he hunts now, she can feel him do it as he lies wakefully beside her in the dark.

"Yes, well tell him the Pembrokes own the house we're in, I should. We're using their name to order things from the shop. Only if asked, naturally."

"Naturally."

"Those two men are still there," says Tom from the door, who turns out to have been part of their conversation all this while.

"What men?" says Mary.

But her skin is pricking on her nape, her body is clammy with panic. How much has Tom heard? Seen?

"The ones who are mending their motorbike by the river. They've got special army sleeping-bags and a torch and a special tent."

"There are campers all over the island," says Mary. "Go back to bed."

"They were on our ship too," says Tom. "Behind the lifeboat, playing cards. Watching us. Speaking German."

"Lots of people were on the ship," says Mary. Why don't you say something, you bastard? she screams at Magnus in her head. Why do you lie dead instead of helping me when I'm still wet from you?

With Tom on one side of her, Magnus on the other, Mary listens to the bells of Plomari tolling out the hours. Four more days, she tells herself. On Sunday, Tom flies back to London for the new school term. And on Monday I'll do it and be damned.

Brotherhood was shaking her. Nigel had said something to him: ask her about the beginning—pin her down.

"We want you to come back a stage, Mary. Can you do that? You're running ahead of yourself."

She heard murmuring, then the sound of Georgie changing a reel on her tape-recorder. The murmuring was her own.

"Tell us how you came to be taking the holiday in the first place, will you, dear? Who proposed it? . . . Oh Magnus, did he? I see. And was that here in this house? . . . It was. . . . Now what time of day would that have been? Sit up, will you?"

So Mary sat up and began again where Jack had told her: on a sweet, early summer evening in Vienna when everything was still absolutely fine and neither Lesbos nor all the islands that came before it were a glint in clever Magnus's eye. Mary was in the basement in her overalls, binding a first edition of *Die letzten Tage der Menschheit*, by Karl Kraus

which Magnus had found in Leoben while meeting a Joe
there and Mary—

"That a regular one—Leoben?"

"Yes, Jack, Leoben was regular."

"How often did he go there?"

"Twice a month. Three times. It was an old Hungarian
he had, no one special."

"He told you that, did he? I thought he kept his Joes to
himself."

"An old Hungarian wine dealer from way back, with
offices in Leoben and Budapest. Mostly Magnus kept his
secrets to himself. Sometimes he told me. Now can I go on?"

Tom was at school, Frau Bauer was out praying, said
Mary. It was some kind of Catholic bean feast, Assumption,
Ascension, Prayer and Repentance, Mary had lost count.
Magnus was supposed to be at the American Embassy. The
new committee had just started meeting and she wasn't
expecting him back till late. She was bang in the middle of
glueing when suddenly, without hearing a sound, she saw
him standing in the doorway—God knows how long he'd
been there—looking very pleased with himself and watching
her the way he liked to.

"How was that, dear? Watched you how?" Brotherhood
cut in.

Mary had surprised herself. She faltered. "Superior,
somehow. Pained superiority. Jack, don't make me hate him,
please."

"All right, he's watching you," said Brotherhood.

He is watching her and when she catches sight of him he
bursts out laughing and shuts her mouth with passionate
kisses doing his Fred Astaire number, then it's upstairs for a
full and frank exchange of views, as he calls it. They make
love, he hauls her to the bath, washes her, hauls her out and
dries her, and twenty minutes later Mary and Magnus are
bounding across the little park on the top of Döbling like the
happy couple they nearly are, past the sandpits and the
climbing-frame that Tom is too big for, past the elephant cage
where Tom kicks his football, down the hill towards the
Restaurant Teheran which is their improbable pub because
Magnus so adores the black-and-white videos of Arab romances they play for you with the sound down while you eat
your couscous and drink your Kalterer. At the table he holds

her arm fiercely and she can feel his excitement racing through her like a charge, as if having her has made him want her more.

"Let's get away, Mabs. Let's really get away. Let's live life for a change instead of acting it. Let's take Tom and all our mid-tour leave and bugger off for the whole of the summer. You paint, I'll write my book, and we'll make love until we fall apart."

Mary says where to, Magnus says who cares, I'll go to the travel agent on the Ring tomorrow. Mary says what about the new committee. He is holding her hand inside his own, touching it with his fingertips into little peaks, and she is going mad for him again, which is what he likes.

"The new committee, Mary," Magnus pronounces, "is the most stupid bloody charade I've been mixed up in, and believe me, I've seen a few. All it is, it's a talking-shop to goose up the Firm's ego and allow them to tell whoever will listen to them that we're hugger-mugger in bed with the Americans. Lederer can't possibly imagine we're going to unveil our networks to him, and as for Lederer, he wouldn't tell me the name of his tailor, let alone his agents—assuming he's got either, which I doubt."

Brotherhood again: "Did he tell you *why* Lederer mightn't be inclined to talk to him?"

"No," said Mary.

Nigel for a change: "And no other reasons offered as to why or how the committee might be a charade?"

"It was a charade, it was a sham, it was makework. That's all he said. I asked about his Joes, he said the Joes could look after themselves and if Jack was bothered about them he could send a locum. I asked what Jack would think—"

"And what *would* Jack think?" said Nigel, all open curiosity.

"He said Jack's a sham too: 'I'm not married to Jack, I'm married to you. The Firm should have retired him ten years ago. Sod Jack.' Sorry. That's what he said."

Hands shoved in his pockets, Brotherhood took a stroll round the little room, poking at Frau Bauer's photographs of her illegitimate daughter, poring over her shelf of paperback romances.

"Anything else about me?" he asked.

"Jack's had too many miles in the saddle. The Boy Scout era's over. It's a new scene and he's not up to it."

"Any more?" said Brotherhood.

Nigel had lowered his chin into his hand and was studying one small but perfectly formed shoe.

"No," said Mary.

"Did he go for a walk that night? Meet P?"

"He'd been the night before."

"I said that night. Answer the bloody question!"

"And I said the night before!"

"With a newspaper. The whole bit?"

"Yes."

His hands still in his pockets, his head high against his shoulders, Brotherhood turned stiffly to Nigel. "I'm going to tell her," he said. "You want to throw a fit?"

"Are you asking me formally?" Nigel asked.

"Not particularly."

"If you are, I'll have to pass it to Bo," said Nigel and looked respectfully at his gold watch as if he took orders from it.

"Lederer knows and we know. If Pym knows too, who's left?" Brotherhood insisted.

Nigel thought about this. "Up to you. Your man, your decision, your tail-end. Frankly."

Brotherhood leaned over Mary and put his head close to her ear. She remembered his smell: tweedy and paternal. "Listening?"

She shook her head. I'm not, I never will be, I wish I never had.

"The new committee that your Magnus derided was shaping up to be a very high-powered outfit. Maybe the best potential working relationship at field level that we've had with the Americans for years. The name of the game was mutual trust. Not as easy to establish these days as it used to be, but we managed it. Are you going to sleep?"

She nodded.

"Your Magnus was not only aware of this, he was one of the prime movers in getting the committee off the ground. If not *the* prime mover. He even went so far as to complain to me, when we were negotiating the deal, that London was being small-minded in its interpretation of the barter terms. He thought we should give the Americans more. In exchange for more. That's number one."

I have absolutely nothing else to say. You can have my

home address, my next of kin and that's your lot. You taught
me that yourself, Jack, in case they ever grabbed me.

"Number two is that for reasons which I regarded at the
time as specious and insulting, the Americans objected to
your husband's presence on that committee not three weeks
after it met, and asked me to replace him with somebody
more to their liking. Since Magnus was kingpin of the Czecho
operation and of several other little shows in Eastern Europe
besides, this was a totally unrealistic demand. They'd raised
the same objections about him in Washington the year before
and Bo had bowed to them, in my view mistakenly. I wasn't
about to let them do it again. I happen not to care for
American gentlemen or anybody else telling me how to run
my shop. I said no and ordered Magnus to take himself off on
mid-tour leave and stay clear of Vienna till I told him to come
back. That's the truth, and I think it's time you heard some."

"It's also very secret," said Nigel.

She waited in vain to be amazed. No surge of protest, no
flash of the celebrated family temper. Brotherhood had taken
himself to the window and was staring out. Morning had
come early because of the snow. He looked old and beaten.
His white hair was fluffed against the light and she could see
the pink skin of his scalp.

"You defended him," she said. "You were loyal."

"Seems as if I was a bloody fool as well."

The house had turned itself upside down. The thump of
shifting furniture came from below them in the drawing-
room. The safest place to be was here. Upstairs with Jack.

"Oh don't be so hard on yourself, Jack," Nigel said.

Brotherhood had sat Mary in the chair and handed her a
whisky. You get one only, he had said; make it last. Nigel
had taken over the bed and was lounging on it with one
suited little leg stuck out in front of him as if he'd sprained it
trying to get up the steps of his club. Brotherhood had turned
his back on both of them. He preferred the view from the
window.

"So first you go to Corfu. Your auntie has a house there.
You borrowed it from her. Tell that bit. Carefully."

"Aunt Tab," said Mary.

"In full, I think," said Nigel.

"Lady Tabitha Grey. Daddy's sister."

"Sometime member of the Firm," Brotherhood murmured to Nigel. "There's hardly a member of her family hasn't been on our books at one time or another, come to think of it."

She had telephoned Aunt Tab as soon as they got back from their drink that evening, and by a miracle there'd been a cancellation and her house was free. They took it, phoned Tom's school and arranged for him to fly there direct when term ended. As soon as the Lederers heard, they wanted to come too of course. Grant said he would drop everything but Magnus wouldn't hear of it. The Lederers are exactly the kind of social prop I need to kick away, he had said. Why the hell should I take my work with me on holiday? Five days later they were settled into Tab's house and everything was absolutely fine. Tom took tennis lessons at the hotel up the road, swam, fed the landlady's goats and pottered around the boat with Costas who looked after it and watered the garden. But his best thing was the crazy cricket matches on the edge of town that Magnus took him to in the evenings. Magnus said the Brits had brought the game to the island when they were defending it against Napoleon. Magnus knew those things. Or pretended to.

At the cricket in Corfu Magnus was closer to Tom than he had ever been. They lay on the grass, munched ice creams, rooted for their favourite players and had those mannish chats that were so crucial to Tom's happiness: for Tom loved Magnus to distraction; he was a man's boy, always had been. As to Mary, she had taken up pastels because Corfu in summer was really too hot for her style of watercolours, the paint just dried on the page before she could get near it. But she was drawing well, getting nice likenesses and shapes, and playing hostess to half the dogs on the island because the Greeks don't feed them or look after them or *anything*. So everyone was happy, everyone absolutely fine and Magnus had a cool conservatory to write in, and inland walks for his restlessness, which came to him first thing in the morning and again in late evening after he had held it off all day. They lunched late, usually in a taverna—and often rather a liquid affair, to be honest, but why not, they were on holiday. Then long sexy siestas while Mary and Magnus made love on the balcony and Tom lay on the beach studying the nudies across the bay with Magnus's binoculars, so as Magnus put it everybody was getting his pound of flesh. Until one day the clock stopped dead and Magnus came back from a late walk and confessed he had hit a bit of a block with his writing. He just strode in, poured himself a stiff ouzo, flung himself into a chair and said it straight out:

"Sorry, Mabs. Sorry, Tom, old chap. But this place is too damned idyllic. I need roughing up a bit. I need *people*, for Christ's sake. Smoke and dirt and a bit of suffering around us. It's like being on the moon here, Mabs. Worse than Vienna. Truly."

He was sweet about it but he was adamant. He'd been drinking, obviously, but that was because he was upset. "I'm going bonkers, Mabs. It's really getting to me. I told Tom. Didn't I, Tom? I said I really can't take much more of this and I feel a shit because you two are having such a good time."

"Yes, he did," said Tom.

"Several times. And today it's just hit me, Mabs. You've got to help me out. Both of you."

So of course they both said they would. Mary rang Tab at once, so that she could put the house back on the market, they all had a bear-hug and went to bed feeling resolved, and next day Mary packed while Magnus went off to town to do tickets and fix the next stage of their odyssey. But Tom, over washing-up which was always a talkative time for him, had a different version of why they were leaving Corfu. Daddy had met this mystery man at cricket. It was a really super match, Mum, the best two teams on the island, a real vendetta. We were watching it like mad and suddenly there was this wise, stringy man with a sad moustache like a conjuror's and a limp, and Dad got all uptight. He came up to Dad smiling, they talked a bit, they walked round and round the ground together with the thin man going slowly like an invalid, but he was terribly kind to Dad although Dad got so emanated.

"Animated," Mary corrected him automatically. "Don't talk too loud, Tom. I think Daddy's working somewhere."

And there was this really incredible batsman, said Tom. Called Phillippi. Just the absolute best batsman Tom had seen *ever*. "He scored eighteen in one over and the crowd went absolutely ape, but Dad didn't notice, he was so busy listening to the kind man."

"How do you know he was so kind?" said Mary with a strange irritation. "Keep your voice down." There was no light in the conservatory, but sometimes Magnus sat there in the dark.

"He was like a father with him, Mum. He's senior to him but sort of calm. He kept offering Dad a ride in his car. Dad kept saying no. But he didn't get angry or anything, he was too wise. He gentled him and smiled."

"What car? It's just a great big romance, Tom. You know it is."

"The Volvo. Mr. Kaloumenos's Volvo. One man was driving and another man in the back. They kept up with them on the other side of the fence when they went round and round talking. Honestly, Mum. The thin man never lost his temper or anything, and he really likes Dad, you can tell. It's not just holding arms. They're friends to each other. Much more than Uncle Grant. More like Uncle Jack."

Mary asked Magnus that night. They'd packed, she was excited to be moving, and really looking forward to the Athens museums.

"Tom says you were harassed by some tiresome man at the cricket match," said Mary while they enjoyed a rather stiff nightcap after their heavy day.

"Was I?"

"Some little man who chased you round and round the ground. Sounded like an angry husband to me. He had a moustache, unless Tom imagined it."

Then vaguely Magnus did remember. "Oh that's right. He was some boring ancient Brit who kept pressuring me to go and see his villa. Wanted to flog it. Bloody little pest actually."

"He spoke German," said Tom, next day at breakfast while Magnus was out walking.

"Who did?"

"Dad's thin friend. The man who picked Dad up at the cricket. And Dad spoke German back to him too. Why did Dad say he was an ancient Brit?"

Mary flew at him. She hadn't been so angry with him for years. "If you want to listen to our conversations, you bloody well come in and listen to them and don't skulk outside the door like a spy."

Then she was ashamed of herself and played tennis with him till the boat left. On the boat Tom was sick as a dog and by the time they reached Piraeus he had a temperature of a hundred and three so her guilt was unconfined. At the Athens hospital a Greek doctor diagnosed shrimp rash which was absurd because Tom loathed shrimps and hadn't touched a single one; by now his face was swollen like a hamster's, so they took expensive rooms and put him to bed with an icepack and Mary read fantasy to him while Magnus listened or sat in Tom's room to write. But mainly he liked to listen because the best thing in his life, he always said, was watching her comfort their child. She believed him.

"Didn't he go out at all?" Brotherhood asked.

"Not to begin with. He didn't want to."

"Make any phone calls?" said Nigel.

"The Embassy. To check in. So that you'd know where he was."

"He tell you that?" said Brotherhood.

"Yes."

"You weren't there when he made them?" Nigel said.

"No."

"Hear him through the wall?" Nigel again.

"No."

"Know who he spoke to?" Still Nigel.

"No."

From his place on the bed Nigel lifted his eyes to Brotherhood. "But he phoned *you*, Jack," he said encouragingly. "Little chats from out-of-the-way places with his old boss now and then? That's practically mandatory, isn't it? Check on the Joes—'How's our old buddy from you-know-where?'"

Nigel is one of the new non-professionals, Mary remembered Magnus telling her. He's one of the idiots who are supposed to be introducing a breath of Whitehall realism. If ever I heard a contradiction in terms, that's it, said Magnus.

"Not a peep," Brotherhood was replying. "All he did was send me a string of stupid postcards saying 'Thank God you're not here' and giving me his latest address."

"When did he start going out?" said Nigel.

"When Tom's temperature went down," Mary replied.

"A week?" said Nigel invitingly. "Two?"

"Less," said Mary.

"Describe," said Brotherhood.

It was evening, probably their fourth day. Tom's face was normal again so Magnus suggested Mary go shopping while he baby-sat Tom to give her a break. But Mary wasn't keen on braving the Athens streets alone so Magnus went instead; Mary would do a museum in the morning. He came back around midnight very pleased with himself saying he'd found this marvellous old Greek travel agent in a basement opposite the Hilton, a tremendously cultured fellow, and how they had drunk ouzo together and solved the problems of the universe. The old man ran a villa-renting service for the islands and hoped to turn up a cancellation in a week or so when they'd all had enough of Athens.

"I thought islands were out," Mary said.

For a moment it seemed that Magnus had forgotten the reason they had left Corfu. He smiled lamely and said something about not every island being the same. After that, she seemed to lose count of the days. They moved to a smaller hotel; Magnus wrote and wrote, went out in the evenings and when Tom was well enough took him swimming. Mary sketched the Acropolis and took Tom to a couple of museums but he preferred swimming. Meanwhile they waited for the old Greek to come up with something.

Brotherhood was once more interrupting. "This writing of his. How much did he talk about it exactly?"

"He wanted to preserve his secrecy. Scraps. That was all he gave me."

"Like his Joes. The same," Brotherhood suggested.

"He wanted to keep me fresh for when he'd really got something to show me. He didn't want to talk it out of himself."

It was a quiet and, as Mary now remembered it, strangely furtive time until one night Magnus vanished. He went out after dinner saying he was going to give the old boy a prod. Next morning he hadn't come back and by lunchtime Mary was scared. She knew she should phone the Embassy. On the other hand she didn't want to start a scare unnecessarily or do anything that might get Magnus into trouble.

Yet again Brotherhood cut in. "What sort of trouble?"

"If he'd gone on a bender or something. It wouldn't exactly have looked well on his file. Just when he was hoping for promotion."

"Had he gone on benders before?"

"Absolutely not. He and Grant got drunk together occasionally but that was as far as it went."

Nigel sharply lifted his head. "But why should he be

expecting promotion? Who said anything about promotion to him?"

"I did," said Brotherhood without a whiff of repentance. "I reckoned after all the messing him around he was about owed it with his reinstatement."

Nigel made a neat little note in his book and smiled mirthlessly as he wrote. Mary went on.

Anyway, she waited till evening then took Tom up to the Hilton and together they explored all the houses opposite until they found the cultured old Greek in his basement, exactly as Magnus had described him. But the Greek hadn't seen Magnus for a week and Mary wouldn't stay for coffee. When they got back to the taverna they found Magnus with two days' beard, dressed in the clothes he had disappeared in, sitting in the courtyard and eating bacon and eggs, drunk. Not silly drunk, he couldn't do that. Not angry drunk, or maudlin, or aggressive, and least of all indiscreet, because drink only ever fortified his defences. Courteous drunk, therefore, and amiable to a fault as ever, and his cover story perfectly intact except for one rare mistake.

"Sorry, gang. Got a bit pissed with Dimitri. Swine drank me clean under the table. Hullo, Tom."

"Hullo," said Tom.

"Who's Dimitri?" Mary asked.

"You know who Dimitri is. Old Greek travel agent who does his beads across the road from the Hilton."

"The cultured one."

"That's him."

"Last night?"

"Far as I can remember, old girl, last night as ever was."

"Dimitri hasn't seen you since last Monday. He told us himself an hour ago."

Magnus considered this. Tom had found a copy of the *Athens News* and was standing at the next table intently studying the film page.

"You checked on me, Mabs. You shouldn't have done that."

"I wasn't checking on you, I was looking for you!"

"Don't make a scene now, girl. Please. Other people eating here, you see."

"I'm not making a scene. You are. It's not me who

disappears for two days and comes back with a lie. Tom, go to your room, darling. I'll be up in a minute."

Tom left, smiling brightly to show he hadn't heard anything. Magnus took a long drink of coffee. Then he grasped Mary's hand and kissed it and gently pulled her down on to the chair beside him.

"Which would you rather I told you, Mabs? I was carousing with a whore or I've got problems with a Joe?"

"Why don't you just tell me the truth?"

The suggestion amused him. Not cruelly or cynically. Merely, he received it with the rueful indulgence that he would show towards Tom when he came through with one of his solutions for ending world poverty or the arms race.

"Know something?" He kissed her hand again and held it against his cheek. "Nothing goes away in life." To her surprise she felt moisture in his stubble and realised he was weeping. "I'm in Constitution Square, right? Coming out of the Grande Bretagne bar. Minding my own business. What happens? I walk straight into the arms of a Czech Joe I used to run. Real tough egg, fabricator, caused us a lot of problems. Holds my arm like this. 'Colonel Manchester! Colonel Manchester!' Threatens to call the police, expose me as a British spy if I don't give him money. Says I'm the only friend he's got left in the world. 'Come and drink with me, Colonel Manchester. Like we used to.' So I did. Drank him right under the table. Then gave him the slip. I'm afraid I got a bit pissed myself. Line of duty. Let's go to bed."

And they do. And make love. The desperate screwing of strangers while Tom reads fantasy next door. And two days later they leave for Hydra, but Hydra is too cramped, too ominous, there is suddenly nowhere to go but Spetsai: at this time of year we'll have no problem. Tom asks if Becky can join them, Magnus says no she absolutely can't because they'll all want to come and he's not going to have a pride of Lederers sitting on his head while he's trying to write. Otherwise, apart from his drinking, Magnus has never been more caring and polite than now.

She had stopped. Like standing back from a painting halfway. Studying the story so far. She drank some whisky, lit a cigarette.

"Christ," said Brotherhood softly. Then nothing.

Nigel had found a bit of dead skin on the back of one undersized finger and was picking it off meticulously.

It is Lesbos again, it is another dawn but the same Greek bed and Plomari is once more waking up though Mary is praying it will go back to sleep again, that the sounds will fade and the sun flop behind the rooftops where it came from, because it is Monday and yesterday Tom went back to school. Mary has the evidence under her pillow where she promised to put the rabbitskin he gave her to keep her safe—and as if she needed it to strengthen her resolve—the terrible memory of his last words to her before he left. Mary and Magnus have driven him to the airport, weighed him in for yet another departure. Tom and Mary are standing about unable to touch each other while they wait for the flight to be called, Magnus is at the bar buying Tom a bag of pistachios for the journey and an ouzo for himself while he's about it. Mary has six times confirmed that Tom has his passport and his money and his letter to Matron about his shrimp rash, and his letter to Granny to be handed to her the *moment* you meet her at London Airport, darling, so that you don't forget. But Tom is even more than usually distracted; he is looking back to the main entrance, watching the people going through the swing doors, and there is something desperate in his face, so desperate that Mary really wonders whether he is thinking of making a dash for it.

"Mums?" Sometimes, when he is distracted, he still calls her that.

"Yes, darling."

"They're here, Mums."

"Who are?"

"Those two campers from Plomari. They're sitting in the airport carpark on their motorbike, watching Dad."

"Now darling just *stop*," Mary retorts firmly, determined to drive away these shadows, one and all. "Just completely stop, okay?"

"Only I've recognised them, you see. I worked it out this morning. I remembered. They're the men who drove the car round the outside of the cricket ground at Corfu while Dad's friend tried to make him come for a drive."

For a moment, though Mary has been through this

agonising procedure a dozen times before, she wants to
scream out: "Stay—don't go—I don't care a damn about your
bloody education—stay with me!" But instead the fool waves
him through the barrier and saves her tears for the journey
back while Magnus is absolutely sweet to her as ever. And
now it is next morning, Tom is just about arriving at his
school, and Mary is staring at the prison bars of Kyria
Katina's rotting shutters while the sky remorselessly whitens
through the cracks and she is trying not to hear the clanking
of the water-pipes beneath her and the rush of water free-
falling onto the flagstones as Magnus celebrates his morning
shower.

"Wowee! Christ! You awake, girl? It's brass monkeys
down here, believe me!"

Believe you, she repeats to herself and draws deeper
into the bedclothes. In fifteen years he never called me girl
till here. Now suddenly she is girl all day as if he has woken
to her gender. A single width of floorboard separates her from
him and if she dares look over the bedside she will glimpse
his stranger's naked body through the gaps between the
planks. Receiving no reply from her, Pym starts singing his
one piece of Gilbert and Sullivan while he sloshes water.

"'Rising early in the morning, We proceed to light the
fire . . .' How'm I doing?" he calls when he has sung all he
knows.

Mary in another life has a small reputation for her music.
In Plush she led a passable group in madrigals. When she
was doing her stint at Head Office she sang solo in the Firm
choir. It's just that nobody's ever played records for you, she
used to tell him in a veiled criticism of his first wife, Belinda.
One day your singing voice will be as good as your spoken
one, darling.

She summons her breath. "Better than Caruso!" she
shouts.

The exchange is accomplished, Magnus can resume his
showering.

"It went well, Mabs. Really well. Seven pages of death-
less prose. Undercoat but good."

"Great."

He has started shaving. She can hear him empty the
kettle into the plastic washing-up bowl. Contour blades, she
thinks: oh God, I forgot to buy him his bloody Contour

blades. All the way to the airport and back she had known there was something she had forgotten, for little things are as dreadful to her as big things these days. Now I will buy cheese for lunch. Now I will buy bread to go with the cheese. She closes her eyes and takes another enormous breath.

"Did you sleep?" she asks.

"Like the dead. Didn't you notice?"

Yes, I noticed. I noticed how you slipped out of bed at two in the morning and crept downstairs to your workroom. How you paced and stopped pacing. I heard the creak of your chair and the whisper of your felt-tipped pen as you began to write. Who to? In what voice? Which one?

A boom of music drowns the sound of his shaving. He has switched on his clever radio for the BBC *World News*. Magnus knows the time to the minute, all through the day and night. If he looks at his watch it is only to confirm the schedules in his brain. She listens numbly to a recitation of events no one is able to control. A bomb has gone off in Beirut. A town has been wiped out in El Salvador. The pound has fallen. Or risen. The Russians are out of the next Olympics— or into them after all. Magnus follows politics like a gambler who is too wise to bet. The noise grows steadily louder as Magnus carries the radio upstairs, slop, slop, naked except for his sandals. He bends over her and she smells his shaving soap and the flat Greek cigarettes he has taken to smoking while he writes.

"Still sleepy?"

"A bit."

"How's Rat?"

Mary has been tending a half-eviscerated rat she found in the garden. It is lying in a straw box in Tom's room.

"I haven't looked," she says.

He kisses her close to the ear, an explosion, and starts to fondle her breast as a sign to her to take him but she grunts an awkward "Later" and rolls over. She hears him slop to the wardrobe, she hears the old door resist and jolt open. If he chooses shorts he's going for a walk. If he chooses jeans he's going into town to drink with the deadbeats. Colonel call-me-Parkie Parker, with my Greek fancy-boy and my Sealyham dog that I hold on the lead like a teapot. Elsie and Ethel, retired dyke schoolteachers from Liverpool. Jock somebody,

I've a wee business in Dundee. Magnus pulls out a shirt and slips it on. She hears him fastening his shorts.

"Where are you going?" she says.

"For a walk."

"Wait for me. I'll come with you. You can tell me about it."

Who was this speaking out of her suddenly—this mature straight-to-the-point woman?

Magnus is as surprised as she is: "About what, for heaven's sake?"

"Whatever it is that's worrying you, darling. I don't mind. Just tell me, whatever it is, so that I don't have to . . ."

"Don't have to what?"

"Bottle it up. Look away."

"Nonsense. Everything's fine. We're just both a bit blue without Tom." He comes to her and lays her back on the pillow as if she were an invalid. "You sleep it off, I'll walk it off. See you at the taverna round three."

Only Magnus can make Kyria Katina's front door close so softly.

Suddenly Mary is strong. His departure has released her. Breathe. She goes to the north window, everything planned. She has done these things before and remembers now that she is good at them, often steadier than the men. In Berlin when Jack needed a spare girl Mary had kept watch, gulled room keys out of concierges, replaced stolen documents in dangerous desks, driven scared Joes to safe flats. I knew the game better than I realised, she thought. Jack used to praise my coolness and my sharp eye. From the window she sees the new tarmac road winding into the hills. Sometimes he goes that way, but not today. Opening the window, she leans out as if savouring the place and morning. That witch Katina has milked her goats early; that means she's gone to market. Only one fleeting glance does Mary allow herself towards the dried-up river bed where, in the shadow of the stone footbridge, the same two boys are tinkering with their German-registered motorbike. If they had appeared outside the house in Vienna like this, Mary would have been on to Magnus in an instant—phoned him if need be at the Embassy. "Looks like the angels are flying rather low today," she'd have said. And Magnus would have done whatever he did—alerted the diplomatic patrol, sent his people down to check them out. But now in their separated lives it is as if they have agreed between them that angels, even suspected ones, are not to be remarked upon.

His workroom is on the ground floor. He does not lock the door on her but there is an ethic between them that she does not enter except at his specific beckoning. She turns the handle and steps inside. The shutters are closed but they do not cover the upper window panes and there is light for her to see by. Tread heavily, she tells herself, remembering her training. If you have to make a noise, make a bold one. The room is sparse, which is what Magnus likes. A desk, a chair, a single bed to crash on between bursts of creative matrix-writing. She pulls back the chair and sends a bottle of vodka skidding. The desk is covered with books and papers but she touches nothing. His old buckram-bound copy of *Simplicissimus* occupies pride of place as usual. His mascot. His something. It is a source of permanent offence to Mary that he will never let her bind it. Because I like it the way it is, he says stubbornly. That's how it was given to me. By some woman no doubt. "For Sir Magnus who will never be my enemy" reads the inscription in German. Screw her. And screw fancy nicknames.

Brotherhood had again interrupted.

"Where's it now, this book?"

With difficulty and a slight resentment Mary returned to time present.

But Brotherhood insisted: "It's not in his desk downstairs. I didn't see it lying about in the drawing-room either. It's not in the bedroom or in Tom's room. Where is it?"

"I told you," she said. "He takes it everywhere."

"You didn't, but thank you," Brotherhood retorted.

She is wearing a pair of cotton gloves against sweat and grime marks. He'll use a trick. He does those things instinctively. His old briefcase lies on the floor, wide open, but she doesn't touch that either. Other books are strewn like paperweights to hold down the manuscript and seemingly at random. She reads a title. It is in German: *Freedom and Conscience* by someone she has never heard of. Beside it, a copy of Madox Ford's *Good Soldier*, which Magnus reads incessantly these days; it has become his Bible. Beside this again, an old photograph album. Gently she lifts the unfamiliar cover and without moving it turns a few pages. Magnus aged eight in football gear, a team group. Magnus aged five in alpine setting holding a toboggan. Magnus at Tom's age already with his overwilling smile, inviting you in but not expecting to be invited. Magnus on honeymoon with Belinda, neither of them looking more than about twelve years old. She has not seen these photographs before. Letting the cover fall, Mary steps back and again surveys the arrangement on the desk. As she does so his bit of tradecraft becomes apparent to her. Each of the three books, lying seemingly haphazardly across the papers, is aligned to the point of the paper scissors at their centre. Going to the kitchen Mary grabs the tablecloth, comes back and lays it on the floor beside the desk, then measures the distances between each object on the desk with her gloved hand. As gently as if she is lifting bandages from a wound she lays them in the same pattern on the tablecloth. The papers on the desk now lie free for her inspection. She has not reckoned with so much dust. Just by crossing the floor she has set up clouds of it. I'm a tomb robber, she thinks, as the dust burns her throat. She is gazing at a wad of handwritten manuscript. The top page is dark with crossings-out. She picks up the wad, leaving everything else lying. She takes it to the little bed, sits down. At Plush when she was a girl they had called it "Kim's Game" and played it every New Year's Eve along with acting games and Murder and reels. At the training house, when she was supposed to be adult, they called it Observation and played it round the sleepy villages of Dedham, Manningtree and Bergholt: who's had their door painted this week, pruned their roses, bought a new car; how many bottles of milk did No. 18 have on its doorstep? But wherever they play it Mary always comes top by miles; she is cursed with a snapshot memory from which very little ever goes away.

Bits of novel, she told Brotherhood, all beginnings.

A dozen Chapter Ones, some typed and some in long-hand, all stiff with crossings-out. Mostly they told about the orphan childhood of a boy called Ben.

Doodles. Drawings of an arm stretched out to steal. A woman's crotch.

Notes to himself, all abusive: "sentimental crap"..."rewrite or destroy"... "You've missed the curse we pass from man to child".... "One day a Wentworth will get us all."

A pink folder marked "Random Passages." Ben gives himself up to the authorities. Ben discovers there is another, real Secret Service, and joins it in the nick of time. A blue folder marked "Final Scenes," several of them addressed to "Poppy, dear bloody Poppy." A sheet of cartridge paper stolen from her sketch block on which Magnus has drawn a pattern of linked think-bubbles to form a flow chart of his ideas, exactly as Tom is taught to prepare his essays at school. Bubble: "If all Nature abhors a vacuum, how does a vacuum feel about all Nature?" Bubble: "Duplicity is when you please one person at the expense of another." Bubble: "We are patriots because we are afraid to be cosmopolitan, cosmopolitan because we are afraid to be patriots."

There was a tapping at the door but Brotherhood shook his head at Georgie, telling her to ignore it.

"It wasn't his true writing," Mary said. "It was all spiky. It ran for a while then seized up. It seemed to hurt him to go on."

Brotherhood didn't give a damn whom it hurt.

"More," he said. "More. Hurry."

"It's me, sir," Fergus called through the door. "Urgent message, sir. Very."

"I said wait," Brotherhood ordered.

"'The systems of Ben's life are all collapsing,'" Mary continued. "'All his life he's been inventing versions of himself that are untrue. Now the truth is coming to get him and he is on the run. His Wentworth is standing at the door.'"

"More," said Brotherhood, towering over her.

"'Rick invented me, Rick is dying. What will happen when Rick drops his end of the string?'"

"Keep going."

"A quotation from Saint Luke. I never saw him open a Bible in his life. 'He who is faithful in a very little is faithful also in much.'"

"And?"

"'He who is dishonest in a very little is dishonest also in much.' He'd illuminated the edges of the page for hours on end. Different inks."

"And?"

"'Wentworth was Rick's Nemesis. Poppy was mine. We each spent our lives trying to put right what we'd done to them.'"

"And again!"

"'Now everyone's after me. The Firm's after me, the

Americans are after me, you're after me. Even poor Mary is after me, and she doesn't know you exist.'"

"*You* being who? Who's *you* in this poem?"

"'Poppy. My destiny. Dearest Poppy, best of best friends, get your bloody dogs off my doorstep.'"

"Poppy like the flowers," Brotherhood suggested, shoving away Georgie's microphone as he knelt beside her. "Like the flowers in the chimney. But singular. One Poppy."

"Yes."

"And Wentworth like the place. Sunny Wentworth, in tasteful Surrey?"

"Yes."

"Know him—her—anyone of that name?"

"No."

"Or Poppy?"

"No."

"On."

"There was a Chapter Eight," she said. "Out of the blue. No Two to Seven, but this Chapter Eight, all in his own handwriting and without a crossing-out. Titled 'Overdue Bills,' whereas the Chapter Ones were untitled. Describing a day when Ben revolts against all his promises. Slipping from third to first person and staying there, whereas the Chapter Ones were 'he' and 'Ben.' The creditors are beating at the door, Wentworth to the fore, but Ben doesn't give a damn. I lower my head and lift my shoulders, I wade at them, I punch and flail and butt them while they smash my face in. But even with no face left I am doing what I should have done thirty-five years ago, to Jack and Rick and all the mothers and fathers, for stealing my life off my plate while I watched you do it. Poppy, Jack, the rest of you, driving me into a lifetime's—a lifetime's—a lifetime's—'"

She had stopped. Iron clamps had squeezed the breath out of her. The door opened and Fergus gatecrashed, a flouting of discipline for which he would surely be punished. Nigel was staring at him expressionlessly. Georgie was rolling her eyes at him, pointing at the door and mouthing Get out, get out, but Fergus stood his ground.

"A lifetime's what, for God's sake?" Brotherhood was shouting in her ear.

She was whispering. She was screaming. She was fighting the word inside her mouth, heaving and pressing at it but nothing came out. Brotherhood shook her, at first gently, then much harder, then very hard indeed.

"Betrayal," she said. "'We betray to be loyal. Betrayal is like imagining when the reality isn't good enough.' He wrote that. Betrayal as hope and compensation. As the making of a better land. Betrayal as love. As a tribute to our unlived lives. On and on, these ponderous aphorisms about betrayal. Betrayal as escape. As a constructive act. As a statement of ideals. Worship. As an adventure of the soul. Betrayal as travel: how can we discover new places if we never leave home? 'You were my Promised Land, Poppy. You gave my lies a reason.'"

And that was the very phrase she had got to in her reading, she explained—the one about Poppy and the Promised Land—when she turned round and saw Magnus in his shorts standing in the open doorway to his workroom, holding a big blue envelope in one hand and the telegram in the other, smiling like the head boy of one of his schools.

"There was someone else inside him," Mary said, shocking herself. "It wasn't him."

"What the hell does that mean? You just said it was Magnus, standing in the doorway. What are you getting at?"

She didn't know either. "It was something that had happened to him when he was young. Someone standing in doorways watching him. He was doing it back somehow. I could see the recognition in his face."

"What did he *say*?" Nigel suggested helpfully.

She had a voice for Magnus, or perhaps it was just a facial expression. Empty yet impenetrable. Tirelessly polite: "Hullo, old love. Catching up with the great novel, are we? Not exactly Jane Austen, I'm afraid, but some of it may be usable when I get a proper run at it."

The tablecloth was spread on the floor, his books and half his papers on it. But his smile flashed victory and relief as he held the telegram towards her. She took it from his hand and walked with it to the window in order to read it. Or to distract his attention from the desk.

"It was from you, Jack," she said, "using your cover name of Victor. Addressed to Pym care of Pembroke. Return at once, you said. All is forgiven. Committee reassembles Vienna Monday 10 a.m. Victor."

Taking his time, Brotherhood had turned to Fergus at last.

"What the hell do you want?" he said.

Fergus spoke the way Tom did when he had been holding back too long, waiting for the grown-ups to let him in.

"Crash message from the Station clerk at the Embassy, sir," he blurted. "He phoned it through in word code. I've just unbuttoned it. The Station burnbox is missing from the strongroom."

Nigel had a funny little gesture designed to ease a charged atmosphere. He raised his beloved hands and, with the fingertips pointing loosely towards Heaven, flapped them as if he were drying his nails. But Brotherhood, still kneeling at Mary's side, seemed suddenly to have been seized by lethargy. He rose slowly, then slowly passed his hand across his mouth as if he had a bad taste on the tip of his tongue.

"Since when?"

"Not known, sir. Not signed out. They've been searching for it for this last hour. They can't find it. That's all they know. There's a diplomatic courier card that goes with it. The card's disappeared too."

Mary had not yet grasped the mood. The synchronisation has gone wrong, she thought. Who is in the doorway, Fergus or Magnus? Jack's gone deaf. Jack who questions in salvoes has run out of ammunition.

"Chancery guard says Mr. Pym called at the Embassy first thing Thursday morning on his way to the airport, sir. The guard hadn't thought to mention it because he hadn't put him into his log. It was upstairs, down again and sorry about your father, sir. But when he came down the stairs he was carrying this heavy black pouch."

"And the guard didn't think to question him at all?"

"Well he wouldn't, sir, would he? Not with his father dead and him being in a hurry."

"Anything else missing?"

"No, sir, just the burnbox, sir, so far as he's got. And the card like I said."

"Where are you going?" said Mary.

Nigel was on his feet, tugging at the points of his waistcoat, while Brotherhood was loading things into his jacket pocket for a long journey on his own. His yellow cigarettes. His pen and notebook. His old German lighter.

"What's a burnbox?" Mary said, close on panic. "Where are you going? I'm talking! Sit down!"

Finally Brotherhood remembered her, and stared down at her where she sat.

"You wouldn't know, would you," he said. "Of course you wouldn't. You were grade nine. You never got high enough to find out." Explaining was a chore but he managed it for old times' sake. "A burnbox is what it says. Little metal box. In this instance it's a diplomatic pouch, steel-lined. Burns whatever is inside it as soon as you tell it to. It's where a Station Chief keeps his crown jewels."

"So what's in it?"

Nigel and Brotherhood exchanged glances. Fergus still had his eyes wide open.

"What's in it?" she repeated as a different and more elusive fear began to grip her.

"Oh. Not much," said Brotherhood. "Agents in place. All our Czechs. A few Poles. Hungarian or two. Just about everything we have that's run from Vienna. Or used to be. Who's Wentworth?"

"You asked. I don't know. A place. What else is in the burnbox?"

"So it is. A place."

She had lost him. Jack. Gone. Lost him as a lover, as a friend, as an authority. His face was her father's face when she took him the news of Sam's death. The love had gone out of him and the last of his faith with it.

"You knew," he said casually. He was halfway to the door, not even looking at her. "You bloody knew, for years and years."

We all did, she thought. But she hadn't the heart to say it to him or, for that matter, the interest.

As if the bell had rung for the end of visiting time, Nigel also prepared to make his exit. "Now, Mary, I'm leaving you Georgie and Fergus for company. They'll agree their cover with you and tell you how to play everything. They'll report to me all the time. From now on, so will you. Only to me. Do you understand? If you need to leave a message or anything like that, I'm Nigel, I'm Head of Secretariat, my P.A. is called Marcia. Don't talk to anybody else in the Firm at all. I'm afraid that's an order. Even Jack," he added, meaning Jack particularly.

"What else is in the burnbox?" she repeated.

"Nothing. Nothing at all. Routine stores. Don't you worry yourself." He came to her and, emboldened by Brotherhood's intimacy with her, placed a hand awkwardly on her shoulder. "Listen. This needn't all be as bad as it sounds. We have to take precautions, naturally. We have to assume the worst and cover ourselves. But Jack does have a rather Gothic way of looking at things sometimes. The less dramatic explanations are often a lot closer to home. Jack's not the only one with experience."

6

A dark sea rain had enveloped Pym's England and he strode in it warily. It was early evening and he had been writing for longer than he had written in his whole life and now he was empty and accessible and afraid. A foghorn sounded—one short, two long—a lighthouse or a ship. Pausing under a lamp he again studied his watch. A hundred and ten minutes to go, fifty-three years gone. Bandstand empty, bowling green awash. Shop-windows still wearing their fly-blown yellow cellophane against the summer's sun.

He was heading out of town. He had bought a plastic cape from Blandy the haberdasher. "*Good* evening, Mr. Canterbury, sir, what can we be doing *you* for?" In the rain its hood pattered round him like a tin roof. Inside its skirts he carried his shopping for Miss Dubber: the bacon from Mr. Aitken, only mind and tell him he's to cut it on number five, give him half a chance he'll make it thicker. And tell that Mr. Crosse three of his tomatoes were rotten last week, not just bad, *rotten*. If I don't have replacements I'll never go to him again. Pym had followed her instructions to the letter, though not with the ferocity she would have wished, for both Crosse and Aitken were recipients of his secret subventions, and for years had been sending Miss Dubber bills for only half what she had spent. From Farways the travel agent he had also obtained details of a senior citizens' tour of Italy departing Gatwick in six days. I'll phone her cousin Melanie in Bognor, he thought. If I offer to pay for Melanie as well, Miss Dubber won't be able to refuse.

A hundred and six minutes. Only four gone. From countless pressing memories in his head clamouring to be acknowledged, Pym selected instead Washington and the balloon. Of all the crazy ways we ever had of talking, really that balloon took the biscuit. You wanted a chat, I wouldn't meet you. I was running scared and had appointed you my unperson. But you wouldn't be put down, you never would. To humour me, you launched a miniature silver-coated gas balloon over the rooftops of Washington, D.C. Half a metre diameter; sometimes Tom gets them free at the supermarkets. As we drove our separate cars on either side of town, you told me in German what a fool I was to do a Garbo on you. Over matched handsets that hopped like bedbugs between the frequencies and must have sent the listeners just as frantic.

He was climbing the cliff path, past lighted bungalows cut from the gardens of a great house. I'll phone that doctor of hers and get him to persuade her that a break is what she needs. Or the vicar, she'd listen to him. Below him the fairy lights of the Amusement Palace glowed like fat berries in the mist. Alongside them he could make out the blue-white neons of the Softa Ice Parlour. Penny, he thought. You'll never see me again unless it's my face in the newspaper. Penny belonged to his secret army of lovers, so secret she didn't know she was a member. Five years ago she was selling fish and chips from a Portacabin on the promenade and was in love with a leather-boy called Bill who beat her up, until Pym ran the licence number of Bill's motorbike across the Firm computer and established he was married and had kids in Taunton. In a disguised hand he sent the details to the local vicar and a year later Penny was married to a jolly Italian ice-cream seller called Eugenio. But not tonight she wasn't. Tonight, as Pym had approached her café for his regular two scoops of Cornish, she was head to head with a burly man in a trilby whom Pym hadn't liked the look of one bit. It was just an ordinary traveller, he told himself as a gust of wind filled his cape. A food salesman, a taxman. Who hunts alone these days apart from Jack? And Jack it isn't, not by thirty years. It was the car, he thought. Those clean wings, the smart aerial. The pitch of his head as he listened.

"Any callers, Miss D?" said Pym, setting out his packages on the sideboard.

Miss Dubber was sitting in the kitchen watching American soap-opera and having her one of the day. Toby sat in her lap.

"They're so wicked, Mr. Canterbury," she said. "There's not one among them we'd have here even for a night, would we, Toby? What's that tea you bought? I said Assam, you silly man, take it back."

"It is Assam," Pym said gently, stooping to show her. "They've put it in a new packing and given you three pence off. Any callers while I was out?"

"Only the gasman for the meter."

"That usual? Or someone new?"

"New, dear. They're all new these days." Lightly kissing her cheek he straightened her new shawl over her shoulders. "Give yourself a nice stiff vodka, darling," she said.

But Pym declined, saying he must work.

Regaining his room he checked the papers on his desk. Stapler to handle of teacup. Book matches to pencil. Burnbox aligned to desk leg, ignore. Miss Dubber is no Mary. Shaving, he caught himself thinking of Rick. I saw your ghost, he thought. Not here but in Vienna. Just as I used to see you in the flesh in Denver, Seattle, San Francisco, Washington. I saw your ghost in every shop-window and autumn doorway while I tried to clear my itchy back. You were wearing your camel-hair coat and smoking the cigar you never drew on without frowning. Following me, you were, and your blue eyes shadowed like a drowned man's, the pupils stuck against the upper lids to scare me. "Where are you off to, old son, where are those fine legs of yours taking you so late at night? Got a nice lady, have you? Someone who thinks the world of you? Come on, old son. You can tell your old man. Give us a hug." In London you were lying on your deathbed but I wouldn't go to you, I wouldn't know about you or talk about you, it was my way of mourning you. "No, I will not. No, I will not," I used to say each time my heel hit the cobble. So you came to me instead. To Vienna and did a Wentworth on me. Every corner I turned you were there. Until I felt your loving stare like a heat on the back I could never clear. Get off me, damn you, I whispered. What death was I wishing you? All of them by turns. Die, I told you. Do it on the pavement where everyone can see. Stop adoring me. Stop believing in me. Did you want money? Not any more. You had waived your claim to it in favour of the greatest claim of all. You wanted Magnus. You wanted my living spirit to enter your dying body and give you back the life I owed you. "Having a bit of fun, are we, son? Old Poppy's crackerjack, I can see that for openers. What are you two hatching up together there? Come on, you can tell your old pal! Got some piece of business, have you? Putting a few bob in your pockets, are you, the way your old man taught you?"

Three minutes. I always like to cut it fine. Pym wiped his face clean and from an inside pocket drew his faithful copy of Grimmelshausen's *Simplicissimus*, bound in worn brown buckram and much travelled. He laid it ready on the desk beside a pad of paper and a pencil, crossed the room and knelt down in front of dear old Winston's wireless, spinning the bakelite tuning dial until he had the wavelength.

Volume down. Switch on. Wait. A man and a woman discussing in Czech the economics of a fruit cooperative. Discussion fades in midsentence. Time signal announces evening news. Stand by. Pym is calm. Operational calm.

But he is also a little bit transported. There is a serenity here that is not quite of this world, a hint of mystical affinity in his youthful loving smile that says "Hullo there" to someone not quite of this earth. Of all those who have known him, other than this extraterrestrial stranger, perhaps only Miss Dubber has seen the same expression.

Item one, harangue against American imperialists following breakdown of latest round of arms talks. Sound of page turning, signal for get ready. Noted. You are going to talk to me. I am thankful. I appreciate this gesture. Item two coming up. Presenter introduces college professor from Brno. Good evening, Professor, and how is the Czech Secret Service this evening? The professor speaks, a passage for translation. All nerves extended, the all of me at full stretch. First sentence: THE TALKS HAVE ENDED IN DEADLOCK. Ignore. IN ANOTHER BID. Write it down. Slowly. Don't rush. Patience again while we wait for the first numeral. Here it is. A FIFTY-FIVE-YEAR-OLD WELDER FROM PLZEŇ. He switched off the wireless and,

pad in hand, returned to his desk, eyes straight ahead of him.
Opening his Grimmelshausen at page 55, he found five lines
down without even counting and on a fresh sheet of paper wrote
out the first ten letters of that line, then converted them to
numerals according to their position in the alphabet. Subtract
without carrying. Don't reason, do it. He was adding again, still
not carrying. He was converting numbers into letters. Don't
reason. NEV...VER...RMI...IND...DEW... There's nothing
here. It's gobbledegook. Tune in again at ten and take a
fresh reading. He was smiling. He was smiling like a saint
when the agony is over. The tears were starting to his eyes.
Let them. He was standing, holding the page in both hands
above his head. He was weeping. He was laughing. He could
scarcely read what he had written. NEVER MIND, E. WEBER LOVE
YOU ALWAYS. POPPY.

"You cheeky sod," he whispered aloud, punching away
more tears. "Oh Poppy. Oh my."

"Is anything wrong, Mr. Canterbury?" Miss Dubber demanded
sternly.

"I came to take that vodka off you, Miss D. Vodka," he
explained. "Vodka and something."

He was already mixing it.

"You've only been upstairs an hour, Mr. Canterbury. We
don't call that working, do we, Toby? No wonder the country's in a fuss."

Pym's smile widened. "What fuss is that?"

"The football crowds. Setting such a bad example to the
foreigners. You'd never have let that happen, would you, Mr.
Canterbury?"

"Of course I wouldn't."

Warm orange juice from the bottle, oh glory! Chalky
water from the tap, where else would you find it? He sat with
her for an hour, bubbling on about the charms of Naples,
before he returned to his task of saving the country.

How Rick won the peace I'll never rightly know, Tom, but
win it he did, overnight as usual, and none of us will ever
have to worry again, son, there's plenty for everyone and
your old man's made it. In the zeal of the new prosperity

father and son took up the profession of country gentleman. With victory in Europe still wet on the hoardings the newly adolescent Pym bought himself a charcoal Harrods suit with its coveted long trousers, a black tie and a stiff white collar, all on the account, and steeled himself to have Sefton Boyd's promised fish-hooks poked through his earlobes. Rick meanwhile in his immense maturity acquired a twenty-acre mansion in Ascot with white fencing down the drive, and a row of tweed suits louder than the Admiral's, and a pair of mad red setters, and a pair of two-toned country shoes for walking them, and a pair of Purdey shotguns for his portrait with them, and a mile-long bar to while away his rustic evenings over bubbly and roulette, and a bronze bust of TP's head on a plinth in the hall beside a larger one of his own. A platoon of displaced Poles was hauled in to staff the place, a new mother wore high heels on the lawn, bawled at the servants and gave Pym tips on the hygiene and diction of the upper classes. A Bentley appeared and was not changed or hidden for several weeks though a Pole with a grudge contrived to fill it with water from a hose-pipe through a crack in the window and drench Rick's dignity when he opened the door next morning. Mr. Cudlove got a mulberry uniform and a cottage in the grounds where Ollie grew geraniums, sang *The Mikado*, and painted the kitchen for his nerves. Livestock and a surly cowman supplied the character of a farm, for Rick had become a taxpayer which I know now marked the summit of his heroic struggle for liquidity: "It's a damn shame, Maxie," he declared proudly to a Major Maxwell-Cavendish who had been brought in to advise on matters of the Turf. "Lord in Heaven if a man can't enjoy the fruits of his labours these days what the devil did we fight the war for?" The major, who wore a tinted monocle, said "What indeed?" and pursed his lips into a holly leaf. And Pym, agreeing wholeheartedly, topped up the major's glass. Still waiting to be sent to school, he was going through a faceless period and would have topped up anything.

Up in London the court commandeered a pillared Reichskanzlei in Chester Street staffed by a troupe of Lovelies who were changed as often as they wore out. A stuffed jockey in the Pym sporting colours waving his little whip at them, photographs of Rick's neverwozzers, and a Tablet of Honour commemorating the unfallen companies of the latest Rick T.

Pym & Son empire completed the Wall of Fame. Their names live in me for ever more, apparently, for it took me years of sworn statements to disown them and I have most of them by heart to this day. The best celebrate the victory at arms that Rick by now was convinced he had obtained for us single-handed: the Alamein Sickness & Health Company, the Military & Permanent Pensions Fund, the Dunkirk Mutual & General, the T.P. Veteran Alliance Company—all seemingly unlimited, yet all satellites of the great Rick T. Pym & Son holding company, whose legal limitations as a receptacle of widows' mites were only gradually revealed. I have enquired, Tom. I have asked lawyers who know things. A hundred pounds of capital was enough to cover the lot. And we had books, fancy! Winfield on Tort, MacGillivray on Insurance, Snell on Equity, somebody else on Rome, hoary old lawyers that they were, they were always the first to disappear in adversity and the first to come back smiling when the struggle was won. And beyond Chester Street lay the clubs, tucked like safe houses around the quieter corners of Mayfair. The Albany, the Burlington, the Regency, the Royalty—their titles were nothing to the glories that awaited us inside. Do such places exist today? Not on the Firm's expenses, Jack, that's for sure. And if so, then in a world already dedicated to pleasure, not austerity. They don't sell you illegal petrol coupons at the bar, illegal steaks in the grill-room or take illegal bets in the illegal sporting room. They don't have illegal mothers in low gowns who swear you'll break a lot of hearts one day. Or real live members of our beloved Crazy Gang leaning gloomily at the bar, an hour before reducing us to tears of laughter in the stalls. Or jockeys scurrying round the snooker table that was too high for them, a hundred quid a corner and Magnus why aren't you at school yet and where's that bloody jigger? Or Mr. Cudlove standing outside in his mulberry, reading *Das Kapital* against the Bentley steering wheel while he waited to whisk us to our next important conference with some luckless gentleman or lady requiring the divine touch.

Beyond the clubs again lay the pubs: Beadles at Maidenhead, the Sugar Island at Bray, the Clock here, the Goat there, the Bell at somewhere else, all with their silver grills and silver pianists and silver ladies at the bar. At one of them Mr. Muspole was called a bloody profiteer by a small waiter he was insulting and Pym contrived to leap in with a funny word in time to stop the fight. What the word was I don't remember, but Mr. Muspole had once shown me a brass knuckleduster he liked to take to the races and I know he had it with him that night. And I know the waiter's name was Billy Craft and that he took me home to meet his underfed wife and children in their Bob Cratchit flat on the edge of Slough, and that Pym spent a jolly night with them and slept on a bony sofa under everybody's woollies. Because fifteen years later at a resources conference at Head Office who should loom out of the crowd but this same Billy Craft, supremo of domestic surveillance section. "I thought I'd rather follow them than feed them, sir," he said with a shy laugh as he shook my hand about fifty times. "No disrespect to your father, mind. He was a great man, naturally." Pym, it turned out, had not been the only one to redress Mr. Muspole's ill-behaviour. Rick had sent him a case of bubbly and a dozen pairs of nylons for Mrs. Craft.

After the pubs, if we were lucky, came a dawn raid on Covent Garden for a nice touch of bacon and eggs to perk us up before the hundred-mile-an-hour dash to the stables where the jockeys put on brown caps and jodhpurs and became the Knights Templar Pym had always known they were, galloping the neverwozzers down frosty runways marked by pine sprigs, till in his loyal imagination they rode off into the sky to win the Battle of Britain for us all over again.

Sleep? I remember it just the once. We were driving to Torquay for a nice weekend's rest at the Imperial, where Rick had set up an illegal game of chemin de fer in a suite overlooking the sea, and it must have been one of those times when Mr. Cudlove had resigned, for suddenly we found ourselves in the middle of a moonlit cornfield that Rick, smelling strongly of the cares of office, had mistaken for the open road. Stretched side by side on the Bentley roof, father and son let the hot moon scorch their faces.

"Are you all right?" Pym asked, meaning, are you liquid, are we on our way to prison?

Rick gave Pym's hand a fierce squeeze. "Son. With you beside me, and God sitting up there with His stars, and the Bentley underneath us, I'm the most all-right fellow in the world." And he meant it, every word as ever, and his proudest day was going to be when Pym was at the Old

Bailey on the right side of the rails wearing the full regalia of
the Lord Chief Justice, handing down the sentences that had
once been handed down to Rick in the days we never owned
to.

"Father," said Pym. And stopped.

"What is it, son? You can tell your old man."

"It's just that—well, if you can't pay the first term's
boarding fees in advance, it's all right. I mean I'll go to day
school. I just think I ought to go somewhere."

"Is that all you've got to say to me?"

"It doesn't matter. Really."

"You've been reading my correspondence, haven't you?"

"No, of course not."

"Have you ever wanted for anything? In your whole
life?"

"Never."

"Well then," said Rick and nearly broke Pym's neck with
an armlock embrace.

"So where did the money come from, Syd?" I insist again and
again. "Why did it ever end?" Even today in my incurable
earnestness I long to find a serious centre to the mayhem of
these years, even if it is only the one great crime that lies,
according to Balzac, behind every fortune. But Syd was never
an objective chronicler. His bright eye mists over, a far smile
lights his birdy little face as he takes a sip of his wet. Deep
down he still sees Rick as a great wandering river which each
of us can only ever know the stretch that Fate assigns to us.
"Our big one was Dobbsie," he recalls. "I'm not saying there
wasn't others, Titch, there was. There was fine projects,
many very visionary, very fantastic. But old Dobbsie was our
big one."

With Syd there must always be the big one. Like gam-
blers and actors he lived for it all his life, does still. But the
Dobbsie story as he told it to me that night over God knows
how many wets can serve as well as any, even if it left the
darkest reaches unexplored.

For some time, Titch—says Syd while Meg gives us a
drop more pie and turns the log fire up—as the ebb and flow
of war, Titch, with God's help, naturally, increasingly favours
the Allies, your dad has been very concerned to find a new

opening to suit those fantastic talents of his that we are all
fully aware of and rightly. By 1945 the shortages cannot be
counted on to last for ever. Shortages have become, let's face
it, Titch, a risk business. With the hazards of peace upon us,
your chocolate, nylons, dried fruit and petrol could flood the
market in a day. The coming thing, Titch, says Syd—out of
whom Rick's cadences ring like tunes I cannot shake off—is
your Reconstruction. And your dad, with that brain of his
he's got, is as keen as any other fine patriot to get his piece of
it, which is only right. The snag, as ever, is to find the
toehold, for not even Rick can corner the British property
market without a penny piece of capital. And quite by
accident, says Syd, this toehold is provided through the
unlikely agency of Mr. Muspole's sister Flora—well *you*
remember Flora! Of course I do. Flora is a good scout, a
favourite with the jockeys on account of her stately breasts
and the generous use she puts them to. But her true allegiance, Syd reminds me, is pledged to a gentleman named
Dobbs, who works for Government. And one evening in
Ascot over a glass—your dad being away at a conference at
the time, Titch—Flora casually lets slip that her Dobbsie is
by vocation a city architect and that he has landed this
important job. What job is that, dear? the court enquires
politely. Flora falters. Long words are not her suit. "Assessing
the compensation," she replies, quoting something she has
not fully understood. Compensation for what, dear? the
court asks, pricking up its ears, for compensation never hurt
anyone yet. "Bomb-damage compensation," says Flora and
glowers round her with growing uncertainty.

"It was a natural, Titch," says Syd. "Dobbsie hops on his
bicycle, slips round to a bombed house, picks up the blower
to Whitehall. 'Dobbs here,' he says. 'I'll have twenty thousand quids' worth by Thursday and no backchat.' And Government pays up like a lady. Why?" Syd jabs my upper knee
with his forefinger—Rick's gesture to the life. "Because Dobbsie
is impartial, Titch, and never you forget it."

Dimly I remember Dobbsie too, a whipped, untruthful
little man plastered on two glasses of bubbly. I remember
being ordered to be nice to him—and when was Pym ever
not? "Son, if Mr. Dobbs here asks you for something—if he
wants that fine picture off the wall there—you give it to him.
Understand?"

Pym eyed the picture of ships on a red sea in a different light from that day on but Dobbsie never asked for it.

With Flora's amazing secret on the table, Syd continues, the wheels of commerce are flung into top gear. Rick is recalled from his conference, a meeting with Dobbsie is arranged, a mutuality established. Both men are Liberals or Masons or the Sons of Great Men, both follow Arsenal, admire Joe Louis, think Noël Coward is a sissy or share the same vision of men and women of all races marching arm in arm towards the one great Heaven which, let's face it, is big enough for all of us, whatever our colour or creed may be—this being one of Rick's set speeches, guaranteed to make him weep. Dobbs becomes an honorary member of the court and within days introduces a loved colleague named Fox, who also likes to do good for mankind, and whose job is selecting building land for the post-war Utopia. Thus the ripples of conspiracy multiply, find each other and spread.

The next to be blessed is Perce Loft. While pursuing a line of business in the Midlands Perce has heard voices about a moribund Friendly Society that is sitting on a fortune, and makes enquiries. The Chairman of the Society, name of Higgs—Destiny has decreed that all conspirators bear monosyllables—turns out to be a lifelong Baptist. So is Rick; he could never have got where he is today without it. The fortune derives from a family trust watched over by a country solicitor named Crabbe, who went off to the war the moment it became available, leaving the trust to watch over itself as it thought best. As a Baptist, Higgs can fiddle no funds without Crabbe to cover him. Rick secures Crabbe's release from his regiment, whisks him by Bentley to Chester Street where he can inspect the Wall of Fame, the law books and the Lovelies, and thence to the dear old Albany where he can have a nice talk and relax.

Crabbe turns out to be a cantankerous, idiotic little man who sticks out his elbow to take his drink, sir, wiggles his moustache to demonstrate his military shrewdness and after a few glasses demands to know what you stripe-arsed civilians were doing while I was taking part in a certain contest, sir, risking one's neck amid shot and shell? At the Goat some drinks later, however, he declares Rick to be the kind of chap he'd have liked to have as commandant and if need be die for, which one damn nearly did a few times but mum's the word.

He even calls Rick "Colonel," thus triggering a bizarre interlude in the great man's rise, for Rick is so taken with the rank
that he decides to award it to himself in earnest, much as in
later life he convinces himself he has been knighted secretly
by the Duke of Edinburgh and keeps a set of calling-cards for
those admitted to this confidence.

Yet none of these added responsibilities holds up Rick's
breathless waltz for one minute. All night long, all weekend,
the house in Ascot receives a pageant of the great, the
beautiful and the gullible, for Rick has become a collector of
celebrities as well as fools and horses. Test cricketers, jockeys, footballers, fashionable Counsel, corrupt parliamentari-
ans, glistening Under Secretaries from helpful Whitehall
Ministries, Greek shipowners, cockney hairdressers, unlisted
maharajahs, drunk magistrates, venal mayors, ruling princes
of countries that have ceased to exist, prelates in suède boots
and pectoral crosses, radio comedians, lady singers, aristocratic layabouts, war millionaires and film stars—all pass
across our stage as the bemused beneficiaries of Rick's great
vision. Lubricious bank managers and building-society chair-
men who have never danced before throw off their jackets,
confess to barren lives and worship Rick the giver of their sun
and rain. Their wives receive unobtainable nylons, perfumes,
petrol coupons, discreet abortions, fur coats and if they are
among the lucky ones, Rick himself—for everyone must have
something, everyone must be taken care of, everyone must
think the world of him. If they have savings, Rick will double
them. If they like a flutter, Rick will get them better odds
than the bookies—slip me the cash, I'll see you right. Their
children are passed to Pym for entertainment, exempted
from National Service by the intervention of dear old somebody, given gold watches, tickets to the Cup Final, red setter
puppies and, if they are ailing, the finest doctors to attend
them. There was a time when such liberality dismayed the
growing Pym and made him envious. Not today. Today I
would call it no more than normal agent welfare.

And among them, casual as cats, stalk the quiet men of
the enlarged court, the men from Mr. Muspole's side, in
broad-shouldered suits and brown pork-pie hats, calling themselves consultants and holding the telephone receiver to their
ear but not speaking into the mouthpiece. Who they were,
how they came there, where they went—to this day only the

Devil and Rick's ghost know, and Syd refuses point-blank to speak of them, though with time I think I have put together a fair idea of what they did. They are the axemen of Rick's tragi-comedy, now yielding at the knees and covered in false smiles, now posted like Shakespearean sentries round his stage, white-eyed in the gloom as they wait to disembowel him.

And tiptoeing between this entire menagerie—as if between their legs, although he was already as tall as half of them—I glimpse Pym again, willing potboy, blank page, Lord Chief Justice designate, clipping their cigars and topping them all up. Pym the credit to his old man, the diplomat in embryo, scurrying to every summons: "Here, Magnus—what have they done to you at that new school of yours, poured fertiliser over you?" "Here, Magnus, who cut your hair then?" "Here, Magnus, tell us the one about the cabbie who puts his wife in the family way!" And Pym—the most compelling raconteur for his age and weight in all of Greater Ascot—obliges, smiles and sidesteps between their anomalous, colliding masses, and for relaxation attends late-night classes in radical politics with Ollie and Mr. Cudlove in their cottage, at which it is heartily agreed over stolen canapés and cocoa that all men are brothers but nothing against your dad. And though political doctrines are at root as meaningless to me today as they were to Pym then, I remember the simple humanity of our discussions as we promised to mend the world's ills, and the truthful goodheartedness with which, as we went off to bed, we wished each other peace in the spirit of Joe Stalin who, let's face it, Titch, and nothing against your dad *ever*, won the war for all these capitalist bastards.

Court holidays are restored to the curriculum, for no man can give of his best without relaxation. St. Moritz is off the map following Rick's unsuccessful bid to buy the resort as a substitute for paying his bills there, but as compensation, now a favourite word, Rick and his advisers have espoused the South of France, sweeping down on Monte in the Train Bleu, banqueting the journey away in a brass-and-velvet dining-car, only pausing to tip the Froggie engine driver, who's a first-rate Liberal, before dashing off to the Casino, illicit currency at the ready. There, standing at Rick's shoulder in the *grande salle*, Pym can watch a year's school fees vanish in seconds and nobody has learned a thing. If he prefers the bar he can exchange views with a Major de Wildman of Lord knew whose army, who calls himself King Farouk's equerry and claims to have a private telephone link to Cairo so that he can report the winning numbers and take royal orders inspired by soothsayers on how to dissipate the wealth of Egypt. For our Mediterranean dawns we have the sombre march to the all-night pawnbroker on the waterfront, where Rick's gold watch, gold cigarette case, gold swizzle-stick and gold cufflinks with the Pym sporting colours are sacrificed to the elusive god liquidity. For our reflective afternoons, we have the *tir aux pigeons* at which the court, well lunched, lies face down in the butts and pots away at luckless doves as they emerge from their tunnels and start out into the blue sky before crashing into the sea in a crumpled swirl. Then home again to London with the bills all taken care of, which meant signed, and the concierges and headwaiters seen right, which meant tipped lavishly with the last of our cash, to resume the ever-mounting cares of the Pym & Son empire.

For nothing may stand still, too much is not enough, as Syd himself admits. No income is so sacrosanct that expenditure cannot exceed it; no expenditure is so great that more loans cannot be raised to hold the dam from breaking altogether. If the building boom is put temporarily out of service by the passing of an unfriendly Building Act, then Major Maxwell-Cavendish has a plan that speaks deeply to Rick's sporting soul: it is to buy up everyone who has drawn a horse in the Irish Sweep and so win first, second and third prizes automatically. Mr. Muspole knows a derelict newspaper proprietor who has got in with a bad crowd and needs to sell out fast; Rick has ever seen himself as a shaper of the human mind. Perce Loft the great lawyer wants to buy a thousand houses in Fulham; Rick knows a building society whose chairman has Faith. Mr. Cudlove and Ollie are on intimate terms with a young dress designer who has acquired the donkey-ride concession for the projected Festival of Britain; Rick likes nothing better than to give our English kids a break, and my God, son, if anybody has earned it they have. An amphibious motorcar has been designed by Morrie Washington's nephew, a National Cricket Pool is envisaged to complement the winter Football Pools, Perce has yet another scheme for contracting an Irish village to grow human hair for the wig market which is expanding fast thanks to the munificence of the newly formed National Health Service. Automatic orange-peelers, pens that can write under water, the spent shell cases of temporarily discontinued wars: each project engages the great thinker's interest, attracts its experts and its alchemists, adds another line to the Pym & Son Tablet of Honour at the house in Chester Street.

So what went wrong? I ask Syd again, glancing ahead to the inevitable end. What quirk of fate, this time round, Syd, checked the great man's stride? My question sparks unusual anger. Syd sets down his glass.

"Dobbsie went wrong, that's what. Flora wasn't enough for him any more. He had to have the lot. Dobbsie went woozy in the head from all his women, didn't he, Meg?"

"Dobbsie done his little self too well," says Meg, ever a stern student of human frailty.

Poor Dobbs, it transpires, became so lulled that he awarded a hundred thousand pounds of compensation to a housing estate that had not been built till a year after the bombing ended.

"Dobbsie spoilt it for everyone," says Syd, bristling with moral indignation. "Dobbsie was selfish, Titch. That's what Dobbsie was. Selfish."

One later footnote belongs to this brief but glorious high point of Rick's affluence. It is recorded that in October 1947 he sold his head. I chanced upon this information as I was standing on the steps of the crematorium covertly trying to puzzle out some of the less familiar members of the funeral. A breathless youth claiming to represent a teaching hospital waved a piece of paper at me and demanded I stop the ceremony. "In Consideration of the sum of fifty pounds cash I, Richard T. Pym of Chester Street W., consent that on my death my head may be used for the purposes of furthering medical science." It was raining slightly. Under cover of the porch I scribbled the boy a cheque for a hundred pounds and told him to buy one somewhere else. If the fellow was a confidence trickster, I reasoned, Rick would have been the first to admire his enterprise.

And always somewhere in this clamour the name of Wentworth ringing softly in Pym's secret ear like an operational codename

known only to the initiated: Wentworth. And Pym—the
outsider, not on the list—struggling to join, to know. Like a
buzzword passed between older hands in the senior officers'
bar at Head Office and Pym the new boy, hearing from the
edge, not knowing whether to pretend knowledge or deafness:
"We picked it up on Wentworth." "Top Secret and Wentworth—
have you been Wentworth-cleared?" Till the very name became to Pym a teasing symbol of wisdom denied, a challenge
to his own desirability. "The bugger's doing a Wentworth on
us," he hears Perce Loft grumble under his breath one
evening. "That Wentworth woman's a tiger," says Syd another
time. "Worse than her stupid husband ever was." Each
mention spurred Pym to renew his searches. Yet neither
Rick's pockets nor his desk drawers, not his bedside table or
his pigskin address book or pop-up plastic telephone book,
not even his briefcase, which Pym reconnoitred weekly with
the key from Rick's Asprey key chain, yielded a single clue.
Nor did the impenetrable green filing cabinet which like a
travelling icon had come to mark the centre of Rick's migrant
faith. No known key fitted it, no fiddling or prising made it
yield.

And finally there was school. The cheque was sent, the
cheque was cleared.

The train lurched. In the window Mr. Cudlove and other
people's mothers dipped their faces into handkerchiefs and
vanished. In his compartment, children larger than himself
whimpered and chewed the cuffs of their new grey jackets.
But Pym with one turn of his head glanced backward on his
life thus far, and forward to the iron path of duty curling into
the autumn mist, and he thought: here I come, your best
recruit ever. I'm the one you need so take me. The train
arrived, school was a mediaeval dungeon of unending twilight, but Saint Pym of the Renunciation was on hand immediately to help his comrades hump their trunks and tuck-
boxes up the winding stone staircases, wrestle with unfamiliar
collar-studs, find their beds, lockers and clothes-pegs and
award himself the worst. And when his turn came to be
summoned before his housemaster for an introductory chat
Pym made no secret of his pleasure. Mr. Willow was a big
homely man in tweeds and a cricket tie, and the Christian

plainness of his room after Ascot filled Pym at once with an assurance of integrity.

"Well, well, what's in here then?" Mr. Willow asked genially as he lifted the parcel to his great ear and shook it.

"It's scent, sir."

Mr. Willow misunderstood his meaning. "Sent? I thought you brought it with you," he said, still smiling.

"It's for Mrs. Willow, sir. From Monte. They tell me it's about the best those Frenchies make," he added, quoting Major Maxwell-Cavendish, a gentleman.

Mr. Willow had a very broad back and suddenly that was all Pym saw. He stooped, there was a sound of opening and closing, the parcel vanished into his enormous desk. If he'd had a nine-foot grappling iron he couldn't have treated Pym's gift with greater loathing.

"You want to watch out for Tit Willow," Sefton Boyd warned. "He beats on Fridays so that you have the weekend to recover."

But still Pym strove, bled, volunteered for everything and obeyed every bell that summoned him. Terms of it. Lives of it. Ran before breakfast, prayed before running, showered before praying, defecated before showering. Flung himself through the Flanders mud of the rugger field, scrambled over sweating flagstones in search of what passed for learning, drilled so hard to be a good soldier that he cracked his collarbone on the bolt of his vast Lee-Enfield rifle, and had himself punched to kingdom come in the boxing ring. And still he pulled a grin and raised his paw for the loser's biscuit as he tottered to the dressing-room and you would have loved him, Jack; you would have said that children and horses needed to be broken, public school was the making of me.

I don't think it was at all. I think it damn near killed me. But not Pym—Pym thought it all perfectly wonderful and shoved out his plate for more. And when it was required of him by the rigid laws of a haphazard justice, which in retrospect seems like every night of the week, he pressed his limp forelock into a filthy washbasin, clutched a tap in each throbbing hand, and expiated a string of crimes he didn't know he had committed until they were thoughtfully explained to him between each stroke by Mr. Willow or his representatives. Yet when he lay at last in the trembling dark of his dormitory, listening to the creaks and kennel coughs of adolescent longing, he still contrived to persuade himself that he was a prince in the making and, like Jesus, taking the rap for his father's divinity. And his sincerity, his empathy for his fellow man flourished unabated.

In a single afternoon, he could sit down with Noakes the groundsman, eat cake and biscuits in his cottage beside the cider factory and bring tears to the old athlete's eyes with his fabricated tales of the antics of the great sportsmen who had let their hair down at the Ascot feasts. All nonsense, yet all perfectly true to him as he spun his magic. "Not the Don?" Noakes would cry incredulously. "The great Don Bradman himself, dancing on the kitchen table? In your house, Pymmie? Go on!" "And singing 'When I Was a Child of Five' while he was about it," said Pym. Then while Noakes was still glowing from these insights, straight up the hill went Pym to faded Mr. Glover, the assistant drawing master, who wore sandals, to help him wash palettes and remove the day's daubs of powder paint from the genitals of the marble cherub in the main hall. Yet Mr. Glover was the absolute opposite of Noakes. Without Pym the two men were irreconcilable. Mr. Glover thought school sports a tyranny worse than Hitler's and I wish they'd throw their bloody football boots into the river, I do, and plough up their games fields and get on with some Art and Beauty for a change. And Pym wished they would as well and swore his father was going to send a donation to rebuild the arts school to twice its size—probably millions, but keep it secret.

"I'd shut up about your father if I were you," said Sefton Boyd. "They don't like spivs here."

"They don't like divorced mothers either," said Pym, biting back for once. But mainly his strategy was to pacify and reconcile, and keep all the threads in his own hands.

Another conquest was Bellog the German master who seemed physically crumpled by the sins of his adopted country. Pym beleaguered him with extra work, bought him an expensive German beer mug on Rick's account at Thomas Goode's, walked his dog and invited him to Monte all expenses paid, which by a mercy he declined. Today I would blush for such an unsophisticated pass and agonise about whether Bellog had gone sour and been turned. Not Pym. Pym loved Bellog as he loved them all. And he needed that German soul, he had been hard on its path since Lippsie's

day. He needed to give himself away to it, right into Mr.
Bellog's startled hands, though Germany meant nothing whatever to him, except escape to an unpopular preserve where
his talents would be appreciated. He needed the embrace of
it, the mystery, the privacy of another side of life. He needed
to be able to close the door on his Englishness, love it as he
might, and carve a new name somewhere fresh. He even
went so far on occasion as to affect a light German accent
which drove Sefton Boyd to paroxysms of fury.

And women? Jack, no one was more alive than Pym to
the potential virtues of a female agent well handled, but in
that school they were the devil to come by and handling
anybody, including yourself, was a beatable offence. Mrs.
Willow, though he was prepared to love her any time, appeared
to be permanently pregnant. Pym's languishing glances were
wasted on her. The house matron was personable enough but
when he called on her late at night with a fictitious headache
in the vague hope of proposing marriage to her, she ordered
him sharply back to bed. Only little Miss Hodges who taught
the violin showed a short-lived promise: Pym presented her
with a pigskin music case from Harrods and said he wished to
turn professional, but she wept and advised him to take up a
different instrument.

"My sister wants to do it with you," said Sefton Boyd
one night as they lay in Pym's bed embracing without enthusiasm. "She read your poem in the school rag. She thinks
you're Keats."

Pym was not altogether surprised. His poem was certainly a masterpiece, and Jemima Sefton Boyd had several times
scowled at him through the windscreen of the family Land
Rover when it came to collect her brother for weekends.

"She's panting for it," Sefton Boyd explained. "She does
it with everybody. She's a nympho."

Pym wrote to her at once, a poet's letter.

"A tale must linger in your soft hair. Do you
ever have the feeling beauty is a kind of sin? Two
swans have settled on the Abbey moat. I watch
them often, dreaming of your hair. I love you."

She replied by return, but not before Pym had suffered
agonies of remorse at his recklessness.

"Thank you for your letter. I get a long exeat from school starting twenty-fifth which is one of your exeat weekends also. How fateful that they coincide. Mama will invite you for Sunday night and obtain Mr. Willow's permission for you to sleep with us. Are you considering elopement?"

A second letter was more precise:

"The servants' staircase is quite safe. I will kindle a light and have wine waiting in case you get thirsty. Bring any work you have in progress and please caress me first. On my door you will find the red rosette I won last holidays for jumping Smokey."

Pym was scared stiff. How could he acquit himself with a woman of such experience? Breasts he knew about and loved. But Jemima appeared to have none. The rest of her was an unintelligible thicket of dangers and disease, and his memories of Lippsie in the bath became hazier by the minute.

A card came:

"We would all be so pleased if you would visit us at Hadwell for the weekend of the twenty-fifth. I am writing separately to Mr. Willow. Don't worry about clothes as we do not dress in the evenings during summer.

Elizabeth Sefton Boyd"

On the hill above Mr. Willow's house stood a girls' school peopled by brown vestals. Boys who penetrated its grounds were flogged and expelled. But Elphick in Nelson House maintained that if you stood beneath the footbridge when the girls were crossing on their way to hockey much could be learned. Alas, all Pym saw when he followed this advice was a few cold knees that looked much like his own. Worse, he had to suffer the coarse humour of a games mistress who leaned over the bridge and invited him to come and play. Disgusted, Pym stalked back to his German poets.

The town library was run by an elderly Fabian, a Pym agent. Pym skipped lunch and hunted his way unchecked through the section marked "Adults Only." *Guidance on Marriage* appeared to be a handbook on mortgages. *The Art of the Chinese Pillow Book* started well but descended into a description of games of darts and leaping white tigers. *Amor and Rococo Woman*, on the other hand, richly illustrated, was a different matter, and Pym arrived at Hadwell expecting naked Graces frolicking with their gallants in the park. At dinner, which to his relief was taken dressed, Jemima cut Pym dead, hiding her face in her hair and reading Jane Austen. A plain girl called Belinda, billed as Jemima's dearest friend, declined speech in sympathy.

"That's how Jem gets when she's horny," Sefton Boyd explained within Belinda's hearing, at which Belinda tried to punch him, then stormed off in a rage.

Dispatched to bed Pym wound his way up the great staircase while a dozen clocks tolled his death knell. How often had Rick not warned him against women who wanted nothing but his money? How dearly he longed for the safety of his bed at school. Crossing the landing he saw a rosette glinting like blood in the low light. He climbed another flight and saw Belinda's head scowling at him round her door. "You can come in here if you like," she said rudely.

"It's all right, thanks," said Pym. He entered his room.

On his pillow lay his eight love letters and four poems to Jemima, bound with ribbon and smelling of saddle soap.

> "Please take back your letters which I find oppressive since I regret we are no longer compatible. I do not know what possessed you to slick down your forelock like an errand boy but henceforth we meet as strangers."

Dashed down by humiliation and despair Pym hastened back to school and the same night wrote to every mother, active or retired, whose name and address he could put his hands on.

"Dearest Topsie, Cherry, darling Mrs. Ogilvie, Mabel, darling Violet, I am being beaten mercilessly for writing poetry and I am very unhappy. Please take me away from this awful place." But when they answered his appeal, the readiness of their love revolted him and he threw away their letters scarcely read. And when one of them, the best, dropped everything and travelled a hundred expensive miles to buy him a mixed grill at the Feathers, Pym met her enquiries with a remote politeness. "Yes, thank you, school is super, everything is absolutely fine. How are *you*?" Then led her an hour early to the railway station so that he could be a good chap at kickabout.

> "Dear Belinda"—he wrote in his poet's cursive hand— "Thanks very much for your letter explaining that Jem is unstable. I know girls are terrifically sensitive at this age and going through all sorts of changes so it's really all right. Our house side won Juniors which is a bit of a sensation here. I often think of your beautiful eyes. Magnus."

> "Dear Father"—he wrote in a gruff Edwardian manner copied from Sefton Boyd—"I am doing lots of essential entertaining here which is very much the thing and gets me on. Everyone is very grateful for what I do, but prices at the tuckshop have risen and I wondered whether you could send me another five pounds to see me right."

To his surprise, Rick sent him nothing, but came down from the mountain in person, bringing not money but love, which was what Pym had written to him for in the first place.

It was Rick's first visit. Until now Pym had forbidden him the place, explaining that distinguished parents were considered bad form. And Rick with unwonted diffidence had accepted his exclusion. Now with the same diffidence he came, looking trim and loving and mysteriously humble. He didn't venture into the school but sent a letter in his own hand proposing a rendezvous on the road to Farleigh Abbott, which was on the sea. When Pym arrived by bicycle as instructed, expecting the Bentley and half the court, round the corner instead rode Rick alone, also on a bicycle, with a lovely smile that Pym could see from miles off and humming "Underneath the Arches" out of tune. In the bicycle basket he had brought a picnic of their favourite things, a bottle of ginger pop for Pym, bubbly for himself and a football left over from Paradise.

They rode their bicycles on the sand and skimmed pebbles on the waves. They lay in the dunes munching foie gras and Ryvita. They wandered through the little town and wondered whether Rick should buy it. They stared at the church and promised never to forget their prayers. They made a goal out of a broken gateway and kicked the football at each other all the way across the world. They kissed and wept and bear-hugged and swore to be pals all their lives and go bicycling every Sunday even when Pym was Lord Chief Justice and married with grandchildren.

"Has Mr. Cudlove resigned?" Pym asked.

Rick just managed to hear, though his face had already acquired the dreamy expression that overcame it at the approach of a direct question.

"Well, son," he conceded, "old Cuddie's been having his ups and downs over the years and he's decided it's time to give himself a bit of a rest."

"How's the swimming-pool coming along?"

"Nearly done. Nearly done. We must be patient."

"Super."

"Tell me, son," said Rick, now at his most venerable. "Have you got a pal or two who might like to do you the favour of supplying you with a bed and some accommodation during the school holidays that are already looming on the horizon?"

"Oh, masses," said Pym, striving to sound careless.

"Well I think you would be well advised to accept their invitations, because with all that rebuilding going on at Ascot, I don't think you're going to enjoy the rest and privacy that fine mind of yours is entitled to."

Pym at once said he would, and made an even greater fuss of Rick in order to persuade him that he did not suspect anything was amiss.

"I'm in love with a rather super girl too," said Pym when it was nearly time to part, in a further effort to persuade Rick of his happiness. "It's quite amusing. We write to each other every day."

"Son, there's no finer thing in this life than the love of a good woman and if anybody's earned it, you have."

"Tell me, boy," said Willow one evening, during an intimate confirmation class. "What does your father do, exactly?"

To which Pym with a natural instinct for the way to Willow's heart replied that he appears to be some kind of, well, free-wheeling businessman, sir, I don't know. Willow changed the subject but at their next session obliged Pym to give an account of his mother. His first instinct was to say she had died of syphilis, an ailment that featured large in Mr. Willow's lectures on Sowing the Seed of Life. But he restrained himself.

"She just sort of vanished when I was young, sir," he confessed with more truth than he intended.

"Who with?" said Mr. Willow. So Pym, for no particular reason he could afterwards think of, said, "With an army sergeant, sir, he was already married so he took her off to Africa to elope."

"Does she write to you, boy?"

"No, sir."

"Why not?"

"I suppose she's too ashamed, sir."

"Does she send you money?"

"No, sir. She hasn't any. He swindled her out of everything she had."

"We are speaking of the sergeant still, I take it?"

"Yes, sir."

Mr. Willow pondered. "Are you familiar with the activities of a company known as The Muspole Friendly and Academic Limited?"

"No, sir."

"You appear to be a director of this company."

"I didn't know, sir."

"Then you also have no knowledge, presumably, as to why this company should be paying your school fees? Or not paying them, perhaps?"

"No, sir."

Mr. Willow pushed up his jaw and narrowed his eyes, indicating a sharpening of his interrogation technique. "And does your father live in some luxury, would you say, by comparison with the kind of standards that apply to other parents here?"

"I suppose he does, sir."

"Suppose?"

"He does, sir."

"Do you disapprove of his life-style?"

"I do a bit, I suppose."

"Does it occur to you that you may one day be obliged to choose between God and Mammon?"

"Yes, sir."

"Have you discussed this with Father Murgo?"

"No, sir."

"Do so."

"Yes, sir."

"Have you ever thought of entering the Church?"

"Often, sir," said Pym, putting on his soulful face.

"We have a fund here, Pym, for impecunious boys wishing to enter the Church. It occurs to the Bursar that you might be eligible to benefit from this fund."

"Yes, sir."

Father Murgo was a toothy, driven little soul whose unlikely task, considering his proletarian origins, was to act as God's itinerant talent-spotter to the public schools. Where Willow was thunderous and craggy, a sort of Makepeace Watermaster without a secret, Murgo writhed inside his habit like a ferret roped into a bag. Where Willow's fearless gaze was unruffled by knowledge, Murgo's signalled the lonely anguish of the cell.

"He's nuts," Sefton Boyd declared. "Look at the scabs on his ankles. The swine picks them while he's praying."

"He's mortifying himself," said Pym.

"Magnus?" Murgo echoed in his sharp northern twang. "Whoever called you that? God's Magnus. You're Parvus." His quick red smile glinted like a stripe that would not heal. "Come this evening," he urged. "Allenby staircase. Staff guest-room. Knock."

"You mad bugger, he'll touch you up!" Sefton Boyd shouted, beside himself with jealousy. But Murgo never touched anyone as Pym had guessed. His lonely hands remained lashed inside his sleeves by invisible thongs, emerging only to eat or pray. For the rest of that summer term Pym floated on clouds of undreamed freedom. Not a week earlier Willow had sworn to flog a boy who had dared to describe cricket as a recreation. Now Pym had only to mention that he proposed to take a stroll with Murgo to be excused what games he wished. Neglected essays were mysteriously waived, beatings vaguely due to him deferred. On breathless walks, on bicycle rides, in little teahouses in the country, or at night crammed into a corner of Murgo's miserable bedroom, Pym eagerly offered versions of himself that alternately shocked and thrilled them both. The shiftless materialism of his home life. His quest for faith and love. His fight against the demons of self-abuse and such tempters as Kenneth Sefton Boyd. His brother-and-sister relationship with the girl Belinda.

"And the holidays?" Murgo proposed one evening as they loped down a bridlepath past lovers fondling in the grass. "Fun, are they? High living?"

"The holidays are a desert," said Pym loyally. "So are Belinda's. Her father's a stockbroker."

The description acted on Murgo like a goad.

"Oh, a desert, are they? A wilderness? All right. I'll go along with that. Christ was in the wilderness too, Parvus. For a bloody long time. So was Saint Anthony. Twenty years he served, in a filthy little fort on the Nile. Perhaps you've forgotten."

"No I hadn't at all."

"Well he did. And it didn't stop him talking to God or God talking to him. Anthony didn't have privilege. He didn't have money or property or fine cars or stockbrokers' daughters. He prayed."

"I know," said Pym.

"Come to Lyme. Answer the call. Be like Anthony."

"What the fuck have you done to the front of your hair?" Sefton Boyd screamed at him the same evening.

"I've cut it off."

Sefton Boyd stopped laughing. "You're going to be a monkey Murgo," he said softly. "You've fallen for him, you mad tart."

Sefton Boyd's days were numbered. Acting on information received—even now I blush to contemplate the source of it—Mr. Willow had decided that young Kenneth was getting a little too old for the school.

So there's yet another Pym for you, Jack, and you had better add him to my file even if he is neither admirable nor, I suspect, comprehensible to you, though Poppy knew him inside out from the first day. He's the Pym who can't rest till he's touched the love in people, then can't rest till he's hacked his way out of it, the more drastically the better. The

Pym who does nothing cynically, nothing without conviction.
Who sets events in motion in order to become their victim,
which he calls decision, and ties himself into pointless relationships, which he calls loyalty. Then waits for the next
event to get him out of the last one, which he calls destiny.
It's the Pym who passes up a two-week invitation to stay with
the Sefton Boyds in Scotland, all found including Jemima,
because he is pledged to hurl himself over the Dorset hills
in the wake of a tortured Mancunian zealot, preparing for a
life he has not the smallest intention of leading, among
people who chill him to the root. It's the Pym who writes
daily to Belinda because Jemima has cast doubts on his
divinity. It's Pym the Saturday night juggler bounding round
the table and spinning one stupid plate after another because
he can't bear to let anyone down for one second and so lose
their esteem. So off he goes and half chokes himself on
incense and sleeps in a cell that stinks like a wet dog and
nearly dies of nettle stew in order to become pious and pay
his school fees and be adored by Murgo. Meanwhile he heaps
fresh promises on old and convinces himself that he is on the
path to Heaven while he digs himself deeper into his own
mess. By the end of a week he is promised to a boys' camp in
Hereford, a pan-denominational retreat in Shropshire, a Trade
Unionists' pilgrimage in Wakefield and a Celebration of Witness in Derby. By the end of two weeks there isn't a county
in England where he hasn't pledged his holiness six different
ways—which is not to deny that intermittently he has visions
of himself as a haggard apostle of the life renounced, converting
beautiful women and millionaires to Christian poverty.

It was a full month before God provided the escape that
Pym was waiting for.

YOUR IMMEDIATE PRESENCE CHESTER STREET ESSEN-
TIAL IN MATTER OF VITAL NATIONAL AND INTERNATION-
AL IMPORTANCE RICHARD T. PYM MANAGING DIRECTOR
PYMCORP.

"You must go," said Murgo with tears of misery rolling
down his hollowed cheeks as he handed him the fatal telegram after Terce.

"I don't think I can face it," said Pym, no less affected.
"It's just money, money all the time."

They walked past the print shop and the basket shop, through the kitchen gardens to the little wicker gate that kept Rick's world at bay.

"You didn't send it to yourself, did you, Parvus?" Murgo asked.

Pym swore he had not, which was the truth.

"You don't understand what a force you are," Murgo said. "I don't think I'll be the same again."

It had never occurred to Pym until now that Murgo was capable of change.

"Well," said Murgo with a last sad writhe.

"Goodbye," said Pym. "And thanks."

But there is cheer in sight for both of them. Pym has promised to be back for Christmas, when the tramps come.

Mad swings, Tom. Mad leaps and loves, madder round the corner. I wrote to Dorothy too somewhere in that time. Care of Sir Makepeace Watermaster at the House of Commons, though I knew he was dead. I waited a week then forgot until one day out of the blue my ploy was rewarded with a tatty little letter, blotchy with tears or drink, on ruled paper torn from a notepad, no address but postmark East London, a country I had never visited. It is before me now.

> "Yours was a voice down many Coridors of Years, my dear, I put it in the kitchen cuboard with my Tableware to view at leasure. I will be at Euston Station the up platform 3 p.m. Thursday without my Herbie and I will be carrying a posy of lavender which you always loved."

Already greatly regretting his decision, Pym arrived at the station late and placed himself in the gunman's corner beneath an iron arch close to some mail bags. Quite a bevy of mothers was milling about, some eligible, some less so, but there was none he wanted and several who were drunk. And one of them seemed to be clutching a posy of flowers wrapped in newspaper but by then he had decided he had the wrong platform. It was his darling Dorothy that Pym had wanted, not some lolloping old biddy in a pantomime hat.

*   *   *

A weekday evening, Tom. The traffic in Chester Street burps and crackles in the rain, but inside the Reichskanzlei it is a Green Hill Sunday. Still pious from his monastery Pym presses the bell but hears no answering chime. He drives the great brass door knocker against its stud. A lace curtain parts and closes. The door opens, but not far.

"Cunningham's the name, squire," says a heavy man in a thick expatriate cockney, as he shuts the door fast after him as if scared of letting in germs. "Half cunning, half ham. You'll be the son and heir. Greetings, squire, Salaams."

"How do you do," says Pym.

"I'm optimistic, squire, thank you," Mr. Cunningham replies with a Middle-European literalness. "I think we're on a road to understanding. Some resistance at first is to be expected. But I believe I see a light begin to shine."

It is more than Pym does for the passage down which Mr. Cunningham leads him with such assurance is pitch black and the only light comes from the pale patches on the wall left by the departed law books.

"You're a German scholar, I understand, squire," says Mr. Cunningham more thickly, as if the exertion has affected his adenoids. "A fine language. The people, I'm not sure. But a lovely tongue in the right hands, you can quote me."

"Why are we going upstairs?" says Pym, who has by now recognised several familiar omens of impending pogrom.

"Trouble with the lift, squire," Mr. Cunningham replies. "I understand an engineer has been sent for and is at this moment hastening on his way."

"But Rick's office is on the ground floor."

"But upstairs has the privacy, squire," Mr. Cunningham explains, pushing open a double door. They enter a gutted State Apartment lit by the glow of street lamps. "Your son, sir, fresh from his worship," Mr. Cunningham announces, and bows Pym ahead of him.

At first Pym sees only Rick's brow glinting in the candlelight. Then the great head forms round it, followed by the broad bulk of the body as it advances swiftly to envelop him in a damp and fervent bear-hug.

"How are you, old son?" he asks urgently. "How was the train?"

"Fine," says Pym who has hitchhiked owing to a temporary problem of liquidity.

"Did they give you a bit to eat then? What did they give you?"

"Just a sandwich and a glass of beer," says Pym who has had to make do on a piece of rocklike bread from Murgo's refectory.

"My own boy, as you see me!" Mr. Cunningham exclaims with zest. "Never satisfied unless he's eating."

"Son, you want to watch that drinking of yours," says Rick in an almost unconscious reflex, as he clutches Pym under the armpit and marches him over bare floorboards towards an imperial-sized bed. "There's five thousand pounds for you in cash if you don't smoke or take liquor until you're twenty-one. All right, my dear, what do you think of this boy of mine?"

A darkly dressed figure has risen like a shade from the bed.

It's Dorothy, thinks Pym. It's Lippsie. It's Jemima's mother lodging a complaint. But as the darkness lifts, the aspiring monk observes that the figure before him is wearing neither Lippsie's headscarf nor Dorothy's cloche hat, nor has she the daunting authority of Lady Sefton Boyd. Like Lippsie she sports the antiquarian uniform of pre-war Europe but there the comparison ends. Her flared skirt has a nipped waist. She wears a blouse with a lace ruff and a feathery bit of hat that makes the whole outfit jaunty. Her breasts are in the best tradition of *Amor and Rococo Woman*, and the dim light flatters their roundness.

"Son, I want you to meet a noble and heroic lady who has known great advantages and misfortunes and fought great battles and suffered cruelly at the hands of fate. And who has paid me the greatest compliment a woman can pay a man by coming to see me in her hour of need."

"Rot-schilt, darling," the lady says softly, lifting her limp hand to a level where Pym may kiss or shake it.

"Heard that name anywhere, have you, son, with your fine education? *Baron* Rothschild? *Lord* Rothschild? *Count* Rothschild? Rothschild's *Bank*? Or are you going to tell me you're not conversant with the name of a certain great Jewish family with all the wealth of Solomon at its fingertips?"

"Well yes, of course I've heard of it."

"Well then. Just you sit yourself here and listen to what she has to say because this is the baroness. Sit down, my

dear. Come here bet... ...im,
Elena?"

"Beautiful, darling...

He's selling me to ... ...ng.
I'm his last desperate d...

So there we all a... ...d
madness here to stay. ...d
buttock to buttock with a ...
director's knocking-shop ...
tricity, and Mr. Cunningh...
guard at the door. An air ...
with later daft conspiracies...
voice embarks on one of t...
that your Uncle Jack and I ...
either of us can remember...
virgin in these matters, and...
cosily against that of the asp...

"I am a humble widow... ...
married happily but oh so b... ...Luigi
Svoboda-Rothschild, the last ... ...Czech line. I was
seventeen, he twenty-one, imagine our pleasure. My greatest
regret is I bore him no child. Our country seat was the Palais
of Nymphs at Brno, which first the Germans then the Russians
rape worse than a woman literally. My Cousin Anna she
marry to the head man from De Beers diamonds Cape Town,
got houses like you not imagine, too much luxury I don't
approve." Pym does not approve either, as he tries to tell her
with a monkish smirk of sympathy. "With my Uncle Wolfram
I never speak and thanks God I say. He collaborate with the
Nazis. The Jews hang him upside down." Pym sets his jaw in
grim approval. "My Granduncle David give all his tapestries
to the Prado. Now he is poor like a kulak, why don't the
museum give him something so he can eat?" Pym rolls his
head in despair at the baseness of the Spanish soul. "My
Auntie Waldorf—" She breaks down beautifully while Pym
wonders whether the agitation of his body is visible to her in
the darkness.

"It's a damn shame!" cries Rick, while the baroness
composes herself. "My God, son, those Bolsheviks could swoop
down on Ascot tomorrow without a by-your-leave and help
themselves to a fortune. Go on, my dear. Son, tell her to go

on. Call her Elena, she likes it. She's not a snob. She's one of us."

"*Weiter, bitte*," says Pym.

"*Weiter*," the baroness echoes approvingly and pats her eyes with Rick's handkerchief. "*Jawohl*, darling. *Sehr gut!*"

"Oh but you should hear his accent," Mr. Cunningham calls from the door. "Not a wrinkle, you can quote me, same as my own boy."

"What does she say, son?"

"She can manage," says Pym. "She can handle it."

"She's a damned gem. I'm going to see her right, you mark my words."

So is Pym. He is going to marry her at least. But meanwhile, to his irritation, he must hear more praise for my dear late husband the baron. My Luigi was not only the proprietor of a great palace, he was a financial genius and until the outbreak of war the Chairman of the House of Rothschild in Prague.

"They were the richest of the lot," says Rick. "Weren't they, son? You've read your history. What's your verdict?"

"They couldn't even count it," Mr. Cunningham confirms from the door with the pride of an impresario. "Could they, Elena? Ask her. Don't be shy."

"We give such concerts, darling," the baroness confides to Pym. "Princes from all countries. We got house from marble. We got mirrors, culture. Like here," she adds graciously, indicating a priceless oil painting of Prince Magnus in his paddock, done from a photograph. "We lose everything."

"Not quite everything," says Rick under his breath.

"When the Germans come, my Luigi he refuse to flee. He face the Nazi pigs from the balcony, got a pistol in his hand, don't never been heard of since."

Another necessary break follows in which the baroness allows herself a delicate sip of brandy from a row of crystal decanters on the floor, and Rick to Pym's fury takes over the story, partly because Rick is already tired of listening, but more particularly because a secret is approaching, and secrets in court etiquette are Rick's alone to divulge.

"That baron was a fine man and a fine husband, son, and he did what any fine husband would do, and believe me, if your mother was in a position to appreciate it, I'd do the same for her tomorrow—"

"I know you would," says Pym hastily.

"That baron got some of the best treasures out of that palace, he put them in a box and he gave that box to certain very good friends of his and friends of this fine lady here, and he gave orders that when the British won the war this same box should be handed over to his lovely young wife, with everything it contained, however much it may have risen in value in the meantime."

The baroness knows the menu from memory and again selects Pym as her audience, for which purpose it is necessary for her to arrest his attention with a delicate hand placed on his wrist.

"One Gutenberg Bible, nice condition, darling, one Renoir early, two Leonardo medical. One first edition Goya caprices, artist annotation, three hundred best gold American dollar, Rubens a couple cartoons."

"Cunningham says it's worth a bomb," says Rick when she seems to have finished.

"It's Hiroshima," says Mr. Cunningham from the door.

Pym contrives an ethereal smile intended to indicate that great art knows no price. The baroness intercepts it and understands.

It is an hour later. The baroness and her protector have departed, leaving father and son alone in the great unlighted room. The traffic below the window has subsided. Shoulder to shoulder on the bed they are eating fish and chips which Pym has been dispatched to buy with precious pound notes from Rick's back pocket. They wash it down with a bottle of Château d'Yquem from a Harrods crate.

"Are they still there, son?" says Rick. "Did they see you? Those men in the Riley. Heavy built."

"I'm afraid they are," says Pym.

"You believe in her, don't you, son? Don't spare my feelings. Do you believe in that fine woman or do you think she's a black-hearted liar and adventuress to boot?"

"She's fantastic," says Pym.

"You don't sound convinced. Spit it out, son. She's our last chance, I'll tell you that for nothing."

"It's just I wasn't quite sure why she hadn't gone to her own people."

"You don't know those Jews the way I do. They're some of the finest people in the world. There's others, they'd have the coat off her back as soon as look at her. I asked her the same question. I didn't pull my punches either."

"Who's Cunningham?" says Pym, barely able to conceal his distaste.

"Old Cunnie's first class. I'm bringing him into the business when this is over. Exports and Foreign. He'll be a tearaway. His sense of humour alone is worth five thousand a year to us. He wasn't on form tonight. He was tense."

"What's the deal?" says Pym.

"Faith in your old man, that's the deal. 'Rickie,' she says to me—that's what she calls me, she doesn't pull her punches either—'Rickie, I want you get that box for me, sell the contents and invest the money in one of your fine enterprises, and I want you to take the cares off my shoulders and give me ten percent a year for life for as long as I'm spared, with all the necessary provisions of insurance and endowment if you go before me. I want that money to be yours to see the world right in whatever way you deem in your wisdom.' That's a big responsibility, son. If I had a passport I'd go myself. I'd send Syd if he was available. Syd would go. Cattle and pigs. That's what I'm going to do after this. Just a few acres and some livestock. I'm retiring."

"What's happened to your passport?" said Pym.

"Son, I'm going to level with you, which I always do. That airy-fairy school of yours are hard bargainers. They want cash and they want it on the due day and that's it. You speak her language, that's the point. She likes you. She trusts you. You're my son. I could send Muspole but I'd never be sure he'd come back. Perce Loft's too legal. He'd scare her. Now slip to the window and see if that Riley's gone. Don't get the light on your face. They can't come in. They haven't got a warrant. I'm an honest citizen."

Half hidden behind the chipped green filing cabinet, Pym squints steeply downward into the street in covert counter-surveillance. The Riley is still there.

There are no blankets for the bed so they make do with curtains and dust-sheets. Pym sleeps fitfully and freezes, dreaming of the baroness. Once Rick's arm falls violently across him, once he is roused by Rick's strangled voice calling out invective against a bitch called Peggy. And some time in

the early hours he feels the soft female weight of Rick's
nether body in silk shirt and underpants backing inexorably
against him, which persuades him it is more restful on the
floor. In the morning Rick still will not leave the house, so
Pym walks alone to Victoria Station carrying his few possessions in a splendid white box-calf suitcase with Rick's initials
in brass underneath the handle. He wears one of Rick's
camel-hair coats though it is too large for him. The baroness,
looking more delectable than ever, is waiting on the platform.
Mr. Cunningham is there to wave them off. In the train
lavatory, Pym opens the envelope Rick gave him and extracts
a wad of white ten-pound notes and his first-ever instructions
for a clandestine encounter.

> "You are to proceed to Bern and take Rooms at
> the Grand Palace Hotel. Mr. Bertl the under-manager
> is first Rate, the Bill is taken care of. Signor Lapadi
> will Contact the Baroness and guide you to the
> Austrian border. When Lapadi has given you the
> Box and you have Confirmed in our Language that
> it's all there, see him right with the Enclosed _and not
> until._ This is going to be the Saving of us, son. That
> Money you are Carrying took a lot of earning, but
> when this is over none of us will ever have to Worry
> again."

I shall be brisk with the operational details of the Rothschild
assignment, Jack—the days of hope, the days of doubt, the
sudden leaps from one to the other. And I truly forget which
street corners or codewords preceded the slow descent into
inconclusion that has been my memory of so many operations
since—just as I forget, if I ever knew, in what quantities of
skepticism and blind faith Pym pursued his mission to its
inevitable end. Certainly I have known operations since that
have been mounted on quite as little likelihood of success,
and have cost a great deal more than money. Signor Lapadi
spoke only to the baroness, who relayed his information with
disdain.
    "Lapadi he talk mit his _Vertrauensmann_, darling." She
smiles indulgently when Pym asks what a _Vertrauensmann_ is.

"The *Vertrauensmann* is man we are trusting. Not yesterday, maybe not tomorrow. But today we are trusting him for ever."

"Lapadi he need one hundred pound, darling"—a day or two later—"the *Vertrauensmann* know a man whose sister know the head from customs. Better he pay him now for friendship."

Remembering Rick's instructions Pym offers token resistance but the baroness already has her hand out and is rubbing her finger and thumb together with delightful insinuation. "You want to paint the house, darling, first you got to buy the brush," she explains and to Pym's amazement lifts her skirts to the waist and pops the banknotes into the top of her stocking. "Tomorrow we buy you nice suit."

"Gave her the money, son?" Rick roars that night across the Channel. "God in Heaven, what do you think we are? Fetch me Elena."

"Don't shout me, darling," the baroness says calmly into the telephone. "You got lovely boy here, Rickie. He very strict with me. I think one day he be great actor."

"The baroness says you're first rate, son. Are you talking our language with her out there?"

"All the time," says Pym.

"Have you had an honest-to-God English mixed grill yet?"

"No, we're sort of saving it."

"Well have one on me. Tonight."

"We will, Father. Thanks."

"God bless you, son."

"And you too, Father," says Pym politely and, butler-like, keeps his knees and feet together while he puts the phone down.

More important to me by far are my memories of Pym's first platonic honeymoon with a wise lady. With Elena beside him, Pym wandered Bern's old city, drank the light small wines of the Valais, watched *thés dansants* in the great hotels and consigned his past to history. In scented, frilly boutiques that she seemed to find by instinct, they exchanged his battered wardrobe for fur capes and Anna Karenina riding boots that slithered on the frosty cobble, and Pym's dismal school habit for a leather jacket and trousers without buttons for his braces. Even in her disarray, the baroness would insist on Pym's judgment, beckoning him into the little mirrored box to help her choose, and permitting him, as if unknowingly, delicious glimpses of her Rococo charms: now a nipple, now the cup of a buttock carelessly uncurtained, now an amazing shadow at the centre of her rounded thighs as she whisked from one skirt to another. She is Lippsie, he thought excitedly; she is how Lippsie would have been if she hadn't thought so much of death.

"*Gefall' ich dir*, darling?"

"*Du gefällst mir sehr.*"

"One day you have pretty girl, you talk to her just like this, she go crazy. You don't think too tarty?"

"I think perfect."

"Okay, we buy two. One for my sister Zsa-Zsa, she my size."

A tilt of the white shoulders, a careless pull at a straying hem of lingerie, the bill was brought, Pym signed it and addressed it to the provident Herr Bertl, turning his back on her and crouching forward in order to conceal the evidence of his perturbation. From a jeweller in the Herrengasse they bought a pearl necklace for another sister in Budapest and as an afterthought a topaz ring for her mother in Paris which the baroness would take to her on her way home. And I see that ring now, winking on her freshly manicured finger as she traces a trout back and forth across the fish tank in the grill-room of our grand hotel while the headwaiter stands above her with his net poised to strike.

"*Nein, nein*, darling, *nicht* this one, *that* one! *Ja, ja, prima.*"

It was at one such dinner, in the event their last, that Pym was so moved by love and confusion that he felt obliged to confide to the baroness his intention of leading a monastic life. She put down her knife and fork with a clatter.

"Don't tell me no more from monks!" she commanded him angrily. "I see too many of monks. I see monks of Croatia, monks of Serbia, Russia. God He ruin the damn world with monks."

"Well, it's not completely certain," said Pym.

It took a lot of funny voices from him, and a lot of intimate fabrications, before the light came cautiously back to her brown eyes.

"And her name was Lippsie?"

"Well that's what we called her. I mustn't tell you her real name."

"And she slept with such a young boy like you? You made love with her so young? She was a whore, I think."

"Probably just lonely," said Pym wisely.

But her thoughtfulness remained and when Pym as usual saw her to her bedroom door she studied him closely before taking his head between her hands and kissing him on the mouth. Suddenly her mouth opened, Pym's also. The kiss became intense, he felt an unfamiliar mound plying irresistibly against his thigh. He felt its warmth, he felt soft hair slipping against silk as she pressed more rhythmically. She whispered "*Schatz*," he heard a squeak and wondered whether he had hurt her somehow. Her head twisted, her neck pressed against his lips. With confiding fingers she handed him the key to her bedroom door and looked away while he opened it. He found the keyhole, turned the key and held the door for her. He put the key into her palm and saw the light in her eyes fade.

"So, my dear," she said. She kissed him, one cheek other cheek, she stared at him as if searching for something she had lost. It was not till next morning that he discovered she had been kissing him goodbye.

> "Darling"—she wrote—"You are good man, got body from Michelangelo but your Papi got bad problems. Better you stay in Bern. Never mind. E. Weber love you always."

In the envelope were the gold cufflinks we had bought for her cousin in Oxford, and two hundred of the five hundred pounds that Pym had given her for the invisible Mr. Lapadi. I wear the cufflinks as I write. Gold with tiny diamonds in a crown. The baroness always loved a touch of royalty.

It was morning at Miss Dubber's also. Through the closed curtains, Pym heard the milk van clinking on its rounds. Pen in hand he drew a pink file towards him marked simply "R.T.P.," licked his forefinger and thumb and began methodically turning through the entries until he had extracted some half dozen.

Copy letter Richard T. Pym to Father Guardian, Lyme Regis, dated 1 October 1948, threatening legal proceedings for the abduction of his son Magnus. (Ex R.T.P.'s files.)

Memorandum of 15 September 1948, Fraud Squad to Passport Control Department, recommending impounding of R.T.P.'s passport pending criminal investigations in the matter of one J.R. Wentworth. (Obtained informally through Head Office police liaison section.)

Letter from school bursar to R.T.P. declining to accept either dried fruit, tinned peaches or any other commodity in part or full payment of fees and regretting that the governing board cannot see its way to educating Pym for nothing. "I note also with regret that you refuse to describe yourself as an impecunious parent whose son is destined for the clergy." (Ex R.T.P.'s files.)

Furious letter from lawyers representing Herr Eberhardt Bertl, sometime under-manager of the Grand Palace Hotel in Bern, addressed to Colonel Sir Richard T. Pym, D.S.O., one of a succession, demanding payment in the order of eleven thousand and eighteen Swiss francs forty centimes, plus interest at four percent per month. (Ex R.T.P's files.)

Extract from London *Chronicle* dated November 8, 1949, declaring personal bankruptcy R.T.P., and compulsory liquidation of the eighty-three companies of the Pym empire including, no doubt, The Muspole Friendly & Academic Ltd.

Extract from *Daily Telegraph* dated October 9, 1948, recording the death in Truro Hospital, Cornwall, of one John Reginald Wentworth, after a long illness resulting from his injuries, beloved husband to Peggy.

And a quaint little cutting, culled from God knows where, recording the arrest at sea, on the cruise ship S.S. *Grande Bretagne*, of the notorious confidence tricksters Weber and Woolfe alias Cunningham, masquerading as the Duke and Duchess of Seville.

One by one, with a red pen, Pym numbered each document in the top right corner, then entered the same numbers at the appropriate points in his text by way of reference. With a bureaucrat's neat manners he stapled the exhibits together and inserted them in a file marked "Annexe." Closing the file he stood up, gave an unrestrained sigh and thrust down his arms behind him like a man slipping off a harness. The ghostly formlessness of adolescence was over. Manhood and maturity beckoned, even if he never made the distance. He was in his beloved Switzerland at last, the spiritual home of natural spies. Crossing to the window he made a last inspection of the square, the tired lights of England fading as he watched. Gravely he undressed, drank a last vodka, gravely took a look at himself in the mirror and prepared to put himself to bed. But lightly, very lightly. Almost on tiptoe. Almost as if he were afraid to wake himself up. On his way he paused at the desk and read again the decoded message that for once he had not bothered to destroy.

Poppy, he thought, stay exactly where you are.

7

Five years ago Jack Brotherhood had shot his Labrador bitch. She was in her basket, rheumatic and shaking; he'd given her the pills but she'd sicked them up, then shamed herself by messing the carpet. And when he threw on his windcheater and took his 12-bore from behind the door, willing her, she looked at him like a criminal because she knew she was finally too sick to find for him. He ordered her to get up but she couldn't. When he yelled "Seek!" she rolled herself on to her forepaws and lay down again with her head stuck stupidly over the basket. So he put down the gun and got a shovel from the shed and dug her a hole in the field behind the cottage, a bit up the slope with a decent view across the estuary. Then he wrapped her in his favourite tweed jacket and carried her up there and shot her in the back of the head, smashing the spinal cord at the nape, and buried her. After that he sat beside her with a half-bottle of scotch while the Suffolk dew settled itself over him and he decided she had probably had the best death anyone was likely to have in a world not distinguished by good deaths. He didn't leave a headstone or a coy wood cross for her but he had taken bearings on the spot, using the church tower, the dead willow tree and the windmill, and whenever he passed it by he'd send her a gruff mental greeting, which was as near as he had ever come to pondering on the afterlife, until this empty Sunday morning as he drove through deserted Berkshire lanes and watched the sun lifting on the Downs. "Jack's had too many miles in the saddle," Pym had said. "The Firm should have retired him ten years ago."

And how long ago should we have retired you, my boy? he wondered. Twenty years? Thirty? How many miles have you had in the saddle? How many miles of exposed film have you rolled into how many newspapers? How many miles of newspaper have you dropped into dead letter boxes and tossed over cemetery walls? How many hours have you listened to Prague radio, seated over your code pads?

He lowered his window. The racing air smelt of silage and wood smoke and it thrilled him. Brotherhood was country stock. His forebears were gypsies and clergymen, gamekeepers and poachers and pirates. With the morning wind pouring into his face, he became a raggedy-arsed boy again, galloping Miss Sumner's hunter bareback across her park and getting the hiding of his life for it. He was freezing to death in the flat mud of the Suffolk fens, too proud to go home without a catch. He was making his first drop from a barrage balloon at Abingdon Aerodrome and discovering how the wind kept his mouth open after he yelled. I'll leave when they throw me out. I'll leave when you and I have had our word, my boy.

He had slept six hours in forty-eight, most of them on a lumpy camp bed in a room set aside for typists with the vapours, but he was not tired. "Can we have you for a minute, Jack?" said Kate, the Fifth Floor vestal, with a look that stayed on him a beat too long. "Bo and Nigel would like another small word." And when he wasn't sleeping or answering the telephone or thinking his usual puzzled thoughts about Kate, he had watched his life go by in a kind of bewildered free fall into enemy territory: so this is what it's like, this is badland and these are my feet spinning towards it like a sycamore twig. He had contemplated Pym in all the stages he had grown up with him, drunk with him and worked with him, including a night in Berlin he had totally forgotten until now when they had ended up screwing a couple of army nurses in adjoining rooms. He had remembered contemplating his own mangled arm on the winter's day in 1943 when it had hung beside him embellished with three German machine-gun bullets, and he had experienced the same feeling of incredulous detachment.

"If you could only have let us know a little earlier, Jack. If only you could have seen it coming."

Yes, I'm sorry, Bo. Careless of me.

"But Jack, he was practically your own son, we used to say."

Yes, we did, didn't we, Bo. Silly really, I agree.

And Kate's reproving eyes, as ever, saying, Jack, Jack, where are you?

There had been other cases in his lifetime, naturally. Ever since the war had ended, Brotherhood's professional life had been regularly turned upside down by the Firm's latest terminal scandal. While he was Head of Station in Berlin, it had happened to him not twice but three times: night tele-grams, flash, for Brotherhood's eyes only. Phone call—where is he? Jack, get off your elbows and get in here *now*. Race through wet streets, dead sober. Telegram one, the subject of my immediately following telegram is a member of this service and has now been revealed as a Soviet Intelligence agent. You will inform your official contacts of this in confi-dence before they read it in the morning papers. Followed by the long wait beside the codebooks while you think: is it him, is it her, is it me? Telegram two, spell a name of six letters, who the hell do I know who's got six letters? First group M—Christ, it's Miller! Second group A—oh my God, it's Mackay! Until up comes a name you never heard of, from a section you didn't know existed, and when the expurgated case history finally arrives on your desk all you have is a vision of an under-welfared little nancy-boy in the cypher room in Warsaw who thought he was playing the world's game when what he really wanted was to shaft his employers.

But these distant scandals had been till now the gunfire of a war he was certain would never come his way. He had regarded them not as warnings but as confirmation of every-thing he disliked about the way the Firm was going: its retreat into bureaucracy and semi-diplomacy, its pandering to American methods and example. By comparison his own hand-picked staff had only looked better to him, and when the

witch-hunters had gathered at his door, led by Grant Lederer
and his nasty little Mormon bag-carriers, baying for Pym's
blood and brandishing fanciful suspicions based on nothing
more than a few computerised coincidences, it was Jack
Brotherhood who had banged his open hand upon the conference table and made the water-glasses hop: "Stop this
now. There's not a man or woman in this room who won't look
like a traitor once you start to pull our life stories inside out.
A man can't remember where he was on the night of the
tenth? Then he's lying. He *can* remember? Then he's too
damn flip with his alibi. You go one more yard with this and
everyone who tells the truth will become a barefaced liar,
everyone who does a decent job will be working for the other
side. You carry on like this and you'll sink our service better
than the Russians ever could. Or is that what you want?"

And God help him, with his reputation and his anger
and his connections and with his section's record, in the
modern jargon that he loathed, of low cost and high produc-
tivity, he had carried the day, never thinking for a moment
that another day might come where he wished he hadn't.

Closing his window Brotherhood stopped the car in a
village where no one knew him. He was too early. He had
needed to get out of London, out of touch, away from Kate's
brown stare. Give him one more hopeless damage-limitation
conference, one more session on how to keep it from the
Americans, one more glance of pity or reproach from Kate, or
of plain hatred from Bo's grey army of suburban mandarins,
and possibly, just possibly, Jack Brotherhood might have said
things that everyone, but most of all himself, would afterwards have regretted. So he had volunteered for this errand
instead, and Bo with rare promptness had said what a good
idea, who better? And he knew as soon as he cleared Bo's
doorway that they were as glad to see him go as he was to
leave. Except for Kate.

"Just do keep phoning in if you don't mind," Bo called
after him. "Three-hourly at most. Kate will know the score.
Won't you, Kate?"

Nigel followed him down the corridor. "When you phone
in, I want you coming through Secretariat. You're not to use
his direct line and I shall need to speak to you first."

"And that's an order," Brotherhood suggested.

"It's a temporary licence and it can be withdrawn at any time."

The church had a wooden porch, a footpath led beside a playing field. He passed a farmyard with brick barns and smelt warm milk on the autumn air.

"We evacuate them in echelons, Jack," Frankel is saying in his hand-pressed Euro-English. "That's if we evacuate them at all."

"And on my say-so," Nigel adds from the wings.

The room is low and windowless and overlit. A uniformed guard mans the peephole. Spaced along the wall sit Frankel's greying female assistants at their trestle desks. They have brought thermos flasks and share each other's cigarettes. They have done it all before, like a day at the races. Frankel is fat and ugly, a Latvian headwaiter. Brotherhood recruited him, Brotherhood promoted him. Now he was taking over Brotherhood's mess. So it goes. It is three in the morning. It is today, six hours ago.

"Day one, Jack, we move only head agents," says Frankel with a doctor's false assurance. "Conger and Watchman in Prague, Voltaire in Budapest, Merryman in Gdansk."

"When do we begin?" says Brotherhood.

"When Bo waves the flag, and not before," says Nigel. "We're still evaluating and we still regard Pym's loyalties as *quite possibly impeccable*," says Nigel, like somebody mastering a tongue-twister.

"We move them very quietly, Jack," says Frankel. "No goodbyes, no flowers for the neighbours, no finding somewhere for the cat. Day two radio operators, day three the cut-outs, subagents. Day four whoever's left."

"How do we reach them?" Brotherhood asks.

"You don't, we do," says Nigel. "If and when the Fifth Floor says it's necessary, which at the moment, I repeat, is pure hypothesis."

Kate has followed them in. Kate is our widowed English spinster, pale and sculptural and beautiful, who at forty mourns the loves she never had. And Kate is still Kate, he can see it as clear as ever in her eyes.

"Maybe we pick them off the street when they go to work," Frankel continues. "Maybe we bang on the door, tell a friend, leave a note somewhere. Just anything we think of, so long as it wasn't done before."

"That's where you'll be able to help if we get that far," Nigel explains. "Telling us what's been done before."

Frankel has paused before a map of Eastern Europe. Brotherhood waits a step behind him. Head agents red, subagents blue. So much easier to kill a pushpin than a man. Still gazing at the map Brotherhood remembers an evening in Vienna. Pym is playing host, Brotherhood is Colonel Peter bringing London's thanks for ten years' service. He remembers Pym's gracious speech in Czech, the champagne and medals, the handshakes, the assurances, the quiet waltzes to the gramophone. And this dumpy couple in brown, he a physicist, she a senior lady in the Czech Ministry of the Interior, lovers in betrayal, their faces glistening with excitement as they whirl round the drawing-room to the strains of Johann Strauss.

"So when do you start?" Brotherhood asks again.

"Jack, that is Bo's judgment," Nigel insists, dangerously patient.

"Jack, the Fifth Floor has ruled that the most important thing is to look busy, act natural, keep everything normal," says Frankel, picking a sheaf of telegrams from his desk. "They use letter boxes? So clear the letter boxes like normal. They got radio? So send radio like normal, stick to all the normal schedules, hope the opposition are listening."

"That's the most important thing at the moment," Nigel says, as if anything Frankel says is invalid until he says it too. "Total normality in all areas. One premature step would be fatal."

"So would a late one," Brotherhood says as his blue eyes start to catch fire.

"They're waiting for you, Jack," Kate says, meaning, come away, there's nothing you can do.

Brotherhood does not move. "Do it now," he tells Frankel. "Take them into the embassies. Broadcast a warning. Abort."

Nigel doesn't say a word. Frankel looks to him for help but Nigel has folded his arms and is looking over the shoulder of one of Frankel's women while she types a signal.

"Jack, no way do we take those Joes into embassies or consulates," Frankel says, making faces in Nigel's direction. "*Verboten*. The most we can do when we get the order from the Fifth Floor is fresh escape papers, is money, transport, a couple of prayers. That right, Nigel?"

"*If* you get the order," Nigel corrects him.

"Conger will head east," Brotherhood says. "His daughter's at university in Bucharest. He'll go to her."

"Okay, so where does he go from Bucharest?" says Frankel.

Brotherhood is nearly shouting. There is nothing Kate can do to stop him. "South into bloody Bulgaria, what do you think! If we give him a date and place, we can put a plane in, hedgehop him into Yugoslavia!"

Now Frankel also lifts his voice. "Jack. Hear me, okay? Nigel, confirm this for me so I don't sound too negative all the time. No little planes, no embassies, no frontier crashes of any kind. This is not the sixties any more. Not the fifties, not the forties. We don't drop planes and pilots around Eastern Europe like birdseed. We are not enthusiastic about reception committees for ourselves or our Joes that are laid on by the opposition."

"He's got it straight," Nigel confirms with just enough surprise.

"I got to tell you this, Jack. Your networks are so contaminated at this moment that the Foreign Office wouldn't even drop them in the trash can, would they, Nigel? You are isolated, Jack. Whitehall's got to cover itself in polythene before it shakes your hand. Is this correct, Nigel?" Frankel hears himself and stops. He looks to Nigel yet again but receives no comforting word. He catches Brotherhood's eye and stares at him with a long and unexpected fearfulness, the way we look at monuments and find ourselves contemplating our own mortality. "I take orders, Jack. Don't look at me that way. Cheers."

Brotherhood slowly climbs the stairs. Climbing them ahead of him, Kate slows down and trails a couple of fingers for him to take hold of. He pretends he hasn't seen.

"When will I see you?" she says.

Brotherhood has gone deaf as well.

The responsibilities that rested on the shoulders of Tom Pym that morning were as heavy as any he had been obliged to face during his first month as a school prefect and captain of Pandas. Today was the first of Pandas' duty week. Today, and for the six awesome days to follow, Tom must ring the morning bell, assist Matron to supervise showers and call the roll before breakfast. Today being Sunday he must keep charge of letter-writing in the day room, read the Lesson in chapel and inspect the changing rooms for untidiness and impropriety. When evening came at last he must preside over the boys' committee that receives suggestions about the management of school life and, after editing, submit them to the agonised consideration of Mr. Caird the Headmaster, for Mr. Caird could do nothing lightly and saw all sides of every argument. And when he had somehow got through all this and rung the bell for lights out, there was Monday to wake up to. Last week it had been Lions' turn for duty and Lions had done well. Lions, Mr. Caird had pronounced in a rare show of conviction, had displayed a democratic approach to power, holding votes and forming committees on every contentious issue. In chapel, waiting for the last lines of the hymn to die, Tom prayed earnestly for his dead grandfather's soul, for Mr. Caird and for victory in Wednesday's squash match against St. Saviour's, Newbury, away, though he feared it would be another humiliating defeat, for Mr. Caird was divided on the merits of athletic competition. But most fervently he prayed that come next Saturday—if Saturday ever did come—Pandas too would earn Mr. Caird's favour, because Mr. Caird's disappointment was actually more than Tom could bear.

Tom was a very tall boy and affected already the British administrator's bobbing walk that characterised his father. His receding hairline gave him an air of maturity that may have accounted for his advancement to high position in the school. To watch him, hands linked behind his back, detach himself from the prefect's pew, step into the aisle, duck his head at the altar and mount the two steps to the lectern, you could have been forgiven for wondering whether this was a pupil at all and not a member of Mr. Caird's impressively youthful staff. Only his froggy voice as he barked the day's text betrayed the changeling inside the senatorial exterior. Tom heard little of what he was reading. The Lesson was the first he had read and he had practised it till he knew it by heart. Yet now that he came to perform it, the red and black print before him had neither sound nor meaning. Only the sight of his chewed thumbs stuck either side of him on the lectern, and the white head floating above them in the back row of the congregation, held him to the world at all. Without them, he decided, he could have taken off, smack through the chapel ceiling and into the sky, and thereafter levitated, like his gas balloon on Commemoration Day, which flew all the way to Maidenhead and landed with his name on it in an old lady's back garden, earning him five pounds in book tokens and a letter from her saying she too had a son called Tom, who worked at Lloyd's.

"I have trodden the winepress alone," he bellowed to his surprise. "And of the people there was none with me: for I will tread them in mine anger and trample them in my fury." The threat alarmed him and he wondered why he had uttered it and to whom. "And their blood shall be sprinkled upon my garments, and I will stain all my raiment."

Still reading, feeling the backs of his knees batting against his trousers, Tom considered a number of other matters that turned out to be weighing on his mind, some of which were new to him until this moment. He had no expectation any more that his mind would be ruled by what was going on around it, even in work. In Friday's gym class he had found himself thinking out a problem of Latin grammar. In yesterday's Latin he had worried about his mother's drinking. And in the middle of French construe he had discovered that he was no longer in love with Becky Lederer, despite their ardent correspondence, but preferred instead one of the Bursar's daughters. Under the pressures of high office his mind had become a slice of undersea cable like the one in the science lab. First there was this bunch of wires, all carrying their proper messages and doing their appointed jobs; and then, swimming around them like a shoal of invisible fish, ran a whole lot more messages which for some reason did not need wires at all. And that was how his mind felt now, while he honked out the sacred words in his deepest possible voice only to hear them tinkling like cracked bells in a distant room.

"For the day of vengeance is in mine heart, and the year of my redeemed is come," he said.

He thought of gas balloons and of the Tom who worked in Lloyd's, and of the forthcoming apocalypse when he failed his common entrance examination, and of the Bursar's daughter when she rode her bicycle with her blouse flattened against her chest by the wind. And he fretted about whether Carter Major, who was Pandas' vice-captain, had the qualities of democratic leadership to handle afternoon kickabout. But there was one thought he refused to have at all because really all these other thoughts were surrogates for it. There was one thought he could not put in words or even pictures, because it was so bad that even thinking it could turn it into truth.

"How's your beef, son?" Jack Brotherhood asked, what seemed about twenty seconds later, over lunch in the Digby Hotel where they always went.

"Super, Uncle Jack, thank you," said Tom.

Otherwise they ate in the silence that they mostly observed till lunch was past. Brotherhood had his *Sunday Telegraph*, Tom a fantasy novel he was reading over and over again, because it was a book in which everything came right and other books could be dangerous. Nobody understands better than Uncle Jack how you take people out from school, Tom decided, while he read and ate and thought of his mother. Not even his father had such a clear idea of how everything should be the same each time yet exquisitely different in tiny ways. How you had to be completely calm and unfussed yet draw out the day by doing masses of different things until the last moment. How school was a place that for most of the day must not exist, so that there was never any question of going back there. Only during the last countdown must it be sufficiently reconstructed to make return a possibility.

"Want a second?"

"No, thank you."

"More Yorkshire?"

"Yes, please. A bit."

Brotherhood lifted his eyebrows to the waiter and the waiter came at once, which was what waiters did for Uncle Jack.

"Heard from your father?"

Tom did not answer at once because his eyes suddenly hurt and he couldn't breathe.

"Here, now," said Brotherhood softly, putting down his newspaper. "What's this, then?"

"It's just the Lesson," said Tom, fighting away his tears. "It's all right now."

"You made a damn good job of reading that Lesson. Anyone tells you different, knock him down."

"It was the wrong day's," Tom explained, still fighting to

get back above water. "I should have turned to the next bookmark and I forgot."

"Bugger the wrong day's," Brotherhood growled, so emphatically that the old couple at the next table swung their heads round at him. "If yesterday's Lesson was any good, it won't do anyone an ounce of harm to hear it twice. Have another ginger beer."

Tom nodded and Brotherhood ordered it before once more taking up his *Sunday Telegraph*. "Probably didn't even understand it the first time anyway," he said with contempt.

But the real trouble was Tom had not read the wrong Lesson; he had read the right one. He knew very well he had, and he had a suspicion Uncle Jack knew it too. He just needed something easier to cry about than the fish that were swimming round the cable in his head and the thought he refused to have.

They agreed to do without pudding so as not to waste the fine weather.

Sugarloaf Hill was a chalky hump in the Berkshire Downs with Ministry of Defence barbed wire round it and a warning to the public to keep out, and probably in all Tom's life there was nowhere better in the world to be, except at home in Plush at lambing time. Not Lech and skiing with his father, not Vienna and riding with his mother: nowhere he had ever been or dreamed of was as private, as amazingly privileged, as this secret hilltop compound with barbed wire to keep out enemies, where Jack Brotherhood and Tom Pym, godfather and godson and the best friends ever, could take turns to loose off clay pigeons from the launcher, and shoot them down or miss them with Tom's 20-bore. The first time they had come here, Tom hadn't believed it. "It's all locked, Uncle Jack," he had objected as Uncle Jack stopped the car. It had been a good day till then. Now suddenly it had gone all wrong. They had driven ten miles by the map and to his chagrin ended at a pair of high white gates that were locked and forbidden by order. The day was over. He had wished he could be back at school again, doing his voluntary-punishment prep.

"Then go over and yell 'Open sesame!' at it," Uncle Jack had advised, handing Tom a key from his pocket. And the next thing was, the white gates of authority had closed again behind them and they were special people with a special pass to be up here on the hilltop with the boot open, pulling out the rusted launcher that Uncle Jack had kept secret all through lunch. And the next thing after *that* was that Tom scored nine clays out of twenty, and Uncle Jack nineteen, because Uncle Jack was the best shot ever, the best at everything, although he was so old, and he wouldn't give away a match to please anybody, not even Tom. If Tom ever beat Uncle Jack, he would beat him fair, which was what they both wanted without needing to say it. And it was what Tom wanted more than anything today: a normal exchange, a normal competition, with normal conversation, the kind that Uncle Jack was brilliant at. He wanted to hide his worst thoughts in a deep hole and not have to show them to anybody ever until he died for England.

It was the outdoors that set Tom free. Uncle Jack had nothing to do with it. He didn't like too much talk and certainly not about things that were private. It was the sense of daytime that was like a resurrection. It was the din of gunfire, the clatter of the October wind that buffeted his cheeks and slid inside his school pullover. Suddenly these things got him talking like a man instead of whimpering under the bedclothes with the stuffed animals which progressive Mr. Caird encouraged. Down in the river valley there had been no wind at all, just a tired autumn sun and brown leaves along the towpath. But up here on the bare chalk hilltop the wind was going like a train through a tunnel, taking Tom with it. It was clanking and laughing in the new Ministry of Defence pylon that had gone up since they had last come here.

"If we shoot the pylon down we'll let the bloody Russians in!" Uncle Jack yelled at him through cupped hands. "Don't want to do that, do we?"

"No!"

"All right, then. What do we do?"

"Pitch the launcher right next to the pylon and shoot away from it!" Tom had shouted back joyfully, and as he shouted he felt the last bits of worry go out of his chest, and his shoulders settle on his back, and he knew that with a wind like this whipping over the hilltop he could tell anything he wanted to anybody. Uncle Jack launched ten clays for him and he brought down eight with eleven cartridges, which was his absolute best yet considering the wind. And when it was Tom's turn to launch, Uncle Jack had a fight on his hands just to match him. But match him he did and Tom loved him for it. He didn't want to beat Uncle Jack. His father maybe, but not Uncle Jack; there would be nothing left. In his second ten Tom did less well but he didn't mind because his arms were aching, which wasn't his fault. But Uncle Jack stayed steady as a castle. Even when he was reloading, the white head stayed forward to meet the rising butt.

"Fourteen eighteen to you," Tom shouted as he galloped about collecting empty cartridges. "Well shot!" And then, just as loud and cheerful: "And Dad's all right, is he?"

"Why wouldn't he be?" Brotherhood shouted back.

"He seemed a bit down when he came to see me after Granddad's funeral, that's all."

"I should think he bloody well *was* down. How would you feel if you had just buried *your* old man?"

Still shouting in the wind, both of them. Small talk while they loaded the 20-bore and cranked back the launcher for another go.

"He talked about freedom all the time!" Tom yelled. "He said nobody could ever give it to us, we've got to grab it for ourselves. I got rather bored with it, actually."

Uncle Jack was so busy reloading that Tom even wondered whether he had heard. Or if he had, whether he was interested.

"He's dead right," said Brotherhood snapping the gun shut. "Patriotism's a dirty word these days."

Tom released the clay and watched it curl and burst to powder under Uncle Jack's perfect aim.

"He wasn't talking about patriotism exactly," Tom explained, delving for another couple of cartridges.

"Oh?"

"I think he was telling me that if I was unhappy I should run away. He said it in his letter too. It's sort—"

"Well?"

"It's as if he wanted me to do something he hadn't done himself when *he* was at the school. It's a bit weird actually."

"I shouldn't think it's weird at all. He's testing you, that's all. Saying the door's open if you want to bolt. More like a gesture of trust by the sound of it. No boy had a better father, Tom."

Tom fired and missed.

"What do you mean letter, anyway?" said Brotherhood.
"I thought he came and saw you."

"He did. But he wrote to me as well. A great long letter.
I just thought it was weird," he said again, unable to get away
from a favourite new adjective.

"All right, he was cut up. What's wrong with that? His
old man dies, he sits down and writes to his son. You should
feel honoured—good shot, boy. Good shot."

"Thanks," said Tom and looked on proudly while Uncle
Jack marked a hit on his scorecard. Uncle Jack always kept
the score.

"That's not what he said, though," Tom added awkwardly.
"He wasn't cut up. He was pleased."

"He wrote that, did he?"

"He said Granddad had gobbled up the natural humanity
in him and he didn't want to gobble it up in me."

"That's just another way of being cut up," said Brotherhood, unbothered. "Your dad ever talk about a secret place,
by the by? Somewhere he could find his well-earned peace
and quiet, ever?"

"Not really."

"He had one though, didn't he?"

"Not really."

"Where is it?"

"He said I was never to tell anyone."

"Then don't," said Uncle Jack firmly.

Suddenly, after that, talking about one's father became
the necessary function of a democratic prefect. Mr. Caird had
said it was the duty of people of privilege to sacrifice what
they held most dear in life, and Tom loved his father beyond
bearing. He felt Brotherhood's gaze on him and was pleased
to have aroused his interest even though it did not seem to
be particularly approving.

"You've known him a very long time, haven't you, Uncle
Jack?" said Tom, getting into the car.

"If thirty-five years is a long time."

"It is," said Tom, for whom a week was still an age.
Inside the car there was suddenly no wind at all. "So if Dad's
all right," he said with false boldness as he buckled on his
seat belt, "why are the police looking for him? That's what *I*
want to know."

*   *   *

"Going to tell our fortunes today, Mary Lou?" Uncle Jack asked.

"Not today, darling, I'm not in the mood."

"You're always in the mood," said Uncle Jack, and the two of them had a huge laugh while Tom blushed.

Mary Lou was a gypsy, Uncle Jack said, though Tom thought her more like a pirate. She was fat-bottomed and black-haired and had false lips drawn over her mouth like Frau Bauer in Vienna. She cooked cakes and served cream teas in a wooden café at the edge of the Common. Tom asked for poached eggs on toast and the eggs were creamy and fresh like the eggs at Plush. Uncle Jack had a pot of tea and a piece of her best fruitcake. He seemed to have forgotten everything Tom had been talking about, which Tom was grateful for, because he was feeling headachey from the fresh air and embarrassed by his own thoughts. It was two hours and eight minutes till he had to ring the bell for evensong. He was thinking he might take his father's advice and run away.

"So what was all this about the police again?" said Brotherhood a little vaguely, long after Tom had decided he had forgotten or not heard.

"They came and saw Caird. Then Caird sent for me."

"*Mr.* Caird, son," Brotherhood corrected him perfectly kindly and took a grateful pull of tea. "When?"

"On Friday. After house rugger. Mr. Caird sent for me and there was this man in a raincoat sitting in Mr. Caird's armchair, and he said he was from Scotland Yard about Dad, and did I by any chance have his leave address because in his absent-mindedness after Granddad's funeral Dad had taken leave and not told anyone where he was."

"Bollocks," Brotherhood said after a long time.

"It's true, sir. It really is."

"You said they."

"I meant he."

"Height?"

"Five foot ten."

"Age?"

"Forty."

"Colour of hair?"

"Like mine."

"Clean-shaven?"

"Yes."

"Eyes?"

"Brown."

It was a game they had played often in the past.

"Car?"

"He took a taxi from the station."

"How do you know?"

"Mr. Mellor brought him. He takes me to cello and works from the station cab-rank."

"Be accurate, boy. He came in Mr. Mellor's car. Did he tell you he'd come by train?"

"No."

"Did Mellor?"

"No."

"So who says he was a policeman?"

"Mr. Caird, sir. When he introduced me."

"What was he wearing?"

"A suit, sir. Grey."

"Did he give his rank?"

"Inspector."

Brotherhood smiled. A wonderful, comforting affectionate smile. "You silly chump, he was a *Foreign Office* inspector. That's just a flunkey from your dad's shop. That's not a *policeman*, son; that's a half-arsed clerk from Personnel Department with too little to do. Caird got it wrong as usual."

Tom could have kissed him. He nearly did. He straightened up and felt about nine feet taller, and he wanted to bury his face in the thick tweed of Uncle Jack's sports coat. Of course he wasn't a policeman! He didn't talk like a policeman, he didn't feel like a policeman, he didn't have big feet or short hair like a policeman, or a policeman's way of being separate from you even when he was being nice. It's all right, Tom told himself in glory. Uncle Jack's made it right, the way he always can.

Brotherhood was holding out his handkerchief and Tom scrubbed his eyes with it.

"So what did you tell him anyway?" Brotherhood said. And Tom explained that he didn't know where his father was either, he'd talked about losing himself in Scotland for a few days before returning to Vienna. Which had made Dad somehow seem at fault, a sort of criminal or worse. And when

Tom had told his Uncle Jack everything else he remembered about the interview, the questions, and the telephone number in case Dad surfaced—Tom didn't have it, but Mr. Caird did—Uncle Jack went to the phone in Mary Lou's parlour and rang Mr. Caird, and got an extension for Tom till nine o'clock, on the grounds that there were family matters that needed talking about.

"But what about my bells?" said Tom in alarm.

"Carter Major's doing them," said Uncle Jack, who understood absolutely everything.

He must have rung London too, because he took a long time and gave Mary Lou an extra five pounds to fill what he called her Christmas stocking, which had them both in fits again, and this time Tom joined in.

How they came to be talking about Corfu, Tom was afterwards never sure and perhaps there was no real path to their conversation any more; it was just chat about what they had both been up to since they had last met, which after all was before the summer holidays so there was masses to talk about if you were in a talking mood. And Tom was; he hadn't talked like this for ages, maybe ever, but Uncle Jack had the ease, he had that mixture of tolerance and discipline that for Tom was the perfect blend, for he loved to feel the strength of Uncle Jack's frontiers as well as the safe ground inside.

"How's your confirmation going?" Brotherhood had asked.

"All right, thanks."

"You're of an age now, Tom. Got to face it. In some countries you'd be in uniform already."

"I know."

"Work still a problem?"

"A bit, sir."

"Still got your eye on Sandhurst?"

"Yes, sir. And my uncle's regiment says they'd take me if I do all right."

"Well you'll have to swot, won't you?"

"I'm really trying actually."

Then Uncle Jack drew nearer and his voice dropped. "I'm not sure I should tell you this, son. But I'm going to anyway because I think you're ready to keep a secret. Can you do that?"

"I've got lots of secrets I've never told to anyone, sir."

"Your father is rather a secret man himself actually. I expect you knew that, didn't you?"

"You are too, aren't you?"

"Quite a great man as well, he is. But he's got to keep it quiet. For his country."

"And for you," said Tom.

"A lot of his life is blocked off completely. You could almost say from human gaze."

"Does Mummy know?"

"In principle, yes, she does. In detail, next to nothing. That's the way we work. And if your father has ever given the impression of lying, or being evasive, less than truthful sometimes, you can bet your boots it was his work and his loyalty that were the reason. It's a strain for him. It is for all of us. Secrets are a strain."

"Is it dangerous?" Tom asked.

"Can be. That's why we give him bodyguards. Like boys on motorbikes who follow him round Greece and hang about outside his house."

"I saw them!" Tom declared excitedly.

"Like tall thin men with moustaches who come up to him at cricket matches—"

"He did, he did! He had a straw hat!"

"And sometimes what your dad does is so secret he has to disappear completely. And not even the bodyguards can have his address. *I* know. But the rest of the world doesn't and it mustn't. And if that inspector comes to you again, or to Mr. Caird, or if anybody else does, you must tell them whatever you know and report to me immediately afterwards. I'm going to give you a special phone number and have a special word with Mr. Caird too. He deserves a lot of help, your father does. And gets it."

"I'm really glad," said Tom.

"Now then. That letter of his he wrote to you. The long one that came after he'd gone. Did it talk about things like that?"

"I don't know. I haven't read it all. There was a whole lot of stuff about Sefton Boyd's penknife and some writing in the staff loo."

"Who's Sefton Boyd?"

"He's a boy in the school. He's my friend."

"Is he your dad's friend too?"

"No, but his father was. His father was in the school too."

"Now what have you done with this letter?"

Punished himself with it. Squidged it up till it was tight and prickly and kept it in his trousers pocket where it jabbed his thigh. But Tom didn't say that. He just handed the remnants gratefully to Uncle Jack, who promised to take proper care of them and talk everything over with him next time—if there was anything that needed talking over, which Uncle Jack very much doubted that there would be.

"Got the envelope, have you?"

Tom hadn't.

"Where did he post it from then? There's a clue there, I expect, if we look for it."

"The postmark was Reading," said Tom.

"What day?"

"The Tuesday," said Tom unhappily, "but it could have been after post on Monday. I thought he was going back to Vienna on Monday afternoon. If he didn't go to Scotland, that is."

But Uncle Jack didn't seem to hear because he was talking about Greece again, playing what the two of them called report writing about this weedy fellow with a moustache who had shown up at the cricket ground in Corfu.

"I expect you were worried about him, weren't you, son? You thought he was up to no good with your dad, I expect, although he was so friendly. I mean, if they knew each other *that* well, why didn't your dad ask him home to meet your mum? I can see that would have bothered you on reflection. You didn't think it very nice your dad should have a secret life on Mum's doorstep."

"I suppose I didn't," Tom admitted, marvelling as ever at Uncle Jack's omniscience. "He held Dad's arm."

They had returned to the Digby. In the great joy of his release from worry, Tom had rediscovered his appetite and was having a steak and chips to fill the gap. Brotherhood had ordered himself a whisky.

"Height?" said Brotherhood, back at their special game.

"Six foot."

"All right, well done. Six foot exactly is correct. Colour of hair?"

Tom hesitated. "Sort of mousy fawny with stripes," he said.

"What the hell's that supposed to mean?"

"He wore a straw hat. It was hard to see."

"I know he wore a straw hat. That's why I'm asking you. Colour of hair?"

"Brown," said Tom finally. "Brown with the sun on it. And a big forehead like a genius."

"Now how the hell does the sun get under the brim of a hat?"

"Grey brown," said Tom.

"Then say so. Two points only. Hatband?"

"Red."

"Oh dear."

"It was red."

"Keep trying."

"It was red, red, red!"

"Three points. Colour of beard?"

"He hasn't got a beard. He's got a shaggy moustache and thick eyebrows like yours but not so bushy, and crinkly eyes."

"Three points. Build?"

"Stoopy and hobbly."

"What the hell's hobbly?"

"Like chumpy. Chumpy's when the sea is choppy and bumpy. Hobbly is when he walks fast and hobbles."

"You mean limps."

"Yes."

"Say so. Which leg?"

"Left."

"One more try?"

"Left."

"Certain?"

"Left!"

"Three points. Age?"

"Seventy."

"Don't be damn stupid."

"He's old!"

"He's not seventy. I'm not seventy. I'm not sixty. Well only just. Is he older than me?"

"The same."

"Carry anything?"

"A briefcase. A grey thing like elephant skin. And he was stringy like Mr. Toombs."

"Who's Toombs?"

"Our gym master. He teaches aikido and geography. He's killed people with his feet, though he's not supposed to."

"All right, stringy like Mr. Toombs, carried an elephant skin briefcase. Two points. Another time, omit the subjective reference."

"What's that?"

"Mr. Toombs. You know him, I don't. Don't compare one person I don't know with another I don't know."

"You said you knew him," said Tom, very excited to catch Uncle Jack out.

"I do. I'm fooling. Did he have a car, your man?"

"Volvo. Hired from Mr. Kaloumenos."

"How do you know that?"

"He hires it to everyone. He goes down to the harbour and hangs about and if anyone wants to hire a car Mr. Kaloumenos gives them his Volvo."

"Colour?"

"Green. And it's got a bashed wing and a Corfu registration and a fox's tail from the aerial and a—"

"It's red."

"It's green!"

"No points," said Brotherhood firmly, to Tom's outrage.

"Why not?"

Brotherhood pulled a wolfish smile. "It wasn't his car, was it? How do you know it was the bloke with the moustache who hired it when two other blokes were riding in it? You lost your objectivity, son."

"He was in charge!"

"You don't *know* that. You're guessing it. You could start a war, making up things like that. Ever met an Auntie Poppy at all, son?"

"No, sir."

"Uncle?"

Tom giggled. "No, sir."

"A Mr. Wentworth a name to you?"

"No, sir."

"No bells at all?"

"No, sir. I thought it was a place in Surrey."

"Well done, son. Never make it up if you think you don't know and ought to. That's the rule."

"You were teasing again, weren't you?"

"Maybe I was at that. When did your dad say he'd see you again?"

"He didn't."

"Does he ever?"

"Not really."

"Then there's no fuss, is there?"

"It's just the letter."

"What about the letter?"

"It's as if he's dead."

"Bollocks. You're imagining. Want me to tell you something else you know? That secret hideaway of your dad's that he's gone to. It's all right. We know about it. Did he give you the address?"

"No."

"Name of the nearest Scottish town?"

"No. He just said Scotland. On the sea in Scotland. A place to write where he's safe from everyone."

"He's told you all he can, Tom. He's not allowed to tell you any more. How many rooms has he got?"

"He didn't say."

"Who does his shopping then?"

"He didn't say. He's got a super landlady. She's old."

"He's a good man. And a wise man. And she's a good woman. One of us. Now don't you worry any more." Uncle Jack glanced sideways at his watch. "Here. Finish that up and order yourself a ginger beer. I need to see a man about a dog." Still smiling, he strode to the door marked toilets and telephone. Tom was nothing if not an observer. Points of happy colour on Uncle Jack's cheeks. A sense of merriness like his own and everybody absolutely fine.

Brotherhood had a wife and a house in Lambeth, and in theory he could have gone to them. He had another wife in his cottage in Suffolk, divorced it was true but given notice willing to oblige. He had a daughter married to a solicitor in Pinner and he wished them both to the devil and it was mutual. Nevertheless they would have had him as a duty. And there was a useless son who scratched a living on the stage and if Brotherhood was feeling charitable towards him, which oddly enough these days he sometimes was, and if he could stomach the squalor and the smell of pot, which he sometimes could, he would have been welcome enough to the heap of greasy coverlets that Adrian called his spare bed. But tonight and for every other night until he had had his word with Pym he wanted none of them. He preferred the exile of his stinking little safe flat in Shepherd Market with sooty pigeons humping each other on the parapet and the tarts doing sentry go along the pavement below him, the way they used to in the war. Periodically the Firm tried to take the place away from him or deduct the rent from his salary at source. The desk jockeys hated him for it and said it was his fuck-hutch, which occasionally it was. They resented his claims for hospitality booze and cleaners he didn't have. But Brotherhood was hardier than all of them and more or less they knew it.

"Research have turned up more stuff about the use of newspapers by Czech Intelligence," Kate said into the pillow. "But none of it's conclusive."

Brotherhood took a long pull of his vodka. It was two in the morning. They had been here an hour. "Don't tell me. The great spy pricks the letters of his message with a pin and posts the newspaper to his spymaster. Said spymaster holds the newspaper to the light, and reads the plans for Armageddon. They'll be using semaphore next."

She lay white and luminous beside him on the little bed, a forty-year-old Cambridge débutante who had lost her way. The grey-pink glow through the grimy curtains cut her into classic fragments. Here a thigh, here a calf, here the cone of a breast or the knifeline of a flank. She had turned her back to him, one leg slightly bent. God damn it, what does she want of me, this sad, beautiful bridge-player of the Fifth Floor, with her air of lost love and her prim carnality? After seven years of her, Brotherhood still had no idea. He'd be out touring the stations, he'd be in Bonga-bonga land. He'd not speak or write to her for months. Yet he'd hardly unpacked his toothbrush before she was in his arms, demanding him with her sad and hungry eyes. Does she have a hundred of us—are we her fighter pilots, claiming her favours each time we limp home from another mission? Or am I the only one who storms the statue?

"And Bo's called in some top shrink to join the feast," she said, in her impeccable vowels. "Somebody who specialises in harmless nervous breakdowns. They've thrown Pym's dossier at him and told him to assemble the profile of a loyal Englishman under severe stress who is arousing anxiety in other people, particularly Americans."

"He'll be calling in a medium next," said Brotherhood.

"They've checked flights to the Bahamas, Scotland and Ireland. That's as well as everywhere else. They've checked ships, car-hire firms and goodness knows what. They've got warrants running on every telephone he ever used and a blanket warrant for the rest. They've cancelled leave and weekends for all transcribers and put the surveillance teams on twenty-four-hour alert, and they still haven't told anybody what it's about. The canteen's a funeral parlour, nobody talking to anybody. They're questioning anyone who shared an office with him or bought a secondhand car from him, they've turned the tenants out of the Pyms' house in Dulwich and stripped the place from top to bottom pretending to be woodworm experts. Now Nigel's talking of moving the whole search team to a safe house in Norfolk Street, it's getting so big. Including the help, that's about a hundred and fifty staff. What's in the burnbox?"

"Why?"

"There's a shadow over it. Not in front of the children. Bo and Nigel clam up as soon as anybody mentions it."

"Press?" said Brotherhood, as if he had answered her question instead of deflecting it.

"Sewn up as usual. From *TitBits* downwards. Bo had lunch with the editors yesterday. He's already written their leaders for them in case anything gets out. How rumours weaken our security. Uninformed speculation as the true Enemy Within. Nigel's been leaning his full weight on the radio and television people."

"All two stone of it. What about the phoney copper?"

"Whoever called on Tom's Headmaster wasn't family. He wasn't from the Firm and he wasn't police."

"Maybe he was from the competition. They don't have to ask us first, do they?"

"Bo's terror is that the Americans are launching their own manhunt."

"If he'd been American there'd have been three of him.

He was a cheeky Czech. That's the way they work. Same as they used to fly in the war."

"The Headmaster describes him as up-market English, not a whiff of foreign. He didn't come or leave by train. He gave his name as Inspector Baring of Special Branch. There isn't one. The taxi bill return between the station and the school was twelve pounds and he didn't ask the driver for a receipt. Imagine a policeman not wanting a receipt for twelve pounds. He left a fake visiting card. They're looking for the printer, the paper-maker and for all I know the ink manufacturers, but they won't bring in police, the competition or liaison. They'll make any enquiry they can think of as long as it doesn't frighten the horses."

"And the London phone number he gave?"

"Bogus."

"I could nearly laugh about that if humour was my mood. What does Bo think about the moustachioed gentleman with a handbag who holds Pym's arm at cricket matches?"

"He refuses to take a view. He says if we all had our friends checked at cricket matches, we'd have no friends and no cricket. He's drafted extra girls to comb the Czech personalities index and he's signalled Athens Station to send someone to Corfu to talk to the car-hire man. It's delay and pray, and Magnus please come home."

"Where do I stand? In the corner?"

"They're terrified you'll pull down the Temple."

"I thought Pym had done that already."

"Then perhaps it's guilty contact," Kate said in her crisp Queen Bee voice.

Brotherhood took another long swallow of vodka. "If they'd get the bloody networks out. If they'd do the obvious thing, just for once."

"They won't do anything that might alert the Americans. They'd rather lie all the way to the grave. 'We've had three major traitors in three minor years. One more and we might as well admit the party's over.' That's Bo speaking."

"So the Joes will die for the Special Relationship. I like that. So will the Joes. They'll understand."

"Will they find him?"

"Maybe."

"Maybe's not enough. I'm asking you, Jack. Will they find him? Will you?"

She sounded suddenly imperious and urgent. She took the glass from his hand and drank the rest of his vodka while he watched her. She leaned over the side of the bed and fished a cigarette from her handbag. She handed him the matches and he lit it for her.

"Bo's put a lot of monkeys in front of a lot of typewriters," Brotherhood said, still watching her intently. "Maybe one of them will come up with the goods. I didn't know you smoked, Kate."

"I don't."

"You're drinking well too, I'm pleased to see. I don't remember you hitting the vodka as hard as this, I'm sure I don't. Who taught you to drink vodka that way?"

"Why shouldn't I?"

"More to the point is why should you? You're trying to tell me something, aren't you? Something I don't think I like at all. I thought you were spying for Bo for a minute there. I thought you were doing a bit of a Jezebel on me. Then I thought, no, she's trying to tell me something. She's attempting a small and intimate confession."

"He's a blasphemer."

"Who is, dear?"

"Magnus."

"Oh he is, is he? Magnus a blasphemer. Now why is that?"

"Hold me, Jack."

"Like hell I will." He pulled away from her and saw that what he had mistaken for arrogance was a stoical acceptance of despair. Her sad eyes stared straight at him, and her face was set in resignation.

"'I love you Kate,'" she said. "'Get me clear of this and I'll marry you and we'll live happily ever after.'"

Brotherhood took her cigarette and drew on it.

"'I'll dump Mary. We'll go and live abroad. France. Morocco. Who cares?' Phone calls from the other end of the earth. 'I rang to say I love you.' Flowers, saying 'I love you.' Cards. Little notes folded into things, shoved under the door, personal for my eyes only in top-secret envelopes. 'I've lived too long with the what-ifs. I want action, Kate. You're my escape-line. Help me. I love you. M.'"

Once again, Brotherhood waited.

"'I love you,'" she repeated. "He kept saying it. Like a

ritual he was trying to believe in. 'I love you.' I suppose he thought if he said it to enough people enough times, one day it might be true. It wasn't. He never loved a woman in his life. We were enemy, all of us. Touch me, Jack!"

To his surprise he felt a wave of kinship overcome him. He drew her to him and held her tightly to his chest.

"Is Bo wise to any of this?" he said.

He could feel the sweat collecting on his back. He could smell Pym's nearness in the crevices of her body. She rolled her head against him but he gently shook her, making her say it aloud: Bo knows nothing. No, Jack. Bo's got no idea.

"Magnus wasn't interested till he was calling the whole game," she said. "He could have had me any time. That wasn't enough for him. 'Wait for me, Kate. I'm going to cut the cable and be free. Kate, it's me, where are you?' I'm here, you idiot, or I wouldn't be answering the phone, would I?. . . He doesn't have affairs. He has lives. We're on separate planets for him. Places he can call while he floats through space. You know his favourite photograph of me?"

"I don't think I do, Kate," Brotherhood said.

"I'm naked on a beach in Normandy. We'd stolen the weekend. I've got my back to him, I'm walking into the sea. I didn't even know he had a camera."

"You're a beautiful girl, Kate. I could get quite hot about a picture like that myself," said Brotherhood, pulling back her hair so that he could see her face.

"He loved it better than he loved me. With my back to him I was anyone—his girl on the beach—his dream. I left his fantasies intact. You've got to get me out of it, Jack."

"How deep in are you?"

"Deep enough."

"Write him any letters yourself?"

She shook her head.

"Do him any little favours? Bend the rules for him? You better tell me, Kate." He waited, feeling the increasing pressure of her head against him. "Can you hear me?" She nodded. "I'm dead, Kate. But you've got a while to go. If it ever comes out that you and Pym so much as had a strawberry milkshake together at McDonald's while you were waiting for your bus home, they will shave your head and post you to Economic Development before you can say Jack anybody. You know that, don't you?"

Another nod.

"What did you do for him? Steal a few secrets, did you? Something juicy out of Bo's own plate?" She shook her head. "Come on, Kate. He fooled me too. I'm not going to throw you to the wolves. What did you do for him?"

"There was an entry in his P.F.," she said.

"So?"

"He wanted it taken out. It was from long ago. An army report from his National Service time in Austria."

"When did you do this?"

"Early. We'd been going for about a year. He was back from Prague."

"And you did it for him. You raided his file?"

"It was trivial, he said. He was very young at the time. A boy still. He'd been running some low-grade Joe into Czechoslovakia. A frontier crosser, I think. Really small stuff. But there was this girl called Sabina who'd got in on the act and wanted to marry him and defected. I didn't listen to it very clearly. He said if anybody picked through his file and came on the episode he'd never make it to the Fifth Floor."

"Well that's not the end of the world now, is it?"

She shook her head.

"Joe have a name, did he?" Brotherhood asked.

"A codename. Greensleeves."

"That's fanciful. I like that. Greensleeves. An all-English Joe. You fished the paper from the file and what did you do with it? Just tell it to me, Kate. It's out now. Let's go."

"I stole it."

"All right. What did you do with it?"

"That's what he asked me."

"When?"

"He rang me."

"When?"

"Last Monday evening. After he was supposed to have left for Vienna."

"What time? Come on, Kate, this is good. What time did he ring you?"

"Ten. Later. Ten-thirty. Earlier. I was watching *News at Ten*."

"What bit?"

"Lebanon. The shelling. Tripoli or somewhere. I turned the sound down as soon as I heard him and the shelling went on and on like a silent movie. 'I needed to hear your voice, Kate. I'm sorry for everything. I rang to say I'm sorry. I wasn't a bad man, Kate. It wasn't all pretend.'"

"Wasn't?"

"Yes. Wasn't. He was conducting a retrospective. Wasn't. I said it's just your father's death, you'll be all right, don't cry. Don't talk as if you're dead yourself. Come round. Where are you? I'll come to you. He said he couldn't. Not any more. Then about his file. I should feel free to tell everyone what I'd done, not try to shield him any more. But to give him a week. 'One week, Kate. It's not a lot after all those years.' Then, had I still got the paper I took out for him? Had I destroyed it, kept a copy?"

"What did you say?"

She went to the bathroom and returned with the embroidered spongebag she kept her kit in. She drew a folded square of brown paper from it and handed it to him.

"Did you give him a copy?"

"No."

"Did he ask for one?"

"No. I wouldn't have done that. I expect he knew. I took it and I said I'd taken it and he should believe me. I thought I'd put it back one day. It was a link."

"Where was he when he rang you on Monday?"

"A phone box."

"Reverse charges?"

"Middle distance. I reckoned four fifty-pence pieces. Mind you, that could still be London, knowing him. We were on for about twenty minutes but a lot of the time he couldn't speak."

"Describe. Come on, old love. You'll only have to do it once, I promise you, so you might as well do it thoroughly."

"I said, 'Why aren't you in Vienna?'"

"What did he say to that?"

"He said he'd run out of small change. That was the last thing he said to me. 'I've run out of small change.'"

"Did he have a place he ever took you? A hideaway?"

"We used my flat or went to hotels."

"Which ones?"

"The Grosvenor at Victoria was one. The Great Eastern at Liverpool Street. He has favourite rooms that overlook the railway lines."

"Give me the numbers."

Holding her against him, he walked her to the desk and scribbled down the two numbers to her dictation, then pulled on his old dressing-gown and knotted it round his waist and smiled at her. "I loved him too, Kate. I'm a bigger fool than you are." But he won no smile in return. "Did he ever talk about a place away from it all? Some dream he had?" He poured her some more vodka and she took it.

"Norway," she said. "He wanted to see the migration of the reindeer. He was going to take me one day."

"Where else?"

"Spain. The north. He said he'd buy a villa for us."

"Did he talk about his writing?"

"Not much."

"Did he say where he'd like to write his great book?"

"In Canada. We'd hibernate in some snowy place and live out of tins."

"The sea—nothing by the sea?"

"No."

"Did he ever mention Poppy to you? Someone called Poppy, like in his book?"

"He never mentioned any of his women. I told you. We were separate planets."

"How about someone called Wentworth?"

She shook her head.

"'Wentworth was Rick's Nemesis,'" Brotherhood recited. "'Poppy was mine. We each spent our lives trying to put right the wrong we'd done to them.' You heard the tapes. You've seen the transcripts. Wentworth."

"He's mad," she said.

"Stay here," he said. "Stay as long as you like."

Returning to the desk, he wiped the books and papers off it with a single sweep of his arm, switched on the reading lamp, sat down and laid the sheet of brown paper beside Pym's crumpled letter to Tom, postmark Reading. The London telephone directories were on the floor at his side. He chose the Grosvenor Hotel, Victoria, first and asked the night porter to put him through to the room number Kate had given him. A drowsy man answered.

"House detective here," Brotherhood said. "We've reason to believe you've got a lady in your room."

"Of course I've got a fucking lady in my room. This is a double room I'm paying for, and she's my wife."

It wasn't any of Pym's voices.

He laughed for her, rang the Great Eastern Hotel and got a similar result. He rang Independent Television News and asked for the night editor. He said he was Inspector Markley of Scotland Yard with an urgent enquiry: He wanted the time of transmission of the item on the Lebanese bombing story on Monday night *News at Ten.* He held on for as long as it took, while he continued to leaf through the pages of Pym's letter. Postmark Reading. Posted Monday night or Tuesday morning.

"Ten-seventeen and ten seconds. That's when he rang you," he said, and glanced round to make sure she was all right. She was sitting up against the pillow, head back like a boxer between rounds.

He rang the post office investigation unit and got the night officer. He gave her the Firm's codeword and she responded with a doom-laden "I hear you," as if the third world war was about to happen.

"I'm asking the impossible and I want it by yesterday," he said.

"We'll try our best," she said.

"I want a backtrack on any cash call to London made from a Reading area telephone box between ten-eighteen and ten-twenty-one on Monday night. Duration around twenty minutes."

"Can't be done," she said promptly.

"I love her," he told Kate over his shoulder. She had rolled over and was lying on her stomach with her face buried in her arm.

He rang off and addressed himself in earnest to Kate's purloined pages from Pym's personal file. Three of them, extracted from the army record of First Lieutenant Magnus Pym, number supplied, of the Intelligence Corps, attached No. 6 Field Interrogation Unit, Graz, described in a footnote as an offensive military intelligence-gathering unit with limited permission to run local informants. Dated 18 July 1951, writer unknown, relevant passage sidelined by Registry. Date of entry to Pym's P.F., 12 May 1952. Reason for entry, Pym's formal candidature for admission to this service. The extract was from his commanding officer's conduct report at the close of Pym's tour of duty in Graz, Austria: ". . . exceptional young officer . . . popular and courteous in the mess . . . earned a high reputation for his skilful running of source GREENSLEEVES who over the last eleven months has supplied this unit with secret and top-secret intelligence on the Soviet Order of Battle in Czechoslovakia."

"You all right there?" he called to Kate. "Listen. You did nothing wrong. Nobody even missed this stuff. Nobody would have been the wiser for it. Nobody ever tried to follow it up."

He turned a page: ". . . close personal relationship established between source and case officer . . . Pym's calm authority during crisis . . . source's insistence on operating through Pym only . . ." He read fast to the end then began again at the beginning more slowly.

"His C.O. was in love with him too," he called to Kate. "'. . . his excellent memory for detail,'" he read, "'. . . lucid report writing, often done in the early hours of the morning after a long debriefing . . . high entertainment value . . .'

"Doesn't even mention Sabina," he complained to Kate. "Can't see what the devil he was so worried about. Why risk his hotline to you to suppress a bit of paper from the Dark Ages that did him nothing but credit? Must be something in his own nasty little mind, not ours at all. That doesn't surprise me either."

The phone was ringing. He glanced round. The bed was empty, the bathroom door closed. Scared, he sprang up and pulled it quickly open. She was standing safely at the basin, chucking water in her face. He closed the door again and hastened back to the telephone. It was a mossy green scrambler with chrome buttons. He picked up the receiver and growled "Yes?"

"Jack? Let's go over. Ready? Now."

Brotherhood pressed a button and heard the same tenor voice trilling in the electronic storm.

"You'll enjoy this, Jack—Jack, can you hear me? Hullo?"

"I can hear you, Bo."

"I've just had Carver on the line." Carver was the American Head of Station in London. "He insists his people have come up with fresh leads concerning our mutual friend. They want to reopen the story on him immediately. Harry Wexler's flying over from Washington to see fair play."

"That all?"

"Isn't it enough?"

"Where do they think he is?" said Brotherhood.

"That's exactly the point. They didn't ask, they weren't worried. They assume he's still coping with his father's affairs," said Brammel, very pleased. "They actually made the point that this would be an excellent time to meet. While our friend is occupied with his personal affairs. Everything is still in its place as far as they're concerned. Except for the new leads of course. Whatever they are."

"Except for the networks," Brotherhood said.

"I'll want you with me at the meeting, Jack. I want you in there punching for me, just like your usual self. Will you do that?"

"If it's an order, I'll do anything."

Bo sounded like someone organising a jolly party: "I'm having everyone we'd normally have. Nobody's to be left out or added. I want nothing to stick out, not a ripple while we go on looking for him. This whole thing could still be a storm in a teacup. Whitehall is convinced of it. They argue that we're dealing with follow-on from the last thing, not a new situation at all. They've got some awfully clever people these days. Some of them aren't even civil servants. Are you sleeping?"

"Not a lot."

"None of us is. We must stick together. Nigel's over at the Foreign Office at this moment."

"Is he though?" said Brotherhood aloud as he rang off. "Kate?"

"What is it?"

"Just keep your fingers away from my razor blades, hear me? We're too old for dramatic gestures, both of us."

He waited a second, dialled Head Office and asked for the night duty officer.

"You got a rider there?"

"Yes."

"Brotherhood. There's a War Office file I want. British Army of Occupation in Austria, old field case. Operation Greensleeves, believe it or not. Where will it be?"

"Ministry of Defence, I suppose, seeing that the War Office was disbanded about two hundred years ago."

"Who are you?"

"Nicholson."

"Well, don't bloody suppose. Find out where it is, fetch it and phone me when it's on your desk. Got a pencil, have you?"

"I don't think I have actually. Nigel has left instructions that any request from you has to be processed by Secretariat first. Sorry, Jack."

"Nigel's at the Foreign Office. Check with Bo. While you're about it, ask Defence to give you the name of the Commandant of Number Six Interrogation, Graz, Austria, on July 18, 1951. I'm in a hurry. Greensleeves, have you got it? Maybe you're not musical."

He rang off and pulled Pym's battered letter to Tom savagely towards him.

"He's a shell," Kate said. "All you have to do is find the hermit crab that climbed into him. Don't look for the truth about him. The truth is what we gave him of ourselves."

"Sure," said Brotherhood. He set a sheet of paper ready to jot on while he silently read: *"If I don't write to you for a while, remember I'm thinking of you all the time."* Maudlin slush. *"If you need help and don't want to turn to Uncle Jack, this is what you do."* He continued reading, writing out Pym's instructions to his son, one by one. *"Don't worry your head so much about religious things, just try to trust in God's goodness."* "Damn the man!" he expostulated aloud for Kate's sake and, slamming down his pencil, pressed both fists against his temple as the phone rang again. He let it ring a moment, recovered and picked it up, glancing at his watch, which was his habit always.

"Anyway the file you want went missing *years* ago," said Nicholson with pleasure.

"Who to?"

"Us. They say it's marked out to us and we never returned it."

"Who of *us* in particular?"

"Czech section. It was requisitioned by one of our own London desk officers in 1953."

"Which one?"

"M.R.P. That would be Pym. Do you want me to ring Vienna and ask him what he did with it?"

"I'll ask him myself in the morning," he said. "What about the C.O.?"

"A Major Harrison Membury of the Education Corps."

"The *what*?"

"He was on secondment to Army Intelligence for the period 1950 to '54."

"Christ Almighty. Any address?"

He wrote it down, remembering, quip of Pym's a paraphrased from Clemenceau: "Military intelligence has about as much to do with intelligence as military music has to do with music."

He rang off.

"They haven't even indoctrinated the poor bloody duty officer!" Brotherhood expostulated, again for Kate.

He went back to his homework better pleased. Somewhere beyond Green Park a London clock was striking three.

"I'm going," Kate said. She was standing at the door, dressed.

Brotherhood was on his feet in a moment.

"Oh no you're not. You're staying here until I hear you laugh."

He went to her and undressed her again. He put her back to bed.

"Why do you think I'm going to kill myself?" she said. "Has somebody done that to you once?"

"Let's just say once would be too often," he replied.

"What's in the burnbox?" she asked, for the second time that night. But for the second time, too, Brotherhood appeared too busy to reply.

8

My memory gets selective here, Jack. More than usual. He's in my sights as I expect he begins to be in yours. But you are in them too. Whatever doesn't point to you both slips by me like landscape through a railway window. I could paint for you Pym's distressing conversations with the luckless Herr Bertl in which, on Rick's instruction, he assured him repeatedly it was in the post, it was taken care of, everybody would be seen right, and his father was on the point of making an offer for the hotel. Or we could have some fun with Pym, languishing for days and nights in his hotel bedroom as a hostage to the mountain of unpaid bills downstairs, dreaming of Elena Weber's milky body reflected in its many delightful poses in the mirrored changing rooms of Bern, kicking himself for his timidity, living off hoarded continental breakfasts, running up more bills and waiting for the telephone. Or the moment when Rick went off the air. He did not ring and when Pym tried his number the only response was a howl, like the cry of a wolf stuck on one note.

When he tried Syd he got Meg, and Meg's advice was strikingly similar to E. Weber's. "You're better off where you are, dear," she said in the pointed voice of someone who is telling you she is overheard. "There's a heat wave here and a lot of people are getting burned." "Where's Syd?" "Cooling himself, darling." Or the Sunday afternoon when everything in the hotel fell mercifully silent and Pym, having packed together his few possessions, stole heart in mouth down the staff staircase and out through a side door into what was suddenly a hostile foreign city—his first clandestine exit, and his easiest.

I could offer you Pym the infant refugee, though I never starved, had a valid British passport and in retrospect seldom wanted for a kindly word. But he did dip tallows for a religious candlemaker, sweep the aisle of the Minster, roll beer barrels for a brewer and unstitch sacks of carpets for an old Armenian who kept urging him to marry his daughter, and come to think of it he might have done worse; she was a beautiful girl and kept sighing and draping herself over the sofa but Pym was too polite to approach her. All those things he did and more. All of them at night, a night animal on the run through that lovely candlelit city with its clocks and wells and cobble and arcades. He swept snow, carted cheeses, led a blind dray-horse and taught English to aspiring travel agents. All under cover while he waited for Herr Bertl's hounds to sniff him out and bring him to justice, though I know now the poor man bore me no grudge whatever, and even at the height of his rage avoided mentioning Pym's part in the affair.

"Dear Father,
        I am really happy out here and you must not worry about me at all as the Swiss are kindly and

hospitable and have all sorts of remarkable bursaries for young foreigners keen on reading law."

I could sing of another great hotel, not a stone's throw from the first, where Pym went to earth as a night waiter and became a schoolboy again, sleeping under avenues of lagged piping in a basement dormitory as big as a factory where the lights never went out; how he took gratefully once more to his little iron bed and how he jollied his fellow waiters as he had jollied his fellow new boys, for they turned out to be peasants from Ticino who wanted only to go home. How he rose willingly with every bell and donned a white dicky that, though thick with last night's grease, was not half as constricting as Mr. Willow's collars. And how he took trays of bubbly and foie gras to ambiguous couples who sometimes wanted him to stay, Amor and Rococo beckoning from their glances. But once again he was too polite and too unknowing to oblige. His manners in those days were a barbed-wire cage. He only lusted when he was alone. Yet even as I allow my memory to brush past these tantalising episodes, my heart is hurtling ahead to the night I met the saintly Herr Ollinger in the third-class buffet of Bern railway station and, through his charity, stumbled into the encounter that altered all my life till here—and I fear your life as well, Jack, though you have yet to learn by how much.

Of the university, how Pym enrolled there and why, my recollections are equally impatient. It was for cover. All for cover as usual, leave it there. He had been working in a circus at its winter home, which was a patch of land just beneath the same railway station where his footsteps so often finished after his all-day walks. Somehow the elephants had drawn him. Any fool can wash an elephant, but he was surprised to learn how hard it was to dip the head of a twenty-foot brush into a bucket when the only light comes in shafts from the spotlights in the apex of the marquee. Each dawn when his work was done he made his way home to the Salvation Army hostel that was his temporary Ascot. Each dawn he saw the green dome of the university rising above him through the autumn mist like an ugly little Rome challenging him to convert. And somehow he had to get inside the place, for he had a second terror, greater than Herr Bertl's hounds: namely that Rick despite his problems of liquidity would appear in a cloud of Bentley and whisk him home.

He had fabricated for Rick handsomely and imaginatively. *I have won that foreigners' scholarship I was talking about. I am reading Swiss law and German law and Roman law and all the other laws there are. I am attending night school on the side to keep myself out of mischief.* He had praised the erudition of his non-existent tutors and the piety of the university chaplains. But Rick's systems of intelligence, though erratic, were impressive. Pym knew he was not safe until he had given substance to his fictions. One morning therefore he found the courage and marched up there. He lied first about his qualifications and then about his age, for the one could not have been earned without an adjustment to the other. He paid out the last of E. Weber's white banknotes to a crew-cut cashier, and in return received a grey cloth-card with his photograph on it, describing him as legitimate. *I have never in my life been so gratified by the sight of a false document.* Pym would have given his whole fortune for it, which was a further seventy-one francs. *Philosophie Zwei* was Pym's faculty and I still have only the sketchiest notion of what it comprised, for Pym had asked for law but somehow been rerouted. He learned more from translating the students' bulletins on the notice-board, which invited him to a string of unlikely forums and gave him his first rumblings of political gunfire since Ollie and Mr. Cudlove had vented their anger against the rich and Lippsie had warned him of the hollowness of possessions. You remember those forums too, Jack, though from a different aspect, and for reasons we shall come to soon enough.

It was from the university notice-board also that Pym discovered the existence of an English church in Elfenau, the diplomatic fairyland. Along he went—he could hardly wait—often two or three Sundays running. He prayed, he hovered outside the doors afterwards, shaking hands with anything that moved, though little did. He gazed soulfully at elderly mothers, fell in love with several, consumed cake and lifeless tea in their thickly curtained houses and charmed them with extravagant accounts of his parentless upbringing. Soon the expatriate in him couldn't get along without its weekly shot of the English banality. The English church with its iron-back diplomatic families, ancient Britons and dubious Anglophiles became his school chapel and all the other chapels he had defected from.

Its counterpart was the third-class railway buffet where, if he wasn't working, he could sit all night smoking himself sick on Disque Bleus over a single beer and fancying himself the most stateless, world-weary globe-trotter he had ever met. Today the station is an indoor metropolis of smart boutiques and plastic-coated restaurants, but in the immediate post-war years it was still an ill-lit Edwardian staging post, with stuffed stages in the concourse and murals of freed peasants waving flags, and a scent of Bockwurst and fried onion that never went away. The first-class buffet was full of gentlemen in black suits with napkins round their necks, but the third class was shadowed and beery, with a whiff of Balkan lawlessness and drunks who sang out of tune. Pym's favourite table was in a panelled corner near the coats where a sacred waitress called Elisabeth gave him extra soup. It must have been Herr Ollinger's favourite also for he homed on it as soon as he entered and having bowed lovingly at Elisabeth, who wore a low-cut *Tracht* with perforated smocking, bowed at Pym too, and fidgeted with his poor briefcase, and hauled at his disobedient hair, and asked, "Do we disturb you?" in a tone of breathless anxiety while he stroked an old yellow chow dog that hung grumbling on its lead. Thus as I now know does our Maker disguise His best agents.

Herr Ollinger was ageless but I guess now fifty. His complexion was doughy, his smile regretful, his cheeks were dimpled and pendulous like an old man's bottom. Even when he did finally allow that his chair was not taken by superior beings, he lowered his round body so gingerly into it that you would think he expected to be shooed away any minute by someone more deserving. With the assurance of an habitué Pym took the brown raincoat from his unresisting arm and threaded a hanger into it. He had decided he needed Herr Ollinger and his yellow chow dog urgently. His life was going through a fallow period at the time and he had not exchanged more than a few words with anyone for a week. His gesture threw Herr Ollinger into a vortex of hopeless gratitude. Herr Ollinger beamed and declared Pym most friendly. He grabbed a copy of *Der Bund* from the rack and buried his face in it. He whispered to the dog to behave itself and tapped it ineffectually on the snout, though it was behaving with

exemplary tolerance. But he had spoken, which gave Pym
reason to explain, in a set sentence, that unfortunately I am
foreign, sir, and not yet equal to your local dialect. So please
be kind enough to speak High German and excuse me. After
this, as he had learned to, he added his surname, "Pym," at
which Herr Ollinger confessed that he was Ollinger, as if the
name implied some frightful slur, and afterwards presented
the chow as Herr Bastl, which for a moment rang uncomfortably of the luckless Bertl.

"But you speak excellent German!" Herr Ollinger
protested. "I would immediately have thought you are from
Germany! You are not? Then where do you come from, if I
may be so impertinent?"

And this was kind of Herr Ollinger for nobody in his
right mind, in those days, could have confused Pym's German with the real thing. So Pym told Herr Ollinger the story
of his life, which was what he had intended from the first,
and dazzled him with tender questions about himself, and in
every way he knew laid upon Herr Ollinger the full burden of
his sensitive charm—which as it later turned out was a totally
needless exertion on Pym's part since Herr Ollinger was
unselective in his acquaintance. He admired everybody, pit-
ied everybody from below—not least for their dreadful misfortune in having to share the world with him. Herr Ollinger
said he was married to an angel, and possessed three angel
daughters who were musical prodigies. Herr Ollinger said he
had inherited his father's factory in Ostermundigen, which
was a great worry to him. And so indeed it should have been,
for in retrospect it is clear that the poor man rose diligently
every morning in order to run it further into the earth. Herr
Ollinger said Herr Bastl had been with him three years but
only temporarily, because he was still trying to find the dog's
owner.

Reciprocating with equal generosity, Pym described his
experiences in the blitz, and the night he had been visiting
his aunt in Coventry when they hit the cathedral; how she
lived but a hundred yards from the main doors and her house
by a miracle was unscathed. When he had destroyed Coventry, he described himself in an imaginative tour de force as an
admiral's son standing at his dormitory window in his dressing-
gown, calmly watching the waves of German bombers flying

over his school and wondering whether this time they were going to drop the parachutists dressed as nuns.

"But did you have no shelters?" Herr Ollinger cried. "That's a disgrace! You were a child, my God! My wife would be completely furious. She is from Wilderswil," he explained, while Herr Bastl ate a pretzel and farted.

Thus Pym skipped on, piling one fiction on another, appealing to Herr Ollinger's Swiss love of disaster, enthralling the neutral in him with the dire realities of war.

"But you were so young," Herr Ollinger protested again when Pym related the rigours of his early military training at the Signals Depot in Bradford. "You had no nest warmth. You were a child!"

"Well, thank God they never had to use us," said Pym in a throwaway voice as he called for his bill. "My grandfather died in the first one, my father was given up for dead in the second, so I can't help feeling it's time our family had a break." Herr Ollinger would not hear of Pym paying. Herr Ollinger might be breathing the free air of Switzerland, he said, but he had three generations of English to thank for the privilege. Pym's sausage and beer were a mere step in the mercurial progress of Herr Ollinger's generosity. It was followed by the offer of a room, for as long as Pym wished to do him the honour, in the narrow little house in the Länggasse that Herr Ollinger had inherited from his mother.

It was not a big room. It was actually a very small room indeed. An attic, one of three, and Pym's was in the middle, and only the middle of it was big enough for him to stand in, and even then he was more comfortable with his head poked through the skylight. In summer the daylight lasted all night, in winter the snow blacked out the world. For heating he had a great black radiator cut into the party-wall, which he heated from a wood stove in the corridor. He had to choose between freezing and boiling, depending on his mood. Yet, Tom, I have not been so content anywhere until I found Miss Dubber. Once in our lives, it is given us to know a truly happy family. Frau Ollinger was tall and luminous and frugal. On a routine patrol of the house Pym once watched her through a crack in a doorway while she slept, and she was smiling. I am sure she was smiling when she died. Her husband fussed round her like a fat tug, upsetting the economy, dumping every waif and sponger on her that he came upon, adoring her. The daughters were each plainer than the next, played musical instruments atrociously, to the fury of the neighbours, and one by one they married even plainer men and worse musicians whom the Ollingers thought brilliant and delightful—and by thinking made them so. From morning till night a trail of migrants, misfits and undiscovered geniuses drifted through their kitchen, cooking themselves omelettes and treading out their cigarettes on the linoleum. And woe if you left your bedroom unlocked, for Herr Ollinger was quite capable of forgetting you were there—or, if need be, of persuading himself you would be out tonight, or that you wouldn't mind a stranger just until he's got somewhere. What we paid I don't remember. What we could afford was next to nothing and certainly not enough to subsidise the factory in Ostermundigen, for the last I heard of Herr Ollinger he was working happily as a clerk in Bern's main post office, enchanted by the erudite company. The only possession I associate with him apart from Herr Bastl is a collection of erotica with which he consoled himself in his shyness. Like everything else about him it was there to be shared, and it was a great deal more revealing than *Amor and Rococo Woman*.

Such then was the household on which Pym's crow's-nest was built. For once his life was as good as complete. He had a bed, he had a family. He was in love with Elisabeth in the third-class buffet and contemplating marriage and early fatherhood. He was locked in a tantalising correspondence with Belinda, who felt it her duty to inform him of Jemima's love affairs, "which I'm sure she only has because you are so far away." If Rick was not extinct he was at least quiescent, for the only sign of him was a flow of homilies on Being Ever True to your Advantages, and avoiding the Foreign Temptations and the Snares of Synicism, which either he or his secretary could not spell. These letters had the distinct air of being typed on the run, and never came from the same place twice: "Write care Topsie Eaton at the Firs, East Grinstead, no need to put my name on envelope." "Write to Colonel Mellow post restaurant the main G.P.O. Hull who obliges by collecting my mail." On one occasion a handwritten love letter varied the diet, beginning: "Annie, my sweet Pet, your body means more to me than Riches of the earth." Rick must have put it into the wrong envelope.

The only thing Pym missed therefore was a friend. He met him in Herr Ollinger's basement on a Saturday at midday, when he took down his laundry for his weekly wash. Upstairs in the street the first snowfall was driving out the autumn. Pym had an armful of damp clothes in front of his face and was concerned about the stone steps. The basement light was operated by a time switch; any second he could be plunged into darkness and trip over Herr Bastl, who owned the boiler. But the light stayed on and as he brushed past the switch he noticed that somebody had ingeniously jammed a matchstick into it, a very sleek matchstick trimmed with a knife. He smelt cigar smoke but Bern was not Ascot—anyone who had a few pence could smoke a cigar. When he saw the armchair he mentally assigned it to the junk Herr Ollinger set aside as a gift to Herr Rubi the rag-and-bone man who came on Saturdays on his horse-drawn float.

"Don't you know it is forbidden for foreigners to hang their clothes in Swiss basements?" said a male voice, not in dialect but in a crisp High German.

"I'm afraid I didn't," said Pym. He peered round for someone to apologise to and saw instead the unclear form of a slender man curled on the armchair, clutching a patchwork blanket to his neck with one long white hand and a book with the other. He wore a black beret and had a drooping moustache. No feet showed, but his body had the look of something spiky and wrongly folded, like a tripod that had stuck halfway. Herr Ollinger's walking-stick was propped against the chair. A small cigar smouldered between the fingers that clutched the blanket.

"In Switzerland it is forbidden to be poor, it is forbidden to be foreign, it is *completely* forbidden to hang clothes. You are an inmate of this establishment?"

"I am a friend of Herr Ollinger's."

"An English friend?"

"My name is Pym."

Discovering the moustache, the fingers of one white hand began stroking it reflectively downward.

"Lord Pym?"

"Just Magnus."

"But you are of aristocratic stock."

"Well, nothing very special."

"And you are the war hero," the stranger said, and made a sucking noise that in England would have sounded skeptical.

Pym did not like the description at all. The account of himself that he had given to Herr Ollinger was obsolete. He was dismayed to hear it revived.

"So who are you, if I may ask?" said Pym.

The stranger's fingers rose to claw at some irritation in his cheek while he appeared to consider a range of alternatives. "My name is Axel and since one week I am your neighbour, so I am obliged to listen to you grinding your teeth at night," he said, drawing on his cigar.

"*Herr* Axel?" said Pym.

"Herr Axel Axel. My parents forgot to give me a second name." He put down the book and held out a slim hand in greeting. "For God's sake," he exclaimed with a wince as Pym grasped it. "Go easy, will you? The war's over."

Too challenged for his comfort Pym left his washing for another day and took himself upstairs.

"What is Axel's other name?" he asked Herr Ollinger next day.

"Maybe he hasn't one," Herr Ollinger replied mischievously. "Maybe that's why he has no papers."

"Is he a student?"

"He is a poet," said Herr Ollinger proudly but the house was stiff with poets.

"They must be very long poems. He types all night," said Pym.

"Indeed he does. And on my typewriter," said Herr Ollinger, his pride complete.

My husband found him in the factory, Frau Ollinger said while Pym helped her prepare vegetables for the evening meal. That is to say, Herr Harprecht the night-watchman found him. Axel was sleeping on sacks in the warehouse and Herr Harprecht wanted to hand him over to the police because he had no papers and was foreign and smelly, but thank goodness my husband stopped Herr Harprecht in time and gave Axel breakfast and took him to a doctor for his sweating.

"Where does he come from?" Pym asked.

Frau Ollinger became uncharacteristically guarded. Axel comes from *drüben*, she said—*drüben* being across the border, *drüben* being those irrational tracts of Europe that were not Switzerland, where people rode in tanks instead of trolley-buses, and the starving had the ill manners to pick their food from rubble instead of buying it from shops.

"How did he get here?" Pym asked.

"We think he walked," Frau Ollinger said.

"But he's an invalid. He's all crippled and thin."

"We think he had a strong will and a great necessity."

"Is he German?"

"There are many sorts of German, Magnus."

"Which sort is Axel?"

"We don't ask. Maybe you should not ask either."

"Can you guess from his voice?"

"We don't guess either. With Axel it is better we are completely without curiosity."

"What's he ill of?"

"Maybe he suffered in the war, as you did," Frau Ollinger suggested with a smile of rather too much understanding. "Don't you like Axel? Is he disturbing you up there?"

How can he disturb me when he doesn't speak to me? thought Pym. When all I hear of him is the clicking of Herr Ollinger's typewriter, the cries of ecstasy from his lady callers in the afternoons and the shuffle of his feet as he hauls himself to the lavatory on Herr Ollinger's walking-stick? When all I see of him is his empty vodka bottles and the blue cloud of his cigar smoke in the corridor and his pale empty body disappearing down the stairs?

"Axel's super," he said.

Pym had already appointed Christmas to be the jolliest of his life and so it was—despite a letter of appalling misery from Rick describing the privations of "a small Private hotel in the wilds of Scotland where the meagrest of life's Necessities are a Godsend." He meant, I discovered later, Gleneagles. Christmas Eve came. Pym as youngest lit the candles and helped Frau Ollinger lay the presents round the tree. It had been wonderfully dark all day and in the afternoon thick snowflakes began swirling in the streetlights and clogging the tramlines. The Ollinger daughters arrived with their escorts, followed by a shy married couple from Basel over whom some shadow hung, I forget what. Next a French genius called Jean-Pierre who painted fish in profile, always on a sepia background. And after him an apologetic Japanese gentleman called Mr. San—enigmatically so since, as I now know, San is itself a term of Japanese address. Mr. San was working at Herr Ollinger's factory as some sort of industrial spy, which in retrospect strikes me as very funny indeed, because if the Japanese ever tried copying Herr Ollinger's methods, they must have set back their industrial output by a decade.

Finally Axel himself came slowly down the wood stairs and made his entry. For the first time Pym could regard him at his leisure. Though desperately thin, his face was by nature rounded. His brow was tall but the hank of brown hair that grew sideways over it gave it a curved and saddening air. It was as if his Maker had put His thumb and forefinger to either temple and yanked the whole face downward as a warning to his frivolity: first the hooped eyebrows, then the eyes, then the moustache which was a shaggy horseshoe. And somehow inside all this was Axel himself, his eyes twinkling out of their own shadows, the grateful survivor of something Pym was not allowed to share. One of the daughters had knitted him a sloppy cardigan which he wore like a cape over his wasted shoulders.

"*Schön guten Abend*, Sir Magnus," he said. He was carrying a straw bonnet upside down. Pym saw parcels in it, beautifully wrapped. "Why do we never speak to each other up there? We could be kilometres apart instead of twenty centimetres. Are you still fighting the Germans? We are allies, you and I. Soon we shall be fighting the Russians."

"I suppose we shall," said Pym feebly.

"Why don't you bang on my door once when you are lonely? We can have a cigar together, save the world a little. You like to talk nonsense?"

"Very much."

"Okay. We talk nonsense." But on the point of shuffling away to greet Mr. San, Axel stopped and turned. And over his caped shoulder he vouchsafed Pym a quizzical, almost challenging glare, as if asking himself whether he had invested his trust too easily.

"*Aber dann können wir doch Freunde sein*, Sir Magnus?" —then we may be friends after all?

"*Ich würde mich freuen!*" Pym replied heartily, meeting his gaze without fear—I would be happy!

They shook hands again, but this time lightly. At the same moment Axel's features broke into such a smile of sparkling good fun that Pym's heart filled for him in response, and he promised himself that he would follow Axel anywhere for all the Christmases that he was spared. The party began. The girls played carols and Pym sang with the best, using English words where he lacked the German. There were speeches and after them a toast to absent friends and relations, at which Axel's long eyelids almost hid his eyes and he fell quiet. But then, as if shaking off bad memories, he stood up abruptly and began unpacking the bonnet he had brought while Pym hovered at hand to help him, knowing that this was what Axel had always done at Christmas, wherever Christmas was. For the daughters he had made musical pipes, each with her name carved along the underneath. How had he carved with such wispy white hands? So exquisitely, without Pym hearing him through the partition? Where had he found his wood, his paint and brushes? For the Ollingers he produced what I later realised was another emblem of prison life, a matchstick model. This one was an ark with painted figures of our extended family waving from the portholes. For Mr. San and Jean-Pierre he had squares of cloth of a sort that Pym had once made for Dorothy on a homemade handloom between nails. For the Basel couple a patterned woollen eye to ward off whatever was afflicting them. And for Pym—I still take it as a compliment that he left me until last—for Sir Magnus he had a much used copy of Grimmelshausen's *Simplicissimus*, bound in old brown buckram, which Pym had not heard of but could not wait to read since it would give him an excuse to bang on Axel's door. He opened it and read the inscription. "For Sir Magnus, who will never be my enemy." And in the top left corner, in an older ink but in a younger version of the same hand: "A.H. Carlsbad August 1939."

"Where is Carlsbad?" Pym asked before he had allowed himself a second's thought, and noticed at once an awkwardness round him as if everybody had heard the bad news except for himself who was deemed not old enough to receive it.

"Carlsbad no longer exists, Sir Magnus," Axel replied politely. "When you have read *Simplicissimus* you will understand why."

"Where was it?"

"It was my home town."

"Then you have given me a treasure from your own past."

"Would you prefer me to give you something I did not value?"

And Pym—what had he brought? God help him, the Chairman and Managing Director's son was not used to ceremonies with meaning, and had thought of nothing better than a box of cigars to see dear old Axel right.

"Why does Carlsbad no longer exist?" Pym asked Herr Ollinger as soon as he could get him alone. Herr Ollinger knew everything except how to run a factory. Carlsbad was in the Sudetenland, he explained. It was a beautiful spa city and everybody used to go there: Brahms and Beethoven, Goethe and Schiller. First it was Austria, then it became Germany. Now it was Czechoslovakia and had a new name and the Germans had all been chucked out.

"So who does Axel belong to?" Pym asked.

"Only to us, I think," said Herr Ollinger gravely. "And we must be careful of him or they will take him away from us, you may be sure."

"He has women in his room," said Pym.

Herr Ollinger's face turned pink with impish pleasure. "I think he has all the women of Bern," he agreed.

A couple of days passed. On the third Pym banged on Axel's door and found him standing smoking at the open window with several heavy-looking books before him on the sill. He must have been freezing but he seemed to need the open air to read by.

"Come for a stroll," said Pym boldly.

"At my speed?"

"Well we can't go at mine, can we?"

"My constitution dislikes crowded places, Sir Magnus. If we are to walk, better we stay out of town."

They borrowed Bastl and wandered with him along the empty towpath beside the racing Aare while Herr Bastl peed and refused to follow and Pym did his best to keep an eye open for anyone who looked like a policeman. In the sunless river valley the frost drifted about in evil clouds and the cold was merciless. Axel seemed not to notice. He puffed at his cigar while he tossed out questions in his soft, amused voice.

If this is how he walked from Austria, thought Pym, shivering in his wake, he must have taken years.

"How did you reach Bern, Sir Magnus? Were you advancing or retreating?" Axel asked.

Never able to resist an opportunity to portray himself on a fresh page, Pym went to work. And though, as was his wont, he took care to improve upon the reality, rearranging the facts to fit his prevailing image of himself, an instinctive caution nevertheless counselled him restraint. True, he endowed himself with a noble and eccentric mother, and true, when he came to describe Rick he awarded him many of the qualities Rick unsuccessfully aspired to, such as wealth, military distinction and daily access to the Highest in the Land. But in other respects he was frugal and self-mocking and when he came to the story of E. Weber, which he had not told anyone till now, Axel laughed so much he had to sit on a bench and light another cigar to get his wind back, while Pym laughed with him, delighted by his success. And when he showed him her very letter saying, "Never mind. E. Weber love you always," he shouted, "*Nochmal!* Tell it again, Sir Magnus! I order you! And make sure it is completely different this time. Did you sleep with her?"

"Of course."

"How many times?"

"Four or five."

"All in one night? You are a tiger! Was she grateful?"

"She was very, very experienced."

"More than your Jemima?"

"Well, jolly nearly."

"More than your wicked Lippsie who seduced you when you were still a little boy?"

"Well, Lippsie was in a class of her own."

Axel slapped him gaily on the back. "Sir Magnus, you are a prince, no question. You are a dark horse, you know that? Such a good little boy, yet you sleep with dangerous adventuresses and young English aristocrats. I love you, hear me? I love all English aristocrats, but you best."

Walking again, Axel had to shove his arm through Pym's to support himself, and from then on used him unashamedly as his walking-stick. For the rest of our lives we have seldom walked in any other way.

*   *   *

Somewhere that evening under a bridge, Pym and Axel
found an empty café and Axel insisted on paying for two
vodkas from the black purse he kept on a leather thong round
his neck. Somewhere on the freezing journey home they
agreed that Axel and Pym must begin the education they had
never had, and that they would appoint tomorrow the first
day of the world, and that Grimmelshausen would be their
first subject because he taught that the world was a mad place
and getting madder by the moment, with everything that
appeared right almost certainly wrong. They agreed that Axel
would take charge of Pym's spoken German and not rest till
he spoke it to perfection. Thus, in a day and an evening, Pym
became Axel's legs and Axel's intellectual companion and,
though it was not initially meant that way, Axel's pupil, for
over the next few months he unveiled for Pym the German
muse. If Axel's knowledge was greater than Pym's, his curiosity was no less, his energy equally relentless. Perhaps by
resuscitating his country's culture for an innocent, he was
reconciling himself to its recent past.

As to Pym, he was gazing at last on the glories of the
kingdom he had dreamed of for so long. The German muse
had no particular draw for him, then or later, for all his loud
enthusiasm. If she had been Chinese or Polish or Indian, it
would have made no earthly odds. The point was, she supplied
Pym with the means, for the first time, to regard himself
intellectually as a gentleman. And for that Pym was eternally
grateful to her. By willing Pym night and day to accompany
Axel on his explorations, she gave him the world inside his
head that Lippsie had said he would be able to take with him
anywhere. And Lippsie was right, because when he went
down to the warehouse in Ostring where Herr Ollinger had
obtained illegal nightwork for him at the hands of a fellow
philanthropist, he neither walked nor took the tram but rode
with Mozart in his coach to Prague. When he washed his
elephants at night he endured the humiliations of Lenz's
Soldaten. When he sat in the third-class buffet bestowing
soulful looks on Elisabeth, he imagined himself as the young
Werther, planning his wardrobe before committing suicide.
And when he considered all his failures and hopes together,
he was able to compare his *Werdegang* with Wilhelm Meister's

years of apprenticeship, and planned even then a great autobiographical novel that would show the world what a noble sensitive fellow he was compared with Rick.

And yes, Jack, the other seeds were there, of course they were: a crash diet of Hegel, as much as they both could swallow at a time, a burst of Marx and Engels and the bad bears of Communism—for after all, said Axel, this was the first day of the world. "If we are to judge Christianity by the misery it has caused mankind, who would ever be a Christian? We accept no prejudices, Sir Magnus. We believe everything as we read it and only afterwards reject it. If Hitler hated these fellows so much, they can't be all bad, I say." Out came Rousseau and the revolutionaries, and *Das Kapital*, and *Anti-Dühring*, and in went the sun for several weeks, though I swear we came to no conclusions that I remember, except that we were glad when it was over. And I honestly doubt now whether the substance of Axel's teaching was of importance beside Pym's joy that he was teaching him at all. What counted was that Pym was happy from the moment he got up until the early hours of the following morning; and that when they finally went to bed on either side of their black radiator, sleeping, to use Axel's phrase, like God in France, Pym's mind went on exploring in his sleep.

"Axel's got the Order of the Frozen Meat," Pym told Frau Ollinger proudly one day, carving bread for family fondue.

Frau Ollinger gave an exclamation of disgust. "Magnus, what nonsense are you talking now?"

"It's true! It's German soldiers' slang for a Russian campaign medal. He volunteered from his *Gymnasium*. His father could have got him a safe post in France or Belgium. A *Druckposten*, somewhere he could keep his head down. Axel wouldn't let him. He wanted to be a hero like his classmates."

Frau Ollinger was not pleased. "Then better you keep quiet about where he fought," she said sternly. "Axel is here to study, not to boast."

"He has women up there," said Pym. "They creep up the stairs in the afternoons and scream when he makes love to them."

"If they give him happiness and help him to study they are welcome. Do you wish to invite your passionate Jemima?"

Furious, Pym stalked to his room and penned a long letter to Rick about the unfairness of the average Swiss in daily matters. "Sometimes I think the law here does duty for common kindness," he wrote stuffily. "Particularly where women are concerned."

Rick wrote back by return, urging chastity: "Better you remain Clean until you have made the choice that is Meant for you."

"Dear Belinda,
   "Things are a bit sticky here at the moment. Some of the foreign students in the house are taking things a bit far with their womenfolk and I have had to step in or I'll never get my work done. Perhaps if you adopted the same firm line with Jem, you might in the long run be doing her a favour."

A day came when Axel fell ill. Pym hurried back from the zoo full of funny stories about his adventures to find him in bed, where he hated most to be. His tiny room was heavy with cigar smoke, his pale head darkened with stubble and shadows. A girl was hanging about but Axel ordered her out when Pym arrived.

"What's wrong with him?" Pym asked Herr Ollinger's doctor, peering over his shoulder, trying to decipher the prescription.

"What is wrong with him, Sir Magnus, is that he was bombed by the heroic British," said Axel savagely from the bed, in a barbed unfamiliar voice. "What is wrong with him is that he got half a British shell up his arse and is having trouble shitting it out."

The doctor was sworn not just to secrecy but to silence and with a friendly pat for Pym departed.

"Maybe it was you who fired it at me, Sir Magnus. Did you land in Normandy, by any chance? Perhaps you led the invasion?"

"I didn't do anything like that at all," said Pym.

So Pym became Axel's legs again, fetching his medicines and cigars and cooking for him and ransacking the university libraries for ever more books which he could read aloud to him.

"No more Nietzsche, thank you, Sir Magnus. I think we

know enough about the cleansing effect of violence. Kleist is not as bad but you don't read him properly. You must bark Kleist. He was a Prussian officer, not an English hero. Get the painters."

"Which ones?"

"Abstractionists. Decadents. Jews. Anyone who was *entartet* or forbidden. Give me a holiday from these mad writers."

Pym consulted Frau Ollinger. "Then you must ask the librarian for whomever the Nazis did not like, Magnus," she explained in her governess voice.

The librarian was an émigré who knew Axel's needs by heart. Pym brought Klee and Nolde, Kokoschka and Klimt, Kandinsky and Picasso. He stood their picture books and catalogues open on the mantelshelf where Axel could see them without moving his head. He turned the pages and read the captions out loud. When women came, Axel again sent them away. "I am being attended to. Wait till I am well." Pym brought Max Beckmann. He brought Steinlen, then Schiele and more Schiele. Next day the writers were reinstated. Pym fetched Brecht and Zuckmayer, Tucholsky and Remarque. He read them aloud, hours of them. "Music," Axel commanded. Pym borrowed Herr Ollinger's wind-up gramophone and played him Mendelssohn and Tchaikovsky until Axel fell asleep. He woke delirious, the sweat falling off him like raindrops while he described a retreat through snow with the blind hanging on to the lame and the blood freezing in the wounds. He talked of a hospital, two to a bed and the dead lying on the floor. He asked for water. Pym fetched it and Axel took the glass in both hands, shaking wildly. He lifted the glass till his hands froze, then he lowered his head in jerks until his lips reached the brim. Then he sucked the water like an animal, spilling it while his fevered eyes kept guard. He drew up his legs and wetted himself and sat shaking and grumpy in an armchair while Pym changed his sheets.

"Who are you afraid of?" Pym asked again. "There's no one here. It's just us."

"Then I must be afraid of you. What's that poodle in the corner?"

"It's Herr Bastl and he's a chow chow, not a poodle."

"I thought it was the Devil."

Till a day when Pym woke to find Axel standing fully dressed at his bedside. "It is Goethe's birthday and it's four in the afternoon," he announced in his military voice. "We must go into town and listen to the idiot Thomas Mann."

"But you're ill."

"Nobody who stands up is ill. Nobody marches who is ill. Dress."

"Was Mann on the forbidden list too?" Pym asked as he pulled on his clothes.

"He never made it."

"Why's he an idiot?"

Herr Ollinger supplied a raincoat that could have gone twice round Axel's body, Mr. San provided a broad black hat. Herr Ollinger drove them to the door in his broken car two hours early and they took their places at the back before the great hall filled. When the lecture was over, Axel marched Pym backstage and hammered on the dressing-room door. Pym had not cared for Thomas Mann till now. He found his prose perfumed and unwieldy, though he had tried his best for Axel's sake. But now, there stood God Himself, tall and angular like Uncle Makepeace. "This young English nobleman wishes to shake your hand, sir," Axel advised him with authority from underneath Mr. San's broad hat. Thomas Mann peered at Pym, then at Axel so pale and ethereal from his fever. Thomas Mann frowned at the palm of his own right hand as if asking himself whether it could take the strain of an aristocratic embrace. He held out his hand and Pym shook it, waiting to feel Mann's genius flow into him like one of those electric shocks you used to be able to buy at railway stations—hold this knob and let my energy revive you. Nothing happened, but Axel's enthusiasm was enough for both of them:

"You touched him, Sir Magnus! You are blessed! You are immortal!"

Within a week, they had saved enough cash to take themselves to Davos to visit the shrine of Mann's diseased souls. They travelled in the lavatory, Pym standing and Axel, in his beret, sitting patiently on the seat. The conductor knocked on the door and yelled, "*Alle Billette, bitte*"; Axel gave a girlish whimper of discomfort and pushed their one ticket under the door. Pym waited, his eyes fixed on the shadows of the conductor's feet. He felt the conductor stoop, heard him grunt as he straightened up. He heard a snap that felt like his own nerve breaking as the ticket reappeared under the door with a hole punched in it. The shadows moved on. This is how you walked here, thought Pym with admiration, as they silently shook hands. These are the tricks that got you to Switzerland. In Davos that evening Axel told Pym all about his nightmare journey from Carlsbad to Bern. Pym felt so proud and rich he decided that Thomas Mann was the best writer in the world.

> "Dear Father"—he wrote jubilantly as soon as he was back in the attic—"I am having a really wizard time here now and getting some first-rate instruction. I cannot tell you how much I miss your worldly counsel and how grateful I am for your wisdom in sending me to Switzerland for my studies. Today I met lawyers who really seem to know life in all its aspects, and I am sure they will be a help in furthering my career."

> "Dear Belinda,
>   "Now that I have put my foot down, things are much better."

Meanwhile there was good old you, wasn't there, Jack? Jack the other war hero, Jack the other side of my head. I will describe to you who you were because I don't expect we know the same person any more. I will describe what you were to me and what I did for you and as best I can why, because there again I doubt whether we share the same interpretation of events and personalities. I doubt it very much. To Jack, Pym was just another baby Joe, one more addition to his private army in the making, not broken and certainly not trained, but with the halter already slipped nicely round his neck and willing to run a long way for his lump of sugar. You probably don't remember—why should you?—how you picked him up or made your overtures to him. All you knew was he was the type the Firm liked, and so did you, and so did part of me. Short back and sides, speaks the King's English, decent linguist, good country public school. A games player, understands discipline. Not an arty chap, certainly not one of your overintellectual types. Level-headed, one of us. Comfortably off but not too grand, father

some sort of minor tycoon—how typical that you never
bothered to check Rick out. And where else should you meet
this paragon of tomorrow's men but at the English church,
where the flag of Saint George fluttered victorious in the
neutral Swiss breeze?

How long you had been tracking Pym I don't know. I'll
bet you don't either. You liked the way he read the Lesson,
you said, so you must have had your eye on him from at least
before Christmas because it was an early Advent text. You
seemed surprised when he told you he was studying at the
university, so I guess your first enquiries were made before
he enrolled there and you hadn't topped them up. It was on
Christmas Day after matins that Pym shook your hand for the
first time. The church porch was like a crowded lift with
everyone rattling umbrellas and making rah-rah English noises,
and the diplomatic kids pelting each other with snowballs in
the street. Pym was wearing his E. Weber jacket, and you,
Jack, you were a tweedy, unscalable English mountain of
twenty-four. In terms of war and peace the seven years
between us were a generation, more like two. Much as they
were with Axel, as a matter of fact; you both had those crucial
years on me, still do.

Do you know what else you wore apart from your good
brown suit? Your Airborne tie. Prancing silver-winged horses
and crowned Britannias on a maroon field, congratulations.
You never told me where you had been for it, but the reality
as I now know it is no less impressive than my imaginings:
with the Partisans in Yugoslavia and the Resistance in Czechoslovakia, behind the lines with the Long Range Desert
Group in Africa and even, if I remember right, in Crete. You
are an inch taller than I, but I remember as if it were
yesterday how, as Pym grasped your great dry hand, that
Airborne tie looked him in the eye. He lifted his head, he
saw your rock jaw and your blue eyes—the ferocious bushy
eyebrows even then—and he knew he was standing face to
face with the character he was supposed to have become at all
his schools, and sometimes in his fancy had: a straight-backed
English brave of the officer class, the one who keeps his head
when all about him are losing theirs. You wished him Happy
Christmas and when you spoke your name he thought you
were making a sort of Everyman's joke to do with Christmas
Day—you are Good Fellowship and I will be Brotherhood.

"No, no, old boy, it's real," you insisted with a laugh. "Why should a nice chap like me use a false name?"

Why indeed, when you had diplomatic cover? You invited him for a glass of sherry before lunch tomorrow, Boxing Day, and you said you would have sent him an invitation if you'd known his address, which was clever of you, because of course you knew it perfectly well: address, date of birth, education and all the other nonsense we imagine gives us ascendancy over those we seek to obtain. Then you did an amusing thing. You took an invitation card from your pocket and in the crammed porch while everyone went on woof-woofing you spun Pym round and, using his back to press on, wrote his name along the middle line and handed it to him: "Captain and Mrs. Jack Brotherhood request the pleasure." You scratched out the "RSVP" to emphasise that the deal was done, and you scratched out the "Captain" to show what pals we were. "If you want to stay on afterwards you can help us eat up the cold turkey. Rough clothes," you added. Pym watched you stride off through the rain exactly as he knew you had carried yourself through the gunfire of all the battle-fields where you had triumphed single-handed over Jerry, while Pym was doing nothing braver than carve Sefton Boyd's initials on the wall of the staff lavatory.

Next day he presented himself punctually at your little diplomatic house, and as he pressed the bell he read your visiting card framed in the panel above it. "Captain J. Brotherhood, Assistant Passport Officer, British Embassy, Bern." You were married to Felicity in those days, you may remember. Adrian was six months old. Pym played with him for hours in order to impress you, a habit that soon became a feature of his dealings with the younger members of your trade. You questioned him in a perfectly agreeable way and, where you left off, Felicity as the good Secret Service squaw took over, God forgive her: "But what *friends* have you got, Magnus, you must be so *lonely* here?" she cried. "What do you do for *fun*, Magnus?" And was there much in the way of an extracurricular life at the university, for instance—she asked—political groups and so forth? Or was it all a bit flat and dreary like the rest of Bern? Pym didn't find Bern flat or dreary at all, but for Felicity he pretended he did. In the chronology, Pym's friendship with Axel was by now twelve hours old, but he didn't give him a thought—why should he when he was so taken up with impressing you both with himself?

I remember asking what crowd you fought with, sir, expecting you to say "Fifth Airborne," or "Artists' Rifles" so that I could look suitably awed. Instead you went a bit gruff and said, "General List." I know now that you were exercising the double standard of diplomatic cover: you wanted it to cover you, but you also wanted Pym to see through it. You wanted him to know you were an irregular, and not one of those intellectual little ponces from the Foreign Office, as you call them. You asked him whether he got around the country and suggested that, on occasions when you were making an official car journey somewhere, he might like to come aboard and amuse himself the other end. The two of us put on boots and went for what you called a bash: meaning a forced march through the Elfenau woods. In the course of it you told Pym he needn't call you "sir," and when we came back, Felicity had fed Adrian, and there was an older, smirking man sitting talking to her. You introduced him as Sandy from the Embassy and Pym sensed you were colleagues and vaguely that Sandy was your boss. I know now that he was your Station Head and you were his number two, and that he was performing his standard task of looking over the property before allowing you to buy your way any further in. But at the time Pym just thought of Sandy as headmaster and you as housemaster, a construction you would not have disapproved of.

"How good's your German, by the by?" Sandy asked Pym through his smirk while the three of us munched Felicity's mince pies. "Bit hard to learn here, isn't it, with all this Swissie dialect about?"

"Magnus knows rather a lot of university émigrés," you explained for me, underlining a selling point. Sandy let out a silly laugh and slapped his knee.

"Does he, does he though? I'll bet there's some rum characters among *that* crowd!"

"He could probably tell us a good deal about them too, couldn't you, Magnus?" you said.

"You wouldn't mind?" said Sandy quizzically, still smirking.

"Why should I?" said Pym.

Sandy forced the card cleverly. He sensed that Pym liked taking rash decisions in front of people, and he used this knowledge to press a commitment out of him before he knew what he was committing to.

"No high-minded scruples about the sanctity of academic study or anything like that?" Sandy insisted.

"None at all," said Pym boldly. "Not if it's for my country," and was rewarded by Felicity's smile.

What version of himself Pym supplied that day, and had to live with for the coming months, I do not remember, which means it must have been a fairly restrained one, short on those awkward story-points that too often had to be paid for later. As best he could, he gave you what he thought you were looking for. He was prudent enough not to admit he was earning money, which went down well with you, for you knew already he was working "black," as the Germans call it—meaning illegally, and at night. Shrewd chap, you thought; resourceful; not above a bit of larceny. He played down family life with the Ollingers since proxy parents undermined his self-image as a mature exile. When you asked him whether he knew any girls—the shadow of homosexuality, is he one of those?—Pym got the message at once, and wove a harmless fantasy around an Italian beauty called Maria whom he had met at the Cosmo Club and was keen on, but only as a stopgap for his regular girlfriend Jemima, back in England.

"Jemima who?" you asked, and Pym said Sefton Boyd, which produced an audible sigh of social satisfaction. A real Maria did indeed exist and was indeed beautiful but Pym's adoration of her was private to himself, for he had never spoken to her.

"Cosmo?" said you. "Don't think I've heard of that one. Have you, Sandy?"

"Can't say I have, old boy. Sounds fishy to me."

Pym explained that the Cosmo was a sort of foreigners' political forum, and Maria was some sort of officer of it, like treasurer.

"Any particular complexion?" Sandy asked.

"Well, she's dark," said Pym ingenuously and you and Felicity and Sandy laughed and laughed, like Little Audrey, and Felicity remarked that it was *quite* clear what Magnus's politics were. After that no meeting was complete without somebody asking after Maria's complexion, and everyone cracking up over such a marvellously healthy misunderstanding. It was evening by the time Pym left your house and you had given him a present of a duty-free bottle of scotch to keep out the cold. Cost to the Firm in those days: I guess around five shillings. You offered to run him home but he said he loved to walk, thus earning further Brownie points. And walk he did, on air. He skipped and laughed and hugged his bottle and himself; he hadn't felt so blessed in all his seventeen years. In a single Christmas, God had dished him up two saints. The one was on the run and couldn't walk, the other was a handsome English warlord who served sherry on Boxing Day and had never had a doubt in his life. Both admired him, both loved his jokes and his voices, both were clamouring to occupy the empty spaces of his heart. In return he was giving to each man the character he seemed to be in search of. His decision to keep them secret from each other was never taken. Let each be the mistress that keeps the other home intact, Pym thought. If he thought at all.

"From whom did you steal it, Sir Magnus?" Axel asked in his formal English, looking curiously at the label.

"The chaplain," said Pym without a second's hesitation. "He's a terrific bloke. Ex-army. I didn't steal it. He gave it me, actually. A free bottle for regular attenders. They get it at diplomatic rates, of course. They don't have to pay like in the shops."

"He didn't offer you cigarettes as well, did he?" said Axel.

"Why should he?"

"A bar of chocolate for a night with your sister?"

"I haven't got a sister."

"Good. Then let's drink it."

Do you remember our car journeys, Jack? I begin to think you do. Have you ever wondered how our forebears managed to run their agents in the days before the motorcar? Our first trip could not have come more handy. You had a date in Lausanne. You would need three hours. You gave no reason why you needed three hours in Lausanne, though you could have given me any cover story under the sun. Once again with the advantage of hindsight I know that you were deliberately admitting me to the secrecy of your work without letting on what the work was. You asked nothing of Pym on that occasion. You were building intimacy. The most you did was give him a rendezvous and a fallback and see whether he managed them. "Look here, it's just possible I'll have to make another call. If I'm not outside the Hotel Dora at three, be at the west side of the main post office at three-twenty." Pym wasn't good at east and west but he asked about six people till one of them got it right for him, and he made the fallback at three-twenty exactly, even if he was panting his heart out. You circled the square and the second time round you kept the car rolling and pushed open the door, and Pym hopped in like an airborne soldier to show you how able he was.

"I've been talking to Sandy," you said as we drove to Geneva a week later. "He wants you to do a job for him. Mind?"

"Of course not."

"You any good at translation?"

"What sort?"

"Can you keep your mouth shut?"

"I think so."

You gave him his first Target for Tonight: "We get technical stuff in from time to time. Mainly about funny little Swissie firms that are manufacturing things we don't much like. Nasty things that blow up," you added with a smile. "It's not exactly secret, but we hire a lot of local labour in the Embassy so we'd rather have it done by someone outside. Preferably a Brit. Someone we trust. You game?"

"Of course."

"We pay. Not much, but it'll buy you a dinner with Maria now and then. Heard from Jemima recently?"

"Jem's fine, thanks."

Pym had never been so scared in his life. You handed him the envelope, he put it in his pocket, you gave him your Master of Intrigue look and said "Good luck, old chap" —Yes, Jack, you did! We talked to each other like that—and Pym walked home changing that damned envelope from one pocket to another so many times he must have looked like a bookie on the run. And what was in it? Don't tell me, I'll tell you: junk. Photocopied junk from out-of-date armaments catalogues. It was Pym's soul you were after, not the piffling translation. He lost the envelope about six times in his attic too. Under the bed, under the mattress, behind the mirror, up the chimney. He translated its contents in hours even Axel didn't know he had. You paid Pym twenty francs. The technical dictionary had cost twenty-five but he knew that gentlemen didn't mention things like that, even if Rick's cheques, if they came at all, tended to meet with failure.

"Been to the Cosmo Club recently?" you enquired lightly as we headed towards Zurich, where you said you had a man to see about a dog. Pym confessed he had not. With Axel and Jack Brotherhood as his cosmos, who needed another?

"I'm told some of the people who go along there are a bit outspoken. Nothing against Maria, mind. Those outfits always have a broad spectrum. Part of democracy. Might be a good idea all the same if you took a closer look," you said. "Don't stick out. If they expect you to be a Leftie, let them think you are one. If they're looking for a Right-of-centre Brit, give 'em one. If necessary give 'em both. But don't go overboard. We don't want you getting into trouble with the Swissies. Any other Brits there, apart from you?"

"There are a couple of Scottish medical students but they told me they come for the girls."

"A few names would help," you said.

With that one conversation, looking back, Pym was Pym no longer. He was our man in the Cosmo, don't use the telephones for anything delicate. He was a symbolised agent, graded semi-conscious, which is our sweet way of saying he sort of half knows what he is sort of doing and sort of why. He was seventeen years old, and if he needed you urgently he was to ring Felicity and say his uncle was in town. If you needed him you'd phone the Ollingers from a callbox and say you were Mac from Birmingham passing through. Otherwise it was meeting-to-meeting, which means we always fix the next one at this one. Float, Magnus, you said. Get in there and be your own charming self, Magnus. Keep your ears and eyes open, see what sticks, but for God's sake don't get us into trouble with the Swissies. And here's your next month's alimony, Magnus. And Sandy sends his love. I tell you, Jack: we reap as we sow, even if the harvest is thirty-five summers in the growing.

The secretary of the Cosmo was a vapid Rumanian royalist called Anka who wept unaccountably in lectures. She was gangly and wild and walked with her wrists turned inside out, and when Pym stopped her in the corridor she scowled at him with red eyes and told him to go away because she had a headache. But Pym was on spy's business and brooked no rejection.

"I'm thinking of starting a Cosmo newsletter," he announced. "I thought we might include a contribution from each group."

"The Cosmo don't got no groups. The Cosmo don't want no newsletter. You are stupid. Go away."

Pym pursued Anka to the tiny office that was her lair.

"All I need is a list of members," he said. "If I have a list of members I can send out a circular and find out who is interested."

"Why don't you come to next meeting and ask them?" Anka said, sitting down and putting her head in her hands as if she were about to be sick.

"Not everyone comes to meetings. I want to test all shades. It's more democratic."

"Nothing is democratic," said Anka. "Is all illusion."

"He is an English," she explained to herself aloud as she hauled open a drawer and began to pick through its chaotic contents. "What does an English know about illusion?" she demanded of some private confessor. "He is mad." She handed him a grimy sheet of names and addresses. Most of them, it turned out later, were misspelt.

"Dearest Father" wrote Pym excitedly—"I am having one or two amazing successes here despite my youth, and I gather the Swissies are considering offering me some kind of academic honour."

"I love you"—he wrote to Belinda—"I've never written that to anyone before."

It is night. It is Bern's darkest winter. The city will never see day again. A smothering brown fog rolls down the wet cobble of the Herrengasse and the good Swiss hurry dutifully through it like reservists headed for the front. But Pym and Jack Brotherhood sit snugly in a corner of their little restaurant and Sandy has sent his extra-special love, together with his absolutely warmest congratulations. It is the first time agent and controller have eaten together in public in their target city. An ingenious cover story has been agreed in the event of a chance encounter. Jack has appointed himself secretary of the Embassy's Anglo-Swiss Christian Society and wishes to attract elements of the university. What more natural than he should turn to Magnus whom he knows from the English church? For deeper cover still he has brought the lovely Wendy who works in Chancery and is honey-haired and well-born, and has a slight but prominent protrusion of the upper lip as if she is permanently blowing out a candle just below her chin. Wendy loves both men equally; she is a natural and spontaneous toucher, with shallow, unfrightening breasts. When Pym has finished describing how he landed his great coup, Wendy cannot resist laying a hand along his cheek and saying, "God, Magnus, that was *so* brave. I mean marvellous. Wouldn't Jemima be proud if she was allowed to know. Don't you think so, Jack?" But all very quietly, in the soft-fall voice that even the horsiest must learn before they are let out of the paddock. And going very near to Jack with her hair to speak to him.

"You did a damn good job," says Brotherhood with his military smile. "Church should be proud of you," he adds, straight at his agent. They drink to Pym's good job for the church.

It is coffee time and Brotherhood has taken an envelope from one jacket pocket and from the other a pair of steel-framed half-moon spectacles which give a mysteriously finite authority to his British-brave face. Not alimony this time, for alimony comes in a white unwatermarked envelope, not a mousy-brown one like this. He does not hand it to Pym but opens it himself in full view of everyone who cares to watch, and asks Wendy for a pencil, dear, your flashy gold one, don't tell me how you earned *that*. And Wendy says, "For you, darling, anything," and drops it into his cupped hands, which close on hers. Jack spreads the paper out before him.

"Just want to check on a few of these addresses," he says. "Don't want to start sending out literature till we're sure. Okay?"

"Okay" meaning: Have you decoded this brilliant *double entendre*?

Pym says absolutely fine and Wendy trails a loving fingernail down the list, stopping at one or two lucky names that are marked with ticks and crosses.

"Only it seems that one or two members of our choir

have been quite unduly modest about their personal particulars. Almost as if they wanted to hide their lights under a bushel," says Brotherhood.

"I didn't really look," says Pym.

Brotherhood's voice drops. "Nor should you. That's our job."

"We couldn't find your lovely Maria *anywhere*," says Wendy, frightfully disappointed. "What have you done with her?"

"I'm afraid she has gone back to Italy," says Pym.

"Not looking for a replacement, Magnus, are you, darling?" says Wendy, and all laugh uproariously, Pym loudest, though he would have given the rest of his life just for the sight of one of her breasts.

Brotherhood mentions names that have no addresses. Pym can help with none of them, cannot put faces to them, cannot supply character descriptions. In other circumstances, he would gladly have made some up but Brotherhood has an uncomfortable way of knowing answers before he asks questions and Pym is getting wise to this. Wendy refills the men's glasses and keeps the dregs for herself. Brotherhood passes to addresses that have no names.

"A.H.," he says carelessly. "Ring a bell? A.—H.?"

Pym confesses it does not. "I really haven't been to enough meetings yet," he says apologetically. "I've been having rather a hard slog at my work before exams."

Brotherhood is still smiling, still perfectly relaxed. Does he know that Pym is sitting no exams? Pym notices that Wendy's pencil has nearly vanished inside his closed fist. Its sharp end peeks out of it like a tiny gun barrel.

"Think a bit," Brotherhood suggests. And says it again, mouthing it slowly like a password: "A.—H."

"Perhaps it's A.H. somebody else," says Pym. "A. H. Smith. Schmidt. I could find a way of asking if you like. It's all quite open really."

Wendy has frozen in the way you freeze in party games when the music stops. Her smile has frozen with her. Wendy has the private secretary's art of suspending her personality until it is required and something has told her it is not required at present. The waiter is clearing plates. Brotherhood's fist is covering the paper so that quite by accident no names are visible to the passer-by.

"Would it help if I told you that A.H., whoever he
is—or she is—shares a certain address in the Länggasse. Or
says he does. Care of Ollinger. That's your place too, isn't it?"

"Oh you mean Axel," says Pym.

Somewhere a cock was crowing but Pym didn't hear it. His
ears were full of a kind of waterfall, his heart was bursting
with a sense of righteous duty. He was in Rick's dressing-
room, looking for a way of stealing back the love he had given
to a wrong cause. He was in the staff lavatory, doing a knife
job on the classiest boy in the school. There were the stories
Axel had told him when he was delirious and spilling his
drinking water with both hands. There were the stories he
had told him in Davos when they went to visit Thomas
Mann's sanatorium. There were the crumbs he had gleaned
for himself on his occasional precautionary inspections of
Axel's room. And there was Brotherhood's clever prompting
that dragged things out of him he hadn't realised he knew.
Axel's father had fought with the Thälmann brigade in Spain,
he said. He was an old-style Social Democrat, so he was
lucky to die before the Nazis could arrest him.

"So he's a Leftie?"

"He's dead."

"I meant the son."

"Well not really, not that he's said. He's just catching up
on his education. He's uncommitted."

Brotherhood pressed his eyebrows together and pen-
cilled "Thälmann" on his choir list. Axel's mother was Catholic but his father had been a member of the anti-Catholic *Los
von Rom* movement, which was Lutheran, Pym said. His
mother lost her right to confession because she had married a
Protestant.

"And a Socialist," Brotherhood reminded Pym, under his
breath, as he wrote.

At the *Gymnasium* Axel's friends all wanted to fly planes
against England but Axel was persuaded by the visiting
recruiting teams to volunteer for the army. He was posted to
Russia, taken prisoner and escaped, but when the Allies
invaded France he was pulled out to fight in Normandy where
he was wounded in the spine and hip.

"Did he tell you *how* he escaped from the Russians?" Brotherhood cut in.

"He said he walked."

"Like he walked to Switzerland," said Brotherhood with a hard smile and Pym began to see a pattern that he had not thought of until Brotherhood suggested it.

"How long was he there?"

"I don't know. But long enough to learn Russian anyway. He's got books in Cyrillic in his room."

Back in Germany he went ill from his wounds but as soon as he was well enough to walk he was sent to fight the Americans. He was wounded again and sent back to Carlsbad where his mother was laid up with jaundice, so he put her on a cart with her possessions and pushed her to Dresden, a beautiful city that the Allies had recently bombed flat. He took his mother to the district where the Silesian refugees had gathered but she died soon after he got her there, so he was alone. By now Pym's head was swimming. The colours on the wall behind Brotherhood's head were merging and sliding. It's not me. It's me. I'm doing my duty for my country. Axel, help me.

"Right-ho, now it's peacetime. 'Forty-five. What does he do?"

"Gets out of the Soviet Zone."

"Why?"

"He was scared the Russians would find him and put him back in prison. He didn't like them and he didn't like prison and he didn't like the way the Communists were taking over Eastern Germany."

"Good story so far. What does he do about it?"

"He burns his paybook and buys another one."

"Where from?"

"A soldier he met in Carlsbad. Somebody who came from Munich who looked fairly like him. He said that in 1945 nobody in Germany looked like their photograph anyway."

"Why didn't this accommodating soldier want his papers?"

"He wanted to stay in the East."

"Why?"

"Axel didn't know."

"Bit thin, isn't it?"

"I suppose it is."

"On we go."

"He boarded the repatriation train to Munich and everything worked fine till he got to the other end, when the Americans pulled him straight off the train and put him into prison and beat him up."

"Why'd they do a thing like that?"

"It was because of his papers. He'd bought the papers of a wanted man. He'd just walked completely into a trap."

"Unless of course they were his own papers in the first place and he never bought them from anybody," Brotherhood suggested, writing again. "Sorry, old boy. Didn't mean to shatter your illusions. Way of the world, I'm afraid. How long did he do?"

"I don't know. He got ill again and they put him into hospital and he escaped from hospital."

"Pretty good at escaping, I must say. You say he walked here?"

"Well, walked and bummed rides on trains. They had to shorten one of his legs. The Germans did. After he came back from Russia. That's why he limps. I should have said that earlier. So I mean even with trains it was quite a walk. Munich to Austria, then Austria over the border at night to Switzerland. Then to Ostermundigen."

"To where?"

"That's where Herr Ollinger has his factory." Pym heard himself trying to make excuses. "He hasn't any papers at all, you see. He destroyed his own in Carlsbad. The Americans kept the ones he bought and he can't find anyone to give him a new set. Meanwhile he's still on the Allied wanted list. He says he'd have confessed everything the Americans asked if only he'd known what he was supposed to have done wrong. But he didn't, so they went on beating him."

"Heard that one before too," said Brotherhood under his breath, once more writing. "How does he spend his days here, Magnus? Who are his buddies?"

Far, far too late, voices were whispering Pym caution.

"He's afraid to go out in case the *Fremdenpolizei* arrest him. If he goes into town he borrows a big hat. It isn't only the *Fremdenpolizei*. If the ordinary Swissies knew about him they'd inform against him too. He says they do that. It's a national sport. He says they do it out of envy and call it civic-mindedness. It's just household gossip I'm telling you."

"Pity you didn't tell it to us earlier."

"It didn't mean anything. It wasn't anything you were interested in. Herr Ollinger told me most of it. He gossips all the time."

Brotherhood had his car outside. Man and boy were sitting in it but Brotherhood didn't drive anywhere. Wendy had gone home. Brotherhood asked about Axel's politics. Pym said Axel despised established attitudes. Brotherhood said, "Describe." He wasn't writing any more and his head was very still in the window frame. Pym said Axel had once remarked that pain was democratic.

"Reading habits?" said Brotherhood.

"Well, everything really. Everything he's missed from the war. He types a lot. Mostly at night."

"What does he type?"

"He says it's a book."

"What does he read?"

"Well, everything. Sometimes when he's ill I get books out of the library for him."

"In your own name?"

"Yes."

"That's a bit rash. What do you get?"

"The whole spectrum."

"Describe."

Pym described and came inevitably to Marx and Engels and the bad bears, and Brotherhood wrote all of them down, asking him who Dühring was when he was at home.

Brotherhood asked about Axel's habits. Pym said he liked cigars and vodka and sometimes kirsch. He didn't mention whisky.

Brotherhood asked about Axel's sex-life. Sweeping aside his own limitations in this respect, Pym declared it mixed.

"Describe," said Brotherhood again.

Pym did his best, though he knew even less about Axel's sexuality than his own, except that whatever form it took, unlike Pym he was on terms with it.

"He does sometimes have women," said Pym deprecatingly, as if that were something all of us did. "Usually she's some token beauty from the Cosmo, cooking for him or polishing his room. He calls them his Marthas. I thought at first he meant martyr."

"Dearest Father"—Pym wrote that night, alone and miserable in his attic—"I am absolutely fine and my head is buzzing from all the seminars and lectures, though I miss you terribly as ever. One bad thing however is that I had a pal who recently let me down."

How Pym loved Axel in the weeks that followed! For a day or so, it was true, he would not go near him, he resented him so much. He resented everything about him, every move on the other side of the radiator. He patronises me. He sneers at my ignorance without respecting my strengths. He is an arrogant German of the worst sort and Jack is right to keep his eye on him. Pym resented the mail he received, Herr Axel care of Ollinger. He resented more than ever the Marthas tiptoeing like shy disciples up the stairs to the great thinker's sanctum, and down again two hours later. He is dissolute. He is unnatural. He is turning their heads for them, exactly as he tried to turn mine. Diligently he kept a log of these developments to give to Brotherhood at their next meeting. He also spent a lot of time in the third-class buffet wearing his clouded look for the benefit of Elisabeth. But these exercises in separation did not endure and the line to Axel grew tighter with every day. He discovered he could gauge his friend's mood from the tempo of his typing: whether he was excited or angry or tired. He is reporting on us, he told himself without conviction. He is selling out the foreign students to his German paymaster. He is a Nazi war criminal turned Communist spy in the image of his Leftie father.

"When do we ever get to read it?" Pym had asked him once shyly in the days when they were close.

"If I ever finish it, and the publisher ever publishes it."

"Why can't I read it now?"

"Because you will take the cream off it for me, and leave me with the curds."

"What's it about?"

"Mysteries, Sir Magnus, and if they are spoken aloud they will never be written down."

He's writing his Wilhelm Meister autobiography, thought Pym indignantly. That was my idea, not his.

He could tell when Axel could not sleep by the striking

of his matches as he lit his cigars. He could tell when his
body was driving him mad. He told it by the altered rhythm
of his movements and the determined gaiety of his singing as
he clomped the wooden corridor to crouch for hours in their
shared lavatory with its porcelain footprints. After several
nights had passed that way Pym was able to loathe Axel for
his incontinence. Why doesn't he go back to hospital? "He
sings German marching songs," he wrote to Brotherhood in
his notebook. "Tonight he sang the whole Horst Wessel Lied
in the lavatory." On the third night, long after Pym had gone
to bed, his door suddenly flew open and there stood Axel
wrapped in Herr Ollinger's dressing-gown.

"Well? Have you forgiven me yet?"

"What have I got to forgive you for?" Pym replied,
discreetly pushing his secret logbook under the bedclothes.

Axel stayed in the doorway. The dressing-gown was
ridiculously large for him. Sweat had made black fangs of his
moustache. "Give me some of your priest's whisky," he said.

After that Pym couldn't let Axel go until he had wiped
the shadows of suspicion from his face. The weeks passed and
spring began and Pym knew that nothing was happening, and
that he had never betrayed Axel in the first place, because if
he had they would have done something long ago. Occasionally Brotherhood asked a couple of follow-up questions but
they had the ring of routine. Once he asked, "Can you tell me
an evening when you know for certain he will be out?" But
Pym was able to answer that there were no certainties in
Axel's life. "Well look here. Why don't you take him out to a
slap-up dinner at our expense?" said Brotherhood. One night
Pym tried. He told Axel he had had a windfall from his father
and wouldn't it be fun to put on disguise again like the time
they called on Thomas Mann? Axel shook his head with a
wisdom Pym dared not explore. After that Pym studied and
strove for Axel in every way he knew, now denying to himself
that Brotherhood existed anywhere but in his mind, now
congratulating himself on Axel's continued survival, which
was owed entirely to Pym's nimble manipulation of irresistible forces.

They came in the small hours of a spring morning, just when
we fear them most: when we want to live the longest and are

most afraid of dying. Soon, unless I make their journey
unnecessary, they will come for me in the same way. If so, I
trust I shall see the justice of it and relish the circularity of
life. They had acquired a key to the front door and some
method of detaching Herr Ollinger's chains which were not
unlike Miss Dubber's. They knew the house inside out
because they had been watching it for months, photographing
our visitors, sending in their bogus meter men and window
cleaners, delaying the mail while they read it and no doubt
listening to Herr Ollinger's forlorn telephone conversations
with his creditors and lame ducks. Pym knew there were
three of them because he could count their stealthy Father
Christmas footsteps on the squeaky top stair. They looked in
the lavatory before they placed themselves outside Axel's
door. Pym knew this because he heard the lavatory door
squeak and stay open. He also heard a rattle as they removed
the lavatory-door key in case their desperate criminal should
attempt to lock himself inside. But Pym could do nothing
personally because at the time he lay deeply dreaming in all
the scared beds of his childhood. He dreamt about Lippsie
and her brother Aaron and how he and Aaron together had
pushed her off the rooftop at Mr. Grimble's school. He
dreamt that an ambulance was waiting outside the house like
the one that called at The Glades for Dorothy, and that Herr
Ollinger was trying to stop the men coming up the stairs but
was being ordered back to his quarters in a fury of Swiss
dialect. He dreamt that he heard a shout of "Pym, you
bastard, where are you?" from the direction of Axel's room
and directly afterwards the awful brief thundering noise of a
man with uneven legs struggling against three healthy intruders and the furious opposition of Bastl whom Axel had once
accused of being his Faustian Devil. But when he lifted his
head from the pillow and listened to the real world, there was
silence and everything was absolutely fine.

I held it against you, Jack, I confess. I argued with you in my
head for years, uphill, downhill, and long after I had joined
the Firm. Why had you done it to him? He wasn't English,
he wasn't a Communist, he wasn't the war criminal the
Americans claimed he was. He was nothing to do with you.
His only crimes were his poverty, his illegal presence and his

lameness—plus a certain freedom in his way of thinking, which in the eyes of some is what we are there to protect. But I did nurse a grudge and I'm sorry. Because now of course I know you hardly gave it a thought. Axel was another bit of barter material. You wrote him up; he came back into your in-tray looking formidable and sinister in Wendy's flawless type. You lit your pipe and admired your handiwork, and you thought: Hullo, I'll bet the old Swissies will like a smell of this one; I'll pop it down to them and earn myself a Brownie point. You made a phone call or two and invited some contact in the Swiss Security Service to join you for an extended luncheon at your favourite restaurant. Over the coffee and the schnapps you slipped him an anonymous brown envelope. As an afterthought you slipped a copy to your American colleague too, because if you're going to earn one favour, why not earn a second while you're about it? After all, it was the Yanks who put him in the cooler, even if they got his record wrong.

You were junior then, too, weren't you? You had your way to make. As we all have. Maturer now, both of us. Sorry to be so lengthy in the remembering, but the episode took me rather a long time to forget. I've got it straight now. Served me right for having a friend outside the service.

"Mr. Canterbury! Mr. Canterbury! You've got a man!"

Pym had put down his pen. He had not looked towards the door. Almost before he was aware of it, he had leapt to his slippered feet and was flying across the room to where the metal-lined black briefcase, still locked, stood against the wall. Dropping to a crouch beside it, he inserted the complicated key in the first lock and sprung it. Then the second: anti-clockwise or it fires.

"What man's that, Miss D?" he said in his softest and most reassuring tone, one hand already in the case.

"With a *cabinet*, Mr. Canterbury," Miss Dubber replied with disapproval through the keyhole. "You've never had a cabinet before. You've never had anything. You've never locked your door either. What's wrong?"

Pym laughed. "Nothing's wrong. It's just a cabinet. I ordered it. How many of them are there?"

Taking the briefcase with him, he tiptoed to the window

and squared his back against the wall while he squinted cautiously through the gap in the curtain.

"Just one—isn't that enough? A great green ugly one made of iron. If you'd wanted a cabinet why didn't you tell me? You could have had Mrs. Tutton's cupboard from room two."

"I meant how many men?"

It was daylight. A yellow taxi-truck was parked outside the house, the driver at the wheel. He glanced round the rest of the square. Fast. Checking everything. Then slowly. Checking everything again.

"What does it matter how many men, Mr. Canterbury? Why do we have to count the men when it's a cabinet?"

Relaxing, Pym replaced the briefcase in its corner and relocked it. Clockwise or it fires. He returned the keys to his pocket. He opened the door.

"Sorry, Miss D. I think I must have been dozing."

She watched him down the stairs, then went after him and watched again as he looked first at the two men, then shyly at the green cabinet, lightly touching its chipped paintwork, up and down, tugging at each drawer in turn.

"It's a bloody weight, governor, I'll tell you," said the first.

"Who's it got in it then?" said the second.

She watched him lead the men up to his room, the cabinet between them, and lead them down again. She watched him pay their bill in cash from his back pocket, and give them an extra five pounds for themselves.

"Sorry about that, Miss D," he said as they drove off. "Some old Ministry archives I'm working on. Here. This is for you." He handed her a travel brochure he had brought down with him from his room. There was a whiff of Rick about the capitals. "Discover Tunisia in the Luxury of our air-conditioned Coach. Seniors a Specialty. Shades of the East in the Mediterranean. Enough to make your mouth Water."

But Miss Dubber would not accept the brochure. "Toby and I aren't going anywhere any more, Mr. Canterbury," she said. "Whatever's troubling you won't go away with us. That's for sure."

9

Brotherhood had bathed and shaved and cut himself and put on a suit. He had listened to the news on the BBC and afterwards tuned to the Deutsche Welle because sometimes the foreign press got hold of stories while Fleet Street was still obediently suppressing them. But he had heard no lighthearted mention of a senior officer of the British Secret Service going walkabout or turning up in Moscow. He had eaten a piece of toast and marmalade, he had made a few phone calls but six till eight of an English morning were the dead hours when nobody except himself was about. On a normal day he would have walked across the park to Head Office and given himself a couple of hours at his desk reading the night's crop of Station reports and preparing himself for the ten-o'clock prayer session in Bo's sanctum. "So how's our Eastern Front this rainy morning, Jack?" Bo would say in a tone of jokey veneration, when Brotherhood's turn came round. And a respectful quiet would follow while the great Jack Brotherhood gave his chief the score. "Some quite nice stuff from Conger on the Comecon trading figures for last year, Bo. We've sent it up to Treasury by special bag. Otherwise it's the silly season. Joes are on holiday, so's the opposition."

But this was not a normal day and Brotherhood was no longer the grand old man of covert operations that Bo cracked him up to be when he introduced him to visiting firemen from Western liaison services. He was the latest unperson in the latest looming scandal and, as he stepped into the street below his flat, his quick gaze was more than usually vigilant. It was eight-thirty. First he headed south across Green Park, walking as fast as ever and perhaps a little faster, so that Nigel's watchers, if they were on him, would either have to gallop or radio for somebody to get ahead of him. The night's rain had stopped. Warm, unhealthy mist hung over the ponds and willows. Reaching the Mall he hailed a cab and told the

driver Tottenham Court Road. He walked again and took a
second cab to Kentish Town. His destination was a grey
hillside of Victorian villas. The lower reaches were still run
down, their windows plugged with corrugated iron against
squatters. But higher up Volvo estate cars and teak-framed
dormer windows testified to the safe arrival of the middle
classes, and the long gardens boasted coloured climbing
frames and half-made dinghies. Here Brotherhood was no
longer in a hurry. He trudged up the hill slowly, noting
everything at his leisure: this is the pace I have earned in
life, this is the smile. A pretty girl passed him on her way to
work and he greeted her indulgently. She winked pertly back
at him, proving for all time that she was not a watcher. At
number 18 he paused and in the manner of a prospective
purchaser stood back and surveyed the house. Bach and a
smell of breakfast issued from the ground-floor kitchen. A
wooden arrow marked "18A" pointed down the basement
steps. A man's bicycle was chained against the railings, a
poster for the Social Democratic Party hung in the bay
window. He pressed the bell. A girl in a blazer opened the
door to him. At thirteen she already wore an air of superiority.

"I'll get Mummy," she said before he could speak, and
turned sharply so that he could watch her skirt swing.
"Mummy. It's a man. For you," she said and, sweeping past
him down the steps, set off for her decent school.

"Hullo, Belinda," Brotherhood said. "It's me."

Coming out of the kitchen, Belinda paused at the foot of
the stairs, drew a breath and yelled up them at a closed door.
"Paul! Come down at once, please. Jack Brotherhood is here.
I assume he wants something."

Which more or less was what he knew she'd shout—
though not quite so loud—because Belinda had always reacted
badly first and put it right rather sweetly later.

They sat in a pine drawing-room on low basketwork chairs
that creaked like swings when you moved. A gigantic lampshade
of white paper rocked crookedly above them. Belinda had
made coffee in hand-thrown mugs and sweetened it with
natural sugar. Her Bach still played defiantly in the kitchen.
She was dark-eyed and angry about something in her
childhood—at fifty her face was still set ready for another

quarrel with her mother. She had greying hair bound in a
sensible bun and wore a necklace of what looked like nutmeg.
When she walked, she waded through her kaftan as if she
hated it. When she sat, she spread her knees and scraped at
the knuckles of one hand. Yet her beauty clung to her like an
identity she was trying to deny and her plainness kept
slipping like a bad disguise.

"They've already been here in case you don't know,
Jack," she said. "At ten at night as a matter of fact. They were
waiting for us on the doorstep when we got back from the
cottage."

"Who's they?"

"Nigel. Lorimer. Two more I didn't know. All men, of
course."

"What did they say they were here for?" Brotherhood
asked, but Paul stopped him.

You could never be angry with Paul. He smiled so wisely
through his pipe smoke even when he was being rude. "What
is this actually, Jack?" he said, taking his pipe from his mouth
and lowering it until it became a hand microphone. "Interrogations about interrogations? You people have no constitu-
tional position, you know, Jack. You're only a chartered body
even under this government, I'm afraid."

"You probably don't know it, but Paul has written
extensively on the rise and rise of the para-military services
under the Tories," Belinda said in a voice that struggled to
be harsh. "You'd know if you'd bother to read *The Guardian*,
but you don't. They gave him a whole page for the last
one."

"So screw you actually, Jack," said Paul just as pleasantly.

Brotherhood smiled. Paul smiled. An old English sheepdog
wandered in and settled at Brotherhood's feet.

"Do you want to smoke, by the way?" said Paul, ever
sensitive to people's needs. "I'm afraid Belinda draws the line
at fags but I can offer you a nifty little brown one if you're
pushed."

Brotherhood pulled out a packet of his foul cigarettes
and lit one. "Screw you too, Paul," he said equably.

Paul had peaked early in life. Twenty years ago he had
written promising plays for fringe theatres. He wrote them
still. He was tall but reassuringly unathletic. Twice, to Brotherhood's knowledge, he had applied to join the Firm. Each

time he had been turned down flat, even without Brotherhood's intervention.

"They came here because they were vetting Magnus for a top appointment, if you want to know," Belinda said all in one breath. "They were in a hurry because they wanted to promote him immediately so that he could get on with the job."

"Nigel?" Brotherhood echoed with an incredulous laugh. "Nigel and Lorimer plus two other men? Doing their own vetting at ten o'clock at night? You've got half the brass of secret Whitehall on your doorstep there, Bel. Not a vetting team of old crocks on half pay."

"It's a senior appointment so he has to be vetted by senior people," Belinda retorted, blushing scarlet.

"Did Nigel tell you that?"

"Yes, he did!" said Belinda.

"Did you believe it?"

But Paul had decided it was time to show his mettle. "Actually, fuck off will you, Jack?" he said. "Get out of the house. Now. Darling, don't answer him. It's all too theatrical and stupid for words. Come on, Jack. Out. You're welcome for a drink any time, as long as you phone first. But not for this nonsense. Sorry. Out."

He had opened the door and was flapping his big soft hand as if scooping water but neither Brotherhood nor the sheepdog stirred.

"Magnus has jumped ship," Brotherhood explained to Belinda, while Paul put on his I-can-be-violent glower. "Nigel and Lorimer sold you a load of cock. Magnus has bolted and gone into hiding while they cook up a case against him as the big traitor of the Western world. I'm his boss so I'm not quite as enthusiastic as they are. I think he's strayed but not lost and I'd like to get to him first and talk to him." Addressing Paul, he didn't even bother to turn his head. He just lifted it far enough to make the difference. "They've put a muzzle on your editor for the time being, same as everybody else, Paul. But if Nigel has his way, in a few days' time your colleagues will be plastering Belinda's previous marriage all over their nasty little columns and taking your picture every time you go to the launderette. So you'd better start thinking about how to get your act together. In the meantime, fetch us some more coffee and leave us in peace for an hour."

* * *

Alone, Belinda was much stronger than when protected by her mate. Her face, though dazed, had relaxed. Her gaze had fixed itself steadfastly on a spot a few feet from her eyes, as if to suggest that although she might not see as far as others, her faith in what she saw burned twice as bright. They sat at a round table in the window bay and the Venetian blind sliced the Social Democratic Party into strips.

"His father's dead," Brotherhood said.

"I know. I read. Nigel told me. He asked me how it might have affected Magnus. I suppose that was a trick."

Brotherhood took a moment to answer this. "Not entirely," he said. "No. Not a complete trick, Belinda. I think they're reasoning that it could have turned his head a little."

"Magnus always wanted me to save him from Rick. I did my best. I tried to explain that to Nigel."

"How save him, Belinda?"

"Hide him. Answer the phone for him. Say he was abroad when he wasn't. I sometimes think that's why Magnus joined the Firm. As a hiding place. Just as he married me because he was scared to risk it with Jemima."

"Who's Jemima?" said Brotherhood, playing ignorant.

"She was a close friend of mine at school." She scowled. "Too close." The scowl softened and became melancholy. "Poor Rick. I only ever saw him once. That was at our wedding. He turned up uninvited in the middle of the reception. I never saw Magnus look happier. Otherwise he was just a voice on the telephone. He had a nice voice."

"Magnus have any other hiding places in those days?"

"You mean women, don't you? You can say it if you want. I don't mind any more."

"Just somewhere he might have hidden. That's all. Little cottage somewhere. An old buddy. Where would he go, Belinda? Who'd have him?"

Her hands, now that she had unlocked them, were elegant and expressive. "He'd have gone anywhere. He was a new man every day. He'd come home one person, I'd try to match him. In the morning he'd be someone else. Do you think he did it, Jack?"

"Do you?"

"You always answer one question with another. I'd forgotten. Magnus had the same trick." He waited. "You could try Sef," she said. "Sef was always loyal."

"Sef?"

"Kenneth Sefton Boyd. Jemima's brother. 'Sef's too rich for my blood,' Magnus used to say. That meant they were equals."

"Could Magnus have gone to him?"

"If it was bad enough."

"Could he have gone to Jemima?"

She shook her head.

"Why not?"

"I understand she's gone off men these days," she said and blushed again. "She's not predictable. She never was."

"Ever heard of anyone called Wentworth?"

She shook her head, still thinking of something different. "Since my time," she said.

"Poppy?"

"My time ended with Mary. If there's a Poppy, that's Mary's bad luck."

"When did you last hear from him, Belinda?"

"That's what Nigel asked me."

"What did you say to Nigel?"

"I said there was no reason to hear from him after we divorced. We'd been married six years. There were no children. It was a mistake. Why relive it?"

"Was that the truth?"

"No. I lied."

"What were you concealing?"

"He rang. Magnus did."

"When?"

"Monday night. Paul was out, thank God." She paused, listening for the sound of Paul's typewriter, which was tapping reassuringly from upstairs. "He sounded strange. I thought he was drunk. It was late."

"What time?"

"It must have been around eleven. Lucy was still doing her homework. I won't let her work after eleven as a rule but she was doing a French mock O-level. He was in a phone box."

"Cash?"

"Yes."

"Where?"

"He didn't say. He just said, 'Rick's dead. I wish we'd had a child.'"

"That all?"

"He said he'd always hated himself for marrying me. Now he was reconciled. He understood himself. And he loved me for trying so hard. Thanks."

"That all?"

"'Thanks. Thanks for everything. And please forgive the bad parts.' Then he rang off."

"Did you tell Nigel this?"

"Why do you keep asking me that? I didn't think it was Nigel's business. I didn't want to say he was being drunk and sentimental on the phone late at night just at the time when they were considering him for promotion. Serves him right for deceiving me."

"What else did Nigel ask you?"

"Just character stuff. Had I ever had any reason to suppose Magnus might have had Communist sympathies. I said Oxford. Nigel said they knew about that. I said I didn't think university politics meant much anyway. Nigel agreed. Had he ever been erratic in any way? Unstable—alcoholic—depressive? I said no again. I didn't reckon one drunken phone call constituted drunkenness, but if it did I wasn't going to tell four of Magnus's colleagues about it. I felt protective of him."

"They ought to have known you better, Belinda," said Brotherhood. "Would you have given him the job yourself, by the way?"

"What job? You said there wasn't one." She was being sharp with him, belatedly suspecting him too of duplicity.

"I meant suppose there had been a job. A high-level, responsible job. Would you give it to him?"

She smiled. Very prettily. "I did, didn't I? I married him."

"You're wiser now. Would you give it to him today?"

She was biting her forefinger, frowning angrily. She could change moods in moments. Brotherhood waited but nothing came so he asked her another question: "Did they ask you about his time in Graz, by any chance?"

"Graz? You mean his army time? Good heavens, they didn't go back *that* far."

Brotherhood shook his head as if to say he would never

be equal to the wicked ways of the world. "Graz is where they're trying to say it all started, Bel," he said. "They've got some grand theory he fell among thieves while he was doing his National Service there. What do you make of that?"

"They're absurd," she said.

"Why are you so sure?"

"He was happy there. When he came back to England he was a new man. 'I'm complete,' he kept saying. 'I've done it, Bel. I've got my other half together.' He was proud he'd done such good work."

"Did he describe the work?"

"He couldn't. It was too secret and too dangerous. He just said I would be proud of him if I knew."

"Did he tell you the name of any of the operations he was mixed up in?"

"No."

"Did he tell you the names of any of his Joes?"

"Don't be absurd. He wouldn't do that."

"Did he mention his C.O.?"

"He said he was brilliant. Everyone was brilliant for Magnus when they were new."

"If I said 'Greensleeves' to you in a loud voice, would that ring any bells?"

"It would mean English traditional music."

"Ever hear of a girl called Sabina?"

She shook her head. "He told me I was his first," she said.

"Did you believe him?"

"It's hard to tell when it's the first for you too."

With Belinda, he remembered, the quiet was always good. If her charges into the lists had something comic about them, there was always dignity to the calm between.

"So Nigel and his friends went away happy," he suggested. "Did you?"

Her face against the window was in silhouette. He waited for it to lift or turn to him, but it didn't.

"Where would you look for him?" he said. "If you were me?"

Still she did not move or speak.

"Some place by the sea somewhere? He had these fantasies, you know. He chopped them up and gave a bit to each person. Did he ever give a version to you? Scotland?

Canada? The migration of the reindeer? Some kind lady who'd take him in? I need to know, Belinda. I really do."

"I won't talk to you any more, Jack. Paul's right. I don't have to."

"Not whatever he's done? Not to save him perhaps?"

"I don't trust you. Specially when you're being nice. You invented him, Jack. He'd have done whatever you told him. Who to be. Who to marry. Who to divorce. If he's done wrong it's as much your fault as his. It was easy to get rid of me—he just gave me the latch key and went to a lawyer. How was he supposed to get rid of you?"

Brotherhood moved towards the door.

"If you find him, tell him not to ring again. And Jack?" Brotherhood paused. Her face was soft again, and hopeful. "Did he write that book he was always on about?"

"Which book was that?"

"The great autobiographical novel that was going to change the world."

"Should he have done?"

"'One day I'm going to lock myself away and tell the truth.' 'Why do you have to lock yourself away? Tell it now,' I said. He didn't seem to think he could. I'm not going to let Lucy marry early. Nor's Paul. We're going to put her on the pill and let her have affairs."

"Lock himself away *where*, Belinda?"

The light once more faded from her face. "You brought it on yourselves, Jack. All of you. He'd have been all right if he'd never met people like you."

Wait, Grant Lederer told himself. They all hate you. You hate most of them. Be a clever boy and wait your turn. Ten men sat in a room inside a room. In the false walls, false windows looked onto plastic flowers. From places like this, thought Lederer, America lost her wars against the little brown men in black pyjamas. From places like this, he thought—from smoked-glass rooms, cut off from humankind—America will lose all her wars except the last. A few yards beyond the walls lay the placid diplomatic backwaters of St. John's Wood. But here inside they could have been in Langley or Saigon.

"Harry, with the greatest *possible* respect," Mountjoy of the Cabinet Office piped with very little respect at all.

"These early indicators of yours could perfectly easily have been dumped on us by an unscrupulous opposition, as some of us have been saying all along. Is it really fair to trot them out yet again? I thought we put all this stuff to bed back in August."

Wexler stared at the spectacles he was holding in both hands. They are too heavy for him, thought Lederer. He sees too clearly through them. Wexler lowered them to the table and scratched his veteran's crew cut with his stubby fingertips. What's holding you up? Lederer demanded of him silently. Are you translating English into English? Are you paralysed by jet-lag after flying Concorde all the way from Washington? Or are you in awe of these English gentlemen who never tire of telling us how they set up our service in the first place and generously invited us to sup at their high table? You're a top man of the best intelligence agency in the world, for Christ's sake. You're my boss. Why don't you stand up and be counted? As if in response to Lederer's silent pleading, Wexler's voice started functioning again with all the animation of a machine that speaks your weight.

"Gentlemen," Wexler resumed—except that he said "junnlemen." Reload, aim again, take your time, thought Lederer. "Our position, Sir Eric," Wexler resumed, with something unpleasantly close to a bow in the direction of Mountjoy's knighthood, "that is—the ah Agency position overall on this thing—at this important meeting, and at this moment in time—is that we have here an accumulation of indicators from a wide range of sources on the one hand, and new data on the other which we consider pretty much conclusive in respect of our unease." He moistened his lips. So would I, thought Lederer. If I'd spoken that mouthful, I'd spit at least. "It looks to us therefore that the ah logistics here require us to go back over the ah course a little distance and—when we've done that—to ah slot the new stuff in where we can all take a good look at it in light of what has—ah latterly gone before." He turned to Brammel and his lined but innocent face broke into an apologetic smile. "You want to do it different in any way, Bo, why don't you just say so and see if we can accommodate you?"

"My dear chap, you must do exactly whatever makes you feel most comfortable," said Brammel hospitably, which was what he had been saying to everybody all his life. So Wexler went back to his brief, first centering the folder before him on the table then tilting it cautiously to the right, as if landing it on one wingtip. And Grant Lederer III, who has the impression that the inside surfaces of his skin have been afflicted by an itchy rash, tries to lower his pulse rate and his blood heat and believe in the high level of this conference. Somewhere, he argues to himself, there is worth and secrecy and an all-knowing intelligence service. The only trouble is, it's in Heaven.

The British had fielded their usual intractable, over-fluent team. Ingram, seconded from the Security Service, Mountjoy from the Cabinet Office and Dorney from the Foreign Office all lolled in varying positions of disbelief or outright contempt. Only the placement had changed, Lederer noticed: whereas Jack Brotherhood had hitherto been placed symbolically at Brammel's side, today that position had gone to Brammel's bagman, Nigel, and Brotherhood had been promoted to head of the table, where he presided like an old grey bird glowering down on his prey. On the American side of the table they were a mere four. How typical that in our Special Relationship the Brits should outnumber the Americans, thought Lederer. In the field the Agency outguns these bastards by about ninety to one. In here we're a persecuted minority. To Lederer's right, Harry Wexler, having cleared his throat not before time, had at last begun wrestling with the intricacies of what he insisted on calling the ongoing ah situation. To Lederer's left lounged Mick Carver, Head of the London Station, a spoilt Bostonian millionaire considered brilliant on no evidence Lederer was aware of. Below him the egregious Artelli, a distraught mathematician from Signals Intelligence, looked as though he had been hauled from Langley by his hair. And, between them, here sit I, Grant Lederer III, unlovable even to myself, the pushy law boy from South Bend, Indiana, whose tireless efforts in the interest of his own promotion have dragged everyone together this one more time to prove what could have been proved six months ago: namely, that computers do not fabricate intelligence, do not sidle over to the opposition in return for favours, do not voluntarily compose slanders against men in high standing in the British service. They tell the disgraceful truth without regard to charm, race or tradition and they tell it to Grant Lederer III, who is busy making himself as unpopular as possible.

As Lederer listened impotently to Wexler's floundering, he decided that it was himself not Wexler who was the alien. Here is the great Harry E. Wexler, he reasoned, who in Langley sits at the right hand of God. Who has been featured in *Time* as America's Legendary Adventurer. Who played a star part in the Bay of Pigs and fathered some of the finest intelligence fuck-ups of the Vietnam War. Who has destabilised more bankrupt economies in Central America than are dreamed of, and conspired with the greatest in the land from the heads of the Mafia downwards. And here is me, an ambitious jerk. And what am I thinking? I am thinking that a man who cannot speak clearly cannot think clearly. I am thinking that self-expression is the companion to logic and that Harry E. Wexler is by this criterion circumcised from the neck up, even if he does hold my precious future in his hands.

To Lederer's relief, Wexler's voice suddenly acquired new confidence. This was because he was reading directly from Lederer's brief. "*In March '81 a reliably assessed defector reported that . . .*" Cover name Dumbo, Lederer remembered automatically, himself becoming the computer: resettled Paris with a hooker supplied by Resources Section. A year later, it was the hooker who defected. "*In May '81 Signals Intelligence reported that . . .*" Lederer glanced at Artelli, hoping to catch his eye, but Artelli was hearing signals of his own. "*In March again of '82 a source inside Polish Intelligence while on a liaison visit to Moscow was advised that . . .*" Cover name Mustapha, Lederer recalled with a fastidious shiver: died of overenthusiasm while assisting Polish security in its enquiries. With a fumble and a near fall the great Wexler delivered his first punchline of the morning and managed not to fluff it. "And the burden of these indicators, junnlemen, is in every case the same," he announced, "namely *that the entire Balkan effort of an unnamed Western intelligence service is being orchestrated by Czech Intelligence in Prague, and that the leak is occurring under the noses of the Anglo-American intelligence fraternity in Washington.*" Nobody leaps in the air however. Colonel Carruthers does not remove his monocle to exclaim "By God, the fiendish cunning!" The sensational force of Wexler's revelation is six months old. The sedge is withered from the case and no spooks sing.

Lederer decided to listen instead to what Wexler does not say. Nothing about my interrupted tennis training, for example. Nothing about my imperilled marriage, my truncated sex-life, my total noncontribution as a father, starting the morning they hauled me off all other duties and assigned me to the great Wexler as his superslave for twenty-five hours a day. "You have a lawyer's training, you have Czech language and Czech expertise," Personnel had told him in as many words. "More appropriately you have a thoroughly sleazy mind. Apply it, Lederer. We expect terrible things of you." Nothing about the night hours in front of my computer while I typed my damned fingers off, feeding in acres of disconnected data. Why did I do it? What got into me? Mom, I just felt my talent striding out inside of me, so I got on its back and rode away to my destiny. Names and records of all Western intelligence officers past or present in Washington with access to the Czech target, whether central or peripheral consumers: Lederer cans the whole ridiculous assembly in four days cold. Names of all their contacts, details of their travel movements, behaviour patterns, sexual and recreational appetites: Lederer nets them all in a manic Friday-to-Monday while Bee does the praying for both of us. Names of all Czech couriers, officials, legal and illegal travellers passing in and out of the United States, plus separately entered personal descriptions to counteract false passports. Dates and ostensible purpose of such journeys, frequency and duration of stay. Lederer delivers them bound and gagged in three short days and nights while Bee convinces herself he is making it with Maisie Morse from Collation, who has pot smoke coming out of her ears.

Still disdaining these and the many other noble sacrifices of his subordinate, Wexler has embarked on a disastrous paragraph about "incorporating our general awareness of the Czechoslovak methodology in regard to the servicing *of* and the ah communication *with* their agents in the field." An impressed silence follows while the meeting mentally paraphrases.

"Ah, you mean *tradecraft*, Harry," says Bo Brammel, who never could resist a quip if he thought it would adorn his reputation, and little Nigel next to him restrains his laughter by patting down his hair.

"Well, yes, sir, I guess that is what I do mean," Wexler confesses, and Lederer to his surprise feels a yawn of nervous excitement pass over him as the tousled Artelli takes the stage.

Artelli uses no notes and has a mathematician's frugality with words. Despite his name, he speaks with a slight French accent that he disguises beneath a Bronx drawl. "As the indicators continued to multiply," he says, "my section was ordered to make a reappraisal of clandestine radio transmissions beamed from the roof of the Czech Embassy in Washington as well as from certain other identified Czech facilities in the United States, throughout the years '81 and '82, notably their consulate in San Francisco. Our people reconsidered skip distances, frequency variations and probable reception zones. They backtracked over all intercepts of that period though we had not been able to break them at the time of their original transmission. They prepared a schedule of such transmissions so that they could be matched against the movements of eligible suspects."

"Hold on a minute, will you?"

Little Nigel's head snaps round like a weathervane in a gale. Even Brammel shows distinct signs of human interest. From his exile at the end of the table, Jack Brotherhood is pointing a .45-calibre forefinger straight at Artelli's navel. And it is symptomatic of the many paradoxes of Lederer's life that of all the people in the room, Brotherhood is the one whom he would most wish to serve, if ever he had the opportunity, even though—or perhaps because—his occasional efforts to ingratiate himself with his adopted hero have met with iron rebuff.

"Look here, Artelli," Brotherhood says. "You people have made rather a lot out of the point that every time Pym left the precincts of Washington, whether on leave or in order to visit another town, a particular series of coded transmissions from the Czech Embassy was discontinued. I suspect you are going to make that point again now."

"With embellishments, yes, I am," says Artelli pleasantly enough.

Brotherhood's forefinger remains trained on its mark. Artelli keeps his hands on the table. "The assumption being that if Pym was out of range of their Washington transmitter, the Czechs wouldn't bother to talk to him?" Brotherhood suggests.

"This is correct."

"Then every time he came back to the capital they'd pop up again. 'Hullo it's you and welcome home.' Correct?"

"Yes, sir."

"Well turn it round for a moment, will you? If you were framing a man, isn't that precisely what you would do too?"

"Not today," he says equably. "And not in 1981 or '82. Ten years ago, maybe. Not in the eighties."

"Why not?"

"I wouldn't be that dumb. We all know it's standard intelligence practice to continue transmitting whether or not the party is listening the other end. It's my hunch they—" He stops. "Maybe I should leave this one to Mr. Lederer," he says.

"No you don't—you tell it to them yourself," Wexler orders without looking up.

Wexler's terseness is not unexpected. It is a feature of these meetings, known to everybody present, that a curse, if not an outright embargo, hangs over the use of Lederer's name. Lederer is their Cassandra. Nobody ever asked Cassandra to preside over a meeting on damage limitation.

Artelli is a chess-player and takes his time. "The communication techniques we were required to observe here were out of fashion even at the time of their use. You get a feel. A smell. A smell of age. A sense of long habituation, one human being to another. Years of it maybe."

"Well now that's *very* special pleading," Nigel exclaims, quite angry, and continues to sit bolt upright before keeling towards his master, who appears to be trying to shake his head and nod at the same time. Mountjoy says "Hear, hear." A couple of Brammel's supporters' club are making similar farmyard noises. There is hostility in the air, and it is forming on national lines. Brotherhood says nothing but has coloured. Whether anyone apart from himself has noticed this, Lederer does not know. He has coloured, he has lowered his fist, and for a second he appears to have dropped his guard entirely. Lederer hears him growl, "Fanciful twaddle," but misses the rest because Artelli has decided to continue.

"Our more important discovery relates however to the types of code in these transmissions. As soon as we had the notion of an older type of system, we subjected the transmissions to different analytical methods. Like you don't immediately look for a steam engine inside the hood of a Cadillac. We decided to read the messages on the assumption they were being received by a man or woman in the field who is of a certain generation of training, and who cannot or dare not store modern coding materials. We looked for more elementary keys. We looked in particular for evidence of non-random texts that would serve as base keys for transposition."

If anybody here understands what he's saying, they are not showing it, thinks Lederer.

"When we did this, we at once began to detect a progression in the structure. Right now it's still algebra. But it's there. It's a logical linguistic progression. Maybe it's a piece of Shakespeare. Maybe it's a Hottentot nursery rhyme. But there is a pattern emerging that is based upon the continuous text of some such analogue. And that analogue is in effect the codebook for those transmissions. And we feel—maybe it's a little mystical—that the analogue is—well, like a bond between the field and base. We see it as having almost a human identity. All we need is one word. Preferably but not necessarily the first. After that it's only a question of time before we identify the rest of the text. Then we'll break those messages wide open."

"So when will that be?" says Mountjoy. "About 1990, I suppose."

"Could be. Could be tonight."

Suddenly it becomes apparent that Artelli means more than he is saying. The hypothetical has become the specific. Brotherhood is the first to take him up on his innuendo.

"So why tonight?" he says. "Why not 1990?"

"There's something very peculiar going on with the Czech transmissions overall," Artelli confesses with a smile. "They're throwing stuff out at random everywhere. Last night Prague Radio put out a world-wide spook call using some phoney professor who doesn't exist. Like a cry for help to somebody who's only in a position to receive spoken word. Then all around the clock we get Mayday calls—for example a high-speed transmission from your Czech Embassy here in London. For four days now, they've been bumping high-speed signals into your mainline BBC transmissions. It's as if the Czechs had lost a kid in the forest and were shouting out any messages that might conceivably get through to him."

Even before Artelli's echoless voice has died, Brotherhood is speaking. "Of *course* there's a London transmission," he declares vehemently, laying his fist on the table like a challenge. "Of course the Czechs are stirring it. My goodness, how many times do we have to put this to you? For two damned years, there have been Czech transmissions in any part of the globe where Pym sets foot and they do, naturally, coincide with his movements. It's a radio game. That's how you play the radio game when you're framing a man. You persist and you repeat and you wait till the other fellow's nerve cracks. The Czechs are not fools. Sometimes I think we are."

Unbothered, Artelli turns his twisted smile to Lederer as if to say, "See if *you* can impress them." At which Grant Lederer allows himself an irrelevant memory of his wife Bee splayed above him in her naked glory, making love to him like all the angels in Heaven.

"Sir Michael, I have to start the other end," Lederer says brightly in a prepared opening, straight at Brammel. "I have to pick up in Vienna just ten days ago, if you don't mind, sir, and track back from there to Washington."

Nobody is looking at him. Start wherever you must, they were saying, and get it over with.

A different Lederer has broken loose inside him and he greets this version of himself with pleasure. I am the bounty hunter, shuttling between London, Washington and Vienna with Pym perpetually in my sights. I am the Lederer who, as Bee vociferously complained when we were safe from microphones, took Pym into bed with us every night, woke sweating with self-doubt in the fitful hours, woke again in the morning with Pym once more firmly between us: "I'll get you, boy. I'll nail you." The Lederer who for the last twelve months—ever since Pym's name began to wink at me from the computer screen—has tracked him first as an abstraction, then as a fellow screwball. Has posed with him on spurious committees as his earnest and admiring colleague. Shared jolly drunken picnics with family Pym in the Vienna woods,

then rushed back to my desk and set to work with fresh
vigour to rip apart what I have just enjoyed. I am the Lederer
who too easily attaches himself, then punishes whatever
holds him tight; the Lederer who is grateful for every wiry
smile and casual pat of encouragement from the great Wexler,
my master, only to round on him minutes later, lampooning
him, degrading him in my overheated mind, punishing him
for being yet another disappointment to me.

Never mind that I am twenty years Pym's junior. What I
recognise in Pym is what I recognise in myself: a spirit so
wayward that, even while I am playing a game of Scrabble
with my kids it can swing between the options of suicide,
rape and assassination. "He's one of *us*, for Christ's sake!"
Lederer wants to scream at the sleeping potentates around
him. "Not one of you. One of *me*. We're howling psycho-
paths, the both of us." But of course Lederer doesn't scream
that or anything else. He talks sanely and wisely about his
computer. And about a man named Petz, also known as
Hampel and Zaworski, who travels almost as much as Lederer
and exactly as much as Pym, but takes more trouble than
either of us to conceal his tracks.

But first, in the same perfectly balanced and dispassion-
ate voice, Lederer describes the situation as it had stood in
August, when it was agreed on both sides—Lederer casts a
respectful glance towards his hero Brotherhood—that the
Pym case should be abandoned and the committee of investigation dissolved.

"But it wasn't abandoned, was it?" Brotherhood says, not
bothering this time to give warning of his interruption. "You
kept a watch going on his house and I don't mind betting you
left a few other meters ticking too."

Lederer glances at Wexler. Wexler scowls into his hands
to say keep me ah out of this. But Lederer has no intention of
fielding that ball, and waits boorishly for Wexler to do it for
him.

"The determination on our side, Jack, was that we
should capitalise the ah existing appropriation of resources,"
Wexler says reluctantly. "We opted here for a gradual reduction of a—ah phased and undramatic running down."

In the silence Brammel gives a sporting smile. "So you
mean you did keep the surveillance going? Is that what
you're saying?"

"On a limited basis only, very low key, very minimal at all levels, Bo."

"I rather thought we said we'd all call off our dogs at once, Harry. We certainly kept *our* half of the bargain, I know."

"The ah Agency decided here to honour that agreement in spirit, Bo, but also in light of what was deemed operationally expedient having regard to ah all the known facts and indicators."

"Thanks," says Mountjoy and tosses down his pencil like a man refusing food.

But this time Wexler bites back and Wexler can do that: "I think you may find your gratitude is well placed, sir," he snaps, and pushes his knuckles combatively across the tip of his nose.

The case of Hans Albrecht Petz, Lederer continues, surfaced six months ago in a context that at first sight had nothing whatever to do with the case against Pym. Petz was simply another Czech journalist who had appeared at an East-West conference in Salzburg and been talent-spotted as a new face. An older man, withdrawn but intelligent, passport details supplied. Lederer put his name on watch and signalled Langley for a routine background check. Langley signalled "nothing recorded against" but warned that it was irregular that a man of Petz's age and profession should not have come to notice. A month later Petz surfaced again in Linz, purportedly to cover an agricultural fair. He didn't hobnob with other journalists, didn't try to ingratiate himself, was seen seldom at the tents and contributed nothing. When Lederer had his press readers comb the Czech press for contributions by Petz, the most they came up with was two paragraphs in the *Socialist Farmer*, signed "H.A.P.," on the limitations of Western heavy tractors. Then, just when Lederer was disposed to forget about him Langley came back with a positive identification. Hans Albrecht Petz was identical with one Alexander Hampel, a Czech intelligence officer, who had recently attended a conference of non-aligned journalists in Athens. Do not approach Petz-Hampel without an authorisation. Stand by for more information.

Hearing himself say "Athens," Lederer has a feeling that the air pressure has dropped inside the safe room.

"Athens *when*?" Brotherhood growls irritably. "How can we follow this stuff without dates?"

Nigel's hair has become a sudden and intense worry to him. He is shaping the greying horns above one ear again and again with his immaculate fingertips while he frowns in pain.

Wexler once more cuts in, and to Lederer's pleasure he is beginning to shed his shyness and respect. "Athens conference was July 15 to 18, Jack. Hampel was sighted on the first day only. He kept his hotel room the three nights but didn't sleep in it once. Paid cash. According to Greek records he arrived Athens on July 14 and never left the country. Most likely he went out on a different passport. Looks like he flew to Corfu. Greek flight lists are the usual pig's breakfast, but looks like he flew to Corfu," he repeats. "By this time we're getting very interested in this man."

"Aren't we running ahead?" says Brammel, whose sense of the proprieties is never sharper than in moments of crisis. "I mean damn it, Harry, it's the same old game. It's guilt by coincidence. It's no different to the radio stuff. If *we* were looking to frame a man, we'd play the same game on them. We'd get some old member of the Firm, a bit tarnished but nothing discreditable, and we'd run him parallel to some poor chap's movements and wait for the opposition to say 'Whoo-hoo, our man's a spy.' Get them to shoot themselves in the foot. Dead easy. All right. Hampel is trailing Pym around. But what's to show that Pym's an active partner?"

"At that point in time nothing, sir," Lederer confesses with false humility, stepping in on Wexler's behalf. "However we had by then established a retrospective link between Pym and Hans Albrecht Petz. At the time of the Salzburg conference, Pym and his wife were attending a music festival there. Petz was staying about two hundred yards from the Pyms' hotel."

"Same story over again," says Brammel doggedly. "It's a set-up. Sticks out a mile. Right, Nigel?"

"It's awfully tenuous actually," Nigel says.

The air pressure again. Maybe the machines kill the oxygen as well as the sound, thinks Lederer. "Do you mind telling us the date when that Athens trace came through?" asks Brotherhood, still on the matter of the timing.

"Ten days ago, sir," says Lederer.

"Bloody slow about advising us, weren't you?"

In anger Wexler finds his words faster: "Well now, Jack,

we were pretty damn reluctant to present you people prematurely with yet another series of computerised coincidences." And to Lederer, his whipping boy: "What the hell are you waiting for?"

It is ten days ago. Lederer is crouched in the communications room in the Station in Vienna. It is night and he has bowed out of two cocktail invitations and one dinner by pretending a light flu. He has phoned Bee and let her hear the excitement in his voice and he has half a mind to rush back and tell her then and there, because he has always told her everything anyway—and sometimes when trade was poor a little more than everything in order to keep the image going. But he holds on to himself. And though his fingers are frozen in the joints from the sheer tension of it, he keeps on typing. First he calls up the most recent schedules of Pym's known movements in and out of Vienna and establishes, almost as a matter of course, that he visited both Salzburg and Linz on precisely the same dates as Petz alias Hampel.

"Linz too?" Brotherhood interrupts sharply.

"Yes, sir!"

"You followed him there, I suppose—contrary to our agreement?"

"No, sir, we did not follow Magnus to Linz. I had my wife Bee call Mary Pym. Bee elicited the information in the course of an innocent conversation, woman to woman, on another matter, Mr. Brotherhood."

"He might still not have gone to Linz. Could have told his wife a cover story."

Lederer is at pains to concede that this is possible but gently suggests that it hardly matters, sir, in view of Langley's signal of that same night, which signal he now reads aloud to his assembled Anglo-American lords of intelligence. "It arrived on my desk five minutes after we had the Linz connection, sir. I quote: 'Petz-Hampel also identical with Jerzy Zaworski, born Carlsbad 1925, West German journalist of Czech origin who made nine legal journeys to United States in 1981, '82.'"

"Perfect," says Brammel under his breath.

"Birthdates are of course approximations in these cases," Lederer continues undaunted. "It is our experience that alias passports have the tendency to give the bearer a year or two."

The signal is hardly on Lederer's desk, he says, before he is typing in the dates and destinations of Herr Zaworski's visits to America. And then it was—says Lederer, though not in as many words—that with one touch of the button everything came together, continents merged, three journalists in their late fifties became a single Czech spy of uncertain age, and Grant Lederer III, thanks to the flawless insulation of the signals room, was able to scream "Hallelujah!" and "Bee, I love you!" to the padded walls.

"Every American city visited by Petz-Hampel-Zaworski in 1981 and 1982 was visited by Pym on the same dates," Lederer intones. "During those dates the relevant clandestine transmissions from the Czech Embassy roof were discontinued, the reason in our estimation being that a personal encounter was occurring between the agent in the field and his visiting controller. Radio transmissions were accordingly superfluous."

"It's beautiful," says Brammel. "I'd like to find the Czech intelligence officer who thought this one up and give him my private Oscar immediately."

With a pained discretion Mick Carver lifts a briefcase gently to the table and extracts a bunch of folders.

"This is Langley's profile as of now on Petz-Hampel-Zaworski, Pym's presumed controller," he explains in the patient manner of a salesman bent on showing off a new technology, despite the obstruction of the older element. "We expect a couple more updates in the next immediate while, maybe even tonight. Bo, when does Magnus return to Vienna, do you mind telling us, please?"

Brammel like all the rest of them is peering into his folder, so it is natural he should not reply at once. "When we tell him to, I suppose," he says carelessly, turning a page. "Not before, that's for certain. As you say, his father's death was rather providential. Old man left quite a mess, I gather. Magnus has a lot to sort out."

"Where is he now?" says Wexler.

Brammel looks at his watch. "Having dinner, I should imagine. Nearly time, isn't it?"

"Where's he staying?" Wexler insists.

Brammel smiles. "Now Harry, I don't think I'm going to tell you that. We do have some rights in our own country, you know, and your chaps have been a bit overeager on the surveillance stakes."

Wexler is nothing if not stubborn. "Last we heard of him, he was at London Airport checking in to his flight to Vienna. Our information is he'd wrapped up his affairs over here and was heading back to his post. What the hell happened?"

Nigel has clasped his hands together. He sets them, still clasped, on the table to indicate that, small or not, he is speaking. "You haven't been following him over here too, have you? That really would be going it."

Wexler rubs his chin. His expression is rueful but undefeated. He turns again to Brammel. "Bo, we need a piece of this. If this is a Czech deception operation it's the damnedest, most ingenious case I ever heard of."

"Pym is a most ingenious officer," Brammel countered. "He's been a thorn in the Czechs' side for thirty years. He's worth a lot of trouble on their part."

"Bo, you've got to pull Pym in and you've got to interrogate the living shit out of him. If you don't, we're going to go around and around this thing till we've all got grey hairs and some of us are in our graves. Those are our secrets he's been fooling with as well as yours. We have some very heavy questions to put to him and some fine people trained to put them."

"Harry, you have my word that when the moment is ripe, you and your people shall have as much of him as you want."

"Maybe the moment's right now," Wexler says, sticking out his jaw. "Maybe we should be there from when he starts to sing. Hit him while he's soft."

"And maybe you should trust sufficiently in our judgment to bide your time," Nigel purrs sleekly in reply, and casts Wexler a very reassuring glance over the top of his reading spectacles.

A most strange impulse, meanwhile, is taking hold of Lederer. He feels it rising in him and can no more check himself than if it were an urge to vomit. In this self-renewing cycle of compromise and double-think he needs to externalise the secret affinity between himself and Magnus. To assert his monopoly of understanding of the man and underline the personal nature of his triumph. To be at the centre still, and not shoved out to the bleachers where he came from.

"Sir, you mentioned Pym's father," he bursts out, talking straight at Brammel. "Sir, I know about that father. I have a father who is not in certain ways dissimilar, only in degree. Mine's a small-time iffy lawyer and honesty is not his strong suit. No, sir. But that father of Pym's was a total crook. A con artist. Our psychiatrists have assembled a really disturbing profile of that man. Do you know that when Richard T. Pym was in New York he faked a whole *empire* of bogus companies? Borrowed money from the most unlikely people, really some important people? I mean listed. There's a serious strain of controlled instability here. We have a paper on this." He was overrunning himself but couldn't stop. "I mean Jesus, do you know Magnus made the most wild pass at my own wife? I don't grudge him that. She's an attractive woman. What I mean is the guy's everywhere. He's all over the place. That English cool of his is just veneer."

Not for the first time Lederer has just committed suicide. Nobody hears him, nobody shouts "Wow, you don't say!" And when Brammel speaks, his voice is as cold as charity and as late in arriving.

"Yes, well, I always assume that businessmen are crooks, don't you, Harry? I'm sure we all do." He glances round the table at everyone but Lederer and comes back to Wexler. "Harry, why don't you and I get our heads together for an hour, shall we? If there's to be a hostile interrogation at some stage, I'm sure we should agree on some guidelines in advance, Nigel, why don't you come along to see fair play? The rest of us—" His gaze falls on Brotherhood and he awards him a particularly confiding smile. "Well, we'll simply say see you all later. You will leave in pairs, won't you, when you've done your reading? Not all at once, it scares the local peasants. Thank you."

Brammel leaves, Wexler waddles boldly after him, a man who has made his point and doesn't care who knows it. Nigel waits till they have all left, then like a busy undertaker hastens round the table and takes Brotherhood's arm in a fraternal gesture.

"Jack," he whispers. "Well put, well played. We absolutely stymied them. A word in your ear away from the microphones, yes?"

*   *   *

It was early afternoon. The safe house where they had met was a pseudo-Regency villa with jewellers' screens across the windows. A warm fog hung over the gravel drive and Lederer loitered in it like a murderer waiting for Brotherhood's hulk to fill the lighted porch. Mountjoy and Dorney passed by him without a word. Carver, accompanied by Artelli and his briefcase, was more explicit. "I have to live here, Lederer. I just hope that this time either you make it stick or they post the hell out of you."

Bastard, thought Lederer.

At last Jack Brotherhood emerged, speaking cryptically to Nigel. Lederer watched them jealously. Nigel turned and went back inside. Brotherhood walked forward.

"Mr. Brotherhood, sir? Jack? It's me. Lederer."

Brotherhood came slowly to a halt. He was wearing his usual grimy raincoat and a muffler, and he had lit one of his yellow cigarettes.

"What do you want?"

"Jack. I want to tell you that whatever happens, and whatever he's done or not done, I'm sorry it's him and I'm sorry it's you."

"Probably hasn't done anything at all. Probably recruited one of the other side and hasn't told us, knowing him. My guess is you've got the story inside out."

"Would he do that, Magnus? Play a lone hand with the enemy and not tell anybody? Jesus, that's dynamite! If I ever tried that, Langley would skin me."

Unbidden, he fell in beside Brotherhood. A policeman stood at the gate. They passed the Royal Horse Artillery Barracks. The sound of hoofs clattered at them from the parade ground but the horses were hidden in the fog. Brotherhood was striding fast. Lederer had difficulty keeping up.

"I feel really bad, Jack," Lederer confessed. "Nobody seems to understand what it's been like for me to have to do this to a friend. It's not just Magnus. It's Bee and Mary and the kids and everybody. Becky and Tom are real sweethearts. It kind of made all of us consider ourselves in many ways. There's a pub right here. Can I buy you a drink?"

"Got to see a man about a dog, I'm afraid."

"Can I drop you somewhere? I have a car and driver right here around the corner."

"Prefer to walk if you don't mind."

"Magnus told me a lot about you, Jack. I guess he broke some of the rules but that's how we were. We really shared. It was a great liaison. That's the crazy thing. We really *were* the Special Relationship. And I believe in that. I believe in the Anglo-Saxon alliance, the Atlantic Pact, the whole bit. You remember that burglary you and Magnus did together in Warsaw?"

"Don't think I do, I'm afraid."

"Oh come on, Jack. How you lowered him through a skylight? Like in the Bible? And you had these fake Polish cops downstairs on the doorstep in case the quarry came home unexpectedly? He said you were like a father to him. You know how he referred to you once? 'Grant,' he said to me. 'Jack is the true champion of the great game.' You know what I feel? I think if Magnus's writing had ever worked for him, he'd have been okay. There's just too much inside him. He has to put it somewhere." He was breathing a little hastily between his words, but he insisted on keeping up; he had to get it right with Brotherhood. "You see, sir, I've read a great deal recently about the creativity of the criminal mind."

"Oh he's a criminal now, is he?"

"Please. Let me quote you something I read." They had reached a crossing and were waiting for the lights. "'What is the difference, in morality, between the totally anarchic criminality of the artist, which is endemic in all fine creative minds, and the artistry of the criminal?'"

"Can't do it, I'm afraid. Too many long words. Sorry about that."

"Hell, Jack, we're licensed crooks, that's all I'm saying. What's our racket? Know what our racket is? It is to place our larcenous natures at the service of the state. So I mean why should I feel different about Magnus just because maybe he got the mix a little wrong? I can't. Magnus is still exactly the same man I spent these great times with! And I'm still the same man who had these times with Magnus. Nothing's changed except we've landed on different sides of the net. You know we talked about defection once? Where we would go if we ever cut and run? Left our wives and kids and work, and just stepped into the blue? We were that close, Jack. We literally thought the unthinkable. We really did. We were amazing."

They had entered St. John's Wood High Street, and were heading towards Regent's Park. Brotherhood's pace had increased.

"Where did he say he'd go, then?" Brotherhood snapped. "Back to Washington? Moscow?"

"Home. He said there was only ever one place. Home. I mean this shows you. The man loves his country, Mr. Brotherhood. Magnus is no renegade."

"Didn't know he had a home," said Brotherhood. "Vagrant childhood, he always told me."

"Home is a little seaside town in Wales. It has a very ugly Victorian church. It has a very strict landlady who shuts him in at 10 P.M. And one of these days Magnus is going to lock himself in that upstairs room and write his ass off till he comes out with all twelve volumes of Pym's answer to Proust."

Brotherhood might not have heard. He strode faster.

"Home is childhood re-created, Mr. Brotherhood. If defection is a self-renewal, it requires also a rebirth."

"That his stupid phrase or yours?"

"Mine and his equally. We discussed all this and we discussed much, much more. Know why so many defectors redefect? We had that one straight too. It's in and out of the womb all the time. Have you ever noticed that about defectors—the one common factor in all that crazy band? They're immature. Forgive me, they are *literally* mother-fuckers."

"Have a name, this place?"

"Pardon?"

"This Welsh paradise place of his. What's it called?"

"He never said a name. All he said was it was near the castle where he grew up with his mother, in an area with great houses, where he and his mother used to go to the hunts, dance at the Christmas balls and mix quite democratically with the servants."

"Have you ever come across Czechs using back numbers of newspapers?" Brotherhood asked.

Momentarily thrown by the change of tack, Lederer was obliged to pause and consider.

"It's a case a colleague of mine is running," Brotherhood said. "He asked me. Czech agent always grubbing around for last week's newspapers before he takes a walk up the road. Why would he do that?"

"I'll tell you why. It's a standard thing," said Lederer, recovering. "Old hat, but standard. We had a Joe like that, a double. The Czechs trained him for days, just in how to roll exposed film into newspaper. Took him out into the streets at night, made him find a dark area. Poor bastard nearly froze his fingers off. It was twenty below."

"I said back numbers," Brotherhood said.

"Sure. There's two ways. One way they use the day of the month, the other way they use the day of the week. Day of the month is a nightmare: thirty-one standard messages to be learned by heart. It's the eighteenth of the month so it's 'Meet me behind the gentleman's convenience in Brno at nine-thirty and don't be late.' It's the sixth so 'Where the hell's my monthly pay cheque?'" He giggled breathlessly but Brotherhood did not reciprocate. "The days of the week, that's a shortened version of the same thing."

"Thanks, I'll pass it on," said Brotherhood, drawing to a halt at last.

"Sir, I can imagine no greater honour than taking you out to dinner tonight," Lederer said, now quite desperate for Brotherhood's absolution. "I cast aspersions on one of your men, that's duty. But if I were ever able to separate the personal and the official sides, I'd be a happy man, sir. Jack?"

The taxi was already drawing up.

"What is it?"

"Do you think you could give Magnus a message for me—a friendly one?"

"What is it?"

"Tell him any time—when it's over—any place. I'll be there as his friend."

With a nod Brotherhood climbed into the taxi and rode away before Lederer could hear his destination.

What Lederer did next should go into history, if not into the larger history of the Pym affair then at least into his own exasperating personal chronicle of seeing everything with perfect vision and being repeatedly dismissed as an unwelcome prophet. Lederer struggled into a phone box intending to call Carver, only to discover he had no English coins. He dived into the Mulberry Arms, fought his way to the bar and bought a beer he did not want in order to have change. He returned to the phone box to find it didn't work, so he pelted back down the road in search of his driver, who, having watched Lederer march by with Brotherhood, had assumed he was no longer required and had driven home to Battersea where he had a friend. At nine o'clock, Lederer burst in upon Carver at the U.S. Embassy, where Carver was drafting a signal on the day's events.

"They're lying!" Lederer shouted.

"Who are?"

"The fucking Brits! Pym's flown the coop. They don't know where he is from the man in the fucking moon. I asked Brotherhood to pass him this totally subversive message and he sweet-mouthed me to keep me off the track. Pym jumped ship at London Airport and they're looking for him the same way we are. Those Czech radio transmissions are kosher. The Brits are looking for him, we're looking for him. And the fucking Czechs are looking for him all over. Listen to me!"

Carver had listened. Carver continued to listen. He took Lederer through his conversation with Brotherhood and concluded it should not have taken place and that Lederer had exceeded his competence. He did not say this to Lederer but he made a note of it, and later that night in a separate telegram to the Agency's personnel people he took care that this note was added to Lederer's file. At the same time he accepted that Lederer might well have stumbled upon the truth, even if by the wrong route, and said this also. Thus Carver covered his back all ways, while at the same time knifing an unpleasing interloper. Never bad.

"The British are not playing this straight," he confided to people he knew at the top. "I am going to have to watch this very carefully."

The Headmaster's study smelt of killing bottles. Mr. Caird, though he hated violence, was a passionate lepidopterist. A grim portrait of our founder G. F. Grimble glowered down on cracked leather chairs. In one of them sat Tom. Brotherhood sat opposite him. Tom was looking at the photograph from the Langley folder on Petz-Hampel-Zaworski. Brotherhood was looking at Tom. Mr. Caird had shaken Brotherhood's hand and left them to it.

"That the one who walked your dad round the cricket ground in Corfu?" said Brotherhood, watching Tom.

"Yes, sir."

"You weren't far wrong with your description then, were you?"

"No, sir."

"I thought you'd be amused."

"I am."

"He doesn't limp in the photograph, so he doesn't look so hobbly. Had any more letters from your dad? Phone calls?"

"No, sir."

"Written to him?"

"Don't know where to send it, sir."

"Why don't you give it to me?"

Tom delved inside his grey pullover and unearthed a sealed envelope with no name or address on it. Brotherhood took it from him and took back the photograph too.

"That inspector fellow hasn't been back to trouble you, has he?"

"No, sir."

"Anyone else been?"

"Not really, sir."

"What does that mean?"

"It's just so odd you coming tonight."

"Why?"

"It's maths prep," said Tom. "It's my worst thing."

"I expect you'd like to get back to it then." He took Pym's crushed letter from his pocket and handed it across the gap. "Thought you might like this back, too. It's a fine letter. You should be proud."

"Thank you, sir."

"Your dad talks there about an Uncle Syd. Who's that? 'If you're ever down on your luck,' he says, 'or if you need a warm meal and a laugh or a bed for the night, don't forget your Uncle Syd.' Who's Uncle Syd, when he's at home?"

"Syd Lemon, sir."

"Where does he live?"

"Surbiton, sir. By a railway."

"Old man, is he? Youngish?"

"He looked after Dad when he was small. He was a

friend of Granddad's. He's got a wife called Meg but she's dead."

They both stood up.

"Dad's still all right, isn't he, sir?" said Tom.

Brotherhood's shoulders stiffened. "You're to go to your mother, d'you hear? Your mother or me. No one else. That's if things get tough." He pulled an old leatherbound box from his jacket pocket. "This is for you."

Tom opened it. A medal lay inside with a piece of ribbon attached to it—crimson with narrow dark blue stripes on either side.

"What did you get it for?" said Tom.

"Sticking out dark nights alone." A bell was ringing. "Now run along and do your job," said Brotherhood.

The night was foul. Gusts of rain tore across the windscreen as Brotherhood negotiated the narrow lane. The car was a souped-up Ford from the Firm's pool and he had only to stroke the accelerator for it to lunge towards the hedge. Magnus Pym, he thought: traitor and Czech spy. If I know, why don't they? How many times, in how many ways, do they need the proof before they act on it? A pup loomed suddenly out of the rain. He pulled into the forecourt and drank a scotch before going to the phone. Call me on my private line, old boy, Nigel had said expansively.

"The man in the picture is our friend from Corfu. No question about it," Brotherhood reported.

"You're sure?"

"I'm sure. The boy's sure. I'm sure he's sure. When are you going to give the order to evacuate?"

A muffled crackle while Nigel put his fist over the mouthpiece the other end. But not, presumably, the earpiece.

"I want those Joes out, Nigel. Get them out. Tell Bo to get his head out of the sand and give the order."

Long silence.

"We're tuning in at 0500 tomorrow," said Nigel. "Come back to London and get some sleep." He rang off.

London was east. Brotherhood headed south, following the signs to Reading. In every operation there is an above the line and a below the line. Above the line is what you do by the book. Below the line is how you do the job.

The letter to Tom was postmarked Reading, he rehearsed. Posted Monday night or first thing Tuesday morning.

He rang me on Monday evening, Kate had said.

He rang me on Monday evening, Belinda had said.

Reading station resembled a low redbrick stable set at one end of a tawdry square. A poster in the concourse gave the times of coaches to and from Heathrow. That's what you did, he thought. That's what I'd do. At Heathrow you put up your smokescreen about planes to Scotland, then you hopped a coach to Reading to keep things nice and private. He considered the coach stop, then cast a long slow look around the square until his eye fell at last on the ticket kiosk. He wandered over to it. The clerk wore a small metal wheel in the buttonhole of his jacket. Brotherhood put five pounds in the tray.

"I'd like some change, please, to telephone."

"Sorry, mate. Can't do," the clerk said, and went on with his newspaper.

"You could do it last Monday night though, couldn't you?" The clerk's head came up fast.

Brotherhood's office pass was green with a red diagonal line drawn in transparent ink across his photograph. A notice on the back said that if found it should be returned to the Ministry of Defence. The clerk looked at both sides of it and gave it back.

"I haven't seen one like that before," he said.

"Tall fellow," Brotherhood said. "Carried a black briefcase. Probably wore a black tie as well. Well spoken, nice manner. Had a lot of calls to make. Remember?"

The clerk vanished, to be replaced a minute later by a tubby Indian with exhausted, visionary eyes.

"Were you on duty here Monday evening?" Brotherhood said.

"Sir, I was the man who was on duty on Monday evening," he replied warily, as if he might not be that man any more.

"A pleasant gentleman in a black tie."

"I know, I know. My colleague has acquainted me with all the details."

"How much change did you give him?"

"Good heavens above, what does that matter? If I elect to give a man change, that is my personal preference, a matter for my pocket and my conscience that has nothing to do with anybody."

"How much change did you give him?"

"Five pounds exactly. Five he wanted, five he got."

"What in?"

"Fifty p's exclusively. He wished to make no local calls at all. I questioned him about this and he was entirely consistent in his answers. I mean where is the hardship in this? Where is the sinister element?"

"What did he pay you with?"

"To my recollection, he gave me a ten-pound note. I cannot be completely certain but that is my imperfect recollection: that he gave me a ten-pound note from his wallet, accompanied by the words 'Here you are.'"

"Did the ten pounds cover his rail ticket too?"

"This was totally unproblematical. The price of a second-class single fare to London is four pounds and thirty pence exactly. I gave him ten fifties and the balance in small change. Now have you further questions? I seriously hope not. Police, police, you know. If it's one enquiry a day, it's half a dozen."

"Is this the man?" said Brotherhood. He was holding a photograph showing Pym and Mary at their wedding.

"But that is you, sir. In the background. I think you are giving the bride away. Are you sure you are engaged in an official enquiry? This is a most irregular photograph."

"Is this the man?"

"Well I'm not saying it is not, put it that way."

Pym would take him off perfectly, thought Brotherhood. Pym would catch that accent to a tee. He stood at the barrier studying the timetable of trains leaving Reading station after eleven o'clock on a weekday night. You went anywhere except to London because London is where you bought your ticket to. You had time. Time to make your maudlin telephone calls. Time to write your maudlin letter to Tom. Your plane left Heathrow at eight-forty without you. By eight o'clock latest you had done your turnaround. By eight-fifteen, according to the testimony of the airport travel clerk, you had put up your little smokescreen about planes to Scotland. After that you hightailed it to the Reading-bound coach, pulled down the brim of your hat and said goodbye to the airport as quickly and quietly as you knew how.

Brotherhood walked back to the coach timetable. Time to kill, he repeated to himself. Say you caught the eight-thirty from Heathrow. Between nine- and ten-thirty there were half a dozen trains in both directions out of Reading but you caught none of them. You wrote to Tom instead. Where from? He went back to the square. In the neon-lit pub there. In the fish-and-chip shop. In the all-night café where the tarts sit. Somewhere in this dowdy square you sat down and told Tom what to do when the world ended.

The telephone box stood at the station entrance, under a bright light that was supposed to deter vandals. Smashed glass and paper cups cluttered the floor. Graffiti and promises of love defaced the awful grey paint. But it was a good telephone, for all that. You could watch the whole square from it while you said your goodbyes. A mail box was let into the wall close by. And that's where you posted it, saying whatever happens, remember that I love you. After which you went to Wales. Or to Scotland. Or you popped over to Norway to watch the migration of the reindeer. Or you hightailed it to Canada and prepared to eat out of tins. Or you did something that was all these things and none of them, in an upstairs room with a view of the church and the sea.

Reaching his flat in Shepherd Market, Brotherhood was still not quite done. The Firm's official police contact was a Detective Superintendent Bellows at Scotland Yard. Brotherhood rang his home number.

"What have you got for me on that ennobled gentleman I mentioned to you this morning?" he asked, and to his relief detected no note of reservation in Bellows's voice as he read him out the details. Brotherhood wrote them down.

"Can you do me another one for tomorrow?"

"It'll be a pleasure."

"Lemon, believe it or not. First name Syd or Sydney. Old chap, widowed, lives in Surbiton, close to a railway."

Reluctantly Brotherhood phoned Head Office and asked for Nigel of Secretariat. Belatedly, and in the teeth of more larcenous instincts, he knew he must conform. Just as he had conformed this afternoon when he poured scorn on the Americans. Just as in the end he had always conformed, not out of slavishness but because he believed in the fight and,

despite everything, the team. A lot of atmospherics followed
while Nigel was located. They went over to scramble.

"What's the matter?" said Nigel rudely.

"The book Artelli was talking about. The analogue, he
called it."

"I thought he was perfectly ridiculous. Bo is going to
take it to the *highest* level."

"Tell them to try Grimmelshausen's *Simplicissimus*. On a
hunch. Tell them to be sure to use an early text."

A long silence. More atmospherics. He's in the bath,
thought Brotherhood. He's in bed with a woman, or whatever he likes.

"Now how are you spelling that?" said Nigel warily.

10

Once again a willed brightness was overtaking Pym as he
listened to the many voices in his mind. To be king, he
repeated to himself. To look with favour on this child that was
myself. To love his defects and his strivings, and pity his
simplicity.

If there was such a thing as a perfect time in Pym's life, a
time when all the versions of himself were appreciated and
playing nicely and he would never want for anything again,
then surely it was his first few terms at Oxford University
whither Rick had dispatched him as a necessary interlude to
having him appointed Lord Chief Justice and thus securing
him a place among the Highest in the Land. The relationship
between the two pals had never been better. Following Axel's
departure, Pym's final lonely months in Bern had seen a
dramatic flowering of their correspondence. With Frau Ollinger
barely speaking to him and Herr Ollinger increasingly absorbed
in the problems of Ostermundigen, Pym walked the city
streets alone, much as he had done at the beginning. But at
night, with the wall beside him silent, he penned long and
intimate letters of affection to Belinda and his one true
anchor, Rick. Stimulated by his attentions, Rick's letters in

reply took on a sudden stylishness and prosperity. The anguished missives from outer England ceased. The stationery thickened, stabilised and acquired illustrious headings. First the Richard T. Pym Endeavour Company wrote to him from Cardiff, advising him that the Clouds of Misfortune which had appeared to Gather had been swept Away one and All by a Providence I can only regard as crackerjack. A month later, the Pym & Partners Property and Finance Enterprise of Cheltenham was advising him that certain Steps were now in Hand for Pym's future with a view to Insuring that he would never want for Anything again. Most recently a printed card of regal elegance was pleased to announce that following a Merger Agreeable to all Parties, matters relating to the above Companies should henceforth be referred to the Pym & Permanent Mutual Property Trust (Nassau), of Park Lane W.

Jack Brotherhood and Wendy treated him to a farewell fondue on the Firm; Sandy came and Jack gave Pym two bottles of whisky and hoped their paths would cross. Herr Ollinger accompanied him to the railway station and they drank a last coffee. Frau Ollinger stayed home. Elisabeth served them but she was distracted. She had put on bulk around the tummy, though she wore no ring. As the train pulled out of the station, Pym took a look downward at the circus and its elephant house, then a look upward at the university and its green dome and by the time he reached Basel he knew that Bern had sunk with all hands. Axel was illegal. The Swiss informed against him. I was lucky to get out myself. Standing in the corridor somewhere south of Paris he observed tears on his cheeks and vowed not to be a spy again. At Victoria Mr. Cudlove was waiting for him with a new Bentley.

"What do we call you now, sir? Doctor or Professor?"

"Just Magnus will do fine," said Pym handsomely as they pumped hands. "How's Ollie?"

The new Reichskanzlei in Park Lane was a monument to prosperous stability. The bust of TP was back in place. Law books, glass doors and a new jockey with the Pym colours winked assurance at him while he waited on leather cushions for a Lovely to admit him to the State Apartments.

"Our Chairman will see you now, Mr. Magnus."

They bear-hugged, both for a moment too proud to speak. Rick palmed Pym's back, moulded his cheeks and wiped away his tears. Mr. Muspole, Perce and Syd were summoned by separate buzzers to pay homage to the returning hero. Mr. Muspole produced a sheaf of documents and Rick read the best bits of them aloud. Pym was appointed International Legal Adviser for life and awarded five hundred pounds a year to be reconsidered as appropriate on the strict understanding he worked for no other firm. His law studies at Oxford were thus taken care of; he need never want for anything again. A second Lovely brought bubbly. She seemed to have nothing else to do. Everybody drank the health of the company's newest employee. "Come on, Titch, let's have it in the parley-voo!" cried Syd excitedly, and Pym obliged by saying something fatuous in German. Father and son hugged again, Rick wept again and said if only he had had the advantages. The same evening, at a mansion in Amersham called The Furlong, his homecoming was again celebrated by an intimate party of two hundred old friends, few of whom Pym had seen before, including the heads of several world-famous corporations, leading stars of stage and screen and several Great Barristers who one by one took him aside and claimed the credit for obtaining a place for him at Oxford. The party over, Pym lay wakefully in his fourposter listening to the expensive slamming of car doors.

"You did a fine job out there in Switzerland, son," said Rick from the dark where he had been standing for some while. "You fought a good fight. It's been noticed. Enjoy your dinner?"

"It was really good."

"A lot of people said to me, 'Rickie,' they said, 'you've got to get that boy back. Those foreigners will make a whore of him.' You know what I said to them?"

"What did you say to them?"

"I said I had faith in you. Have you got faith in me, son?"

"Masses."

"What do you think of the house?"

"It's wonderful," said Pym.

"It's yours. It's in your name. I bought it from the Duke of Devonshire."

"Thank you very much, anyway."

"Nobody can ever take it away from you, son. You can be twenty. You can be fifty. Where your old man is, that's home. Did you talk to Maxie Moore at all?"

"I don't think I did."

"The fellow who scored the winning goal for Arsenal against Spurs? Go on. Of course you did. What did you think of Blottsie?"

"Which one was he?"

"G. W. Blott? One of the most famous names in the retail grocery world you'll ever meet. That marvellous dignity. He'll be a lord one day. So will you. What do you think of Sylvia?"

Pym recalled a bulky, middle-aged woman in blue with an aristocratic smile that could have been the bubbly.

"She's nice," he said cautiously.

Rick seized on the word as if he had been hunting for it half his life. "*Nice*. That's what she is. She's a damned nice woman with two first-class husbands to her credit."

"She's really attractive, even for my age."

"Did you get yourself involved out there? There's nothing can't be put right in this world by good pals."

"Just the odd affair. Nothing serious."

"No woman's ever going to come between us, son. Once those Oxford girls know who your old man is, they'll be after you like a pack of wolves. Promise you'll keep yourself clean."

"I promise."

"And learn your law as if your life depended on it? You're being paid, remember."

"I promise."

"Well, then."

The stealthy weight of Rick's body landed like a sixteen-stone cat at Pym's side. He pulled Pym's head towards his own until their two cheeks were pressed stubble to stubble. His fingers found the fatty parts of Pym's chest under his pyjama top and kneaded them. He wept. Pym wept too, thinking again of Axel.

The next day Pym moved hastily into his college, claiming a variety of urgent reasons for going up two weeks early. Declining the services of Mr. Cudlove, he travelled by bus and gazed in mounting wonder on flowing hills and mown cornfields glowing in the autumn sunlight. The bus passed through country towns and villages, down lanes of russet beech trees and dancing hedgerows, till slowly the golden stone of Oxford replaced the Buckinghamshire brick, the hills flattened and the city's spires lifted into the thickening rays of afternoon. He dismounted, thanked the driver, and drifted through the enchanted streets, asking his way at every corner, forgetting, asking again, not caring. Girls in bell skirts skimmed past him on their bicycles. Dons in billowing gowns clutched their mortarboards against the wind; bookshops beckoned to him like houses of delight. He was lugging a suitcase but it weighed no more than a hat. The college porter said staircase five, across the Chapel Quad. He climbed the winding wooden stairs until he saw his name written on an old oak door: M. R. Pym. He pushed the door and saw darkness and another door beyond. He pushed the second door and closed the first. He found the switch and closed the second door on his whole life till now. I am safe inside the city walls. Nobody will find me, nobody will recruit me. He tripped over a case of legal tomes. A vaseful of orchids wished him "Godspeed, son, from your best pal." A Harrods invoice debited them to the newest Pym consortium.

University was a conventional sort of place in those days, Tom. You would have a good laugh at the way we dressed and talked and the things we put up with, though we were the blessed of the earth. They shut us in at night and let us out in the morning. They gave us girls for tea but not for dinner and God knows not for breakfast. The college scouts doubled as the Dean's Joes and ratted on us if we broke the rules. Our parents had won the war—or most people's had—and since we couldn't beat them our best revenge was to imitate them. Some of us had done national service. The rest of us dressed like officers anyway, hoping no one would notice the difference. With his first cheque, Pym bought a dark blue blazer with brass buttons. With his second, a pair of cavalry twill trousers and a blue tie with crowns that radiated patriotism. After that there was a moratorium because the third cheque took a month to clear. Pym polished his brown shoes, sported a handkerchief in his sleeve, and groomed his hair like a gentleman's. And when Sefton Boyd, who was a year ahead of him, feasted him in the exalted Gridiron Club, Pym made such strides with the language that in no time he was talking it like a native, referring to his inferiors as Charlies, and to our own lot as the Chaps, and pronouncing bad things Harry

Awful, and vulgar things Poggy, and good things Fairly Decent.

"Where did you pick up that Vincent's tie, by the by?" Sefton Boyd asked him kindly enough as they sauntered down the Broad for a game of shove-ha'penny with some Charlies at the Trinity pub. "Didn't know you were a boxing blue in your spare time."

Pym said he had admired it in the window of a shop called Hall Brothers in the High Street.

"Well, put it on ice for a bit, I should. You can always get it out again when they elect you." Carelessly he put a hand on Pym's shoulder. "And while you're about it, get your scout to sew some ordinary buttons on that jacket. Don't want people thinking you're the Pretender to the Hungarian throne, do we?"

Once more Pym embraced everything, loved everything, stretched every sinew to excel. He joined the societies, paid more subscriptions than there were clubs, became college secretary of everything from the Philatelists to the Euthanasians. He wrote sensitive articles for university journals, lobbied distinguished speakers, met them at the railway station, dined them at the society's expense and brought them safely to empty lecture halls. He played college rugger, college cricket, rowed in his college eight, got drunk in college bar and was by turn rootlessly cynical towards society and stalwartly British and protective of it, depending on whom he happened to be with. He threw himself afresh upon the German muse and scarcely faltered when he discovered that at Oxford she was about five hundred years older than she had been in Bern, and that anything written within living memory was unsound. But he quickly overcame his disappointment. This is quality, he reasoned. This is academia. In no time he was immersing himself in the garbled texts of mediaeval minstrels with the same energy that, in an earlier life, he had bestowed on Thomas Mann. By the end of his first term he was an enthusiastic student of Middle and Old High German. By the end of his second he could recite the *Hildebrandslied* and intone Bishop Ulfila's Gothic translation of the Bible in his college bar to the delight of his modest court. By the middle of his third he was romping in the Parnassian fields of comparative and putative philology, where youthful creativity has ever had its fling. And when he found himself briefly transported into the perilous modernisms of the seventeenth century, he was pleased to be able to report, in a twenty-page assault on the upstart Grimmelshausen, that the poet had marred his work with popular moralising and undermined his validity by fighting on both sides in the Thirty Years' War. As a final swipe he suggested that Grimmelshausen's obsession with false names cast doubt upon his authorship.

I shall stay here for ever, he decided. I shall become a don and be hero to my pupils. To entrench this ambition he worked up a selective stammer and a self-denying smile, and at night sat long hours at his desk keeping himself awake on Nescafé. When daylight came he ventured downstairs unshaven so that all might see the lines of study etched upon his eager face. It was on one such morning that he was surprised to find a case of vintage port waiting for him, accompanied by a note from the Regius Professor of Law:

> "Dear Mr. Pym,
>
>   "Yesterday, Messrs. Harrods delivered the enclosed to me, together with a charming letter from your father which appears to commend you to me as my pupil. While it is not my habit to turn away such generosity, I fear that the gesture is better directed to my colleague in the Modern Languages school, since I understand from your Senior Tutor that you are reading German."

For half the day, Pym did not know where to put himself. He turned up his collar, wandered miserably in Christ Church Meadows, cut his tutorial for fear of being arrested and wrote letters to Belinda who was working as an unpaid secretary to a London charity. In the afternoon he sat in a dark cinema. In the evening, still in despair, he carted his guilty parcel to Balliol, determined to tell Sefton Boyd the whole story. But by the time he got there he had thought of a better version.

"Some rich shit in Merton is trying to get me to go to bed with him," he protested, in the tone of healthy exasperation he had been practising all the way to the gates. "He sent me a Harry great case of port to buy me over."

If Sefton Boyd doubted him he did not let it show.

Between them they carried their booty to the Gridiron Club where six of them drank it at a sitting, fitfully toasting Pym's virginity till morning. A few days later Pym was elected a member. When the vacation came he took a job selling carpets at a shop in Watford. A lawyers' vacation course, he told Rick. Similar to the holiday seminars he had attended in Switzerland. In reply Rick sent him a five-page homily, warning him against airy-fairy intellectuals, and a cheque for fifty pounds that bounced.

A summer term was devoted entirely to women. Pym had never been so in love. He swore his love to every girl he met, he was so anxious to overcome what he assumed would be their poor opinion of him. In intimate cafés, on park benches or strolling beside the Isis on glorious afternoons, Pym held their hands and stared into their puzzled eyes and told them everything he had ever dreamed of hearing. If he felt awkward today with the one, he swore he would feel better tomorrow with the next, for women of his own age and intelligence were a novelty to him and he became disconcerted when they did not assume a subordinate position. If he felt awkward with all of them he wrote to Belinda, who never failed to reply. His love-talk was never duplicated; he was not a cynic. To one he spoke of his ambitions to return to the Swiss stage, where he had been such a runaway success. She should learn German and come with him, he said; they would act together. To another he painted himself as a poet of the futile and described his persecution at the hands of the murderous Swiss police.

"But I thought they were so terrifically neutral and humane!" she cried, appalled by his descriptions of the beatings he had received before being marched over the border into Austria.

"Not if you're different," Pym said grimly. "Not if you refuse to conform with the bourgeois norm. Those Swissies have two laws that really matter out there. Thou shalt not be poor and thou shalt not be foreign. I was both."

"You've really been through it," she said. "It's fantastic. I haven't done anything at all."

And to a third he portrayed himself as a novelist of the tortured life, with work that he had yet to show his publishers, all stashed away in an old filing cabinet at home.

One day Jemima came. Her mother had sent her to an Oxford secretarial college to learn typing and go to dances. She was long-legged and distraught like someone always late. She was more beautiful than ever.

"I love you," Pym told her, handing her bits of fruitcake in his room. "Wherever I was, whatever I was having to endure, I loved you all the time."

"But what were you having to endure?" Jemima asked.

For Jemima an extra kind of specialness was needed. Pym's reply took him by surprise. Afterwards, he decided that it had been lying in wait inside him and leapt out before he could prevent it. "It was for England," he said. "I'm lucky to be alive. If I tell anyone about it they'll kill me."

"Why ever will they do that?"

"It's secret. I swore never to tell."

"Then why are you telling me?"

"I love you. I had to do awful things to people. You can't imagine what it's like, carrying secrets like that alone."

As Pym heard himself saying this he remembered something that Axel had told him shortly before the end: There is no such thing as a life that does not return.

The next time he met Jemima, he described a brave girl he had worked with when he was doing his terribly secret work. He had in mind one of those muddy war photographs of beautiful women who win George Medals for being parachuted weekly into France.

"Her name was Wendy. We did secret missions into Russia together. We became partners."

"Did you do it with her?"

"It wasn't that kind of relationship. It was professional." Jemima was fascinated. "You mean she was a tart?"

"Of course she wasn't. She was a secret agent like me."

"Have you ever done it with a tart?"

"No."

"Kenneth has. He's done it with two. One each end."

Each end of what? thought Pym, in rampant indignation. Me a secret hero, and she talks to me about sex! In his despair he wrote Belinda a twelve-pager about his platonic love for her, but by the time her reply came he had forgotten the context of his feelings. Sometimes Jemima came uninvited, wearing no make-up and her hair shoved behind her ears. She lay on the bed and read Jane Austen on her tummy, while she kicked a bare leg in the air or yawned.

"You can put your hand up my skirt if you like," she said.

"I'm fine, thanks," said Pym.

Too polite to disturb her further he sat in the chair and read *A Handbook of Old High German Literature* till she made a grimace and left. For a while after that, she didn't visit him. He kept glimpsing her in cinemas of which there were seven so he got round them nicely in a week. Always she was with another man and once, like her brother, she had two. Once during this same period Belinda came to stay with her, but told Pym she should keep away from him because it wasn't fair on Jem. Pym's need to impress Jemima now took on wild dimensions. He ate his meals alone and looked haunted, but she still didn't come to him. One evening, passing a brick wall, he deliberately dashed his knuckles against it until they bled, then hurried to her expensive lodgings in Merton Street, where he found her drying her long hair before the electric fire.

"Who've you been fighting?" she asked as she dabbed on iodine.

"I can't talk about it. Some things never go away."

Laying the fire on its back she cooked him toast while she went on brushing her hair and watching him through the strands.

"If *I* were a man," she said, "I wouldn't waste my energy hitting anybody. I wouldn't play rugger, I wouldn't box, I wouldn't spy for people. I wouldn't even ride. I'd save everything I had for fucking, again and again and again."

Pym departed, once more smouldering at the frivolity of those who failed to perceive his higher calling.

"Dearest Bel,
    "Is there nothing you can do for Jemima? I simply cannot bear to see her go to the devil like this."

Did Pym know that he had tempted God? Certainly I know it now, this blowy night beside the sea as I try to write it so many years later. Whom else but his Maker was he provoking

as he spun his stupid stories? Pym was calling down his fate
on himself as surely as if he had begged for it by name in his
prayers, and God dealt him the favour as God often did.
Pym's fantasy version of himself waited out there like a decoy
that no celestial eye could overlook, and the divine response
was lying in his cubbyhole in the porter's lodge not twenty-
four hours later when he came down to see who loved him
this Saturday morning before breakfast. Ah! A letter! Blue in
colour! Can it be perhaps from Jemima? Or is it from the
virtuous Belinda, Jemima's friend? Is it from Lalage, perhaps—
or Polly, or Prudence, or Anne? The answer, Jack, was none
of them. It came, like so many bad things, from you. You
were writing to Pym from Oman, care of the Trucial-Oman
Scouts, though the stamp was true-blue British and the
postmark Whitehall, because it had come to England by bag.

> "My dear Magnus,
>   "As you will see from the letter heading, I have
> abandoned the fleshpots of Bern for harsher fare and
> am presently attached to the Military Mission here,
> where life is certainly a little more exciting! I still do
> the odd spot of church work, and I must say some of
> these Arabs sing pretty nicely. The purpose of my
> letter is twofold.
>   "1. To wish you all the best with your studies
> and to repeat my interest in your progress.
>   "2. To tell you that I have passed your name to
> our sister church back in the old country, since I
> gather they are a bit short of tenors in your region.
> So if you should chance to hear from a chap called
> Rob Gaunt, who tells you he is a friend of mine, I
> trust you will allow him to buy you a meal on my
> behalf, and make sure he does you proud! Inciden-
> tally, he is a Lieutenant Colonel, nominally a Gunner."

Pym had not long to wait, though every minute seemed
a year. On the following Tuesday, returning from a testing
tutorial on the theory of Ablaut, he found a second envelope
waiting for him. This one was brown and of exceptional
thickness, of a type I never saw in later years. Faint lines ran
across it, giving it the appearance of corrugated cardboard
though the texture was oily and smooth. There was no crest

on the back, no address of sender. Even the manufacturer
was secret. Yet Pym's name and address were immaculately
typed, the stamp perfectly centred, and when he probed at
the flap in the safety of his room, he discovered that it was
stuck down with a rubberised bonding, which smelt of acid
drops and parted in sticky threads like chewing gun. Inside
lay a single sheet of thick white paper that was not so much
folded as ironed. Prising it open the great spy observed at
once the absence of a watermark. The type was large, as if for
the partially sighted, the alignment faultless:

Box 777
The War Office
Whitehall S.W. 1

My dear Pym,
    Our mutual friend Jack tells me excellent things
about you and I would greatly like the opportunity
to get to know you, as there are important matters
of mutual interest that you might help us out with.
Unfortunately I have a full programme at the moment, and shall be abroad by the time you receive
this letter. I wonder therefore whether as an interim
measure you would care to have a conversation with
a colleague of mine who will be down your way on
Monday of next week. If you are willing, why not
take the bus to Burford and be in the saloon bar of
the Monmouth Arms a little before midday? For
ease of recognition he will be carrying a copy of
Rider Haggard's *Allan Quatermain*, and I suggest
you provide yourself with a *Financial Times*, which
has a distinctive pink. His name is Michael, and,
like Jack, he had a valuable war. I have no doubt the
two of you will hit it off famously.
    With all good wishes,

Yours sincerely,
R. Gaunt
(Lt. Col., R.A., ret.)

For the next five days Pym abandoned work. He paced
the back streets of the city, turning in his tracks to see who
was following him. He bought a sheath knife and practised
throwing it at trees until the blade broke. He wrote a Will

and sent it to Belinda. When he entered his rooms he did so with circumspection, never descending or climbing his staircase without first listening for unfamiliar sounds. Where should he hide the secret letters? They were far too precious to throw away. Remembering something he had read, he gouged out the centre of his brand-new copy of Kluge's *Etymological Dictionary* to make a nest for them. From then on, his eviscerated Kluge became the first thing his eye fell upon when he returned from his sorties. To buy his copy of the *Financial Times* without attracting notice, he walked all the way to Littlemore but the village post office had never heard of it. By the time he returned to Oxford everything was shut. After a sleepless night he made a dawn raid on the Junior Common Room before anyone was up, and stole a back number from the racks.

Two buses went to Burford on weekday mornings but the second left him only twenty minutes to find the Monmouth Arms, so he took the first and got there at nine-forty, only to discover that the bus dropped him at the door. In his overalert condition the inn sign with its bold lettering struck him as a breach of national security and he strode past it with averted eyes. The rest of the morning crawled by on feet of lead. By eleven o'clock his notebook was already crammed with the number of every parked car in Burford, as well as copious notes on suspicious passers-by. By two minutes to twelve, duly seated in the saloon bar of the Monmouth Arms, he was seized by panic. Was he in the Monmouth Arms or the Golden Pheasant? Had Colonel Gaunt said the Horn of Plenty? In the furnace of Pym's mind these possibilities fused themselves into a brilliant and appalling alloy. He stepped into the forecourt and covertly reread the inn sign before hastening to the outdoor gentlemen's to throw cold water in his face. Standing at a stall he heard the sound of wind breaking and divined a bulky figure in a navy-blue mackintosh standing at his side. The body was tilted backwards and sideways, the eyes were cast upward in agony. For a frightful moment Pym feared the man was shot, until he realised that these contortions were caused by the difficulties of retaining a thick volume wedged under his armpit. Unable to perform, Pym buttoned himself, hurried back to the saloon and, laying *Financial Times* on the bar, ordered himself a bitter.

"Make that two, will you, sport?" a breezy voice told the

barman. "Uncle's in the chair today. How are you? What about over there in the corner? Don't forget your paper."

I won't give you much of our courtship, Jack. When two people have decided to go to bed with each other, what passes between them before the event is a matter of form rather than of content. Nor do I remember very clearly what justifications we cooked up, for Michael was a shy man who had spent most of his life at sea, and his rare snatches of philosophy came out of him like escaping steam signals while he pummelled his mouth with a check handkerchief. "Somebody's got to dredge the drains, o' boy—fire with fire, only way. Unless we want the buggers to steal the ship from under us, which I *don't*, thank you." This last being a tensely underplayed statement of personal faith, which he at once smothered with a swig of beer. Michael was the first of your surrogates, Jack, so let him do duty for the rest. After Michael, if I remember, came David, and after David an Alan, and after Alan I forget. Pym would see no flaw in any of them. Or if he did, he translated it at once into a fiendishly clever piece of deception. Today of course I know the poor souls for what they were: members of that large, lost family of the British unprofessional classes that seems to wander by right between the secret services, the automobile clubs and the richer private charities. Not bad men by any means. Not dishonest men. Not stupid. But men who see the threat to their class as synonymous with the threat to England and never wandered far enough to know the difference. Modest men, practical, filling in their expense accounts and collecting their salaries, and impressing their Joes with their quiet expertise beneath the banter. Yet still, in their secret hearts, nourishing themselves on the same illusions that in those days nourished Pym. And needing their Joes to help them do it. Worried men, touched with an odour of pub meals and club squash, and a habit of looking round them while they paid, as if wondering whether there was a better way to live. And Pym, as he was passed from hand to hand, did his best to honour and obey each one of them. He believed in them; he cheered them with witty stories from his ever-increasing store. He strained to give them treats and make their day exciting. And when it was time for them to go he was always careful to have saved for them some last nugget of information to take home to their parents, even if he sometimes had to make it up.

"How's the colonel?" Pym ventured one day, belatedly recalling that Michael was still officially the stand-in for a Colonel Gaunt.

"Not a question I ever ask, personally, old boy," said Michael and to Pym's surprise began snapping his fingers as if he were summoning a dog.

Did Rob Gaunt exist? Pym never met him and later, when he was in a better position to ask, he could find nobody who would admit to having heard of him.

Now the brown envelopes flow in thick and fast, often two or three a week. The college porter grows so used to them he chucks them into Pym's pigeonhole without reading the address and Pym has to gouge out the centre of another dictionary to accommodate them. Always they contain instructions, and sometimes they contain small sums of cash, which the Michaels call his hard-lying money. Better still is Pym's float for operational expenses, which is kept at a fabulous twenty pounds: to entertaining secretary O. U. Hegelian Society, seven and ninepence... contribution to Peace in Korea campaign, five shillings... bottle of sherry for Society of Cultural Relations with the USSR get-together, fourteen shillings... coach trip to Cambridge for goodwill visit to C.U. Branch members, plus entertainment, one pound fifteen shillings and ninepence. At first Pym is timid of these claims, fearing that by making them he is straining his masters' indulgence. The colonel will find someone cheaper, someone richer, someone who knows that gentlemen do not count the cost. But slowly he comes to realise that, far from displeasing his masters, his expenditures are taken as evidence of his industry.

"Dear Old Friend," wrote Michael—observing his own dictum that names must be avoided lest the enemy intercept our correspondence—

"Eleven. Thanks for your Eight safely to hand, a pearl as usual. I took the liberty of passing your rendering of the clans' latest choral to our lord and master upstairs and I haven't seen the old boy laugh so much since his aunt caught her left doodah in the you've-got-it. Brilliant and informative, dear sir, and be advised that the great man himself remarked upon your perseverance. Now to the usual shopping list.

"1. Are you certain that our distinguished clan treasurer spells his name with a Z and not an S? The Doomsday Book contains an Abraham S, mathematician, late of Manchester Grammar School who fits the bill, but definitely no Z. (Though it's always possible of course that a gentleman of his tartan spells it both ways anyway . . .) Don't force it, as the Bishop said, but if Lady Luck pushes the answer your way, let us know. . . .

"2. Please keep your Eversharp ear open for talk about our gallant Scottish brethren getting up a delegation to attend the Sarajevo Youth Festival in July. The powers that be are getting unaccountably miffed about gents who accept large government grants only to oil off abroad and spit on said government's shadow.

"3. Regarding the distinguished visiting vocalist from Leeds University who is slated to address the clan on March 1st, do please keep an eye and an ear open for his faithful spouse, Magdalene (God bless us!), who by repute is quite as musical as her old man, but prefers to keep her head down owing to her delicate scientific interests. All comments gleefully received . . ."

Why did Pym do it, Tom? In the beginning was the deed. Not the motive, least of all the word. It was his own choice. It was his own life. No one forced him. Anywhere along the line, or right at the start of it, he could have yelled no and surprised himself. He never did. It took another ten university generations before he threw in the sponge, and by then the lines were drawn for good, all the lines. Why chuck away his freedom and good luck, you will ask, his good looks and good humour and good heart, just when they were coming into their own at last? Why befriend a bunch of grimy and unhappy people of alien background and mentality, press himself upon them, all smiling and obliging—because, believe me, there was no glamour to the university Left by then; Berlin and Korea had put paid to that for good—merely in order to be able to betray them? Why sit whole nights away in back rooms among sullen girls from the provinces who scowled and ate nut cutlets and took Firsts in Economics, in order to profess a view of the world that he had to learn as he went along, twisting his mind inside out, killing himself on cheap cigarettes while passionately agreeing that everything that was fun in life was a damn shame? Why do a Father Murgo on them, offering his bourgeois origins for their condemnation, abasing himself, revelling in their disapproval, yet gaining no absolution from it—only to rush off and bang the scales down the other way in a gush of embellished reports of the night's proceedings? I should know. I have done it and I have made others do it, and I was never less than cogent in my persuasion. For England. So that the free world can sleep safely in its bed at night while the secret watchers guard her in their rugged care. For love. To be a good chap, a good soldier.

Abie Ziegler's name, whether with a Z or an S, was written, you may be sure, in capitals on every left wing poster in every college lodge of the university. Abie was a publicity-crazed pipe-smoking sex maniac about four feet high. His one ambition in life was to be noticed and he saw the depleted Left as a fast lane to this end. There were a dozen painless ways in which Michael and his people could have found out whatever they wanted about Abie, but Pym had to be their man. The great spy would have walked all the way to Manchester just to look up Siegler or Ziegler in the phone book, such was the drive with which he had flung himself into his secret mission. This is not betrayal, he told himself when he was being the Michaels' man; this is the real thing. These strident men and women with their college scarves and funny accents who refer to me as our bourgeois friend are my own countrymen planning to upset our social order.

For his country, or whatever he called it, Pym addressed envelopes and memorised the addresses, played steward at public meetings, marched in dispirited processions, and afterwards wrote down whoever came. For his country he took any menial job going if it earned him favour. For his country or for love or for the Michaels, he stood at street corners late at night, offering unreadable Marxist pamphlets to passers-by who told him he ought to be in bed. Then dumped the

surplus copies in a ditch and put his own money into the
Party kitty because he was too proud to reclaim it from the
Michaels. And if occasionally, as he sat up still later writing
his meticulous reports on tomorrow's revolutionists, the ghost
of Axel materialised before him and Axel's cry of "Pym you
bastard where are you" whispered in his ear, Pym had only to
wave him away with a combination of the Michaels' logic and
his own: "You were my country's enemy even if you were my
friend. You were unsound. You had no papers. Sorry."

"Hell are you running with all those Reds for?" Sefton Boyd
asked drowsily one day, face downward in the grass. They had
driven out to Godstow in his sports car for lunch, and were
lying in a meadow above the weir. "Somebody told me they'd
seen you at the Cole Group. You made a piss-awful speech
about the madness of war. Hell's the Cole Group when it's at
home?"

"It's a discussion group run by G.D.H.Cole. It explores
avenues of Socialism."

"Are they queer?"

"Not that I know of."

"Well, explore somebody else's avenue. I also saw your
nasty name on a poster. College secretary of the Socialist
Club. I mean, Christ, you're supposed to be in the Grid."

"I like to see all sides," said Pym.

"They're not all sides. We are. They're one side. They've
pinched half Europe and they're a band of absolute shits.
Take my words for it."

"I'm doing it for my country," Pym said. "It's secret."

"Bollocks," said Sefton Boyd.

"It's true. I get instructions from London every week.
I'm in the Secret Service."

"Like you were in the German Army at Grimble's,"
Sefton Boyd suggested. "Like you were Himmler's aunt at
Willow's. Like you fucked Willow's wife and your father
carried messages for Winston Churchill."

A day came, long spoken of and frequently postponed,
when Michael took Pym home to meet his family. "Double
First material," Michael warned him in an advance write-up
of his spouse. "Mind like a dart. No mercy." Mrs. Michael
turned out to be a ravenous, fast-fading woman in a slashed

skirt and a low blouse over an unappetising chest. While her husband did things in his shed, where he appeared to live, Pym inexpertly mixed the Yorkshire pudding and fought off her embraces until he was obliged to take refuge with the children on the lawn. When it rained he marched them to the drawing-room and posted them round him in self-defence while he pushed their Dinky toys.

"Magnus, what are your father's initials?" Mrs. Michael said bossily from the doorway. I remember her voice, querulous and interrogative, as if I had just eaten her last chocolate instead of refusing to pop upstairs with her to bed.

"R.T.," said Pym.

She was trailing a copy of a Sunday newspaper in her hand and must have been reading it in the kitchen.

"Well, it says here that there's an R. T. Pym standing as Liberal Candidate for Gulworth North. He's described as a philanthropist and property broker. There can't be two, can there?"

Pym took the paper from her. "No," he agreed, staring at Rick's Portrait of Self with Red Setter. "There can't."

"Only you could have told us. I mean you're terribly rich and superior, I know, but a thing like that is jolly exciting if you're people like us."

Sick with apprehension Pym returned to Oxford and forced himself to read, if only glancingly, the last four letters from Rick that he had tossed unopened in his desk drawer, next to Axel's copy of Grimmelshausen and other unpaid bills.

Inside his camel-hair dressing-gown Pym at fifty-three was shivering. It had come over him suddenly, as it sometimes did, a fever without a temperature. He had been writing for as long as he had been awake, which to judge by his beard was a long time. The shiver turned to a shake, which was how it went. It twisted his neck muscles and gnawed at the backs of his thighs. He started to sneeze. The first sneeze was long and speculative. The second followed it like an answering shot. They're fighting over me, he thought: the good guys and the bad guys are shooting it out inside me. Whoops: O God receive my soul. Whoops: O Lord forgive him, for he knew not what he did. Rising, he held one hand over his mouth and with the other turned up the gas fire. Clutching himself, he began a prisoner's tour of the room's perimeter, dipping into his knees with each stride. From a corner of Miss Dubber's carpet he paced ten feet, made a right angle and paced eight more. He stopped and surveyed the rectangle he had measured. How did Rick endure it? he asked himself. How did Axel? He raised his arms, comparing the cell's breadth with his own wingspan. "Christ," he whispered aloud. "I'll hardly fit."

Picking up the reinforced briefcase which he had still not opened, he carried it to the fire and sat there, brows drawn, eyes glowering at the flames while the shaking grew more violent. Rick should have died when I killed him. Pym whispered the words out loud, daring himself to hear it. "You should have died when I killed you." He returned to his desk and took up his pen. Every line written is a line behind me. You do it once, then die. He wrote fast. And as he wrote, he began to smile again. Love is whatever you can still betray, he thought. Betrayal can only happen if you love.

Mary too was praying. She was kneeling on her school hassock with her eyes plunged into the night-time of her palms and she was praying that she was not at school any more but at their little Saxon church in Plush that went with the estate, with her father and brother kneeling protectively to either side of her and their Colonel the Reverend High Anglican vicar barking out his fire orders and rattling the incense like a mess-gong. Or that she was kneeling at her own bedside in her own room in her nightdress with her hair brushed and her bottom pushed out, praying that nobody would make her go to boarding-school again. Yet however much Mary prayed and begged, she knew that she wasn't going anywhere but where she was: in the English church in Vienna where I come every Wednesday for early service, in common with the usual band of upwardly mobile Christians led by the British Ambassadress and the American Minister's wife and supported by Caroline Lumsden, Bee Lederer and a heavy contingent of Dutch, Norwegians and also-rans from the German Embassy next door. Fergus and Georgie are roosting in the pew behind me without a pious thought between them, it's Tom not me who is at boarding-school and it is Magnus not God who is all-pervasive, all-knowing yet invisible and who holds the keys to all our destinies. So Magnus you bastard, if there is any truth left in you at all, do me a favour will you and lean out of your firmament and advise me, of your infinite goodness and wisdom—just for once with no lies, evasion or decoration—what the hell I am supposed to do about your dear old friend from Corfu cricket ground who is sitting not praying in the same pew as myself just across the aisle on the bride's side—is slender and drooping with a pepper-and-salt moustache and bottleneck shoulders, exactly as Tom described him right down to the cobwebby lines of laughter round his eyes and the grey raincoat wrapped around his shoulders like a cape. For this is neither the first appearance of your grey angel nor the second. It is the third and the most imaginative in two days, and each time that I do nothing about it I feel him draw a step nearer to me, and if you don't come back soon and tell me what to do, you may very well find us in bed together, because after all, as you used to assure me in Berlin, you can't beat a little sex for breaking the tension and removing social barriers.

Giles Marriott the English chaplain was inviting all those of a pure heart and humble mind to draw near with faith. Mary stood up, straightened her skirt and stepped into the aisle. Caroline Lumsden and her husband were ahead of her but the ethics of piety required that they greet one another after and not before the Sacrament. Georgie and Fergus stayed firmly in their pew, too high-minded to sacrifice their agnosticism for cover. More likely they just don't know what to do, thought Mary. Clasping her hands to her chin, she quickly ducked her head again in prayer. Oh God, oh Magnus, oh Jack, tell me what to do now! He is standing a foot behind me, I can smell his stale cigar smoke. Tom had mentioned that too. At the airport, as an afterthought: "He smoked little cigars, Mum, like Dad used to when he was giving up cigarettes!" And he has *limped* along his pew. He has *limped* into the aisle. A dozen people or more had fallen in behind Mary, including the Ambassadress, her spotty daughter and a flock of Americans. Yet a limp is a limp and good Christians stop for it and smile and let it go ahead, and there he was behind her, the privileged recipient of everybody's charity. And still each time the queue takes a pace nearer to the altar he *limps* as intimately as if he were patting me on the bum. Mary had never known such an insinuating, impudent, fla-

grant limp in all her life. His merry eyes were burning her
back, she could feel them. She could feel her neck burning
and her face heating as the moment of divine consummation
approached. At the altar rail Jenny Forbes, the Administration Officer's wife, was genuflecting before retiring to her
seat. As well she might, the way she's carrying on with the
new young Chancery guard. Mary stepped forward gratefully
and kneeled in her place. Get off my back you creep, stay
your own side. The creep did, but by then his softly murmured words were bellowing inside her head like a bullhorn.
"I can help you find him. I will send a message to the
house."

In choral unison the questions were shrieking inside
Mary's head. Send how? A message saying what? To instruct
her in the causes of her disloyalty? To explain to her why, as
she was leaving yesterday's International Ladies' bunfight,
she had not flung out an accusing arm at him as he smiled at
her from across the street? Why she had not screamed "Arrest
that man!" to Georgie and Fergus who were parked not forty
feet from the doorway he emerged from—jauntily, no hood
was ever like that? Or again when he appeared not six yards
from her at Swab's supermarket?

Giles Marriott was gazing down at her in puzzlement,
offering her for the second time the body of Christ which was
given for her. Hastily Mary placed her hands as she had been
taught since childhood—right over left and make a cross with
them. He laid the wafer on her palm. She raised it to her lips
and felt it stick, then lie like a log on her dry tongue. No, I
am not worthy, she thought wretchedly as she waited for the
chalice. It's true. I am not worthy to come to this Thy table or
anybody else's table either. Every moment I fail to denounce
him is another moment of disloyalty. He is tempting me and I
am hearing him for all I am worth. He is drawing me to him
and I am saying yes please. I am saying, "I will come to you
for the sake of Magnus and my child." I am saying, "I will
come to you if you are clarity, even if you are evil. Because I
am searching for a light, any light at all, and going half off my
head in the darkness. I will come to you because you are
the other half of Magnus, and therefore the other half of
me."

As she walked back to her seat she caught Bee Lederer's
eye. They exchanged pious smiles.

11

There was never a by-election like it, Tom, there was never an election like it. We are born, we get married, we divorce, we die. But somewhere along the way, if we get the chance, we should also stand as Liberal Candidate for the ancient fishing and weaving constituency of Gulworth North situated in the remoter fens of East Anglia in the unlit post-war years before television replaced the Temperance Hall, and communications were such that a man's character could be born again by removing it a hundred and fifty miles north-east of London. If we do not have the luck to stand ourselves, then the least we can do is drop everything from crypto-Communism to unconsummated sexual exploration and, forgetting the later *Minnesänger*, hasten to our father's side in the Hour of his Greatest Test to shiver on icy doorsteps for him, and charm votes out of old ladies in the manner in which he has instructed us, and see them right if it kills us, and tell the world by loudspeaker what a crackerjack fellow he is, and that they will never want for anything again, and promise ourselves, and mean it, that as soon as polling day is over we will forsake all other lives and take our place among the working classes where our hearts and origins have always been, as witness our clandestine espousal of the workers' cause during the formative years of our studentship.

It was deep winter when Pym arrived and it is winter still, for I have never been back, I never dared. The same snow lies over the fens and marshes and freezes Quixote's windmills to a standstill against the cindery Flemish sky. The same steepled towns dangle from the sea's horizon, the Brueghel faces of our electorate are as pink with zeal as they were those three decades ago. Our Candidate's convoy, led by the lifelong Liberal Mr. Cudlove and his precious cargo, still bears the message from chalky schoolroom to paraffin-heated hall, skidding and cursing over country lanes while

Our Candidate broods and downs another wet, and Sylvia
and Major Maxwell-Cavendish fight in undertones over the
Ordnance Survey map. In my memory our campaign is a
drama tour of the theatre of the politically absurd as we
advance across snow and marshland upon Gulworth's majestic
Town Hall itself—hired against all advice from those who said
we'd never fill it, but we did—for Our Candidate's Positively
Last Appearance. There suddenly the comedy stops dead.
The masks and fools' bells come clattering to the stage as God
in one simple question presents us with His bill for all our
fun till here.

Evidence, Tom. Facts.

Here is Rick's rosette of yellow silk that he wore for his
great night. It was run up for him by the same luckless tailor
who made his racing colours. Here is the centre-page spread
from the *Gulworth Mercury* next day. Read all about it for yourself. CANDIDATE DEFENDS HIS HONOUR. SAYS LET GULWORTH
NORTH BE THE JUDGE. See the picture of the podium with its
illuminated organ pipes and curving staircase? All we need is
Makepeace Watermaster. See your grandfather, Tom, centre
stage, hacking at the speckled beams of the spotlights, and
your father peeking coyly from behind him, forelock at the
slope? Hear the thunder of the great saint's piety rising into
the wagon roof, do you? Pym knows every word of Rick's
speech by heart, every hammy gesture and inflection. Rick is
describing himself as an honest trader who will devote "my
life for as long as I am spared, and as long as you deem in
your wisdom that you require me," to the service of the
constituency, and he's about five seconds from making a
swipe with his left forearm to cut off the heads of the
Unbelievers. Fingers closed and slightly curled as ever. He is
telling us that he's a humble Christian and a father and a
straight dealer, and he's going to rid Gulworth North of the
twin heresies of High Toryism and Low Socialism, though
sometimes in his teetotal fervour he gets them the wrong way
round. He also hates excess. It really churns him up. Now
comes the good news. You can hear it from the faith in his
voice. With Rick as its Member of Parliament, Gulworth
North will undergo a Renaissance beyond its dreams. Its
moribund herring trade shall rise from its bed and walk. Its

decaying textile industry shall bring forth milk and honey. Its farms shall be freed of Socialist bureaucracy and become the envy of the world. Its crumbling railways and canals shall be miraculously cut loose from the toils of the Industrial Revolution. Its streets shall run with liquidity. Its aged shall have their savings protected against Confiscation by the State, its menfolk shall be spared the ignominies of conscription. Pay-As-You-Earn taxation shall go and so shall all the other iniquities that are featured in the Liberal Manifesto which Rick has partly read but believes in totally.

So far so good, but tonight is our final curtain and Rick has worked up something special. Daringly he turns his back to the punters and addresses his faithful supporters ranged behind him on the dais. He is about to thank us. Watch. "First my darling Sylvia, without whom nothing could have been accomplished—thank you, Sylvia, thank you! Let's have a big hand for Sylvia my Queen!" The punters oblige with enthusiasm. Sylvia pulls the gracious smile for which she is retained. Pym is expecting to be called next but he is not. Rick's blue gaze has steel in it tonight, the glow is on him. More voice and less breath to his bombast. Shorter sentences but the champ throws them harder. He thanks the Chairman of the Gulworth Liberal Party and *his* very lovely lady wife—Marjory, my dear, don't be shy, where are you?—He thanks our miserable Liberal agent, an unbeliever called Donald Somebody, see the caption, who since the court's arrival on his territory has retired into a fuming sulk from which he has only tonight emerged. He thanks our transport lady whom Mr. Muspole claims to have favoured in the snooker room, and a Miss Somebody Else who made sure Your Candidate was never once late for a meeting—laughter—though Morrie Washington swears she isn't safe to be sat with in the back. He passes "to these other gallant and faithful helpers of mine." Morrie and Syd leer like a pair of reprieved murderers from the back row, Mr. Muspole and Major Maxwell-Cavendish prefer to scowl. It is there in the photograph, Tom, look for yourself. Next to Morrie roosts an inebriated radio comedian whose failing reputation Rick has contrived to harness to our campaign, just as in the last weeks he has wheeled in witless cricketers and titled owners of hotel chains and other so-called Liberal personalities, marching them through town like prisoners and tossing them back to London when they have served their brief span of usefulness.

Now take another look at Magnus seated on the right hand of his maker. Rick arrives at him last and every word he shouts at him is replete with secret knowledge and reproach. "He won't tell you himself so I will. He's too modest. This boy of mine here is one of the finest students of law this country has yet seen and not only this country either. He could hold this speech in five different languages and do it better than I can in any one of them." Laughter. Cries of "Shame!" and "No, no." "But that never stopped him from working his feet off for his old man throughout this campaign. Magnus, you've been crackerjack, old son, and your old man's best pal. Here's to you!"

But the dinning ovation does nothing to alleviate Pym's anguish. In the lonely reality of being Pym and listening to Rick resume his speech, his heart is beating in terror while he counts off the clichés and waits for the explosion that will destroy the candidate and his bold tissue of deceptions forevermore. It will blow the wagon roof and its gilded bearings into the night sky. It will smash the very stars that provide the grand finale of Rick's speech.

"People will say to you," cries Rick, on a note of ever-mounting humility, "and they've said it to me—they've stopped me in the street—touched my arm—'Rick,' they say, 'what is Liberalism except a package of ideals? We can't *eat* ideals, Rick,' they say. 'Ideals don't buy us a cup of tea or a nice touch of English lamb chop, Rick, old boy. We can't put our ideals in the collection box. We can't pay for our son's education with ideals. We can't send him out into the world to take his place in the highest law courts of the land with nothing but a few ideals in his pocket. So what's the point, Rick?' they say to me, 'in this modern world of ours, of a party of ideals?'" The voice drops. The hand, till now so agitated, reaches out palm downward to cup the head of an invisible child. "And I say to them, good people of Gulworth, and I say to you too!" The same hand flies upward and points to Heaven as Pym in his sickly apprehension sees the ghost of Makepeace Watermaster leap from its pulpit and fill the Town Hall with a dismal glow. "I say this. Ideals are like the stars. We cannot reach them, but we profit by their presence!"

Rick has never been better, more passionate, more sincere. The applause rises like an angry sea, the faithful rise with it. Pym rises with the faithful, pummelling his hands together loudest of us all. Rick weeps. Pym is on the brink. The good people have their Messiah, the Liberals of Gulworth North have too long been a flock without a shepherd; no Liberal candidate has stood here since the war. At Rick's side our local Liberal Party Chairman is smacking his yeoman's paws together and rhubarbing ecstatically into Rick's ear. At Rick's back, the whole court is following Pym's example, standing, clapping, rah-rahing "Rick for Gulworth!" Thus reminded, Rick turns to them yet again and, taking his cue from any number of the variety shows he loves, indicates the court to the people, saying: "You owe it to them, not to me." But once more his blue eyes are on Pym, saying, "Judas, patricide, murderer of your best pal."

Or so it seems to Pym.

For this is exactly the moment, this is exactly where everyone is standing and beaming and clapping, when the bomb that Pym has planted goes off: Rick with his back to the enemy, his face upon Pym and his beloved helpers, half ready, I think, to break into a rousing song. Not "Underneath the Arches," it is too secular, but "Onward, Christian Soldiers" will be first rate. When suddenly the din takes sick and dies on its feet in front of us, and a freezing silence slips in after it as if somebody has flung open the great doors of the Town Hall and let in the vengeful angels of the past.

Someone unreliable has spoken from under the minstrel gallery where the press sits. At first the acoustics are so lousy they do not allow us more than a few querulous notes, but already the notes are subversive. The speaker tries again but louder. She is not a person yet, merely a damned woman, with the kind of piping, strident Irish voice that menfolk instinctively detest, wheedling you with its impotence in the same breath as its cause. A man shouts "Silence, woman," then "Be quiet," and then "Shut up, you bitch!" Pym recognises the port-fed voice of Major Blenkinsop. The major is a Free-Trader and a rural Fascist from the embarrassing Right of our great movement. But the scratchy Irish voice prevails like a door squeak that will not go away, and no amount of slamming or oiling seems able to silence it. Some tiresome Home-Ruler probably. Ah good, somebody has got hold of her. It is the major again—see his bald head and yellow rosette of office. He is calling her "My good *madame*," of all things, and manhandling her towards the door. But the freedom of the press prevents him. The hacks are leaning over the balcony shouting "What's your name, miss?" and even "Yell it at him again!" Major Blenkinsop is suddenly neither a gentleman nor an officer but an upper-class lout with a screaming Irishwoman on his hands. Other women are yelling "Leave her be!" and "Get your hands off her, you dirty swine." Somebody shouts "Black and Tan bastard!"

Then we hear her, then we see her, both clearly. She is small and furious in black, a widowed shrew. She wears a pill-box hat. A bit of black veil hangs from it by a corner, ripped aside by herself or someone else. With the perversity of a crowd, everybody wants to hear her. She begins her question for perhaps the third time. Her brogue comes from the front of the mouth and appears to be spoken through a smile, but Pym knows it is no smile but the grimace of a hatred too powerful to be kept inside her. She speaks each word as she has learned it, in the order she has arranged them. The formulation is offensive in its clarity.

"I wish to know please—whether it is true—if you would be so kind, sir—that the Liberal Parliamentary Candidate for the Constituency of Gulworth North—has served a prison sentence for swindle and embezzlement. Thank you very much for your consideration."

And Rick's face on Pym while her arrow shoots him in the back. Rick's blue eyes opening wide on impact, but still steady on Pym—exactly as they were five days ago, when he lay in his ice-bath with his feet crossed and his eyes open, saying, "Killing me is not enough, old son."

Come back ten days with me, Tom. The excited Pym has arrived from Oxford light of heart, determined as a protector of the nation to throw his changeful weight behind the democratic process and have some fun in the snow. The campaign is in full cry but the trains to Gulworth have a way of petering out at Norwich. It is weekend and God has ruled that English by-elections be held on Thursdays, even if He has long forgotten why. It is evening: the Candidate and his cohorts are on the stomp. But as Pym alights bag in hand at Norwich's imposing railway station, there stands faithful Syd

Lemon at the barrier with a campaign car plastered with the Pym regalia waiting to whisk him to the main meeting of the evening, scheduled for nine o'clock in the village of Little Chedworth-on-the-Water, where according to Syd the last missionary was eaten for tea. The car's windows are darkened with posters saying "PYM THE PEOPLE'S MAN." Rick's great head—the one, as I now know, that he had quite likely sold—is pasted to the boot. A loudspeaker bigger than a ship's cannon is wired to the roof. A full moon is up. Snow covers the fields and Paradise is all around.

"Let's drive to St. Moritz," Pym says as Syd hands him one of Meg's meat pies, and Syd laughs and musses Pym's hair. Syd is not an attentive driver but the lanes are empty and the snow is kind. He has brought a ginger ale bottle filled with whisky. As they meander between the laden hedges they swallow big mouthfuls. Thus fortified, Syd briefs Pym on the state of the battle.

"We favour free worship, Titch, and we're mustard for Home Ownership for All with Less Red Tape."

"We always were," says Pym, and Syd gives him the hairy eyeball in case he's being cheeky.

"We take a poor view of ubiquitous High Toryism in all its forms—"

"Iniquitous," Pym corrects him, sipping again from the ginger ale bottle.

"Our Candidate is proud of his record as an English Patriot and Churchman. He's a Merchantman of England who has fought for his country, Liberalism being the only right road for Britain. He's been educated in the University of the World, he's never touched a drop of the hard stuff in his life, nor have you, and don't forget it." He grabbed back the ginger ale bottle and took a long, teetotal draught.

"But will he win?" said Pym.

"Listen. If you'd have come in here with ready money on the day your dad announced his intention, you could have had fifty to one. By the time me and Lord Muspole showed up he was down to twenty-fives and we took a ton each. Next morning after he done his adoption you couldn't get tens. He's nine to two now and shrinking and I'll have a small wager with you that come polling day he's evens. Now ask me whether he'll win."

"What's the competition?"

"There isn't any. The Labour boy's a Scottish schoolmas-

ter from Glasgow. Got a red beard. Small bloke. Looks like a
mouse peering out of a red bear's backside. Old Muspole sent
a couple of the lads round the other night to cheer up one of
his meetings. Put them in kilts and gave them football rattles
and had them roaring round the streets till morning. Gulworth
doesn't hold with rowdiness, Titch. They take a very poor
view of the Labour Candidate's drunken friends singing
'Little Nellie of the Glen' at three in the morning on the
church steps."

The car slides gracefully towards a windmill. Syd rights
it and they proceed.

"And the Tory?"

"The Tory is everything a Tory candidate should be with
knobs on. He's a landed pukka sahib who toils one day a week
in the City, rides to hounds, gives beads to the natives and
wants to bring back the thumbscrew for first offenders. His
wife opens garden fêtes with her teeth."

"But who's our traditional mainstay?" asks Pym, remembering his social history.

"The God-thumpers are solid for him, so's the Masons,
so's the Old Nellies. The teetotallers are a cakewalk, so's
the anti-betting league so long as they don't read the form
books and I'll thank you not to mention the neverwozzers,
Titch, they've been put out to grass for the duration. The
rest are a pig in a poke. The sitting member was a Red but
he's dead. The last election gave him five thousand ma-
jority on a straight race with the Tory, but look at the Tory.
The total poll was thirty-five thousand but since then
another five thousand juvenile delinquents have been
enfranchised and two thousand geriatrics have passed on to
a better life. The farmers are nasty, the fishermen are
broke and the hoi polloi don't know their willies from their
elbows."

Switching on the interior light Syd allows the car to steer
itself while he reaches into the back and fishes out an
imposing red-and-black pamphlet with a photograph of Rick
on the front cover. Flanked by somebody's adoring spaniels,
he is reading a book before an unfamiliar fireside, a thing he
has never done in his life. "A Letter to the Electorate of
Gulworth North," runs the caption. The paper, in defiance of
the prevailing austerity, is high gloss.

"We are also supported by the ghost of Sir Codpiece

Makewater, V.C.," Syd adds with particular relish. "Peruse our rear page."

Pym did so and discovered a ruled box resembling a Swiss obituary notice:

A FINAL NOTE

Your Candidate derives his proudest political inspiration from his childhood Mentor and Friend, Sir Makepeace Watermaster, M.P., the World Famous Liberal and Christian Employer whose stern but Fair hand following his Father's untimely Death guided him past Youth's many Pitfalls to his present Highly consolidated position which brings him into daily Contact with the Highest in the Land.

Sir Makepeace was a man of God-fearing Family, an Abstainer, an orator who knew no Equal without whose Shining inspiration it is safe to say Your Candidate might never have presumed to put myself forward for the Historic Judgment of the people of Gulworth North which has already become a Home from home for me, and if elected I shall obtain a Major property here at the earliest convenience.

Your Candidate proposes to Dedicate himself to your interests with the same Humility as was ever displayed by Sir Makepeace, who went to his grave preaching Man's Moral right to Property, free Trading and a fair Crack of the Whip for Women.

Your future Humble Servant,

Richard T. Pym

"You've got the learning, Titch. What do you think of it?" asks Syd, with vulnerable earnestness.

"It's beautiful," says Pym.

"Of course it is," says Syd.

A village, then a church spire glide towards them. As they enter the main street a yellow banner proclaims that Our Liberal Candidate will be speaking here tonight. A few old Land Rovers and Austin Sevens, already snowbound, stand dejectedly in the carpark. Taking a last pull from the ginger ale bottle, Syd carefully parts his hair before the mirror. Pym notices that he is dressed with unaccustomed sobriety. The frosted air smells of cow dung and the sea. Before them rises the archaic Temperance Hall of Little Chedworth-on-the-Water. Syd slips him a peppermint and in they go.

The ward chairman has been speaking for some time but only to the front row, and those of us at the back hear nothing. The rest of the congregation either stares into the rafters or at the display cards of the Common Man's Candidate: Rick at Napoleon's desk with his law books ranged behind him. Rick on the factory floor for the first and only time in his life, sharing a cup of tea with the Salt of the Earth. Rick as Sir Francis Drake gazing towards the misted armada of Gulworth's dying herring fleet. Rick the pipe-sucking agriculturalist intelligently appraising a cow. To one side of the ward chairman, under a festoon of yellow bunting, sits a lady officer of the ward committee. To the other runs a row of empty chairs waiting for the Candidate and his party. Periodically, while the chairman labours on, Pym catches a stray phrase like the Evils of Conscription or the Curse of Big Monopolies—or worse still an apologetic interjection such as "as I was saying to you only a moment ago." And twice, as nine o'clock becomes nine-thirty, then ten past ten, an elderly Shakespearean messenger hobbles painfully from a vestry, clutching his earlobe to tell us in a quavering voice that the Candidate is on his way, he has a busy schedule of meetings tonight, the snow is holding him up. Till just when we have given up hope, Mr. Muspole strides in accompanied by Major Maxwell-Cavendish, both prim as beadles in their greys. Together the two men march up the aisle and mount the dais, and while Muspole shakes hands with the chairman and his lady, the major draws a sheaf of notes from a briefcase and lays them on the table. And though Pym by the end of the campaign had heard Rick speak on no less than twenty-one occasions between that night and his Eve of Poll address in the Town Hall, he never once saw him refer to the major's notes or so much as recognise their presence. So that gradually he concluded they were not notes at all, but a piece of stage business to prepare us for the Coming.

"What's Maxie done with his moustache?" Pym whispers excitedly to Syd, who has sat up with a jolt after a bit of a nap. "Mortgaged it?" If Pym expects a witticism in return, he is disappointed.

"It's not deemed appropriate—that's what he's done with it," says Syd shortly. In the same moment Pym sees the light of pure love suffuse Syd's face as Rick sweeps in.

The order of appearance never changed, neither did the allocation of duties. After Muspole and the major come Perce Loft and poor Morrie Washington who is already getting bother with his liver. Perce holds open the door. Morrie steps through and sometimes, as tonight, gets a bit of a clap because the uninitiated mistake him for Rick, which is not surprising since Morrie, though a third Rick's size, spends most of his life and all his money in an effort to achieve Total Assumption with his idol. If Rick buys a new camel-hair coat, Morrie rushes off and buys two like it. If Rick is in two-tone shoes, so is Morrie, and white socks as well. But tonight Morrie has dressed like the rest of the court in churchy grey. For love of Rick he has even managed to get some of the booze out of his complexion. He steps in, he takes up his place across the door from Perce and fiddles with his rosette to make sure it is working properly. Then Morrie and Perce together crane their heads back in the direction they have come from, straining, as the audience is, to catch a first sight of their champion. And look!—they are clapping! And look, so are we!—as enter Rick, at a spanking pace, for we statesmen have no time to lose, and even as he comes striding up the aisle he is earnestly conferring with the Highest in the Land. Is that Sir Laurence Olivier with him?—looks more like Bud Flanagan to me. It is neither, as we shall quickly learn. It is none other than the great Bertie Tregenza, the Radio Bird Man, a lifelong Liberal. On the dais Muspole and the major present the other notables to the chairman and guide them to their seats. At last the moment we have come for is upon us when the only man left standing is the man in the photographs around him. Syd leans forward, listening with

his eyes. Our Candidate begins speaking. A deliberate,
unimpressive opening. Good evening and thank you for
coming here in such numbers on this cold winter's night. I
am sorry to have had to keep you waiting. A joke for the
Nellies: they tell me I kept my mother waiting a whole week.
Laughter from the Nellies as the joke is turned to account.
But I'll promise you this, people of Gulworth North: nobody
here is going to be kept waiting by your next Member of
Parliament! More laughter and some applause from the faithful as the Candidate's tone stiffens.

"Ladies and Gentlemen, you have ventured out on this
inhospitable night for one reason only. Because you care
about your country. Well that makes two of us, because I care
about it too. I care about the way it's run and the way it's not
run. I care because Politics are People. People with hearts to
tell them what they want, for themselves and for one another.
People with minds to tell them how to achieve it. People with
the Faith and Guts to send Adolf Hitler back to where he
came from. People like ourselves. Gathered here tonight.
The Salt of the Earth and make no bones about it. English
people, root and bough, worried about their country, and
looking for the man to see them right."

Pym peers round the little hall. Not a face but is turned
flowerlike towards Rick's light. Save one, a little woman in a
veiled pill-box hat, sitting like her own shadow, all apart and
the black veil hiding her face. She is in mourning, Pym
decides, moved at once to sympathy. She has come here for a
spot of company, poor soul. On the dais Rick is explaining the
meaning of Liberalism for the benefit of those unfamiliar with
the differences between the three great parties. Liberalism is
not a dogma but a way of life, he says. It is faith in the
essential goodness of man regardless of colour, race or creed
in a spirit of all pulling together to one end. The fine points of
policy thus dispatched, he can proceed to the solid centre of
his speech, which is himself. He describes his humble origins
and his mother's tears when she heard him vow to follow in
the footsteps of the great Sir Makepeace. If only my father
could be here tonight, seated among you good people. An
arm lifts and points to the rafters, as if picking out an aeroplane, but it is God whom Rick is indicating.

"And let me say this to the voters of Little Chedworth
tonight. Without a certain person up there acting night and

day for me as my senior partner—laugh if you will, because I would rather be the object of your mockery than fall prey to the cynicism and Godlessness that is sweeping through our country—without a certain person's helping hand and you all know who I mean, oh yes you do!—I wouldn't be where I am today, offering myself—be it never so humbly—to the people of Gulworth North." He speaks of his understanding of the export market and his pride at selling British products to those foreigners who will never know how much they owe us. His arm strikes out at us again and he issues a challenge. He is British to the core and he doesn't care who knows it. He can bring British common sense to every problem you throw at him. "Bar none," says Syd approvingly under his breath. But if we know a better man for the job than Rickie Pym, we had better speak up now. If we prefer the airy-fairy class prejudices of the High Tories who think they own the people's birthright, whereas in reality they are sucking the people's blood, then we should stand up here and now and say so without fear or favour and let's have it out once and for all. Nobody volunteers. On the other hand, if we would rather hand over the country to the Marxists and Communists and the bully-boy trade unions who are bent on dragging this country to its knees—and let's face it, that's what the Labour vote is all about—then better to come out with it in the full glare of the public gaze of the voters of Little Chedworth and not skulk in the dark like miserable conspirators.

Once again, nobody volunteers, though Rick and everyone on the dais glowers around the room in search of a miscreant hand or guilty face.

"Now press button B for Beautiful," Syd whispers dreamily and closes his eyes for extra pleasure as Rick starts the long climb towards the stars, which like Liberal ideals we cannot reach but can only profit from their presence.

Again Pym looks round. Not a face but is wrapt in love for Rick, save the one bereaved woman in her veil. This is what I came for, Pym tells himself excitedly. Democracy is when you share your father with the world. The applause fades but Pym goes on clapping until he realises he is the only one. He seems to hear his name being called, and observes to his surprise that he is standing. Faces turn to him, too many. Some are smiling. He makes to sit but Syd shakes him back to his feet with a hand under his armpit. The ward chairman is speaking and this time he is recklessly audible.

"I understand our candidate's celebrated young son Maggus is among us here tonight, having interrupted his legal studies at Oggsford in order to assist his father in his great gampaign," he says. "I'm sure we'd all appreciate a word from you, Maggus, if you'll favour us. Maggus? Where is he?"

"Over 'ere, governor!" Syd yells. "Not me. Him."

If Pym is resisting, he is not aware of it. I have fainted. I am an accident. Syd's ginger ale has knocked me out. The crowd separates, strong hands bear him towards the dais, floating voters gaze down on him. Pym ascends, Rick seizes him in a bear-hug; a yellow rosette is nailed to Pym's collarbone by the ward chairman. Pym is speaking, and a cast of thousands is staring up at him—well, sixty, at least—smiling at his first brave words.

"I expect you are all asking yourselves," Pym begins long before anything has occurred to him. "I expect that many of you here tonight, even after that fine speech, are asking yourselves, what manner of man my father is."

They are. He can see it in their faces. They want the confirmation of their faith, and Maggus the Oggsford lawyer supplies it without a blush. For Rick, for England, and for fun. As he speaks he believes as usual every word he says. He paints Rick as Rick has painted himself, but with the authority of a loving son and legal brain who picks his words but never splits them. He refers to Rick as the plain man's honest friend—"and I should know, he's been the best friend I've had these twenty years or more." He depicts him as the reachable star in his childlike firmament, shining before him as an example of chivalrous humility. The image of the singer Wolfram von Eschenbach wanders through his mind and he considers offering them Rick as Little Chedworth's soldier-poet, wooing and jousting his way to victory. Caution prevails. He describes the influence of our patron saint TP, "marching on long after the old soldier has fought his last fight." How whenever we had to move house—a nervous moment—TP's portrait was the first thing to be hung up. He speaks of a father blessed with a fair man's sense of justice. With Rick as my father, he asks, how could I have contemplated any other calling than the law? He turns to Sylvia, who roosts at Rick's side in her rabbitskin collar and stay-press smile.

With a choke he thanks her for taking up the burdens of motherhood where my own poor mother was obliged to lay them down. Then, as quickly as it all began, it is over, and Pym is hastening after Rick down the aisle towards the door, brushing away his tears and clasping hands in Rick's wake. He reaches the door and takes a misty look back. He sees again the woman in the veiled pill-box hat, seated by herself. He catches the glint of her eye inside the mask and it seems to him baleful and disapproving just when everyone else is being so admiring. A guilty fret replaces his elation. She is not a widow, she is the risen Lippsie. She is E. Weber. She is Dorothy, and I have wronged them all. She is an emissary of the Oggsford Communist Party here to observe my treacherous gonversion. The Michaels sent her.

"How was I, son?"

"Fantastic!"

"So were you, son. By God, if I'm spared to be a hundred, I'll never be a prouder man. Who cut your hair?"

Nobody has cut it for a long time, but Pym lets this go. They are crossing the carpark with difficulty for Rick is holding Pym's arm in an ambulant bear-hug and they are advancing at an angle like a pair of crookedly hung overcoats. Mr. Cudlove has the Bentley door open and is weeping a teacher's tears of pride.

"Beautiful, Mr. Magnus," he says. "It was Karl Marx come alive, sir. We shall never forget it."

Pym thanks him distractedly. As so often when on the crest of a phoney triumph, he is gripped by an unfocussed sense of God's approaching retribution. What have I done wrong to her? he keeps asking himself. I'm young and fluent and Rick's son. I'm wearing my new unpaid-for suit from Hall Brothers, the tailor. Why won't she love me like the rest of them? He is thinking, like every artist before or since him, of the only member of the audience who did not applaud.

It is the following Saturday, it is approaching midnight. Campaign fever is mounting fast. In a few minutes, it will be Eve of Poll Day minus three. A new poster saying "He Needs YOU on Thursday" is stuck to Pym's window, yellow bunting with the same message is strung from the sash, across the street to the pawnbroker's opposite. Yet Pym is lying fully dressed and smiling on his bed, and not a thought of the campaign is going through his mind. He is in Paradise with a girl called Judy, the daughter of a Liberal farmer who has lent her to us to drive Old Nellies to the booths, and Paradise is the front of her parked van on the way to Little Kimble. The taste of Judy's skin is on his lips, the smell of her hair is in his nostrils. And when he cups his hands over his eyes they are the same hands that for the first time in human history enclosed a young girl's breasts. The bedroom is on the first floor of a run-down corner house called Mrs. Searle's Temperance Rest, though rest and temperance are the last things it sells. The pubs have closed, the shouts and sighs have taken themselves to another part of town. A woman's voice shrieks from the alley, "Got a bed for us, Mattie? It's Jessie. Come on, you old bugger, we're freezing." An upper window bangs open and the blurred voice of Mr. Searle advises Jessie to take her client behind the bus shelter. "What do you think we are, Jess?" he complains. "A bloody doss house?" Of course we aren't. We are the Liberal Candidate's campaign headquarters and dear old Mattie Searle our landlord, though he didn't know it till a month ago, has been a Liberal all his life.

Careful not to wake himself from his erotic reverie, Pym tiptoes to the window and squints steeply downward into the hotel courtyard. To one side the kitchen. To the other the residents' dining room, now the campaign's committee rooms. In its lighted window Pym makes out the bowed grey heads of Mrs. Alcock and Mrs. Catermole, our tireless helpers, as they determinedly seal the last envelopes of the day.

He returns to his bed. Wait, he thinks. They can't stay up all night. They never do. His conquest in one field is inspiring him to conquest in another. Tomorrow being the sabbath, Our Candidate rests his troops and contents himself with pious appearances at the best-attended Baptist churches where he is disposed to preach on simplicity and service. Tomorrow at eight o'clock Pym will stand at the bus stop for Nether Wheatley and Judy will meet him there in her father's van and in the boot she will have the toboggan the gamekeeper made for her when she was ten. She knows the hill, she knows the barn beside it, and it is agreed between them without fallbacks that somewhere around ten-thirty, depending on how much tobogganing they do, Judy Barker will take Magnus Pym to the barn and anoint him her full and consummated lover.

But in the meantime Pym has a different slope to scale or descend. Beyond the committee rooms lies a staircase to the cellar, and in the cellar—Pym has seen it—stands the chipped green filing cabinet that he has aspired to for three-quarters of his life and too often tried in vain to penetrate. In Pym's wallet beneath his pillow nestles the pair of blue steel dividers with which the Michaels have taught him to spring cheap locks. In Pym's mind, heated by voluptuous ambitions, is the calm conviction that a man who can gain access to Judy's breasts can burst open the fortress of Rick's secrets.

His hands over his face once more, he relives each delicious moment of the day. He was bounced from sleep as usual by Syd and Mr. Muspole, who have taken to shouting Crazy Gang obscenities through his bedroom door.

"Come on, Magnus, give it a rest. You'll go blind, you know."

"It'll drop off, Magnus, dear, if you don't let it grow. Doctor will have to strap it up with a matchstick. What will Judy say then?"

Over early breakfast, Major Maxwell-Cavendish bawls out Saturday's orders to the court. Pamphlets are obsolete, he announces. The only thing we can hit them with now is loudspeakers and more loudspeakers, backed by frontal attacks on their own doorsteps. "They know we're here. They know we mean business. They know we've got the best candidate and the best policy for Gulworth. What we're after now is every single, individual vote. We're going to pick them off one by one and drag them to the polls by sheer force of will. Thank you."

Now the detail. Syd will take number one loudspeaker and two ladies—laughter—down to that bit of scrubland beside the race course where the gyppos hang out—gyppos have votes same as everyone else. Shouts of "Put a fiver on Prince Magnus for us while you're about it!" Mr. Muspole and another lady will take loudspeaker number two and pick up Major Blenkinsop and our miserable agent from the Town Hall at nine. Magnus will take Judy Barker again and cover Little Kimble and the five outlying villages.

"You can cover Judy too while you're about it," says
Morrie Washington. The joke, though brilliant, receives only
token laughter. The court is uneasy about Judy. It distrusts
her composure and resents her claim on their mascot. Barker
looks down her nose at you, they complain behind her back.
Barker's not the good scout we thought she was. But Pym
these days cares less than he used to about the court's
opinion. He shrugs off their gibes and, while the committee
rooms are unguarded, slips down the steps to the cellar
where he inserts the Michaels' dividers in the lock of the
chipped green filing cabinet. One prong to hold back the
spring, one to turn the chamber. The lock pops open. I am in
the presence of a miracle and the miracle is me. I will
return. Quickly relocking the cabinet he hastens back
upstairs and not one minute after establishing his ascendancy
over life's secrets he is standing innocently on the hotel
doorstep in time for Judy's van to pull up beside him, the
loudspeaker fixed to its roof with harvest twine. She smiles
but does not speak. This is their third morning together
but on the first they were accompanied by another lady
helper. Nevertheless Pym contrived several times to brush
his hand against Judy's as she changed gear or passed him
the microphone, and when they parted at lunchtime and
he made to kiss her cheek, she boldly redirected him to
her lips by placing a long hand on the back of his neck. She
is a tall, sunny girl with fair skin and an agricultural voice.
She has a long mouth and playful eyes inside her serious
spectacles.

"Vote for Pym, the People's Man," Pym booms into the
loudspeaker as they head through Gulworth's suburbs towards
open country. He is holding Judy's hand quite openly, first on
her lap and now, at Judy's instigation, on his own. "Save
Gulworth from the scourge of party politics." Then he recites
a limerick about Mr. Lakin the Conservative Candidate,
composed by Morrie Washington the great poet, which the
major vows is winning votes everywhere.

> *"There's a bossy old buffer called Lakin,*
> *Whose manners are frightfully takin'.*
> *But if he thinks Rickie Pym*
> *Can be beaten by him,*
> *It's a deuce of a bloomer he's makin'."*

Reaching across him, Judy switches off the instrument. "I think your dad's got a cheek," she says cheerfully when the city is safely behind them. "Who does he think we are? Bloody idiots?"

Steering the car into an empty side lane, Judy turns off the engine, unbuttons her jacket and then her blouse. And where Pym had been expecting more impediments he discovers only her small and perfect breasts with nipples rigid from the cold. She watches him proudly as he puts his hands over them.

For the rest of the day, Pym walked on clouds of light. Judy had to return to the farm to help her father with the milking, so she dropped him at an inn on the road to Norwich, where he had agreed to meet up with Syd and Morrie and Mr. Muspole for a discreet wet on neutral territory clear of the constituency. With polling day so near, an end-of-term hilarity has infected the gathering and, having remained upright until closing time, the four of them piled into Syd's car and sang "Underneath the Arches" over the loudspeaker all the way to the border, where they once more put on their jackets and their pious faces. In the early evening Pym attended Rick's final Saturday pep talk to his helpers. Henry V on the eve of Agincourt could have done no better. They should not flinch from the final push. Remember Hitler. They should carry a straight bat to victory, they should keep the left elbow up through life, praise God and give her the whip in the final straight. Their ears ringing with these exhortations, the team scrambled for the cars. By now Pym's speech is a fully incorporated feature of the programme. The punters love him and inside the court he has the status of a star. In the Bentley, the two champions can squeeze each other's hands and exchange notes over a glass of warm bubbly to keep them going between triumphs.

"That gloomy woman was there again," said Pym. "I think she's following us round."

"What woman's that, son?" said Rick.

"I don't know. She wears a veil."

And somewhere, amid these pressures and activities, Pym contrived to undertake the most perilous foray of his sexual career till now. Having located an all-night chemist in Ribsdale on the other side of town, he took a tram there and made a series of passes to check his back before marching

boldly to the counter and purchasing a packet of three
contraceptive sheaths from an old reprobate who neither
arrested him nor asked whether he was married. And there is
his prize now, winking at him in its mauve-and-white wrap-
ping from its hiding place at the centre of a stack of "Vote
Pym" circulars as he tiptoes once more to his bedroom
window and looks down.

The committee rooms are in darkness. Go.

The way is clear but Pym is too old a hand to make straight
for his target. Time spent on reconnaissance is never time
wasted, Jack Brotherhood used to say. I will fight my way to
the heart of the enemy and earn her. He begins in the hall,
affecting to read the day's notices. The ground floor is by now
deserted. Mattie's filthy office is empty, the front door chained.
He begins his slow ascent. Two doors past his own on the
next floor lies the residential lounge. Pym opens the door and
smiles in. Syd Lemon and Morrie Washington are playing a
four of snooker against a couple of dear old friends of Mattie
Searle who look like horse thieves but they could be sheep
rustlers. Syd wears his hat. Two locally obtained Lovelies are
chalking cues and dispensing comfort. The mood is fraught.

"What are you playing?" says Pym as if hoping for a
game.

"Polo," says Syd. "Piss off, Titch, and don't be funny."

"I meant how many frames."

"Best of nine," says Morrie Washington.

Syd misses his shot and swears. Pym closes the door.
They are settled. No danger there for at least an hour. He
continues his patrol. Another flight upwards the atmosphere
tightens, as it will in any secret building. Here is the quiet
room where invited guests may kick off their shoes and take
part in a relaxing hand of poker with Our Candidate and his
circle. Pym enters without knocking. At a table strewn with
cash and brandy glasses, Rick and Perce Loft are locked in a
sharp piece of betting with Mattie Searle. The pot is a stack
of petrol coupons, which in the court are preferred as hard
currency. Mattie raises Rick and Rick sees him. Rick looks on
with forbearance while Mattie scoops the pool.

"They tell me you and Colonel Barker had a crack at
Little Kimble this morning, old son."

I forget exactly why Rick called Judy Colonel. I have an idea it was a reference to a celebrated lesbian who had been involved in a court case. Whatever the reason, Pym did not care for it.

"The boy had them kissing the ground, Rickie," Perce Loft confirms.

"Not the only thing he's been kissing, if you ask me," says Rick and everybody laughs because it is Rick's joke.

Pym leans in for the good-night bear-hug and hears Rick sniff his cheek, which has Judy's smell on it.

"Just you keep that old mind of yours on the election, son," he says, patting the same cheek in warning.

Down the corridor lies Morrie Washington's publicity department which doubles as disinformation section. Cases of whisky and nylons are stacked against the wall waiting to pave the way to the last electoral favours. It was from Morrie's desk that the baseless rumours went out regarding the Tory Candidate's support of Sir Oswald Mosley, and the Labour Candidate's overaddiction to his pupils. Springing the locks with his dividers, Pym flicks quickly through the drawers. One bank statement, one set of indecent playing cards. The statement is in the name of Mr. Morris Wurzheimer and is overdrawn by a hundred and twenty pounds. The playing cards would be impressive if Judy's reality did not eclipse them. Relocking everything neatly after him Pym climbs halfway up the last flight, then hovers listening to Mr. Muspole murmuring on the telephone. The top floor is the sanctum. It is safe room, cypher room and operations centre combined. At the end of the corridor lie Our Candidate's State Apartments which not even Pym has penetrated so far, for Sylvia now spends erratic hours in bed having headaches or trying to grill herself brown with a mysterious hand lamp she has bought from Mr. Muspole. He can therefore never be sure of a safe run. Next door resides the so-called Action Committee, where big money and support are mustered and promises traded. What promises is still half a mystery to me, though Syd once spoke of a plan to fill the ancient harbour with cement and make a carpark of it, to the pleasure of many influential contractors.

Abruptly Mr. Muspole rings off. Without a sound, Pym swivels on his heel and prepares to beat an orderly retreat down the stairs. He is saved by the whirr of Mr. Muspole dialling again. He is talking to a lady, asking tender questions and purring at the answers. Muspole can carry on like this for hours. It is his little pleasure.

Having waited till his voice has settled to a reassuring flow Pym returns to the ground floor. The darkness of the committee rooms smells of tea and deodorant. The door to the courtyard is locked from the inside. Pym softly turns the key and pockets it. The cellar staircase stinks of cat. Boxes are stored on the steps. Groping his way down, unwilling to put on the light lest it be visible from the courtyard, Pym has an unmistakable mental reprise of a day in Bern when he carried his damp washing down the stone steps to another cellar and was scared of tripping over Herr Bastl. And as he reaches the bottom step he does indeed miss his footing. Lurching forward he falls heavily on to the cellar door and pushes it open with both hands as he tries to steady himself. The door screeches in the grime. The impetus of his body is enough to carry him into the cellar which to his surprise is lit by a pale light. By its glow Pym makes out the green filing cabinet and standing before it a woman holding what appears to be a chisel, examining its locks by the ailing beam of a bicycle lamp. Her eyes, which are turned to him, are dark and pugnacious. There is not a flicker of guilt about her. And it is a thing I wonder at still that it never seriously occurred to him to doubt that she was the same woman, with the same gaze, and the same intense and disapproving quietness, whose veiled face had fixed on him after his triumph on the hustings of Little Chedworth, and stalked him through a dozen meetings since. Even asking her name Pym realises that he knows it already though he is blessed with no faculty of premonition. She wears a long skirt that could have been her mother's. She has a hard, pebble face and young hair turned to grey. Her eyes are disconcertingly straight and bright, even in the gloom.

"My name is Peggy Wentworth," she replies defiantly in a tough Irish brogue. "Shall I spell it for you, Magnus? Peggy short for Margaret, have you heard that? Your father, Mr. Richard Thomas Pym, killed my husband John, and as good as killed me too. And if it takes me the rest of my living death till they put me in the grave beside him, I'll find the proof of it, and bring the brute to justice."

Seeing a flicker of moving light Pym glances sharply behind him. Mattie Searle is standing in the doorway with a blanket over his shoulders. His head is hung sideways to favour his good ear while he squints first at Pym then at Peggy over the top of his spectacles. How much has he heard? Pym has no idea. But his mind is made fertile by alarm.

"This is Emma from Oxford, Mattie," he says boldly "Emma, this is Mr. Searle who owns the hotel."

"Pleased to meet you," says Peggy calmly.

"Emma and I are in a college play next month, Mattie. She came up to Gulworth so that we could rehearse together. We thought we'd be out of your way down here."

"Oh yes," says Mattie. His eyes slip from Peggy to Pym and back again, with a knowledge that makes nonsense of Pym's lies. They hear his lazy shuffle going up the stairs.

I can't tell you very accurately any more, Tom, which bits she told Pym where. His first thought on escaping the hotel was to keep going, so they hopped a bus and went as far as it took them, which turned out to be the oldest, most broken-down bit of waste dockland you could imagine: gutted warehouses with windows you could see the moon through, idle cranes that rose like gallows straight out of the sea. A bunch of roving knife-bladers had pitched camp there, they must have worked at night and slept by day, because I remember their Romany faces rocking over their wheels as they trod their treadles, and the sparks gushing over the watching children. I remember girls with men's muscles flinging fish baskets while they yelled ribaldries at each other, and fishermen strutting among them in their oilskins, too grand to be bothered with anyone but themselves. I remember with a leap of gratitude every flash of face or voice outside the windows of the prison she had locked me in with her relentless monologue.

At a tea-stall on the waterfront while they stood shivering with a crowd of down-and-outs, Peggy told Pym the story of how Rick had stolen her farm. She had begun it the moment they got on the bus, for the benefit of anyone who'd care to hear it, and had continued it without a comma or a full stop since, and Pym knew that it was all true, all terrible, even if quite often the sheer venom in her drove him secretly to Rick's protection. They walked to get warm but she didn't stop talking for one second. When he bought her beans and egg at a Seamen's Mission hut called the Rover, still she went on talking as she spread her elbows and sawed the toast and used her teaspoon to get up the sauce. It was at the Rover that she told Pym about Rick's great trust fund that took possession of the nine thousand pounds of insurance money paid to her husband John after he fell into the thresher and lost both legs below the knee and all the fingers of one hand. As she told this part she drew the lines of amputation on her own scant limbs without looking at them, and Pym sensed her obsession again and was scared of it. The one voice I never did for you, Tom, is Peggy's Irish brogue dropping into Rick's chapel cadences as she repeated his silver-tongued promises: twelve and a half percent plus profits, my dear, year in and year out, enough to see dear old John right for as long as he's spared, and enough for yourself when he's gone, and enough left over after that, my dear, to put some by for that first-rate boy of yours for when he goes to college and reads his law just the way my own son will—they're birds of a feather. It was a Thomas Hardy story that she told, full of casual disasters that seemed to have been timed by an angry God to obtain the maximum of misfortune. And she was Hardy's woman to go with it: lured forward by her obsession, and only her own destiny left to deal with.

John Wentworth, as well as being a victim, was an ass, she explained, and was ready to be swayed by the first charmer who walked into the room. He went to his grave convinced that Rick was a saviour and a pal. His farm was a Cornish manor called Tamar Rose where every grain of wheat had to be wrestled from the sea wind. He had inherited it from a wiser father, and Alastair their son was his only heir. When John died there was not a penny for anybody. Everything signed away, every bloody thing mortgaged to the neck, Magnus—on which word Peggy passed her bean-stained knife across her throat. She told about Rick visiting John in hospital soon after his accident and the flowers and the chocolates and the bubbly—and Pym in his mind's eye saw the basket of black-market fruit beside his own hospital bed when he woke up after his operation. He remembered Rick's noble caring for the aged and decrepit that he had helped him with during the war years of the great crusade. He remembered Lippsie's sobbing voice calling Rick a *teef*, and Rick's letters to her promising to see her right.

"And a free train ticket for myself," Peggy is saying, "to come up to Truro Hospital to visit him. And your father driving me home after, Magnus, nothing too much trouble for him until he has our man's money." The documents he made John sign, Magnus, always witnessed by the prettiest nurses. How your father always had the patience for John, always explaining to him whatever he couldn't understand, over and again if necessary, but John won't listen, the deluded man is too trusting and lazy in his mind.

A fit of fury seizes her: "Me up at four in the morning for the milking and falling asleep over my accounts at midnight!" she shouts as sleepy heads turn to her from other tables. "And that stupid husband of mine lying warm in his bed in Truro signing it all away behind my back while your father sits by his bedside playing the saint to him, Magnus. And my Alastair needing a pair of shoes to walk to school in, while you're living on the hog there with your fine schools and your fine clothes, Magnus, God save you!" For it turns out, of course, on John's death, that for reasons outside everyone's control the great trust fund has suffered a purely temporary problem of liquidity and can't pay the twelve and a half percent plus profits after all. It can't refund the capital either. And that to tide everyone over this sticky patch, John Wentworth took the wise precaution, just before his death, of mortgaging the farm and land and livestock, and bloody nearly his wife and child as well, so that nobody will ever want for anything again. And had given the proceeds to his dear old pal Rick. And that Rick has brought down a distinguished lawyer, name of Loft, all the way from London with him, just to explain the implications of this smart move to John on his deathbed. And John, to please everyone as usual, has written out a special long letter all in his own hand, assuring whom it may concern that his decision has been taken while he was of sound mind and in full possession of his mental faculties and was not in any manner subjected to undue influence by a saint and his lawyer while he was lying gasping out his last. All this in case Peggy, or for that matter Alastair, should later have the bad manners to dispute the document in court or try to get John's nine thousand pounds back, or should otherwise show a lack of faith in Rick's selfless stewardship of John's ruin.

"When did all this happen?" says Pym.

She tells him the dates, she tells him the day of the week and the hour of the day. She pulls a wad of letters from her handbag signed by Perce and regretting that "our Chairman, Mr. R. T. Pym, is unavailable, being absent indefinitely on a mission of national necessity," and assuring her that "the documents relating to the Freehold of Tamar Rose are at present being processed with a view to acquiring a large Figure in your interest." And she watches him with her mad cold eyes as he reads them by the light of a street lamp while they sit huddled on a broken bench. She takes back the letters and returns them to their envelopes lovingly, careful of the edges and the folds. As she continues talking, Pym wants to close his ears or slap a hand over her mouth. He wants to get up and run to the sea-wall and throw himself over. He wants to scream "Shut up!" But all he does is ask her, please, I beg you, if you would be so kind, don't continue with your story.

"Why not, pray?"

"I don't want to hear it. It's not my business, this part. He robbed you. The rest doesn't make any difference," says Pym.

Peggy doesn't agree. She is flailing her Irish back with her Irish guilt and using Pym's presence as the excuse to do it. She is talking in a gush. It is what she has been waiting to tell him best.

"And why not—seeing as the bloody man possesses you anyway? If he's already got his filthy arms around you sure as if he had you in his fancy bed with the frills and the fancy mirrors"—it is Rick's bedroom in Chester Street she is describing—"seeing as he's already got the power of life and death over you and you're a foolish lonely woman in the world with a sickly boy to care for and a bankrupt farm to mind, and not a soul but the stupid bailiff to say nice day to for a week at a time?"

"It's enough to know he's done you wrong," Pym insists. "Please, Peggy. The rest is private."

"Seeing as he can beckon you up to London first-class,

send the tickets, just with a flick of his fingers the moment he gets back from his national necessity, because he thinks you're going to put the lawyers on him? Well you go, don't you? If you haven't had a man for two years and more and only your own body to look at withering in the mirror every day, you go!"

"I'm sure you do. I'm sure there was every reason," Pym says. "Please don't tell me any more."

She is doing Rick's voice again: "'Let's sort this matter out once and for all, Peggy my dear. I'm not having a sour bit of business come between us when all I ever wanted was to see you right.' Well, you go, don't you?" Her voice is echoing in the empty square and out over the water. "My God, you go. You pack your bag, you take your boy and lock the door because you're off to get your money and some justice. You scurry up there bursting to have the fight of your life just the moment you set eyes on him. You leave the washing and the dishes and the milking and the penny-pinching life he's put you to. And you tell the stupid bailiff to mind the shop for you, me and Alastair we're going up to London. And when you arrive, instead of a business conference with Mr. Percy Loft and Mr. Bloody Muspole and the gang of them, the man buys you fine clothes in Bond Street and treats you like a princess, with the limousines and the restaurants and the fancy petticoats and silks—well you can always have your row with him later, can't you?"

"No," says Pym. "You can't. You've got to have it then or never."

"If he's trodden you into the mud these years the least you can do is get a bit back from him, in exchange for all the misery, take him for every penny he's robbed you of." Yet again she does Rick's voice: "'I always fancied you, Peggy, you know that. You're a good scout, the best. Always had my eye on that pretty Irish smile of yours and not only the smile either.' So all right, he's got a treat prepared for the boy as well. Takes him to the Arsenal and we sit up there like gods in the special box with the lords and grandees, and dinner at Quaglino's after, him the People's Man, with a two-foot cake with the boy's name written on it, you should see Alastair's face. And next day a Harley Street specialist laid on to listen to his cough and a gold watch for the boy after, for being the brave one, with his initials on it, 'From RTP to a fine young man.' Come to think of it, it's not at all unlike the one you're wearing now—is that a gold one too? So when a man's done all that for you and been a bastard—well you have to admit to yourself after a couple of days of it, there's many worse bastards than him in the world. Most of them wouldn't split their bloody Bath bun with you, let alone a two-foot cake at Quaglino's and somebody to take the boy home to bed after, so that the grown-ups can go to a nightclub and have a bit of fun—why not if he always fancied me? There's not many women wouldn't put off a fight for a day or two for some of that, I suppose—so why not?"

She is speaking as if Pym is no longer there and she is right. She has deafened him but he can still hear her. As I hear her still, an endless, needling babble of destruction. She is speaking to the derelict cattle market with its broken pens and stopped clock, but Pym is numb and dead and anywhere but here. He is in the Overflow House at his prep school and Rick's raised voice and Lippsie's weeping keep waking him in his sleep. He is on Dorothy's bed at The Glades and bored to bloody death, with his head against her shoulder staring at the white sky through the window all day long. He is in an attic somewhere in Switzerland, wondering to God why he has killed his friend to please an enemy.

She is describing Rick's madness with her own. Her voice is a nagging querulous torrent and he hates it to distraction. The way the man boasted. He'd not a foot on the earth when he started with his lying. How he had been Lady Mountbatten's lover and she'd assured him he was better than Noël Coward. How they'd wanted him for Ambassador in Paris but he'd turned it down; he'd no patience with the airy-fairies. And about the stupid green filing cabinet with his rotten secrets in it, imagine the madness of a fellow who spends his hours weaving the rope they ought to hang him with! How he'd led her barefoot to it in her nightdress, look at this my child. The record, he called it. All the rights and the wrongs he'd done. All the evidence of his innocence—his bloody righteousness. How, when he was judged, as judged he would surely be, everything in this stupid cabinet would be put into the balance, rights and wrongs together, and we would see him for what he was, up alongside of the angels while us poor sinners down here bleed and starve for the glory of him. It's what he's put together to con the Almighty with and that's the short of it—imagine the impertinence, and him a bloody Baptist too!

Pym asks her how she has known where to find it. I saw the stupid thing being delivered, she says. I was keeping a watch on Searle's hotel the first day of the campaign. The pansy Cudlove drove it up specially in his limousine, the cost alone. The bastard Loft helped him carry it to the cellar, first time he's got his hands dirty. Rick didn't dare leave it in London while they were all up here. "I have to put the proof on him, Magnus," she keeps repeating as he leads her through the dawn to her miserable lodging-house, her voice whining and insisting in his ear like a machine that nobody can stop. "If he's got the proof there like he says, I'll have it off of him and turn it back on him, I swear I will. All right, I've taken a drop of money off him, it's true. But what's the money when he's cheated me in love? What's the money when he can walk down the street a grandee and there's my John rotting in his grave? And the people in the street all clapping for him, for Rickie boy? And con his way to Heaven into the bargain? What's the use of a poor deluded victim like me who let him have his will with her and will burn in Hell for it, if she won't do her duty by the world and point him up for the devil that he is? Where's the proof? I'm asking."

"Please stop," said Pym. "I know what you want."

"Where's the justice? If he's got it there I'll have it from him, thank you. I've no letters above a couple of procrastinators from Perce Loft, and what do they say? It's like trying to nail a raindrop to the wall, I tell you."

"Try to be calm now," Pym said. "Please."

"I took myself to that stupid Lakin, the Tory. Half a day it took of waiting but I got to him. 'Rick Pym's a shark,' I tell him. What's the good of telling that to a Tory when they're all sharks anyway? I told the Labour but they kept saying 'What's he done?' They said they'll enquire and thank you, but what will they find, the poor innocents?"

Mattie Searle is sweeping the courtyard. Pym is indifferent to his scrutiny. Pym carries himself with authority, using the same walk that got him to Lippsie's bicycle and past the policeman to the Overflow House. I am authority. I am British. Will you kindly get out of my way.

"I left something in the cellar," he says carelessly.

"Oh yes," says Mattie.

Peggy Wentworth's bandsaw voice is cutting into his soul. What dreadful echoes has it woken in him? In what empty house of his childhood is it nagging and whining at him? Why is he so abject before its dredging insistence? She is the risen Lippsie, speaking out from the grave at last. She is the world inside my head made strident. She is the sin I can never expiate. Put your head in the basin, Pym. Hold these taps and listen to me while I explain why no punishment will ever be enough for you. Put him on bread and water, his father's child. Why do you wet your bed, old son? Don't you know there's a thousand quid in cash waiting for you at the end of your first dry year? He switches on the committee-room lights, throws open the door to the cellar steps and stomps heavily down them. Cardboard boxes. Commodities. A glut to fill the shortages. The Michaels' dividers to the fore again, better than a Swiss penknife. He trips the lock of the green cabinet and pulls out the first drawer as the glow begins to spread over him.

Lippschitz first name Anna, two volumes only. Why Lippsie, it's you at last, he thinks calmly. Well it was a short life, wasn't it? No time now, but rest where you are and I'll come back and claim you later. Watermaster Dorothy, Marital, one volume only. Well it was a short marriage too, but wait for me, Dot, for I've other ghosts I must attend to first. He closes the first drawer and pulls open the second. Rick, you bastard, where are you? Bankruptcy, the whole drawer full of it. He opens the third. The imminence of his discovery is setting his body on fire: the eyelids, the surfaces of his back and waist. But his fingers are light and quick and agile. This is what I was born for, if I was born at all. I am God's detective, seeing everybody right. Wentworth, a dozen of them, tagged in Rick's handwriting. Foremost in his mind Pym has the dates of Muspole's letter regretting Rick's absence for his national necessity. He remembers the Fall and Rick's long healthy holiday while he and Dorothy were sweating out their imprisonment in The Glades. Rick you bastard where were you? "Come on, old son, we're pals, aren't we?" In a minute I shall hear Herr Bastl barking.

He opens the last drawer and sees Rex versus Pym 1938, three fat files, and beside it Rex versus Pym 1944, one only. He pulls out the first of the 1938 batch, replaces it and selects the last instead. He turns to the final page first and reads the judge's summing-up, verdict, sentence, the immediate disposal of the prisoner. In calm ecstasy he turns back to the beginning and starts again. No camera in those days. No copier, no tape-recorders. Only what you can see and hear and memorise and steal. He reads for an hour. A clock strikes eight but it means nothing to him. I am following my vocation. Divine service is in progress. You women want nothing but to drag us down.

Mattie is still sweeping the courtyard but his outlines are blurred.

"Find it then?" says Mattie.

"Eventually, thanks, yes."

"That's the way then," says Mattie.

He gains his bedroom, turns the key in the lock, pulls a chair to the washstand, starts writing at once, from the memory straight on to the paper, not a thought for style. A clock strikes again and once he hears a knock, first timid then louder. Then a soft and pessimistic "Magnus?" before the feet slowly descend the stairs. But Pym is at the heart of things, women are temporarily abhorrent to him, even Judy is irrelevant to his destiny. He hears her feet clip across the forecourt and the sound of her van driving away, slow at first, then suddenly much faster. Good riddance.

"Dear Peggy"—he is writing—"I hope that the enclosed will be of use to you."

"Dear Belinda"—he is writing—"I really must own to being fascinated by this glimpse of the democratic process at work. What seems at first to be such a rough instrument turns out to be equipped with all sorts of refined checks and balances. Do let's meet as soon as I return to London."

"Dearest Father"—he is writing—"Today is Sunday and in four days we shall know our fate and yours. But I do want you to know how much I have learned

to admire the courage and conviction with which
you have fought your arduous campaign."

On the dais, Rick had not moved. His flick-knife stare was
still fixed on Pym. Yet he appeared quite calm. Nothing had
happened behind him in the hall that could not be dealt with,
apparently. His preoccupation was with his son, whom he was
regarding with dangerous intensity. He was wearing his statesman's silver tie that night and a handmade shirt of cream
silk with double cuffs and the great big RTP links from
Asprey's. He had had his hair cut earlier in the day, and Pym
could smell the barber's lotion as father and son continued to
face each other. Once, Rick's gaze switched to Muspole and it
was Pym's later impression Muspole nodded to him in some
signal. The silence in the hall was absolute. No coughs or
creaks that Pym could hear, not even from the Old Nellies
whom Rick, as always, had appointed to the front row where
they could remind him of his dear mother and his beloved
father who had died so many heroes' deaths.

At last Rick turned, and advanced towards the audience
with the dutiful Goodman Pym walk that so often preceded
an act of particular hypocrisy. He reached the table but did
not stop. He reached the microphone and switched it off: let
no machine come between us at this moment. He went on
walking till he had reached the edge of the dais, at the point
where it meets the fine curving staircase. He set his jaw, he
looked out over the faces, he allowed his features to betray a
moment's soul-searching before he set himself to speak.
Somewhere on his way between Pym and the audience he
had unbuttoned his jacket. Strike me here, he was saying.
Here is my heart. At last, he spoke. His voice higher than
usual. Hear the emotion clenching it.

"Would you mind repeating that question, please Peggy?
Very loudly, my dear, so that everyone can hear?"

Peggy Wentworth did as she was bidden. But as Rick's
guest now as well as his accuser.

"Thank you, Peggy." Then he asked for a chair for her so
that she could sit down like everybody else. It was brought
by Major Blenkinsop himself. Peggy sat on it in the aisle,
obediently, a child in disgrace, waiting to hear some home
truths. So it seemed to Pym, and still does, for I have long

believed that everything Rick did this night was prepared in advance. If they had popped a dunce's cap on her head Pym would not have been surprised. I believe they had seen Peggy haunting them and Rick had laid out his mental defences in advance of her, as he had often done before. Muspole's people could have snatched her for the evening. Major Blenkinsop could have been advised she was not welcome inside the hall. There were a dozen ways in the court's book to keep a crazed and penniless little blackmailer like Peggy at bay for a crucial night. Rick used none of them. He wanted the trial, as ever. He wanted to be judged and found spotless.

"Ladies and gentlemen. This lady's name is Mrs. Peggy Wentworth. She is a widow whom I have known and tried to help for many years, who has been desperately wronged in life, and who blames me for her misfortune. I hope that after this meeting you will all hear whatever Peggy has to tell you, give her every indulgence at your command, show her every patience. And in your wisdom judge for yourselves where the truth may lie. I hope you will show charity to Peggy, and to me, and remember how hard it is for all of us to accept misfortune without pointing the finger of blame."

He placed his hands behind his back. His feet were close together.

"Ladies and gentlemen, my old friend Peggy Wentworth is quite right." Not even Pym, who thought he knew all the instruments in Rick's orchestra, had heard him so straight and simple in his delivery, so bereft of rhetoric. "Many years ago, ladies and gentlemen, when I was a very young man, striving to get on in life—as we all were once, overeager, ready to cut a few corners—I found myself in the position of the office boy who had borrowed a few stamps from the till and been caught before he had a chance to put them back. I was a first offender, it is true. My mother, like Peggy Wentworth here, was a widow. I had a great father to live up to and only sisters in the family. The responsibilities that weighed upon me, I will admit, blew me across the borders of what Justice, in her blind wisdom, deemed right. Justice exacted her penalty. I paid it in full measure. As I shall pay for it all my life."

Then the jaw went up and the thick hands untied

themselves, and one arm struck out towards the Old Nellies in the front while his eyes and voice reached into the darkness at the back.

"My friends—Peggy, my dear, I still count you as one too—my loyal friends of Gulworth North, I see among you here tonight men and women still young enough to be impulsive. I see others with the experience of life upon them, whose children and grandchildren have gone out into the world to follow their impulses, to strive and make mistakes and overcome them. I want to ask you older people this. If one of these young people—children, grandchildren, or if this son of mine who sits behind me here, poised to collect some of the highest prizes the law of this country can offer—if one of them should ever make a mistake, and pay the price that society exacts, and come home and say, 'Mum, it's me. Dad, it's me'—which one of you sitting here among us tonight is going to slam the door in his face?"

They were standing. They were calling his name. "Rickie— good old Rickie—you get our vote, Rickie boy." On the dais behind him we were standing too, and Pym saw through his own tears that Syd and Morrie were embracing each other. For once Rick did not acknowledge the applause. He was casting round theatrically for Pym and calling "Magnus, where are you, son?" though he knew perfectly well where he was. Affecting to find him he seized his arm, raised it and drew him forward, almost lifting him off the ground even as he offered him as champion to the jubilant crowd, shouting "Here's one, here's one!" I suppose he meant a penitent who has paid the price and come home, though I'll never be certain because of the roar, and perhaps he said, "Here's my son." As to Pym, he could no longer contain himself. He had never adored Rick more. He was choking and clapping, he was shaking Rick's hand for them with both of his, bear-hugging him and patting his great shoulder for them and telling him he was crackerjack. As he did so, he thought he saw Judy's pale face and big pale eyes behind their serious spectacles, watching him from the centre of the crowd. My father needed me, he wanted to explain to her. I forgot where the bus stop was. I lost your phone number. I did it for my country. The Bentley was waiting at the front steps, Cudlove at the door. Riding away at Rick's side, Pym imagined he heard Judy calling out his name: "Pym. You bastard. Where are you?"

It was dawn. Unshaven, Pym sat at his desk, not wanting the daylight. Chin in hand he stared at the last page he had written. Change nothing. Don't look back, don't look forward. You do it once, then die. A miserable vision assailed him of the women in his life vainly waiting at every bus stop along his chaotic path. Rising quickly he mixed himself a Nescafé and drank it while it was still too hot for him. Then took up his stapler and marker pen and set himself busily to work—I am a clerk, that is all I am—stapling his cuttings and cross-indexing the helpful references.

Extracts from *Gulworth Mercury* and *Evening Star* reporting Liberal Candidate's fighting stand on Eve of Poll night in the Town Hall. For libel reasons writers omit direct reference to Peggy Wentworth's accusations, referring only to Candidate's spirited self-defence against personal attack. Enter at 21a. Bloody stapler doesn't work. This sea air rusts everything.

Cutting from London *Times* giving results of Gulworth North by-election:

McKechnie (Labour) 17,970
Lakin (Cons.) 15,711
Pym (Lib.) 6,404
Semi-literate leader ascribes victory to "miscalculated intervention" of Liberals. Enter at 22a.

Extract from Oxford University *Gazette* notifying waiting world that Magnus Richard Pym has been awarded a B.A. Hons. degree in Modern Languages, Class I. No reference to night hours spent studying previous examination papers, or informal exploration of tutor's desk drawers with the aid of the Michaels' ever-handy steel dividers. Entered at 23a.

But actually not entered at all, for in the act of marking this cutting, Pym set it down before him and stared at it, head in hands, with an expression of revulsion.

Rick knew. The bastard knew. His head still between his hands, Pym returns himself to Gulworth later the same night. Father and son are riding in the Bentley, their favourite place. The Town Hall lies behind them, Mrs. Searle's Temperance Rest is approaching. The tumult of the crowd still rings in their ears. It will be another twenty-four hours before the world will learn the name of the winning candidate, but Rick knows it already. He has been judged and applauded for all his life till now.

"Let me tell you something, old son," he says in his mellowest and kindest voice. The passing streetlights are switching his wise features on and off, making his triumph appear intermittent. "Never lie, son. I told them the truth. God heard me. He always does."

"It was fantastic," says Pym. "Could you possibly let go of my arm, please?"

"No Pym was ever a liar, son."

"I know," says Pym, taking back his arm anyway.

"Why couldn't you have come to me, son? 'Father,' you could have said—'Rickie' if you like; you're old enough—'I'm not reading law any more. I'm building up my languages because I want the gift of tongues. I want to go out into the world like my best pal, and be heard wherever men gather regardless of colour, race or creed.' Because do you know what I'd have answered if you'd come to me and said that to your old man?"

Pym is too mad, too dead to care.

"You'd have been super," he says.

"I'd have said: 'Son, you're grown up now. You take your own decisions. All your old man can do is play wicket-keeper while Magnus here bats and God does the bowling.'" He grasps Pym's hand, nearly breaking the fingers. "Don't shrink away from me like that, old son. I'm not angry with you. We're pals, remember? We don't have to tiptoe round each other looking in one another's pockets, poking in drawers, talking to misguided women in hotel cellars. We come out with it straight. On the table. Now dry those old peepers of yours and give your old pal a hug."

With his monographed silk handkerchief the great statesman magnanimously wipes away the tears of Pym's rage and impotence.

"Want a good English steak tonight, son?"

"Not much."

"Old Mattie's cooking us one with onions. You can invite

Judy if you like. We'll all have a game of chemmy afterwards.
She'd like that."

Raising his head, Pym recovered his marker pen and
went back to work.

Extract of Branch minutes of Oxford University Communist
Party regretting departure of Comrade M. Pym, tireless
worker on behalf of cause. Fraternal thanks for his tremen-
dous efforts. Entered at 24a.

Pained letter from Bursar of Pym's college enclosing
his cheque for his last term's battles, marked "Refer to
Drawer." Similar letters and cheques from Messrs. Blackwell,
Parker (Booksellers), and Hall Brothers (Tailors), entered
at 24c.

Pained letter from Pym's bank manager regretting that
following return of cheque drawn in Pym's favour by the
Magnus Dynamic & Astral Company (Bahamas) Ltd., in the
sum of two hundred and fifty pounds, he has had no alternative but to refer to drawer the cheques as at 24c.

Extract from London *Gazette* dated March 29, 1951,
appointing official receiver in yet another petition for bankruptcy
of R.T.P. and eighty-three associated companies.

Letter from Director of Public Prosecutions inviting Pym
to present himself for interview on named date in order to
explain his relationship with above companies. Entered at 36a.

Military call-up papers offering Pym sanctuary. Grabbed
with both hands.

"If I could just sit with you for a bit, Miss D," said Pym,
softly pushing open her kitchen door.

But her chair was empty and the fire out. It was not
evening as he had thought, but dawn.

12

It was the same dawn. It was time minus ten minutes. It was
the moment Brotherhood had lain wakeful and alone for in

his rotten flat that was becoming a solitary cell for him, staring at the images of his past in the restless London sky. It was an outdoor game being played by indoor people who didn't know they were awake. How many times had he sat like this, in rubber boats, on arctic hillsides, pressing the headphones into his ears with kapok mittens to catch the whisper that meant life was not extinct? Here in the communications room on the top floor of the Head Office there were no headphones, no subzero winds to rip through sodden clothing and freeze the operator's fingers off, no bicycle generator that some poor bastard had to pump at till his legs failed. No aerial that collapsed on you when you most needed it. No two-ton suitcase to be cached in iron-hard soil while the Huns were breathing down your neck. Up here we have dimpled grey-green boxes freshly dusted, with pretty pinlights and shiny switches. And tuners and amplifiers. And dials to cut out atmospherics. And comfortable chairs for the barons here assembled to rest their candy arses on. And a mysterious compression of the air that clenches your scalp while you watch the green numerals sliding through their prison window as quickly as the later years of life: now I am forty, now I am forty-five, now I am seventy, now I am ten minutes to being dead.

On the raised platform two boys in headphones were patrolling the dials. They'll never know what it was like, thought Brotherhood. They'll go to their graves thinking life came out of a packet. Bo Brammel and Nigel sat below them like producers at a preview. Behind them a dozen shadows that Brotherhood had barely bothered with. He noticed Lorimer, Head of Operations. He saw Kate and thought thank heaven she's alive. At the edge of the stage, Frankel was lugubriously reporting a string of failures. His mid-European accent has thickened.

"Nine-twenty yesterday morning local time, Prague Station has its chief cut-out dial the Watchman household from a callbox, Bo," he said. "Number engaged. He makes five calls in two hours from round town. Still engaged. He tries Conger. Number out of order. Everybody vanished, everybody out of touch. Midday the Station sends a little girl they own to the canteen where Conger's daughter goes for lunch. Conger's daughter is conscious so maybe she knows where her father is. Our little girl is a sixteen-year-old kid, very

small, very hardy. She hangs around two hours, checks both
sittings, checks the queue. No daughter. She checks the
attendance sheets at the factory gate, tells the guards she is
the daughter's room-mate. She's so innocent they let her.
Conger's daughter is not reported present, is not reported
sicklisted. Vanished."

In the tension nobody spoke to anybody. Everyone
spoke to himself. The room was still filling up. How many
people does it take to give a network a decent burial? thought
Brotherhood. Eight minutes to go.

Frankel continued his dirge. "Seven o'clock yesterday
morning local time, Gdansk Station puts two of their local
boys to mend a telegraph pole at the end of the street where
Merryman lives. His house is in a cul-de-sac. He's got no
other way out. Every day normally he goes to work by car,
leaves his house seven-twenty. But yesterday his car is not
outside his house. Every other day it is parked outside his
house. Not yesterday. From where the boys work they can
see his front door. The front door stays closed. No Merryman,
nobody at all leaves or enters that house by that door.
Downstairs is curtained, no lights, no fresh tracks in the drive.
Merryman's good friend is an architect. Merryman likes to
take a coffee with him sometimes on his way to work. This
architect is not a Joe, he is not whitelisted."

"Wenzel," said Brotherhood.

"Wenzel is the architect's name, Jack. One of the boys
calls up Mr. Wenzel and tells him Merryman's mother is ill.
'Where can I get hold of him to give him this bad news?' he
says. Mr. Wenzel says try the laboratory, how ill? The boy
says she's maybe dying, Merryman ought to get to her fast.
'Give him this message,' the boy says. 'Tell him please that
Maximilian says he better get to his mother's bedside fast.'
Maximilian, that's the codeword for it's all over. Maximilian
means abort, means run, means get the hell out by any
known means, don't bother with customary procedures, run.
The boy is resourceful. When he has ceased to speak to Mr.
Wenzel, he calls the laboratory where Merryman works. 'This
is Mr. Maximilian. Where's Merryman? It's urgent. Tell him
Maximilian got to speak to him about his mother.' Merryman
don't come in today, they tell him. Merryman got a conference in Warsaw."

Brotherhood was already objecting. "They wouldn't say that," he growled. "The labs don't give out details of staff movements. They're a top-secret installation, for Christ's sake. Somebody's playing games with us."

"Sure, Jack. My own reaction entirely. You want I go on?"

A couple of heads turned to locate Brotherhood at the back of the room.

"When the line to Merryman went dead we instructed Warsaw to try to reach Voltaire direct," Frankel continued. He paused. "Voltaire is sick."

Brotherhood let out an angry laugh. "Voltaire? He hasn't had a day's sickness in his life."

"His Ministry says he's sick, Jack, his wife says he's sick, his mistress says he's sick. He ate some bad mushrooms, gone to hospital. He's sick. Official. They all say the same."

"I'll say it's official."

"What do you want me to do, Jack? Tell me something I should do that you would do yourself and I have not done. Okay? It's a blackout, Jack. Like a silence everywhere. Like a bomb fell."

"You said you'd keep filling the letter boxes," Brotherhood said.

"We filled for Merryman yesterday. Money and instructions. We filled."

"So what happened?"

"Still there. Money and instructions so much he want. Fresh papers, maps, you name it. For Conger we put up two visuals, one for call us, one for evacuate. One curtain on a first floor, one light in a basement window. Is that correct, Jack? Does that accord with the agreed procedures?"

"It accords."

"Okay. So he doesn't answer. He doesn't call, he doesn't write, he doesn't run."

For five minutes there was no sound but the sounds of waiting: the sighing of soft chairs, the striking of lights and matches and the squeaky-soled footsteps of the boys. Kate glanced at Brotherhood and he smiled confidence back. Bo said, "We're thinking of you, Jack," but Brotherhood did not reply and he was certainly not thinking of Bo. A bell rang. From the platform a boy said, "Conger, sir, on schedule," and trimmed some dials. A white pin-light winked above his head. The second boy dropped a switch. Nobody clapped, nobody got to his feet or cried, "they're alive!"

"Conger operator's come in and say he's ready to send, Bo," Frankel said gratuitously. Behind him, the boys were moving automatically, deaf to everything outside their headphones. "Now we make our first transmission. We use all tape, no handwriting. Conger does the same. Accelerated Morse, we unroll it both ends. Transmission takes maybe one and a half minutes, two. Unroll and decode takes maybe five. . . . See that? . . . 'We are ready to receive you. Talk.' —this is what we say to him. Now Conger is talking again. Watch the red light left, please. It burns, he's talking—he's finished."

"Wasn't very long, was it?" Lorimer drawled, not to anyone in particular. Lorimer had buried agents before.

"Now we wait for the decode," Frankel told his audience a little too brightly. "Three minutes, maybe five. Time to smoke a cigarette, okay? Everybody relax. Conger's alive and well."

The boys were transferring spools, resetting instruments.

"Let's just be grateful he's alive," said Kate, and several heads turned sharply, remarking this unaccustomed display of feeling from a Fifth Floor lady.

The grey spools were rolling, one on to the other. For a moment they heard the unrhythmic piping of Morse code. It stopped.

"Hey," said Lorimer softly.

"Run it through again," said Brotherhood.

"What's happened?" said Kate.

The boys rewound the spools and switched again to forward. The Morse resumed and stopped as before.

"Could it be a fault the other end?" Lorimer asked.

"Sure," Frankel said. "Possible his winder's on the blink, possible he hit some bad ionosphere. In a minute he comes through again. No problem."

The taller of the two boys was pulling off his headphones. "Mind if we decode, Mr. Frankel?" he said. "Sometimes when they've got a hitch they tell us about it in the message."

On a nod from Frankel he shifted a spool to a machine at the far end of the bank. The printer began chattering immediately. Nigel and Lorimer moved quickly towards the

platform. The printer stopped. Nigel magisterially ripped out
the sheet and held it for Lorimer and himself to read.
Brotherhood was already striding down the aisle. Mounting
the platform, he snatched the script from their unresisting
hands.

"Jack, don't," said Kate under her breath.

"Don't what?" Brotherhood said, suddenly out of patience with her. "Don't care about my agents? Don't do what
exactly?"

"Tell them to print another copy, will you, Frankel?"
Nigel said smoothly. "Then we can all look at it together
without shoving."

Brotherhood was holding the sheet before him. Nigel
and Lorimer had meekly arranged themselves to either side
of him and were reading it over his shoulder.

"Routine intelligence report, Bo," Nigel announced reading aloud. "Promised length, three hundred and seven groups.
Actual length so far forty-one. Subject, restationing of Soviet
missile bases in mountains north of Pilsen. Subsource Mirabeau
reporting ten days ago. Mirabeau in turn reporting her Soviet
Army boyfriend codename Leo—Leo's done us rather well in
the past, I seem to remember. Message reads as follows:
Subsource Talleyrand confirms empty low-loaders leaving area—
message ends in midsentence. Obviously the winder. Unless,
as you say, his signal hit freak conditions."

Frankel was already giving orders to the taller boy.
"Send them 'Your signal garbled.' Do it immediately. Tell
them we want a rerun. Tell them if they can't transmit now
we'll remain on standby till they can. Tell them we want a
roll-call of all members of the network. You got set phrases for
that or you want I draft something?"

"Tell them damn all," Brotherhood ordered very loud.
"And stop crying everybody. No one's hurt."

He had thrust his hands into his raincoat pockets. He
was halfway down the aisle. Nigel and Lorimer were still on
stage, a pair of choirboys clutching their hymn sheet between
them. Brammel sat stoically upright in the auditorium. Kate
was staring at him, not stoical at all.

"You can tell them you want a roll-call or a rerun, you
can tell them to abort, you can tell them to jump in the
Vistula. It doesn't make a dime of difference," said Brotherhood.

"Poor man," said Nigel to Lorimer. "They're his Joes, you see. It's the strain."

"They're not my Joes and they never were. You can have them with my blessing." He looked around him for men with sense. "Frankel. For Christ's sake. Lorimer. When this service catches someone else's Joe, if it ever does these days, what does it do? If he's willing to be played, we play him back. If he's not we send him to the Tower. Is it different now? I wouldn't know."

"So?" said Nigel, humouring him.

"If we decide to play him back, we do it as naturally and as fast as we can. Why? Because we want to show the opposition that nothing has changed. We want it seamless. We don't hide his car and close his house. We don't let him or his daughter or anybody else vanish into thin air. We don't ignore dead letter boxes or invent fatuous stories about people eating bad mushrooms. We don't sandbag radio operators in the middle of their high-speed transmissions. That is the last, the very last thing we do. Unless."

"I don't read you, Jack, old boy," Nigel said, whom Brotherhood had deliberately ignored. "I don't think anybody does, to be truthful. I think you are very naturally upset and you are getting a bit metaphysical, if you don't mind my saying."

"Unless what, Jack?" said Frankel.

"Unless we *want* the opposition to know we're rolling up their network."

"But why would anybody want that, Jack?" Frankel asked earnestly. "Explain to us. Please."

"Why not explain it another time?" said Nigel.

"There never was a bloody network. They owned those networks from day one. They paid the actors, wrote the script. They owned Pym and near enough they owned me. They owned all of you as well. You just haven't woken up to it."

"Then why do they bother to tell us anything at all?" Frankel objected. "Why send us a fake interrupted signal? Why rig the disappearance of the Joes?"

Brotherhood smiled. Not kindly, not with humour. But he did turn to Frankel and he did smile at him. "Because, old boy, they want us to think they've got Pym when they haven't," he said. "That is the only lie they've got left to sell

us. They want us to call off the hunt and go home to our high
tea. They want to find him for themselves. That's the good
news of the day. Pym is still on the run and they want him as
much as we do."

They watched him turn and stride down the aisle and
slide the locks back on the padded door. Poor old Jack, they
said to each other with their eyes as the light went up: his
life's work. Lost all his Joes and can't face it. Dreadful to see
him so cut up. Only Frankel seemed to wish he hadn't gone.

"Have you ordered the rerun yet?" said Nigel. "I said
have you ordered a rerun?"

"I'll do it now," said Frankel.

"Good man," said Bo appreciatively from the stalls.

In the corridor, Brotherhood paused to light himself a
cigarette. The door opened and closed again. It was Kate.

"I can't go on," she said. "It's mad."

"Well it's going to get a damn sight madder," snapped
Brotherhood, still angry. "That was just the trailer."

It was night once more and Mary had got through another
day without throwing herself politely from a top-floor window
or scrawling filthy words on the dining-room walls. Seated on
her bed still moderately sober, she stared at the book and
then at the phone. The phone had a second wire fed into it.
The wire led to a grey box and seemed to stop. Since my
time, she thought. Can't be doing with these modern gad-
gets. She poured another generous tot of whisky and set the
glass on the table at her elbow in order to end the argument
she had been having with herself for the last ten minutes.
There you are, damn you. If you want one, have one. If you
don't, leave the bloody thing where it is. She was fully
dressed. She was supposed to have a headache but the
headache was a lie to escape the excruciating company of
Fergus and the girl Georgie who had begun to treat her with
the deference of warders before her hanging. "How about a
nice game of Scrabble, Mary? . . . Not in the mood are we?
Never mind. . . . I say, that shepherd's pie *did* go down a
treat, didn't it, Georgie? I haven't had a shepherd's pie like
that since my nan went. Do you think it's the freezing that
does it? Sort of ripens it, does it, the freezing?" At eleven
o'clock, screaming inside, she had left them to the washing-

up and brought herself up here to the book and to the note that had accompanied it. A deckled card. Silver-edged, my wedding anniversary. In a deckled envelope. Vile cherub blowing trumpet top left.

> "Dear Mary,
>   "So sorry to hear about M's calamity. Picked this up for pennies this morning and wondered whether you would like to bind it for me, same as all the others, full hide, buckram and the title printed in gold capitals between the first and second band on the spine. The end-papers look kind of new to me, maybe just rip them out? Grant's away too so I guess I know how you feel. Could you do it quickly, as a surprise for him? Usual fee, of course!
>   "My love, darling,
>   Bee"

Keeping her hand away from the whisky and her mind clear of thoughts of a certain moustached phantom, Mary applied her training to the note. The handwriting was not Bee Lederer's. It was a forgery and to anyone who knew the game a dismal one. The writer had paid lip-service to Bee's all-American copperplate but the Germanic influence was clear in the spiky "u"s and "n"s and the "t"s without tails. "Whether" instead of "if," she thought: when did an American write "whether"? The spelling wasn't Bee's either: a word like "calamity." Bee couldn't spell for toffee. She doubled every consonant on sight. Her letters to Mary in Greece, penned on similar stationery, had contained such family gems as menipullate and phallassy. As to "full hide": Mary had bound just three books for Bee, and Bee hadn't known from green apples how she wanted them, except she thought they looked great on Grant's shelf, just like the old libraries you have in England. Full hide, buckram, the placing of the lettering: these were the writer talking, not Bee. And if Bee suspected that the end-papers might not be original—well bully for Bee because a month ago she had asked Mary wherever had she bought that cute wallpaper stuff she stuck on the inside of her covers?

The note was so bad, Mary concluded—and so unlike Bee—that it was almost deliberately bad: good enough to fool

Fergus when it was delivered to the door this afternoon, bad enough to be a signal to Mary that it meant something different.

Something she had been warned of, for instance.

She had read the clues from the moment she opened the door to the vanman, while Fergus the idiot lurked in the coat cupboard with a bloody great Howitzer in his hand in case the vanman turned out to be a Russian in disguise—which perhaps on reflection he was, because Bee had never used a private delivery service in her life. Bee would have dropped the book in herself on the way back from Becky's school, cooeeing through the letter box. Bee would have buttonholed Mary at the International Ladies on Tuesday, leaving her to hump the damn thing home as best she could.

"Mind if I read the card, Mary?" Fergus had said. "It's just routine, only you know what they're like in London. Bee. That'll be Mrs. Lederer, wife of the American gentleman?"

"That's who it will be," Mary had confirmed.

"Well it's a nice book, I will say. In English too. Looks really old, it does." He was turning through it with practised fingers, pausing at pencil marks, holding occasional pages to the light.

"It's 1698," Mary had said, pointing to the Roman numerals.

"My goodness, you can read that stuff."

"Can I have it back now, please?"

The grandfather clock in the hall was striking twelve. Fergus and Georgie were by now no doubt lying blissfully in each other's arms. Over the interminable days of her secret imprisonment Mary had watched their romance ripen. Tonight when she came down to dinner Georgie had the indisguisable glow of someone who had been screwing minutes before. In a year's time the two of them would become yet another his-and-hers couple in one of the resources sections where the Other Ranks held sway: surveillance, microphone installation, sweeping, steaming mail. A year later when they had pooled their fiddled overtime and their cooked-up mileage and inflated their out-of-town subsistence they would make a down payment on a house in East Sheen, have two children and become eligible for the Firm's subsidised education scheme. I'm being a jealous bitch, thought Mary, unrepentant. Right now, I wouldn't mind an hour with Fergus myself. She picked up the receiver and waited.

"Who are you ringing, Mary?" said Fergus's voice immediately.

Wherever he was in his love-life just then, Fergus was very awake indeed when it came to cutting in on Mary's outgoing phone calls.

"I'm lonely," Mary replied. "I want to have a chat with Bee Lederer. Anything wrong with that?"

"Magnus is still in London, Mary. He's been delayed."

"I know where he is. I know the story. I am also grown up."

"He's been contacting you regular by phone, you've had nice chats with him, he'll be back in a day or two. Head Office has nabbed him for a briefing while he's over there. That's all that happened."

"I'm all right, Fergus. I'm word perfect."

"Would you normally ring her as late as this?"

"If both Magnus and Grant are away, yes I would."

Mary heard a click and then the dialling tone. She dialled the number and Bee started moaning at once. She was having her damned period, she said, a real bastard, cramps, the bends, you name it. It always grabbed her this way in winter, specially when Grant wasn't there to service her. Giggle. "Oh shit, Mary, I really miss it. Does that make me a whore?"

"I've had a lovely long letter from Tom," said Mary. A lie. It was a letter and it was long but it was not lovely. It was an account of the great time Tom had had with Uncle Jack last Sunday and it had made Mary's flesh creep.

Bee declared that Becky just adored Tom so much it was indecent. "Can you imagine what is going to happen the day those kids wake up and discover *la différence*?"

Yes, I can, thought Mary. They're going to hate each other's guts. She took Bee through her day. Hell, just screwing around, said Bee. She'd had a squash date with Cathie Krane from the Canadian Embassy but they'd agreed on a coffee instead because of Bee's condition. Salad at the Club, and Jesus somebody *really* ought to teach these damned Austrians how to make a decent salad. This afternoon a cruddy Bring and Buy at the Embassy in aid of the Contras in Nicaragua and who gives a fly's elbow about the Contras in Nicaragua?

"You should go out and buy yourself something," Mary suggested. "A dress or an antique or something."

"Listen, I can't even *move*. You know what he did, the little runt? He turned the Audi in for servicing on his way to the airport. I don't get the car, I don't get a lay."

"I'd better ring off," Mary said. "I've got a feeling Magnus is going to pull one of his dead-of-night calls and there'll be all hell if the number is engaged."

"Yeah, how's he taken it?" said Bee vaguely. "Is he all weepy or is he sort of reconciled? Some men, I think they really want to castrate their fathers all their lives. You should hear Grant sometimes."

"I'll know when he's back," said Mary. "Before he left he hardly spoke a word."

"Too cut up, huh? Grant never gets cut up about anything, the creep."

"It hit him badly at first," Mary confessed. "He sounds much better now." She had scarcely rung off before the phone gave its in-house buzz.

"Why didn't you mention the beautiful book she sent you, Mary?" Fergus complained. "I thought that was why you'd be ringing."

"I told you why I was ringing. I was ringing because I was lonely. Bee Lederer sends me about fifteen books a week. Why should I talk to her about a bloody book to please you?"

"I wasn't meaning to offend, Mary."

"She didn't mention the book so why should I? She gave me all the necessary instructions in her bloody note." I'm protesting too much, she thought, cursing herself. I'm putting questions in his mind. "Listen, Fergus. I'm tired and liable to bite, okay? Leave me alone and go back to what you both do best."

She picked up the book. Nothing, not a book on earth, could have authenticated the sender so perfectly. "De Arte Graphica. The Art of Painting by C. A. DU FRESNOY with REMARKS. Translated into English together with an Original Preface containing a Parallel between Painting and Poetry. By Mr. DRYDEN." She drained the glass of whisky. It was the same book. She had no doubt. The same book Magnus brought to me in Berlin when I still belonged to Jack. Came bounding up the stairs with it. Knocking on the steel door of Special Ordnance which was our cover while he clutched it in his hand. "Hey, Mary, open up!" It was before we had

become lovers. Before he had started to call me Mabs.
"Listen I want you to do a rush job for me. Can you put a CD
into the binding of this? It's to take one standard sheet of
code cloth. Can you do it by tonight?" Then I staged a
misunderstanding because we were already flirting. I pretended I hadn't heard of CDs except on diplomatic cars,
which allowed Magnus to explain to me in his earnest way
that CD meant concea' ,nt device and Jack Brotherhood
had told him Mary was the best person for the job. "We're
using a bookshop as a dead letter box," Magnus explained.
"I've got this Joe who's an antiquarian-book fiend." Case
officers were not usually so generous about their operations.

And I took off the end-paper, she remembered as she
began gently prodding the covers. I scraped away a patch of
cover board until I was nearly at the hide. Other people
would have taken off the hide and gone under it from the
front. Not our Mary. For Magnus nothing but perfection
would do. Next night he gave me dinner. The night after that
we went to bed together. Next morning I told Jack what had
happened and he was gallant and sweet and said we were
both very lucky, and that he'd withdraw from the field and let
us get on with it, if that was what I wanted. I said it was. And
I told Jack in my happiness that what had brought me and
Magnus together was de Arte Graphica, a Parallel between
Painting and Poetry, which was rather extraordinary when
you remembered that I was mad about painting and Magnus
was hell-bent on writing the great novel of his life.

"Where are you going, Mary?" Fergus said, looming
before Mary in the corridor. She had the book in her hand.
She shoved it at him. "I can't sleep. I'm going down to the
cellar to fool around with this. Now go back to your nice lady
and leave me alone."

Closing the cellar door she went quickly to the work-
bench. In minutes Georgie is going to saunter in with a nice
cup of tea for me in order to make sure I haven't defected or
cut my wrists. Filling a bowl with warm water she damped a rag
and set to work soaking off the end-paper. The writer she of
the note knew what he was talking about. On a book of that
age the original glue was animal and would have crystallised.
Mary, when she had doctored it for Magnus, had used animal
glue too. But the new paper had been stuck on with flour
paste which responded quickly to water. She was using a

cloth and scrubbing. Normally she would have used blotting
paper and a pressing tin. The end-paper came away. The
board remained. Taking a scalpel she began scuffing it with
the blade. If they've used rope board, I've had it. Rope board
was made of real old rope taken from a man-of-war. It was
tarred and twisted and packed solid. To scrape into it would
take hours. She need not have worried. It was modern
millboard and disintegrated like dry earth. She kept scuffing
and suddenly the code cloth lay before her, flat against the
inside of the hide, exactly where she had put it for Magnus.
Except that this one had capital letters instead of figure
groups. This one began "Dear Mary." She stuffed it quickly
down her front, retrieved the scalpel, and set about removing
the rest of the end-paper as if she were going to rebind from
the beginning, full hide as Bee had requested.

"I just thought I *had* to come and see how you do it,"
Georgie explained, sitting down beside her. "I really *need* a
hobby like that myself, Mary. I just don't ever seem able to
relax."

"Poor you," said Mary.

It was night and Brotherhood was angry. Though he was out
in the streets and away from the Firm and the Firm's ken,
though he had work to do and action to relieve him, he was
angry. His anger had been mounting for two days. This
morning's outburst about the Joes was not the start of it. It
had been kindled yesterday, like a slow-burning fuse, as he
was leaving the conference room in St. John's Wood after
perjuring himself to save Brammel's neck. It had stuck with
him like a faithful friend through his meeting with Tom and
his excursion to Reading station: Pym has broken the moral
laws. He has outlawed himself by choice. It had touched
flashpoint in the signals room this morning and gathered
more heat with every pointless conference and frittered hour
since. From his position of half-pitied and wholly blamed
has-been, Brotherhood had listened to his own arguments
being used against him and had looked on as, under his very
eyes, his old defence of Pym had been adopted and updated
into a policy of institutionalised inertia.

"But, Jack, it's all so circumstantial—you said so yourself," Brammel brayed, never stronger than when demon-

strating that two positives made a negative. "'If you run any succession of coincidences through a computer, you will find that everything looks possible and most things look highly likely.' Who said that, pray? I'm quoting you deliberately, Jack. We're sitting at your feet, remember? Good heavens, I never thought I'd have to defend Pym against *you*!"

"I was wrong," said Brotherhood.

"But who says you were? Only you, I think. So Pym has a Czech code pad in his chimney place," Brammel conceded. "He has a camera we didn't know about with a document-copying attachment or whatever. Good heavens, Jack, think of all the bits of equipment you've picked up in your time, just in the ordinary way of playing agents back and forth! Gold bars, cameras, microdot lenses, concealment devices, I don't know what. You could have started your own pawnbroker's shop with them. All right I grant you he should have turned the stuff in. I see him as being rather in the position of a police detective who has taken a lot of swag off one of his informants. He shoves it in a drawer—or in the fireplace— hides it from his family and one day it's all discovered. But it doesn't make him a burglar. It makes him an efficient police-man who's been cavalier or at worst careless."

"He's not careless," said Brotherhood. "He's not a risk taker."

"All right, so now he is. The fellow's had a nervous breakdown, he's acting clean out of character, he's hidden himself away somewhere, he's putting out the usual cries for help," Brammel reasoned, in a note of saintly tolerance. "Probably a girlfriend, knowing him. We shall find out soon enough. But look at the scenario, Jack. His father dies. He's the artistic type of officer, always wanting to write the great novel, paint, sculpt, take sabbaticals, I don't know what. He's hit a menopausal age in life. He's been living under a cloud of suspicion for far too long. Do you wonder he's had a bit of a crack-up? Be a wonder if he hadn't, if you ask me. All right, I don't condone it. And I shall want to know why he took that burnbox, though you tell me he knew everything that was in it anyway and wrote most of it himself, so what's the difference? And when we find him, I may pull him out of the field for a while. There is still no justification for me to raise a public hue and cry. To go to my Minister and say 'We've found another one.' Least of all to the Americans. Bang go the barter treaties. Bang goes the intelligence pooling and the private line to

Langley that often means so much more than normal diplomatic links. Do you want me to risk all that until we *know*?"

"Bo feels you should stop flying solo," Nigel said when they were back on the servants' side of Brammel's door. "I'm afraid I agree. From now on you'll make no field enquiries without my personal authority. You're to remain on call and you're to start nothing. Is that clear?"

It is clear, thought Brotherhood, examining the house from across the road. It is clear that the rewards of my old age are dangerously threatened. He tried to remember who it was in mythology who was cursed to live long enough to witness the consequences of his bad advice. The house was in the best of Chelsea's many beautiful backwaters, set at the end of a long garden only partly visible above the gate. An air of decadence pervaded its genteel shabbiness, an unworldly languor inhabited its flaking stucco. Brotherhood walked past it several times, checking the upper windows, studying the skyline for sight of a church, for Pym's mental substitutions were becoming rooted in his mind like spy talk. On the fourth floor a dormer window was lit and curtained. As he watched he saw a figure pass across it, too quickly and too far away for him to tell whether it was man or woman.

He took a last look up and down the road. A brass bellpush was set into the gatepost. He pressed it and waited but not long. He shoved the gate, it creaked and opened, he stepped inside and closed it after him. The garden was a secret patch of English countryside walled on three sides. Nothing overlooked it. The sounds of traffic ceased miraculously. The flagstone path was slippery with unswept leaves. Home, he rehearsed again. Home in Scotland, home in Wales. Home by the sea. Home as an upper window and a church. Home as an aristocratic mother who took him visiting great houses. He passed the statue of a draped woman, one stone breast offered to the autumn night. Home as a series of concentric fantasies, all with the same truth at the centre. Who had said that?—Pym or himself? Home as promises to women he didn't love. The front door was opening as he reached it. A young manservant was watching him approach. His monkey jacket had a regimental cut. Behind him, unrestored gilt mirrors and a chandelier glinted against dark wallpaper. "He's got a boy name of Stegwold living there," Superintendent Bellows of police liaison had reported. "If you were old enough, I'd read you his record of convictions."

"Sir Kenneth in, son?" said Brotherhood pleasantly as he wiped his shoes on the mat and shook off his raincoat.

"I don't know, do I? Who shall I say?"

"Mr. Marlow, son, and I'd like ten minutes with him alone on a mutual matter."

"From?" said the boy.

"His constituency, son," said Brotherhood just as pleasantly.

The boy tripped quickly upstairs. Brotherhood's gaze skimmed the hall. Hats, idiosyncratic. Coaching overcoat, green with age. One Guards bowler, ditto. Army service cap with Coldstream badge. Blue china urn stuffed with ancient golf clubs, walking-sticks and warped tennis racquets. The boy came mincing down the stairs again, trailing one hand on the banisters, unable to resist an entrance.

"He'll see you now, Mr. Marlow," he said.

The stairs were lined with portraits of rude men. In a dining-room, two places were laid with enough silver for a banquet. A decanter, cold meats, and cheeses lay on the sideboard. It was not till Brotherhood noticed a couple of dirty plates that he realised the meal was already over. The library smelled of mildew and the fumes of paraffin from a stove. A gallery ran along three walls. Half the balustrade was missing. The stove had been shoved into the fireplace and in front of it stood a clothes-horse hung with socks and underpants. In front of the clothes-horse stood Sir Kenneth Sefton Boyd. He wore a velvet smoking jacket and an open-necked shirt and old satin slippers with gold-stitched monograms worn away. He was burly and thick-necked, with uneven pads of flesh round his jaw and eyes. His mouth was bent to one side as if by a clenched fist. He spoke with the bent side while the other stayed still.

"Marlow?"

"How do you do, sir," said Brotherhood.

"What do you want?"

"I'd like to speak to you alone if I may, sir."

"Policeman?"

"Not quite, sir. Something like."

He handed Sir Kenneth a card. This is to certify that the bearer is engaged in enquiries affecting the national security. For confirmation please ring Scotland Yard extension so-and-so. The extension led to Superintendent Bellows's depart-

ment, which knew all Brotherhood's names. Unimpressed,
Sir Kenneth handed the card back.

"So you're a spy."

"Of a sort, I suppose. Yes."

"Want a drink? Beer? Scotch? What do you want to drink?"

"A scotch would be very welcome, sir, now you mention it."

"Scotch, Steggie," said Sir Kenneth. "Get him a scotch,
will you? Ice? Soda? What do you want in your scotch?"

"A little water would be welcome."

"All right. Give him water. Bring him a jug. Put it on the
table. Over there by the tray. Then he can help himself. You
can go away. And top mine up, while you're about it. Want to
sit down, Marlow? Over there do you?"

"I thought we were going to the Albion," said Steggie
from the door.

"Can't now. Got to talk to this chap."

Brotherhood sat. Sir Kenneth sat opposite him; his gaze
was yellowed and unresponsive. Brotherhood had seen dead
men whose eyes were more alive. His hands had fallen into
his lap and one of them kept flipping like a beached fish. On
the table between them lay a backgammon board with the
pieces in mid-battle. Who was he playing with? thought
Brotherhood. Who dined with him? Who was sharing his
music with him? Who warmed my chair before I sat in it?

"You surprised to see me, sir?" said Brotherhood.

"Take a bit more than that to surprise me, old boy."

"Anyone else been here recently, making funny enquiries?
Foreign gentlemen? Americans?"

"Not that I know of. Why should they?"

"There's a bunch going round from our own vetting side
as well, I'm told. I wondered whether any of them had been
here. I tried to find out before I left the office but there's a
lack of coordination, it's all moving so fast."

"What is?"

"Well, sir, it seems that your old school friend Mr.
Magnus Pym has disappeared. They're looking into everyone
who might have knowledge of his whereabouts. That will
include you naturally."

Sir Kenneth's eye lifted to the door.

"Something out there bothering you, sir?" said Brotherhood.

Sir Kenneth rose, went to the door and pulled it open.

Brotherhood heard a scuffle of footsteps on the stairs but he was too late to see who it was, though he jostled Sir Kenneth aside in his haste to look.

"Steggie, I want you to go to the Albion ahead of me," Sir Kenneth called into the well. "Go now. I'll join you later. I don't want him hearing this stuff," he told Brotherhood as he closed the door. "What he doesn't know can't hurt him."

"With his record I don't blame you," said Brotherhood. "Mind if I look upstairs now we're standing?"

"Yes I damn well do. And don't lay hands on me again. I don't fancy you. Got a warrant?"

"No."

Resuming his chair, Sir Kenneth took a spent matchstick from the pocket of his smoking jacket and set to work on his fingernails with its charred end. "Get a warrant," he advised. "Get a warrant and I might let you look. Other hand I mightn't."

"Is he here?" said Brotherhood.

"Who?"

"Pym."

"Don't know. Didn't hear. Who's Pym?"

Brotherhood was still standing. He was unnaturally pale, and it took him a moment to steady his voice before he spoke again.

"I've got a deal for you," he said.

Sir Kenneth still did not hear.

"Hand him over to me. You go upstairs. Or you ring him. You do whatever you've agreed to do between you. And you hand him over to me. In return I'll keep your name out of it, and Steggie's name out of it. The alternative is 'Baronet M.P. shelters very old friend on the run.' It's also a serious possibility that you will be charged as an accomplice. How old is Steggie?"

"Old enough."

"How old was he when he started here?"

"Look it up. Don't know."

"I'm Pym's friend too. There are worse people than me coming looking for him. Ask him. If he agrees, I agree. I'll keep your name out of it. Just give him to me and you and Steggie need never hear from him or me again."

"Sounds to me as though you've more to lose than we have," said Sir Kenneth, surveying the results of his manicure.

"I doubt it."

"Question of what we've all got left, I suppose. Can't lose

what you haven't got. Can't miss what you don't care about. Can't sell what isn't yours."

"Pym can, apparently," said Brotherhood. "He's been selling his nation's secrets by the looks of it."

Sir Kenneth continued to admire his fingernails. "For money?"

"Probably."

Sir Kenneth shook his head. "Didn't care about money. Love was all he cared about. Didn't know where to find it. Clown really. Tried too hard."

"Meanwhile he's wandering around England with a lot of papers that aren't his to give away, and you and I are supposed to be patriotic Englishmen."

"Lot of chaps do a lot of things they shouldn't do. That's when they need their chums."

"He wrote to his son about you. Do you know that? Some drivel about a penknife. Does that ring a bell?"

"Matter of fact it does."

"Who's Poppy?"

"Never heard of her."

"Or him?"

"Nice thought, but no."

"Wentworth?"

"Never been there. Hate the place. What about it?"

"There was a girl called Sabina he apparently got caught up with in Austria. He ever mention her?"

"Not that I remember. Pym got caught up with a lot of girls. Not that it did him much good."

"He rang you, didn't he? On Monday night, from a callbox."

With startling abruptness, Sir Kenneth flung up one arm in pleasure and gave a hoot of merriment. "Pissed out of his skull," he declared, very loud. "Ossified. Haven't heard him so pissed since Oxford when six of us put away a case of his father's port. Pretended some queen from Merton gave it to him, I don't know why. There weren't any queens in Merton in those days. Not rich ones. We were all at Trinity."

It was after midnight. Back in the confinement of his Shepherd Market flat with the pigeons on the parapet Brotherhood poured himself another vodka and added orange juice from a carton. He had thrown his jacket on the bed, his pocket tape-recorder lay before him on the desk. He was jotting as he listened.

". . . don't go to Wiltshire a lot as a rule while Parliament's in session but Sunday was my second wife's birthday and our boy was down from school so I went and did my stuff and thought I'd stay on for a day or two and see what gives in the constituency. . . ."

Forward again: ". . . don't normally answer the phone in Wiltshire but Monday's her bridge night and I was in the library playing a game of backgammon so when the phone rang I thought I might as well take it rather than spoil her four. Half past eleven it must have been but Jean's bridge nights go on for ever. Chap's voice. Must be her boyfriend, I thought. Bloody cheek, really, this time of night. 'Hullo? Sef? That Sef?' 'Who the hell's that?' I said. 'It's me. Magnus. My father's died. Over here to bury him.' I thought, Poor old chap. Nobody likes to have his old man die on him. . . . That right for you? More water? Help yourself."

Brotherhood hears himself roar "Thanks" as he leans towards the water jug. Then the sounds of a flood as he pours.

"'How's Jem?' he says. Jemima's my sister. They had a ding-dong once, never came to much. Married a florist. Extraordinary thing. Chap grows flowers all along the road to Basingstoke. Puts his name up on a board. Doesn't seem to bother her. Not that she sees much of him. Navigational problems, our Jem. Same as me."

Forward again: ". . . pissed. Couldn't tell whether he was laughing or crying. Poor chap, I thought. Drowning his sorrows. I'd do the same. Next thing I know, he's prosing on about our private school. I mean Christ, we'd done two or three schools together, Oxford, not to mention a couple of holidays, yet all he wants to talk about forty years later, on the blower middle of the night, party going on, is how he carved my initials in the staff loo at our private and got me flogged for it. 'Sorry I carved your initials, Sef.' All right. He did it. He carved 'em. I never doubted he carved 'em. Cocked it up too. He would. Know what he did? Bloody fool put a hyphen between the 'S' and the 'B' where we don't have one. I told old Grimble, the headmaster. 'Why would I put a hyphen in?' I said. 'Not how I spell my name,' I said. 'No hyphen in it. Look at the school list.' Not a blind bit of difference, flogged me. Way it goes, you see. No justice. I don't know I minded much. Everybody flogged everybody in those days. Besides, I wasn't very nice to him myself. Always ragging him about his people. Father was a con man, you know. Nearly ruined my aunt. Had a go at my mother too. Tried to bed her but she was too fly. Some scheme to build a new airport in Scotland somewhere. He'd squared the locals, all he needed was buy the land, get the formal permission, make a fortune. Cousin of mine owns half Argyll. I asked him about it. Hokum, the whole thing. Extraordinary. I stayed with 'em once. Tarts' parlour in Ascot. All these crooks hanging about and Magnus calling them 'sir.' Father tried to get into Parliament once. Pity he didn't. He'd have been good company. . . ."

Forward again: ". . . banging in the cash. I asked him where he was, he said London but he had to use phone boxes, he was being followed. I said, 'Whose initials have you been carving now?' Joke actually, but he didn't see it. I was sorry about his old man, you see. Didn't want him moping. Dramatic chap, always has been. Nothing going on in his life unless he's got some frightful problem on his hands. You could have sold him the Egyptian pyramids long as you said they were falling down. I said, give me the number of your phone, I'll ring you back. He said somebody must have told me to say that. I said 'Absolute bilge, hell are you talking about? Half my friends are on the run.' He said his father was dead and he was looking at his life for the first time. Fundamental. Always has been. Then he went back to these initials he'd carved. 'I'm really sorry, Sef.' I said, 'Look here, old boy, I always knew it was you and I don't think we should go through life wearing hairshirts about what we did at our private. Do you need cash? Want a bed? Take a cottage on the estate.' 'I'm really sorry, Sef. Really sorry.' I said, 'You tell me what I can do, I'll do it. I'm in the book in London, give me a buzz if I can help.' Well I mean damn it, he'd been on for twenty minutes. I put the phone down and half an hour later he's back. 'Hullo, Sef. Me again.' Jean was pretty shirty this time. Thought it was Steggie having a tantrum. 'Got to talk to you, Sef. Listen to me.' Well, you can't ring off on an old chum when he's down, can you?"

Brotherhood heard Sir Kenneth's clock chime twelve. He was jotting fast. Concentric fantasies, he repeated to

himself, defining the truth at the centre. He had reached the
passage he was waiting for.

"... said he was in secret work. That didn't surprise me,
who isn't these days?... Said there was this Englishman he
worked for, called him the Brotherhood. I don't think I
listened to all of it, to be honest. There was the Brotherhood
and there was this other chap. Said he was working for both
of 'em. They were like two parents for him. Kept him going.
I said bully for you, if they keep you going, you stick to them.
Said he had to write this book about them, put the record
right. What record? God knows. He'd write to the Brotherhood, write to the other chap, then he'd take himself off to a
secret place and do his number." Brotherhood heard his own
patient murmur in the background. "... Well maybe I got
that one a bit wrong then. Maybe he was going to hunker
down in his secret place first and write to them from there. I
wasn't listening to all of it. Drunks bore me. I'm one myself."

Prompt from Brotherhood.

Long pause.

Renewed prompt from Brotherhood.

Sir Kenneth indistinct: "Said he was his runner."

"Who was whose runner?"

"Pym was t'other chap's runner. Not the Brotherhood's.
The other fellow's. Said he'd crippled him somehow. Pissed, I
told you."

Brotherhood again, riding him a little harder: "... name
for this person?"

"Don't think so. Don't think it stuck. Sorry. No, it
didn't."

"And the secret place? Where was that?"

"Didn't say. His business."

Brotherhood let the tape continue. Avalanche as Sefton
Boyd lights himself a cigarette. Cannon-blast of the front door
being slammed open and shut again, signalling Steggie's
petulant return.

Brotherhood and Sir Kenneth are on the landing.

"What's that, old boy?" Sir Kenneth very loud.

"I said, so where do you think he might be?" says
Brotherhood.

"Upstairs, old boy. That's what you said." In his memory's eye, Brotherhood sees Sir Kenneth's pouch face approach
close to his own, smiling its downward twist. "Get a warrant,

maybe you can have a look. Maybe you can't. Don't know. Have to see."

Brotherhood heard his own heels clumping down Sir Kenneth's stairs. He heard himself reach the hall and Steggie's lighter footsteps mingle with his own. He heard Steggie's pointed "Good night" and the clatter of bolts as he unlocks the door for him. Followed by Steggie's muffled shriek as Brotherhood hauls him out of the house, one hand over his mouth, the other at the back of his head. Then the thump as he taps Steggie's head against the plaster pillar of Sir Kenneth's gracious porch, and his own voice, very near to Steggie's ear.

"Have they done this before to you, have they? Put you up against a wall?"

A whimper for an answer.

"Who else is living in the house, son?"

"No one."

"Who was on the top floor this evening, back and forth in front of the window."

"Me."

"Why?"

"It's my room!"

"I thought you two would share the bridal chamber."

"I've still got my own room, haven't I? I'm entitled to my privacy, same as he is."

"Nobody else in the house at all?"

"No!"

"Not all week?"

"No. I told you. Hey, stop!"

"What's the matter?" says Brotherhood, already halfway down the path.

"I haven't got my key. How do I get back in?"

A clang as Brotherhood slams the gate.

He phoned Kate. No answer.

He phoned his wife. No answer.

He phoned Paddington and wrote down the times and places along the route of the night sleeper from Paddington to Penzance via Reading.

For an hour he tried to sleep, then returned to his desk, pulled Langley's folder towards him and stared yet again at the eaten-out features of Herr Petz-Hampel-Zaworski, Pym's pre-

sumed controller, lately of Corfu. ". . . Real name unknown . . .
query member Czech archaeological team visiting Egypt
1961 (Petz) . . . query 1966 att. Czech Military Mission East
Berlin (Hampel) . . . height 6 ft., stoops, limps slightly with
left leg . . ."

"There was the Brotherhood and there was this other
chap," Sefton Boyd had said. "They were like two parents for
him. Said he was his runner."

"You brought it on yourselves," he heard Belinda say.
"You invented him."

He continued to stare at the photograph. The down-
turned eyelids. The down-turned moustache. The twinkly
eyes. The hidden Slav smile. Who the devil are you? Why do
I recognise you when I have never set eyes on you?

Grant Lederer had never stood so high in the world, or felt
so rounded as a human being. Justice lives! he assured
himself in the perfect peacefulness of his triumph. My masters are worthy of their authority. A noble service has tried
me to the limit and found me worthy of my hire. All round
him the sealed operations room on the sixth floor of the
American Embassy in Grosvenor Square was filling up with
people he had not known existed. They came from the remote
corners of London Station, yet each as he entered appeared
to bestow a glance of kinship on him. As fine a looking bunch
of Americans as you'd wish to meet, he thought. The Agency
really knows how to pick us these days. They had hardly
settled before Wexler began speaking.

"Time to wrap this thing up," he said grimly as the door
was locked. "Meet Gary, everybody. Gary's head of SISURP.
He's here to report an important breakthrough on Pym and
discuss action."

SISURP, Lederer had recently learned, was the acronym
for Surveillance Intelligence, Southern Europe. Gary was
your typical Kentuckian—tall, spare and amusing. Lederer
already admired him intensely. An aide sat at his elbow with
a heap of papers, but Gary did not refer to them. Our quarry,
he said baldly, was Petz-Hampel-Zaworski, now known to the
indoctrinated familiarly as PHZ. A SISURP team picked him up
Tuesday 10:12 a.m. emerging from the Czech Embassy in
Vienna. Lederer listened enthralled as Gary noted each tiny

detail of PHZ's day. Where PHZ took his coffee. Where PHZ
took his leaks. The bookshops where PHZ browsed. Who
PHZ lunched with. Where. What he ate. PHZ's limp. His
ready smile. His charm, particularly with women. His cigars,
where he lit them, bought them. PHZ's ease of association,
his apparent unawareness that he was being observed by a
field force eighteen strong. The two occasions when "wittingly
or otherwise" PHZ placed himself in the vicinity of Mrs.
Mary Pym. On one of these occasions, said Gary, eye contact
was confirmed. On the other, surveillance was inhibited by
the presence of a British pair believed to be the escorts of
Mrs. Pym. And thence at last to the crowning moment of the
operation and the high point of Grant Lederer's brilliant
marriage and dazzling career so far, when at 8 a.m. local time
today three members of Gary's team found themselves stuck
in the rear pews of the English church in Vienna, while
twelve more were staked out around the outside of it—mobile
units, necessarily, because this was diplomatic-land where
loiterers were not well regarded—and PHZ and Mary Pym
were placed either side of the aisle. Lederer's cue had
arrived. Gary was looking expectantly towards him.

"Grant, I guess you should take over here. We're a little
out of our depth," he said, with pleasing gruffness.

As heads at the table shifted in curiosity, Lederer felt the
warmth of their interest bear him to new heights. He began
speaking at once. Modestly.

"Well hell, I mean I see this whole thing as Bee's
achievement and not mine. Bee is Mrs. Lederer," he explained
to an older man across the table from him, then realised too
late that it was Carver, Head of London Station, never a
Lederer fan. "She's Presbyterian. Her parents were Presbyterian too. Mrs. Lederer latterly has been able to reconcile
her spirituality with organised religion and has been attending
regularly at the Christchurch Anglican church, Vienna, known
as the English church, and frankly just the sexiest little
church you ever saw. Right, Gary? Cherubs, angels—more
like a religious boudoir than a regular church at all. You know,
Mick, if anybody's name is going up in lights at Langley over
this, I guess it should be Bee's," he added, still somehow not
quite able to get to his story.

The rest came out faster. It was Bee after all and not the
surveillance team who had managed to slide out into the aisle

after PHZ and stand in line right behind him as he and Mary queued for the Sacrament. It was Bee who from a distance of maybe five feet had watched as PHZ leaned forward and whispered real words into Mary's ear, and watched again as Mary first leaned back to catch them, then went ahead with her devotions as if nothing in the world had happened.

"So I mean it was actually my wife, my helpmate throughout all of this long operation, who witnessed the spoken contact." He shook his head in marvel. "And it was Bee again who, the first moment the service ended, raced back to our apartment to phone me right here at the Embassy and describe the whole amazing occurrence, using the domestic codewords the two of us had hashed out together for just such a contingency. And I mean Bee did not even *know* that an Agency surveillance team was present in that church at all. She just went because Mary was going, as much as anything. Yet she scooped SISURP single-handed by like six *hours*, more. Harry," said Lederer a little breathlessly, finding Wexler as he put the finishing touch to his narrative, "my only regret is that Mrs. Lederer never learned to lip-read."

Lederer had not expected applause. It was in the nature of the community he had joined that there should be none. The pregnant silence struck him as a more fitting tribute.

Artelli the cryptographer was the first to break it. "Here at the Embassy," he repeated, not quite as a question.

"Pardon me?" said Lederer.

"Your wife called you here at the Embassy? From Vienna? Directly after the happening in the church? On the open phone from your apartment?"

"Yes, sir, and I took her news straight upstairs to Mr. Wexler. He had it on his desk by 9 a.m."

"Nine-thirty," Wexler said.

"And what were these domestic codewords that she used, please?" said Artelli while he wrote.

Lederer was happy to explain: "Well really what we did in *fact* was borrow the names of Bee's aunts and uncles. We have always considered there was a similarity in the psychological profiles of Mary Pym and Bee's Aunt Edie. So we kind of worked it up from there. 'You know what Aunt Edie did in church today?' . . . Bee is very subtle."

"Thanks," said Artelli.

Next Carver spoke, and his question did not seem entirely friendly.

"You mean your wife is *conscious* to this operation, Grant? I thought the Pym case was strictly a no-wives thing. Harry, didn't we make a ruling on that a little while back?"

"Strictly it is no wives," Lederer agreed handsomely. "However since Mrs. Lederer has effectively been out in the field with me on this one it would be somewhat illusory to suppose she would not be aware of the general level of suspicion in relation to the Pyms. Well, to Magnus anyway. And I may add that it was always Bee's contention that somewhere at the bottom of this heap we are going to find Mary playing a very deep and laid-back rôle. Mary is a rôle-player."

Carver again. "Is Mrs. Lederer also conscious to PHZ? He's a pretty hot addition to the cast, Grant. He could be a big fish. But she's in on that, huh?"

There was nothing Lederer could do to stop the colour rushing to his face, or his voice developing its strident edge: "Mrs. Lederer had an instinct regarding that encounter and she acted on it. You want to censure her for that, Carver, you censure me first, okay?"

Artelli again, with his damned French drawl. "What was your domestic codename for PHZ?"

"Uncle Bobby," Lederer snapped.

"But then Bobby is more than instinct, Grant," Carver objected. "Bobby is an agreed thing between you. How could you have agreed Bobby if you hadn't given her the story on Petz-Hampel-Zaworski?"

Wexler had taken back the meeting. "Okay, okay, okay," he growled unhappily. "Cope with that later. Meantime what do we do? SISURP splits and stays with the both of them. PHZ and Mary. That right, Gary? Wherever they go."

"I'm calling for fresh horses right now," said Gary. "Should have two full teams by this time tomorrow."

"Next question, what the hell do we tell the Brits and when and how?" said Wexler.

"Looks like we told them already," said Artelli, with a lazy glance at Lederer. "That's unless the Brits have given up tapping U.S. Embassy telephone lines these days, which I tend to doubt."

Justice lives, but justice, as Grant Lederer discovered before morning, also dies. His health was found to have suffered a sudden lapse, his appointment in Vienna terminated for him in his absence. His wife, far from receiving the commendations Lederer dreamed of, was ordered to follow him back to Langley, Virginia, at once.

"Lederer overheats and overrelates," wrote one of the Agency's ever-expanding team of house psychiatrists. "He requires a less hysterical environment."

The prescribed calm was eventually found for him in Statistics, and it drove him nearly mad.

13

The green cabinet stood in the centre of Pym's room like a discarded fieldpiece that had once been its regiment's pride. Its chrome was peeling from the handles, a heavy boot or fall had stove in one corner, so that the slightest touch could set it trembling and worrying. The chips had rusted into sores, the rust had spread to the screw holes and underneath the paintwork, causing it to lift in humiliating pimples. Pym walked round it with the awe and loathing of a primitive. It has arrived from Heaven. It is destined to return there. I should have put it in the incinerator with him so that he can show it to his Maker as he intended. Four dense drawers of innocence, the Gospel according to Saint Rick.

He gave the cabinet a push and heard a sagging sound from inside as the files slipped obediently to his command.

I should write you witches along his path, Tom. The full moon should be turning red and the owl doing whatever the owl did that was so unnatural when foul murder was afoot. But Pym is deaf and blind to them. He is Second Lieutenant Magnus Pym riding in his private train across occupied Austria, entering by way of that very border town where, long ago, in the less mature existence of a different Pym, E. Weber's fictitious crock of gold had supposedly awaited Mr. Lapadi's collection. He is a Roman conqueror on his way to taking up his first appointment. He is oven-fired against human frailty and his own destiny, as you may observe from the scowls of military abstinence he bestows upon the bare breasts of the Barbarian peasant women harvesting corn in the sunlit fields. His preparation has passed with the ease of an English Sunday, not that Pym ever asked for ease. The privileged English assets of good manners and bad learning have never been more to his advantage. Even his murky political affiliations at Oxford have turned out to be a blessing. "If the Pongos ask you whether you are now or ever have been a member of the clan, look 'em slap in the eye and tell 'em *never*," the last of the Michaels advised him over a sporting lunch beside the swimming-pool at the Lansdowne, as they watched the pure bodies of suburban girls wriggle through the disinfected water.

"Pongos?" said Pym, mystified.

"Licentious soldiery, old boy. The War Office. Wood from here up. The Firm is fixing your clearance direct. Tell them to mind their damn business."

"Thanks terribly," said Pym.

The same evening, glowing from the best of nine games of squash, Pym was led to the presence of a Very Senior Member of the service, in a plain, forgettable office not far from Rick's newest Reichskanzlei. Was this the Colonel Gaunt who had first approached him? He's higher, Pym was told. Don't ask.

"We want to thank you," said the Senior Member.

"I really enjoyed it," said Pym.

"It's a filthy job, mixing with those people. Somebody has to do it."

"Oh, it's not that bad, sir."

"Look here. We're leaving your name on the books. I can't promise you anything, we've got a selection board these days. Besides, you belong to those chaps across the park and we make it a rule not to fish in one another's preserves. All the same if you ever do decide that protecting your country at home is more to your liking than playing Mata Hari abroad, let us know."

"I will, sir. Thank you," said Pym.

The Very Senior Member was crisp and brown and ostentatiously nondescript like one of his own envelopes. He had the testy manners of a country solicitor, which was what he had been before answering the Great Call. Leaning across his desk he pulled a puzzled smile. "Don't tell me if you don't want. How ever did you get mixed up with that crowd in the first place?"

"The Communists?"

"No, no, no. Our sister service."

"In Bern, sir. I was a student there."

"In Switzerland," said the great man, consulting a mental map.

"Yes, sir."

"My wife and I went skiing near Bern once. Little place called Mürren. The British run it so there aren't any cars. We rather liked it. What did you do for them?"

"Much the same as for you, sir, really. It was just a bit more dangerous."

"In what way?"

"You don't feel you have the protection out there. It's eyeball to eyeball, I suppose."

"Seemed such a peaceful spot to me. Well good luck to you, Pym. Look out for those chaps. They're good but they're slippery. We're good but we've got a bit of honour left. That's the difference."

"He's brilliant," Pym told his guide. "He pretends to be completely ordinary but he sees right into you."

His elation had not left him when a few days later he presented himself, suitcase in hand, at the guardroom of his basic-training regiment where for two months he reaped the plentiful rewards of his upbringing. While Welsh miners and Glaswegian cut-throats wept unashamedly for their mothers, went absent without leave and were carted off to a place of punishment, Pym slept soundly and wept for no one. Long before reveille had dragged his comrades smoking and cursing from their beds, he had polished his boots and belt-brasses and cap badge, made his bed and dressed his bedside locker, and was all ready, should anybody ask it of him, to take a cold shower, dress again, and read the first of the Day Hours with Mr. Willow before a disgusting breakfast. On the parade ground and the football ground he excelled. He neither took fright at being shouted at nor expected logic of authority.

"Where's Gunner Pym?" the colonel barked one day, in the middle of a lecture on the battle of Corunna, and looked up angrily as if someone else had spoken. Every sergeant in the drill hall screamed Pym's name until he stood.

"Are you Pym?"

"Sir!"

"See me after this lecture."

"Sir!"

Company Headquarters lay on the other side of the parade ground. Pym marched there and saluted. The colonel's aide-de-camp left the room.

"At ease, Pym. Sit down."

The colonel spoke carefully, with a soldier's mistrust of words. He had a soft honey-coloured moustache and the limpid gaze of an entirely stupid man.

"It has been put to me by certain people that, assuming you are commissioned, you would do well to attend a certain training course at a certain establishment, Pym."

"Yes, sir."

"I am therefore to submit a personal report on you."

"Yes, sir."

"Which I shall do. Favourable, as a matter of fact."

"Thank you, sir."

"You are keen. You are not cynical. You are not marred, Pym, by the luxuries of peace. You are somebody this country needs."

"Thank you, sir."

"Pym."

"Yes, sir."

"If ever those people you're mixed up with happen to be looking for a rather fit retired army colonel with a certain amount of *je ne sais quoi*, I trust you to remember me. I speak some French. I ride decently. I know my wines. Tell them that."

"I shall, sir. Thank you, sir."

Possessing little in the way of memory, the colonel had a habit of returning to conversations as if they were new to him.

"Pym."

"Yes, sir."

"Pick your moment. Don't rush in with it. They don't like that. Be subtle. That's an order."

"I will, sir."

"You know my name?"

"Yes, sir."

"Spell it."

Pym did.

"I'll change it if they want. They've only to let me know. I hear you took a First, Pym."

"Yes, sir."

"Carry on."

In the evenings, seated beside lonely men, Pym the ever-willing obliged by dictating letters of love to their girlfriends. Where the physical feat of writing eluded them, he acted as their amanuensis, adding personalised endearments to their specification. Sometimes, fired by his own rhetoric, he would burst into song on his own account, in the lyrical style of a Blunden or a Sassoon:

> "Dearest Belinda,
> "I cannot tell you what fun and simple human goodness are to be found among one's working-class comrades. Yesterday—great excitement—we drove our twenty-five-pounders to a remote firing range Somewhere in England for our first Shoot, embussing before dawn and not reaching the r.v. till eleven. The slatted seats of a fifteen-hundredweight are designed to split the spine in several places. We had no cushions and only iron rations to munch. Yet the chaps whistled and sang in tremendous spirits all the way, acquitted themselves superbly and endured the journey back with only the most cheerful grumbles. I felt privileged to be one of them and am seriously considering refusing a commission. . . ."

When a commission came his way, however, Pym contrived without difficulty to accept it, as witness the erogenous hillocks of khaki thread backed on green cloth, one to each shoulder of his battledress, whose existence he covertly confirms whenever the train enters another tunnel. The bare breasts of the peasant girls are his first since the election. With each new valley, he strains his disapproving gaze to see more of them and is seldom disappointed. "We'll send you to Vienna first," his commanding officer at the Intelligence Depot had said. "Chance to get the feel of the place before you're pushed out into the field."

"It sounds ideal, sir," said Pym.

Austria in those days was a different country from the one we have come to love, Tom, and Vienna was a divided city like Berlin or your father. A few years later to everyone's lasting amazement the diplomats agreed they wouldn't bother with a sideshow while there was Germany to squabble over, so the occupying powers signed a treaty and went home, thus notching up the British Foreign Office's one positive achieve-

ment in my lifetime. But in Pym's day the sideshow was
going great guns. The Americans had Salzburg as their capital, the French Innsbruck and the Brits Graz, and everyone
had a piece of Vienna to play with. At Christmastime the
Russians gave us wooden buckets of caviar and we gave the
Russians plum puddings, and there was a story still going the
rounds when Pym arrived that when the caviar was served to
the men as a prelude to their dinner, a corporal of Argylls
complained to the duty officer that the jam tasted of fish. The
brains of British Vienna was a sprawling villa called Div. Int.,
and that was where Second Lieutenant Pym was launched
upon his duties, which consisted of reading reports on the
movements of everything from Soviet mobile laundries to
Hungarian horse cavalry, and pushing coloured pins into
maps. His most exciting map showed the Soviet Zone of
Austria which began a mere twenty minutes' drive from
where he worked. Pym had only to look at its borders to feel
intrigue and danger prickle on his skin. At other times, when
he was tired or forgot himself, his eye would lift to the western
tip of Czechoslovakia, to Karlovy Vary formerly Carlsbad, the
charming eighteenth-century spa once favoured by Brahms
and Beethoven. But he knew of no personal connection with
the place and his interest was purely historical.

He lived an odd life those first months, for his destiny
did not lie in Vienna, and it seems to me in fanciful moments
now that the capital was itself waiting to release him to the
sterner laws of nature. Too lowly to be taken seriously by his
brother officers, prevented by protocol from mixing with the
Other Ranks, too poor to revel in the swagman's restaurants
and nightclubs, Pym floated between his commandeered
hotel room and his maps, much as he had floated round Bern
in the days of his illegality. And I will admit now but never
then that, more than once, listening to the Viennese chattering
their zany German on the pavements, or taking himself to
one of the struggling small theatres that were cropping up in
cellars and bombed houses, he had a pang of nostalgic
longing to turn his head and discover a good friend limping at
his side. But he knew of none. It is merely my German soul
reviving, he told himself; it is the German nature to feel
incomplete. On other nights, the great secret agent would
take himself on reconnaissance through the Soviet Sector
disguised in a green Tyrolean hat he had bought specially for

the purpose, to observe from beneath its brim the stubby Russian sentries with their submachine guns posted outside the Soviet headquarters at twenty-yard intervals down the street. If they challenged him Pym had only to show his military pass for their Tartar faces to crack in friendly recognition as they took a pace back in their soft leather boots and tossed up a grey-gloved hand in salute.

"English good."

"But Russian good too," Pym would insist with a laugh. "Russian very good, honestly."

"*Kamarad!*"

"*Tovarich. Kamarad,*" the great internationalist responded.

He would offer a cigarette and take one. He would light them with his big-flamed American Zippo lighter obtained from one of the many clandestine merchants operating inside Div. Int. He would let it glow on the sentry's features and his own. Then Pym in his goodheartedness had half an urge, though fortunately not the language, to explain that although he had spied on the Communists at Oxford, and was spying on them again in Vienna, he was still a Communist at heart and cared more for the snows and cornfields of Russia than ever he did for the musical cocktail cabinets and roulette wheels of Ascot.

And sometimes, very late, returning through empty squares to his monkish little bedroom with its army fire extinguisher and photograph of Rick, he would pause, and drink the clean night air in gusts until he was elated, and gaze down misted cobble streets, and pretend that he saw Lippsie walking towards him through the lamplight in her refugee's headscarf, carrying her cardboard suitcase. And he would smile at her and valiantly congratulate himself that, whatever his outward longings, he was still living in the world inside his head.

He had been in Vienna three months when Marlene asked him for his protection. Marlene was a Czech interpreter and celebrated beauty.

"You are Mr. Pym?" she enquired one evening with a civilian's delightful shyness as he descended the great staircase behind a bevy of high-ranking officers. She wore a baggy mackintosh nipped at the waist and a hat with little horns.

Pym confessed that he was.

"You are walking to the Weichsel Hotel?"

Pym said that he did so every evening.

"You allow I walk with you, please, once? Yesterday a

man tried to rape me. You will guide me to my door? I am not trouble?"

Soon the intrepid Pym was guiding Marlene to her door each evening and collecting her from it in the mornings. His day unfolded between these radiant interludes. But when he invited her to have dinner with him after payday, he was summoned by a furious captain of Fusiliers who had charge of new arrivals.

"You are a lecherous little swine, do you hear?"

"Yes, sir."

"Div. Int. subalterns do not, repeat not, fraternise in public with civilian personnel. Not unless they've put a lot more service in than you have. D'you hear?"

"Yes, sir."

"Do you know what a shit is?"

"Yes, sir."

"No, you don't. A shit, Pym, is an officer whose tie is of a lighter khaki than his shirt. Have you seen your tie recently?"

"Yes, sir."

"Have you seen your shirt?"

"Yes, sir."

"Compare them, Pym. And ask yourself what sort of young officer you are. That woman isn't even cleared above restricted."

It's all training, thought Pym, as he changed his tie. I'm being hardened for the field. Nevertheless it worried him that Marlene had asked him so many questions about himself and he wished that he had not been quite so frank in his replies.

Not long after this, Pym was mercifully deemed to have got the feel of the place. Before departing he was again summoned by the captain who showed him two photographs. One depicted a pretty young man with soft lips, the other a chubby drunk with a sneer.

"If you see either of these men you will report that information to a senior officer immediately, do you hear?"

"Who are they?"

"Hasn't anyone taught you not to ask questions? If you can't find a senior officer, arrest them yourself."

"How?"

"Use your authority. Be courteous but firm. 'You men

are under arrest.' Then bring them to the nearest senior officer."

Their names, Pym learned a few days later from the *Daily Express*, were Guy Burgess and Donald Maclean and they were members of the British Foreign Service. For several weeks, he continued to look for them everywhere, but he never found them because they had already defected to Moscow.

So which of us is responsible, Tom, tell me? Is it Pym's wistful soul or God's wry humour that contrives to deal him a spell of Paradise before every Fall? I told you of the Ollingers in Bern that it was given to us once only in a lifetime to know a truly happy family, but I had forgotten Major Harrison Membury, formerly of the British Library in Nairobi and one-time officer in the Education Corps, who had strayed by a delicious caprice of military logic into the ragtag ranks of Field Security. I had forgotten his beautiful wife and their many grimy daughters who were Fräulein Ollingers in the making, except that they kept goats and a boisterous piglet in preference to making music, which made mayhem of their military hiring, to the rage of the garrison Administration officer, who was powerless because the Memburys were Intelligence and immune. I had forgotten Number 6 Field Interrogation Unit, Graz, a pink baroque villa in a wooded cleft of hills a mile from the city's edge. Bunches of telephone cable led into it, aerials desecrated the spired roof. It had a gateway with a gatehouse and a wild-eyed blond mess waiter called Wolfgang who rushed down the steps in a pressed white coat to hand you out of your jeep. But the best thing about it as far as Membury was concerned was the lake, which he spent his days stocking, for he was mad on fish and lavished a sizable part of our secret imprest on encouraging rare breeds of trout. You must imagine a big, genial man, quite strengthless, with the elegant gestures of an invalid. And of a dreamy religious eye and disposition. A civilian to his soft fingertips if ever I met one, yet when I see him now it is always in army battledress with worn suède boots and a webbing belt either above his belly or below it, standing amid the dragonflies at the edge of his beloved lake in the heat of a scorching afternoon, exactly as Pym discovered him on the day he reported for duty, poking a thing like a shrimping net into the water while he muttered shy imprecations against a marauding pike.

"Oh my goodness. You're Pym. Yes, well, so glad you've come. Look here, I'm going to clear away the weed and drag the whole bed to see exactly what we've got. What do you think of that?"

"It sounds great, sir," said Pym.

"I'm so glad. Are you married?"

"No, sir."

"Marvellous. Then you'll be free at weekends."

And I think of him for some reason as one of a pair of brothers, though I don't recall ever hearing he had a brother. His home-based staff consisted of a sergeant whom I barely remember and a cockney driver called Kaufmann who had a degree in Economics at Cambridge. His second in command was a pink-cheeked young banker named Lieutenant McLaird who was returning to the City. In the cellars, dutiful Austrian clerks tapped telephones, steamed open mail and dumped their unread product in a row of army dustbins which were emptied by the Graz authorities punctiliously once a week because it was a nightmare of Membury's that some fish-hating vandal would tip them in the lake. On the ground floor he kept his stable of locally recruited lady interpreters who ranged from the maternal to the nubile, and Membury, when he remembered their existence, admired them all. And finally he had his wife Hannah, a painter of trees, and Hannah, as is so often the way with the wives of very large men, was as fragile as a wisp. Hannah made painting attractive to me, and I remember her best seated at her easel in a low white dress while the girls roll shrieking down a grass bank and Membury and myself in bathing costumes toil in the brown water. Even today it is impossible to imagine her as the mother of all those daughters.

The rest of Pym's life could scarcely have been more to his liking. For commodities he had Naafi whisky at seven shillings a bottle and cigarettes at twelve shillings a hundred. He could barter or, if he preferred, convert them without effort into the local currency, though it was safest to rely on the services of an elderly Hungarian Rittmeister who sat around Registry reading secret files and gazing lovingly at Wolfgang, much as Mr. Cudlove liked to gaze at Ollie. All of it was familiar, all of it was necessary to Pym for the continuation of his unlived orthodox childhood. On Sundays, he escorted the Memburys to mass and over lunch looked down the front of Hannah's dress. Membury is a genius, Pym exulted as he moved his desk into the great man's anteroom. Membury is Renaissance Man made spy. Within weeks he had his own imprest. Within a few more he had a second pip for Wolfgang to sew on his shoulder, for Membury said he looked silly with only one.

And he had his Joes.

"This is Pepi," McLaird explained with a droll smile, over a discreet dinner out of town. "Pepi fought the Reds for the Germans and now he's fighting them for us. You're a fanatic anti-Communist, aren't you, Pepi? That's why he takes his motorbike into the Zone and sells pornographic photographs to the Russian soldiery. Four hundred Players Medium a month. In arrears."

"This is Elsa," McLaird said, presenting a dumpy Carinthian housewife with four children, in the grill-room of the Blue Rose. "Her boyfriend runs a café in St. Pölten. Sends her the registration numbers and insignia of the Russian lorries that go past his window, doesn't he, Elsa? All in secret writing on the back of his love letters. Three kilos of medium-roast coffee a month. In arrears."

There were a dozen of them and Pym set to work immediately to develop and welfare them in every way he knew. Today when I play them through my memory they are as fine a bunch of neverwozzers as ever came the way of an aspiring spymaster. But to Pym they were simply the best scouts ever and he would see them right if it killed him.

And I have left till last Sabina, Jack, who like her friend Marlene in Vienna was an interpreter, and like Marlene was the most beautiful girl in the world, plucked straight from the pages of *Amor and Rococo Woman*. She was small like E. Weber, with broad, fluid hips and intense demanding eyes. Her breasts in summer or winter were high and very strong and, like her buttocks, pushed their way through the most workaday clothes, insistently demanding Pym's attention. Her features were those of a gloomy Slav elf haunted by sadness and superstition but capable of amazing bursts of sweetness, and if Lippsie had been reincarnated and made twenty-three

again, she could have done a great deal worse than take
Sabina's form.

"Marlene says you are respectable," she informed Pym
with contempt as she clambered aboard Corporal Kaufmann's
jeep, not bothering to conceal her Rococo legs.

"Is that a crime?" Pym asked.

"Don't worry," she replied ominously, and away they
drove to the camps. Sabina spoke Czech and Serbo-Croat as
well as German. In her spare time she was studying economics at Graz University, which gave her an excuse to talk to
Corporal Kaufmann.

"You are believing in mixing agrarian economy, Kaufmann?"

"I don't believe in any of it."

"You are Keynesian?"

"I wouldn't be one with my own money, I'll tell you
that," said Kaufmann.

Thus the conversation went back and forth while Pym
searched for ways of brushing carelessly against her white
shoulder, or causing her skirt to open a fraction further to the
north.

Their destination on these journeys was the camps. For
five years the refugees of Eastern Europe had been pouring
into Austria through every fast-closing gap in the barbed
wire: crashing frontiers in stolen cars and lorries, across
minefields, clinging to the underneath of trains. They brought
their hollow faces and their shorn children and their puzzled
old and their frisky dogs, and their Lippsies in the making, to
be corralled and questioned and decided over in their thousands, while they played chess on wooden packing cases and
showed each other photographs of people they would never
see again. They came from Hungary and Rumania and Poland
and Czechoslovakia and Yugoslavia and sometimes Russia,
and they hoped they were on their way to Canada and
Australia and Palestine. They had travelled by devious routes
and often for devious reasons. They were doctors and scien-
tists and bricklayers. They were truck drivers, thieves, acro-
bats, publishers, rapists and architects. All passed across
Pym's vision as he rode in his jeep from camp to camp with
Kaufmann and Sabina, questioning, grading and recording,
then hastening home to Membury with his booty.

At first his sensitivity was offended by so much misery

and he had a hard time disguising his concern for everyone he spoke to: yes, I will see you to Montreal if it kills me; yes, I will send word to your mother in Canberra that you are safely here. At first Pym was also embarrassed by his lack of suffering. Everyone he questioned had had more experience in a day than he had in his whole young life and he resented them. Some had been crossing borders since they were children. Others spoke of death and torture so casually that he became indignant at their unconcern, until his disapproval sparked their anger and they flung back at him with mockery. But Pym the good labourer had work to do, and a commanding officer to please and, when he armed himself, a quick and covert mind to do it with. He had only to consult his own nature to know when someone was writing in the margin of his memory and excluding the main text. He knew how to make small talk while he was watching, and how to read the signals that came back to him. If they described a night crossing over the hills, Pym crossed with them, lugging their Lippsie suitcases and feeling the icy mountain air cutting through their old coats. When one of them told a lie direct, Pym rapidly took back-bearings on likely versions of the truth with the aid of his mental compass. Questions teemed in him and, budding lawyer that he was, he learned quickly to shape them into a pattern of accusation. "Where do you come from? What troops did you see there? What colour shoulder boards did they wear? What did they drive around in, what weapons did they have? Which route did you take, what guards, obstructions, dogs, wire, minefields did you meet along your way? What shoes were you wearing? How did your mother manage, your grandmother, if the mountain pass was so steep? How did you cope with two suitcases and two small children when your wife was so heavily pregnant? Is it not more likely that your employers in the Hungarian secret police drove you to the border and wished you luck as they showed you where to cross? Are you a spy and if so, would you not prefer to spy for us? Or are you merely a criminal, in which case you would surely like to take up spying, rather than be tossed back across the border by the Austrian police?" Thus Pym drew from his own criss-cross lives in order to unravel theirs, and Sabina with her scowls and moods and occasional gorgeous smiles became the sultry voice in which he did it. Sometimes he let her translate into German for him, in order to give himself the secret advantage of hearing everything twice.

"Where you learn to play these stupid games?" she asked him sternly one evening as they danced together at the Hotel Wiesler, to the disapproval of the army wives.

Pym laughed.

On the brink of manhood, with Sabina's thigh riding against his own, why should he owe anything to anybody? So he invented a story for her about this cunning German he'd known at Oxford who had turned out to be a spy.

"We had a rather weird battle of wits," he confessed, drawing upon hastily created memories. "He used all the tricks in the book and to start with I was as innocent as a babe and believed everything he told me. Gradually the contest got a bit more even."

"He was Communist?"

"As it turned out, yes. He made a show of hiding it, but it slipped out when you really went for him."

"He was hommsexual?" Sabina asked, voicing an ever-ready suspicion as she squirmed more deeply into him.

"Not so far as I could see. He had women in regiments."

"He slept only with military women?"

"I meant he had large quantities of them. I was using a metaphor."

"I think he was wishing to disguise his hommsexuality. This is normal."

Sabina spoke of her own life as if it belonged to someone she hated. Her stupid Hungarian father had been shot at the border. Her fool mother had died in Prague attempting to produce a baby for a worthless lover. Her older brother was an idiot and studying to be a doctor in Stuttgart. Her uncles were drunkards and had got themselves shot by the Nazis and the Communists.

"You want I give you Czech lesson Saturday?" she asked him one evening in an even stricter tone than usual, as they drove home three abreast.

"I would like that very much," Pym replied, holding her hand at her side. "I'm really beginning to enjoy it."

"I think we make love this time. We shall see," she said severely, at which Kaufmann nearly drove into a ditch.

Saturday came and neither Rick's shadow nor Pym's terrors could prevent him from ringing Sabina's doorbell. He

heard a footstep softer than her usual practical tread. He saw
the lightspots of her eyes regard him through the eye-slit in
the door, and did his best to smile in a rugged, reassuring
manner. He had brought enough Naafi whisky to banish the
guilt of ages, but Sabina had no guilt and when she opened
the door to him she was naked. Incapable of speech he stood
before her clutching his carrier bag. In a daze he watched her
reset the security chain, take the bag from his lifeless hands,
stalk to the sideboard and unpack it. The day was warm but
she had lit a fire and turned back the bedcovers.

"You have had many women, Magnus?" she demanded.
"Women in regiments like your bad friend?"

"I don't think I have," said Pym.

"You are hommsexual like all English?"

"I'm really not."

She led him to the bed. She sat him down and unbuttoned his shirt. Severely, like Lippsie when she needed
something for the laundry van outside. She unbuttoned the
rest of him and arranged his clothes over a chair. She guided
him on to his back and spread herself over him.

"I didn't know," said Pym aloud.

"Please?"

He started to say something, but there was too much to
explain and his interpreter was already occupied. He meant:
I didn't know, for all my longing, what I was longing for till
now. He meant: I can fly, I can swim on my front and on my
back and on my side and on my head. He meant: I'm whole
and I've joined the men at last.

It was a balmy Friday afternoon in the villa six days later. In
the gardens below the windows of Membury's enormous
office, the Rittmeister in his lederhosen was shelling peas for
Wolfgang. Membury sat at his desk, his battledress unbuttoned to the waist while he drafted a questionnaire for trawler
captains that he proposed to send in hundreds to the major
fishing fleets. For weeks now he had set his heart on tracing
the winter routes of sea trout, and the unit's resources had
been hard pressed to accommodate him.

"I've had a rather rum approach made to me, sir," Pym
began delicately. "Somebody claiming to represent a potential defector."

"Oh but how interesting for you, Magnus," Membury
said politely, prising himself with difficulty from his preoccu-
pations. "I hope it's not another Hungarian frontier guard. I've
rather had my fill of them. So has Vienna, I'm sure." Vienna
was a growing worry to Membury, as Membury was to Vienna.
Pym had read the painful correspondence between them that
Membury kept safely locked at all times in the top left drawer
of his flimsy desk. It might be only a question of days before
the captain of Fusiliers arrived in person to take charge.

"He's not Hungarian, actually, sir," said Pym. "He's
Czech. He's attached to HQ Southern Command based outside Prague."

Membury tilted his large head to one side as if shaking
water out of his ear. "Well that's heartening," he remarked
doubtfully. "Div. Int. would give their eye-teeth for some
good stuff about Southern Czecho. Or anywhere else in
Czecho for that matter. The Americans seem to think they
have a monopoly of the place. Somebody said as much to me
on the telephone only the other day, I don't know who."

The telephone line to Graz ran through the Soviet Zone.
In the evenings Russian technicians could be heard on it,
singing drunken Cossack music.

"According to my source he's a disgruntled clerk sergeant
working in their strongroom," Pym persisted. "He's supposed
to be coming out tomorrow night. If we're not there to
receive him he'll go to the Americans."

"You didn't hear of him through the Rittmeister, did
you?" said Membury nervously.

With the skill of long habituation, Pym entered the risky
ground. No, it was not the Rittmeister, he assured Membury.
At least it didn't sound like the Rittmeister. The voice sounded
younger and more positive.

Membury was confused. "Could you possibly explain?"
he said.

Pym did.

It was just an ordinary Thursday evening, he said. He'd
been to the movies to see *Liebe 47*, and on his way back he
thought he'd drop in at the Weisses Ross for a beer.

"I don't think I know the Weisses Ross."

"It's just another pub, sir, really, but the Czech émigrés
use it a lot and everyone sits at long tables. I'd been there
literally two minutes when the waiter called me to the phone.

'*Herr Leutnant, für Sie.*' They know me a bit there so I wasn't too surprised."

"Good for you," said Membury, impressed.

"It was a man's voice, speaking High German. 'Herr Pym? Here is an important message for you. If you do exactly as I tell you, you will not be disappointed. Have you pen and paper?' I had, so he started reading to me at dictation speed. He checked it back with me and rang off before I could ask him who he was."

From his pocket Pym produced the very sheet of paper, torn from the back of a diary.

"But if this was last night, why on earth didn't you tell me earlier?" Membury objected, taking it from him.

"You were at the Joint Intelligence Committee meeting."

"Oh my hat, so I was. He asked for you by name," Membury remarked with pride, still looking at the paper. "'Only Lieutenant Pym will do.' That's rather flattering, I must say." He pulled at a protruding ear. "Well look here, you take jolly good care," he warned, with the sternness of a man who could refuse Pym nothing. "And don't go too near the border in case they try and haul you over."

This was not by any means the first advance tip-off of a defector's arrival that had come Pym's way in recent months, not even the sixth, though it was the first that had been whispered to him by a naked Czech interpreter in a moonlit orchard. Only a week before, Pym and Membury had sat out a night in the Carinthian lowlands waiting to receive a captain of Rumanian Intelligence and his mistress who were supposedly approaching in a stolen aeroplane crammed with priceless secrets. Membury had the Austrian police close off the area, Pym fired coloured Very lights into the empty air as they had been instructed in secret messages. But when dawn came no aeroplane had arrived.

"What are we supposed to do now?" Membury had complained with pardonable irritation as they sat shivering in the jeep. "Sacrifice a bloody goat? I do wish the Rittmeister were more precise. It makes one look so silly."

A week before that, disguised in green loden coats, they had taken themselves to a remote inn on the Zonal border in search of a Heimkehrer from a Soviet uranium mine who was expected any moment. As they pushed open the door the conversation in the bar stopped dead and a score of peasants gawped at them.

"Billiards," Membury ordered with rare decisiveness, from under his hand. "There's a table over there. We'll get a game going. Fit in."

Still in his green loden, Membury stooped to play his ball, only to be interrupted by the resounding clang of heavy metal striking the tiled floor close at hand. Glancing down, Pym saw his commanding officer's .38 service revolver lying at his large feet. He had recovered it for him in a moment, never quicker. But not quick enough to prevent the stampede to the door as the terrified peasants scattered in the darkness and the landlord locked himself in the cellar.

"Can I go back now, sir?" said Kaufmann. "I'm not a soldier at all, you see. I'm a coward."

"No you can't," said Pym. "Now be quiet."

The barn stood by itself as Sabina had said it would, at the centre of a flat field lined with larches. A yellow path led to it; behind it lay a lake. Behind the lake a hill and on the hill, as the evening darkened, a single watchtower overlooked the valley.

"You will wear civilian clothes and park your car at the crossroads to Klein Brandorf," Sabina had whispered to his thighs as she kissed and fondled and revived him. The orchard had a brick wall and was occupied by a family of large brown hares. "You will leave sidelights burning. If you cheat and bring protection he will not appear. He will stay in the forest and be angry."

"I love you."

"There is a stone, painted white. This is where Kaufmann must stand. If Kaufmann passes the white stone, he will not appear, he will stay in the forest."

"Why can't you come too?"

"He does not wish it. He wishes only Pym. Perhaps he is hommsexual."

"Thanks," said Pym.

The white stone glinted ahead of them.

"Stay here," Pym ordered.

"Why?" said Kaufmann.

Evening mist lay in strips across the field. The surface of the lake popped with rising fish. With the sun setting, the larches threw mile-long shadows across the golden meadow. Sawn logs lay beside the barn door, boxes of geraniums adorned the windows. Pym thought again of Sabina. Her enfolding flanks, the broad spaces of her back. "What I tell you I have not told to any Englishman. In Prague I have a younger brother who is called Jan. If you tell this to Membury he will already dismiss me immediately. The British do not allow us to have close family inside a Communist country. Do you understand?" Yes, Sabina, I understand. I have seen the moonlight on your breasts, your moisture is on my lips, it is sticking to my eyelids. I understand. "Listen. My brother sends me this message for you. Only for Pym. He trusts you because of me and because I have told him only good things about you. He has a friend who wishes to come out. This friend is very gifted, very brilliant, top access. He will bring you many secrets about the Russians. But first you must invent a story for Membury to explain how you received this information. You are clever. You can invent many stories. Now you must invent one for my brother and his friend." Yes, Sabina, I can invent. For you and your beloved brother I can invent a million stories. Get me my pen, Sabina. Where did you put my clothes? Now tear me a piece of paper from your diary and I will invent a story about a strange man who telephoned me at the Weisses Ross and made me an irresistible proposal.

Pym unbuttoned his loden. "Always draw across the body," his weapons instructor had advised at the sad little depot in Sussex where they had taught him how to fight Communism. "It gives you better protection when the other laddie shoots first." Pym was not sure this was good advice. He reached the door and it was closed. He walked round the barn, trying to find a place to peep in. "His information will be good for you," Sabina had said. "It will make you very famous in Vienna, Membury also. Good intelligence from Czechoslovakia is extremely rare at Div. Int. Mostly it comes from the Americans and is therefore corrupt."

The sun had set and the dusk was gathering fast. From across the lake Pym heard the yelping of a fox. Rows of chicken coops stood at the back of the barn and the straw in them was clean. Chickens in no-man's-land, he thought frivolously. Stateless eggs. The chickens tucked their necks at him and blew out their feathers. A grey heron lifted from the lake and set course towards the hills. He returned to the front of the barn.

"Kaufmann!"

"Sir?"

A hundred metres lay between them but their voices were as close as lovers in the evening stillness.

"Did you cough?"

"No, sir."

"Well, don't."

"I expect I was sobbing, sir."

"Keep guard, but whatever you see, don't come any nearer unless I order you."

"I'd like to desert, if I may, sir. I'd rather be a defector than this, honestly. I'm a sitting target. I'm not a human being at all."

"Do some mental sums or something."

"I can't. I've tried. Nothing comes."

Pym lifted the door latch, stepped inside and smelt cigar smoke and horse. St. Moritz, he thought, lightheaded in his apprehension. The barn was cavernous and beautiful and raised at one end like an old ship. On the dais stood a table and on the table, to Pym's surprise, a lighted oil lamp. By its glow he admired the ancient beams and roof. "Wait inside and he will come," Sabina had said. "He will want to see you go in first. My brother's friend is very cautious. Like many Czechs, he has a great and cautious mind." Two high-backed wooden chairs were pulled to the table and magazines were strewn on it like in a dentist's waiting-room. Must be where the farmer does his paperwork. At the end of the barn, he noticed a rustic ladder leading to a loft. At the weekend I'll bring you here. I'll bring wine and cheese and bread, and blankets in case it's prickly, and you can wear your flouncy skirt with nothing underneath. He climbed halfway up the ladder and peered over. Sound floor, dry hay, no sign of rats. An admirable location for rustic Rococo. He returned to the ground floor and made his way towards the dais where the light burned, intending to settle down in one of the chairs. "You must be patient, if necessary all night," Sabina had said. "Crossing the border is extremely dangerous now. It is late summer and the doubters are coming over before the passes

close. Therefore they have many guards and spies." A stone
pathway ran between two cattle drains. His feet echoed
thickly in the roof. The echo stopped, his feet with it. A
slender figure was seated at the head of the table. He was
leaning alertly forward, posing for something. He held a cigar
in one hand and an automatic pistol in the other. His gaze,
like the barrel of the automatic, was fixed on Pym.

"Keep walking towards me, Sir Magnus," Axel urged in
a tone of considerable anxiety. "Put your arms up and for
heaven's sake don't go imagining you are a great cowboy or a
war hero. Neither of us is a member of the shooting classes.
We put our guns away and we have a nice chat. Be reasonable. Please."

It would take our Maker himself, Tom, with help from all of
us, to describe the range of thoughts and emotions charging
at that moment through Pym's poor head. His first response,
I am sure, was disbelief. He had encountered Axel very often in
the last few years and this was merely another example of the
phenomenon. Axel watching him in his sleep, Axel standing
at his bedside with his beret on—"Let's take another look at
Thomas Mann." Axel laughing at him for his addiction to Old
High German and remonstrating with him for his bad habit of
protesting loyalty to everyone he met: to the Oxford
Communists, to all women, to the Jacks and Michaels and to
Rick. "You are a serious fool, Sir Magnus," he had warned
him once, when Pym returned to his rooms after a particularly deft night of juggling girls and social opposites. "You think
that by dividing everything you can pass between." Axel had
limped at his side along the Isis towpath and watched him
dash his knuckles against the wall in order to impress Jemima.
At the election Pym could not have told you how often Axel's
glistening white dome had popped up in the audience, or his
long, restive hands flapped in sarcastic applause. With Axel
so much upon his conscience, therefore, Pym knew for a fact
that Axel did not exist. And with this certainty in his head it
was perfectly reasonable that his next response to seeing Axel
was downright indignation that someone so thoroughly forbidden, someone who had been literally, for whatever reason,
banished out of sight or mention over the borders of Pym's
kingdom, should presume to be sitting here, smoking and

smiling and pointing a pistol at him—at me, Pym, a bullet-proof, fornicating member of the British Occupational classes gifted with supernatural powers. And after that, of course, paradoxical as ever, Pym was more exultant, more thrilled and more happy to see Axel than anyone since the day Rick rode round the corner on his bicycle singing "Underneath the Arches."

Pym walked then ran to Axel's side. He kept his arms above his head as Axel ordered him. He waited impatiently while Axel flashed his army revolver from his waistband and laid it with his own respectfully at the further end of the table. Then at last he dropped his arms far enough to fling them round Axel's neck. I don't remember that they had ever embraced before or did so afterwards. But I remember that evening as the last of childish sentiments between them, the last day of Bern, because I see them hugging and laughing chest to chest, Slav style, before they hold one another at a distance to see what damage the years of separation have done to each of them. And we may assume from contemporary photographs and from my own memories of the mirror in those days, which still played a large part in the young officer's contemplations, that Axel saw the typical, uncut Anglo-Saxon features of a good-looking, fair young man still trying hard to put on the mantle of experience, whereas in Axel's face Pym witnessed at once a hardening, a hollowing-out, a shaping that was there for ever. Axel would look like this for the rest of his days. Life had had its say. He had the manly, human face that he deserved. The softer contours had gone, leaving an etched jauntiness and assurance. His hair-line had retreated but consolidated. Streaks of grey had joined the black, giving it a practical and military appearance. The clown's moustache, the clown's hooped eyebrows had acquired a sadder humour. But the twinkling dark eyes, peering beneath their languid eyelids, were as merry as ever, while everything around them seemed to give depth to their perception.

"You look well, Sir Magnus!" Axel declared exuberantly, still holding him. "You are a fine fellow, my God. We should buy you a white horse and give you India."

"But who are you?" Pym cried in equal excitement. "Where are you? What are you doing here? Should I arrest you?"

"Maybe I arrest you. Maybe I did already. You put your hands up, do you remember? Listen. We are in no-man's-land here. We can arrest each other."

"You're under arrest," Pym said.

"You too," said Axel. "How's Sabina?"

"Fine," Pym said with a grin.

"She knows nothing, you understand? Only what her brother told her. You will protect her?"

"I promise I will," Pym said.

Here a slight pause as Axel pretended to clap his hands over his ears. "Don't promise, Sir Magnus. Just don't promise."

For a frontier crosser Axel had come well equipped, Pym noticed. There was not a trace of mud on his boots, his clothes were pressed and official-looking. Releasing Pym, he grabbed a briefcase, plonked it on the table and drew from it a pair of glasses and a bottle of vodka. Then gherkins, sausage and a loaf of the black bread he used to send Pym out to buy in Bern. They toasted each other gravely, the way Axel had taught him. They refilled their glasses and drank again, a drink for each man. And it is my recollection that by the time they separated they had finished the bottle, for I remember Axel chucking it out into the lake to the outrage of about a thousand moorhens. But if Pym had drunk a case of the stuff it would not have affected him, such was the intensity of his feeling. Even while they began to talk, Pym kept secretly blinking into corners to make sure everything was how it was when he had last looked, so eerily similar at times was the barn to the Bern attic, right down to the soft wind that used to whirr in the skylights. And when he heard the fox again in the distance, he had the certain feeling it was Bastl barking on the wooden staircase after everyone had gone. Except that, as I say, those sentimental days were over. Magnus had killed them dead; the manhood of their friendship was beginning.

Now it is the way of old friends when they bump into each other, Tom, to put aside the immediate cause of their meeting until last. They prefer as a prelude to account for the years between, which gives a kind of rightness to whatever they have met to discuss. And that is what Pym and Axel did, though you will understand, now that you are familiar with the workings of Pym's mind, that it was he and not Axel who led this passage of the conversation, if only in order to show to himself as well as to Axel that he was totally without sin in the tricky matter of Axel's disappearance. He did it well. He was a polished performer these days.

"Honestly, Axel, nobody ever went out of my life so abruptly," he complained in a tone of jocular reproach as he sliced sausage, buttered the bread and generally occupied himself with what actors call business. "You were there all safely tucked up in the evening, we'd got a bit drunk, said good night. Next morning I hammered on your wall, no answer. I go downstairs and walk into poor old Frau O crying her heart out. 'Where's Axel? They've taken away our Axel! The Fremdenpolizei carried him down the stairs and one of them kicked Bastl.' From all they said, I must have been sleeping like the dead."

Axel smiled his old warm smile. "If we only knew how the dead sleep," he said.

"We held a sort of wake, hung around the house, half expecting you to come back. Herr Ollinger made some useless phone calls and got absolutely nowhere, naturally. Frau O remembered she had a brother in one of the Ministries, *he* was no good. In the end I thought, To hell with it, what have we got to lose? So I went down to the Fremdenpolizei myself. Passport in hand. 'My friend's missing. Some men dragged him from the house early this morning, said they came from you. Where is he?' I banged the table a bit and got nowhere. Then two rather creepy gentlemen in raincoats took me into another room and told me that if I made any more trouble the same thing would happen to me."

"That was brave of you, Sir Magnus," said Axel. Reaching out a pale fist he tapped Pym lightly on the shoulder to say thanks.

"No, it wasn't. Not really. I mean I did have somewhere to go. I was British and I had rights."

"Sure. And you knew people at the Embassy. That's true also."

"And they'd have helped me out too. I mean they tried to. When I went to them."

"You did?"

"Absolutely. Later, of course. Not immediately. Rather as a last resort. But they had a go. . . . So anyway, back I went to the Länggasse and we—honestly, we buried you. It was awful. Frau O was up in your room still crying, trying to sort out whatever you'd left behind without looking at it. Which wasn't much. The Fremdenpolizei seemed to have pinched most of your papers. I took your library books back. Your gramophone records. We hung your clothes in the cellar. Then we sort of wandered round the house as if it had been bombed. 'To think this could happen in Switzerland,' we kept saying. Really just like a death."

Axel laughed. "It was good of you to mourn me at least. Thank you, Sir Magnus. Did you hold a funeral service also?"

"With no body and no forwarding address? All Frau O wanted to do was look for the culprit. She was convinced you'd been informed against."

"Who did she think did it?"

"Everyone in turn really. The neighbours. The shop-keepers. Maybe someone from the Cosmo. One of the Marthas."

"Which one did she choose?"

Pym picked the prettiest and frowned. "I seem to remember there was a leggy blonde one who was reading English."

"*Isabella?* Isabella informed against *me?*" said Axel incredulously. "But she was in love with me, Sir Magnus. Why would she do that?"

"Maybe that was the reason," said Pym boldly. "She came round a few days after you'd gone, you see. Asked for you. I told her what had happened. She howled and wept and said she was going to kill herself. But when I mentioned to Frau O that she'd called, she promptly said, 'Isabella is the one. She was jealous of his other women so she informed against him.'"

"What did you think?"

"Seemed a bit far-fetched to me, but then everything else did too. So yes, maybe Isabella did it. She did seem a bit crazy sometimes, to be honest. I could sort of imagine her doing something awful out of jealousy—on an impulse, you know—then persuading herself she hadn't done it in the first place. It's a sort of syndrome, isn't it, with jealous people?"

Axel took his time to reply. For a defector in the throes of negotiating his terms, Pym reflected, he was remarkably relaxed. "I don't know, Sir Magnus. I don't have your gifts of imagination sometimes. Do you have any other theories?"

"Not really. It could have happened so many ways."

In the silence of the night, Axel replenished their glasses, smiling broadly. "You all seem to have thought about it far more than I have," he confessed. "I'm very touched." He lifted his palms, Slav style, languidly. "Listen. I was illegal. I was a bum. No money, no papers. On the run. So they caught me, they threw me out. That's what happens to illegals. A fish gets a hook in its throat. A traitor gets a bullet in his head. An illegal gets marched across the border. Don't frown so much. It's over. Who gives a damn who did it? To tomorrow!"

"Tomorrow," Pym said, and they drank. "Hey—how did the great book go by the way?" he asked in the secret euphoria of his absolution.

Axel laughed louder. "Go? My God, it went! Four hundred pages of immortal philosophising, Sir Magnus. Imagine the Fremdenpolizei wading their way through that!"

"You mean they kept it—stole it? That's outrageous!"

"Maybe I was not too polite about the good Swiss burghers."

"But you've written it again since?"

Nothing could quench his laughter. "Written it again? It would have been twice as bad next time. Better we bury it with Axel H. You still have *Simplicissimus*? You haven't sold him?"

"Of course not."

A pause intervened. Axel smiled at Pym. Pym smiled at his hands, then raised his eyes to Axel.

"So here we both are," said Pym.

"That's right."

"I'm Lieutenant Pym and you're Jan's intelligent friend."

"That's right," Axel agreed, still smiling.

Having thus, in his own estimation, skilfully circumvented the one awkwardness that might have stood between them, the intelligence predator in Pym now artfully advanced upon the pertinent question of what had become of Axel since his eviction, and what his access had been, and so by extension— as Pym hoped—what cards he held, and what price he proposed to put on them as a reward for favouring the British over the Americans or even—dreadful thought—the French.

In this he met at first with no unpleasant inhibition on Axel's part since, doubtless out of deference to Pym's position of authority, he seemed resigned to take the passive rôle. Nor could Pym fail to notice that his old friend in rendering account of himself assumed the familiar meekness of the displaced person in the presence of his betters. The Swiss had marched him across the German border, he said—and for ease of reference he mentioned the frontier point in case Pym wished to check. They had handed him over to the West German police who, having dealt him a ritual beating, handed him to the Americans, who beat him again, first for escaping, then for returning, and finally of course for being the red-toothed war criminal that he was not, but whose identity he had unwisely purloined. The Americans put him in prison while they prepared a fresh case against him, they brought in fresh witnesses who were too frightened not to identify him, they set a date to try him, and still Axel could reach nobody who would vouch for him or say he was just Axel from Carlsbad and not a Nazi monster brother. Worse still, as the rest of the evidence began to look increasingly thin, said Axel with an apologetic smile, his own confession became increasingly important, so they had naturally beaten him harder in order to obtain it. No trial was held, however. War crimes, even fictitious ones, were becoming out of date, so one day the Americans had thrown him on another train and handed him over to the Czechs who, not to be outdone, beat him for the double crime of having been a German soldier in the war and an American prisoner after it.

"Then one day they stopped beating me and let me out," he said smiling and opening his hands once more. "For this, it seems, I had my dear dead father to thank. You remember the great Socialist who had fought in the Thälmann brigade in Spain?"

"Of course I do," said Pym, and it occurred to him as he watched Axel's quick hands gesticulating and his dark eyes twinkling that Axel had put aside the German in him and put on the Slav for good. "I had become an aristocrat," he said. "In the new Czechoslovakia I was Sir Axel suddenly. The old Socialists had loved my father. The new ones had been my friends at school and were already in the Party apparatus. 'Why do you beat up Sir Axel?' they asked my guards. 'He's got a good brain, stop hitting him and let him out. Okay, so he fought for Hitler. He's sorry. Now he'll fight for us, won't you, Axel?' 'Sure,' I said. 'Why not?' So they sent me to university."

"But what did you study?" said Pym amazed. "Thomas Mann? Nietzsche?"

"Better. How to use the Party to advance oneself. How to rise in the Youth Union. Shine in the committees. How to purge the faculties and students, climb over the backs of friends and the reputation of one's father. Which arses to kick and which to kiss. Where to talk too much and where to shut your mouth. Maybe I should have learned that earlier."

Feeling he was close to the heart of things, Pym wondered whether it was time for him to take notes but decided not to destroy Axel's flow.

"Somebody had the nerve to call me a Titoist the other day," Axel said. "Since '49 it's the latest insult." Pym secretly wondered whether this was why Axel had come over. "Know what I did?"

"What?"

"I informed against him."

"No! What for?"

"I don't know. Something bad. It's not what you say, it's who you say it to. You should know that. You're a big spy, I hear. Sir Magnus of the British Secret Service. Congratulations. Is Corporal Kaufmann all right out there? Maybe you should take him something?"

"I'll deal with him later, thank you."

There was a hiatus while each in his separate way savoured the effect of this disciplinary note. They drank another toast, shaking their heads at one another over their luck. But inside himself Pym was less at ease than he let on. He had a sense of slipping standards and complicated undertones.

"So what work have you actually been up to these last days?" Pym asked, struggling to reclaim the ascendancy. "How does a sergeant from HQ Southern Command come to be wandering round the Soviet Zone of Austria, planning his defection?"

Axel was lighting himself a fresh cigar so Pym had to wait a minute for his answer.

"A sergeant I don't know. In my unit we have only

aristos. Like you, I am also a great spy, Sir Magnus. It's a boom industry these days. We did well to select it."

Needing suddenly to tend his outward appearance, Pym smoothed his hair back in a reflective gesture he was working on. "But you are still proposing to come over to us—assuming that we can offer you the right sort of terms of course?" he asked, with hard-edged courtesy.

Axel waved away such a stupid idea. "I've paid my ticket same as you. So it's not perfect but it's my country. I've crossed my last frontier. They've got to put up with me."

Pym had a sensation of dangerous disconnection. "Then why are you here—if you don't want to defect—if I may ask."

"I heard about you. The great Lieutenant Pym of Div. Int., more latterly of Graz. Linguist. Hero. Lover. I was so excited to think of you spying on me. And me spying on you. It was so beautiful to think we were back in our old attic together, just that little thin wall between us—knock, knock! 'I've got to get in touch with this fellow,' I thought. Shake his hand. Give him a drink. Maybe we can set the world to rights, same as we used to in the old days."

"I see," said Pym. "Great."

"'Maybe we can put our heads together. We are reasonable men. Maybe he doesn't want to fight any more wars. Maybe I don't. Maybe we are tired of being heroes. Good men are scarce,' I thought. 'How many people in the world have shaken hands with Thomas Mann?'"

"Nobody but me," said Pym with a burst of real laughter and they drank again.

"I owe you so much, Sir Magnus. You were so generous. I never knew a better heart. I yelled at you, cursed you. What did you do? Held my head when I threw up. Cooked me tea, cleaned the vomit and the shit off me, fetched me books—back and forth to the library—read to me all night. I owe this man, I thought. I owe this man a step or two forward in his career. I should make him a gesture that is painful to me. If I can help him achieve a position of influence in the world, that's rare, that's already good. For the world as well as for him. Not many good men achieve a position of influence today. So I'll play a little trick and go and see him. And shake his hand. And say, thank you, Sir Magnus. And take him a gift to pay my debt to him and help him in his career, I thought. Because I love this man, do you hear?"

He had brought no straw hat filled with coloured packages but from the briefcase at his side he drew a folder and
handed it to Pym across the table.

"You have landed a great coup, Sir Magnus," he declared
proudly as Pym lifted the cover. "Took me a lot of spying to
get it for you. A lot of risks. Never mind. It's better than
Grimmelshausen, I think. If they ever find out what I've
done, I can bring you my balls as well."

Pym closes his eyes and opens them again, but it is the same
night in the same barn. "I'm a little fat Czech sergeant who
loves his vodka," Axel is explaining while Pym continues in a
dream to turn the pages of his gift. "I'm a good soldier
Schweik. Did we read that book? My name is Pavel. Hear
me? Pavel."

"Of course we read it. It was great. Is this genuine, Axel?
It isn't a joke or anything?"

"You think fat Pavel takes a risk like this to bring you a
joke? He has a wife who beats him, kids who hate him,
Russian bosses who treat him worse than a dog. Are you
listening?"

With half his head, yes, Pym is listening. He is reading
too.

"Your good friend Axel H, he doesn't exist. You never
met him tonight. In Bern long ago, sure, you met a sickly
German soldier who was writing a great book and maybe his
name was Axel, what's a name? But Axel vanished. Some bad
guy informed against him, you never knew what happened.
Tonight you are meeting fat Sergeant Pavel of Czech Army
Intelligence who likes garlic and screwing and betraying his
superiors. He speaks Czech and German, and the Russians
use him as a dogsbody because they don't trust the Austrians.
One week he's hanging around their headquarters in Wiener
Neustadt playing messenger boy and interpreter, the next
he's freezing his arse off on the zonal border looking for small
spies. The week after that he's back in his garrison in
Southern Czecho being kicked around by more Russians."
Axel is tapping Pym's arm. "See this? Pay attention. Here's a
copy of his paybook. Look at it, Sir Magnus. Concentrate. He
brought it for you because he doesn't expect anybody ever to
believe anything he says unless it is accompanied by *Unterlagen*.

You remember *Unterlagen*? Papers? They are what I didn't have in Bern. Take it with you. Show it to Membury."

Reluctantly Pym lifts his eyes from his reading long enough to notice the wad of glossy paper Axel is holding up for him to admire. A photocopy in those days is a big matter: plate photographs, tied into a looseleaf book with bootlaces through the holes. Axel presses it upon Pym and again rouses him sufficiently from the material in the folder to make him study the portrait of the bearer: a piggy, part-shaven little man with puffy eyes and a pout.

"That is *me*, Sir Magnus," Axel says, and bangs Pym on the shoulder quite hard to assure his attention, exactly as he used to in Bern. "Look at him, will you? He's a greedy, grubby fellow. Farts a lot, scratches his head, steals his Commandant's chickens. But he doesn't like his country to be occupied by a bunch of sweating Ivans who swagger round the streets of Prague and tell him he's a stinking little Czech, and he doesn't like being packed down to Austria at some-body's whim to play toady to a lot of drunk Cossacks. So he's brave too, you follow me? He's a brave little greasy coward."

Pym again pauses in his reading, this time to register a bureaucratic complaint which later causes him some shame. "It's all very well inventing this delightful character, Axel, but what am I to do with him?" he reasons in an aggrieved tone. "I'm supposed to produce a defector, not a paybook. They want a warm body back there in Graz. I haven't got one, have I?"

"You idiot!" cries Axel, pretending to be exasperated by Pym's obtuseness. "You guileless English baby! Have you never heard of a defector in place? Pavel *is* a defector! He's defecting but staying where he is. In three weeks' time he'll come here again, bring you more material. He'll defect not just once but if you are sensible twenty times, a hundred. He's an intelligence clerk, a courier, a low-grade fieldman, a bottlewasher, a coding sergeant and a pimp. Don't you under-stand what that means in terms of access? He will bring you wonderful intelligence again and again. His friends in the frontier unit will help him cross. Next time we meet you will have Vienna's questions for him. You will be at the centre of a fantastic industry: 'Can you get us this, Pavel? What does this mean, Pavel?' If you're polite to him, if you come alone, bring him a nice present, maybe he'll answer them."

"And will it be you—will I see you?"

"You will see Pavel."

"And will you be Pavel?"

"Sir Magnus. Listen." Pushing aside the briefcase that lay between them, Axel bangs his glass beside Pym's and yanks his chair so close that his shoulder is nudging against Pym's shoulder and his mouth is at Pym's ear. "Are you being very, very attentive now?"

"Of course I am."

"Because I think you are so fantastically stupid you better not play this game at all. Listen." Pym is grinning exactly as he used to grin when Axel was explaining why he was a *Trottel* for not understanding Kant. "What Axel is doing for you tonight, he can never undo in his whole life. I am risking my bloody neck for you. Like Sabina gave you her brother, Axel gives you Axel. Do you understand? Or are you too shit-stupid to recognise that I am putting my future in your hands?"

"I don't want it, Axel. I'd rather give it back."

"It's too late. I have stolen the papers, I have come over, you have seen them, you know what they contain. Pandora's box cannot be closed again. Your nice Major Membury—those clever aristos in Div. Int.—none of them ever saw such information. Do you follow this?"

Pym nods, Pym shakes his head. Pym frowns, smiles, and tries to look in every way he can the worthy and mature custodian of Axel's destiny.

"In return, you must swear me one thing. I told you earlier you must not promise. Now I tell you you must. To me, Axel, you must promise loyalty. Sergeant Pavel, he's a different matter. Sergeant Pavel you can betray and invent as much as you like—he is an invention anyway. But I Axel—this Axel here—look at me—*I do not exist*. Not for Membury, not for Sabina, not even for yourself. Even when you are lonely and bored and you need to impress somebody or buy somebody or sell somebody, I am not a creature in your game. If your own people threaten you, if they torture you, you must still deny me. If they put you on the cross in fifty years from now, will you lie for me? Answer."

Pym finds time to marvel that after energetically denying Axel's existence for so long he should be promising him to deny it for still longer. And that it must be a very rare thing indeed to be offered a second chance to prove one's loyalty after failing so miserably at the first attempt.

"I will," says Pym.

"What will you?"

"I will keep you secret. I'll lock you in my memory and give you the key."

"For always. Sabina's brother Jan also?"

"For always. Jan too. That's the whole Soviet Order of Battle in Czechoslovakia you've given me," says Pym in a trance. "If it's genuine."

"It's a little bit old, but you British know how to value antiquity. Your maps in Vienna and Graz are older. And they are not so genuine. You like Membury?"

"I think so. Why?"

"Me too. You are interested in fish? You are helping him to restock the lake?"

"Sometimes. Yes."

"That's important work. Do it with him. Help him. It's a lousy world, Sir Magnus. A few happy fish will make it better."

It was six in the morning when Pym left. Kaufmann had long ago put himself to bed in the jeep. Pym could see his boots sticking over the tailboard. Pym and Axel walked as far as the white stone, Axel leaning on his arm the way he used to when they walked beside the Aare. As they reached it Axel stooped and picked a harvest poppy and handed it to Pym. Then he picked another for himself which on reflection he handed to Pym also.

"There is one of me and one of you, Sir Magnus. There will never be another of either of us. You are the keeper of our friendship. Give my love to Sabina. Tell her that Sergeant Pavel sends her a special kiss to thank her for her help."

A man with a highly regarded source is an admired man and a well-fed one, Tom, as Pym quickly discovered in the next few weeks. Visiting Very Senior Officers from Vienna take him to dinner just for the touch of him and the vicarious feel of his achievement. Membury comes too, a grinning, loping Caesar dwarfing his Antony, hauling on his ear, dreaming of fish and smiling at the wrong people. Other officers less senior but still substantial alter their opinion of Pym overnight and send

him smarmy notes by interzonal bag. "Marlene sends her
love and is so sad that you had to leave Vienna without saying
goodbye to her. It looked for a moment as if I might become
your C.O. but fate decreed otherwise. M and I hope to be
engaged as soon as we get clearance from the War Office." He
is a cult of one and to know him is to be an insider: "The
fantastic work young Pym is doing—if I had my way, I'd give
him a third pip, national serviceman or not." "You should have
heard London on the scrambler, they're sending it to the
top." On London's orders, no less, Sergeant Pavel receives
the codename Greensleeves and Pym a commendation. Voluptuous Czech interpreters are proud of him, and demonstrate their pleasure in refined ways.

"You must never tell me what happened, it is a rule,"
Sabina ordered him, biting him half to death between her
deep sad lips.

"I never will."

"He is handsome, Jan's friend? He is beautiful? Like
you? I would love him immediately, yes?"

"He is tall and beautiful and very intelligent."

"Sexy also?"

"Very sexy."

"Hommsexual like you?"

"Totally."

The description pleased her in some deep and satisfying
way.

"You are good man, Magnus," she assured him. "You
have good taste that you protect this man like my brother."

The due day came round when Sergeant Pavel was to
make his second appearance. As Axel had predicted, Vienna
had prepared a dense crop of follow-up questions for him
concerning his first offering. Pym arrived with them written
out in a shorthand notebook. He also brought brown smoked-
salmon sandwiches and an excellent Sancerre from Membury.
He brought cigarettes and Naafi mint chocolates and everything else the gastronomic experts of Div. Int. could think of
to fill the tummy of a brave defector in place. While they ate
the smoked salmon and drank vodka, they cleared up the
outstanding points.

"So what have you got for me this time round?" Pym
enquired cheerfully when they had reached a natural break in
the proceedings.

"Nothing," Axel replied comfortably, helping himself to more vodka. "We let them starve a little. Gives them a better appetite next time."

"Pavel's having a crisis of conscience," Pym reported next day to Membury, obeying Axel's instructions to the letter. "He's having wife trouble and his daughter is going to bed with a no-good Russian officer every time Pavel is sent down to Austria. I didn't press him. I told him we were there and he could trust us and we're not adding to his pressures. I believe in the long run he's going to thank us for that. But I did ask him our questions about the concentrated armour east of Prague and he was interesting."

A visiting colonel from Vienna was sitting in. "What did he say?" asked the colonel, following Pym closely.

"He said he thinks it's guarding something."

"Any idea what?"

"Weaponry of some sort. Could be rockets."

"Stay with him," the colonel advised, and Membury puffed out his cheeks and looked like the proud father he had become.

At their third meeting source Greensleeves solved the mystery of the concentrated armour and produced in addition a breakdown of the total Soviet air strength in Czechoslovakia as of November last. Or nearly total. Vienna was in any case amazed, and London authorised the payment of two small gold bars on condition that the British assay marks first be removed for reasons of deniability. Sergeant Pavel was thus characterised as a greedy man which made everybody feel easier. For several months after this Pym scampered back and forth between Axel and Membury like a butler serving two masters. Membury wondered whether he should meet Greensleeves in person: Vienna seemed to think it would be a good idea. Pym tried for him but came back with the sad news that he would treat only with Pym. Membury resigned himself. It was the breeding season for trout. Vienna summoned Pym and dined him. Colonels, air commodores, and naval persons vied to stake their claim to him. But it was Axel, as it turned out, who was his true proprietor and parent company.

"Sir Magnus," Axel whispered. "Something very terrible has happened." His smile had lost its bounce. His eyes were haunted and there were heavy shadows under them. Pym had brought any number of Naafi delicacies but he refused them all. "You have to help me, Sir Magnus," he said, darting scared looks towards the barn door. "You're my only hope. Help me, for Christ's sake. Do you know what they do to people like me? Don't look at me like that! Think of something for a change! It's your turn!"

I am in the barn at this moment, Tom. I have lived there these thirty and more years. Miss Dubber's stippled ceiling has rolled away, leaving the old rafters and the upside-down bats dangling from the roof. I can smell his cigar smoke as I sit here and I can see the holes of his dark eyes in the lamplight as he whispers Pym's name like the invalid he used to be: get me music, get me painting, get me bread, get me secrets. But there is no self-pity in his voice, no supplication or regret. That was never Axel's way. He demands. His voice is sometimes soft, it is true. But it is never less than powerful. He is his man, as ever. He is Axel, he is owed. He has crossed frontiers and been beaten. Of myself I am thinking nothing at all. Not now, not then.

"They are arresting my friends back home, did you hear? Two of our group were dragged from their beds yesterday morning in Prague. Another vanished on his way to work. I had to tell them about us. It was the only way."

The import of this statement takes a moment to penetrate Pym's worried understanding. Even when it has done so, his voice remains mystified: "About us? Me? What did you say? Who to, Axel?"

"Not in detail. In principle. Nothing bad. Not your name. It's okay, just more complicated, takes more handling. I've been more cunning than the others. In the end it may be better."

"But what did you tell them about *us*?"

"Nothing. Listen. For me it's different. The others, they work in factories, in the universities, they've no back door. When they're tortured they tell the truth and the truth kills them. But me, I'm a big spy, I've got a strong position, same as you. 'Sure,' I say to them. 'I go over the border. That's my job. I collect intelligence, remember?'... I act indignant, I demand to see my senior officer. He's not bad, this senior officer. Not a hundred percent, maybe sixty. But he hates the

Ivans too. 'I'm cultivating a British traitor,' I tell him. 'He's a big fish. An army officer. I have kept it secret from you because of the many Titoists inside our organisation. Get the secret police off my back and you can share his product with me when I put the heat on him.'"

Pym has given up speech by now. He doesn't bother to ask what the senior officer says in reply, or to what extent the real life of Axel may be compared with the fictitious life of Sergeant Pavel. The cells are dying all over him, in his head, his groin, his bone marrow. His loving thoughts about Sabina are as old as childhood memories to him. There is only Pym and Axel and disaster in the world. He is changing into an old man even while he listens. The ignorance of ages is descending on him.

"He says I've got to bring him proof," says Axel a second time.

"Proof?" Pym mumbles. "What sort of proof? Proof? I don't follow you."

"Intelligence." Axel rubs his finger against his thumb, exactly as E. Weber once did. "Pinka-pinka. Product. Money. Something a British traitor like you could give me when I blackmailed him. It doesn't have to be the secrets of the atom bomb but it has to be good. Good enough to keep him quiet. No junk, you understand? He's got senior officers too." Axel smiles, though it is not a smile I care to recollect even now. "There's always one guy higher up the ladder, isn't there, Sir Magnus? Even when you think you're at the top. Then when you reach the top, there they are again below you, swinging on your boots. That's how it is in a system like ours. 'No fabrication,' he says to me. 'Whatever it is, it's got to have quality. Then we can fix it.' Steal for me, Sir Magnus. As you love my freedom, get me something wonderful."

"You look as though you've been seeing things," Corporal Kaufmann says as Pym returns to the jeep.

"It's my stomach," says Pym.

But on the journey back to Graz he began to feel better. Life is duty, he reflected. It's just a question of establishing which creditor is asking loudest. Life is paying. Life is seeing people right if it kills you.

There were half a dozen reconstructed Pyms wandering the streets of Graz that night, Tom, and there isn't one of them I need now feel ashamed of, or wouldn't happily embrace as a long-lost son who had paid his debt to society and come home, if he knocked on Miss Dubber's door at this moment and said, Father, it's me. I don't think there was a night in his life when he thought less about himself and more about his obligation to others than when he was patrolling his city kingdom under the shadows of crumbling Hapsburg glories, pausing now at the leafy gates of Membury's spacious married quarters, now at the doorway to Sabina's unprepossessing apartment house, while he made his plan and flashed them reassuring promises. "Don't worry about a thing," he told Membury in his heart. "You will suffer no humiliation, your lake will continue to be stocked and your post will be safe for as long as you care to adorn it. The Highest in the Land will continue to respect you as the presiding genius of the Greensleeves operation." "Your secrets are in my hands," he whispered to Sabina's unlit window. "Your employment by the British, your heroic brother Jan, your exalted opinion of your lover Pym are all secure. I shall cherish them as I cherish your soft warm body sleeping its troubled sleep."

He took no decisions because he had no doubts. The lone crusader had identified his mission, the skilled spy would take care of the detail, the loyal attacher would never again betray his friend in exchange for the illusion of being a servant of national necessity. His loves, his duties and allegiances had never been clearer. Axel, I owe you. Together we can change the world. I will bring you gifts as you brought gifts to me. I will never again send you to the camps. If he contemplated alternatives, then it was only to reject them as disastrous. Over the last months the inventive Pym had built Sergeant Pavel into a figure of joy and admiration in the secret corridors of Graz, Vienna and Whitehall. Under his skilful hand the choleric little hero's drinking, womanising and quixotic bursts of courage had become a legend. Even if Pym were prepared to break Axel's trust a second time, how could he go to Membury and say: "Sir. Sergeant Pavel does not exist. Greensleeves is my friend Axel, who requires that we give him genuine British secrets"? Membury's kindly eyes would pop open, his innocent face would collapse in lines of sadness and despair. His trust in Pym would wither, his reputation with it: Membury to the lantern, sack Membury;

Membury, his wife and all his daughters, go home. An even worse disaster would result if Pym were to strike a compromise by visiting Axel's dilemma upon the fictitious Sergeant Pavel. He had played that scene, too, in his imagination: "Sir. Sergeant Pavel's frontier-crossings have been noticed. He has told the Czech secret police that he has a British agent in play. We must therefore give him chickenfeed to back his story." Div. Int. had no mandate to run double agents. Graz even less so. Even a defector in place was stretching things. Only Greensleeves' insistence on being handled by Pym personally had prevented a takeover by London long ago, and there was already a lot of earnest talk going on about who would get Pavel when Pym's military service expired. To place Sergeant Pavel in the position of a double agent would unloose a string of immediate consequences, all frightful: Membury would lose Greensleeves to London; Pym's successor would discover the deception in five minutes; Axel would once more be betrayed and his chances of survival forfeit; the Memburys would be posted to Siberia.

No, Tom. As Pym walked the momentous night away under a canopy of unreachable ideals, eschewing Sabina's bed in his purity of soul, he was not tormenting himself over great choices. He was not examining his immortal spirit in anticipation of what purists might call a treasonable act. He did not consider that tomorrow was the day set for his irrevocable execution—the day on which all hope for Pym would die and your father would be born. He was watching the dawn rise on a day of beauty and harmony. A day when a bad record could be put straight, when the fate of everyone he was responsible for rested in his care, when the electors of his secret constituency would go down on their knees and thank Pym and his Maker that he had been born to see them right. He was glowing and exulting. He was letting his goodwill and self-faith fill him up with courage. The secret crusader had placed his sword upon the altar and was transmitting fraternal messages to the God of Battles.

"Axel, come over!" Pym had begged him. "Forget about Sergeant Pavel. You can be an ordinary defector. I'll look after you. I'll get you everything you need. I promise."

But Axel was as fearless as he was determined. "Do not advise me to betray my friends, Sir Magnus. I am the only one who can save them. Did I not tell you I have crossed my last frontier? If you help me, we can win a great victory. Be here on Wednesday at the same time."

Briefcase in hand Pym makes quickly for the top floor of the villa and unlocks the door to his office. I am a morning man, it is known of me. Pym is an early riser, Pym is keen, Pym has done a day's work while most of us are still shaving. Membury's office is linked to his own by a pair of grand doors. Pushing them open, Pym steps inside. As he does so, his sense of well-being becomes unbearable: a dizzying blend of resolution, rightness and release. I am blessed. Membury's tin desk is no Reichstag desk. It has an old tin back and Pym's Swiss Army penknife knows the four screws well. In the third drawer down, on the left side, Membury keeps his basic works of reference: standing orders for the unit, *Brown Fish of the World*, classified telephone directory, *Lakes and Waterways of Austria*, Order of Battle of Military Intelligence in London, a list of leading aquaria and a chart for Div. Int., Vienna, showing units and their functions but no names. Pym reaches a hand in. Not an invasion. Not a retribution. No initials are being carved into the panelling. I am here to administer a caress. Folders, loose-leaf manuals. Signals instructions marked "Top Secret, Guard" which Pym has never seen. I am here to borrow, not to steal. Opening his briefcase he extracts an army-issue Agfa camera with a one-foot measuring chain fastened to the lens front. It is the same camera that he uses when Axel brings out raw material and Pym has to photograph it on the spot. He cocks it and sets it on the desk. This is what I was born for, he thinks, not for the first time. In the beginning was the spy.

From a file with the word "Vertebrates" crossed out on the cover, he selects the Order of Battle of Div. Int. Axel knows it anyway, he reasons. Nevertheless, there are impressive "Top Secret" stamps at top and bottom, and a distribution stamp to guarantee authenticity. As you love my freedom, get me something wonderful. He photographs it once, then again, and is left with a feeling of anticlimax. There are thirty-six frames on this film. Why do I cheesepare and give him only two? I could do something for our mutual understanding. Axel, you deserve better. He remembers a recent War Office assessment of the Soviet threat. If they will read that, they'll read anything. It is in the top drawer, beside *A Handbook of Water Mammals*, and begins with a summary of conclusions. He photographs each page and finishes the film nicely. Axel, I've done it! We're free. We've put the world to rights, exactly as you said we would! We are men of the middle ground—we have founded our own country with a population of two!

"Promise you will never bring me anything so good again, Sir Magnus," said Axel at their next meeting. "If you do, they will make me a general and we shall not be able to meet any more."

> "Dear Father"—Pym wrote to the Majestic Hotel, Karachi, where Rick appeared to be living for his health—"Thanks for your two letters. I am so glad to hear you are hitting it off with the Aga Khan. I believe I am doing good work out here and you would be proud of me."

14

When Mary Pym at the age of sixteen decided it was time to lose her virginity she faked a heavy dose of adolescent vapours and had herself put to bed by Matron instead of playing hockey. There she lay in the sick wing staring at the wall till the three-o'clock bell rang, telling her that Matron was off duty until five. She waited five more minutes exactly by her Confirmation watch, held her breath for thirty seconds which always helped to get her courage up, then tiptoed down the stone back stairs past the kitchens and the laundry and across a bit of sour grass to an old brick potting shed where the under-gardener had made a provisional bed of blankets and old sacking. The results were more spectacular than she had reason to hope, but what she relished after-wards was not the event so much as the anticipation of it: the lying boldly in the bed with her skirt rucked round her waist knowing nothing was going to stop her now she had made up

her mind; the sense of freedom as she took herself across the
border into a state of sin.

And that was the feeling she had now, sitting demurely
in the centre row in Caroline Lumsden's overfurnished drawing-
room, with her hideous Thai tables and her garish Chinese
paintings and her shelf full of factory-made Buddhas, listening to Caroline trying to sound like the Queen as she moaned
out the minutes of the last meeting of the Vienna Branch of
the Diplomatic Wives Association in her plummy swansong.
I'll do it, Mary told herself, dead calm. If it doesn't work one
way, I'll make it work another. She glanced to the window. In
their hired Mercedes across the street, Georgie and Fergus
were sitting with their heads together, two lovers pretending
to study a street map while they kept an eye on the front
door and her Rover parked in Caroline's drive. I'll take the
back way out. It worked then, it'll work now.

"It was therefore *unanimously* agreed," Caroline was
lamenting, "that the Foreign Office Inspectors' *report* on the
local cost of living was both distorted *and* unfair, and that a
Finance subcommittee would be formed *immediately*, headed, I am pleased to say, by *Mrs.* McCormick"—respectful
hush. Ruth McCormick was the wife of the Economic Minister and therefore a financial genius. Nobody mentioned that
she was screwing the Dutch military attaché. "The subcommittee will itemise *all* our points and, having done so, submit
a *written* objection to our association in London for submission *through* the proper channels to the Head of the Inspectorate
himself."

Patter of soprano applause from fourteen pairs of female
hands, Mary's included. Great, Caroline, great. In another
life, it will be your turn to be the rising young diplomat and
your husband's to stay home and imitate you.

Caroline had turned to Any Other Business. "Next *Monday*,
our weekly transatlantic lunch at Manzi's. Twelve-thirty *sharp*
and four hundred schillings a head, cash, please, to include
two glasses of wine, and please *don't* be late as Herr Manzi
took an *awful* lot of persuading to give us a private *room.*"
Pause. Say it, you fool, Mary urged her. Caroline didn't. Not
yet. "Then on Friday, one week today, please, Marjory de
Weever will be giving her really *fascinating* lantern lecture
here on aerobics which she taught *very* successfully to an

all-ranks class in the Sudan where her husband was second *man*. Right, Marjory?"

"Well, chargé really," Marjory roared from the front row. "The Ambassador was only there for three months out of fourteen. Not that Brian got paid for it but that's beside the point."

For pity's sake! thought Mary furiously. *Now!* But she had forgotten about Penny Sharlow's bloody husband landing a medal.

"And I'm sure we'd *all* like to congratulate Penny on the fantastic support she's given to James over the years, without which I'll bet he wouldn't have got anything at *all*."

This was apparently a joke because there was hysterical laughter by too few voices, which Caroline quelled with a mournful stare into the middle distance. She put on her Official Mourning voice.

"And Mary darling—you did say you wouldn't mind if I mentioned it." Mary looked hastily downward to her lap. "I'm sure *everyone* would like me to say how *sorry* we are about the death of your *father*-in-law. We know Magnus has been hit *very* hard and we do hope he will get over it *soon*, and be back among us in his usual *high* spirits that we *all* find so refreshing."

Sympathetic murmurs. Mary whispered "Thank you" and keeled forward not too far. She sensed the anxious pause while everyone waited for her head to come up, but it didn't. She began to shake and was impressed to see real tears flopping on to her clenched hands. She let out a little choke and from her willed darkness heard cheerful Mrs. Simpson, wife of the Chancery guard, say "Come here, lovey," as she put an enormous arm round Mary's back. She choked again, pushed Mrs. Simpson halfheartedly away and struggled to her feet, tears everywhere: tears for Tom, tears for Magnus, tears for being deflowered in the potting shed and I bet I'm pregnant. She let Mrs. Simpson take her arm, she shook her head and stammered "I'm fine." She reached the hall to find that Caroline Lumsden had followed her out. "No thanks . . . really I don't want to lie down. Far rather just take a walk . . . get my coat, please? . . . Blue with a foul fur collar . . . Rather be alone if you don't mind. . . . You've been so kind. Oh Christ, I'm going to cry again. . . ."

Once in the Lumsdens' long back garden, she wandered,

still hunched, along the path until it dropped out of sight behind the trees. Then she moved fast. Training, she thought gratefully, as she unlatched the back gate; nothing quite like it for cooling the blood. She headed quickly for the bus stop. There was one every fourteen minutes. She had looked them up.

"How terribly good of them!" cried Mrs. Membury, with the greatest satisfaction, as she topped up Brotherhood's glass with her homemade elderflower wine. "Oh I do think that's farsighted and sensible. I'd never supposed the War Office would have *half* the wit. Would *you*, Harrison? Not deaf," she explained to Brotherhood while they waited. "Just slow-thinking. Would you, darling?"

Harrison Membury had come up from the stream at the end of the garden where he had been cutting reeds, and he was still wearing his waders. He was large and loping and at seventy still boyish, with pink immature cheeks and silk white hair. He sat at the far end of the table washing down homemade cake with tea from a huge pottery mug with "Gramps" written on it. He moved, Brotherhood reckoned, at exactly half his wife's pace and spoke at half the volume.

"Oh I don't know," he said when everyone else had forgotten the question. "There were some quite clever chaps scattered around the place. Here and there."

"Ask him about fish and you'll get a *far* quicker answer," said Mrs. Membury, hurtling off to the corner of the room and pulling out some albums from among the collected works of Evelyn Waugh. "How are the trout, Harrison?"

"Oh they're all right," said Membury with a grin.

"We're not allowed to eat them, you know. Only the pike can do that. Now would it be fun to look at my photographs? I mean is it going to be an *illustrated* history? Don't tell me. It doubles the cost. It said so in the *Observer*. Pictures double the cost of a book. But then I do think they double the attractiveness too. Specially with biographies. I can't be doing with biography if I can't *look* at the people who are being biogged. Harrison can. He's cerebral. I'm visual. Which are you?"

"I think I must be more your way," said Brotherhood with a smile, playing his ponderous role.

The village was one of those half-urbanised Georgian settlements on the edge of Bath where English Catholics of a certain standing have elected to gather in their exile. The cottage lay at the country end of it, a tiny sandstone mansion with a steep narrow garden descending to a stretch of river, and they sat in the cluttered kitchen on wheelback chairs, surrounded by washing-up, and vaguely votive bric-a-brac: a cracked ceramic plaque of the Virgin Mary from Lourdes; a disintegrating rush cross jammed behind the cooker; a child's paper mobile of angels rotating in the draught; a photograph of Ronald Knox. While they talked, filthy grandchildren wandered in and stared at them before tall mothers swept them off. It was a household in permanent and benevolent disorder, pervaded by the gentle thrill of religious persecution. A white morning sun was poking through the Bath mist. There was a sound of slow water dripping in the gutters.

"You an academic chap?" Membury enquired suddenly, from the end of the table.

"Darling, I *told* you. He's an *historian*."

"Well, more a retired trooper, I suppose, sir, to be honest," Brotherhood replied. "I was lucky to get the job. I'd have been on the shelf by now, if this hadn't come along."

"Now when will it come out?" Mrs. Membury shouted, as if everyone were deaf. "I've got to know *months* in advance so that I can put my name down with Mrs. Lanyon. Tristram, don't tug. We have a mobile library here, you know. Magda darling, do something about Tristram, he's trying to tear a page out of history. They come once a week and they're an absolute godsend as long as you don't mind waiting. Now this is Harrison's villa where he had his office and everyone worked for him. The main bit's 1680, the wing's new. Well nineteenth. This is his pond. He stocked it from scratch. The Gestapo had thrown grenades into it and blown up all the fish. They would. Pigs."

"From what my masters say, it will start out as a work of internal reference," Brotherhood said. "Then afterwards they'll publish a sanitised version for the open market."

"You're not M. R. D. Foot, are you?" said Mrs. Membury. "No, you can't be. You're Marlow. Well I think they're inspired, anyway. So sensible to get hold of the actual people before they peg out."

"Who did you troop with?" Membury said.

"Let's just say I did a little of this and a little of that," Brotherhood suggested with deliberate coyness, while he pulled on his reading glasses.

"There he is," said Mrs. Membury, stabbing a tiny finger at a group photograph. "There. That's the young man you were asking about. Magnus. He did all the really brilliant work. That's the old Rittmeister, he was an absolute darling. Harrison, what was the mess waiter's name—the one who ought to have become a novice but didn't have the gump?"

"Forget," said Membury.

"And who are the girls?" said Brotherhood, smiling.

"Oh my dear, they were all sorts of trouble. Each one dottier than the next and if they weren't pregnant they were running off with unsuitable lovers, cutting their wrists. I could have opened a Marie Stopes clinic for them full time if we'd believed in birth control in those days. Now we're hybrids. Our girls are on the pill, but they still get pregnant by mistake."

"They did the interpreting for us," Membury said, filling himself a pipe.

"Was there an interpreter involved in the Greensleeves operation?" Brotherhood said.

"No need," said Membury. "Chap spoke German. Pym handled him alone."

"Completely alone?"

"Solo. Greensleeves insisted on it. Why don't you talk to Pym?"

"But who took him over when Pym left?"

"I did," said Membury proudly, brushing wet tobacco from the front of his disgraceful pullover.

There is nothing like a red-backed notebook to instill order into desultory conversation. Having spread one very deliberately among the débris of several meals, and shaken out his big right arm as a prelude to becoming what he called a little bit official, Brotherhood drew a pen from his pocket with as much ceremony as a village policeman at the scene of the occurrence. The grandchildren had been removed. From an upper room came the sounds of someone trying to coax religious music from a xylophone.

"If we could get it all down first I can come back to the individual specifics later," said Brotherhood.

"Jolly good idea," said Mrs. Membury sternly. "Harrison, darling, listen."

"Unfortunately, as I have already told you, most of the raw material on Greensleeves has been destroyed, lost or misplaced, which puts even greater responsibility on the shoulders of surviving witnesses. That's you. Now then."

For a while after this forbidding warning there was relative sanity while Membury with surprising accuracy recalled the dates and content of Greensleeves' principal triumphs and the part played by Lieutenant Magnus Pym of the Intelligence Corps. Brotherhood wrote diligently and prompted little, only pausing to wet his thumb and turn the pages of his notebook.

"Harrison, darling, you're being slow again," Mrs. Membury interposed occasionally. "Marlow hasn't got all day." And once: "Marlow's got to get back to *London*, darling. He's not a fish."

But Membury continued swimming at his own good pace, now describing Soviet military emplacements in southern Czechoslovakia; now the laborious procedure for prising small gold bars out of the Whitehall war chests which Greensleeves insisted on receiving in payment; now the fights he had had with Div. Int. to protect his pet agent from being overused. And Brotherhood, despite the little tape-recorder that nestled once more in his wallet pocket, set it all out for them to see, dates left, material centre.

"Greensleeves didn't have any other codename at any time, did he?" he asked casually as he jotted. "Sometimes a source gets rechristened for security reasons or because the name's already been bagged."

"Think, Harrison," Mrs. Membury urged.

Membury took his pipe from his mouth.

"Source Wentworth?" Brotherhood suggested, turning a page.

Membury shook his head.

"There was also a source"—Brotherhood faltered slightly as if the name had nearly escaped him—"Serena, that was it—no it wasn't—Sabina. Source Sabina, operating out of Vienna. Or was it Graz? Maybe it was Graz before your time. Used to be a popular thing that, anyway, mixing up the sexes with the cover names. A quite general trick of disinformation, I'm told."

"Sabina?" cried Mrs. Membury. "Not *our* Sabina?"

"He's talking about a source, darling," Membury said firmly, coming in much more quickly than was his habit. "Our Sabina was an interpreter, not an agent. Quite different."

"Well *our* Sabina was an absolute—"

"She wasn't a source," said Membury firmly. "Now, come on, don't tittle-tattle. Poppy."

"I beg your pardon?" said Brotherhood.

"Magnus wanted to call him Poppy. We did for a bit. Source Poppy. I rather liked it. Then up came Remembrance Day and some ass in London decided Poppy was derogatory to the fallen—poppies are for heroes, not traitors. Absolutely typical of those chaps. Probably got promoted for it. Total buffoon. I was furious, so was Magnus. 'Poppy *is* a hero,' he said. I liked him for that. Nice chap."

"That's the bare bones done, then," said Brotherhood, surveying his handiwork. "Now let's flesh them out, can we?" He was reading from the subject headings he had written at the beginning of his notebook before he came. "Personalities, well, we're touching on that. Value or otherwise of national servicemen to the peacetime intelligence effort, were they a help or a hindrance—we'll come to it. Where they all went afterwards—did they attain positions of interest in their chosen walk of life? Well, you may have kept up with them, and there again you may not. That's more for us to worry about than you."

"Yes, well now, whatever *did* happen to Magnus?" Mrs. Membury demanded. "Harrison was so upset he never wrote. Well so was I. He never even told us whether he converted. He was awfully *close*, we felt. All he needed was one more shove. Harrison was exactly like that for years. It took a jolly good talking to from Father D'Arcy before Harrison saw the light, didn't it, darling?"

Membury's pipe had gone out and he was peering disappointedly into the bowl.

"I never liked the chap," he explained with a kind of embarrassed regret. "Never thought much of him."

"Darling, don't be silly. You adored Magnus. You practically adopted him. You know you did."

"Oh Magnus was a splendid chap. The other chap. The source. The Greensleeves chap. I thought he was a bit of a fraud, to be honest. I didn't say anything—it didn't seem useful. With Div. Int. and London waving their caps in the air, why should we complain?"

"Nonsense," said Mrs. Membury, very firmly indeed. "Marlow, don't listen. Darling, you're being far too modest, as usual. You were the linchpin of the operation, you know you were. Marlow's writing a *history*, darling. He's going to write about *you*. You mustn't spoil it for him, must he, Marlow? That's the fashion these days. Put down, put down. I get absolutely sick of it. Look at what they did to poor Captain Scott on the television. Daddy knew Scott. He was a marvellous man."

Membury continued as if she hadn't spoken. "All the brigadiers from Vienna beaming away like sand boys. Roars of applause from the War Office. No point in me killing the golden goose if they were all happy, was there? Young Magnus cock-a-hoop. Well I didn't want to spoil *his* fun."

"*And* he was taking instruction," said Mrs. Membury pointedly. "Harrison had arranged for him to go to Father Moynihan twice a week. *And* he was running garrison cricket. *And* he was learning Czech. You can't do that in a day."

"Ah now, that's interesting. About the learning Czech, I mean. Was this because he had a Czech source then?"

"It's because Sabina set her cap at him, the little minx," said Mrs. Membury, but this time her husband actually spoke through her.

"His stuff was all so flashy, somehow," he was saying, undeterred. "Always looked good on the plate, but when you came to chew it over, nothing really there. That's how it seemed to me." He gave a puzzled giggle. "Same as trying to eat a pike. All bones. You'd get a report in, look it over. I say, that's jolly good, you'd think. But when you took a closer look it was boring. Yes, that's true because we already know it. . . . Yes, that's possible but we can't verify it because we've nothing on that region. I didn't like to say anything, but I think the Czechs could have been batting and bowling at the same time. I always thought that was why Greensleeves didn't show up after Magnus went back to England. He wasn't so sure he could hoodwink an older chap. Mean of me, I expect. I'm just a failed fish freak, aren't I, Hannah? That's what she calls me. Failed fish freak."

The description pleased them both so much that they broke out laughing for some while, so that Brotherhood had to laugh with them and keep back his question until Membury was able to hear him clearly.

"You mean you never met Greensleeves? He never came to the rendezvous? I'm sorry, sir," he said, returning to his notebook, "but didn't you say just now you yourself took over source Greensleeves when Pym left Graz?"

"I did."

"And now you say you never met him."

"Perfectly true. I didn't. Stood me up at the altar, didn't he, Hannah? She got me into my best suit, packed together all these stupid special foods he was supposed to like—how that started, God knows—he never turned up."

"Harrison probably got the wrong night," said Mrs. Membury, with a fresh gust of laughter. "Harrison's frightful about time, aren't you, darling? He was never *trained* for Intelligence, you know. He was librarian in Nairobi. A jolly good one too. Then he met someone on the ship and got roped in."

"And out," said Membury cheerfully. "Kaufmann came along. He was the driver. Charming chap. Well he knew the meeting place like the back of his hand. I didn't get the wrong night, darling. I got the right one, I know I did. Sat in an empty barn all night. No word from him, nothing. We'd no means of getting hold of him, it was all one way. Ate a bit of his stupid food. Drank some of his booze, I enjoyed that. Went home. Same again the next night and the next. I waited for a message of some sort, phone call like the first time. Absolute blank. Chap was never heard of again. We should have had a formal handover with Pym present, of course, but Greensleeves wouldn't allow it. Prima donna, you see, like all agents. 'One chap at a time.' Iron rule." Membury absently helped himself from Brotherhood's glass. "Vienna was furious. Blamed it all on me. Then I told them he was no good anyway and that didn't help." He gave another rich laugh. "I should think it got me sacked if truth were known. They didn't say so, but I'll bet it jolly well helped!"

Mrs. Membury had made a tuna-fish risotto because it was Friday, and a trifle with cherries on it which she refused to let Membury eat. When lunch was over she and Brotherhood stood on the river bank watching Membury hacking cheerfully at the reeds. Nets and fine wires were stretched all ways across the water. Among the breeding boxes, an old punt was sinking at its mooring. The sun, freed of the mist, beat brightly.

"So tell us about the wicked Sabina," Brotherhood suggested artfully, out of Membury's earshot.

Mrs. Membury couldn't wait. An absolute minx, she repeated: "One look at Magnus and she saw herself with a British passport, a jolly good British husband and nothing to worry about for the rest of her life. But Magnus was a bit too sly for her, I'm pleased to say. He must have stood her up. He never said so, but that was the way we read it. In Graz one day. Gone the next."

"Where did she go then?" Brotherhood said.

"Home to Czechoslovakia, that was the story. With her tail between her legs was our theory. Left a note for Harrison saying she was homesick and she was going back to her old boyfriend, despite the beastly régime. Well *that* didn't please London, as you can imagine. It didn't raise Harrison's stock one bit. They said he should have seen it coming and done something about it."

"I wonder what became of her," Brotherhood mused with an historian's dreaminess. "You don't remember her other name, do you?"

"Harrison. What was Sabina's other name?"

With surprising swiftness the answer rang back across the water. "Kordt. K-O-R-D-T. Sabina Kordt. Very beautiful girl. Charming."

"Marlow says what became of her?"

"God knows. Last we heard she'd changed her name and landed herself a job in one of the Czech Ministries. One of the defectors said she'd been working for 'em all along."

Mrs. Membury was not so much astonished as proved right. "Now there you are! Married getting on for fifty years, thirty-something years since Austria, and he doesn't even tell me she turned up in Czechoslovakia working for one of the Ministries! I expect Harrison had an affair with her himself if truth were known. Practically everybody did. Well my dear she must have been a spy, mustn't she? It sticks out a mile. They'd never have taken her back if they hadn't their hooks on her all along, they're far too vindictive. So Magnus was well rid of her then, wasn't he? Are you sure you won't stay for tea?"

"If I could take a few of those old photographs," Brother-hood said. "We'll give you a credit in the book, naturally."

Mary knew the technique exactly. In Berlin she had watched Jack Brotherhood use it a dozen times, and helped him often. At training camp they had called it paperchasing: how to make an encounter with someone you don't trust. The only difference was, today it was Mary who was the subject of the operation, and the anonymous writer of the note who didn't trust her:

> "I have information that could lead us both to Magnus. You will please do the following. Any morning between ten and twelve, you will sit in the lobby of the Hotel Ambassador. Any afternoon between two and six you will take a coffee at the Café Mozart. Any evening between nine and midnight, the lounge of the Hotel Sacher. Mr. König will collect you."

The Mozart was half empty. Mary sat at a centre table where she could be seen and ordered herself a coffee and a brandy. They've watched me arrive and now they're watching to see whether I am followed. Pretending to consult her diary, she took covert note of the people round her and the parked charabancs and fiacres in the street outside the big windows, looking for anything that could resemble a stake-out. When you've got a conscience like mine, everything stinks anyway, she thought: from the two nuns frowning at the stock exchange prices in the window of the bank to the huddle of bowler-hatted young coachmen stamping their feet and watching the girls go by. In a corner of the café, a fat Viennese gentleman was expressing interest in her. I should have worn a hat, she thought. I'm not a respectable single woman. She got up, went to the newspaper rack and without thinking chose *Die Presse*. Now I suppose I roll it up and take it for a walk in my stockinged feet, she thought stupidly, as she opened it at the film page.

"Frau Pym?"

A woman's voice, a woman's bosom. A woman's deferen-tially smiling face. It was the girl from the cash desk.

"That's right," said Mary, smiling in return.

From behind her back she produced an envelope with "Frau Pym" written on it in pencil. "Herr König left this message for you. He is very sorry."

Mary gave her fifty schillings and opened the envelope.

> "Please pay your bill and leave the café at once,
> turning right into the Maysedergasse, and remaining
> on the right-hand pavement. When you reach the
> pedestrian precinct turn left, and keep to the left
> side, walking slowly and admiring the shop windows."

She wanted the loo but she didn't like to go in case he thought she was tipping someone off. She put the note in her handbag, finished her coffee and took her bill to the cash desk where the girl gave her another smile.

"These men are all the same," the girl said while the change rattled down the chute.

"You're telling me," said Mary. They both laughed.

As she left the café a young couple entered and she had a feeling they were disguised Americans. But then a lot of Austrians were. She turned right and came at once to the Maysedergasse. The two nuns were still at their stock prices. She kept to the right-hand pavement. It was twenty past three and the Wives' meeting was sure to end by five so that they could all get home to change into halter dresses and sequin handbags for the evening cattle market. But even when everyone had gone and only Mary's car remained in the Lumsdens' drive, Fergus and Georgie might well assume she had stayed on for a quiet drink with Caroline on her own. If I make it back by quarter to six I stand a chance, she reckoned. She paused before a woman's lingerie shop and found herself admiring a pair of tart's black cami-knickers in the window. Who buys that stuff anyway? Bee Lederer, a pound to a penny. She hoped something would happen soon, before the Ambassadress came out with an armful of the stuff, or one of the many unattached men tried to pick her up.

"Frau Pym? I am from Herr König. Please come quickly."

The girl was pretty and badly dressed and nervous. Following her Mary had an overwhelming memory of being back in Prague visiting a painter the authorities did not approve of. The side street was one minute packed with shoppers, the next empty. All Mary's senses were alight. She smelt delicatessen, frost and tobacco. She glanced into a shop doorway and recognised the man from the Café Mozart. The girl turned left then right, then left again. Where am I? They entered a paved square. We're in the Kärtnerstrasse. We're not. A hippie boy took Mary's photograph and tried to press a card on her. She brushed him aside. A red plastic bear was holding his mouth open for contributions to some charity. An Asian pop group was singing Beatles music. Across the square lay a dual carriageway and at the near side of it a brown Peugeot waited with a man at the wheel. As they approached, he pushed the back door open at them. The girl grabbed the door and said, "Get in, please." Mary got in and the girl followed. Must be the Ring, she thought. If so it was not a part of the Ring she recognised. She saw a black Mercedes dawdling behind them. Fergus and Georgie, she thought, knowing that it wasn't. Her driver glanced both ways, then pointed the car straight at the central reservation—bump, it's the front tyres, bump, that was my backside you just broke. Everything hooted and the girl peered anxiously through the back window. They left the carriageway and shot down a side street, across a square and as far as the Opera where they stopped. The door on Mary's side opened. The girl ordered her out. Mary had hardly made the pavement before a second woman squeezed past her and took her place. The car drove away at speed, as neat a substitution as Mary had seen. A black Mercedes followed it but she didn't think it was the same one. A dapper, embarrassed young man was guiding her through a wide doorway to a courtyard.

"Take the lift, please, Mary," said the young man, in Euro-American, handing her a piece of paper. "Apartment six, please. Six. You go up alone. You have that?"

"Six," Mary said.

He smiled. "Sometimes when we are scared we kind of forget everything."

"Sure," she said. She walked to the doorway and he smiled and waved at her. She pushed it open and saw an old lift waiting with its doors open, and an old janitor smiling too. They've all been to the same charm school, she thought. She got into the lift and told the janitor, "Six, please," and the janitor launched her on her climb. As the doorway sank below her she had a last glimpse of the boy standing in the courtyard still smiling and a couple of well-dressed girls standing behind him, consulting some bit of paper. The bit of paper in her own hand read "Six, Herr König." Odd, she thought as she slipped it into her handbag. With me it works the other way. When I'm scared I don't forget a damn thing. Like the car number. Like the number of the second Mercedes behind us. Like the fringe of dyed black hair on the driver's neck. Like the Opium perfume that the girl was wearing and Magnus always insists on bringing me when he goes on air journeys. Like the fat gold ring with the red seal on the boy's left hand.

The door to number 6 stood open. A brass plate beside it read "Interhansa Austria A.G." She walked in and the door closed behind her. A girl again but not pretty. A sullen, strong girl with a flat Slav face and resentful, anti-Party manner. With a scowl she nodded Mary forward. She entered a dark drawing-room and saw nobody. At the far end of it stood another pair of doors, also open. The furnishings were old Vienna, phoney. Phoney old chests and oil paintings slipped by her as she advanced. Phoney lamp brackets reached at her from phoney imperial wallpaper. As she kept walking she had a reprise of the erotic expectation she had felt at the Wives' meeting. He's going to order me to undress and I shall obey. He's going to lead me to a red fourposter and have me raped by footmen for his pleasure. But the second room contained no fourposter, it was a drawing-room like the first, with a desk and two armchairs and a heap of out-of-date *Vogues* on the coffee table. It was otherwise empty. Angry, Mary swung round intending to say something rude to the flat-faced Slav. Instead she found herself staring at him. He was standing in the doorway smoking a cigar and for a second she was puzzled she couldn't smell it, but in some eerie way she knew that nothing about him was ever going to surprise her. The next moment the aroma had reached her and she was shaking his lazy hand as if this was the way they always greeted each other when they met fully dressed in Viennese apartments.

"You are a courageous woman," he remarked. "Are they expecting you back soon or what is the arrangement? What can we do to make life easier for you?"

That's perfectly right, she thought in absurd relief. The first thing you always ask your agent is how long you've got him for. The second is whether he needs immediate help. Magnus is in good hands. But she knew that already.

"Where is he?" she said.

He had the authority that enabled him to own to failure. "If only we knew, how happy we would both be!" he agreed as if her question had been a statement of despair, and with his long hand showed her to the chair that he required her to sit on. We, she thought. We are equals yet you are in command. No wonder Tom fell in love with you on sight.

They were sitting opposite one another, she on the gilded sofa, he on the gilded chair. The Slav girl had brought a tray of vodka and some gherkins and black bread and her devotion to him was obscene, she preened and smirked so. She's one of his Marthas, thought Mary, which was what Magnus called his Station secretaries. He poured two stiff ones, holding each glass carefully by turn. He drank to her, looking over the brim. That's what Magnus does, she thought. And it's you he learned it from.

"Has he telephoned?" he asked.

"No. He can't."

"Of course not," he agreed sympathetically. "The house is bugged and he knows that. Has he written?"

She shook her head.

"He's wise. They are watching for him everywhere. They are immoderately angry with him."

"Are you?"

"How can I be angry when I owe the man so much? His last message to me was that he didn't want to see me any more. He said he was free and goodbye. I felt a genuine pang of jealousy. What freedom has he found so suddenly that he cannot share it with us?"

"He said the same to me—I mean about being free. I think he said it to several people. To Tom as well."

Why do I talk to you as if you were an old lover? What sort of whore am I that I can throw off my loyalties with my clothes? If he had reached out to her and taken her hand she would have let him. If he had drawn her to him—

"He should have come to me when I told him," he said in the same philosophically reproachful tone. "'It's over, Sir

Magnus,' I said to him. That's my name for him. Forgive me.''

"In Corfu," she said.

"In Corfu, in Athens, everywhere I could speak to him. 'Come with me. We are passé, you and I. It's time for us oldies to leave the field to the next anguished generation.' He wouldn't see it. 'Do you want to be like one of those poor old actors one has literally to drag from the stage?' I said. He wouldn't listen. He was so adamant they would clear him.''

"They almost did. Maybe they did. He thought so.''

"Brotherhood won a little time and that was all. Not even Jack could sweep back the tide for ever. Besides—Jack has joined the bad guys now. Hell hath no fury like a deceived protector.''

He taught Magnus his style, she thought, in another spurt of recognition. The style he was always wanting for his novel. He taught him how to be superior to human foibles and how to give a Godlike laugh at himself as a way of fending off morbidity. He did all the things for him that a woman is grateful for, except that Magnus is a man.

"His father seems to have been quite a mystery man,'' he said, lighting himself another cigar. "What's all that about, do you think?''

"I don't know. I never met him. Did you?''

"Many times. In Switzerland when Magnus was a student, his father was a great British sea captain who had gone down with his ship.''

She laughed. Heaven help me, I'm actually laughing. Now it's me who's found the style.

"Oh yes. Then when I next heard of him he was a great financial baron. His tentacles extended to every banking house in Europe. He had miraculously recovered from being drowned.''

"Oh Christ,'' she said. And burst out again in cathartic, uncontrollable laughter.

"Since I was German at the time I naturally felt greatly relieved. I had had a really bad conscience about sinking his father until then. What is it about your husband, do you know, that gives us such a bad, bad conscience?''

"His potential,'' she said unthinkingly, and took a long pull of vodka. She was trembling and her cheeks were burning hot. He watched her calmly, helping her to steady.

"You're his other life," she said.

"He always told me I was his oldest friend. If you know different, please don't destroy my illusions."

She was getting it back. Her head. The room was clearing and her head with it. "I understood that position was reserved for somebody called Poppy," she said.

"Where did you hear that name?"

"It's in the great book he's been writing. 'Poppy, my dearest, oldest friend.'"

"Is that all?"

"Oh no. There's much more. Poppy gets a big hand on every fifth page. Poppy this, Poppy that. When they found the camera and the codebook they found dried poppies with them, as a keepsake."

She had hoped to disconcert him, but all she drew from him was a smile of gratification.

"I'm flattered. Poppy is the fanciful codename he awarded me many years ago. I have been Poppy for most of our lives."

Somehow she stayed in there fighting. "So what is he?" she demanded. "Is he a Communist? He can't be. It's too ridiculous."

He opened his long hands. He smiled again, infectiously, offering an immediate bond of his bewilderment. He was invulnerable. "I've asked myself the same question many times. And then I think—well, who believes in marriage these days? He's a searcher. Isn't that enough? In our profession I am sure we should not ask for more. Can you imagine being married to a sedentary ideologist? I had an uncle once who was a Lutheran pastor. He bored us all to death."

She was getting stronger. Less mad. More indignant. "What did Magnus do for you?" she asked.

"He spied. Selectively, it is true. But treasonably it is also true. And often very energetically—something you will understand about him. When his life is happy he believes in God and wants everyone to have a gift. When he is down he will sulk and refuse to go to church. Those of us who run him have to live with that."

Nothing had happened to her. She was upright and drinking vodka in a stranger's safe flat. He has pronounced the sentence, she thought calmly, as if she were attending someone else's trial. Magnus is dead. Mary is dead. Their marriage is dead. Tom is an orphan with a traitor for a father. Everybody's absolutely fine.

"But then I don't run him," she objected, answering his point quite calmly.

He appeared not to notice the new coldness in her voice. "Allow me to sell myself to you a little. I am fond of your husband."

And so you should be, she thought. After all, he sacrificed us to you.

"I also owe him," he continued. "Whatever he wants for the rest of his life, I can give it to him. I am greatly to be preferred to Jack Brotherhood and his service."

You're not, she thought. You are absolutely not.

"Did you say something?" he asked.

She smiled sadly for him and shook her head.

"Brotherhood wishes to catch your husband and punish him. I am the opposite. I wish to find him and reward him. Whatever he will allow us to give, we will give it." He drew on his cigar.

You're a sham, she thought. You seduce my husband and call yourself his friend and mine.

"You know this trade, Mary. I don't need to tell you that a man in his position is a most desirable commodity. Put more frankly, we cannot afford to lose him. The last thing we want is to have him sitting in an English prison for the rest of his useful life, telling the authorities what he's been doing these thirty and more years. Nor do we particularly want him to write a book."

You want, she thought. What about us?

"We would much prefer him to enjoy a well-earned retirement with us—distinction, medals, his family around him if they wish it—where we can still consult him as we need. I can't guarantee that we will permit him to lead the double life he is accustomed to but in every other respect we shall do our best to meet his needs."

"He doesn't want you any more though, does he? That's why he's hiding."

He puffed at his cigar, flapping a hand between them to stop the smoke from bothering her. But it bothered her anyway. It would shame and disgust and accuse her for the rest of her life. He was talking again. Reasonably.

"I am at my wits' end, to be frank. I have done all I can

to put Brotherhood and everyone else off the scent and to find your husband ahead of them. I still have not the least idea where he is and I feel a complete fool."

"What happened to the people he betrayed?" she said.

"Magnus? Oh he hates bloodshed. He always made that clear."

"That never stopped anybody yet from shedding blood."

Once more a pause for his private gravity. "You are right," he agreed. "And he chose a hard profession. I'm afraid it's a little late for us all to ponder our moralities."

"Some of us are rather new to them," she said. But she could not move him. "Why did you ask me here?"

She met his gaze and saw that though nothing had changed in his expression his face was different, which was what happened sometimes when she looked at Magnus.

"Before you came I had ideas that you and your son might care to start a new life in Czechoslovakia and that Magnus would therefore be strongly tempted to join you." He indicated a briefcase at his side. "I brought passports for you and all that nonsense. I was absurd. Having met you, I realise you are not defector material. However, it still occurs to me as a possibility that you do know where he is, and that you have managed, because you are a capable woman, not to tell anybody. You cannot suppose he is better off with his pursuers than he would be with me. So if you do know, I think you should tell me now."

"I don't know where he is," she said. And closed her mouth before she could add: and if I did, you would be the last person on earth I would ever tell.

"But you have theories. You have ideas. You have been thinking of nothing else night and day ever since he left, surely. Magnus, where are you? It's your one thought, isn't it?"

"I don't know. You know more about him than I do."

She was beginning to hate his sanctimony. His manner of pondering before he spoke to her, as if wondering whether she was up to his next question.

"Did he ever talk to you about a woman called Lippsie?"

"No."

"She died when he was young. She was Jewish. All her friends and relations had been killed by the Germans. It seems she adopted Magnus as some kind of support. Then changed her mind and killed herself instead. The reasons, as usual with Magnus, are clouded. It was a curious example for a child, nonetheless. Magnus is a great imitator, even when he doesn't know it. Really I sometimes think he is entirely put together from bits of other people, poor fellow."

"He never told me about her," she repeated doggedly.

He brightened. Just as Magnus might. "Come, Mary. Do you not have the consoling feeling there is someone looking after him? I am sure there is. My understanding of him has always been that he is attracted only to human beings, not to ideas at all. He hates to be alone because then his world is empty. So who is looking after him? Let us try to think whom he would like—I'm not talking of women, you see. Only of friends."

She was smoothing her skirt, looking for her coat. "I'll take a cab," she said. "You don't need to ring for one. There's a stand just on the corner. I saw it as I came."

"Why not his mother? She would be a good person."

She stared at him, unable for a moment to believe her ears.

"Not long ago he talked to me about his mother for the first time," he explained. "He said he had taken to visiting her again. I was surprised. Also flattered, I confess. He unearthed her somewhere and put her in a house. Does he see her much?"

She had the wit. Still in the nick of time she felt her cunning come rushing back to take command of her. Magnus hasn't got a mother, you idiot. She's dead, he hardly knew her, and he doesn't care. The one true thing I know of him, and will swear for him on the Last Day, is that Magnus Pym is not now and never has been the adult son of any woman. But Mary kept her head. She didn't fling insults at him, or sneer at him, or laugh out loud in relief that Magnus had lied to his oldest, dearest friend with the same precision with which he had lied to his wife, his child and his country. She spoke reasonably and sensibly as a good spy always does.

"He likes to chat with her now and then, certainly," she conceded. Picking up her handbag she peered inside it as if to make sure she had money for her taxi.

"Then might he not have taken himself off to Devon and stayed with her? She was so grateful to have her bit of sea air at last. And Magnus was so proud he had been able to work the magic for her. He spoke interminably of the wonderful walks they had together on the beach. How he took her to church on Sundays and fixed her garden for her. Maybe he is doing something as innocent as that?"

"Her house was the first place they looked," Mary lied, closing her handbag. "They frightened the poor old lady out of her skin. How do I get in touch with you if I need you? Throw a newspaper over the wall?"

She stood up. He stood up also, though not so easily. His smile was still in place, his eyes were still as wise and sad and merry in the style that Magnus envied so.

"I don't think you will need me, Mary. And perhaps you are right that Magnus does not want me any more either. Just as long as he wants someone. That's all we must worry about if we love him. There are so many ways of taking vengeance on the world. Sometimes literature is simply not enough."

The alteration in his tone momentarily halted her in her hurry to get out.

"He'll find an answer," she said carelessly. "He always does."

"That's what I'm afraid of."

They walked towards the front door, slowing in order to allow for his limp. He summoned the lift for her and held back the grille. She got in. Her last sight of him was through the bars, still watching her. By then she was liking him again, and frightened stiff.

She had worked out what she would do. She had her passport and she had her credit card. She had checked both when she looked inside her handbag. She had her plan, because it was the one she had used on training exercises in little English towns, and later with modifications in Berlin. In the world of ordinary mortals it was dusk. In the courtyard, two priests were talking in low voices with their heads together, swinging their rosaries behind their backs. The street was packed with shoppers. A hundred people could have been watching her, and when she began to count the possibilities in her mind, a hundred seemed about the likely figure. She imagined a kind of Vienna Quorn, with Nigel as Master and Georgie and Fergus as Whips, and bearded little Lederer heading up the bunch, and teams of Czech hoods in hot pursuit. And poor old Jack, unhorsed, plodding over the horizon after them.

She chose the Imperial which Magnus loved for its pomp.

"I've no luggage, I'm afraid, but I'd like a room for the night," she said to the silver-haired receptionist, handing him the credit card, and the receptionist, who recognised her at once, said, "How is your husband, madam?"

A chasseur showed her to a magnificent bedroom on the first floor. Room 121 that everybody asks for, she thought; the very room I brought him to on his birthday for dinner and a night of love. The memory did not move her in the least. She phoned down to the same receptionist and asked him to book her on tomorrow morning's flight to London: "Of course, Frau Pym." Smoke, she remembered. Smoke was what we called deception. She sat on the bed listening to the footsteps go quiet in the corridor as the dinner hour drew nearer. Double doors, twelve foot high. Painting called *Evening on the Bosphorus* by Eckenbrecher. "I'll love you till we're both too old," he'd said, with his head on that very pillow. "Then I'll go on loving you." The phone rang. It was the concierge to say only club class was available. Mary said, then take club. She kicked her shoes off and held them in her hand while she softly opened the door and peered out. If I think I'm being watched I'll put my shoes out to be cleaned. Burble and canned music from the bar. A whiff of dill sauce from the dining-room. Fish. They have such good fish. She stepped onto the landing, waited but still no one came. Marble statues. Portrait of bewhiskered nobleman. She pulled her shoes on, climbed one staircase, called the lift and descended to the ground floor, emerging in a side corridor out of sight of the reception area. A darkened passage led towards the rear of the hotel. She followed it, heading for a service door at the far end. The door was ajar. She pushed it, already smiling apologetically. An elderly waiter was adding the finishing touches to a private dinner table. Another door stood open behind him, leading to a side street. With a jolly *"Guten Abend"* to the waiter, Mary stepped quickly into the fresh air and hailed a cab. "Wienerwald," she told the driver and heard him announce it over the intercom: "Wienerwald." Nothing was following. Approaching the Ring she gave him a hundred schillings, hopped out at a pedestrian crossing and took a second cab to the airport where she sat reading in the ladies' loo for an hour until the last flight to Frankfurt.

It was earlier on the same evening.

The house was semi-detached and backed on to a railway embankment exactly as Tom had described. Once again Brotherhood reconnoitred it before making his approach. The road was as straight as the railway and seemingly as long. Nothing but the setting autumn sun disturbed the skyline. There was the road, there was the embankment with its telegraph lines and water tower, and there was the huge sky of Brotherhood's raggedy-arsed childhood which was always filled with white cloud left by the stop-go trains as they trundled across the fens to Norwich. The houses were all of the same design, and as he studied them their symmetry became beautiful to him without his understanding why. This was the order of life, he thought. This line of little English coffins is what I thought I was preserving. Decent white men in ordered rows. Number 75 had replaced his wooden gate with a wrought-iron one, with "Eldorado" done in curly handwriting. Number 77 had laid himself a concrete path with seashells bedded in it. Number 81 had faced himself in rustic teak. And number 79, upon which Brotherhood now advanced, was resplendent with a Union Jack fluttering from a fine white flagpole planted just inside his territory. The tyre marks of a heavy vehicle were cut into the little gravel drive. An electric speaker was set beside the polished doorbell. Brotherhood pressed and waited. A gasp of atmospherics greeted him, followed by a wheezing male voice.

"Who the bloody hell's that?"

"Are you Mr. Lemon?" Brotherhood said into the microphone.

"What if I am?" said the voice.

"My name is Marlow. I wondered whether I might have a quiet word with you on a private matter."

"I've got two of them and they both work. Piss off."

In the window bay the net curtain parted far enough for Brotherhood to glimpse a bronzed, shiny little face. very wrinkled, observing him from the darkness.

"Let me put it this way," said Brotherhood more softly, still into the microphone. "I'm a friend of Magnus Pym."

A further crackling while the voice the other end seemed to regather strength. "Well why the hell didn't you say so in the first place? Come in and have a wet."

Syd Lemon was a tiny, thickset old man these days, dressed all in brown like a rabbit. His brown hair, without a fleck of grey, was parted down the centre of his skull. His brown tie had horses' heads looking doubtfully at his heart. He wore a trim brown cardigan and pressed brown trousers and his brown toecaps shone like conkers. From amid a maze of sun-baked wrinkles two bright animal eyes shone merrily, though his breath came hard to him. He carried a blackthorn stick with a rubber ferrule, and when he walked he swung his little hips like a skirt to get himself along.

"The next time you press that bell, just say you're an Englishman," he advised as he led the way down the tiny, spotless hall. On the walls Brotherhood saw photographs of racehorses, and a younger Syd Lemon wearing Ascot rig. "After that you state your business clearly and I'll tell you to piss off again," he ended with a gush of laughter and pivoted awkwardly on his stick so that he could wink at Brotherhood and show him it was just his joke.

"How is the young tyke then?" said Syd.

"In excellent shape, thank you," said Brotherhood.

Without warning Syd sat himself abruptly on a high-backed chair, then leaned cautiously forward on his stick like a tiny dowager until he had the angle that cost him least discomfort. Brotherhood saw dark shadows under his eyes and a film of sweat on his forehead.

"You'll have to do the honours for us today, squire, I'm not myself," he said. "It's in the corner. Lift the lid. I'll take a drop of the scotch one for my health and you'll please yourself."

A thick maroon carpet ran wall to wall. A lurid painting of a Swiss scene hung above the tiled fireplace, to one side of which stood a fine burr-walnut cocktail cabinet. As Brotherhood lifted the lid, a music box began playing a tune, which was what Syd had been waiting for it to do.

"Know that one, do you?" said Syd. "Listen to it. Put the lid down again—that's right—now pull it up. There we go."

"It's 'Underneath the Arches,'" Brotherhood said with a smile.

"Course it is. His dad give it me. 'Syd,' he says, 'I can't

afford a gold watch just now, and I'm afraid there's a temporary problem of liquidity about your pension. But there's an article of furniture I possess which has given us a lot of fun down the corridor of years which is worth a bob or two and I'd like you to have it as a small token.' So we run the van up, me and Meg, before the repossession artists got their hands on it. Five years ago that was. He'd bought six of them from Harrods to see his contacts right. There was this one left. He never asked for it back, not once. 'Still playing, is she, Syd?' he'd say. 'Many a good tune played on an old fiddle, you know. I can still surprise them myself.' He could too. The bloody keyholes wasn't safe when he was around. Right till the end. I couldn't get to the funeral. I was indisposed. How was it?"

"I'm told it was beautiful," said Brotherhood.

"Well it would be. He'd made his mark. They weren't burying just anybody, you know. That man had shaken hands with some of the Highest in the Land. He called the Duke of Edinburgh 'Philip.' Did they write about him when he died? I looked in a few papers but I didn't see a lot. Then I thought, Well they're probably saving it up for the Sundays. Of course you can never tell with Fleet Street. I'd have slipped up there if I'd been well, offered them a few bob to make sure. Are you a bogey, sir?"

Brotherhood laughed.

"You look like a bogey. I did time for him, you know. A lot of us did as a matter of fact. 'Lemon,' he says—always called me by my surname when he wanted something very badly, I never knew why—'Lemon, they'll get me on my signature on those documents. Now if I was to deny it was my signature, and you was to say you'd forged it, nobody would be the wiser, would they?' 'Well,' I said, 'I would. I'd do a lot of time for it,' I said to him. 'If doing time makes you wise, I'm going to be as wise as Methuselah,' I said. I still did it, mind. I don't know why. He said I'd have fifty grand when I come out. I knew I wouldn't. I suppose you could call it friendship really. A cocktail cabinet like that, you couldn't get one to save your life these days. Here's to him. Mud in your eye."

"Cheers," said Brotherhood and drank while Syd looked on approvingly.

"So what are you if you're not a bogey? Are you one of

his airy-fairy Foreign Office friends? You don't look like an airy-fairy. More like a boxer to me, if you're not a bogey. Ever do that at all, did you, the fight game? Ringside seats we used to have, every time. We was there the night Joe Baksi said goodbye to poor old Bruce Woodcock. We had to have a bath afterwards, get the blood off. Then round to the Albany Club and there was Joe standing at the bar without a mark on him, a couple of Lovelies beside him there, and Rickie says to him, 'Why didn't you finish him off, Joe? Why did you spin it out like that, round after round?' Wonderful way with words he had. 'Rickie,' says Joe, 'I couldn't do it. I hadn't got the heart and that's a fact. Every time I hit him he was going "oooh—oooh"—like that—I couldn't put the finisher in and that's a fact.'"

While he continued to listen, Brotherhood allowed his eye to fall idly upon the imprint of an absent piece of furniture in a corner of the room. The shape of it was square, perhaps two foot by two, and it had cut through the carpet pile to the canvas backing underneath. "Did Magnus come along that night as well?" he enquired jovially, turning the conversation delicately back upon the purpose of his visit.

"He was too young, sir," Syd replied stoutly. "Too tender he was. Rickie would have took him but Meg she said no. 'You leave him with me,' she said. 'You boys can go out, you can have your fun. But Titch stays here with me and we'll go to a flick and have a nice evening and that's it.' Well, you didn't quarrel with Meg when she said a thing like that, not twice you didn't. I'd be broke today without her. I'd have given him every penny I had. But Meg, she put a bit away. She knew her Syd. Knew her Rickie too—a bit too well, I thought sometimes. Still you can't blame her. He was bent, you see. We was all bent, but Titch's dad was very bent indeed. Took me a long time to realise that. Still, if he came back, I suppose we'd all do the same." He laughed though it hurt him to do so. "We'd do the same and more, I'll bet we would. Is Titch in trouble, then?"

"Why should he be?" said Brotherhood, lifting his gaze away from the corner of the room.

"You tell me. You're the bogey, not me. You could run a prison with a face like that. I shouldn't be talking to you. I can feel it. I'd walk into the office one day. Audley Street. Mount Street. Chester Street. Old Burlington. Conduit. Park

Lane. Always the best addresses. Nothing altered. Everything nice and tidy. Receptionist there, sitting at her desk
like the Mona Lisa. 'Morning, Mr. Lemon.' 'Morning, sweetheart.' But I'd know. I'd see it in her face. I'd hear the quiet.
Hullo, I'd say to myself. It's the bogies. They've been having
a word with Rickie. Off you go, Syd, it's out the back door
fast. I was never wrong. Not once. Even if it was another
twelve months without the option when they nicked me, I
always had the nose for when the trouble started."

"When did you last see him then?"

"Couple of years ago. Maybe more. He stayed away after
Meg went, I don't know why. I'd have thought he'd come
more but he didn't like it. Didn't like people dying on him, I
suppose. Didn't like people being poor, or no-hopers. He
stood for Parliament once, you know. He'd have got in too if
we'd started a week earlier. Same as his horses. Always
leaving it too late at the finish. He'd ring up of course. Loved
the telephone, always did. Never happy if the blower wasn't
ringing."

"I was meaning Magnus," said Brotherhood patiently.
"Titch."

"I thought you might be," said Syd. He began coughing.
His whisky stood on the table in front of him but he hadn't
touched it although it was in reach. He doesn't drink any
more, thought Brotherhood. It's there for the decorum. The
coughing ended and left him breathless.

"Magnus came and saw you," said Brotherhood.

"Did he? I didn't notice. When was that?"

"On his way to see Tom. After the funeral."

"How did he do that then?"

"Drove out here. Sat with you. Chatted about old times.
He was pleased he came. He told young Tom afterwards. 'I
had a lovely talk with Syd,' he said. 'It was just like old
times.' He wanted everyone to know."

"Did he tell you that?"

"He told Tom."

"Didn't tell you though. Or you wouldn't need to come
here. I always reasoned that. I was never wrong. 'If the
bogies ask, it's because they don't know. So don't tell them. If
they ask and they do know, they're trying to catch you out. So
don't tell 'em either.' I used to say the same to Rickie but he
wouldn't listen. It was being a Mason partly. It made him feel

immune if he talked enough. That's how they got him, nine times out of ten. He talked himself into it." He barely paused. "Listen, squire. I'll do a deal with you. You tell me what you want and I'll tell you to piss off. How's that?"

A long silence followed but Brotherhood's patient smile did not tire. "Tell me something. What's that Union Jack doing out there?" he suggested. "Does it have a meaning at all, or is it just a big flower for the garden?"

"It's a scarecrow for keeping off foreigners and bogies."

As if he were producing a photograph of his family, Brotherhood drew out his green card, the one he had shown to Sefton Boyd. Syd drew a pair of spectacles from his pocket to read it back and front. A train thundered past but he appeared not to hear it.

"Is this a con?" he asked.

"I'm in the same business as that flag," Brotherhood said. "If that's a con."

"Could be. Everything could be."

"You were Eighth Army, weren't you? I understand you picked up a small medal at Alamein as well. Was that a con, too?"

"Could have been."

"Magnus Pym is in a little bit of trouble," said Brotherhood. "To be perfectly honest with you, which I always am with people, he seems to have temporarily disappeared."

Syd's small face had tightened. His breathing became harsh and quick. "Who's disappeared him, then? You? He hasn't been messing with Muspole's boys, has he?"

"Who's Muspole?"

"Friend of Rickie's. He knew people."

"He may have been lifted, he may have gone into hiding. He was playing a dangerous game with some very bad foreigners."

"Foreigners eh? Well he had the parley-voo, didn't he?"

"He was working under cover. For his country. And for me."

"Well he's a silly little bugger then," said Syd angrily and, hauling a perfectly ironed handkerchief from his pocket, dusted his shiny face. "I've no patience with him. Meg saw it. 'He'll go to the bad,' she said. 'There's a copper in that boy, you mark my words. He's a natural grass. Born to it.'"

"This wasn't grassing, this was risking his neck," said Brotherhood.

"That's what you say. That's what you think perhaps. Well you're wrong. Never satisfied, that boy wasn't. God wasn't half good enough for him. Ask Meg. You can't. She's gone. She was a wise one, Meg was. She was a woman, but she had more sense in one eye than you and me and half the world together. He's been playing both ends against the middle, *I* know. Meg always said he would."

"How did he look when he came and saw you?"

"Healthy. Everyone does. Roses in his nasty little cheeks. I always know when he wants something. He's charming, like his dad. I said, 'A bit more mourning would become you by the look of you.' He wouldn't hear of it. 'It was a beautiful service, Syd,' he says. 'You'd have loved it.' Well that was smoke up my arse for a start. 'They was packed together like sardines and there still wasn't room for them in the church.' 'Moonshine,' I said. 'They was in the square outside, they were queuing down the street, Syd. There must have been a thousand people there. If the Irish had let a bomb off, they'd have deprived this country of its finest brains.' 'Was Philip there?' I said. 'Course he was.' Well, I mean he couldn't have been, could he, or they'd have had it in the papers and the telly. Well, I suppose he could have gone incognito. I'm told they do that a lot these days, thanks to the Irish. He had a friend once. Kenny Boyd. His mum was a lady. Rick had a how d'you do with his aunt. Maybe he went to young Kenny. He might."

Brotherhood shook his head.

"Belinda? She was straight, always, although he bilked her. He could go to Belinda any time."

Brotherhood shook it again.

"I mean, a thousand mourners," Syd objected. "*Creditors*, if you like. Not mourners. You don't mourn Rick. Not really. You heave a bit of a sigh of relief, to be frank. Then you look in your wallet and thank old Meg there's still a bit left over for yourself. I didn't tell Titch that. It wouldn't have been appropriate. . . . Did Philip go? Did *you* hear anything about Philip going?"

"It was a lie," said Brotherhood.

Syd was shocked. "Ah now, that's a bit hard, that is.

That's copper's talk. Magnus was conning me, put it that way, same as his dad did."

"Why?" said Brotherhood.

Syd didn't hear.

"What did he want?" said Brotherhood. "Why would he take so much trouble to con you?"

Syd was overacting. He frowned. He pursed his lips. He dusted the tip of his brown nose. "Wanted to see me right, didn't he?" he said too brightly. "Flannel me along. 'I'll go and chat up old Syd. Make him feel nice.' Oh we was always friends. Great friends. A father to him I was, quite often. And Meg was a truly incredible mother." Perhaps with old age he had lost the liar's art. Or perhaps he had never quite had it in the first place. "He just wanted a social, that's all. Comfort, that's what it comes down to. I'll comfort you, you comfort me. He was always fond of Meg, you see. Even when she saw through him. Loyal. I'll say that."

"Who's Wentworth?" Brotherhood said.

Syd's face had slammed tight as a prison door. "Who's who, old boy?"

"Wentworth?"

"No. No, I don't think so. I don't think I know a Wentworth. More a place. Why, is a Wentworth giving him trouble then?"

"Sabina. Did he ever mention a Sabina?"

"That's a racehorse, isn't it? Wasn't there a Princess Sabina who was fancied for the Gold Cup last year?"

"Who's Poppy?"

"Here. Is Magnus playing the Lovelies again? Mind you, he wouldn't be his dad's son if he didn't."

"What did he come here for?"

"I told you. Comfort." Then, by a kind of cruel magnetism, Syd's gaze slid to the spot where a piece of furniture had stood, before returning, too brazenly, to Brotherhood.

"Well then," said Syd.

"Tell us something, do you mind?" said Brotherhood. "What was in that corner there?"

"Where?"

"There."

"Nothing."

"Furniture? Keepsakes?"

"Nothing."

"Something of your wife's you've sold?"

"Meg's? I wouldn't sell anything of Meg's if I was starving."

"What made those lines then?"

"What lines?"

"Where I'm pointing. In the carpet. What made them?"

"Fairies. What's it to do with you?"

"What's it to do with Magnus?"

"Nothing. I told you. Don't repeat things. It annoys me."

"Where is it?"

"Gone. It isn't anything. It's nothing."

Leaving Syd sitting in his chair, Brotherhood ran up the narrow stairs two at a time. The bathroom was ahead of him. He looked inside then stepped to the main bedroom left. A frilly pink divan filled most of the room. He looked under it, felt beneath the pillows, looked under them. He pulled open the wardrobe and swept aside rows of camel-hair coats and costly women's dresses. Nothing. A second bedroom lay across the landing but it contained no piece of heavy furniture two feet by two, just heaps of very beautiful white hide suitcases. Returning to the ground floor he inspected the dining-room and kitchen and, from the rear window, the tiny garden leading to the embankment. There was no hut, no garage. He returned to the parlour. Another train was passing. He waited for the sound of it to fade before he spoke. Syd was sitting hard forward in his chair. His hands were clasped over the handle of his blackthorn, his chin rested passively upon them.

"And the tyre marks in your drive," said Brotherhood. "Did the fairies make them too?"

Then Syd spoke. His lips were tight and the words seemed to hurt him. "Do you swear to me, Scout's honour, copper, that this is for his country?"

"Yes."

"Is what he done, which I don't believe and don't want to know, unpatriotic or could be?"

"It could be. The most important thing for all of us is to find him."

"And may you rot if you're lying to me?"

"And may I rot."

"You will, copper. Because I love that boy but I never did wrong by my country. He come here to con me, that's true. He wanted the filing cabinet. Old green filing cabinet

Rick gave me to look after when he went off on his travels. 'Now Rick's dead, you can release his papers. It's all right,' he says. 'It's legal. They're mine. I'm his heir, aren't I?'"

"What papers?"

"His dad's life. All his debts. His secrets, you might say. Rickie always kept them in this special cabinet. What he owed us all. One day he was going to see everybody right, we'd never want for anything again. I said no at first. I'd always said no when Rickie was alive, and I didn't see nothing had changed it. 'He's dead,' I said. 'Let him have his peace. Nobody never had a better pal than your old dad and you know it, so just you stop asking questions and get on with your own life,' I says. There's some bad things in that cabinet. Wentworth was one of them. I don't know the other names you said. Maybe they're in there too."

"Maybe they are."

"He argued around and so finally I said 'Take it.' If Meg had been here, he'd never have had it off me, legal heir or not, but she's gone. I couldn't refuse him, that's the truth. I never could, no more than what I could his dad. He was going to write a book. I didn't like that either. 'Your dad never held with books, Titch,' I said. 'You know that. He was educated in the university of the world.' He didn't listen. He never would when he wanted something. 'All right,' I said. 'Take it. And maybe that'll get him off your back. Shove it in the car and piss off,' I said, 'I'll get the big Mick from next door to help you lift it.' He wouldn't. 'The car's not right for it,' he says. 'It's not going where the cabinet's going.' 'All right,' I says, 'then leave it here and shut up.'"

"Did he leave anything else here?"

"No."

"Was he carrying a briefcase?"

"A black airy-fairy job with the Queen's badge on it and two keyholes."

"How long did he stay?"

"Long enough to con me. An hour, half an hour, what do I know? Wouldn't even sit down. Couldn't. He walked back and forth all the time in his black tie, smiling. Kept looking out of the window. 'Here,' I said, 'which bank have you robbed, then? I'll go and take my money out.' He used to laugh at jokes like that. He didn't, but he was smiling all the time. Well, funerals, they take you in a lot of ways, don't they? I could have done without his smiling all the same."

"So then he left. With the cabinet?"

"Course he didn't. He sent the lorry, didn't he?"

"Of course he did," said Brotherhood, cursing himself for his stupidity.

He was seated close to Syd and he had put his whisky beside Syd's on the beaten-brass Indian table that Syd kept polished till it shone like the Eastern sun. Syd was speaking very reluctantly, and his voice had almost died.

"How many?"

"Two blokes."

"Did you give them a cup of tea?"

"Course I did."

"See their lorry?"

"Course I did. I was looking out for them, wasn't I? That's a major entertainment, that is, round here, a lorry."

"What was the firm?"

"I don't know. It wasn't written, was it? It was a plain lorry. More like a hired one."

"Colour?"

"Green."

"Hired from who?"

"How should I know?"

"Did you sign anything?"

"Me? You're daft. They had a tea, loaded up, and buggered off."

"Where were they taking it?"

"The depot, weren't they?"

"Where's the depot?"

"Canterbury."

"You sure?"

"Course I'm sure. Canterbury. Package for Canterbury. Then they complained about the weight. They always do that, they think it gets them more dropsy."

"Did they say package for Pym?"

"Canterbury. I told you."

"Did they have a name at all?"

"Lemon. Call at Lemon's, get the package for Canterbury. I'm Lemon. The answer is a Lemon."

"Did you see the number of the lorry?"

"Oh yes. Wrote it down. I mean that's my hobby, lorry numbers."

Brotherhood managed a smile. "Well, can you at least remember what make of lorry it might have been?" he asked. "Distinguishing marks and whatnot?"

It was a harmless enough question, harmlessly put. Brotherhood himself had little expectation of it. It was the kind of question that unasked leaves a gap, but asked produces no dividend: part of the necessary luggage of the interrogator's trade. Yet it was the last that Brotherhood put to Syd on that dying autumn evening, and as a matter of fact it was the last in his short but desperate search for Magnus Pym, because after it he had only answers to concern him. Yet Syd refused point-blank to address himself to it. He started to speak, but then he changed his mind and clapped his mouth shut with a little pop. His chin came off his hands, his head lifted, then by degrees his whole little body lifted too, painfully but strictly from the chair, as if a distant bugle had summoned him to a last parade. His back arched, he held his stick to his side.

"I don't want that boy doing prison," he said with a husk to his voice. "Do you hear me? And I'm not going to help you put him there. His dad did prison. I did prison. And I don't want the boy there. It bothers me. Nothing personal, copper, but on your way."

It's over, thought Brotherhood calmly, staring round the crowded conference table in Brammel's suite on the Fifth Floor. This is my last feast with you. I shall walk out of this door a gamekeeper's son of sixty. A dozen pairs of hands lay under the downlight like corpses waiting to be identified. To his left languished the tailor-made worsted sleeves of the Foreign Office representative named Dorney. Heraldic lions postured on his gold cufflinks. Beyond Dorney reposed the unspoiled fingertips of his master Brammel, whose mid-Surrey heredity needed no advertisement. Beyond Bo sat Mountjoy from Cabinet. Then the rest. In his mood of increasing alienation Brotherhood found it difficult to put the voices to the hands. Not that it mattered any more because tonight they were one voice and one dead hand. They are the body corporate I once believed was greater than the sum of its

parts, he thought. In my lifetime I have witnessed the birth
of the jet airplane and the atom bomb and the computer, and
the demise of the British institution. We have nothing to
clear away but ourselves. The musty midnight air smelt of
decay. Nigel was reading the death certificate.

"They waited outside the Lumsden house till six-twelve,
then telephoned the house from a callbox down the road.
Mrs. Lumsden replied that she and her maid were looking
for Mrs. Pym at this moment. Mary had taken herself for a
walk in the back garden and not returned. She'd been out
more than an hour. The garden was empty. Lumsden himself
was at the Residence. The Ambassador apparently required
him."

"I hope nobody's going to try and blame the Lumsdens
for this," said Dorney.

"I'm sure not," said Bo.

"She left no note, no word to anyone," Nigel continued.
"She'd been preoccupied during the day but that was natural.
We checked the airlines and found she was booked to
London on tomorrow morning's British Airways flight club
class. She gave her address as the Imperial Hotel, Vienna."

"This morning's," somebody corrected, and Brotherhood
saw Nigel's gold watch tilt sharply towards him.

"This morning's flight then," Nigel agreed testily. "When
we checked the Imperial she wasn't in her room and when we
tried the airport a second time we established she'd taken a
standby seat on the last flight of the day, Lufthansa to
Frankfurt. Unfortunately we did not come by this information
until after the Frankfurt flight had landed at its destination."

She diddled you, thought Brotherhood with a satisfaction
bordering on pride. She's a good girl and knows the game.

"Isn't it rather a pity you couldn't have found out about
Frankfurt the *first* time you went to the airport?" said an
unbeliever boldly from the end of the table.

"Of course it's a pity," Nigel snapped. "But if you had
been listening a little more closely, I think you would have
heard me say that she took a standby seat. The official flight
list bearing her name was therefore not complete until literally the moment when the plane took off."

"Sounds a bit of a muddle all the same," said Mountjoy.
"What about the unofficial flight list?"

No, thought Brotherhood. It is not a muddle. To make a

muddle you must first have order. This is inertia, this is normality. What was once a great service has become an immovable hybrid—half bureaucrat, half freebooter, and using the arguments of the one to negate the other.

"So where is she?" somebody asked.

"We don't know," said Nigel with satisfaction. "And short of asking the Germans—and incidentally of course the Americans—to search every hotel in Frankfurt, which seems a long shot to say the least, I fail to see what more we can do. Or could have done. Frankly."

"Jack?" said Brammel.

Brotherhood heard an older version of his own voice ebb into the darkness. "God knows," he said. "Probably sitting on her backside in Prague by now."

Nigel again. "She's done nothing *wrong* as far as anyone knows. We can't keep her prisoner against her will, you know. She's a free citizen. If her son wants to join her there next week there's not much we can do about *that* either."

Mountjoy voiced a previous worry. "I do think the telephone intercept from the American Embassy *is* fairly extraordinary. This woman Lederer, sitting in Vienna, screaming to her husband in London about two people exchanging messages in church. That was our church she was talking about. Mary was *there*. Couldn't we have made a few deductions from that?"

Nigel had his answer pat: "Only long after the event, I'm afraid. Perfectly understandably, the transcribers saw nothing dramatic in the intercept and passed it to us twenty-four hours after the phone call had taken place. The information that *would* have put us on the alert—namely that Mary had been seen *possibly* emerging from a Czech safe flat where this man Petz and so forth had previously been housed—therefore reached us *before* the intercept. You can hardly blame us because we didn't put the cart before the horse, can you?"

Nobody seemed to know whether they could or couldn't.

Mountjoy said it was time to take a view. Dorney said they really must decide whether to call in the police and circulate Pym's photograph, and be damned. At this Brammel came sharply to life.

"If we do that, we may as well put up the shutters," he

said. "We're so nearly there. We're so *warm*, aren't we, Jack?"

"I'm afraid we're not," said Brotherhood.

"But of course we are!"

"It's guesswork. Still. We need the furniture van. That won't be a simple job either. He'll have used cut-outs, halfway houses. The police know how to do those things. We don't have a chance. He's using the name of Canterbury. Or we think he is. That's because in the past all his worknames have been places—he's got a tic about that. Colonel Manchester, Mr. Hull, Mr. Gulworth. On the other hand they just may have taken the cabinet to Canterbury and Canterbury is where he is. Or they've taken it to Canterbury and Canterbury is where he isn't. We need a square beside the sea and a house with a woman in it whom he apparently loves. She's not in Scotland or Wales because that's where he says she is. We are not in a position to comb every seaside town in the United Kingdom. The police are."

"He's mad," said a ghost.

"Yes, he's mad. He's been betraying us for more than thirty years and so far we have failed to certify him. Our error. So we may as well agree that he makes a pretty decent show of being sane when he needs to, and that his tradecraft is damn good. Is anybody nearer to him than I am?"

The door opened and closed. Kate was standing before them with an armful of red striped folders. She was pale and very steady, like a sleepwalker. She laid one folder before each guest.

"These have just come up from Sig. Int.," she said, to Bo only. "They ran the *Simplicissimus* bookcode across the Czech transmissions. The results are positive."

At seven in the morning the London streets were empty but Brotherhood marched in them as if they were full, keeping a straight back among the falterers and weaklings, a man of bearing in a crowd. A solitary policeman wished him good morning. Brotherhood was the kind of man policemen greeted. Thank you, Officer, he thought, striding yet more purposeful-ly. You have just smiled on the man who befriended tomor-row's newest traitor—the man who fought off criticism of him until the case became unanswerable, then fought off his apologists when it became unfaceable. Why do I begin to

understand him? he wondered, marvelling at his own tolerance. Why is it that in my heart if not my intellect I sense a
stirring of sympathy for the man who all his life has made a
failure of my successes? What I made him do, he made me
pay for.

You brought it on yourself, Belinda had said. Then why
was it that, as with his dangling arm at the moment it was
shot to pieces, he had yet to feel the pain?

He's in Prague, he thought. The chase game of the last
few days was a Czech fan dance to keep us looking the wrong
way while they smuggled him to safety. Mary would never
have gone there unless Magnus was ahead of her. Mary
would never have gone there, period.

Would she? Wouldn't she? He didn't know and he wouldn't
have trusted anybody who said they did. To leave Plush and
all her Englishness behind? For Magnus now?

She'd never do it.

She'd do it for Magnus.

Tom will come first for her.

She'll stay.

She'll take Tom with her.

I need a woman.

An all-night coffee shop stood at the corner of Half Moon
Street and on other early mornings Brotherhood might have
stopped there and let the tired whores make a fuss of his dog,
and Brotherhood in return would have made a fuss of the
whores, bought them a coffee and chatted them up, because
he liked their tradecraft and their guts and their mixture of
human canniness and stupidity. But his dog was dead and so
for the time being was his sense of fun. He unlocked his door
and headed for the sideboard where the vodka was. He
poured himself a warm half tumbler and drank it down. He
ran a bath, switched on his transistor radio and took it to the
bathroom. The news reported disasters everywhere but no
British diplomatic couple surfacing in Prague. If the Czechs
want to blow the whistle they'll do it at midday in order to
catch the evening television and tomorrow's papers, he thought.
He began shaving. The phone was ringing. It's Nigel saying
we've found him, he was at his club all the time. It's the duty
officer reporting that the Prague Foreign Ministry has put out
a midday press call for foreign correspondents. It's Steggie,
saying he likes strong men.

He switched off the radio, walked naked to the drawing-room, snatched up the receiver, said "Yes?" and heard a ping, then nothing. He pressed his lips together as a warning to himself not to speak. He was praying. He was definitely praying. Speak, he prayed. Say something. Then he heard it: three short taps of a coin or a nail-file on the drum of the mouthpiece: *Prague procedures*. Casting round for something metal, he saw his fountain pen on the writing table and managed to seize it without relinquishing the telephone. He tapped once in return: *I am reading you*. Two more taps, then three again. *Stay where you are*, said the message. *I have information for you*. With his pen he gave four taps to the mouthpiece and heard two in reply before the caller rang off. He ran his fingers through his stubble hair. He took his vodka to the desk and sat down, put his face in his hands. Keep alive, he prayed. It's the networks. It's Pym, putting it all right. Keep clever. I'm here, if that's what you're asking. I'm here and waiting for your next signal. Don't call again until you're ready.

The phone screamed a second time. He lifted the receiver but it was only Nigel. Pym's description and photograph were on their way to every police station in the country, he said. The Firm was switching to the operational telephone lines only. Bo had ordered the Whitehall lines disconnected. The press contacts were already beating down the doors. Why is he talking to me? Brotherhood wondered. Is he lonely or is he giving me a chance to say I've just had this funny phone call from a Joe using Prague procedures? It's the funny call, he decided.

"Some joker just phoned me with a Czech call sign," he said. "I gave him the signal to speak but he wouldn't. God alone knows what it was about."

"Well if anything comes through, let us know at once. Use the operational line."

"So you said," said Brotherhood.

Waiting again. Thinking of every Joe who had ever come through badland. Take your time. Move carefully and with confidence. Don't panic. Don't run. Take your time. Pick your phone box. He heard a knock at the door. It's some bloody hawker. Kate's taken her overdose. It's that fool Arab boy who lives downstairs and always thinks my bathroom's leaking on him. He pulled on a dressing-gown, opened the door and saw Mary. He hauled her inside and slammed the door. Whatever seized him after that he didn't know. Relief or fury, remorse or indignation. He slapped her once, then he slapped her again and on a clear day he would have taken her straight to bed.

"There's a place called Farleigh Abbott near Exeter," she said.

"What of it?"

"Magnus told him he'd put his mother in a house beside the sea in Devon."

"Told who?"

"Poppy. His Czech controller. They were students together in Bern. He thinks Magnus is going to kill himself. I suddenly realised. That's what's in the burnbox with the secrets. The Station gun. Isn't it?"

"How do you know it's Farleigh Abbott?"

"He talked about his mother in Devon. He hasn't got a bloody mother. His only place in Devon is Farleigh Abbott. 'When I was in Devon,' he'd say. 'Let's go to Devon for a holiday.' It was Farleigh Abbott, always. We never went and he stopped talking about it. Rick used to take him there from school. They used to picnic and bicycle on the beach. It's one of his ideal places. He's there with a woman. I know he is."

15

You will imagine, Tom, with what glory in his youthful heart the brilliant intelligence officer and lover celebrated the completion of his two years of devoted service to the flag in distant Austria and set about returning to civilian England. His leave-taking from Sabina was not as heart-rending as he had feared, for as the day approached she feigned a Slav indifference to his departure.

"I shall be happy woman, Magnus. Your English wives will not make sour faces at me. I shall be economist and free woman, not the courtesan of a frivolous soldier." Nobody had ever called Pym frivolous before. She even took herself on leave ahead of him to forestall the agony of parting. She is being brave, Pym told himself. His farewell from Axel, though haunted by rumours of fresh purges, had a similarly rounded feel to it.

"Sir Magnus, whatever happens to me, we have done a great work together," he said as, in the evening light, they faced each other outside the barn that had become Pym's second home. "Never forget you owe me two hundred dollars."

"I never will," Pym said.

He began the long walk back to Sergeant Kaufmann's jeep. He turned to wave but Axel had vanished into the forest.

The two hundred dollars were a reminder of their increasing closeness during the final months of their relationship.

"My father's pressing me for money again," Pym had said one evening while they photographed a codebook he had borrowed from Membury's cricket locker. "The Burmese police are proposing to arrest him."

"Then send it to him," Axel had replied, winding back the film of his camera. He slipped the film in his pocket and inserted a fresh one. "How much does he want?"

"Whatever it is, I haven't got it. I'm a subaltern on thirteen shillings a day, not a millionaire."

Axel had appeared to pay no further interest, and they turned instead to the topic of Sergeant Pavel. Axel said it was time to stage a fresh crisis in Pavel's life.

"But he had a crisis only last month," Pym had objected. "His wife threw him out of his apartment for drunkenness and we had to help him buy his way in again."

"We need a crisis," Axel had repeated firmly. "Vienna is beginning to take him for granted and I do not care for the tone of their follow-up questions."

Pym found Membury sitting at his desk. The afternoon sun was shining on one side of his friendly head while he read a fish book.

"I'm afraid Greensleeves wants a bonus of two hundred dollars cash," he said.

"But my dear chap, we've paid him a pot of money this month already! What on earth can he want two hundred dollars for?"

"He's got to buy his daughter an abortion. The doctor only takes U.S. dollars and it's getting urgent."

"But the child's a mere fourteen. Who's the man? They ought to throw him into prison."

"It's that Russian captain from headquarters."

"The pig. The utter swine."

"Pavel's a Roman Catholic too, you know," Pym reminded him. "Not a very good one, I agree. But it's not easy for him either."

The next night Pym counted two hundred dollars across the barn table. Axel tossed them back at him.

"For your father," he said. "A loan from me to you."

"I can't do that. Those are operational funds."

"Not any more. They belong to Sergeant Pavel." Pym still did not pick up the money. "And Sergeant Pavel lends them to you as your friend," Axel said, tearing a sheet of paper from his notebook. "Here—write me an I.O.U. Sign it and one day I shall make you pay it back."

Pym rode away in good heart, confident that Graz and all its responsibilities, like Bern, would cease to exist the moment he entered the first tunnel.

Laying down his arms at the Intelligence Corps Depot in Sussex, Pym was handed the following PRIVATE & CONFIDENTIAL letter by the demobilisation officer:

> The Government Overseas Research Group
> P. O. Box 777
> The Foreign Office
> London, S.W. 1
>
> Dear Pym,
>   Mutual friends in Austria have passed your name to me as someone who might be interested in longer term employment. If this is so, would you care to lunch with me at the Travellers' Club for an informal chat on Friday the nineteenth at 12:45?
>   (Signed) Sir Alwyn Leith, C.M.G.

For several days a mysterious squeamishness held Pym back from replying. I need new horizons, he told himself. They are good people but limited. Feeling strong one morning, he wrote regretting he was considering a career in the Church.

*   *   *

"There's always Shell, Magnus," said Belinda's mother, who had taken Pym's future much to heart. "Belinda's got an uncle in Shell, haven't you, darling?"

"He wants to do something *worthwhile*, Mummy," Belinda said, stamping her foot and making the breakfast table rattle.

"Time somebody did," said Belinda's father from behind his *Telegraph*, and for some reason found this very funny, and went on laughing through his gapped teeth while Belinda stormed into the garden in a rage.

A more interesting contender for Pym's services was Kenneth Sefton Boyd, who had come into an inheritance and was proposing that he and Pym should open a nightclub. Keeping this intelligence from Belinda, who had views on nightclubs and the Sefton Boyds, Pym pleaded an engagement at his old school and took himself to the family estate in Scotland, where Jemima met him at the station. She was driving the very Land Rover from which she had glowered at him when they were children. She was more beautiful than ever.

"How was Austria?" she asked as they bumped cheerfully over purple Highlands towards a monstrous Victorian castle.

"Super," said Pym.

"Did you box and play rugger all the time?"

"Well not all the time, actually," Pym confessed.

Jemima cast him a look of protracted interest.

The Sefton Boyds lived in a parentless world. A disapproving retainer served them dinner. Afterwards they played backgammon until Jemima was tired. Pym's bedroom was as large as a football field and as cold. Sleeping lightly, he woke without stirring to see a dismembered red spark switching like a firefly across the darkness. The spark descended and disappeared. A pale shape advanced on him. He smelt cigarette and toothpaste and felt Jemima's naked body arrange itself softly around him, and Jemima's lips find his own.

"You won't mind if we turf you out on Friday, will you?" said Jemima while the three breakfasted in bed from a tray brought in by Sefton Boyd. "Only we've got Mark coming for the weekend."

"Who's Mark?" said Pym.

"Well I'm going to sort of marry him, actually," said

Jemima. "I'd marry Kenneth if I could, but he's so conventional about those things."

Renouncing women, Pym wrote to the British Council offering to distribute culture among primitives, and to his old housemaster, Willow, asking for a position teaching German. "I greatly miss the school's discipline and have felt a keen loyalty towards it ever since my father failed to pay my fees." He wrote to Murgo booking himself in for an extended retreat, though he had the prudence to be vague about dates. He wrote to the Catholics of Farm Street asking to continue the instruction he had begun in Graz. He wrote to an English school in Geneva and an American school in Heidelberg, and to the BBC, all in a spirit of self-negation. He wrote to the Inns of Court about opportunities for reading law. When he had thus surrounded himself with a plethora of choices, he filled in an enormous form detailing his brilliant life till now and followed it to the Oxford Appointments Board in search of more. The morning was sunny; his old university city dazzled him with carefree memories of his days as a Communist informer. His interlocutor was whimsical if not downright fey. He pushed his spectacles to the top of his nose. He shoved them into his greying locks like an effeminate racing driver. He gave Pym sherry and put a hand on his backside in order to propel him to a long window that gave on to a row of council houses.

"How about a life in filthy industry?" he suggested.

"Industry would be fine," said Pym.

"Not unless you like eating with the crew. Do you like eating with the crew?"

"I'm really not very class-conscious actually, sir."

"How charming. And do you like having grease up to your elbows?"

Pym said he didn't mind grease either, actually, but by then he was being guided to a second window that gave on to spires and a lawn.

"I've a menial librarianship at the British Museum and a sort of third assistant clerkship to the House of Commons, which is the proletarian version of the Lords. I've bits and bobs in Kenya, Malaya, and the Sudan. I can do you nothing in India, they've taken it away from me. Do you like abroad or hate it?"

Pym said abroad was super, he had been to university in Bern. His interlocutor was puzzled. "I thought you went to university here."

"Here too," said Pym.

"Ah. Now do you like danger?"

"I love it, actually."

"You poor boy. Don't keep saying 'actually.' And will you give unquestioning allegiance to whoever is rash enough to employ you?"

"I will."

"Will you adore your country right or wrong so help you God and the Tory Party?"

"I will again," said Pym, laughing.

"Do you also believe that to be born British is to be born a winner in the great lottery of life?"

"Well, yes, to be honest, that too."

"Then be a spy," his interlocutor suggested and drew from his desk yet another application form and handed it to Pym. "Jack Brotherhood sends his love, and says why on *earth* haven't you been in touch with him, and why won't you have lunch with his nice recruiter?"

I could write whole essays for you, Tom, on the voluptuous pleasures of being interviewed. Of all the arts of affiliation Pym mastered, and throughout his life improved upon, the interview must stand in first place. We didn't have Office trick-cyclists in those days, as your Uncle Jack likes to call them. We didn't have anybody who wasn't himself a citizen of the secret world, blessed with the unlined innocence of privilege. The nearest they had come to life's experience was the war, and they saw the peace as its continuation by other means. Yet in the terms of the world outside their heads they had led lives so untested, so childlike and tender in their simplicities, so inward in their connections, that they required echelons of cut-outs to reach the society they honestly believed they were protecting. Pym sat before them, calm, reflective, resolute, modest. Pym composed his features in one mould after another, now of reverence, now of awe, zeal, passionate sincerity or spiritual good humour. He paraded pleasurable surprise when he heard that his tutors thought the world of him, and a stern-jawed pride on learning that the army loved him too. He modestly demurred or modestly boasted. He weeded out the half-believers from the believers and did not rest until he had converted the pack of them to paid-up life membership of the Pym supporters' club.

"Now tell us about your father, will you, Pym?" said a man with a droopy moustache uncomfortably reminiscent of Axel's. "Sounds a bit of a colourful sort of type to me."

Pym smiled ruefully, sensing the mood. Pym delicately faltered before rallying.

"I'm afraid he's a bit *too* colourful sometimes, sir," he said amid a hubble-bubble of male laughter. "I don't see a lot of him to be honest. We're still friends, but I rather steer clear of him. I have to, actually."

"Yes. Well, I don't think we can hold you responsible for the sins of your old man, can we?" said the same questioner indulgently. "It's you we're interviewing, not your papa."

How much did they know of Rick, or care? Even today I can only guess, for the question was never raised again and I am sure that in any formal way it went forgotten within days of Pym's acceptance. English gentlemen, after all, do not discriminate against each other on the grounds of percentage, only of breeding. Occasionally they must have read of one of Rick's more lurid collapses, and perhaps allowed themselves an amused smile. Here and there, presumably, word trickled down to them by way of their commercial contacts. But my suspicion is that Rick was an asset. A healthy streak of criminality in a young spy's background never did him any harm, they reasoned. "Grown up in a hard school," they told one another. "Could be useful."

The last question of the interview and Pym's answer echo for ever in my head. A military man in tweeds put it.

"Look here, young Pym," he demanded, with a thrust of his bucolic head. "You're by way of being a Czech buff. Speak their language a bit, know their people. What d'you say to these purges and arrests they're having over there? Worry you?"

"I think the purges are quite appalling, sir. But they are to be expected," said Pym, fixing his earnest gaze upon a distant, unreachable star.

"Why *expected*?" demanded the military man, as if nothing ought to be.

"It's a rotten system. It's superimposed on tribalism. It can only survive by the exercise of oppression."

"Yes, yes. Granted. So what would you do about it—*do*?"

"In what capacity, sir?"

"As one of us, you fool. Officer of this service. Anyone can talk. We *do*."

Pym had no need to think. His patent sincerity was out there speaking for him already.

"I'd play their game, sir. I'd divide them against themselves. Spread rumour, false accusation, suspicion. I'd let dog eat dog."

"You mean you wouldn't mind getting innocent chaps chucked into prison by their own police, then? Being a bit harsh, aren't you? Bit immoral?"

"Not if it shortens the life of the system. No, sir, I don't think I am. And I'm not persuaded about the innocence of these men of yours either, I'm afraid."

In life, says Proust, we end up doing whatever we do second best. What Pym might have done better, I shall never know. He accepted the Firm's offer. He opened his *Times* and read with a similar detachment of his engagement to Belinda. That's me taken care of, then, he thought. With the Firm getting one half of me and Belinda the other, I'll never want for anything again.

Turn your eye to Pym's first great wedding, Tom. It occurs largely without his participation, in his last months of training, in a break between silent killing and a three-day seminar entitled Know Your Enemy, led by a vibrant young tutor from the London School of Economics. Imagine Pym's enjoyment of this unlikely preparation for his married state. The fun of it. The free-wheeling unreality! He has chased Buchan's ghost across the moors of Argyll. He has messed about in rubber boats, made night landings on sandy shores, with hot chocolate awaiting him in the vanquished enemy's headquarters. He has fallen out of aeroplanes, dipped into secret inks, learned Morse and tapped scatological radio signals into the bracing Scottish air. He has watched a Mosquito aeroplane glide a hundred feet above him through the darkness, dropping a boxful of boulders in place of genuine supplies. He has played secret games of fox-and-geese in the streets of Edinburgh, photographed innocent citizens without their knowledge, fired live bullets at pop-up targets in simulated drawing-rooms, and plunged his dagger into the midriff of a swinging sand-bag, all for England and King Harry. In spells of quiet he has been dispatched to genteel Bath to improve his Czech at the feet of an ancient lady called Frau Kohl, who lives in a crescent house of impoverished splendour. Over tea and muffins, Frau Kohl shows him albums of her childhood in Carlsbad, now called Karlovy Vary.

"But you know Karlovy Vary very well, Mr. Sanderstead!" she cries when Pym shows off his knowledge. "You have been there, yes?"

"No," says Pym. "But I have a friend who has."

Then back to base camp Somewhere in Scotland to resume the red thread of violence that has been spun into every new thing he is learning. This violence is not only of the body. It is the ravishment that must be done to truth, friendship and, if need be, honour in the interest of Mother England. We are the chaps who do the dirty work so that purer souls can sleep in bed at night. Pym of course has heard these arguments before from the Michaels, but now he must hear them again, from his new employers, who make pilgrimages from London in order to warn the uncut young of the wily foreigners they will one day have to tangle with. Do you remember your own visit, Jack? A gala night it was, close to Christmas: the great Brotherhood is coming! We had streamers hanging from the rafters. You sat at the directing staff's table in the excellent canteen, while we young 'uns craned our necks to catch a glimpse of one of the great players of the Game. After dinner we gathered round you in a half circle, clutching our subsidised port, and you told us tales of derring-do until we crept off to bed and dreamed of being like you—though alas we could never really have your lovely war, even if that was what we were rehearsing for. Do you remember how in the morning, before you left, you called on Pym while he was shaving, and congratulated him on a damn good showing so far?

"Nice girl you're marrying, too," you said.

"Oh, do you know her, sir?" said Pym.

"Just good reports," you said complacently.

Then off you went, confident you had scattered a pinch more stardust in Pym's eyes. Which you had, Jack. You had.

Except that what goes up with Pym has a way of coming down, and it annoyed him to discover that his impending marriage had received the Firm's approval while it still awaited his.

"So what *exactly* are you doing for a living, old boy? Don't quite understand," Belinda's father asked, not for the first time, during a discussion about whom to invite.

"It's a government-sponsored language lab, sir," said Pym, in accordance with the Firm's sketchy guidelines on cover. "We work out exchanges of academics from various countries and arrange courses for them."

"Sounds more like the Secret Service to me," said Belinda's father, with that queer cracked laugh of his that always seemed to know too much.

To his future spouse, on the other hand, Pym told everything he knew about his work, and more. He showed her how he could break her windpipe with a single blow, and put her eyes out with two fingers easily. And how she could smash the small bones in someone's foot if they were annoying her under the table. He told her everything that made him a secret hero of England, seeing the world right single-handed.

"So how many people have you killed?" Belinda asked him grimly, discounting those that he had merely maimed.

"I'm not allowed to say," said Pym, and with a crisping of the jaw stared away from her towards the stark wastelands of his duty.

"Well don't then," Belinda said. "And don't tell Daddy *anything*, or he'll tell Mummy."

"Dear Jemima"—Pym wrote on an off chance, a week before his great day—

"It seems so odd we are both getting married within a month of each other. I keep wondering whether we are doing the right thing. I'm sick of the boring work I'm doing, and considering a change. I love you. Magnus."

Pym waited eagerly for the mail and scanned the moors around the training camp for a sight of her Land Rover as she dashed over the horizon to save him. But nothing came, and by the eve of his wedding he was left with himself again, walking the night streets of London, and pretending they reminded him of Karlovy Vary.

And what a husband he was, Tom! What a match was celebrated! Priests of upper-class humility, the great church famed for its permanence and previous successes, the frugal reception in a tomblike Bayswater hotel, and there at the centre of the throng, our Prince Charming himself, chatting brilliantly to the crowned heads of suburbia. Pym forgot no one's name, was fluent and informative on the subject of government-sponsored language laboratories, vouchsafed Belinda long and tender glances. All this, at least, until somebody switched off the soundtrack, Pym's included, and the faces of his audience turned mysteriously away from him, looking for the cause of breakdown. Suddenly the interconnecting doors at the far end of the room, until now locked, were flung open by unseen hands. And Pym knew in his toes at once, just by the timing and the pause, and by the way people parted before the empty space, that somebody had rubbed the lamp. Two waiters entered with the grace of well-tipped men, bearing trays of uncorked bubbly and chargers of smoked salmon, though Belinda's mother had not ordered smoked salmon, and had decreed that no champagne be served before the toast to the bride and groom. After that it was the Gulworth election all over again, because first Mr. Muspole appeared, followed by a thin man with a razor slash, and each commandeered a doorpost as Rick swept between them in full Ascot rig, leaning backwards and holding his arms wide, and smiling everywhere at once. "Hello, old son! Don't you recognise your old pal? Have this one on me, boys! Where's that bride of his? By Jove, son, she's a beauty! Come here, my dear. Give your old father-in-law a kiss! My God, there's some flesh here, son. Where have you been hiding her all these years?"

One on each arm, Rick marched the nuptial pair to the hotel forecourt, where a brand-new Jaguar car, painted Liberal yellow, stood parked in everybody's way, with white wedding ribbons tied to the bonnet, and a mile-high bunch of Harrods gardenias crammed into the passenger seat, and Mr. Cudlove at the wheel with a carnation in his mulberry buttonhole.

"Seen one of those before then, son? Know what it is? It's your old man's gift to both of you and nobody will ever take it away from you as long as I'm spared. Cuddie's going to drive you wherever you want to go and leave it with you, aren't you, Cuddie?"

"I wish you both all good fortune in your chosen walk of life, sir," Mr. Cudlove said, his loyal eyes filling with tears.

Of Rick's long speech, I remember only that it was beautiful and modest, and free of all hyperbole, and rested upon the theme that when two young people love each other, us old 'uns who have had our day should stand aside, because if anyone has deserved it, they have.

Pym never saw the car again, and it was a long while before he saw Rick either, because when they went back outside Mr. Cudlove and the yellow Jaguar had vanished, and two very obvious plainclothes police detectives were talking in low tones to the confused hotel manager. But I have to tell you, Tom, that it was the best of our wedding presents, barring perhaps the posy of red poppies, thrust into Pym's arms, without a card of explanation, by a man in a Polish-looking Burberry raincoat as Pym and Belinda rode into the sunset for a week at Eastbourne.

"Put him into the field while he's unsullied," says Personnel, who has a way of speaking about people as if they weren't seated across the desk from him.

Pym is trained. Pym is complete. Pym is armed and ready and only one question remains. What mantle shall he wear? What disguise shall cover the secret frame of his maturity? In a series of unconsummated interviews reminiscent of the Oxford Appointments Board, Personnel unlocks a bedlam of possibilities. Pym will be a freelance writer. But can he write and will Fleet Street have him? With disarming openness Pym is marched through the offices of most of our great national newspapers, whose editors inanely pretend they do not know where he has come from, or why, though henceforth they will know him for ever as a creature of the Firm, and he them. He is already halfway to stardom with the *Telegraph* when a Fifth Floor genius has a better plan: "Look here, how would you like to join up with the Coms again, trade on your old allegiances, get yourself a billet in the international left wing set? We've always wanted to chuck a stone into that pond."

"It sounds fascinating," says Pym as he sees himself selling *Marxism Today* on street corners for the rest of his life.

A more ambitious plan is to get him into Parliament where he can keep an eye on some of these fellow-travelling M.P.s: "Any particular preference as to party, or aren't we fussy?" asks Personnel, still in tweeds from his weekend in Wiltshire.

"I'd rather prefer it not to be the Liberals if it's all the same to you," says Pym.

But nothing lasts long in politics and a week later Pym is destined for one of the private banks whose directors wander in and out of the Firm's Head Office all day long, moaning about Russian gold and the need to protect our trade routes from the Bolsheviks. At the Institute of Directors, Pym is lunched by a succession of captains of finance who think they may have an opening.

"I knew a Pym," says one, over a second brandy or a third. "Kept a dirty great office in Mount Street somewhere. Best man at his job I ever knew."

"What was his job, sir?" Pym asks politely.

"Con man," says his host with a horsy laugh. "Any relation?"

"Must be my distant wicked uncle," says Pym, laughing also, and hurries back to the sanctuary of the Firm.

On goes the dance, how seriously I'll never know, for Pym is not yet privy to these backstage deliberations, though it isn't for want of peeking into a few desk drawers and locked steel cupboards. Then suddenly the mood changes.

"Look here," says Personnel, trying to hide his aggravation. "Why the devil didn't you remind us you spoke Czech?"

Within a month, Pym is attached to an electrical-engineering company in Gloucester as a management trainee, no previous experience necessary. The managing director, to his lasting regret, was at school with the Firm's reigning Chief, and has made the mistake of accepting a series of valuable government contracts at a time when he needed them. Pym is given

to the exports department, charged with opening up the East
European market. His first mission is nearly his last.

"Well, why don't you just sort of take a general swing
through Czecho and test the market?" says Pym's notional
employer wanly. And beneath his breath: "And do *please*
remember that whatever else you get up to is *nothing* to do
with *us*, will you?"

"A quick in and out," Pym's controller tells him gaily, in
the safe house in Camberwell where cub agents receive their
operational briefing before cutting their milk-teeth. He hands
Pym a portable typewriter with hidden cavities in the carriage.

"I know it seems silly," says Pym, "but I can't actually
type."

"Everyone can type a *bit*," says Pym's controller. "Prac-
tise over the weekend."

Pym flies to Vienna. Memories, memories. Pym hires a
car. Pym crosses the border without the smallest difficulty,
expecting to see Axel waiting for him the other side.

The countryside was Austrian and beautiful. Many barns lay
beside many lakes. In Plzeň Pym toured a despondent factory
in the company of square-faced men. In the evening he kept
the safety of his hotel, watched by a pair of secret policemen
who drank one coffee apiece until he went to bed. His next
calls were in the north. On the road to Ústí he saw army
lorries and memorised their unit insignia. To the east of Ústí
lay a factory that the Firm suspected of producing isotope
containers. Pym was unclear what an isotope was, or what it
should be contained in, but he drew a sketch of the main
buildings and hid it in his typewriter. Next day he continued
to Prague and at the arranged hour sat himself in the famous
Tyn church, which has a window looking into Kafka's old
apartment. Tourists and officials wandered about unsmiling.

"*So K. began to move off slowly,*" Pym read as he sat in
the south aisle, third row from the altar, pretending to study
his guidebook. "*K. felt forlorn and isolated as he advanced
between the rows of empty pews, with the priest's eyes fixed
on him for all he knew. . . .*"

Needing a rest, Pym knelt down and prayed. With a
grunt and a puff, a heavy man shuffled in beside him and sat
down. Pym smelt garlic and thought of Sergeant Pavel.

Through a crack in his fingers, he identified the recognition signals: smear of white paint on left fingernail, splash of blue on left cuff, a mass of disgraceful black hair, black coat. My contact is an artist, he realised. Why didn't I think of that before? But Pym did not sit back, he did not ease the little package from his pocket as a prelude to laying it between them on the pew. He remained kneeling and soon discovered why he had done so. The sound of trained feet was crunching towards him down the aisle. The footsteps stopped. A male voice said, "Come with us, please," in Czech. With a sigh of resignation, Pym's neighbour clambered wearily to his feet and followed them out.

"Sheer coincidence," Pym's controller assured him, much amused, when he got back. "He's already been on to us. They were pulling him in for a routine questioning. He comes up for one every six weeks. Never even crossed their minds he might be making a clandestine pick-up. Let alone with a chap your age."

"You don't think he's—well, told them?" Pym said.

"Old Kyril? Blown *you*? You must be joking. Don't worry. We'll give you another shot in a few weeks' time."

Rick was not pleased to hear of Pym's contribution to the British export drive, and told him so on one of his secret visits from Ireland, where he had established his winter quarters while he cleared up certain misunderstandings with Scotland Yard, and fought his way into the crowded new profession of West End property evictions.

"Working as a commercial traveller—my own boy?" he exclaimed, to the alarm of the adjoining tables. "Selling electric shavers to a bunch of foreign Communists? We *did* all that, son. It's over. What did I pay your education for? Where's your patriotism?"

"They're not electric shavers, Father. I sell alternators, oscillators and sparking plugs. How's your glass?"

Hostility towards Rick was a new and giddying notion for Pym. He vented it cautiously, but with growing excitement. If they ate a meal, he insisted on paying in order to savour Rick's disapproval at seeing his own boy put down good money where a signature would have done the trick.

"You're not mixed up with some racket out there, are

you?" said Rick. "The doors of tolerance only open a certain distance, you know, son. Even for you. What are you up to? Tell us."

The pressure on Pym's arm was suddenly dangerous. He made a joke of it, smiling broadly. "Hey, Father, that hurts," he said, awfully amused. It was Rick's thumbnail that he was most aware of, boring into an artery. "Could you possibly stop doing that, Father?" he said. "It really is uncomfortable." Rick was too busy pursing his lips and shaking his head. He was saying it was a damned shame when a father who had given up everything for his own son was treated like a "poor ayah." He meant pariah but the notion had never properly formed in him. Placing his elbow on the table, Pym relaxed his whole arm and let it ride about with Rick's pressure—flop one way, flop the other. Then abruptly stiffened it and, exactly as he had been taught, smacked the fat of Rick's knuckles on to the table-edge, causing the glasses to jump and the cutlery to dance and slide off the table. Taking back his bruised hand, Rick turned away to bestow a resigned smile on his subjects feasting around him. Then with his good hand he lightly pinged the edge of his Drambuie glass to indicate that he required another nice touch. Just as, by unlacing his shoes, he used to let it be known that somebody should fetch his bedroom slippers. Or by rolling on to his back, after a lengthy banquet, and spreading his knees, he declared a carnal appetite.

Yet, as ever, nothing is one thing for long with Pym, and soon a strange calm begins to replace his early nervousness as he continues his secret missions. The silent, unlit country that at first sight appeared so threatening to him becomes a secret womb where he can hide himself, rather than a place of dread. He has only to cross the border for the walls of his English prisons to fall away: no Belinda, no Rick—and very nearly no Firm either. I am the travelling executive of an electronic company. I am Sir Magnus, roving free. His solitary nights in unpeopled provincial towns, where at first the yapping of a dog had been enough to bring him sweating to his window, now inspire him with a sense of protection. The air of universal oppression that hangs over the entire country enfolds him in its mysterious embrace. Not even the prison walls of his public school had given him such a sense of security. On car and train rides through river valleys, over hills capped by Bohemian castles, he drifts through realms of such inner contentment that the very cattle seem to be his friends. I shall settle here, he decides. This is my true home. How foolish of me to have supposed that Axel could ever leave it for another! He begins to relish his stilted conversations with officials. His heart leaps when he unlocks a smile from their faces. He takes pride in his slowly filling order book, feels a fatherly responsibility for his oppressors. Even his operational detours, when he is not blocking them from his mind, can be squeezed beneath the broad umbrella of his munificence: "I am a champion of the middle ground," he tells himself, using an old phrase of Axel's, as he prises a loose stone from a wall, fishes out one package and replaces it with another. "I am giving succour to a wounded land."

Yet even with all this preliminary self-conditioning, it takes another six journeys on Pym's part before he can coax Axel out of the shadows of his perilous existence.

"Mr. Canterbury! Are you all right, Mr. Canterbury? Answer!"

"Of course I'm all right, Miss D. I'm always all right. What is it?"

Pym pulled back the door. Miss Dubber was standing in the darkness, her hair in papers, holding Toby for protection.

"You thump so, Mr. Canterbury. You grind your teeth. An hour ago you were humming. We're worried that you're ill."

"Who's *we*?" said Pym sharply.

"Toby and me, you silly man. Do you think I've got a lover?"

Pym closed the door on her and went swiftly to the window. One parked van, probably green. One parked car, white or grey, Devon registration. An early milkman he had not seen before. He returned to the door, put his ear to it and listened intently. A creak. A slippered footstep. He pulled the door open. Miss Dubber was halfway down the corridor.

"Miss D?"

"Yes, Mr. Canterbury?"

"Has anybody been asking you questions about me?"

"Why should they, Mr. Canterbury?"

"I don't know. Sometimes people just do. Have they?"

"It's time you slept, Mr. Canterbury. I don't mind how much the country needs you, it can always wait another day."

The town of Strakonice is more famous for its manufacture of motorcycles and Oriental fezzes than for any great cultural gem. Pym made his way there because he had filled a dead letter box in Pisek, nineteen kilometres to the north-east, and Firm tradecraft required he should not register his presence in a target town where a dead letter box was waiting to be cleared. So he drove to Strakonice feeling flat and bored, which was how he always felt after a bit of Firm's business, and booked himself into an ancient hotel with a grand staircase, then drifted round the town trying to admire the old butchers' shops on the south side of the square, and the Renaissance church which, according to his guidebook, had been changed to baroque; and the church of St. Wenceslaus which, though originally Gothic, had been altered in the nineteenth century. Having exhausted these excitements, and feeling even wearier from the long heat of the summer's day, he trudged up the stairs to his bedroom thinking how pleasant it would be if they were leading him to Sabina's apartment in Graz, in the days when he had been a penniless young double agent without a care in the world.

He put his key in the keyhole but it was not locked. He was not unduly surprised by this for it was still the evening hour when servants turned back bedcovers, and secret policemen took a last look round. Pym stepped inside and discerned, half hidden behind a sloping shaft of sunlight from the window, the figure of Axel, waiting as the old wait, his domed head propped against the chair's back, pitched a little sideways so that he could make out, among the lights and shades, who was coming in. And not in all the Firm's unarmed combat lessons, and dagger-play lessons, and close-contact shooting lessons, had anybody thought to teach Pym how to terminate the life of an emaciated friend seated behind a sunbeam.

Axel was prison-pale and a stone lighter. Pym could not have supposed, from his parting memory of him, that he had more flesh to give. But the purgers and interrogators and gaolers had managed to find it, as they usually do, and they had helped themselves to it in handfuls. They had taken it from his face, his wrists, his finger-joints and ankles. They had drained the last blood from his cheeks. They had also helped themselves to one of his teeth, though Pym did not discover this immediately, because Axel had his lips tight shut, and one twiglike forefinger raised to them in warning while he waved the other at the wall of Pym's hotel bedroom, indicating microphones at work. They had smashed his right eyelid too, which drooped over its parent eye like a cocked hat, adding to his piratical appearance. But his coat, for all that, still hung over his shoulders like a musketeer's cape, his moustache flourished, and he had inherited a marvellous pair of boots from somewhere, rich as timber, with soles like the running-boards of a vintage car.

"Magnus Richard Pym?" he demanded with theatrical gruffness.

"Yes?" said Pym after a couple of unsuccessful attempts to speak.

"You are charged with the crimes of espionage, provocation of the people, incitement to treason and murder. Also sabotage on behalf of an imperialist power."

Still slouched languidly in his chair, Axel drove his hands together with improbable vigour, producing a thwack that echoed round the great bedroom, and no doubt impressed the microphones. After it, he offered the prolonged grunt of a man coming to terms with a heavy punch in the stomach. Delving in his jacket pocket, he then detached a small automatic pistol from the lining and, finger to his lips again, waved it about so that Pym got a healthy sight of it.

"Face the wall!" he barked, clambering with difficulty to his feet. "Place your hands on your head, you Fascist swine! March."

Laying a hand gently round Pym's shoulder, Axel guided him towards the door. Pym stepped ahead of him into the gloomy corridor. Two burly men in hats ignored him.

"Search his room!" Axel commanded them. "Find what you can but do not remove anything! Pay attention to the typewriter, his shoes and the lining of his suitcase. Do not leave his room until you receive orders from me personally. Walk slowly down the stairs," he told Pym, prodding him in the small of the back with the gun.

"This is an outrage," Pym said lamely. "I demand to see a British consul immediately."

At the reception desk the female concierge sat knitting like a hag at the guillotine. Axel prodded Pym past her to a waiting car outside. A yellow cat had taken shelter underneath it. Pulling open the passenger door, Axel nodded Pym to get in and, having shooed the cat into the gutter, climbed in after him and started the engine.

"If you collaborate completely you will not be harmed," Axel announced in his official voice, indicating a patch of crude perforations in the dashboard. "If you attempt to escape you will be shot."

"This is a ridiculous and scandalous act," Pym muttered. "My government will insist that those responsible be punished."

But once again, his words had none of the confident ring they had possessed in the cosy barrack hut in Argyll where he and his colleagues had practised the skills of resisting interrogation.

"You have been watched from the moment you arrived here," said Axel loudly. "All your movements and contacts have been observed by the protectors of the people. You have no alternative but to make an immediate admission of your guilt on all charges."

"The free world will see this senseless act as the latest evidence of the brutality of the Czech régime," Pym declared, with increasing strength. Axel nodded approvingly.

The streets were empty, the old houses also. They entered what had once been a rich suburb of patrician villas. Sprawling hedges hid the lower windows. The iron gateways, wide enough to ride a coach through, were blocked with ivy and barbed wire.

"Get out," Axel commanded.

The evening was young and beautiful. The full moon shed a white, unearthly light. Watching Axel lock the car, Pym smelt hay and heard the clamour of insects. Axel guided him down a narrow path between two gardens until they came to a gap in the yew hedge to his right. Grabbing Pym's wrist, he led him through it. They were standing on the terrace of what had once been a great garden. A many-towered castle lifted into the sky behind them. Ahead, almost lost to a thicket of roses, stood a decrepit summerhouse. Axel wrestled with the door but it refused to yield.

"Kick it for me, Sir Magnus," he said. "This is Czecho-slovakia."

Pym drove his foot against the panel. The door gave, they stepped inside. On a rusted table stood the familiar bottle of vodka and a tray of bread and gherkins. Grey stuffing was bleeding from the ripped covers of the wicker chairs.

"You are a very dangerous friend, Sir Magnus," Axel complained as he stretched out his thin legs and surveyed his fine boots. "Why in God's name couldn't you have used an alias? Sometimes I think you have been put on earth in order to be my black angel."

"They said I would be better being me," Pym replied stupidly as Axel twisted the cap from the vodka bottle. "They call it natural cover."

For a long time after that, Axel appeared unable to think of anything useful to say at all, and Pym did not feel it was his place to interrupt his captor's reverie. They were sitting legs parallel and shoulder to shoulder like a retired couple on the beach. Below them, squares of cornfield stretched towards a forest. A heap of broken cars, more than Pym had ever seen on the Czech roads, littered the lower end of the garden. Bats wheeled decorously in the moonlight.

"Do you know this was my aunt's house?" said Axel.

"Well, no, I didn't, actually," said Pym.

"Well, it was. My aunt was a witty woman. She once described to me how she broke the news to her father that she wished to marry my uncle. 'But why do you want to marry him?' said her father. 'He has no money. He is very small and you are small too. You will have small children. He is like the encyclopedias you make me buy you every year. They look pretty but once you have opened them and seen inside, you don't bother with them any more.' He was wrong. Their children were large and she was happy." He scarcely paused. "They want me to blackmail you, Sir Magnus. That is the only good news I have for you."

"Who do?" said Pym.

"The aristos I work for. They think I should show you the photographs of the two of us coming out of the barn together in Austria, and play you the recordings of our conversations. They say I should wave the I.O.U. in your face that you signed to me for the two hundred dollars we tricked out of Membury for your father."

"How did you answer them?" said Pym.

"I said I would. They don't read Thomas Mann, these guys. They're very crude. This is a crude country, as you no doubt noticed in your journeys."

"Not at all," said Pym. "I love it."

Axel drank some vodka and stared into the hills. "And you people don't make it any better. Your hateful little department has been seriously interfering in the running of my country. What are you? Some kind of American butler? What are you doing, framing our officials, sowing suspicion, and seducing our intellectuals? Why do you cause people to be beaten unnecessarily, when a few years in prison would be enough? Do they teach you no reality over there? Have you no reality at all, Sir Magnus?"

"I didn't know the Firm was doing that," said Pym.

"Doing what?"

"Interfering. Causing people to be tortured. That must be a different section. Ours is just a sort of postal service for small agents."

Axel sighed. "Maybe they're not doing it. Maybe I have been brainwashed by our own stupid propaganda these days. Maybe I'm blaming you unfairly. Cheers."

"Cheers," said Pym.

"So what will they find in your room?" Axel asked when he had lit himself a cigar and puffed at it several times.

"Pretty well everything, I suppose."

"What's everything?"

"Secret inks. Film."

"Film from your agents?"

"Yes."

"Developed?"

"I assume not."

"From the dead letter box in Pisek?"

"Yes."

"Then I wouldn't bother to develop it. It's cheap pedlar material. Money?"

"A bit, yes."

"How much?"

"Five thousand dollars."

"Codebooks?"

"A couple."

"Anything I might have forgotten? No atom bomb?"

"There's a concealed camera."

"Is that the talcum-powder tin?"

"If you peel the paper off the lid, it makes a lens."

"Anything else?"

"A silk escape map. In one of my neckties."

Axel drew on his cigar again, his thoughts seemingly far away. Suddenly he drove his fist on to the iron table. "We have got to get ourselves *out* of this, Sir Magnus," he exclaimed angrily. "We have got to get ourselves *out*. We've got to rise in the world. We've got to help each other until we become aristos ourselves and we can kick the other bastards goodbye." He stared into the gathering darkness. "You make it so difficult for me, you know that? Sitting in that prison, I had bad thoughts about you. You make it very, very difficult to be your friend."

"I don't see why."

"Oh, oh! He doesn't see why! He does not see that when the bold Sir Magnus Pym applies for a business visa, even the poor Czechs can look in their card index and discover there was a gentleman of the same name who was a Fascist imperialist militarist spy in Austria, and that a certain running dog named Axel was his fellow conspirator." His anger reminded Pym of the days of his fever in Bern. His voice had acquired the same unpleasant edge. "Are you really so ignorant of the manners of the country you are spying on that you do not understand what it means these days for a man like me even to have been in the same continent as a man like you, let alone his fellow conspirator in a spying game? Do you really not know that in this world of whisperers and accusers, I may literally die of you? You've read George Orwell, haven't you? These are the people who can rewrite yesterday's weather!"

"I know," said Pym.

"Do you also know then, that I may be fatally contaminated like all those poor agents and informers you are showering with money and instructions? Do you not know that you are delivering them to the scaffold, unless they belong to us already? You know at least what they will do with you, I assume, unless I make them hear me, these aristos of mine, if we can't satisfy their appetites by other means? They mean to arrest you and parade you before the world's press with your stupid agents and associates. They plan to have another show trial, hang some people. When they start to do that, it will be sheer oversight if they don't hang me too. Axel, the imperialist lackey who spied for you in Austria! Axel, the revanchist Titoist Trotskyist typist who was your accomplice in Bern! They would prefer an American but in the meantime they will stretch a point and hang an Englishman until they can get hold of the real thing." He flopped back, his fury exhausted. "We've got to get *out* of this, Sir Magnus," he repeated. "We've got to rise, rise, *rise*. I am sick of bad superiors, bad food, bad prisons and bad torturers." He drew angrily on his cigar again. "It's time I looked after your career and you looked after mine. And this time properly. No bourgeois shrinking back from the big scoops. This time we are professionals, we make straight for the biggest diamonds, the biggest banks. I mean it."

Suddenly, Axel turned his chair until it was facing Pym, then sat on it again and laughed, and tapped Pym smartly on the shoulder with the back of his hand to cheer him up.

"You got the flowers okay, Sir Magnus?"

"They were super. Someone handed them into our cab as we were leaving the reception."

"Did Belinda like them?"

"Belinda doesn't know about you. I never told her."

"Who did you say the flowers were from?"

"I said I'd no idea. Probably for another wedding altogether."

"That was good. What's she like?"

"Super. We were childhood sweethearts together."

"I thought Jemima was your childhood sweetheart."

"Well, Belinda was too."

"At the same time—both of them? That's quite a childhood you had," Axel said with a fresh laugh as he refilled Pym's glass.

Pym managed to laugh too, and they drank together.

Then Axel began speaking, kindly and gently without irony or bitterness, and it seems to me that he spoke for about thirty years because his words are as loud in my ear now as they ever were in Pym's then, never mind the din of the cicadas and the cheeping of the bats.

"Sir Magnus, you have in the past betrayed me but, more important, you have betrayed yourself. Even when you are telling the truth, you lie. You have loyalty and you have affection. But to what? To whom? I don't know all the reasons for this. Your great father. Your aristocratic mother. One day maybe you will tell me. And maybe you have put your love in some bad places now and then." He leaned forward and there was a kindly, true affection in his face and a warm long-suffering smile in his eyes. "Yet you also have morality. You search. What I am saying is, Sir Magnus: for once nature has produced a perfect match. You are a perfect spy. All you need is a cause. I have it. I know that our revolution is young and that sometimes the wrong people are running it. In the pursuit of peace we are making too much war. In the pursuit of freedom we are building too many prisons. But in the long run I don't mind. Because I know this. All the junk that made you what you are: the privileges, the snobbery, the hypocrisy, the churches, the schools, the fathers, the class systems, the historical lies, the little lords of the countryside, the little lords of big business, and all the greedy wars that result from them, we are sweeping that away for ever. For your sake. Because we are making a society that will never produce such sad little fellows as Sir Magnus." He held out his hand. "So. I've said it. You are a good man and I love you."

And I remember that touch always. I can see it any time by looking into my own palm: dry and decent and forgiving. And the laughter: from the heart as it always was, once he had ceased to be tactical and become my friend again.

16

How appropriate, Tom, that looking back over all the years that follow our meeting in the Czech summerhouse, I see nothing but America, America, her golden shores glittering on the horizon like the promise of freedom after the repressions of our troubled Europe, then leaping towards us in the summer joy of our attainment! Pym still has more than a quarter of a century in which to serve his two houses according to the best standards of his omnivorous loyalty. The trained, married, case-hardened, elderly adolescent has still to become a man, though who will ever break the genetic code of when a middle-class Englishman's adolescence ends and his manhood takes over? Half a dozen dangerous European cities, from Prague to Berlin to Stockholm to the occupied capital of his native England, lie between the two friends and their goal. Yet it seems to me now they were no more than staging places where we could provision and refurbish and watch the stars in preparation for our journey. And consider for a moment the dreadful alternative, Tom: the fear of failure that blew like a Siberian wind on our unprotected backs. Consider what it would have meant, to two men such as ourselves, to have lived out our lives as spies without ever having spied on America!

It must be said quickly, lest there is any doubt of it left in your mind, that after the summerhouse Pym's path was set for life. He had renewed his vow and in the terms your Uncle Jack and I have always lived by, Tom, there was no way out. Pym was owned and hooked and pledged. Finish. After the barn in Austria, well, yes, there had been a little latitude still, though never any prospect of redemption. And you have seen how, if feebly, he did try to jump clear of the secret world and brave the hazards of the real one. Not with any conviction, true. But he made a stab at it, even if he knew he would be about as much use out there as a beached fish dying of too much oxygen. But after the summerhouse, God's brief to Pym was clear: no more dithering; stay put in your proper station, in the element to which nature has appointed you. Pym needed no third telling.

"Make a clean breast of it," I hear you cry, Tom. "Hurry home to London, go to Personnel, pay the penalty, begin again!" Well now, Pym thought of that, naturally he did. On the drive back to Vienna, on the aeroplane home, on the bus to London from Heathrow, Pym did a lot of energetic agonising along those lines, for it was one of the occasions when the whole of his life was pinned up in a vivid strip cartoon inside his skull. Begin where? he asked himself, not unreasonably. With Lippsie, whose death, in his gloomier hours, he was still determined to take upon himself? With Sefton Boyd's initials? With poor Dorothy whom he had driven off her head? With Peggy Wentworth, screaming her dirt at him, another victim for sure? Or with the day he first picked the locks of Rick's green cabinet or Membury's desk? How many of the systems of his life exactly are you proposing that he bare to the guilt-bestowing gaze of his admirers?

"Then resign! Bolt to Murgo! Take the teaching job at Willow's." Pym thought of that too. He thought of half a dozen dark holes where he could bury his leftover life and hide his guilty charm. Not one of them attracted him for five minutes.

Would Axel's people really have exposed Pym if he had cut and run? I doubt it, but that isn't the point. The point is, Pym quite frequently loved the Firm as much as he loved Axel. He adored its rough, uncomprehending trust in him, its misuse of him, its tweedy bear-hugs, flawed romanticism and cock-eyed integrity. He smiled to himself each time he stepped inside its Reichskanzleis and safe palaces, accepted the unsmiling salute of its vigilant janitors. The Firm was home and school and court to him, even when he was betraying it. He really felt he had a lot to give it, just as he had a lot to give to Axel. In his imagination, he saw himself with cellars full of nylons and black-market chocolate, enough to see everybody right in every shortage—and intelligence is nothing if not an institutionalised black market in perishable commodities. And this time Pym himself was the hero of the fable. No Membury stood between himself and the fraternity.

"Suppose that on a lonely drive to Plzeň, Sir Magnus, you stopped your car to give a lift to a couple of workmen on their way to work. You would do that?" Axel had suggested, in the small hours of the morning in the summerhouse, when he had put Pym back together again.

Pym conceded that he might.

"And suppose, Sir Magnus, that as simple fellows will, they had confided to you, as you drove along, their fears about handling radioactive material without sufficient protective clothing. You would prick up your ears?"

Pym laughed and agreed that he would.

"And suppose also that as a great operator and a generous spirit, Sir Magnus, you had written down their names and addresses and promised to bring them a pound or two of good English coffee next time you visited their region?"

Pym said he would certainly have done this.

"And suppose," Axel continued, "that having driven these fellows to the outer perimeter of the protected area where they work, you had the courage, and the initiative, and the officer qualities—as you assuredly have—to park your car in a discreet spot and climb this hill." Axel was indicating the very hill on a military map he happened to have brought along with him and spread over the iron table. "And from its apex you photographed the factory, using the convenient protection of a thicket of lime trees whose lower branches are later discovered to have slightly marked the pictures? Your aristos would admire your enterprise? They would applaud the great Sir Magnus? They would instruct him to recruit the two loquacious workmen and obtain further details of the factory's output and purpose?"

"They surely would," said Pym vigorously.

"Congratulations, Sir Magnus."

Axel drops the very film into Pym's waiting palm. The Firm's own issue. Wrapped in anonymous green. Pym secretes it in his typewriter. Pym hands it to his masters. The wonder does not stop there. When the product is rushed to the Whitehall analysts, the factory turns out to be the very plant recently photographed from the air by an American overflight! With a show of reluctance, Pym supplies the personal particulars of his two innocent and, thus far, fictitious informants. The names are filed, carded, checked, processed and bandied round the senior officers' bar. Until finally, under the divine laws of bureaucracy, they are the subject of a special committee.

"Look here, young Pym, what makes you think these chaps aren't going to turn you in next time you show up on their doorstep?"

But Pym is in interview mode, he has a large audience and is invincible: "It's a hunch, sir, that's all." Count two slowly. "I think they trusted me. I think they're keeping their mouths shut and hoping I'll show up one evening exactly as I said I would."

And events prove him right, as they would, wouldn't they, Jack? Braving all, our hero returns to Czecho and repairs, regardless of risk, to their very doorsteps—how can he fail to, since he is escorted there by Axel, who makes the introductions? For this time there will be no Sergeant Pavels. A loyal, bright-eyed repertory company of actors has been born, Axel is its producer and these are its founder-members. Painfully and dangerously, the network is built upon. By

Pym, a cool number if ever we knew one. Pym, the latest hero of the corridors, the chap who put Conger together.

The Firm's system of natural selection, accelerated by Jack Brotherhood's promptings, can no longer be resisted.

"Joined the *Foreign Office*?" Belinda's father echoes, in heavy, artificial mystification. "Posted it to *Prague*? How do you do *that* from a deadbeat electronics firm? Well, well, I must say."

"It's a contract appointment. They need Czech speakers," says Pym.

"He's boosting British trade, Daddy. You wouldn't understand. You're just a stockbroker," says Belinda.

"Well they might at least give him a decent cover story, mightn't they?" says Belinda's father, laughing his infuriating laugh.

In the Firm's newest and most secret safe flat in Prague, Pym and Axel drink to Pym's instatement as Second Secretary Commercial and Visa Officer at the British Embassy. Axel has fattened, Pym observes with pleasure. The lines of suffering are clearing from his haggard features.

"To the land of the free, Sir Magnus."

"To America," says Pym.

"My dearest Father,

"I am so glad you approve of my appointment. Unfortunately, I am not yet in a position to persuade Pandit Nehru to grant you an audience so that you can put your football pool scheme to him, though I can well imagine the boost it might give to the struggling Indian economy."

So were there no genuine Joes at all? I hear you asking, Tom, in a tone of disappointment. Were they *all* pretend? Indeed there were genuine Joes. Never fear! And very good they were too, the best. And every one of them profited from Pym's improved tradecraft, and looked up to Pym as he looked up to Axel. And Pym and Axel looked up to the genuine Joes also, in their fashion, regarding them as the unwitting ambassadors of the operation, testifying to its smooth running and integrity. And used their good offices to shield and advance them, arguing that every improvement in their circumstances brought glory to the networks. And smuggled them to Austria for clandestine training and rehabilitation. The genuine Joes were our mascots, Tom. Our stars. We made sure they would never want for anything again, so long as Pym and Axel were there to see them right. Which, as a matter of fact, is how it all went wrong. But later.

I wish I could adequately describe to you, Jack, the pleasure of being really well run. Of jealousy, of ideology, nothing. Axel was as keen for Pym to love England as he was to direct him at America, and it was part of his genius throughout our partnership to praise the freedoms of the West while tacitly implying that Pym had it within his reach, if not his duty as a free man, to bring some of this freedom to the East. Oh, you may laugh, Jack! And you may shake your grey hairs at the depths of Pym's innocence! But can you not imagine how easily it came to Pym to take a tiny, impoverished country into his protection, when his own was so favoured, so victorious and wellborn? And, from where he saw it, so absurd? To love poor Czecho like a rich protector through all her terrible vicissitudes, for Axel's sake? To forgive her lapses in advance? And blame them on the many betrayals that his parent England had perpetrated against her? Does it honestly amaze you that Pym, by making bonds with the forbidden, should be once more escaping from what held him? That he who had loved his way across so many borders should not be loving his way across another, with Axel there to show him how to walk and where to cross?

"I'm sorry, Bel," Pym would say to Belinda as he abandoned her yet again to the Scrabble board in their dark apartment in Prague's diplomatic ghetto. "Got to go up country. May be a day or two. Come on, Bel. Kiss-kiss. You wouldn't rather be married to a nine-till-five man, would you?"

"I can't find *The Times*," she said, shaking him aside. "I suppose you left it at the bloody Embassy again."

But however frayed Pym's nerves when he arrived at the rendezvous, Axel reclaimed him every time they met. He was never hasty, never importunate. He was never anything but respectful of the pains and sensibilities of his agent. It was not stasis one side and all movement the other either,

Tom, far from it. Axel's ambitions were for himself as well as Pym. Was not Pym his ricebowl, his fortune in all its meanings, his passport to the privileges and status of a paid-up Party aristo? Oh, how he studied Pym! Such obsessive, flattering concentration on a single man! How delicately he coaxed and gentled him! How meticulous he was, always to put on the clothes Pym needed him to wear—now the mantle of the wise and steady father Pym had never had, now the bloody rags of suffering that were the uniform of his authority, now the soutane of Pym's one confessor, his Murgo absolute. He had to learn Pym's codes and evasions. He had to read Pym faster than ever he could read himself. He had to scold and forgive him like the parents who would never slam the door in his face, laugh where Pym was melancholy and keep the flame of all Pym's faiths alive when he was down and saying, I can't, I'm lonely and afraid.

Above all, he had to keep his agent's wits constantly alert against the seemingly limitless tolerance of the Firm, for how could we ever dare believe, either of us, that the dear, dead wood of England was not a cladding for some masterly game being played inside? Imagine the headaches Axel had, as Pym went on producing his mountains of intelligence material, to persuade his masters they were not the victims of some grand imperialist deception! The Czechs admired you so much, Jack. The old ones knew you from the war. They knew your skills and respected them. They knew the dangers, every day, of underestimating their wily adversary. Axel had to fight toe to toe with them, more than once. He had to argue with the very henchmen who had tortured him, in order to prevent them from pulling Pym out of the field and giving him a little of the medicine they periodically dished out to one another, on the off chance of extracting a true confession from him: "Yes, I am Brotherhood's man!" they wanted him to scream. "Yes, I am here to plant disinformation on you. To distract your eye from our anti-Socialist operations. And yes, Axel is my accomplice. Take me, hang me, anything but this." But Axel prevailed. He begged and bullied and slammed the table, and when still more purges were planned to explain the chaos left behind by the last ones, he scared his enemies into silence by threatening to expose them for their insufficient appreciation of the historically inevitable imperialist decay. And Pym helped him every inch of the distance. Sat again at his sickbed—if only metaphorically—gave him nourishment and courage, held up his spirits. Ransacked the Station files. Armed him with outrageous examples of the Firm's incompetence worldwide. Until, fighting thus for their mutual survival, Pym and Axel drew still closer together, each laying the irrational burdens of his country at the other's feet.

And once in a while, when a battle was over and won, or a great scoop had been achieved on one side or the other, Axel would put on the play clothes of the libertine and arrange a midnight dash to his frugal equivalent of St. Moritz, which was a small white castle in the Giant Mountains, set aside by his service for people they thought the world of. The first time they went there was for an anniversary celebration, in a limousine with blackened windows. Pym had been in Prague two years.

"I have decided to present you with an excellent new agent, Sir Magnus," Axel announced as they zigzagged contentedly up the gravel road. "The Watchman network is lamentably short of industrial intelligence. The Americans are pledged to the collapse of our economy, but the Firm is providing nothing to support their optimism. How would you regard a middle executive from our great National Bank of Czechoslovakia, with access to some of our most serious mismanagements?"

"Where am I supposed to have found him?" Pym countered cautiously, for these were delicate decisions, requiring lengthy correspondence with Head Office before the approach to a new potential source was licensed.

The dinner table was laid for three, the candelabra lit. The two men had taken a long, slow walk in the forest and now they were drinking an apéritif before the fire, waiting for their guest.

"How is Belinda?" said Axel.

This was not a subject they often discussed, for Axel had little patience with unsatisfactory relationships.

"Fine, thank you, as always."

"That's not what our microphones tell us. They say you fight like two dogs day and night. Our listeners are becoming thoroughly depressed by you both."

"Tell them we'll mend our ways," said Pym with a rare flash of bitterness.

A car was coming up the hill. They heard the footsteps of the old servant crossing the hall, and the rattle of bolts.

"Meet your new agent," Axel said.

The door banged open and Sabina marched in. A little more matronly, perhaps, at the hips: one or two hard lines of officialdom around the jaw; but his delicious Sabina all the same. She was wearing a stern black dress with a white collar, and clumpy black court shoes that must have been her pride, for they had green brilliants on the straps and the sheen of imitation suède. Seeing Pym, she drew up sharply and scowled at him in suspicion. For a moment, her manner reflected the most radical disapproval. Then to his delight she burst out laughing her crazy Slav laugh, and ran to cover him with her body, much as she had done in Graz when he took his first faltering lessons in Czech.

And so it was, Jack. Sabina rose and rose until she became the head agent of the Watchman network, and the darling of her successive British case officers, though you knew her either as Watchman One or as the intrepid Olga Kravitsky, secretary to the Prague Internal Committee on Economic Affairs. We retired her, if you remember, when she was expecting her third baby by her fourth husband, at a special dinner for her in West Berlin while she was attending her last conference of Comecon bankers in Potsdam. Axel kept her on a little longer, before he decided to follow your example.

"I've been posted to Berlin," Pym told Belinda, in the safety of a public park, at the end of his second tour in Prague.

"Why are you telling me?" said Belinda.

"I wondered whether you'd like to come," Pym replied, and Belinda began coughing again, her long unquenchable cough that she must have picked up from the climate.

Belinda went back to London and took an Open University course in journalism, though none in silent killing. Eventually, in her thirty-seventh year, she launched herself upon the hazardous path of fashionable liberal causes, where after encountering several Pauls, she married one, and had an unruly daughter who criticised her for everything she did, which gave Belinda the feeling of being reconciled with her own parents. And Pym and Axel embarked on the next leg of their pilgrims' voyage. In Berlin, a brighter future awaited them, and a maturer treason.

c/o Colonel Evelyn Tremaine, D.S.O.
Pioneer Corps, ret.
P.O. Box 9077
MANILA

To His Excellency Sir Magnus Richard Pym,
Decorations
The British High Mission
BERLIN

My dearest Son,
    Merely a note which I hope does not Inconvenience you on your way to the Top, since none should expect gratitude until it is his turn to stand before the Father of us all which I expect to be doing at an early Date. Medical Science being still at a primitive Stage here, it appears notwithstanding that this Cruel summer is likely to be the writer's Last, despite Sacrifice of Alcohol and other Comforts. If you are Sending for Treatment or Funeral be sure to make out cheque and envelope to the Colonel, not Self, as the name of Pym is Persona non Gratis to the natives, and anyway may be Dead.
        Praying to be Spared,
            Rick T. Pym
P.S. Am advised that 916 Gold may be had in Berlin at knockdown price, the Diplomatic Bag being available to those in High Position seeking opportunity for informal Reward. Perce Loft is at old Address and will assist for ten percent but watch him.

Berlin. What a garrison of spies, Tom! What a cabinet full of useless, liquid secrets, what a playground for every alchemist, miracle-worker, and rat-piper that ever took up the cloak and turned his face from the unpalatable constraints of political reality! And always at the centre, the great good American heart, bravely drumming out its honourable rhythms

in the name of liberty, democracy, and setting the people
free.

In Berlin, the Firm had agents of influence, agents of
disruption, subversion, sabotage and disinformation. We even
had one or two who supplied us with intelligence, though
these were an underprivileged crowd, kept on more out of a
traditional regard than any intrinsic professional worth. We
had tunnellers and smugglers, listeners and forgers, trainers
and recruiters and talent-spotters and couriers and watchers
and seducers, assassins and balloonists, lip-readers and disguise artists. But whatever the Brits had, the Americans had
more, and whatever the Americans had the East Germans
had five of it and the Russians ten of it. Pym stood before
these marvels like a child let loose in a sweet shop, not
knowing what to grab first. And Axel, slipping in and out of
the city on any number of false passports, padded softly
behind him with his basket. In safe flats and dark restaurants,
never the same one twice, we ate quiet meals, exchanged our
goods and gazed upon each other with the incredulous contentment that passes between mountaineers when they are
standing on the peak. But even then, we never forgot the
bigger peak that lay ahead of us as we raised our vodka
glasses to each other and whispered, "Next year in America!"
across the candlelight.

And the committees, Tom! Berlin was not safe enough to
contain them. We assembled in London, in gilded imperial
chambers appropriate to players of the world's game. And
such a bold, diverse, brilliantly inventive cross-section of our
society's leaders we were, for these were the new years of
England, when the country's hidden talent would be winkled
from its shell and harnessed to the nation's service. Spies are
blinkered! went the cry. Too incestuous. For Berlin we must
open the doors to the real world of dons, barristers and
journalists. We need bankers and trade unionists and indus-
trialists, chaps who put their money where their mouths are
and know what makes the world tick. We need Members of
Parliament who can supply a whiff of the hustings and utter
stern words about taxpayers' money!

And what happened to these wise men, Tom, these
shrewd no-nonsense outsiders, watchdogs of the secret war?
They rushed in where even the spies might have feared to
tread. Too long frustrated by the limitations of the overt

world, these brilliant, unfettered minds fell overnight in love with every conspiracy, skulduggery and short cut you can imagine.

"Do you know what they're dreaming up now?" Pym raged, pacing the carpet of the service flat in Lowndes Square which Axel had rented for the duration of an Anglo-American conference on unofficial action.

"Calm yourself, Sir Magnus. Have another drink."

"Calm myself? When these lunatics are seriously proposing to plug themselves into the Soviet ground control, talk a MiG over American airspace, blow it out of the sky and, if the pilot by any chance survives, offer him the choice of being put on trial for espionage or staging a public defection in front of the microphones? That's the defence editor of the *Guardian* newspaper speaking, for Christ's sake! He'll start a war. He wants to. It will give him something to report at last. He was backed by a nephew of the Archbishop of Canterbury and a deputy director general of the BBC."

But Axel's love of England would not be spoiled by Pym's prissiness. Through the passenger window of a self-drive Ford from the Firm's carpool, he gazed at Buckingham Palace and softly clapped his hands when he saw the royal pennant fluttering in its arclight.

"Go back to Berlin, Sir Magnus. One day it will be the Stars and Stripes."

His Berlin apartment was in the centre of the Kurfürstendamm, on the top floor of a sprawling Biedermeier house that had miraculously survived the bombing. His bedroom was on the garden side so he didn't hear their car pull up, but he heard their spongy footsteps on the stairs and had a memory of the Fremdenpolizei stealing up Herr Ollinger's wooden staircase in the early hours of the morning that policemen like the best. Pym knew it was the end, though of all the ways he had imagined the end he hadn't expected it to come this way. Fieldmen feel those things and learn to trust them, and Pym was a fieldman twice over. So he knew it was the end and in a quiet way he was neither surprised nor disconcerted. He was out of bed and into the kitchen in a second, because the kitchen was where he had been concealing the rolls of film for his next rendezvous with Axel. By the time they pressed the doorbell he had unrolled six reels and exposed them, and touched off the instant-ignition code pad that he had hidden in an oilskin inside the lavatory cistern. In his clear-eyed acceptance of his fate, he even contemplated something rather more drastic, for Berlin was no Vienna and he kept a pistol in his bedside locker and another in a drawer in the hall. But something about the apologetic way they murmured "Herr Pym, wake up, please," through the letter box discouraged him, and when he looked through the peephole and saw the amiable shape of Police Lieutenant Dollendorf and the young sergeant at his side, a shaming awareness came over him of the shock he would cause them if he took that path. So they're pulling a soft entry, he thought as he opened the door: first you spread your wolf-children round the building, then you put in Mr. Nice Guy by the front door.

Lieutenant Dollendorf, like most people in Berlin, was a client of Jack Brotherhood, and earned a small retainer by looking the other way when agents were being hustled back and forth across the profitable stretch of Wall in his district. He was a cosy Bavarian fellow with all the Bavarian appetites, and his breath smelt permanently of *Weisswurst*.

"Forgive us, Herr Pym. Excuse the disturbances, so late," he began, smiling too broadly. He was in uniform. His gun was still in its holster. "Our Herr Kommandant asks that you come immediately to headquarters on a personal and urgent matter," he explained, still not touching his gun.

There was resolution in Dollendorf's voice as well as embarrassment, however, and his sergeant was peering sharply up and down the stairwell. "The Herr Kommandant assures me that everything can be arranged discreetly, Herr Pym. He wishes at this stage to be delicate. He has made no approach to your superiors," Dollendorf insisted, as Pym still hesitated. "The Kommandant has high respect for you, Herr Pym."

"I have to dress."

"But quickly, if you are so kind, Herr Pym. The Kommandant would like the matter dealt with before he has to hand it over to the day shift."

Pym turned and walked carefully to his bedroom. He waited to hear the policemen following him, or a barked order, but they preferred to remain in the hall, looking at the Cries of London prints, courtesy of the Firm's accommodation section.

"May I use your telephone, Herr Pym?"

"Go ahead."

He dressed with the door open, hoping to overhear the conversation. But all he heard was: "Everything in order, Herr Kommandant. Our man is coming immediately."

They walked down the broad stairs three abreast, to a parked police car with its light flashing. Nothing behind it, no late-night loiterers in the street. How typical of the Germans to disinfect the entire area before arresting him. Pym sat in the front with Dollendorf. The sergeant sat tensely behind. It was raining and two in the morning. A red sky was seething with black cloud. Nobody spoke any more.

And at the police station Jack will be waiting, thought Pym. Or the Military Police. Or God.

The Kommandant rose to receive him. Dollendorf and his sergeant had faded away. The Kommandant considered himself a man of supernatural subtlety. He was tall and grey and hollow-backed, with staring eyes and a narrow rattling mouth that operated at self-destructive speed. He leaned back in his chair and put his fingertips together. He spoke in an anguished monotone to an etching of his birthplace in East Prussia that was hanging on the wall above Pym's head. He spoke, in Pym's calm estimation, for about six hours without a break and without appearing to draw breath, which for the Kommandant was the equivalent of a quick warm-up before they got down to a serious discussion. The Kommandant said that he was a man of the world and a family man, conversant with what he called the "intimate sphere." Pym said he respected this. The Kommandant said he was not didactic, he was not political, though he was a Christian Democrat. He was Evangelical but Pym could rest assured that he had no quarrel with Roman Catholics. Pym said he would have expected no less. The Kommandant said that misdeeds were a spectrum that ran between pardonable human error and calculated crime. Pym agreed, and heard a footfall in the corridor. The Kommandant begged Pym to bear in mind that foreigners in a strange country frequently felt a sense of false security when contemplating what might strictly be regarded as a felonious act.

"I may speak frankly, Herr Pym?"

"Please do," said Pym, in whom by now a fearful premonition was beginning to form that it was Axel, not himself, who was under arrest.

"When they brought him to me, I looked at him. I listened to him. I said, 'No, this cannot be. Not Herr Pym. The man is an impostor,' I said. 'He is trading upon a distinguished connection.' However as I continued to listen to him, I detected a sense of, shall I say, vision? There is an energy here, an intelligence, I may say also a charm. Possibly, I thought, this man is who he says he is. Only Herr Pym can tell us, I thought." He pressed a button on his desk. "I may confront him with you, Herr Pym?"

An old turnkey appeared, and waddled ahead of them down a painted brick corridor that stank of carbolic. He unlocked a grille and closed it behind them. He unlocked another. It was the first time I had seen Rick in prison, Tom, and I have made sure ever since that it was the last. In future times, Pym sent him food, clothes, cigars, and, in Ireland, Drambuie. Pym emptied his bank account for him, and if he had been a millionaire he would have bankrupted himself rather than see him there again, even in his mind's eye. Rick sat in the corner and Pym knew at once that he did this in order to give himself a bigger view of the cell, for ever since I had known him he always needed more space than God had given him. He sat with his great head tipped forward, scowling with a convict's sullenness, and I swear he had closed off his hearing with his thinking and hadn't heard us coming.

"Father," said Pym. "It's me."

Rick came to the bars and put a hand each side and his face between. He stared first at Pym, then at the Kommandant and the turnkey, not understanding Pym's position. His expression was sleepy and bad-tempered.

"So they got you too, did they, son?" he said—not, I thought, without a certain satisfaction. "I always thought you were up to something. You should have read your law like I told you." Slowly the truth began to dawn on him. The turnkey unlocked his door, the good Kommandant said, "Please, Herr Pym," and stood aside for Pym to enter. Pym went to Rick, and put his arms round him, but delicately, in case they had been beating him and he was sore. Gradually the puff began to fill Rick up again.

"God in heaven, old son, what the devil are they doing

to me? Can't an honest fellow do a bit of business in this country? Have you seen the food they give you here, these German sausages? What do we pay our taxes for? What did we fight the war for? What's the good of a son who's head of the Foreign Office if he can't keep these German thugs away from his old man?"

But by then Pym was bear-hugging Rick, slapping his shoulders and saying it was good to see him in whatever circumstances. So Rick took to weeping also, and the Kommandant delicately removed himself to another room while, reunited, each pal celebrated the other as his saviour.

I don't mean to disappoint you, Tom, but I do honestly forget, perhaps deliberately, the details of Rick's Berlin transactions. Pym was expecting his own judgment at the time, not Rick's. I remember two sisters and that they were of noble Prussian stock and lived in an old house in Charlottenburg, because Pym called on them to pay them off for the usual missing paintings Rick was selling for them, and the diamond brooch he was getting cleaned for them, and the fur coats that were being remodelled by a first-rate tailor friend of his in London who would do it free because he thought the world of Rick. And I remember the sisters had a bent nephew who was involved in a shady arms racket, and that somewhere in the story Rick had an aeroplane for sale, the finest, best-preserved fighter-bomber you could wish for, in mint condition inside and out. And for all I know it was being painted by those lifelong Liberals, Balham's of Brinkley, and guaranteed to fly everyone to Heaven.

It was in Berlin also that Pym courted your mother, Tom, and took her away from his boss and hers, Jack Brotherhood. I am not sure that you or anybody else has a natural right to know what accident conceived you, but I'll try to help you as best I can. There was mischief in Pym's motive, I won't deny it. The love, what there was of it, came later.

"Jack Brotherhood and I seem to be sharing the same woman," Pym remarked impishly to Axel one day, during a callbox-to-callbox conversation.

Axel required to know immediately who she was.

"An aristo," said Pym, still teasing him. "One of ours. Church and spy Establishment, if that means anything to you. Her family's connections with the Firm go back to William the Conqueror."

"Is she married?"

"You know I don't sleep with married women unless they absolutely insist."

"Is she amusing?"

"Axel, we are talking of a lady."

"I mean is she social?" Axel demanded impatiently. "Is she what you call diplomatic geisha? Is she bourgeois? Would Americans like her?"

"She's a top Martha, Axel. I keep telling you. She's beautiful and rich and frightfully British."

"Then maybe she is the ticket that will get us to Washington," said Axel, who had recently been expressing anxieties about the number of random women drifting through Pym's life.

Soon afterwards, Pym received similar advice from your Uncle Jack.

"Mary has told me what's going on between you, Magnus," he said, taking him aside in his most avuncular manner. "And if you ask me you could travel further and fare a damned sight worse. She's one of the best girls we've got, and it's time you looked a little less disreputable."

So Pym, with both his mentors pushing in the same direction, followed their advice and took Mary, your mother, to be his truly wedded partner at the High Table of the Anglo-American alliance. And really, after all that he had given away already, it seemed a very reasonable sacrifice.

"Hold his hand, Jack"—Pym wrote—"He's the dearest thing I had."

"Mabs, forgive"—Pym wrote—"Dear, dear Mabs, forgive. If love is whatever we can still betray, remember that I betrayed you on a lot of days."

He began a note to Kate and tore it up. He scribbled "Dearest Belinda" and stopped, scared by the silence around him. He looked sharply at his watch. Five o'clock. Why hasn't the clock chimed? I've gone deaf. I'm dead. I'm in a padded cell. From across the square the first chime sounded. One. Two. I can stop it any time I want, he thought. I can stop it at one, at two, at three. I can take any part of any hour and stop

it dead. What I cannot do is make it chime midnight at one
o'clock. That's God's trick, not mine.

A shocked stillness had descended over Pym and it was the
literal stillness of death. He was standing at the window once
more, watching the leaves drift across the empty square. An
ominous inactivity marked everything he saw. Not a head in a
window, not an open doorway. Not a dog or cat or squirrel or
a single squawking child. They have taken to the hills. They
are waiting for the raiders from the sea. But in his head he is
standing in the cellar flat of a run-down office block in
Cheapside, watching the two faded Lovelies on their knees as
they tear open the last of Rick's files and lick their crabbed
fingertips to speed them in their paperchase. Paper lies in
growing mounds around them, it flutters through the air like
swirling petals as they rummage and discard what they have
vainly plundered: bank statements written in blood, invoices,
furious solicitors' letters, warrants, summonses, love letters
dripping with reproach. The dust of them is filling Pym's
nostrils as he watches, the clang of the steel drawers is like the
clang of his prison grilles, but the Lovelies heed nothing;
they are avid widows ransacking Rick's record. At the centre
of the débris, drawers and cupboard askew, stands Rick's last
Reichskanzlei desk, its serpents twining themselves round its
bombé legs like gilded garters. On the wall hangs the last
photograph of the great TP in mayoral regalia and on the
chimney piece, above a grate stuffed with false coals and the
last of Rick's cigar butts, stands the bronze bust of your
Founder and Managing Director himself, beaming out the
last of his integrity. On the open door at Pym's back hangs
the memorial tablet to Rick's last dozen companies, but a sign
beside the bell reads "Press here for attention," because
when Rick has not been saving his nation's faltering economy,
he has been working as night porter for the block.

   "What time did he die?" says Pym, before remembering
that he knows.

   "Evening, dearie. The pubs was just opening," says one
of the Lovelies through her cigarette as she heaves another
batch of paper on to the rubbish heap.

   "He was having a nice drop next door," says the other,
who like the first has not for one moment relaxed her labours.

"What's next door?" says Pym.

"Bedroom," says the first Lovely, tossing aside another spent file.

"So who was with him?" Pym asks. "Were you with him? Who was with him, please?"

"We both were, dearie," says the second. "We was having a little cuddle, if you want to know. Your dad loved a drink and it always made him amorous. We'd had a nice tea early because of his commitments, steak with onion, and he'd had a bit of a barney on the blower with the telephone exchange about a cheque that was in the post to them. He was depressed, wasn't he, Vi?"

The first Lovely, if reluctantly, suspends her researches. The second does likewise. Suddenly they are decent London women, with kindly faces and puffed, overworked bodies.

"It was over for him, dearie," she says, pushing away a hank of hair with her chubby wrist.

"What was?"

"He said if he couldn't have that phone no more, he'd have to go. He said that phone was his lifeline and if he couldn't have it, it was a judgment on him, how would he do his business without a blower and a clean shirt?"

Mistaking Pym's silence for rebuke, her companion flares at him. "Don't look at us like that, darling. He'd had all we've got long ago. We done the gas, we done the electric, we cooked his dinners, didn't we, Vi?"

"We done all we could," says Vi. "And given him the comfort, too."

"We pulled tricks for him more than was natural, didn't we, Vi? Three a day for him, sometimes."

"More," says Vi.

"He was very lucky to have you," says Pym sincerely. "Thank you very much for looking after him."

This pleases them, and they smile shyly.

"You haven't got a nice bottle in that big black briefcase of yours, I suppose, dearie?"

"I'm afraid not."

Vi goes to the bedroom. Through the open doorway Pym sees the great imperial bed from Chester Street, its upholstery ripped and stained with use. Rick's silk pyjamas lie sprawled across the coverlet. He smells Rick's body lotion and Rick's hair oil. Vi returns with a bottle of Drambuie.

"Did he talk about me at all, in the last days?" says Pym while they drink.

"He was proud of you, dear," says Vi's friend. "Very proud." But she seems dissatisfied with her reply. "He was going to catch you up, mind. That was nearly his last words, wasn't it, Vi?"

"We was holding him," says Vi, with a sniff. "You could see he was going from the breathing. 'Tell them I forgive them at the telephone exchange,' he says. 'And tell my boy Magnus we'll both be ambassadors soon.'"

"And after that?" says Pym.

"'Give us another touch of the Napoleon, Vi,'" says Vi's friend, now weeping also. "It wasn't Napoleon though, it was the Drambuie. Then he says: 'There's enough in those files, girls, to see you right till you join me.'"

"He just nodded off really," says Vi, into her handkerchief. "He mightn't have been dead at all, if it hadn't been for his heart."

There is a rustle at the door. Three knocks. Vi opens it an inch, then all the way, then stands back disapprovingly to admit Ollie and Mr. Cudlove, armed with buckets of ice. The years have not been kind to Ollie's nerves, and the tears at the corners of his eyes are stained with mascara. But Mr. Cudlove is unchanged, down to his chauffeur's black tie. Transferring the bucket to his left side, Mr. Cudlove seizes Pym's right hand in a manly grip. Pym follows them down a narrow corridor lined with photographs of neverwozzers. Rick is lying in the bath with a towel round his middle, his marbled feet crossed over each other as if in accordance with some Oriental ritual. His hands are curled and cupped in readiness to harangue his Maker.

"It's just that there wasn't the funds, sir," Mr. Cudlove murmurs while Ollie pours in the ice. "Not a penny piece anywhere, to be frank, sir. I think those ladies may have taken a liberty."

"Why didn't you close his eyes?" says Pym.

"We did, sir, to be frank, but they would open again, and it didn't seem respectful."

On one knee before his father, Pym writes out a cheque for two hundred pounds, and nearly makes it dollars by mistake.

Pym drives to Chester Street. The house has been in

other hands for years but tonight it stands in darkness, as if once more waiting for the Distraining Bailiffs. Pym approaches gingerly. On the doorstep, a nightlight burns despite the rain. Beside it like a dead animal lies an old boa in the mauve of half mourning, similar to the one belonging to Aunt Nell that he had used to block the lavatory at The Glades so long ago. Is it Dorothy's? Or Peggy Wentworth's? Is it some child's game? Is it put there by Lippsie's ghost? No card attaches to its dew-soaked feathers. No sequestrator has pinned his claim to it. The only clue is the one word "Yes," scrawled in trembling chalklines on the door, like a safety signal in a target town.

Turning his back on the deserted square Pym strode angrily to the bathroom and opened the skylight that years ago he had daubed with green paint for Miss Dubber's greater decency. Through a gun slit, he examined the gardens at the side of the house and concluded that they too were unnaturally empty. No Stanley, the Alsatian, tethered to the rain tub of number 8. No Mrs. Aitken, the butcher's wife, who spends every waking hour at her roses. Closing the skylight with a bang, he stooped over the basin and sluiced water in his face, then glowered at his reflection till it gave him a false and brilliant smile. Rick's smile, put on to taunt him, the one that is too happy even to blink. The one that cuddles up against you and presses into you like a thrilled child. The one Pym hated most.

"Fireworks, old son," said Pym, mimicking Rick's cadences at their holy worst. "Remember how you loved a firework? Remember dear old Guy Fawkes night, and the great setpiece there, with your old man's initials on it, RTP, going up in lights all over Ascot? Well then."

Well then, Pym echoed in his soul.

Pym is writing again. Joyously. No pen can take the strain of this. Reckless free letters are careering over the paper. Light-paths, rocket tails, stars and stripes are zipping above his head. The music of a thousand transistor radios plays around him; the bright faces of strangers laugh into his own, and he is laughing back at them. It is July 4th. It is Washington's

night of nights. The diplomatic Pyms have arrived a week ago
to take up his appointment as Deputy Head of Station. The
island of Berlin is sunk at last. They have a spell in Prague
behind them, Stockholm, London. The path to America was
never easy, but Pym has gone the distance, Pym has made it,
he is assumed and almost risen into the reddened dark that is
repeatedly blasted into whiteness by the floodlights, fireworks and searchlights. The crowd is bobbing round him and
he is part of it, the free people of the earth have taken him
among them. He is one with all these grown-up happy
children celebrating their independence of things that never
held them. The Marine Band, the Breckenridge Boys Choir
and the Metropolitan Area Symposium Choral Group have
wooed and won him unopposed. At party after party Magnus
and Mary have been celebrated by half the intelligence
aristos of Georgetown, have eaten swordfish by candlelight in
red-brick yards, chatted under lights strung in overhanging
branches, have embraced and been embraced, shaken hands
and filled their heads with names and gossip and champagne.
Heard a lot about you, Magnus—Magnus, welcome aboard!
Jesus, is that your wife? That's *criminal*! Till Mary, worried
about Tom—the fireworks have over excited him—is determined to go home and Bee Lederer has gone with her.

"I'll join you soon, darling," Pym murmurs as she leaves.
"Must pop in on the Wexlers or they'll think I'm cutting
them."

Where am I? In the Mall? On the Hill? Pym has no idea.
The bare arms and thighs and unhampered breasts of young
American womanhood are brushing contentedly against him.
Friendly hands make space for him to pass; laughter, potsmoke,
din pack the scalding night. "What's your name, man?" "You
British? Here, let's shake your hand—take a swig of this."
Pym adds a mouthful of bourbon to the impressive mixture
he has already taken in. He is climbing a slope, whether of
grass or tarmac he cannot determine. The White House
glistens below him. Before it, erect and floodlit, the white
needle of the Washington Monument cuts its light-path to the
unreachable stars. Jefferson and Lincoln, each in his eternal
patch of Rome, lie to either side of him. Pym loves them both.
All the patriarchs and founding fathers of America are mine.
He crests the slope. A black man offers him popcorn. It is salt
and hot like his own sweat. Further up the valley, the

harmless battles of other firework shows boom and splash into the sky. The crowd is denser up here but still they smile at him and part for him while they ooh and aah at the fireworks, call friendship to each other, break into patriotic song. A pretty girl is teasing him. "Hey, man, why won't you dance?" "Well, thank you, I will with pleasure but just let me take off my coat," Pym replies. His answer is too woody, she has found another partner. He is shouting. At first he does not hear himself but as he enters a quieter place his own voice bursts on him with startling distinctness. "Poppy! Poppy! Where are you?" Helpfully, the good people round him take up the cry. "Hurry on over, Poppy, your boyfriend's here!" "Come on, Poppy, you bad bitch, where you bin?" Behind and above him the rockets become a ceaseless fountain against the swirling crimson clouds. Before him a gold umbrella opens, embracing the whole white mountain and lighting the emptying street. Instructions are ringing remotely in Pym's head. He is reading the numbers of the streets and doorways. He finds the door and with a final surge of joy feels the familiar bony hand close round his wrist and the familiar voice admonishing him.

"Your friend Poppy cannot come tonight, Sir Magnus," says Axel softly. "So will you please stop shouting her name?"

Shoulder to shoulder the two men sit on the steps of the Capitol, gazing down into the Mall on the uncountable thousands they have taken into their protection. Axel has a basket containing a thermos flask of ice-cold vodka, and the best gherkins and brown bread America can supply.

"We made it, Sir Magnus," he breathes. "We are home at last."

"My dearest Father,
    "I am very pleased to be able to tell you of my new appointment. Cultural Counsellor may not sound much to you, but it is a post that commands a deal of respect among the highest circles here, and even gets me into the White House. I am also the proud owner of what is called a Cosmic Pass, which means literally that no doors are closed to me any more."

17

Oh my heaven, Tom, the fun we had! The glorious free-wheeling last honeymoon, even as the clouds gathered!

You would be pardoned for thinking that the duties of a Deputy Head of Station, though elevated, are inferior to those of his boss. Not so. The Head of Station in Washington floats in the upper air of intelligence diplomacy. His task is to massage the corpse of the Special Relationship and convince everybody, including himself, that it is alive and well. Every morning, poor Hal Tresider rose early, put on his old Shirburnian tie and sweat-patched tropical suit, and pedalled his pushbike earnestly away to the sodden dreamland of the committee rooms, leaving your father free to ransack the Station Registry, supervise the outstations in San Francisco, Boston, and Chicago, or dart off to welfare a field agent in transit to Central America, China, or Japan. Another chore was shepherding grey-faced British boffins through the battery farms of American high technology, where the scientific secrets that are traded in Washington have their artificial conception. Dining the poor souls, Tom, where others would have left them mouldering in their motels. Consoling them in their womanless, under-financed foreign exile. Chatting hastily memorised jargon at them, about nose cones, turning radius, underwater communication and captive-carry. Borrowing their working documents from them to give back in the morning. "Hullo—*that* looks interesting. Mind if I sneak a sight of that for our Naval Attaché? He's been badgering the Pentagon about that one for years, but they've been holding out on him."

The Naval Attaché had a sight, London had a sight, Prague had a sight. For what use is a Cosmic Pass without a Cosmic readership?

Poor stolid, worthy Hal! How meticulously Pym misused your trust and torpedoed your innocent ambitions! Never mind. If the National Trust won't have you, you can always count on the Royal Automobile Club or a favoured City company.

"I say, Pymmie, there's some ghastly group of physicists visiting the Livermore weapons laboratory next month," you would say, all apology and diffidence. "You don't think you could pop down there and feed and water a few of them and see they don't blow their noses on the tablecloth, could you? Why on earth this service has to behave like a lot of flat-footed security officers these days, I really don't know. I've a good mind to do a letter to London about it, if I can squeeze a moment."

No country was ever easier to spy on, Tom, no nation so open-hearted with its secrets, so quick to air them, share them, confide them, or consign them too early to the junk heap of planned American obsolescence. I am too young to know whether there was a time when Americans were able to restrain their admirable passion to communicate, but I doubt it. Certainly the path has been downhill since 1945, for it was quickly apparent that information which ten years ago would have cost Axel's service thousands of dollars in precious hard currency could by the mid-seventies be had for a few coppers from the *Washington Post*. We could have resented this sometimes, if we had been smaller natures, for there are few things more vexing in the spy world than landing a great scoop for Prague and London one week, only to read the same material in *Aviation Weekly* the next. But we did not complain. In the great fruit garden of American technology, there were pickings enough for everyone and none of us need ever want for anything again.

Cameos, Tom, little tiles for your mosaic are all I need to give you now. See the two friends romping under a darkening sky, catching the last rays of the sunlight before the game is over. See them thieving like children, knowing the police are round the corner. Pym did not take to America in a night, not in a month, for all the splendid fireworks of the Fourth. His love of the place grew with Axel's. Without Axel he might never have seen the light. Pym set out, believe it or not, determined to disapprove of everything he saw. He found no holding point, no stern judgment to revolt against. These vulgar pleasure-seeking people, so frank and clamorous, were too uninhibited for his shielded and involuted life. They loved their prosperity too obviously, were too flexible and mobile, too little the slaves of place, origin and class. They had no sense of that hush which all Pym's life had been the background music of his inhibition. In committee, it was true, they reverted soon enough to type, and became the warring princelings of the European countries they had left behind. They could run you up a cabal that would make mediaeval Venice blush. They could be Dutch and stubborn, Scandinavian and gloomy, Balkan and murderous and tribal. But when they mixed with one another they were American and loquacious and disarming, and Pym was hard put to find a centre to betray.

Why had they done him no harm? Why had they not cramped him, frightened him, forced his limbs into impossible positions from the cradle up? He found himself longing for the empty, darkened streets of Prague and the reassuring embrace of chains. He wanted his dreadful schools back. He wanted anything but the marvellous horizons that led to lives he had not lived. He wanted to spy upon hope itself, look through keyholes at the sunrise and deny the possibilities he had missed. And all this time, ironically, Europe was coming to get him. He knew that. So did Axel. Not a year had passed before the first insidious whispers of suspicion began to reach their ears. Yet it was this very intimation of mortality that shook Pym out of his reluctance, and inspired him to take the upper hand in their relationship just as Axel was saying, "End it, get out." A mysterious gratitude for America the Just and her impending retribution seized him as, like a ponderous, puzzled giant, she bore steadily down on him, clutching in her great soft fist the multiplying evidence of his duplicity.

"Certain aristos in Langley and London are getting worried about our Czecho networks, Sir Magnus," Axel warned him in his stiff, dry English at a crash meeting at the carpark of the Robert F. Kennedy Stadium. "They have begun to discern certain unfortunate patterns."

"What patterns? There are no patterns."

"They have noticed that the Czecho networks provide better intelligence when we are running them and almost nothing when we are not. That is the pattern. They have computers these days. It takes them five minutes to turn everything upside down and wonder what is the right way up. We have been careless, Sir Magnus. We were too greedy. Our parents were right. If you want a thing done well, you must do it yourself."

"Jack Brotherhood can run those networks as well as we can. The head agents are genuine, they report whatever they can get hold of. All networks go moribund now and then. It's normal."

"These networks only go moribund when we are not there, Sir Magnus," Axel repeated patiently. "That is Langley's perception. It bothers them."

"Then give the networks better material. Signal Prague. Tell your aristos we need a scoop."

Axel sadly shook his head. "You know Prague, Sir Magnus. You know my aristos. The man who is absent is the man they conspire against. I have no power to persuade them."

Calmly Pym contemplated the option that remained to him. Over dinner in their smart house in Georgetown, while Mary played gracious hostess, gracious English lady, gracious diplomatic geisha, Pym wondered whether it was time to persuade Poppy to cross one more frontier after all. He saw himself free of taint, a husband, son and father in good standing at last. He remembered an old Revolutionary farmhouse he and Poppy had admired in Pennsylvania, set among rolling fields and stone fences, with thoroughbred horses that loomed at them out of the sun-stained morning fog. He remembered the whitewashed churches, so sparkling and hopeful after the musty crypts of his childhood, and imagined the resettled family Pym at work and prayer there, and Axel rocking on the garden swing while he drank vodka and shelled peas for lunch.

I shall sell Axel to Langley and buy my freedom, he thought as he dazzled a pearly-toothed matron with a witty anecdote. I shall negotiate an administrative amnesty for myself, and put the record straight.

He never did, he never would. Axel was his keeper and his virtue, he was the altar on which Pym had laid his secrets and his life. He had become the part of Pym that was not owned by anybody else.

Do I need to tell you, Tom, how bright and dear the world looks when we know our days are numbered? How all life swells and opens to you, and says "Come in" just when you had thought you were unwanted? What a paradise America became once Pym knew the writing was on the wall. All his childhood, rushing back to him! He took Mary to point-to-points at Winterthur in the château country and dreamed of Switzerland and of Ascot. He wandered Georgetown's beautiful Oak Hill Cemetery and imagined he was with Dorothy at The Glades, confined to the dripping orchard where his guilty face could be hidden from the passers-by. Minnie Wilson was our letter box at Oak Hill, Tom. Our first in all America—go and take a look at her one day. She lies on a curled plinth a short way down the terraced bowl, a small dead Victorian girl in marble drapes. We left our messages in a leafy recess between Minnie's backside and her protector, one Thomas Entwistle, who had died in later age. The doyen of the graveyard rested higher up, near the gravel sweep where Pym parked his diplomatic car. Axel found him, Axel made sure Pym found him too. He was Stefan Osusky, co-founder of the Czechoslovak Republic, died in exile, 1973. No concealed offering to Axel seemed complete without a silent prayer of greeting to our brother Stefan. After Minnie, as the volume of our business grew, we were obliged to appoint postmen nearer to the centre of the town. We selected forgotten bronze generals, mostly French, who had fought on the American side in order to annoy the British. We relished their soft hats and telescopes and horses, and the flowers in red uniform at their feet. Their battlefields were grass squares filled with lounging students, our letter boxes anything from the stubby cannon that protected them to the stunted conifers whose inner branches made convenient brown nests of pine needles. But Axel's favourite place of all was the newly opened Air and Space Museum, where he could gaze his heart out at the *Spirit of St. Louis* and John Glenn's *Friendship 7*, and touch the Moon Relic with his forefinger as devoutly as if he were taking water from a holy shrine. Pym never saw him do these things. He could only hear about them afterwards. The trick was to leave their packages in separate lockers in the cloakroom, and swap keys in the darkness of the Samuel P. Langley projection theatre while the audience gasped and clutched the handrails as the screen dazzled them with the thrills of flight.

And away from the eyes and ears of Washington, Tom? What shall I give you first? Silicon Valley, perhaps, and the little Spanish village south of San Francisco where Murgo's monks sang plainsong to us after dinner. Or the Dead Sea landscape of Palm Springs, where the golf carts had Rolls-Royce grilles, and the Mountains of Moab looked down on the pastel stucco and artificial-rock pools of our walled motel while illegal Mexicans wandered the lawns with backpacks, blowing away unsightly leaves that could offend the sensibilities of our fellow millionaires. Can you imagine Axel's ecstasy as he beheld the outdoor air-conditioning machines that moistened the desert air and blew micro-mist over the sunbathers with faces covered in green mud? Shall I tell you of the Palm Springs Humane Society's dog-adoption dinner we attended to celebrate Pym's acquisition of the very latest blueprint for the nose cone of the Stealth bomber? How the dogs were led on stage groomed and ribboned, to be auctioned to humane ladies, while everybody wept as if they were Vietnamese orphans? Of the all-day Bible-thumpers' radio channel that portrayed the Christian God as the champion of wealth, since wealth was the enemy of Communism? "God's waiting room" is what they call Palm Springs. It has one swimming-pool for every five inhabitants, and lies a couple of hours' drive from the biggest killing factories in the world. Its industries are charity and death. That night, unknown to the retired bandits and senile comedians who made up its geriatric court, Pym and Axel added espionage to the list of its accomplishments.

"We shall never fly so high again, Sir Magnus," Axel said as he reverently surveyed Pym's offering in the silence of their six-hundred-dollar-a-night suite. "I think we may retire also."

Shall I give you Disneyland and another projection room, with a circular screen that showed us the American dream? Can I convince you that Pym and Axel wept sincere tears as they watched the refugees from European persecution set foot on American soil while the commentator spoke of a Nation of Nations and the Land of the Free? We believed it, Tom. And Pym believes it still. Pym never felt more free in his life until the night Rick died. Everything he still contrived to love in himself was here to love in the people round him. A willingness to open themselves to strangers. A guile that was only there to protect their innocence. A fantasy that fired but never owned them. A capacity to be swayed by everything, while still remaining sovereign. And Axel loved them too, but he was not so confident that his affection was reciprocated.

"Wexler is setting up an investigation team, Sir Magnus,"

he warned one night in Boston as they dined in the Colonial dignity of the Ritz Hotel. "Some bad defector has been telling stories. It's time we got out."

Pym said nothing at all. They walked through the park and watched the swan boats on the pond. They sat in a tense, bare Irish pub that seethed with crimes the English had forgotten. But Pym still refused to speak. A few days later, however, visiting an English don at Yale who occasionally supplied the Firm with tidbits, he found himself in front of the effigy of the American hero Nathan Hale, who was hanged by the British as a spy. His hands were bound behind his back. Below him were inscribed his last words: "I only regret that I have but one life to lose for my country." For several weeks after this, Pym went to ground.

Pym was talking. Pym was on the move. Pym was somewhere in the room, arms locked at his sides, palms splayed like someone wishing to fly or swim. He was sinking into his knees, rolling his shoulders against the wall. He was clutching the green cabinet and shaking it and the cabinet was hobbling in his grasp like an old grandfather clock about to flatten him with its embrace, and the burnbox was bobbing and swaying on top of it saying, "Take me." He was swearing, all in his head. He was talking, all in his head. He wanted calm from his surroundings but they wouldn't give it him. He was at his desk again and the sweat was patting on the paper round him. He was writing. He was calm, but the damned room still wouldn't settle, it was interfering with his prose.

Boston again.

Pym has been visiting the golden semicircle that lies along Route 128. Welcome to America's Technological Highway. It is a place like a crematorium without a smokestack. Discreet, low-lying factories and laboratories crouch amid shrubberies and landscaped mounds. He has picked the brains of a British delegation and taken a few forbidden photographs with a concealed camera in his briefcase. He has lunched privately at the home of a great American patriarch of industry named Bob, whom he has befriended for his indiscretion. They have sat on the verandah, they have gazed across a garden of descending lawns which a black man is sedately mowing with a triple cutter. After lunch Pym drives to Needham, where Axel is waiting for him beside a bend in the Charles River, which serves them as their local Aare. A heron skims over the blue-green rushes. Red-tailed hawks eye them from dead trees. Their path climbs deep into the woods, along a raised esker.

"So what's the matter?" says Axel finally.

"Why should anything be the matter?"

"You are tense and you are not speaking. It is reasonable to assume something is the matter."

"I'm always tense for a debriefing."

"Not tense like this."

"He wouldn't talk to me."

"Bob wouldn't?"

"I asked him how the *Nimitz* refitting contract was going. He replied that his corporation was making great strides in Saudi Arabia. I asked him about his discussions with the Admiral of the Pacific Fleet. He asked me when I was going to bring Mary up to Maine for the weekend. His face has changed."

"How?"

"He's angry. Somebody's warned him about me. I think he's more angry with them than he is with me."

"What else?" says Axel patiently, knowing that with Pym there is always one more door.

"I was followed to his house. A green Ford, smoked windows. There's nowhere to hang around and American watchers don't walk, so they left again."

"What else?"

"Stop asking what else!"

"What else?"

Suddenly a great gulf of caution and mistrust separated them.

"Axel," said Pym finally.

It was unusual for Pym to address him by name; the proprieties of espionage normally restrained him.

"Yes, Sir Magnus."

"When we were in Bern together. When we were students. You weren't, were you?"

"Not a student?"

"You weren't spying on anyone. On the Ollingers. On the Cosmo. On me. You hadn't got people running you in those days. You were just you."

"I was not spying. Nobody was running me. Nobody owned me."

"Is that true?"

But Pym knew already that it was. He knew it by the rare glow of anger that shone in Axel's eyes. By the solemnity and distaste in his voice.

"It was your idea that I was a spy, Sir Magnus. It was never mine."

Pym watched him light a fresh cigar and noticed how the flame of the match trembled.

"It was Jack Brotherhood's idea," Pym corrected him.

Axel drew on the cigar and his shoulders slowly relaxed. "It doesn't matter," he said. "It is simply unimportant at our age."

"Bo's authorised a hostile interrogation," said Pym. "I'm flying back to London on Sunday to face the music."

Who should talk to Axel of interrogation? And of a hostile one at that? Who should dare compare the nocturnal posturings of a couple of the Firm's tame barristers in a safe house in Sussex with the beatings and electric shocks and deprivations that for two decades had been Axel's irregular fare? I blush now to think I used the word to him at all. In '52, as I learned later, Axel had denounced Slansky and demanded the death sentence for him—not very loud because he was half dead himself.

"But that's terrible!" Pym had cried. "How can you serve a country that does that to you?"

"It was not terrible at all, thank you. I should have done it earlier. I secured my survival and Slansky would have died whether I denounced him or not. Give me another vodka."

In '56 he went down again: "That time it was less problematic," he explained, lighting himself a fresh cigar. "I denounced Tito and nobody even bothered to go and kill him."

In the early sixties, while Pym was in Berlin, Axel had rotted for three months in a mediaeval dungeon outside Prague. What he promised that time has always been unclear to me. It was the year when the Stalinists themselves were purged, if only halfheartedly, and Slansky was declared alive again, if only posthumously. (Though he was still ruled to be guilty of his offences, you will remember, if only innocently.) In any case, Axel came back looking ten years older, and for some months had a soft "r" in his speech that was very like a stammer.

Beside experience like this, the inquisition of Pym was watery stuff indeed. Jack Brotherhood was there to defend him. Personnel fussed over him like an old hen, assuring him it was just a matter of answering a few questions. Some chinless flunkey from Treasury kept warning my persecutors they were in danger of exceeding their brief, and my two gaolers insisted on talking to me about their children. After five days and nights of it, Pym felt as spry as if he had been taking a country holiday, and his interrogators were out on their feet.

"Good trip, darling?" Mary asked, back in Georgetown, after a morning in bed in which Pym had temporarily slaked the tension.

"Great," said Pym. "And Jack sends love."

But on his walk to the Embassy he saw a new white arrow chalked on the brickwork of the Fayre-deal wine shop, which was Axel's warning to attempt no contact until further notice.

And here, Tom, it is time for me to tell you what Rick was doing, for your grandfather had one last trick to play before the end. It was his best, as you would suppose. Rick shrank. He abandoned monstrosity as a way of life, and came weeping and cringing to me like a whipped animal. And the smaller and more encompassable he became, the less secure Pym felt. It was as if the Firm and Rick were closing in on him from either side, each with his regretful, hangdog banality, and Pym, like an acrobat on the high wire between them, suddenly had nothing to support him. Pym implored him in his mind. He screamed at him: Stay bad, stay monstrous, keep your distance, don't give up! But on Rick came, shuffling and smirking like a pauper, knowing his power was greatest now that he was weak. "I did it all for you, son. It's thanks to me you've taken your place among the Highest in the Land. Got a few coppers for your old man, have you? How about a nice mixed grill, or are you ashamed to take your old pal out?"

He struck first one Christmas Day, not six weeks after Pym had received a formal apology from Head Office. Georgetown had two feet of snow and we had asked the Lederers to lunch. Mary was putting the food on the table as the phone rang. Will Ambassador Pym accept a collect call from New Jersey? He will.

"Hullo, old son. How's the world using you?"

"I'll take this upstairs," says Pym grimly to Mary, and everybody looks understanding, knowing that the secret world never sleeps.

"Happy Christmas, old son," says Rick as Pym picks up the bedroom phone.

"And Happy Christmas to you, too, Father. What are you doing in New Jersey?"

"God's the twelfth man on the cricket team, son. It's God who tells us to keep the left elbow up through life. No one else."

"So you always said. But it's not the cricket season. Are you drunk?"

"He's umpire, judge and jury rolled into one and never you forget it. There's no conning God. There never was. Are you glad I paid for your education, then?"

"I'm not conning God, Father, I'm trying to celebrate with my family."

"Say hullo to Miriam," says Rick, and there is muffled protest before Miriam comes on the line.

"Hullo, Magnus," says Miriam.

"Hullo, Miriam," says Pym.

"Hullo," says Miriam a second time.

"They feed you all right in that Embassy of yours, son, or is it all Thousand Island and French fries?"

"We have a perfectly decent canteen for the lower staff but at the moment I'm trying to eat at home."

"Turkey?"

"Yes."

"English bread sauce?"

"I expect so."

"That grandson of mine all right then, is he? He's got the forehead, has he, the one I gave you that everybody talks about?"

"He's got a very good brow."

"Blue eyes, same as mine?"

"Mary's eyes."

"I hear she's first class, son. I hear first-rate reports of her. They say she's got a fine piece of property down in Dorset that's worth a bob or two."

"It's in trust," says Pym sharply.

But Rick has already begun drowning in the gulf of his own self-pity. He weeps, the weep becomes a howl. In the background, Miriam is weeping, too, in a high-pitched whimper, like a small dog locked in a big house.

"But darling," says Mary as Pym resumes his place as head of the family. "Magnus. You're upset. What's the matter?"

Pym shakes his head, smiling and crying at once. He grabs his wineglass and lifts it.

"To absent friends," he calls out. "To *all* our absent friends!" And later, for a wife's ears only: "Just an old, old Joe, darling, who managed to track me down and wish me happy bloody Yule."

Would you ever have supposed, Tom, that the greatest country in the world could be too small for one son and his old man? Yet that is what happened. That Rick should head for wherever he could use his son's protection was, I suppose, only natural and after Berlin, probably inevitable. He went first, as I now know, to Canada, unwisely trusting in the bonds of Commonwealth. The Canadians quickly tired of him and when they threatened to repatriate him he made a small down payment on a Cadillac and headed south. In Chicago, my enquiries show that he succumbed to the many enticing offers from property companies to move into new developments on the edge of town and live rent-free for three months as an inducement. A Colonel Hanbury resided at Farview Gardens, a Sir William Forsyth graced Sunleigh Court, where he extended his tenancy by conducting protracted negotiations to buy the penthouse for his butler. What either of them did for liquidity is, as ever, a mystery, though no doubt there were grateful Lovelies in the background. The one clue is a prickly letter from the stewards of a local turf club, advising Sir William that his horses will be welcome when his stable fees have been settled. Pym was still only vaguely aware of these distant rumblings, and his absences from Washington gave him a false sense of protection. But in New Jersey something changed Rick for ever, and whatever it was, from then on Pym became his only industry. Was the same wind of reckoning blowing over both men simultaneously? Was Rick really ill? Or was he, like Pym, merely conscious of impending judgment? Certainly Rick thought he was ill. Certainly he thought he ought to be:

"Am obliged to use strong walking-stick (twenty-nine dollars cash) at all times owing to Heart and other more sinister Ailments"—he wrote—"My doctor keeps the Worst from me and recommends that Frugal diet (plain foods and Champagne only, no Californian) could Prolong this Meagre existence and enable me to Fight back for a few more Months before I am Called."

Certainly he took to wearing liver-coloured spectacles like Aunt Nell. And when he fell foul of the law in Denver, the prison doctor was so impressed by him that he was released the moment Pym had paid the medical fees.

And after Denver you decided you were already dead, didn't you, and set·out to haunt me with your smallness? Every town I went to, I walked in fear of your pathetic ghost. Every safe house I entered, I expected to see you waiting at the gate, parading your willed, deliberate littleness. You knew where I would be before I got there. You would con a ticket and travel five thousand miles just to show me how small you had become. And off we'd go to the best restaurant in town, and I would buy you your treat and boast to you about my diplomatic doings and listen to your boastings in return. I would shower you with all the money I could afford, praying that it would enable you to add a few more Wentworths to the green cabinet. But even while I fawned on you and exchanged radiant smiles with you and held hands with you and bolstered you in your idiotic schemes, I knew that you had pulled the best con of them all. You were nothing any more. Your mantle had passed to me, leaving you a naked little man, and myself the biggest con I knew.

"Why don't those fellows give you your knighthood, then, old son? They tell me you ought to be Permanent Under Secretary by now. Got a skeleton in your cupboard, have you? Maybe I should slip over to London and have a word with those Personnel boys of yours."

How did he find me? How could it be that his systems of intelligence were better than those of the Agency's leash dogs who were fast becoming my regular, unwelcome companions? At first I thought he was using private detectives. I began collecting the numbers of suspicious cars, noting the times of dead-end phone calls, trying to distinguish them from Langley's. I bearded my secretary: has someone calling himself my sick father been pestering you for information? Eventually I discovered that the Embassy travel clerk had an addiction to playing English snooker at some Masonic hostel in the dirty part of town. Rick had found him there and pitched him a fatuous cover story: "I've got this dicky heart," he'd said to the fool. "It could get me any time, you see, but don't you go telling my boy. I don't like to bother him when he's got enough on his plate as it is. What you're to do, you're to get on the blower to me and give me the wink whenever that boy of mine leaves town, so that I know where to find him when the end comes." And no doubt there was a gold watch in it somewhere. And tickets for next year's Cup Final. And seeing the boy's dear old mother right next time Rick slipped home for a drop of English air.

But my discovery had come too late. We had had San Francisco by then, and Denver, and Seattle, and Rick had homed on every one of them, weeping and shrinking before my very eyes, until all that was left of Rick was what he owned of Pym; and all that was left of Pym, it seemed to me, as I wove my lies and blandished, and perjured myself before one kangaroo court after another, was a failing con man tottering on the last legs of his credibility.

And that's how it was, Tom. Betrayal is a repetitious trade and I will not bother you with more of it. We have reached the end, though it seems from here to look quite like the beginning. The Firm pulled Pym out of Washington and sent him to Vienna so that he could take back his networks and so that his growing army of accusers could draw its wretched computer pattern tighter round his neck. There was no saving him. Not in the end. Poppy knew that. So did Pym, though he would never admit it, even to himself. Just one more con, Pym kept saying to himself; one more con will see me right. Poppy pressed him, begged him, threatened him. Pym was adamant: Leave me in place, I'll win through, they love me, I've given my life to them.

But the truth is, Tom, that Pym preferred to test the limits of the tolerance of those he loved. He preferred to sit here in Miss Dubber's upper room and wait for God to come, while he looked down the gardens to the beach where the best pals ever had kicked a football from one end of the world to the other, and ridden their Harrods bicycles across the sea.

18

It's fireworks night at Plush, thought Mary, staring into the
darkness of the square. It's an unlit bonfire waiting for Tom.
Through the windscreen of their parked car she gazed at the
empty bandstand and pretended she saw the last of her
family and retainers crammed into the old cricket pavilion.
The muffled footsteps were the footsteps of the gamekeepers
as they gathered to her brother Sam, back for his last leave.
She pretended she could hear her brother's voice, a little too
parade-ground for her liking, still scratchy from the strain of
Ireland. "Tom?" he calls. "Where's old Tom?" . . . Not a move.
Tom is stuck inside Mary's sheepskin coat, his head jammed
against her thigh and nothing short of Christmas is going to
lure him out. "Come on, Tom Pym, you're the youngest!"
cries Sam. "Where is he? . . . You'll be too old next year, you
know, Tom." Then his brutal dismissal. "Fuck it. Let's have
someone else." Tom is shamed, the Pyms are disgraced, Sam
as usual is angry that Tom has no taste for blowing up the
universe. A braver child puts the match and the world
ignites. Her brother's military rockets race over it in perfect
salvoes. Everyone is small, looking at the night sky.

   She sat at Brotherhood's side and he was holding her
wrist the way the doctor held it when she was about to bear
her little coward. To reassure her. To steady her. To say "I am
in charge here." The car was parked in a side street and
behind them stood the police van and behind the police van
stood a caravan of about six hundred parked police cars and
radio vans and ambulances and bomb lorries, all occupied by
Sam's familiars who spoke soundlessly to one another without
moving their eyes. Beside her was a shop called Sugar
Novelties with a neon-lit window and a plastic gnome pushing
a wheelbarrow laden with dusty sweets, and next to it a
granite workhouse with "Public Library" engraved over a
funereal door. Across the street stood a hideous Baptist

church that told you God was no fun either. Beyond the
church lay God's square and His bandstand and His monkey-
puzzle trees, and between the fourth and fifth tree from the
left, as she had counted twenty times, and three-quarters of
the way up, hung an arched lighted window with the orange
curtains drawn, which my officers advise me is where your
husband's room is situated, madam, though our enquiries
indicate that he is known locally by the name of Canterbury
and is well liked in the community.

"He's always liked," Mary snapped.

But the superintendent was saying this to Brotherhood.
He was speaking through Brotherhood's window and defer-
ring to Brotherhood as her keeper. And Mary knew that the
superintendent had been ordered to speak to her as little as
possible, which came hard to him. And that Brotherhood had
given himself the job of answering for her, which the superintendent seemed to accept was as near to godliness as he was
likely to get without having his ears blasted off. The superintendent was a Devon man, and ponderously traditional. I'm
so *frightfully* glad he's being arrested by a *Devon* man, she
thought cruelly, in Caroline Lumsden's Sloane-Ranger twit-
ter. I always think it's *so* much *nicer* to be taken prisoner by a
man of the soil.

"Are you quite sure you wouldn't like to come into the
Church Hall, madam?" the superintendent was saying for the
hundredth time. "It's much warmer in the Church Hall and
there's some quite fine company. Cosmopolitan, counting the
Americans."

"She's best here," Brotherhood murmured in reply.

"Only we can't allow the gentleman to switch on the
engine, you see, to be truthful, madam. And if he can't
switch on the engine, well you can't have the heating, if you
see what I mean."

"I'd like you to go away," Mary said.

"She's all right as she is," said Brotherhood.

"Only it could be all night, you see, madam. Could be
all tomorrow too. If our friend decides to stick it out, kind of
thing, to be truthful."

"We'll play it as it comes," Brotherhood said. "When you
need her, this is where she'll be."

"Well I'm afraid she won't, sir, to be truthful, not when
we go in, if we have to. I'm afraid she'll have to withdraw to a

somewhat safer position, to be truthful, same as you. Only the rest of them are back in the Church Hall, if you follow me, sir, and the chief constable says that's where all non-combatants have got to be at that stage in the proceedings including the Americans."

"She doesn't want to be with the rest of them," said Mary before Brotherhood could speak. "And she's not American. She's his wife."

The superintendent went away and came back almost immediately. He's the go-between. They've chosen him for his bedside manner.

"Message from the roof, sir," he began apologetically, crouching yet again to Brotherhood's window. "Do you happen to know, please, the precise type and calibre of the weapon our friend is alleged to have in his possession?"

"Standard Browning three-eight automatic. An old one. Shouldn't think it's been cleaned for years."

"Any theories regarding the type of ammunition at all, sir? Only it would be nice for them to know the carry, you see."

"Short nose, I should think."

"But not a stopper, for instance, or a dumdum?"

"Why the hell should he want a dumdum?"

"I don't know, sir, do I? Information is gold dust on this one, the way it's being passed around, if I may say so. I haven't seen so many tight lips in one room for, oh, a long time. How many rounds has our friend got, do you think?"

"One magazine. Maybe a spare."

Mary was suddenly furious. "For God's sake. He's not a maniac! He's not going to start a—"

"Start a what?" said the superintendent, whose country manners had a way of slipping when he wasn't spoken to respectfully.

"Just assume it's one magazine and one spare," Brotherhood said.

"Well, then, perhaps you can tell us how our friend's marksmanship is," the superintendent suggested as if stepping on to safer ground. "You can't blame them for asking that, can you?"

"He's been trained and topped up all his life," said Brotherhood.

"He's good," Mary said.

"Now how do you know that, madam, if I may be allowed to ask a simple question?"

"He shoots Tom's air pistol with him."

"Rats and that? Or something larger?"

"Paper targets."

"Does he now? And gets a high score then, does he, madam?"

"Tom says so."

She glanced at Brotherhood and knew what he was thinking. Just let me go in and get him, gun or no. She was thinking much the same herself: Magnus, come out of there and stop making yourself so bloody ridiculous. The superintendent was speaking again, this time to Brotherhood directly.

"Now there's a query from our disposal people this time, sir," he said, as if it were all a little bit unreasonable but we must humour them. "Regarding this box device our friend is carrying with him. I've tried them in the Church Hall but they're all a bit above the technicalities like, and they said to ask you. Our boys do appreciate they're not allowed to know too much about it, but they would like the benefit of your wisdom regarding the charge it contains."

"It's self-consuming," Brotherhood replied. "It's not a weapon."

"Ah, but could it be used as a weapon, put it that way, if it got into the hands of one who might for instance have lost the balance of his mind?"

"Not unless he put somebody inside it," Brotherhood replied and the superintendent let out a mellow country laugh.

"I'll tell that one to the boys," he promised. "They like a joke up there, the boys do, it gets the tension out of them." His voice fell and he spoke to Brotherhood alone. "Has our friend ever fired his gun in anger, sir?"

"It's not his gun."

"Ah, now you didn't quite answer the question there, sir, did you?"

"To my knowledge he's never been in a shoot-out."

"Our friend doesn't get angry," Mary said.

"Has he ever taken anybody prisoner, sir?"

"Us," Mary said.

Pym had made the cocoa and Pym had put the new shawl over Miss Dubber's shoulders although she said she didn't feel the chill. Pym had chopped up the piece of chicken for

Toby that he had bought at the supermarket as a treat for
him, and if she had let him he would have cleaned out the
canary's cage as well; for the canary was his secret pride ever
since a night when he had found it dead after Miss Dubber had
gone to bed, and contrived, unknown to her, to exchange it for a
live one with Mr. Loring of the pet shop. But Miss Dubber
wanted no more fussing from him. She wanted him sitting beside
her where she could keep an eye on him and listen to him reading Aunt Al's latest letter from distant Sri Lanka, which came
in yesterday, Mr. Canterbury, but you never had the interest.

"Is that Ali the dhobi who stole her lace last year?" she
enquired sharply, interrupting him. "Why does she go on
employing him if he stole from her? I thought we'd seen the
last of Ali long ago."

"I expect she forgave him," said Pym. "He had all those
wives, if you remember. She probably couldn't bear to chuck
him into the street." His voice was very clear to him and
beautiful. It was good to speak aloud.

"I do wish she'd come home," Miss Dubber said. "It
can't be good for her, the heat, after all these years."

"Ah but then she'd have to do her own washing, wouldn't
she, Miss D?" said Pym. And his smile warmed him as he
knew it was warming her.

"You're better now, aren't you, Mr. Canterbury? I'm so
glad. It's got out of you, whatever it is. You can have a nice
rest now."

"What from?" said Pym gently, still smiling at her.

"Whatever you've been doing all these years. You can let
somebody else run the country for a while. Did he leave you
a lot of work to do, the poor gentleman who died?"

"I suppose he did really. It's always difficult when you
don't have a proper handover."

"But you'll be all right now, won't you? I can see."

"I will when you say you'll take that holiday, Miss D."

"Only if you come."

"I can't *do* that. I told you! I've run out of leave!"

His voice had lifted more than he intended. She looked
at him and he saw the scare in her face, which was how he
had caught her looking at him ever since the green cabinet had
arrived, or when he had smiled and pampered her too much.

"Well I'm not going," she replied tartly. "I don't like
putting Toby into prison and Toby doesn't like going to prison

and we're not going to do it just to please you, are we, Toby? You're very kind but don't mention it again. Is that all she says?"

"The rest is about the race riots. She thinks there are more on the way. I didn't think you'd like it."

"You're quite right, I would *not*," said Miss Dubber firmly and her eyes stayed on him as he crossed the room, folded the letter and put it in the ginger jar. "You can read it to me in the morning when I don't mind so much. Why's the square quiet? Why isn't Mrs. Peel playing her television next door? She should be watching that announcer she's in love with."

"Probably gone to bed," said Pym. "More cocoa, Miss D?" he asked, taking the mugs to the scullery. The curtains were drawn, but beside the window was an extractor fan that Pym had built into the wooden wall and it was made of transparent plastic. Putting his eye to it he quickly surveyed the square but saw no sign of life.

"Don't be so silly, Mr. Canterbury," Miss Dubber was saying. "You know I never have a second cup. Come back and watch the news."

At the far end of the square, in the shadow of the church, a small light went on and off.

"Not tonight, Miss D, if you don't mind," he called to her. "I've had nothing but politics all week." He ran the tap and waited till the Crimean war geyser caught before he rinsed the mugs. "I'm going to put myself to bed and give the world a rest, Miss D."

"Well you'd better answer the telephone first," she replied. "It's for you."

She must have lifted the receiver at once for he had not heard it above the sobbing of the geyser. It had never rung for him before. He returned to the kitchen and she was holding the receiver out to him and he saw the scare in her face again, accusing him, as he reached out a steady hand to take it. He put the phone to his ear and said "Canterbury." The line went dead but he kept the phone to his ear and gave a quick bright smile of recognition to the middle distance of Miss Dubber's kitchen, somewhere between the picture of Pilgrim slogging up the hill past the hookers, and the picture of the little girl in bed with her hair brushed, about to eat her boiled egg.

"Thank you," he said. "Well thank you very much indeed, Bill. Well that's very handsome of you. And of the

Minister. Thank him for me, will you, Bill? Let's have lunch about it next week. On me."

He rang off. There was a lot of heat in his face and he was no longer quite sure, now that he looked at Miss Dubber, what her expression was doing, or whether she was aware of the pains he was getting around the shoulders and neck and in the right knee, which he had ricked when he was skiing at Lech with Tom.

"Apparently the Minister's rather pleased with the work I did for him," he explained to her a little blindly. "He wanted me to know that my efforts hadn't been in vain. That was his private secretary. Bill. Sir William Wells. Friend of mine."

"I see," Miss Dubber said. But she was not enthusiastic.

"The Minister's not terribly appreciative as a rule, to be honest. Doesn't let it show. Hard man to please. Practically never been known to hand out a compliment in his life. But we're all rather devoted to him. Warts and all, as you might say. We do all rather tend to be a bit fond of him notwithstanding, if you follow. We've all rather decided to accept that he's part of life's rich pageant, and not some sort of monster. Yes, well I'm tired, Miss D. Let's put you to bed."

She had not moved. He talked harder.

"It wasn't Himself of course. He's in all-night session. Liable to be there on and off for a long while. This was his private secretary."

"So you told me."

"'That's medal material, Pym dear boy,' he said. 'The old man actually smiled.' The old man, that's what we call the Minister. Sir William to his face, but 'the old man' behind his back. Be nice to have a gong, wouldn't it, Miss D? Put it over the fireplace. Polish it at Easter and Christmas. Our own private medal. Earned on the premises. If anyone's deserved it, you have."

He stopped speaking for a while because he was blurting a bit and his mouth was dry and he had the worst ear-and-throat thing he could remember. I really ought to go to one of those private health clinics and have the complete sheep-dip. So instead of speaking he stood over her with his hands dangling so that he could haul her to her feet and give her the old good-night bear-hug that meant so much to her. But Miss Dubber did not oblige. She did not want the hug.

"Why do you call yourself Canterbury if your name is Pym?" she demanded sternly.

"That's my first name. Pym. Like Pip. Pym Canterbury."

She had thought for a long time about that. She studied his dried-up eyes and his cheek muscles that were writhing for no known reason. And he noticed that she didn't like much what she saw, and was disposed to quarrel. But as he strained his smile at her, and willed her with all the life that was left in him, he was rewarded by a strict nod of acceptance.

"Well we're both too old for Christian names now, Mr. Canterbury," she said. After which she did finally hold out her arms and he did gently take hold of them above the elbows, and he did have to remember not to pull too hard, because he was so keen to have her against him and get himself off to bed where he belonged.

"Now I'm glad about that medal," she announced as he led her along the passage. "I've always admired a man who gets a medal, Mr. Canterbury. Whatever he's done."

The stairs belonged to the houses of his childhood so he skipped up them lightly and forgot his aches and pains. The star-of-Bethlehem lampshade on the landing, though it shed a lousy light, was an old friend from The Glades. Everything is kind to me, he noticed. When he pushed open the door of his room, everything winked and laughed at him like a surprise party. The parcels were all as he had prepared them but it never did any harm to check. So he checked them now. Envelope for Miss Dubber, lots of money and apologies. Envelope to Jack, no money and come to think of it, precious few apologies. Poppy, how odd that you are such a distant sound at last. That stupid filing cabinet, I don't know why I bothered with it all these years. I haven't even looked inside. The burnbox, what a weight it is for so few secrets. Nothing to Mary but he'd really nothing much more to say to her: "Sorry I married you for cover. Glad I managed a bit of love along the way. Hazards of the trade, m'dear. You're a spy too, remember? Rather better than Pym was, come to think of it. Class will tell in the end." Only the envelope to Tom bothered him, and he tore open the sealed flap feeling that a last word of explanation was after all required.

"You see, Tom, I am the bridge," he wrote in a hand that was irritatingly sluggish. "I am what you must walk over to get from Rick to life."

Then he added his initials, as one always should with a postscript, and addressed a fresh envelope and put the old one in the waste-paper basket because he had been taught from early in his life that untidiness was the sister of insecurity.

Then he hauled the burnbox from the top of the cabinet to the desk and with the two keys from his chain disarmed it and fished out first the files which were too secret to be classified at all and which gave a lot of bogus information about the networks he and Poppy had so painstakingly composed. He chucked them in the waste-paper basket too. When he'd done that he pulled out the gun and loaded it and cocked it, all rather swiftly, and set it on the desk thinking of the many times he had carried a gun and not fired it. He heard a scraping sound from the roof, and said to himself: must be a cat. He shook his head as if to say those damned cats, they get everywhere these days, don't give the birds a chance. He glanced at his gold watch, a wide gesture, remembering that Rick had given it to him and that he might forget to take it off in the bath. So he took it off now and laid it on Tom's envelope and drew a cheerful moon face right next to it, the sign they drew for one another to say "Smile." He undressed and laid his clothes neatly by the bed, then he put on his dressing-gown and took both his towels from the clothes-horse, the big one for the bath, the small one for hands and face. He slipped the gun into the dressing-gown pocket, leaving the safety catch in the "off" position because it was the laborious ethic of the trainers that a safed gun was more dangerous than a live one. He was only going across the corridor but it's a violent world these days and you can't be too careful. About to open the bathroom door he was annoyed to discover that the porcelain knob had stiffened up and scarcely turned. Damned doorknob. Look at that. It took him all the strength of both his hands to twist it and, more annoying still, some idiot must have left soap on it, because his hands kept slithering and he had to use a towel to get a grip. It's probably dear old Lippsie, he thought with a smile: always living in that world inside her head. Placing himself for the last time before the shaving mirror, he arranged the towels around his head and shoulders, making a bonnet of the small one and a cape of the large one, because if there was one thing Miss Dubber hated above another, it was mess. Then he held the gun to where his right ear was, forgetting, as anybody might in the circumstances, whether the trigger of your Browning .38 automatic had two pressures or just the one. And he noticed how he was leaning: not away from the gun, but into it, like someone a little deaf, straining for a sound.

Mary never heard the shot. The superintendent was crouching at Brotherhood's window again, this time to tell him that Magnus's presence inside the house had now been positively confirmed by a ruse and that he had orders to assemble non-combatants in the Church Hall without delay. Brotherhood was contesting this, and Mary still had her eye on the four men playing Grannie's Footsteps among the chimney-pots across the square. For half an hour now they had been reeling out rope to one another and adopting classic postures of stealth, and Mary loathed the lot of them more than she could have imagined possible. A society that admires its shock troops had better be bloody careful about where it's going, Magnus liked to say. The superintendent was confirming that there were no other male lodgers on the premises apart from the said Canterbury, and he was asking Mary whether she would hold herself in readiness to speak to her husband on the telephone in a conciliatory manner if this became necessary during the course of operations. And Mary was retorting: "Of *course* I will," in an overbold whisper intended to deflate all this theatrical nonsense. All those things in her later memory were taking place or had just done so as Brotherhood shoved open the driver's door, sending the superintendent flying to one side, one boot for ever frozen in the window frame. After that she had a forward image of Jack pelting towards the house at a young man's pace because sometimes she had a dream of him doing exactly that, and the house was always Plush and he was coming to make love to her. But with the clamour all around him he was standing still. Lights had come on, ambulances were racing to the spot without apparently knowing where the spot was, police and plainclothesmen were falling over each other and the fools on the roof were shouting at the fools in the square and England was being saved from things it didn't know were threatening it. But Jack Brotherhood was standing to attention like a dead centurion at his post, and everyone was watching a dignified little lady in a dressing-gown coming down the steps of her house.

ABOUT THE AUTHOR

JOHN LE CARRÉ was born in 1931. After attending
the universities of Bern and Oxford, he taught at
Eton and spent five years in the British Foreign
Service. *The Spy Who Came In from the Cold*,
his third book, secured him a world-wide reputation. He divides his time between England and
the Continent.